Louise Mühlbach

Andreas Hofer

Louise Mühlbach

Andreas Hofer

ISBN/EAN: 9783741149290

Manufactured in Europe, USA, Canada, Australia, Japa

Cover: Foto ©Andreas Hilbeck / pixelio.de

Manufactured and distributed by brebook publishing software
(www.brebook.com)

Louise Mühlbach

Andreas Hofer

THE WORKS OF
LOUISE MÜHLBACH

ANDREAS HOFER

FRONTISPIECE IN COLOR FROM PAINTING BY
WALTER H. EVERETT

NEW YORK
P. F. COLLIER & SON

15

CONTENTS.

ANDREAS HOFER

ANDREAS HOFER.

THE year 1809 had come; but the war against France, so intensely longed for by all Austria, had not yet broken out, and the people and the army were vainly waiting for the war-cry of their sovereign, the Emperor Francis. It is true, not a few great things had been accomplished in the course of the past year: Austria had armed, organized the militia, strengthened her fortresses, and filled her magazines; but the emperor still hesitated to take the last and most decisive step by crowning his military preparations with a formal declaration of war.

No one looked for this declaration of war more intensely than the emperor's second brother, the Archduke John, a young man of scarcely twenty-seven. He had been the soul of all the preparations which, since the summer of 1808, had been made throughout Austria; he had conceived the plan of organizing the militia and the reserves; and had drawn up the proclamation of the 12th of May, 1808, by which all able-bodied Austrians were called upon to take up arms. But this exhausted his powers; he could organize the army, but could not say to it, "Take the field against the enemy!" The emperor alone could utter this word, and he was silent.

"And he will be silent until the favorable moment has passed," sighed the Archduke John, when, on returning from a very long interview with the emperor, he was alone with his friend, General Nugent, in his cabinet.

He had communicated to this confidant the full details of his interview with the emperor, and concluded his report by saying, with a deep sigh, "The emperor will be silent until the favorable moment has passed!"

Count Nugent gazed with a look of heart-felt sympathy into the archduke's mournful face; he saw the tears filling John's large blue eyes; he saw that he firmly compressed his lips as if to stifle a cry of pain or rage, and that he clinched his hands in the agony of his despair. Animated by tender compassion, the general approached the archduke, who had sunk into a chair, and laid his hand gently on his shoulder. "Courage, courage!" he whispered; "nothing is lost as yet, and your imperial highness—"

"Ah, why do you address me with 'imperial highness'?" cried the archduke, almost indignantly. "Do you not see, then, that this is a miserable title by which Fate seems to mock me, and which it thunders constantly, and, as it were, sneeringly into my ears, in order to remind me again and again of my deplorable powerlessness? There is nothing 'imperial' about me but the yoke under which I am groaning; and my 'highness' is to be compared only with the crumbs of Lazarus which fell from the rich man's table. And yet there are persons, Nugent, who envy me these crumbs—men who think it a brilliant and glorious lot to be an 'imperial highness,' the brother of a sovereign emperor! Ah, they do not know that this title means only that I am doomed to everlasting dependence and silence, and that the emperor's valet de chambre and his private secretary are more influential men than the Archduke John, who cannot do anything but submit, be silent, and look on in idleness."

"Now your imperial highness slanders yourself," exclaimed Count Nugent. "You have not been silent, you have not looked on in idleness, but have worked incessantly and courageously for the salvation of your people and your country. Who drew up the original plan for the organization of the militia and the reserves? Who elaborated its most minute details with admirable sagacity? It was the Archduke John —the archduke in whom all Austria hopes, and who is the last refuge and comfort of all patriots!"

"Ah, how much all of you are to be pitied, my friend, if you hope in me!" sighed John. "What am I, then? A poor

atom which is allowed to move in the glare of the imperial
sun, but which would be annihilated so soon as it should pre-
sume to be an independent luminary. Pray, Nugent, do not
speak of such hopes ; for, if the emperor should hear of it, not
only would my liberty be endangered, but also yours and that
of all who are of your opinion. The emperor does not like
to see the eyes of his subjects fixed upon me ; every kind word
uttered about me sours him and increases the ill-will with
which he regards me."

"That is impossible, your highness," exclaimed the count.
"How can our excellent emperor help loving his brother, who
is so gifted, so high-minded and learned, and withal so modest
and kind-hearted ? How can he help being happy to see that
others love and appreciate him too ? "

"Does the emperor love my brother Charles, who is much
more gifted and high-minded than I am ? " asked John, shrugging his shoulders. "Did he not arrest his victorious career,
and recall him from the army, although, or rather *because*, he
knew that the army idolized him, and that all Austria loved
him and hoped in him ? Ah, believe me, the emperor is distrustful of all his brothers, and all our protestations of love
and devotedness do not touch him, but rebound powerlessly
from the armor of jealousy with which he has steeled his
heart against us. You see, I tell you all this with perfect
composure, but I confess it cost me once many tears and inward struggles, and it was long before my heart became calm
and resigned. My heart long yearned for love, confidence, and
friendship. I have got over these yearnings now, and resigned
myself to be lonely, and remain so all my life long. That is
to say," added the archduke, with a gentle smile, holding out
his hand to the count, "lonely, without a sister, without a
brother—lonely in my family. However, I have found a
most delightful compensation for this loneliness, for I call you
and Hormayr friends ; I have my books, which always comfort, divert, and amuse me ; and last, I have my great and
glorious hopes regarding the future of the fatherland. Ah,
how could I say that I was poor and lonely when I am so rich
in hopes, and have two noble and faithful friends ? I am sure,
Nugent, you will never desert me, but stand by me to the end

—to the great day of victory, or to the end of our humiliation and disgrace ? "

"Your imperial highness knows full well that my heart will never turn from you ; that I love and revere you ; that you are to me the embodiment of all that is noble, great, and beautiful ; that I would be joyfully ready at any hour to suffer death for you ; and that neither prosperity nor adversity could induce me to forsake you. You are the hope of my heart, you are the hope of my country—nay, the hope of all Germany. We all need your assistance, your heart, your arm ; for we expect that you will place yourself at the head of Germany, and lead us to glorious victories ! "

"God grant that the hour when we shall take the field may soon come ! Then, my friend, I shall prove that I am ready, like all of you, to shed my heart's blood for the fatherland, and conquer or die for the liberty of Austria, the liberty of Germany. For in the present state of affairs the fate of Germany, too, depends on the success of our arms. If we succumb and have to submit to the same humiliations as Prussia, the whole of Germany will be but a French province, and the freedom and independence of our fatherland will be destroyed for long years to come. I am too weak to survive such a disgrace. If Austria falls, I shall fall too ; if German liberty dies, I shall die too." *

"German liberty will not die ! " exclaimed Count Nugent, enthusiastically ; "it will take the field one day against all the powerful and petty tyrants of the fatherland. Then it will choose the Archduke John its general-in-chief, and he will lead it to victory ! "

"No, no, my friend," said John, mournfully ; "Fate refuses to let me play a decisive part in the history of the world. My role will always be but a secondary one ; my will will always be impeded, my arm will be paralyzed forever. You know it. You know that I am constantly surrounded by secret spies and eavesdroppers, who watch me with lynx-eyed vigilance, and misrepresent every step I take. It was always so, and will remain so until I die or become a decrepit old

* The Archduke John's own words.—See "Forty-eight Letters from Archduke John of Austria to Johannes von Müller," p. 90.

man, whose arm is no longer able to wield the sword or even the pen. That I am young, that I have a heart for the sufferings of my country, a heart not only for the honor of Austria, but for that of Germany—that is what gives umbrage to them, what renders me suspicious in their eyes, and causes them to regard me as a revolutionist. I had to suffer a good deal for my convictions ; a great many obstacles were raised against all my plans ; and yet I desired only to contribute to the welfare of the whole ; I demanded nothing for myself, but every thing for the fatherland. To the fatherland I wished to devote my blood and my life ; for the fatherland I wished to conquer in the disastrous campaign of 1805. However, such were not the plans of my adversaries ; they did not wish to carry on the war with sufficient energy and perseverance ; they would not give my brother Charles and me an opportunity to distinguish ourselves and gain a popular name. Whenever I planned a vigorous attack, I was not permitted to carry it into effect. Whenever, with my corps, I might have exerted a decisive influence upon the fortunes of the war, I was ordered to retreat with my troops to some distant position of no importance whatever ; and when I remonstrated, they charged me with rebelling against the emperor's authority. Ah, I suffered a great deal in those days, and the wounds which my heart received at that juncture are bleeding yet. I had to succumb, when the men who had commenced the war at a highly unfavorable time, conducted it at an equally unfavorable moment, and made peace. And by that peace Austria lost her most loyal province, the beautiful Tyrol, one of the oldest states of the Hapsburgs ; and her most fertile province, the territory of Venetia and Dalmatia, for which I did not grieve so much, because it always was a source of political dissensions and quarrels for the hereditary provinces of Austria. What afflicted me most sorely was the loss of the Tyrol, and even now I cannot think of it without the most profound emotion. It seemed as though Fate were bent on blotting out from our memory all that might remind us of our ancestors, their virtues, their patriotism, and their perseverance in the days of universal adversity ; and as though, in consequence of this, the spirit of the Hapsburgs had almost become extinct,

and we were to lose all that they had gained in the days of
their greatness.* But now Fate is willing to give us another
opportunity to repair our faults and show that we are worthy
of our ancestors. If we allow this to pass too, all is lost, not
only the throne of the Hapsburgs, but also their honor ! "

"This opportunity will not pass ! " exclaimed the count.
"The throne of the Hapsburgs will be preserved, for it is protected by the Archdukes John and Charles, a brave army that
is eager for a war with France, and a faithful, intrepid people,
which is sincerely devoted to its imperial dynasty, which
never will acknowledge another ruler, and which never will
desert its Hapsburgs."

"Yes, the people will not desert us," said John, "but worse
things may happen ; we may desert ourselves. Just look
around, Nugent, and see how lame we have suddenly become
again ; how we have all at once stopped half way, unable to
decide whether it might not be better for us to lay down our
arms again and surrender at discretion to the Emperor of the
French."

"Fortunately, it is too late now to take such a resolution ;
for Austria has already gone so far that a hesitating policy at
this juncture will no longer succeed in pacifying the Emperor
of the French. And it is owing to the efforts of your imperial
highness that it is so ; we are indebted for it to your zeal, your
energy, and your enthusiasm for the good cause, which is now
no longer the cause of Austria, but that of Germany. And
this cause will not succumb ; God will not allow a great and
noble people to be trampled under foot by a foreign tyrant,
who bids defiance to the most sacred treaties and the law of
nations, and who would like to overthrow all thrones to convert the foreign kingdoms and empires into provinces of *his*
empire, blot out the history of the nations and dynasties, and
have all engulfed by his universal monarchy."

"God may not decree this, but He may perhaps allow it if
the will of the nations and the princes should not be strong
enough to set bounds to such mischief. When the feeling of
liberty and independence does not incite the nations to rise

* John's own words.—See " Forty-eight Letters from Archduke John to
Johannes von Müller," p. 103.

enthusiastically and defend their rights, God sends them a tyrant as a scourge to chastise them. And such, I am afraid, is our case. Germany has lost faith in herself, in her honor ; she lies exhausted at the feet of the tyrant, and is ready to be trampled in the dust by him. Just look around in our German fatherland. What do you see there ? All the sovereign princes have renounced their independence, and become Napoleon's vassals ; they obey his will, they submit to his orders, and send their armies not against the enemy of Germany, but against the enemies of France, no matter whether those enemies are their German brethren or not. The German princes have formed the Confederation of the Rhine, and the object of this confederation is not to preserve the frontier of the Rhine to Germany, but to secure the Rhine to France. The German princes are begging for honors and territories at the court of Napoleon ; they do not shrink from manifesting their fealty to their master, the Emperor of the French, by betraying the interests of Germany ; they are playing here at Vienna the part of the meanest spies ; they are watching all our steps, and are shameless enough to have the Emperor Napoleon reward their infamy by conferring royal titles on them, and to accept at his hands German territories which he took from German princes. Bavaria did not disdain to aggrandize her territories at our expense ; Wurtemberg accepts without blushing the territories of other German princes at the hands of Napoleon, who thus rewards her for the incessant warnings by which the King of Wurtemberg urges the Emperor of the French to be on his guard against Austria, and always distrust the intentions of the Emperor Francis * In the middle of the German empire we see a new French kingdom, Westphalia, established by Napoleon's orders ; it is formed of the spoils taken from Prussia and Hanover ; and the German princes suffer it, and the German people bow their heads, silently to the disgraceful foreign yoke ! Ah, Nugent, my heart is full of grief and anger, full of the bitterness of despair ; for I have lost faith in Germany, and see shudderingly that she will decay and die, as Poland died, of her own weakness. Ah, it would be dreadful, dreadful, if we too, had to fall, as the unfortunate

* Schlosser, " History of the Eighteenth Century," vol. vii., p. 488.

Kosciusko did, with the despairing cry of '*Finis Germa-niæ!*'"

"No, that will never happen!" cried Nugent. "No, Germany will never endure the disgrace and debasement of Poland; she will never sink to ruin and perish like Poland. It is true, a majority of the German princes bow to Napoleon's power, and we may charge them with infidelity and treason against Germany; but we can not prefer the same charge against the German people and the subjects of the traitorous German princes. They have remained faithful, and have not yet lost faith in their fatherland. They are indignantly champing the bit with which their despots have shut their mouth; and, in silence, harmony, and confidence in God, they are preparing for the great hour when they will rise, for the sacred day when they will break their shackles with the divine strength of a united and high-minded people. Everywhere the embers are smouldering under the ashes; everywhere secret societies and leagues have been formed; everywhere there are conspirators, depots of arms, and passwords; everywhere the people of Germany are waiting only for the moment when they are to strike the first blow, and for the signal to rise. And they are in hopes now that Austria will give the signal. Our preparations for war have been hailed with exultation throughout Germany: everywhere the people are ready to take up arms so soon as Austria draws the sword. The example of Spain and Portugal has taught the Germans how the arrogant conqueror must be met; the example of Austria will fill them with boundless enthusiasm, and lead them to the most glorious victories!"

"And we are still temporizing and hesitating," exclaimed John, mournfully; "we are not courageous enough to strike the first blow! All is ready; the emperor has only to utter the decisive word, but he refuses to do so!"

"The enthusiasm of his people will soon compel him and his advisers to utter that word," said Nugent. "Austria can no longer retrace her steps; she must advance. Austria must lead Germany in the sacred struggle for liberty; she can no longer retrace her steps."

"God grant that your words may be verified!" cried John, lifting his tearful eyes to heaven; "God grant that—"

A low rapping at the door leading to the small secret corridor caused the archduke to pause and turn his eyes with a searching expression to this door.

The rapping was repeated, more rapidly than before.

"It is Hormayr," exclaimed the archduke, joyfully ; and he hastened to the secret door and opened it quickly.

A tall young man, in the uniform of an Austrian superior officer, appeared in the open door. The archduke grasped both his hands and drew him hastily into the cabinet.

"Hormayr, my friend," he said, breathlessly, "you have returned from the Tyrol ? You have succeeded in fulfilling the mission with which I intrusted you ? You have carried my greetings to the Tyrolese ? Oh, speak, speak, my friend ! What do my poor, deserted Tyrolese say ? "

Baron von Hormayr fixed his flashing dark eyes with an expression of joyful tenderness on the excited face of the archduke.

"The Tyrolese send greeting to the Archduke John," he said ; "the Tyrolese hope that the Archduke John will deliver them from the hateful yoke of the Bavarians ; the Tyrolese believe that the hour has arrived, when they may recover their liberty ; and to prove this—"

"To prove this ? " asked the archduke, breathlessly, when Hormayr paused a moment.

"To prove this," said Hormayr, in a lower voice, stepping up closer to the prince, "some of the most influential and respectable citizens of the Tyrol have accompanied me to Vienna ; they desire to assure your imperial highness of their loyal devotedness, and receive instructions from you."

"Is Andreas Hofer, the landwirth, among them ? " asked the archduke, eagerly.

"He is, and so are Wallner and Speckbacher. I bring to your imperial highness the leading men of the Tyrolese peasants, and would like to know when I may introduce them to you, and at what hour you will grant a private audience to my Tyrolese friends ? "

"Oh, I will see them at once ! " exclaimed John, impatiently. "My heart longs to gaze into the faithful, beautiful eyes of the Tyrolese, and read in their honest faces if they really are still devoted and attached to me. Bring them to me, Hormayr ; make haste—but no, I forgot that it is broad daylight, and that the spies watching me have eyes to see, ears to hear, and tongues to report to the emperor as dreadful crimes all that they have seen and heard here. We must wait, therefore, until the spies have closed their eyes, until dark and reticent night has descended on earth, and—. Well, Conrad, what is it ? " the archduke interrupted himself, look-ing at his valet de chambre, who had just entered hastily by the door of the anteroom.

" Pardon me, your imperial highness," said Conrad ; " a messenger of her majesty the empress is in the anteroom. Her majesty has ordered him to deliver his message only to the archduke himself."

" Let him come in," said the archduke.

Conrad opened the door, and the imperial messenger ap-peared on the threshold.

" Her majesty the Empress Ludovica sends her respects to the archduke," said the messenger, approaching the archduke respectfully. " Her majesty thanks your imperial highness for the book which you lent her ; and she returns it with sin-cere thanks."

An expression of astonishment overspread John's face, but it soon disappeared, and the archduke received with a calm smile the small sealed package which the messenger handed to him.

" All right," he said ; " tell her majesty to accept my thanks."

The messenger returned to the anteroom, and Conrad closed the door behind him.

" Place yourself before the door, Nugent, that nobody may be able to look through the key-hole," whispered John, " for you know that I do not trust Conrad. And you, Hormayr, watch the secret door."

The two gentlemen hastened noiselessly to obey. The archduke cast a searching glance around the walls, as if afraid that even the silken hangings might contain somewhere an opening for the eyes of a spy, or serve as a cover to an ear of Dionysius.

"Something of importance must have occurred," whispered John ; "otherwise the empress would not have ventured to send me a direct message. I did not lend her a book, and you know we agreed with the ladies of our party to communicate direct news to each other only in cases of pressing necessity. Let us see now what it is."

He hastily tore open the sealed package and drew from it a small prayer-book bound in black velvet. While he was turning over the leaves with a smile, a small piece of paper fluttered from between the gilt-edged leaves and dropped to the floor.

"That is it," said John, smiling, picking up the paper, and fixing his eyes on it. "There is nothing on it," he then exclaimed, contemplating both sides of the paper. "There is not a word on it. It is only a book-mark, that is all. But, perhaps, something is written in the book, or there may be another paper."

"No, your imperial highness," whispered Nugent, stepping back a few paces from the door. "The Princess Lichtenstein whispered to me yesterday, at the court concert, that she had obtained an excellent way of sending a written message to her friends and allies, and that, if we received a piece of white paper from the ladies of our party, we had better preserve it and read it afterward near the fireplace."

"Ah, sympathetic ink," exclaimed John ; "well, we will see."

He hastily approached the fireplace, where a bright fire was burning, and held the piece of paper close to the flames. Immediately a number of black dots and lines appeared on the paper ; these dots and lines assumed gradually the shape of finely-written words.

The archduke followed with rapt attention every line, every letter that appeared on the white paper, and now he read as follows :

"The French ambassador has requested the emperor to grant him an audience at eleven o'clock this morning. A courier from Metternich in Paris has arrived, and, I believe, brought important news. The decisive hour is at hand. Hasten to the emperor ; leave nothing undone to prevail on him to take a bold stand. Send somebody to the Archduke Charles ; request him to repair likewise to the emperor and influence him in the same direction. I have paved the way for you. I hope the French ambassador will, in spite of himself, be our ally, and by his defiant and arrogant bearing, attain for us the object which we have hitherto been unable to accomplish by our persuasion and our arguments. Make haste ! Burn this paper."

The archduke signed to his two confidants to come to him, and pointed to the paper. When they had hastily read the lines, he threw the paper into the flames, and turned to the two gentlemen who stood behind him.

"Well, what do you think of it ?" he inquired. "Shall I do what these mysterious lines ask of me ? Shall I go to the emperor without being summoned to him ?"

"The empress requests you to do so, and she is as prudent as she is energetic," said Count Nugent.

"I say, like the empress, the decisive hour is at hand," exclaimed Baron von Hormayr. "Hasten to the emperor ; try once more to force the sword into his hand, and to wrest at length the much-wished-for words, 'War against France !' from his lips. The Tyrolese are only waiting for these words, to rise for their emperor and become again his loving and devoted subjects. All Austria, nay, all Germany, is longing for these words, which will be the signal of the deliverance of the fatherland from the French yoke. Oh, my lord and prince, hasten to the emperor ; speak to him with the impassioned eloquence of the cherubim, break the fatal charm that holds Austria and the Tyrol enthralled !"

At this moment the large clock standing on the mantelpiece commenced striking.

"Eleven o'clock," said the archduke—"the hour when the emperor is to give an audience to the French ambassador. It is high time, therefore. Nugent, hasten to my brother ; implore him to repair forthwith to the emperor, and to act this time at least in unison with me. Tell him that everything is at stake, and that we must risk all to win all. But you, Hormayr, go to my dear Tyrolese ; tell them that I will receive them here at twelve o'clock to-night, and conduct them to me at that hour, my friend. We will hold a council of war at midnight."

"And your imperial highness does not forget that you promised to go to the concert to-night?" asked Nugent. "Your highness is aware that our friends not only intend to-night to give an ovation to the veteran master of German art, Joseph Haydn, but wish also to profit by the German music to make a political demonstration; and they long for the presence of the imperial court, that the emperor and his brothers may witness the patriotic enthusiasm of Vienna."

"I shall certainly be present," said the archduke, earnestly, "and I hope the empress will succeed in prevailing on the emperor to go to the concert.—Well, then, my friends, let us go to work, and may God grant success to our efforts!"

CHAPTER II.

THE EMPEROR FRANCIS.

THE Emperor Francis had to-day entered his study at an earlier hour than usual, and was industriously engaged there in finishing a miniature cup which he had commenced cutting from a peach-stone yesterday. On the table before him lay the drawing of the model after which he was shaping the cup; and Francis lifted his eyes only from time to time to fix them on the drawing, and compare it with his own work. These comparisons, however, apparently did not lead to a cheering result, for the emperor frowned and put the cup rather impetuously close to the drawing on the table.

"I believe, forsooth, the cup is not straight," murmured the emperor to himself, contemplating from all sides the diminutive object which had cost him so much labor. "Sure enough, it is not straight, it has a hump on one side. Yes, yes, nothing is straight, nowadays; and even God in heaven creates His things no longer straight, and does not shrink from letting the peach-stones grow crooked. But no matter—what God does is well done," added the emperor, crossing

himself devoutly ; " even an emperor must not censure it, and
must not grumble when his cup is not straight because God
gave the peach-stone a hump.   Well, perhaps, I may change
it yet, and make the cup straight."

He again took up the little cup, and commenced industriously working at it with his sharp files, pointed knives, and
gimlets. It was hard work : large drops of sweat stood on the
emperor's forehead ; his arms ached, and his fingers became
sore under the pressure of the knives and files ; but the emperor did not mind it, only from time to time wiping the sweat
from his brow, and then continuing his labor with renewed zeal.

Close to the small table containing the tools stood the emperor's large writing-table. Large piles of documents and
papers lay on this table, and among them were scattered also
many letters and dispatches with broad official seals. But the
emperor had not yet thought of opening these dispatches or
unsealing these letters. The peach-stone had engrossed his
attention this morning, and he had unsealed only one of the
papers ; the emperor had read only the report of the secret
police on the events of the previous day. These reports of the
secret police and the *Chiffre-Cabinet* were the favorite reading
matter of the Emperor Francis, and he would have flown into
a towering passion if he had not found them on his writing-
table early every morning.

Thanks to these reports, the emperor knew every morning
all that had occurred in Vienna during the previous day ;
what the foreign ambassadors had done, and, above all things,
what his brothers, the Archdukes Charles, Ferdinand, Joseph,
and John, had said, done, and perhaps only thought. To-day's
report had not communicated many important things to the
emperor ; it had only informed him that, at daybreak, a courier
from Paris had arrived at the house of the French ambassador, Count Andréossi, and that there were good reasons to
believe that he had brought highly important news.

It was exactly for the purpose of dispelling the anxiety
with which this unpleasant intelligence had filled him, that
Francis had laid aside the report and recommenced his work
on the cup ; and by this occupation he had succeeded in forgetting the burdensome duties of his imperial office.

He was just trying very hard to plane one side of his cup, when a low rap at the small door leading to the narrow corridor, and thence to the apartments of the empress, interrupted him. The emperor gave a start and looked toward the door, listening and hoping, perhaps, that his ear might have deceived him. But no, the rapping was heard once more : there could no longer be a doubt of it—somebody sought admittance, and intended to disturb the peaceful solitude of the emperor.

"What does the empress want?" murmured Francis. "What does she come here for ? I am afraid something unpleasant has happened again."

He rose with a shrug from his chair, put his miniature cup hastily into the drawer of his table, and hurried to open the door.

Francis had not been mistaken. It really was the Empress Ludovica, the third consort of the emperor, who had married her only a few months ago. She wore a handsome dishabille of embroidered white muslin, closely surrounding her delicate and slender form, and trimmed with beautiful laces. The white dress reached up to the neck, where a rose-colored tie fastened it. Her beautiful black hair, which fell down in heavy ringlets on both sides of her face, was adorned with a costly lace cap, from which wide ribbons of rose-colored satin flowed down on her shoulders. But the countenance of the empress did not correspond to this coquettish and youthful dress. She was young and beautiful, but an expression of profound melancholy overspread her features. Her cheeks were transparently white, and a sad, touching smile quivered round her finely-chiselled, narrow lips ; her high, expansive forehead was shaded, as it were, by a cloud of sadness ; and her large black eyes shot, from time to time, gloomy flashes which seemed to issue from a gulf of fiery torture. But whatever passions might animate her delicate, ethereal form, the empress had learned to cover her heart with a veil, and her lips never gave utterance to the sufferings of her soul. Only her confidantes were allowed to divine them ; they alone knew that twofold tortures were racking Ludovica's fiery soul, those of hatred and wounded pride. Napoleon ! it was he whom the empress hated with indescribable bitterness ; and the neg-

lect with which her consort, the Emperor Francis, treated her
cut her proud heart to the quick. Thanks to the intrigues and
immense riches of her mother, Beatrix of Este, Duchess of Modena, she had become the wife of an emperor, and herself an
empress; but she had thereby obtained only an august position, not a husband and partner. She was an empress in name
only, but not in reality. Francis had given her his hand, but
not his heart and his love. He disdained his beautiful, lovely
wife ; he avoided any familiar intercourse with her with
anxious timidity ; only in the presence of the court and the
public did he treat the empress as his consort, and tolerate her
near his person. At first Ludovica had submitted to this
strange conduct on the part of her husband with proud indifference, and not the slightest murmur, not the mildest reproach, had escaped her lips. For it was not from love that
she had chosen this husband, but from ambition and pride.
She had told herself that it would be better for her to be Empress of Austria than Princess of Modena and Este ; and even
the prospect of being the *third* wife of Francis of Austria, and
the stepmother of the ten children whom his second wife had
borne to him, had not deterred her. She meant to marry the
emperor, and not the man ; she wished to play a prominent
part, and exert a powerful influence on the destinies of the
world. But these hopes were soon to prove utterly futile.
The emperor granted her publicly all the privileges of her exalted position by his side ; but in the privacy of her apartments
he never made her his confidante ; he refused to let her have
any influence over his decisions ; he never consulted her as to
the measures of his administration ; nay, he avoided alluding
to such topics in her presence.

Such was the grief that was gnawing at the heart of the
young empress—the wound from which her proud and lofty
soul was bleeding. But for a few weeks past she had overcome her silent grief, and the presence of her mother, the
shrewd and intriguing Duchess of Modena, seemed to have imparted fresh strength to the empress, and confirmed her in her
determination to conquer the heart and confidence of her husband. Whereas she had hitherto met his indifference by
proud reticence, and feigned not to notice it, she was now

kind and even affectionate toward him; and it often happened that, availing herself of the privilege of her position, she traversed the private corridor separating her rooms from those of her husband, and, without being summoned to him, entered his cabinet to talk politics with him in spite of his undisguised aversion to doing so.

The emperor hated these interviews from the bottom of his heart; a shudder pervaded his soul, and a cloud covered his brow, whenever he heard the low rap of the empress at his private door. To-day, too, the dark cloud covered his forehead even after the empress had entered his cabinet. Ludovica noticed it, and a mournful smile overspread her pale face for a moment.

"As your majesty did not come to me to bid me good-morning, I have come to you," she said, in a gentle, kind voice, holding out her beautiful white hand to the emperor.

Francis took it and pressed it to his lips. "It is true," he said, evidently embarrassed, "I did not come this morning to pay my respects to you, but time was wanting to me. I had to go at once to my cabinet and work; I am very busy."

"I see," said Ludovica; "your majesty's dress still bears the traces of your occupation."

The emperor hastened to brush away with his hands the small particles of the peach-stone that had remained on his shirt-bosom and his sleeve; but while he was doing this his brow darkened still more, and he cast a gloomy and defiant glance on the empress.

"Look, empress," he said; "perhaps you belong to the secret police, and have been employed to watch me in order to find out what I am doing when I am alone in my cabinet. Why, if I found out that that was so, I should be obliged to be on my guard and have this door walled up, so that my esteemed consort might no longer be able to surprise and watch me."

"Your majesty will assuredly not do that," said Ludovica, whose voice was tremulous, and whose cheeks had turned even paler than before. "No, your majesty will not make me undergo the humiliation of making known to the world the deplorable secret with which we alone have hitherto been acquainted. Your majesty will not deprive me of the only privilege which I enjoy in common with your former consorts, and thereby proclaim to the world that I am in this palace a stranger who has not even access to the rooms of her husband."

"I do not say that I intend to do it," said Francis, shrugging his shoulders; "I say only that it is highly repugnant to me to have my steps dogged and watched in any manner. It is true, my former consort had also the keys of this private corridor, but—pardon me for this remark, your majesty—the empress never used these keys, but always waited for me to open the door."

"And she did not wait in vain," said the empress, quickly; "your majesty never failed to come, for you loved your consort, and I have been told you never suffered even a few hours to pass by without leaving your cabinet and crossing the secret corridor to repair to the rooms of the empress."

"But the good Empress Theresa," exclaimed the emperor, "when I was with her, never endeavored to talk to me about politics and state affairs."

"I understand that," said Ludovica; "you had both so many mutual interests to converse about. You had your mutual love, your children, to talk about. I, who am so unhappy as not to be able to talk with you about such matters, how intensely soever my heart longs for it, must content myself with coversing with my husband on different subjects; and I desire to share at least his cares when I cannot share his love. My husband, I beseech you, do not disdain my friendship; accept a friend's hand, which I offer to you honestly and devotedly."

"My God, that is precisely what I long for!" exclaimed the emperor fervently, again pressing to his lips the hand which the empress held out to him. "My fondest wish is fulfilled when your majesty will give me your friendship, and confide in me as your best, most devoted, and faithful friend!"

"But this confidence must be reciprocated, my dearest friend," said Ludovica, putting her hand on the emperor's shoulder, and gazing long and ardently into his eyes. "Your majesty must confide in me too, and count implicitly on my fidelity."

"That is what I do," said Francis, hastily; "never should

I dare to doubt the fidelity of the purest, chastest, and most virtuous empress and lady—the fidelity of my wife."

"I did not refer to the wife's fidelity," said Ludovica, sighing, "but to the fidelity of my friendship, which is joyously ready to share all your cares and afflictions."

"Well, then," said the emperor, nodding to her smilingly, "I will give you a proof of my faith in your friendship. Yes, you shall share my cares and afflictions."

"Oh, my husband, how happy you make me by these words!" exclaimed Ludovica, and a faint blush beautified her noble face.

"I will let you participate in my work to-day, and you shall give me your advice," said the emperor, nodding to the empress, and stepping to the writing-table, from whose drawer he took the little cup. "Look, my dear friend," added the emperor, handing the cup to his consort, "I wished to make a little cup from this peach-stone and give it to Maria Louisa, who delights in such things; but when I had nearly finished it, I discovered suddenly that the peach-stone was crooked and not equally round on both sides. Now give me your advice, my fair friend; tell me what I am to do in order to straighten the cup. Look at it, and tell me how to fix it. It would be an everlasting disgrace for an emperor to be unable to straighten a thing which he himself made crooked."

The empress had turned pale again; her dark eyes shot fire for a moment, and she compressed her lips as if to stifle a cry of indignation. But she overcame her agitation quickly, and hastily took the little cup which the emperor still held out to her.

"Your majesty is right," she said; the "cup is really crooked, and will not stand erect when you put it on the table. As your majesty has asked me what ought to be done about it, I advise you to get rid of the thing, declare war against the little cup, and remove it forever by touching it in this manner with your little finger."

She upset the miniature cup with her slender little finger, so that it rolled to the other end of the table.

"That is very energetic advice, indeed," said Francis, smil-

ing, "but I do not like it. To upset a thing that is not well
done is no way of improving it."

"Yes, your majesty, to destroy what is not well done is
paving the way for something better," exclaimed Ludovica.
"You yourself said just now it would be an everlasting disgrace for an emperor to be unable to straighten anything
which he himself made crooked. It seems to me, now, an
emperor should extricate himself from any position imposing
on him the necessity of doing anything crooked and unworthy
of his imperial dignity. If such is his duty in regard to a
thing so insignificant as a peach-stone, how much more urgent is this duty, when there is at stake something so great
and sacred as the independence and honor of your empire and
policy!"

"See, see!" said the emperor, scratching his head with
an expression of ludicrous surprise ; "then we have really
got back from the peach-stone to political affairs and the
war-question. Now, this war-question is a hard peach-
stone to crack, and the mere thought of it sets my teeth on
edge."

"Ah," said Ludovica, "your teeth are firm and strong, for
they are composed of three hundred thousand swords, and
thousands of cannon and muskets. If the lion is determined
to use his teeth, he will easily succeed in destroying the were-
wolf ; for this rapacious and bloodthirsty were-wolf is brave
and invincible only when he has to deal with lambs ; only the
feeble and disarmed have reason to fear him."

"In speaking of a were-wolf, I suppose you refer to the
Emperor Napoleon?" asked the emperor, smiling. "I must
tell you, however, that, in your warlike enthusiasm, you do
him injustice. It seems to me he is brave not alone when he
has to deal with lambs, and not alone the feeble and disarmed
have reason to fear him. I think I did not march lambs
against him at Austerlitz, but brave men, who were not feeble
and disarmed, but strong and well-armed. Nevertheless,
Bonaparte overpowered them ; he gained the battle of Austerlitz over us, and we had to submit to him, and accept the terms
of peace which he imposed on us."

"Yes, your majesty had to submit to him," cried the empress, ardently; "you were obliged to repair to the proud usurper's camp and beseech him to grant you peace!"

"I was not obliged to go to him, but I did so in order to restore peace to my people, and prevent all Austria from sinking into ruin. It is true, it was a dreadful walk for me, and when I saw the Emperor of the French at his camp-fire, he became utterly distasteful to me.* Nevertheless, the truth cannot be gainsaid, and the truth is that the Emperor Napoleon is more than a were-wolf killing only lambs; he is a lion whose furious roar causes all thrones to tremble, and who, when he shakes his mane, shakes all Europe to its foundations."

"The more is it incumbent on us then to put an end to this unnatural state of affairs," exclaimed the empress, vehemently; "to strengthen the thrones, and restore at length tranquillity to Europe. And there is only one way of doing this, my lord and emperor, and that is war! We must destroy the lion in order to restore tranquillity to the peaceable nations."

"But what if, instead of destroying the lion, we should be destroyed by him?" asked the emperor, with a shrug. "What if the lion should a second time place his foot on our neck, trample us in the dust, and dictate to us again a disgraceful and humiliating peace? Do you think that the present position of the King of Prussia is a pleasant and honorable one, and that I am anxious to incur a similar fate? No, madame! I am by no means eager to wear a martyr's crown instead of my imperial crown, and I will rather strive to keep my crown on my head, regardless of the clamor of the German war-party. These German shriekers are nice fellows. They refuse to do any thing, but think it is enough for them to cry, 'War! war!' and that that will be sufficient to conquer Bonaparte. But, empress, a great deal more is required for that purpose than the fanatical war-clamor of the aristocratic saloons, and the scribblings of the journalists and patriotic poets; in order to attain so grand an object, it is indispensable that all Germany should rise, take up arms, and attack the enemy with united forces."

* The emperor's own words.—See "Lebensbilder aus dem Befreiungskriege," vol. i.

" It is as your majesty says," exclaimed Ludovica, enthusiastically ; " all Germany is ready for the struggle against the enemy. The nation is only waiting for Austria to give the signal, draw the sword, and advance upon France, when all Germany will follow her."

" I know these fine phrases," said Francis, shrugging his shoulders ; " I hear them every day from my brothers, who are eager for war, and who manage to gain a great deal of popularity in so comfortable a manner. But after all, they are phrases with very little sense in them. For just tell me, empress, where is the Germany which, you say, is only waiting for Austria to give the signal ? Where are the German armies which, you say, are only waiting for Austria to advance, when they will follow her ? I have good sound eyes, but I cannot see such armies anywhere. I am quite familiar with the geography of Germany, I know all the states that belong to it, but among them I vainly look for those which are waiting for us to give such a signal. Prussia is utterly powerless, and cannot do any thing. The princes of the Rhenish Confederacy, it is true, are waiting for the signal, but Bonaparte will give it to them, and when they march, they will march against Austria and strive to fight us bravely in order to obtain from the French Emperor praise, honors, titles, and grants of additional territories. No, no, I cannot be blinded by brave words and bombastic phrases ; I know that Austria, in case a war should break out, would stand all alone, and that she must either conquer or be ruined. In 1805, when, in consequence of the disastrous battle of Austerlitz, I lost half my states, I was not alone, Russia was my ally. But Russia has recently declared that, in case a war should break out, she would not assist us against Napoleon, but observe a strict neutrality as long as possible ; if she should, however, be obliged to take a decided stand, she would be on the side of France and against us. Consequently, I am entirely isolated, and Napoleon has numerous allies."

" But your majesty has a powerful ally in the universal enthusiasm of the Austrians and Germans, in the universal indignation of the nations against Napoleon. You have public opinion on your side, and that is the most powerful ally."

"Ah, let me alone with that abominable ally," cried the emperor, vehemently ; "I do not want to hear of it nor to have anything to do with it. Public opinion is the hobby which my brother, the popular Archduke John, is riding all the time ; but it will throw him one day into the mire, and then he will find out what it really amounts to. Pray, never speak to me again of public opinion, for I detest it. It smells of revolution and insurrection, and, like a patient donkey, suffers itself to be led by whosoever offers it a thistle as a bait. I renounce once for all the alliance of public opinion, and I do not care whether it blesses or crucifies me, whether it calls me emperor or blockhead. You see now, empress, that I am entirely isolated, for the ally which you offer to me will do me no good ; I do not want it, and I have no other allies. I thought it necessary to arm, in view of the formidable armaments of France, and show our adversary that I am not afraid of him, but am prepared for every thing. I therefore put my army on the war footing, and showed Bonaparte that Austria is able to cope with him, and that money and well-disciplined armies are not wanting to her. But just now I shall not proceed any further, and, unless something important should occur, all this war-clamor and all importunities will make no impression on me. The important event to which I alluded would be Napoleon's defeat in Spain, whereby he would be compelled to keep his armies there. In that event, I should no longer be isolated, but Spain would be my ally, and I should probably declare war. But if matters should turn out otherwise, if fortune should favor Napoleon there as everywhere else, necessity alone will determine my course. I shall not attack, and thereby challenge fate of my own accord ; but I shall wait, sword in hand, for Napoleon to attack me. If he does, God and my good right will be on my side, and whatever may be the result of the struggle, people will be unable to say that I rashly plunged into war and broke the peace. If we succumb, it is the will of God and the Holy Virgin, and not, our fault. And now, empress," said the emperor, drawing a deep breath, "I have complied with your wishes and talked politics with you. I think it will be enough once for all, and you and you political friends will perceive that you cannot do any

thing with me, and that it will be best for you to let me entirely alone ; for I am so stubborn as not to allow others to
lead me, but pursue my own course. You have promised me,
empress, to be a faithful friend to me. I ask you now to give
me a proof of your friendship. Let us speak of something
else than politics ; that is all that I ask of your friendship."

"Well, then, let us drop the subject," said the empress,
with a deep sigh. "Your majesty will be kind enough to
permit me now to ask a favor of you ?"

"Ah, you speak as if there were anything that I could
refuse you," exclaimed the emperor, smiling.

Ludovica bowed slightly. "I pray you, therefore," she
said, "to be kind enough to accompany me to the concert
which is to be given at the university hall. Haydn's 'Creation' will be performed there, and I believe the old *maestro*
himself will be present to receive the homage of his admirers."

"H'm, h'm ! I am afraid there is something else behind
it," said the emperor, thoughtfully, "and the audience will
not content itself with merely offering homage to old Haydn.
But no matter, your majesty wishes to go to the concert, and
it will afford me pleasure to accompany my empress."

At this moment they heard a low rap at the door leading
from the emperor's cabinet into the conference-room, where
the officers of the private imperial chancery were working.

"Well, what is it ?" exclaimed the emperor. "Come
in !"

The emperor's private chamberlain slipped softly through
the half-opened door, and, on beholding the empress, he stood
still without uttering a word.

"Never mind, the empress will excuse you," said Francis.
"Just tell me what you have come in for."

"Your majesty," said the chamberlain, "the French ambassador, Count Andréossi, has just arrived, and requests your
majesty to grant him an audience. He says he wishes to
communicate information of great importance to you."

"Why did he not apply to my minister of foreign affairs ?"
asked the emperor, indignantly.

"Your majesty, the ambassador begs your pardon, but he

says the Emperor Napoleon gave him express orders to endeavor if possible to speak with your majesty."

"And he is already in the anteroom, and waits for an immediate audience ? "

" Yes, your majesty."

" Well, then, I will receive him," said the emperor, rising. " Conduct the ambassador to the small audience-room.— Well ? " asked the emperor, wonderingly, when the chamberlain did not withdraw. " You do not go ? Do you wish to tell me any thing else ? "

" I do, your majesty. A courier has just arrived from Paris with pressing dispatches from Count Metternich to your majesty."

"Ah, that changes the matter !" exclaimed the emperor. " Tell the ambassador that I can not receive him now, but that he is to come back in an hour, at eleven precisely, when I shall be ready to receive him. Tell the courier to come to me at once."

The chamberlain slipped noiselessly out of the door, and the emperor turned again to the empress

" Empress," he said, " do me the honor of permitting me to offer you my arm, and conduct you back to your rooms. You see I am a poor, tormented man, who is so overwhelmed with business that he cannot even chat an hour with his wife without being disturbed. Pity me a little, and prove it to me by permitting me henceforth to rest in your presence from the cares of business, and not talk politics."

" The wish of my lord and emperor shall be fulfilled," said the empress, mournfully, taking the arm which the emperor offered to her to conduct her back to her rooms.

Just as she crossed the threshold of the imperial cabinet, and stepped into the corridor, she heard the voice of the chamberlain, who announced : " The courier from Paris, Counsellor von Hudelist."

" All right, I shall be back directly ! " exclaimed the emporor, and he conducted the empress with a somewhat accelerated step through the corridor. In front of the door at its end he stood still and bowed to the empress with a pleasant smile.

" I have conducted you now to the frontier of your realm,"
said Francis ; " permit me, therefore, to return to mine.
Farewell ! We shall go to the concert to-night. Farewell ! "

Without waiting for the reply of the empress, he turned
and hastily re-entered his cabinet.

Ludovica entered her room and locked the door behind
her. " Closed forever ! " she said, with a sigh. " At least I
shall not try again to avail myself of this door, and shall not
expose myself again to the sneers of the emperor. I must,
then, bear this disgrace ; I must submit to being disdained and
repudiated by my husband ; I——But hush ! " the empress
interrupted herself, " this is no time for bewailing my personal fate, for the fate of all Austria is at stake at this juncture Highly important events must have occurred at Paris,
else Metternich would not have sent his confidant and assistant Hudelist, nor would Andréossi demand an audience in so
impetuous a manner. Perhaps this intelligence may at length
lead to a decision to-day, or we may at least contribute to such
a result. I will write to the Archduke John, and ask him to
see the emperor. Perhaps he will succeed better than I did
in persuading my husband to take a determined stand."

She hastened to her writing-desk, and penned that mysterious little note which she sent to the Archduke John in the
book which she pretended he had lent to her.

CHAPTER III.

THE COURIER AND THE AMBASSADOR.

THE emperor, in returning to his cabinet, like the empress,
carefully locked the door behind him. He then turned
hastily to the courier, who was standing near the opposite
door, and was just bowing most ceremoniously to his majesty.

" Hudelist, it is really you, then ? " asked the emperor.
" You left your post by the side of Metternich without obtain-

ing my permission to come to Vienna ? Could you not find
any other man to bring your dispatches ? I had commis-
sioned you to remain always by the side of Metternich, watch
him carefully, and inform me of what he was doing and
thinking."

"Your majesty, I have brought my report with me," said
Hudelist ; "and as for your majesty's order that I should
always remain by the side of Count Metternich, I have hardly violated it by coming to Vienna, for I believe the Count
will follow me in the course of a few days. Unless your majesty recalls him to Vienna, the Emperor Napoleon, I think,
will expel him from Paris."

"You do not say so !" exclaimed Francis, shrugging his
shoulders. "You think he will issue a manifesto against
Metternich, as he did against the Prussian minister Von
Stein ? Well, let me hear the news. What have you to tell
me ?"

"So many important things, your majesty, that the count
and myself deemed it expedient to report to your majesty
verbally, rather than send a dispatch which might give
you only an unsatisfactory idea of what has occurred.
Hence I came post-haste to Vienna, and arrived here only a
quarter of an hour since ; I pray your majesty therefore to
pardon me for appearing before you in my travelling-
dress."

"Sit down, you must be tired," said the emperor, good-na-
turedly, seating himself in an arm-chair, and pointing to the
opposite chair. "Now tell me all !"

"Your majesty," said Hudelist, mysteriously, while a
strange expression of mischievous joy overspread his ugly,
pale face, "the Emperor Napoleon has returned from Spain to
France."

The Emperor Francis gave a start and frowned. "Why ?"
he asked.

"Because he intends to declare war against Austria," said
Hudelist, whose face brightened more and more. "Because
Napoleon is distrustful of us, and convinced that Austria is
intent on attacking him. Besides, he felt no longer at ease in
Spain, and all sorts of conspiracies had been entered into in

Paris, whereby his return might have been rendered impossible if he had hesitated any longer."

"Who were the conspirators?"

"Talleyrand and Fouché, the dear friends and obedient
servants of the Emperor Napoleon. He knows full well what
their friendship and devotedness amount to. Hence he had
the two gentlemen well watched, and it seems his spies sent
him correct reports, for, after returning from Spain, he rebuked them unmercifully ; he told them, with the rage of
a true Corsican, and regardless of etiquette, what miserable
fellows they were, and how high he stood above them."

"And yet he would like so much to be an emperor in strict
accordance with court etiquette," said the emperor, laughing.
"He is anxious to have such a court about him as Louis XIV.
had. But the lawyer's son always reappears in the emperor,
and, if it please God, He will one day deprive him of all his
power and splendor."

"And, if it please God, your majesty will be His instrument in putting an end to Napoleon's power and splendor," cried Hudelist, with a smile which distorted his face
strangely, and caused two rows of large yellow teeth to appear
between the pale lips of his enormous mouth. "It is true
he stands firm as yet, and rebukes his ministers as Nero did
his freedmen. Talleyrand was still thunderstruck at what the
emperor had told him, when he had an interview with Count
Metternich and myself in Fouché's green-house. To be sure,
the phrases which he repeated to us were well calculated to
make even the blood of a patient minister boil. Napoleon
sent for the two ministers immediately after his arrival ; when
they came to him, he let them stand at the door of his cabinet
like humble suppliants, and, running up and down before
them, and casting fiery glances of anger upon them, he up-
braided them with their conduct, and told them he was aware
of all their intrigues, and knew that they were conspiring
with Austria, Spain, and, through Spain, with England. Then
he suddenly stood still in front of them, his hands folded on
his back, and his glances would have crushed the two ministers if they had not had such a thick skin 'You are impudent
enough to conspire against me !' he shouted, in a thundering

voice. ' To whom are you indebted for every thing—for your honors, rank, and wealth ? To me alone ! How can you preserve them ? By me alone ! Look backward, examine your past. If the Bourbons had reascended the throne, both of you would have been hanged as regicides and traitors. And you plot against me ? You must be as stupid as you are ungrateful, if you believe that anybody else could promote your interest as well as I have done. Had another revolution broken out, on whatever side you might have placed yourselves, you would certainly have been the first to be crushed by it.' " *

"That is very plain talk, indeed," said Francis, laughing. "But Talleyrand and Fouché have sound stomachs ; they will digest it, and not get congestions in consequence of it provided the emperor does not punish them in a different manner."

" For the time being, he only punished Talleyrand, whom he deprived of the position and salary of lord chamberlain. Fouché remained police minister, but both are closely watched by Napoleon's secret police. Nevertheless, they succeeded in holding a few unobserved interviews with us. Count Metternich learned also from another very well-informed quarter, many accurate details regarding the plans and intentions of the Emperor Napoleon."

"What do you mean ? What well-informed quarter do you refer to ? " asked the emperor.

"Your majesty," said Hudelist, with a significant grin, "Count Metternich is a very fine-looking man ; now, Queen Caroline of Naples, Murat's wife, and Napoleon's favorite sister, is by no means insensible to manly beauty, and she accepted with evident satisfaction the homage which the count offered to her. For the rest, Napoleon winked at and encouraged this flirtation ; for, previous to his departure for Spain, he said to his sister loud enough to be overheard by some of our friends, ' *Amusez-nous ce niais, Monsieur de Metternich. Nous en avons besoin à present !* ' " † Madame Caroline

---

* Napoleon's own words.—See Schlosser, " History of the Eighteenth Century," vol. viii., p. 488.

† Hormayr, " The Emperor Francis and Metternich, a Fragment, p. 55.

Murat told Count Metternich, for instance, that it is the Kings
of Bavaria and Würtemburg that keep their spies for Napoleon here in Vienna, and that they urged Napoleon vehemently
to return from Spain in order to declare war against Austria.
And Napoleon is determined to comply with their wishes.
He travelled with extraordinary expedition from Madrid to
Paris, stopping only at Valladolid, where he shut himself up
for two days with Maret, his minister of foreign affairs, and
dispatched eighty-four messages in different directions, with
orders to concentrate his forces in Germany, and call out the
full contingents of the Rhenish Confederacy. His own troops
and these German Contingents are to form an army to which
he intends to give the name of 'the German Army of the Emperor Napoleon.' Although Count Metternich was aware of
all this, he hastened to attend the great reception which took
place at the Tuileries after Napoleon's return, in order to assure him again of the friendly dispositions of the imperial
court of Austria. But Napoleon gave him no time for that.
He came to meet him with a furious gesture, and shouted to
him in a thundering voice : 'Well, M. de Metternich ! here is
fine news from Vienna. What does all this mean ? Have
they been stung by scorpions ? Who threatens you ? What
would you be at ? Do you intend again to disturb the peace of
the world and plunge Europe into numberless calamities ? As
long as I had my army in Germany, you conceived no disquie-
tude for your existence ; but the moment it is transferred to
Spain, you consider yourselves endangered ! What can be the
end of these things ? What, but that I must arm as you arm,
for at length I am seriously menaced ; I am rightly punished
for my former caution." *

"What an impudent fellow !" murmured the Emperor
Francis to himself. "And Metternich ? What did he reply ? "

"Nothing at all, your majesty. He withdrew, returned
immediately to the legation, and I set out that very night to
convey this intelligence to your majesty. Your majesty, we
can no longer doubt that Napoleon has made up his mind to
wage war against Austria. His exasperation has risen to the

* Napoleon's own words.—See Schlosser, vol. vii., p. 490.

highest pitch, and the events in Spain have still more inflamed his rage and vindictiveness."

"Then he is unsuccessful in Spain ?" asked the emperor,
whose eyes brightened.

"Spain is still bidding him defiance, and fighting with the
enthusiasm of an heroic people who will suffer death rather
than be subjugated by a tyrant. She will never accept King
Joseph, whom Napoleon forced upon her ; and as they see
themselves deserted and given up by their royal family, the
Spanish patriots turn their eyes toward Austria, and are ready
to proclaim one of your majesty's brothers king of Spain, if
your majesty would send him to them with an auxiliary
army."

"That would be a nice thing !" cried the emperor, angrily.
"Not another word about it! If my brothers should hear it,
their heads would be immediately on fire, for they are very ambitious; hence, it is much better that they should not learn
anything of these *châteaux en Espagne.* Tell me rather how
it looks in France. Are the French still satisfied with their
emperor by the grace of the people !"

"They are not, your majesty. Let me tell you that not only
Napoleon's own officers, his marshals and ministers, are dissatisfied with him; but the whole people, those who possess
money as well as those who own no other property than their
lives, are murmuring against the emperor. He robs the mon-
eyed men of their property by heavy taxes and duties, and
those who have nothing but their lives he threatens with death
by forcing muskets into their hands, and compelling them to do
military service. Another conscription has been ordered, and
as the population of France is decreasing, youths from sixteen
to eighteen years old have to be enrolled. France is tired of
these everlasting wars, and she curses Napoleon's insatiable
bloodthirstiness no longer in secret only, but loud enough to
be heard by the emperor from time to time."

"And the army ?"

"The army is a part of France, and feels like the rest of the
French people. The marshals are quarrelling among themselves, and some of them hate Napoleon, who never gives them
time to repose on their laurels and enjoy the riches which they

have obtained during their campaigns. The army is a perfect hotbed of conspiracies and secret societies, some of which are in favor of the restoration of the republic, while others advocate the restoration of the Bourbons. Napoleon, who is served well enough at least by his spies, is aware of all these things. He is afraid of the discontent and disobedience of his marshals and generals, conspiracies in the army, the treachery of his ministers, and the murmurs of his people; and he fears, besides, that the fanaticism of the Spaniards may dim his military glory; hence, he feels the necessity of arousing the enthusiasm of his people by fresh battles, of silencing the malcontents by new victories, and of reviving the heroic spirit of his army. He hopes to gain these victories in a war between his German army and the Austrian forces. He is, therefore, firmly resolved to wage war, and the only question now is, whether your majesty will anticipate him, or await a declaration of war on his part. This is about all I have to communicate to your majesty; the vouchers and other papers I shall have the honor to deposit at the imperial chancery."

The emperor made no reply, but gazed into vacancy, deeply absorbed in his reflections. Hudelist fixed his small sparkling eyes on the bent form of the emperor; and as he contemplated his care-worn, gloomy face, his flabby features, his protruding under-lip, his narrow forehead, and his whole emaciated and fragile form, an expression of scorn overspread the face of the counsellor; and his large mouth and flashing eyes seemed to say, "You are the emperor, but I do not envy you, for I am more than you are; I am a man who knows what he wants."

At this moment the clock commenced striking slowly, and its shrill notes aroused the emperor from his contemplation.

"Eleven o'clock," he said, rising from his chair, "the hour when I am to give an audience to the French ambassador. Hudelist, go to the chancery and wait there until I call you. You will not return to Paris anyhow, but resume your former position in the chancery of state. I am glad that you have returned, for I consider you a faithful, able, and reliable man, with whom I have good reason to be content, and who, I hope, will not betray my confidence. I know, Hudelist, you are ambitious, and would like to obtain a distinguished position.

Well, serve me—do you hear?—serve none but me honestly and faithfully; watch everything and watch closely; never think of obtaining the friendship and good graces of others, nor seeking for any other protectors, save me; and I shall always be favorably disposed toward you, and see to it that the cravings of your ambition are satisfied. Go then, as I said before, to the chancery of state; and on hearing me re-enter the room, step in again. There are many other things which I wish to tell you."

"I see through him," said Hudelist, looking with a smile after the emperor, who closed the door of the cabinet behind him, to repair to the small reception-room; "yes, I see through the emperor. He is glad of my return, for I am a good spy for him in regard to the doings of his brothers, of whom he is jealous, and whom he hates with all his heart. If I succeed one day in communicating to him things capable of rendering the archdukes suspicious to him, or even convicting them of a wrong committed against him, the emperor will reward and promote me, and, as he says, satisfy the cravings of my ambition. Well, well, we shall see. If you watch a man very closely and are really intent on spying out something suspicious in his conduct, you will in the end surely find some little hook or other by which you may hold him, and which you may gradually hammer out and extend until it becomes large enough to hang the whole man on it. In the first place, I shall pay particular attention to the Archduke John, for his brother is particularly jealous of and angry with him. Ah, if I could discovery such a little hook by which to hold him, the emperor would reward my zeal with money, honors, and orders, and he would henceforward repose the most implicit confidence in my fidelity. Well, I shall think of it; the idea is a good one, and worthy of being matured. I shall form a scheme to make the good and munificent Archduke John the ladder by which I shall rise. I must conquer, and if I can do it only by pulling down others, it is the duty of self-preservation for me not to shrink from the task. I will now go to the chancery and wait there for the emperor's return. Ah, how his old limbs trembled when he heard of Napoleon's return. How hard and unpleasant it was for him to swallow the bad

news which I communicated to him! There is no more interesting spectacle than that presented by a human face passing
through all the various stages of excitement, and involuntarily
performing in its features the five acts of a tragedy. And all
the better when this human face is that of an emperor. During my whole journey from Paris to Vienna I was enjoying,
by anticipation, the moment when I should deliver this Pan-
dora's box to the emperor. He is opposed to war, and must
nevertheless wage it; that is the best part of the joke. Aha!
it is a fine sight to behold the gods of this earth a prey to such
human embarrassments! I felt like bursting into loud laughter at the woe-begone appearance of the emperor. But hush,
hush! I will go to the chancery until he returns."

In the meantime the emperor had repaired to the small
reception-room, where Count Andréossi, the French ambassador, was already waiting for him.

Francis responded to the respectful greeting of the ambassador by a scarcely perceptible nod, and strode, with head
erect, into the middle of the room. There he stood still, and
casting a stern and almost defiant glance on the ambassador,
he said in a cold, dignified tone: "You requested an audience
of me in a very unusual manner. I granted it to prove to
you my desire to remain at peace with France. Now speak;
What has the ambassador of the Emperor of the French to
say to the Emperor of Austria?"

"Your majesty, I have to present to you, in the first place,
the respects of my master, who has returned from Spain to
Paris."

Francis nodded his head slowly. "What next?" he asked.

"Next, my sovereign has charged me with a very difficult
commission, for the execution of which I must first, and above
all things, beg your majesty's pardon."

"You are your master's servant, and it is your duty to obey
him," said the emperor, dryly. "Say, therefore, what he
ordered you to tell me."

"Well, then, as your majesty has granted me permission,
I will say that my master, the Emperor of the French, has
taken deep umbrage at the hostile course which Austria has of
late pursued toward him."

"And what is it that your emperor complains of ?" asked the emperor, with perfect composure.

"In the first place, the Emperor Napoleon has taken deep umbrage at Austria's still hesitating to recognize King Joseph as King of Spain, and to send a minister plenipotentiary to his court."

"I did not know where to send my ambassador, and where he would find M. Joseph Bonaparte, King of Spain, for the time being—whether at Madrid or at Saragossa; in the camp, on the field of battle, or in flight. Hence I did not send an ambassador to his court. So soon as the Spanish nation is able to inform me where I may look for the king it has elected and recognized, I shall immediately dispatch a minister plenipotentiary to this court. State that to your monarch."

"Next, his majesty the Emperor Napoleon complains bitterly that Austria, instead of being intent on maintaining friendly relations with France, has left nothing undone to reconcile the enemies of France who were at war with each other, and to restore peace between them; and that Austria, by her incessant efforts, has really succeeded now in bringing about a treaty of peace between Turkey and England. Now, my master the emperor must look upon this as a hostile act on the part of Austria against France; for to reconcile England with Turkey is equivalent to setting France at variance with Turkey, or at least neutralizing entirely her influence over the Sublime Porte."

"Turkey is my immediate neighbor, and it is highly important to Austria that there should be no war-troubles and disturbances on all her frontiers. Every independent state should be at liberty to pursue its own policy; and while this policy does not assume a hostile attitude toward other independent states, no one can take umbrage at it. Are you through with your grievances ?"

"No, your majesty," said Andréossi, almost mournfully. "The worst and most unpleasant part remains to be told; but, as your majesty was gracious enough to say, I must obey the orders of my master, and it is his will that I shall now communicate to your majesty the emperor's views in his own words. It has given great offence to the Emperor Napoleon that Austria should place herself in a posture of open hostility against France, when France has given her so many proofs of her forbearance, and has hitherto always spared Austria, notwithstanding the numerous acts of duplicity and evident hostility of the Austrian court. The Emperor Napoleon informs your majesty that he is well aware of the ambitious schemes of Austria, but that he thinks your majesty is not strong enough to carry them into effect. He requests your majesty never to forget the magnanimity which the Emperor Napoleon manifested toward you after the battle of Austerlitz. The Emperor Napoleon has instructed me to remind you of the fact, well known to you, that you can confide in his generosity, and that he is firmly resolved to observe the treaties. Naples, Prussia, and Spain, would stand erect, yet, if their rulers had relied on their own sagacity, and not listened to the fatal advice of their ministers, or even of courtiers, women, and ambitious young princes. His majesty beseeches the Emperor of Austria not to listen to such insidious advice, nor to yield to the wishes of the war-party, which is intent only on gratifying its passionate ambition, and whose eyes refuse to see that it is driving Austria toward the brink of an abyss where she must perish, as did Prussia, Naples, and Spain."[*]

"It is very kind in his majesty the Emperor Napoleon to give me such friendly advice," said the Emperor Francis, smiling. "But I beg his majesty to believe that, in accordance with his wishes, I rely only on my own individual sagacity; that I am influenced by no party, no person, but am accustomed to direct myself the affairs of my country and the administration of my empire, and not to listen to any insinuations, from whatever quarter they may come. I request you to repeat these words to his majesty the Emperor Napoleon, with the same accuracy with which you communicated his message to me. And now, Count Andréossi, I believe you have communicated to me all that your master instructed you to say to me."

"Pardon me, your majesty, I am instructed last to demand in the emperor's name an explanation as to the meaning of the formidable armaments of Austria, the organization of the

* Hormayr, " Allgemeine Geschichte," vol. iii., p. 205.

militia, and the arming of the fortresses on the frontiers, and to inquire against whom these measures are directed. The emperor implores your majesty to put a stop to these useless and hurtful demonstrations, and orders me expressly to state that, if Austria does not stop her armaments and adopt measures of an opposite character, war will be inevitable." *

"In that case, Mr. Ambassador of the Emperor Napoleon, war *is* inevitable," cried Francis, who now dropped the mask of cold indifference, and allowed his face to betray the agitation and rage filling his bosom, by his quivering features, flashing eyes, and clouded brow. "I have calmly listened to you," he added, raising his voice; "I have received with silent composure all the arrogant phrases which you have ventured to utter here in the name of your emperor. I look on them as one of the famous proud bulletins for which your emperor is noted, and to whose overbearing and grandiloquent language all Europe is accustomed. But it is well known too that these bulletins are not exactly models of veracity, but sometimes the very reverse of it. An instance of the latter is your emperor's assertion that he observes the treaties, and that he gave me proofs of his magnanimity after the battle of Austerlitz. No, the emperor did no such thing; he made me, on the contrary, feel the full weight of his momentary superiority. He was my enemy, and treated me as an enemy, without magnanimity, which, for the rest, I did not claim at the time. But he has proved to me, too, that he does not observe the most sacred treaties. He violated every section of the peace of Presburg; he did not respect the frontiers as stipulated in that treaty; he forced me, in direct violation of the treaties, to allow him the permanent use of certain military roads within the boundaries of my empire; he hurled from their thrones dynasties which were related to me, and whose existence I had guaranteed; he deprived, in violation of the law of nations, the beloved and universally respected head of Christendom of his throne, and subjected him to a most disgraceful imprisonment; he exerted on all seas the most arbitrary pressure on the Austrian flag. And now, after all this has happened, after Austria has endured

* Napoleon's own words.—See " Lebensbilder," vol. ii., and Hormayr, "All-gemeine Geschichte," vol. iii.

all these wrongs so long and silently, the Emperor Napoleon undertakes even to meddle with the internal administration of my empire, and forbids me what he, ever since his accession, has incessantly done, to wit: to mobilize my army, levy conscripts for the troops of the line and the reserves, and arm the fortresses. He asks me to put a stop to my armaments; else, he says, war will be inevitable. Well, Mr. Ambassador, I do not care if the Emperor Napoleon looks at the matter in that light, and I shall not endeavor to prevent him from so doing, for I shall not stop, but continue my preparations. I called out the militia, just as the Emperor of the French constantly calls new levies of conscripts into immediate activity; and if war should be inevitable in consequence thereof, I shall bear what is inevitable with firmness and composure."

"Your majesty, is this your irrevocable resolution?" asked Andréossi. "Is this the answer that I am to send to my master, the Emperor Napoleon?"

"I think it will be better for you to convey this answer in person to your emperor," said Francis, calmly. "As no one has witnessed our interview, only you yourself can repeat my words with perfect accuracy; and it is therefore best for you to set out this very day for Paris."

"That is to say, your majesty gives me my passports, and war will immediately break out between France and Austria!" sighed Andréossi. "Your majesty should graciously consider—"

"I have considered every thing," interrupted Francis, vehemently, "and I request you not to speak to me again in the style of your French bulletins. I will hear the bulletins of the Emperor Napoleon on the field of battle rather than in my cabinet. Set out, therefore, for Paris, Mr. Ambassador, and repeat to the emperor what I have said to you."

"I will comply with your majesty's orders," said Andréossi, with a sigh; "I will set out, but I shall leave the members of my legation here as yet, for I do not yet give up the hope that it may be possible for the two courts to avoid a declaration of war, and to spare such a calamity to two countries that have such good reasons to love each other."

"Let us quietly await the course of events," replied the

emperor. "Farewell, Count Andréossi. If you will accept
my advice, you will set out this very day; for so soon as my
dear Viennese learn that war is to break out in earnest, they
will probably give vent to their enthusiasm in the most tumultuous and rapturous demonstrations, and I suppose it
would be disagreeable to you to witness them. Farewell,
sir!"

He waved his hand toward the ambassador, bent his head ·
slowly and haughtily, and left the reception-room without
vouchsafing another glance to Count Andréossi.

"Now my brothers will be in ecstasies," said the emperor
to himself, slowly walking up and down, his hands folded on
his back, in the sitting-room adjoining the reception-room.
"They will be angry, though, because I did not consult them,
and decided the whole affair without listening to their wisdom."

"Your majesty," said a footman, who entered the room
at this moment, "their imperial highnesses, the Archdukes
Charles and John, request an audience of your majesty."

"They are welcome," said the emperor, whose features
were lit up by a faint smile. "Show my brothers in."

CHAPTER IV.

THE EMPEROR AND HIS BROTHERS.

A FEW minutes afterward the two archdukes entered the
room of the emperor, who slowly went some steps to meet
them, and greeted them with a grave, cold glance.

"Why, this is a rare spectacle," said Francis, sneeringly,
"to see my brothers side by side in such beautiful harmony.
In truth, it was only wanting to me that even you two should
be of the same opinion, and come to me for the purpose of
inviting me, as Schiller says, to be the third in your league."

"Your majesty would always be the first in this league,"
said the Archduke John, in his clear, ringing voice; "my
brother would be the second, and I only the third."

"See, see, my brother is very modest and humble to-day,"
said Francis, smiling. "This means doubtless that you have
come to ask a favor of me, and that, by your kindness and
devotedness, you wish to induce me to comply with your request, as a dog is decoyed with cakes and sweets by the thief
who intends to steal something from the dog's master."

"Oh, your majesty, we do not intend to steal any thing
from our master!" exclaimed John, laughing. "But there is
really an attack to be made on our master's property; only he
who intends to make it does not decoy us with cakes and
sweets, but assails us with the sword and coarse invectives."

"It was very shrewd in you to mention at once the subject
on which you wished to speak with me," said the emperor,
with a slight sneer. "But permit me first to say a word to my
brother Charles there, and bid welcome to his imperial highness, the illustrious captain, the generalissimo of our army,
the hope and consolation of Austria."

"Your majesty wishes to mock me," said the Archduke
Charles, in a mournful voice.

"I repeat only what I read every day in the newspapers,
and what the dear Viennese are singing and shouting in every
street!" exclaimed the emperor. "Yes, yes, my dear brother,
you must consent to be the hope and consolation of Austria,
and to be praised as the august and invincible hero of our immediate future."

So saying, the emperor gazed with a long and searching
look at his brother's form, and a scornful expression overspread his features.

Indeed, the epithets which the emperor had applied to his
brother corresponded but little to the appearance of the Archduke Charles. His small, bent form, with its weak, shrivelled
limbs, was not the form of a hero ; his pale, wan face, with
the hollow cheeks ; the dim eyes deeply imbedded in their
sockets, and the clouded brow, on which thin tufts of hair
hung down, was not the face of a bold captain, confident of
achieving brilliant triumphs by his heroic deeds, and deserv-
ing of the name of the hope and consolation of Austria. But
the Austrians did call him by that name, and the glory of his
military achievements, which filled not only Austria but the

whole of Germany, caused them really to build their hopes on the Archduke Charles, despite his very feeble health. The Emperor Francis was aware of this; he knew that the Archdukes Charles and John were by far more popular than he was; hence he was jealous of and angry with them—nay, he almost hated them.

"You look very pale and sick to-day, my dear Archduke Charles," said the emperor, after a pause, during which he had contemplated the archduke with a searching expression.

"I am very feeble and unwell, your majesty," sighed Charles; "and but for the special request of my brother, the Archduke John, I should not have dared to come here this morning. However, I am afraid that I can do but little to comply with his wishes, and that my brother John will soon think it would have been better for him not to ask me to accompany him to your majesty."

"Ah, then, you are after all not so harmonious as I thought when I saw you entering here together!" exclaimed the emperor, laughing. "There are still differences of opinion, then, between the two pillars of my throne, and were I to lean on one, the other would totter and give way. Well, what do you want? What brought you here?"

"Your majesty, only the intense desire to dedicate our services to Austria and our emperor!" exclaimed John, enthusiastically. "We wished to implore your majesty to utter at length the word that will deliver Austria and all Germany. Your majesty, this hesitation and silence rests like a nightmare on every heart and every bosom; all eyes are fixed hopefully on your majesty. Oh, my lord and emperor, one word from your lips, and this nightmare will disappear; all hearts will rejoice in blissful ecstasy, and every bosom will expand and breathe more freely when your majesty shall utter this word: 'War! war!' We hold the sword in our hands; let the will of my august emperor give us the right now to draw the sword against him who, for years past, has swept like a destructive hurricane through all Germany, all Europe, and who tramples alike on princes and peoples, on liberty and law. Your majesty, in the name of your people, in the name of all German patriots, I bend my knees here be-

fore my lord and emperor, and thus, kneeling and full of reverence, I implore your majesty to let the hour of deliverance
strike at length ; let us, with joyful courage, expel the enemy
who has already so long been threatening our frontiers with
defiant arrogance : let us take the field against the impudent
usurper, and wrest from him the laurels which he gained at
Austerlitz, and of which he is so proud. Your majesty, your
people are filled with warlike ardor ; your faithful Tyrolese
are waiting only for a signal to break their chains and rise
for their beloved emperor. Your Italian provinces are longing for the day when war shall break out, in order to avenge
themselves on the tyrant who promised them liberty and
brought them only slavery. The hour of retribution has
come for Napoleon ; may your majesty consult our best interests by saying that we are to profit by this hour, and that war,
a mortal struggle, is to begin now against the Emperor of the
French ! "

And, still bending his knees before the emperor, John
looked up to him with longing, beseeching eyes.

Francis looked down on him with a gloomy air, and the
noble and enthusiastic face of his brother, who was ten years
younger, and much stronger and better-looking, made a disagreeable impression on him.

"Rise, brother," he said, coldly ; "your knees must ache,
and I, for my part, do not like such theatrical scenes at all,
and such fine phrases make but little impression on my cold
and prosy heart. I am accustomed to follow always my convictions, and when I advance a step, I must be sure not to fall
into an abyss which some poetical hero may perhaps have
merely covered for me with his flowery phrases. That I am
aware of the dangers threatening us on the part of France I
have proved by putting the army on the war footing, by in-
trusting you, Archduke John, with organizing the militia and
the reserves in accordance with the plan you drew up for that
purpose ; and by placing you, Archduke Charles, at the head
of my army and appointing you generalissimo."

"An honor, your majesty, which I accepted with reverent
gratitude, although it almost crushes me at the present time,"
said the Archduke Charles, with a sigh. "Permit me now,

your majesty, to open my heart to you, and lay my innermost
thoughts at your feet. To do so, I accompanied my brother
John to you. He said he would implore your majesty once
more to postpone the declaration of war no longer, but utter
at length the decisive word. I implored him not to do so,
and not to force us to engage prematurely in a war that could
not but bring the greatest calamities on Austria. But my dear
brother would not listen to my remonstrances and prayers ;
he called me a secret friend and admirer of Napoleon ; he demanded that I should at least speak out freely and openly in
your majesty's presence, and refute him if I could, or yield to
him if my arguments should prove untenable. Your majesty,
I have therefore complied with the wishes of my brother, the
Archduke John ; I have come to you, but only to say to my
lord and emperor : Your majesty, I implore you, in the name
of your people and your throne, do not yet unsheath the
sword ! Wait until our army is ready for the contest, and
until our armaments are completed. Do not plunge rashly into war, lest victory escape us. A great deal remains
to be done yet before we can say that our armaments are
completed ; and only after being fully prepared can we dare
to take the field against the Emperor Napoleon and his hitherto victorious legions."

"Ah, do you hear our Fabius Cunctator, brother John,
the Lion-hearted !" exclaimed the emperor, sarcastically.
" Which of you is right, and whose wise advice shall I follow
now—I, the poor emperor, who is not strong and sagacious
enough to be his own adviser and advance a step without his
brothers ? John, the learned soldier, beseeches me to declare
war, and Charles, the intrepid hero, implores me not to do so.
What am I, the poor emperor, who cannot advise himself, and
who receives too much advice from others, to do under such
circumstances ? Whose will must I submit to ?"

" Your majesty," cried John, in dismay, " it is we that must
submit ; it is your will on which depends the decision. I implore your majesty to declare war, because I deem it necessary ;
but, if your majesty should take a different resolution, I shall
submit silently and obediently."

"And I," said Charles, "requested you to postpone the

declaration of war, because I do not believe that we are sufficiently prepared for the contest ; but, like my brother, I shall
submit silently if your majesty should take a different resolution."

"Indeed, will you do so, archdukes ?" asked the emperor,
in a scornful tone. "Will you be mindful of your duties as
subjects, and, instead of giving me unnecessary advice, obey
me silently ?"

The two archdukes bowed to indicate their submissiveness.
The emperor advanced a few steps, and proudly raising his
head, he looked at his two brothers with a stern and imperious
expression.

"Let me tell you, then, archdukes, what I, your lord and
emperor, have resolved," said Francis, sternly. "I have resolved to declare war !"

Two loud cries resounded with one accord ; a cry of joy
burst from John's lips, a cry of dismay from those of Charles.
Pale, reeling like a drunken man, the generalissimo approached the emperor and held out his hands to him with a
beseeching expression.

"Your majesty," he said, "you have resolved to declare
war, but you do not mean to say that it is to commence immediately ?"

"That is what I mean to say," replied the emperor, sarcastically.

The Archduke Charles turned still paler than before ; a
strange tremor passed through his frame, his head dropped on
his bosom, and a deep groan issued from his breast.

The Archduke John, forgetful of his quarrel with his
brother Charles, at the sight of the latter's profound grief,
hastened to him, and tenderly grasped both his hands.

"Brother," he asked, anxiously, "what is the matter ? Are
you unwell ?"

"I am," said Charles, wiping from his forehead the large
drops of sweat standing on it. "I am unwell, but I must say
a few additional words to the emperor. I must disclose to
him a melancholy secret of which I heard only an hour ago.
—Your majesty, I implore you once more, postpone the war
as long as possible ; for—hear my terrible secret—we have

been infamously defrauded by Commissary-General von Fass-bender."

"Your intimate friend?" interposed the emperor, with a scornful laugh.

"Yes, my intimate friend," exclaimed the archduke, in a loud, shrill voice; "he deceived me most shamefully. All the army contracts had been intrusted to him, and he assured me he had filled them in the most conscientious manner. I believed him, and it is only now that I find out that he has shamefully deceived me and his emperor. All his bills for the supplies which he pretended to have furnished are in my hands, but the troops did not get the supplies. The scoundrel sent only sour flour, bad linen, and moth-eaten uniform cloth to the regiments, and yet he drew enormous sums of money for the full amount of his contracts."

"We shall compel the thief to disgorge his ill-gotten gains," cried the emperor.

"No, your majesty," said Charles, with a groan; and lean-ing more firmly on his brother's arm, in order not to sink to the floor, he added: "no, your majesty, the criminal is be-yond the reach of your power. He escaped from human justice by committing suicide an hour ago. The criminal has fled from his judges, but his crimes remain, and our army suffers in consequence of them. Now your majesty knows all, you will take back your word, and say no longer that you will declare war. You will be gracious enough to give me time to repair the injury resulting from the crimes of the commissary-general, and to provide the army with all that is unfortunately wanting to it as yet."

"No," cried the emperor vehemently, "I will not! I will not take back my word, and I had already made up my mind before you, my brothers, entered here to assist me so generous-ly by your wisdom. War will be declared immediately; my resolution is irrevocable. I have already informed the French ambassador of it, and ordered him to leave Vienna this very day. Your warnings come just as much too late as did John's entreaties. I did what I myself deemed best; and I deemed it best to declare war against Bonaparte, in reply to his in-tolerable arrogance. Every thing is fixed and settled; war

will commence without delay : and you, Archduke Charles,
are the generalissimo of my army."

The Archduke Charles made no reply ; he uttered a painful groan and sank to the floor by John's side. All his limbs
trembled and quivered ; his pale face became distorted, he
clinched his fists, and his eyes were glassy as though he were
dying.

" He has one of his fits," said the emperor calmly, looking
down on his brother.   " Call his servants and his doctor,
Archduke John, that they may remove the generalissimo to
another room and administer medicine to him."

John rushed to the door, and soon the servants and the
physician, who always accompanied the Archduke Charles,
hastened into the room. They lifted with practised hands the
archduke, who was still writhing in convulsions, and carried
him tenderly out of the room.

John, who, with touching solicitude, had remained near
the sufferer, would have accompanied him ; but a word from
the emperor called him back.

" Stay a moment, archduke," said Francis ; " the Archduke
Charles only has his fits, and his servants will take care of
him. I have yet to speak a few words with you. This will
be a formidable war, brother, and we must see to it that it
breaks out at the same time in all quarters of our empire, and
that the people rise with one accord and take up arms. We
have made our preparations everywhere, and our emissaries
have done their duty ; they have everywhere enlisted friends
of our cause, and established committees which have made
all necessary dispositions for the defence of the country. You
yourself sent your emissary, Baron von Hormayr, to your
beloved Tyrol ; if I am correctly informed, he has already
returned to Vienna."

" Your majesty, he arrived here this morning," said John,
looking at his brother with an air of surprise and even terror.

This did not escape the emperor, and a smile of satisfaction
lit up his face.

" You see, my agents serve me very well, and I am aware
of all that is going on," said Francis, gravely. " I know, too,

that Baron von Hormayr has returned to Vienna not alone, but accompanied by some good friends. I believe you did not come here to give me your advice, but to beg permission to receive your Tyrolese friends at your palace to-night."

"What !" asked John, surprised ; "your majesty is aware of this, too ? "

"I have told you already that my agents serve me very well. Let this be a warning to you not to do or undertake any thing that you would like to conceal from me. I know that Andreas Hofer is here, to concert with you some sort of plan for the insurrection of the Tyrol. Under the present circumstances I permit you to do so, for it is really important that the German and Italian Tyrol should rise ; and as we are going to have war, we will strive to recover our Tyrol. But we must proceed cautiously, and the world must not find out that we instigated the Tyrolese to rise in arms. That would be setting a bad example to the other nations of our empire. We may at times profit by popular insurrections, but must beware of letting the world know that we ourselves brought them about. Hence, I do not want to know any thing of your Tyrolese, and shall not grant them an audience. But I permit you to do so, and you may tell these brave Tyrolese, too, that I should be glad if they would become again my dear subjects."

"Your majesty," exclaimed John, joyously, "these words of their emperor will be the signal for them to rise as one man, take their rifles, and expel the Evil One, that is to say, the Bavarians."

"I shall be glad to see the Tyrolese do so, and, moreover, do it in time," said the emperor, nodding his head. "Repeat my words to Andreas Hofer, brother John, and pledge him my word that, if we recover the Tyrol this time, we shall never give it up again. But Andreas Hofer must behave with great prudence, and not show himself to the public here, but keep in the background, that the police may wink at his presence in Vienna, and act as though they did not see him and his friends. And now, brother, farewell, and inquire if the generalissimo has recovered from his fit. It would be bad, indeed, if these fits should befall him once in the midst of a bat-

tle. Well, let us hope for the best for us all, and especially
for the Tyrol. You have now a great task before you, John,
for you will receive a command ; you shall assist the Tyrolese
in shaking off the foreign yoke."

"Oh, my lord and emperor," exclaimed John, with a radiant face and fiery glance, "how kind and gracious you are
to-day ! It is the heart of a brother that speaks out of your
mouth—of a brother who wishes to make me happy, and
knows how to do so. Yes, send me with a corps to the assistance of the Tyrolese ; let me bring freedom and salvation to
my beloved mountaineers. That is a task which fills me with
boundless ecstasy, and for which I shall always be grateful
and devoted to you, brother."

"Be devoted to your emperor, archduke," said Francis,
smiling ; "the brothers will get along well enough ; they
have nothing to do with politics and public affairs. Farewell, John. But, remember, we shall meet again to-day, for
I shall summon the ministers and generals to a consultation,
and you will, of course, be present. Once more, then, farewell !"

He nodded repeatedly to the archduke and left the room
with unusual quickness. The emperor walked hastily and
with a gloomy face through the adjoining room, and entered
his cabinet, the door of which he closed rather noisily.

"I am to let him bring freedom and salvation to his beloved mountaineers," murmured Francis to himself—"to *his*
mountaineers ! I believe he would be glad if they really were
his, and if he could become King of the Tyrol. Well, we
shall see. I have lulled his suspicion by permitting him to
hold intercourse with the Tyrolese, and concert plans with
them. We shall see how far my brother will go, and what his
gratitude and devotion will amount to. It is a troublesome
burden for me to have such dangerously ambitious and re-
nowned brothers, against whom I must be constantly on my
guard. I would I could pick them off as quickly as I remove
the flies from this wall."

So saying, he took from the table the fly-flap which had always to lie on it in readiness, and entered upon his favorite
amusement, the pursuit of the flies on the wall and furniture,

which his servants took good care not to drive from the emperor's cabinet, because Francis would never have pardoned them for spoiling his sport.

Walking along the walls with a rapid step, the emperor commenced killing the flies.

" Ha ! " he exclaimed, striking a fly, " ha ! brother Charles, this stroke is intended for you. Really, there lies the fly writhing, as the generalissimo did, on the floor. But he has a tougher life than the fly ; for the fly will writhe until it is dead, but the generalissimo always revives ; and when he has no fits, he is a very brave and illustrious man, before whom his emperor must humbly stand aside. I cannot take the fly-flap and strike his writhing limbs as I do this miserable fly, the little Archduke Charles, that is writhing on the floor there. So, now you are dead, confounded little brother Charles, and we will hunt for your brother John. See, see, there he sits on the wall, cleaning his wings and making himself tidy and pretty. There ! There is an affectionate blow from your imperial brother, and you are done for. Now you will never fly to *your* mountaineers and *bring* them freedom and salvation. You will, on the contrary, stick to the wall of your emperor's room, and learn that your brother is your master. Why, this is most amusing sport to day ! I shall not stop before killing a dozen Archdukes Charles and John ! "

And Francis hunted eagerly on the walls and the furniture for other flies, which he pursued and killed with his fly-flap, always applying the name of Charles to one, and that of John to the next.

In the excitement of this strange sport he had not noticed that, soon after he entered the cabinet, the door had opened, and Counsellor von Hudelist had come in. Francis did not remember at that moment that he had given express orders to Hudelist to re-enter the cabinet as soon as he heard the emperor return to it ; he had fixed his thoughts exclusively on the cruel pleasure of killing the flies Charles and John, and Hudelist took good care not to disturb him in this pleasant pastime. He stood leaning against the wall close to the door ; his small, flashing eyes followed every motion of the emperor with rapt attention, and whenever Francis, on killing a fly, pronounced the name of either of his brothers in a triumphant tone, a malicious smile overspread the pale and ugly face of the counsellor.

Now, however, Francis, in hunting for flies, had arrived at the extreme end of the room. Until then, his back had been turned to Hudelist. If he should turn now and continue his sport on the other side of the room, he would discover him, and be disagreeably surprised at his presence. Therefore, before the emperor turned, Hudelist opened once more the door near which he was standing, and closed it rather noisily.

The emperor turned and asked gayly : " Well, what is it, Mr. Counsellor ? "

" Your majesty ordered me to return to the cabinet as soon as you should be back."

" But I returned some time ago," said Francis, casting a distrustful, searching glance on Hudelist.

"Pardon me, your majesty, I believed I heard you only just now close the door, and had until then vainly waited for some sound in the cabinet," replied Hudelist, with a perfectly innocent expression of countenance. " The second door separating the conference-room from your majesty's cabinet is so heavily lined with cushions as to render it almost impervious to sound, and I beg your pardon again for not having heard despite the most eager attention."

The emperor's face had again entirely cleared up. "Never mind," he said; " I am glad that those in the adjoining room cannot hear what is going on here. I like to have ears for all, but do not like anybody to have ears for me. Now let me hear what you have brought for me from Paris."

" Above all things, your majesty, I succeeded in obtaining, for a considerable sum of money, the receipt for making Spanish sealing-wax, from a Spanish refugee, who was formerly employed at the royal sealing-wax factory of Madrid, and was perfectly familiar with the formula for making it. Your majesty knows that this receipt is a secret, and that the officers and workmen employed at the factory must even · wear an oath not to divulge it."

"And you obtained the receipt nevertheless, and brought it with you ?" inquired the emperor.

"Here it is, your majesty."

Francis hastily seized the paper which Hudelist handed to him with a respectful bow.

"See, see, this is a very kind service which you have rendered me, and I shall be grateful for it !" he exclaimed. "You shall test the receipt with me alone; we will try it right away. But hold on; I must first tell you some grave news. We shall declare war. I have already told the French ambassador to leave Vienna to-day, and Metternich can come home too. I will hold a council of the ministers and generals to-day. Tell the functionaries at the chancery to inform the ministers, archdukes, and generals that I wish to see them in the conference-room at four. Make haste, and then come to my laboratory. We will try the Spanish receipt."

CHAPTER V.

THE PERFORMANCE OF "THE CREATION."

A BRILLIANT festival was to take place to-night in the large *aula* of the Vienna University. All the composers, musicians, *dilettanti*, and amateurs of Vienna, had joyously consented to participate in it. The most distinguished names of the aristocracy and the artistic circles of Vienna were at the head of the committee of arrangements. Among those names were those of the Princes Lichnowsky and Lichtenstein, the Countesses Kaunitz and Spielmann, of Beethoven and Salieri, Kreutzer and Clementi, and finally, those of the poets Collin and Carpani.

Every one wished to participate in this festival, which was to render homage to the veteran German composer, the great Joseph Haydn, on the occasion of the twenty-fifth performance of the maestro's great work, " The Creation." Ten years had elapsed since the first performance of " The Creation " at Vienna, and already the sublime composition had made the

tour of Europe, and had been performed amid the most enthusiastic applause in London and Paris, in Amsterdam and
St. Petersburg, in Berlin, and all the large and small cities of
Germany. Everywhere it had excited transports of admiration; everywhere delighted audiences had greeted with rapturous enthusiasm this beautiful music, so full of holy ardor and
childlike piety, this great work of the German composer,
Joseph Haydn.

To-day the twenty-fifth performance of "The Creation"
was to take place at Vienna, and Joseph Haydn himself was
to be present at the concert. The committee of arrangements
had invited him, and he had accepted the invitation. Although his seventy-seven years were resting heavily on his
head, and had paralyzed his strength, he could not withstand
the honorable request of his friends and admirers, and he had
replied with a touching smile to the committee of arrangements, whose delegates had conveyed the invitation to him :
"I shall come to take leave of the world with my 'Creation,'
and bid a last farewell to my dear Viennese. *You* will often
yet sing my 'Creation,' but *I* shall hear it for the last time !"

"For the last time !" These were the words which had
thrilled all the friends and admirers of the maestro, and filled
them with the ardent desire to greet him once more, and render him homage for the last time. For all felt and knew that
Haydn had spoken the truth, and that his end was drawing
near. All, therefore, longed to take part in this last triumph of the composer of "The Creation," whom death had
already touched with its inexorable finger.

Hence, there was a perfect jam in front of the university
building; the equipages of the high nobility formed two immense lines down the long street; like a black, surging stream,
rising from moment to moment, the part of the audience
arriving on foot moved along the houses and between the
double line of carriages toward the entrance of the building.

Thousands had vainly applied for admission at the ticket-
office; there was room only for fifteen hundred persons in the
aula and the adjoining rooms, and perhaps as many thousands
had come to hear the concert. As they could not be admitted
into the hall, they remained in the street in front of the build-

ing; as they could not hear Haydn's music, they wished at least to see his face and cheer him on his arrival at the door.

But there was a surging crowd also in the festively-decorated university hall. All had come in their holiday attire, and joy and profound emotion beamed from all faces. Friends shook hands and greeted each other with radiant eyes; and even those who did not know each other exchanged kindly greetings and pleasant smiles on seating themselves side by side, and looked at each other as though they were friends and acquaintances, and not entire strangers.

For all felt the great importance of this hour; all felt themselves Germans, owing to the homage which they were to render to the German maestro and to German music; and all knew that this festival would be looked upon beyond the Rhine as a hostile demonstration of the Germans against French pride and arrogance. They wished to show to France that, although Germany was dismembered, the heart of the Germans throbbed for Germany and German art, and that they did not feel at all alarmed at the grandiloquent threats of the Emperor of the French, but yielded with undisturbed equanimity to the enjoyment of German art. While the threatening words of the Emperor Napoleon were resounding, like ringing war-fanfares, from Paris, the Viennese desired to respond to him by the beautiful notes of sublime music; and, regardless of the growls of the lion beyond the Rhine, they wished to delight in the soul-stirring harmonies of "The Creation."

All preparations were now completed. The hall was all ablaze with the wax-lights which were beaming down from those gigantic lustres, and whose rays were reflected in the large mirrors covering the walls. The imperial box was splendidly festooned with rare flowers, and decorated with carpets and gilt candelabra, whose enormous wax-lights filled the interior of the spacious box with broad daylight.

Opposite the imperial box, on the other side of the hall, rose the large tribune destined for an orchestra of eighty performers and a choir of one hundred singers. All the latter, too, were in joyous spirits; all were animated to-day, not by the envy and jealousy so often to be found among artistes, but by the one great desire to contribute their share to the homage to be rendered to German art. They did not wish to-day to exhibit themselves and their artistic skill, but desired only to render homage to the music of the great maestro, and to German art.

And now the hour was at hand when the concert was to commence. The audience had taken their seats, the orchestra ceased tuning their instruments, the singers were in readiness, and the committee of arrangements had gone down to the street-door to await Haydn's arrival.

The door of the imperial box opened at this moment, and the emperor and empress entered, followed by the archdukes and their suites. To-day for the first time the audience took no notice of these august persons; they did not rise to greet the imperial couple and the archdukes. No one had perceived their arrival, for all eyes were steadfastly fixed on the large folding-doors by which Joseph Haydn was to enter the hall.

He had been expected already for some time, and the audience began to whisper anxiously : " Will he, perhaps, not come, after all ? Will his physician not permit him to go to the concert because the excitement might be injurious to him ? "

But all at once the silence was broken by a noise in the street, which sounded like the roar of the stormy ocean ; it rent the air, and caused the windows of the hall to rattle. And the audience was joyfully moved ; all faces became radiant, all turned their eyes toward the door.

Now this door opened, and a beautiful though strange group appeared in it. In its midst, on the shoulders of eight strong young men, arose an easy chair, festooned with flowers, and in this chair sat the small, bent form of an old man. His face was pale and wan, and in his forehead the seventy-seven years of his life had drawn deep furrows ; but from his large blue eyes beamed the eternal fire of youth, and there was something childlike and touching in the smile of his mouth. On the right side of his easy-chair was seen the imposing form of a gentleman, plainly dressed, but with a head full of majestic dignity, his face gloomy and wild, his high forehead, surrounded by dense dishevelled hair, his eyes now gleaming

with sombre fires, now glancing mildly and amiably.   It was
Louis von Beethoven, whom Haydn liked to call his pupil, and
whose fame had at that time already penetrated far beyond
the frontiers of Austria.   On the left side of the easy-chair
was seen the fine, expressive face of Salieri, who liked to call
himself Gluck's pupil ; and side by side with these two walked
Kreutzer and Clementi, and the other members of the committee of arrangements.

Thundering cheers greeted their appearance ; the whole
audience rose ; even the Empress Ludovica started up from
her gilded chair and bowed smilingly ; and the Archduke
John advanced close to the railing of the box to greet again
and again with pleasant nods of his head and waves of his
hand Joseph Haydn, thus borne along above the heads of the
audience.   But the Emperor Francis, who was standing by
the side of his consort, looked with a somewhat sneering expression on the crowd below, and, turning to the empress, he
said : "Perhaps my dear Viennese may consider Haydn on
his easy-chair yonder their emperor, and I myself may abdi-
cate and go home.   They did not even look at us to-night, and
are raising such a fuss now as though God Almighty had entered the hall ! "

In effect, the exultation of the audience increased at every
step which the procession advanced, and endless cheers accompanied the composer to the seat which had been prepared for
him on an estrade in front of the orchestra.

Here two beautiful ladies of high rank came to meet him,
and presented to him, on cushions of gold-embroidered velvet,
poems written by Collin and Carpani, and printed on silken
ribbons.   At the same time many hundred copies of these
poems flittered through the hall, and all shouted joyously,
"Long live Joseph Haydn, the German maestro ! "   And the
orchestra played a ringing flourish, and the cheers of the audience rent the air again and again.

Joseph Haydn, quite overcome, his eyes filled with tears,
leaned his head against the back of his chair.   A mortal pallor overspread his cheeks, and his hands trembled as though
he had the fever.

"Maestro, dear, dear maestro ! " said the Princess Esterhazy, bending over him tenderly, "are you unwell ? You tremble, and are so pale ! Are you unwell ?"

"Oh, no, no," said Haydn, with a gentle smile, "my soul is in ecstasies at this hour, which is a precious reward for a long life of arduous toils. My soul is in ecstasies, but it lives in such a weak and wretched shell ; and because the soul is all ablaze with the fires of rapturous delight, the whole warmth has entered it, and the poor mortal shell is cold and trembling."

The Princess Esterhazy took impetuously from her shoulders the costly Turkish shawl in which her form was enveloped ; she spread it out before Haydn and wrapped it carefully round his feet. Her example was followed immediately by the Princesses Lichtenstein and Kinsky, and the Countesses Kaunitz and Spielmann. They doffed their beautiful ermine furs and their Turkish and Persian shawls, and wrapped them around the old composer, and transformed them into cushions which they placed under his head and his arms, and blankets with which they covered him.*

Haydn allowed them smilingly to do so, and thanked, with glances of joyful emotion, the beautiful ladies who manifested so much tender solicitude for him.

"Why can I not die now ?" he said to himself in a low voice. "Why does not Death kiss my lips at this glorious hour of my triumph ? Oh, come, Death ! waft me blissfully into the other world, for in this world I am useless henceforth ; my strength is gone, and my head has no more ideas. I live only in and on the past ! "

"And yet you live for all time to come," said the Princess Esterhazy, enthusiastically, "and while German art and German music are loved and honored, Joseph Haydn will never die and never be forgotten."

Hushed now was every sound. Salieri had taken his seat as conductor of the concert, and signed now to the orchestra.

The audience listened in breathless silence to the tumultuous notes depicting in so masterly a manner the struggle of light and darkness, the chaos of the elements. The struggle of the elements becomes more and more furious, and the music depicts it in sombre, violent notes, when suddenly the

* See " Zeitgenossen," third series, vol. vi., p. 32.

horizon brightens, the clouds are rent, the dissonant sounds pass into a sublime harmony, and in glorious notes of the most blissful exultation resound through the struggling universe the grand, redeeming words, "Let there be light !" And all join in the rapturous chorus, and repeat in blissful concord, "Let there be light !"

The audience, carried away by the grandeur and irresistible power of these notes, burst into long-continued applause.

Haydn took no notice of it; he heard only his music; his soul was entirely absorbed in it, and lifting both his arms to heaven, he said devoutly and humbly, "It comes from above !" *

The audience had heard these loud and enthusiastic words ; it applauded no longer, but looked in reverent silence toward the aged composer, who, in the midst of his most glorious triumph, rendered honor to God alone, and bowed piously and modestly to the work of his own genius.

The performance proceeded. But Joseph Haydn hardly heard much of the music. His head leaned against the back of the chair; his face, lit up by a blissful smile, was deathly pale; his eyes cast fervent glances of gratitude toward heaven, and seemed, in their ecstatic gaze, to see the whole heavens opened.

"Maestro," said the Princess Esterhazy, when the first part of the performance was ended, "you must no longer remain here, but return to your quiet home."

"Yes, I shall return to the quiet home which awaits us all," said Haydn, mildly, "and I feel sensibly that I shall remain no longer among men. A sweet dream seems to steal over me. Let the performers commence the second part, and my soul will be wafted to heaven on the wings of my music."

But the Princess Esterhazy beckoned to his friends. "Take him away," she said, "the excitement will kill him, if he stays any longer."

They approached his chair and begged permission to escort him home. Haydn nodded his assent silently and smilingly, and his eyes glanced dreamily round the hall.

Suddenly he gave a start as if in great terror, and rose so impetuously that the furs and Turkish shawls, which had been wrapped round him, fell to the floor. His face crimsoned

* "Zeitgenossen," ibid.

as if in the light of the setting sun ; his eyes looked up with a
radiant expression to the box yonder—to his emperor, whom
he had loved so long and ardently, for whom he had wept in
the days of adversity, for whom he had prayed and sung at all
times.   Now he saw him who, in his eyes, represented fatherland, home, and human justice ; he felt that it was the last time
his eyes would behold him, and he wished to bid farewell at
this hour to the world, his fatherland, and his emperor.

With a vigorous hand he pushed back the friends who
would have held him and replaced him in his chair.   Now he
was no longer a weak and decrepit old man ; he felt strong
and active, and he hastened forward with a rapid step through
the orchestra toward the conductor's seat and the piano in
front of it.   He laid his hands, which trembled no longer, on
the keys, and struck a full concord.   He turned his face toward the imperial box ; his eyes beamed with love and exultation, and he began to play his favorite hymn with impressive
enthusiasm—the hymn which he had composed ten years ago
in the days of Austria's adversity, and which he had sung
every day since then,—the hymn, *" Gott erhalte Franz den
Kaiser, unsern guten Kaiser Franz ! "*   And the audience
rose and gazed with profound emotion upon Joseph Haydn's
gleaming face, and then up to the emperor, who was standing
smilingly in his box, and the empress, from whose eyes two
large tears rolled down her pale cheeks ; and with one accord
the vast crowd commenced singing :

> " Gott erhalte Franz den Kaiser,
>   Unsern guten Kaiser Franz !
>   Lange lebe Franz der Kaiser
>   In des Glückes hellem Kranz !
>   Ihm erblühen Lorbeerreiser,
>   Wo er geht, zum Ehrenkranz.
>   Gott erhalte—" *

> * " God preserve the emperor,
>   Francis, our good emperor !
>   Long live Francis, brightest gem
>   In fair Fortune's diadem !
>   O'er him see the laurel wave,
>   Honoring the true, the brave !
>   God preserve—"

Haydn's hands dropped exhausted from the keys ; his form rocked to and fro, and, half fainting, he sank back into the arms of Salieri and Kreutzer.

The audience paused ; all forgot the imperial hymn, and looked only at the venerable old maestro, whom Salieri and Kreutzer lowered now softly into the easy-chair, which had been brought to them.

"Take me home, dear ones," he said, faintly, "sing on, my 'Creation' ; my soul will remain with you, but my body can no longer stay. Old age has broken its strength. Farewell, farewell, all of you ! My soul will always be among you when you sing my music ; my body will go, but the soul will remain. Farewell !"

And the votaries of art who had conveyed him to the hall now placed the maestro's chair again on their shoulders, and carried it slowly through the hall toward the entrance.

The audience stood in silent reverence and looked up to Haydn's passing form, and durst not break this profound still-ness by uttering a sound. They bade farewell to the univer-sally beloved and revered maestro only by bowing their heads to him and shedding tears of emotion—farewell for evermore !

The solemn procession had now arrived at the door. Jo-seph Haydn lifted his weary head once more ; his spirit gleamed once more in his eyes ; an expression of unutterable love beamed from his mild face ; he stretched out his arms toward the orchestra as if to bless it, and greeted it with his smile, with the nodding of his head, and the tears which filled his eyes.*

A low rustling and sobbing passed through the hall ; no one was courageous enough to clap his hands ; all hearts were profoundly moved, all eyes filled with tears.

But now he disappeared, and the door closed behind Joseph Haydn. The German maestro had to-day celebrated his apo-theosis amidst the enthusiastic people of Vienna. Life had dedicated to him the laurel-wreath which usually only death grants to poets and artists.

The audience was still silent, when all at once a powerful voice exclaimed : "Let us sing the second verse of Haydn's

* "Zeitgenossen," third series, vol. iv., p. 33.

favorite hymn—the second verse of ‘ *Gott erhalte Franz den Kaiser !* ’ ”

“ Yes, yes,” shouted all, enthusiastically, “ the second verse ! the second verse ! ”

And hundreds of voices shouted to the orchestra beseechingly, imperiously, thunderingly, that it should play the accompaniment ; and the musicians complied with this tumultuous request.

The audience expressed their gratitude by an outburst of applause, and sang thereupon the second verse :

> “ Lass von seiner Fahne Spitzen
> Strahlen Sieg und Furchtbarkeit !
> Lass in seinem Rathe sitzen
> Weisheit, Klugheit, Redlichkeit,
> Und mit seiner Hoheit Blitzen
> Schalten nur Gerechtigkeit.
> Gott erhalte Franz den Kaiser,
> Unsern guten Kaiser Franz ! ” *

The emperor bowed his thanks to the audience, the orchestra commenced again playing the air, and the audience sang anew :

> “ Lass von seiner Fahne Spitzen
> Strahlen Sieg und Furchtbarkeit ! ”

And arms and hands were lifted here and there beseechingly toward the emperor ; in vain the orchestra tried to play on ; the audience, with rare unanimity, as if seized with one sentiment and one wish, sang again and again :

> “ Lass von seiner Fahne Spitzen
> Strahlen Sieg und Furchtbarkeit ! ”

And then all shouted loudly, beseechingly, and withal an-

---

* “ Before his banner floating high
Let victory shout and foemen fly!
In his counsels let preside
Wisdom, prudence, noble pride !
And in loftiness enshrined
Homely justice dwelling find !
God preserve the emperor,
Francis, our good emperor !”

grily and courageously, "War ! war ! *Lass von seiner Fahne Spitzen strahlen Sieg und Furchtbarkeit !* "

The excitement of the audience grew constantly bolder and more impetuous. The men left their seats and crowded around the imperial box, repeating again and again the words :

> " Lass von seiner Fahne Spitzen
> Strahlen Sieg und Furchtbarkeit ! "

The emperor withdrew in confusion into the background of his box, and whispered quickly a few words to the Archduke John. The archduke advanced to the railing of the box, and commanded silence by waving his hand to the audience. The singers paused immediately, and amidst the breathless silence which ensued, the Archduke John shouted in a loud and powerful voice : " The emperor announces to his dear Viennese that he is determined to submit no longer to the arrogance of France, and that war is irrevocably resolved on."

A cry of rapture burst from all lips ; all shouted exultingly, " War ! war ! We shall at length bid defiance to the arrogance of the French emperor ! We shall have war with France ; we shall avenge the wrongs which we have suffered so long, and set bounds to the encroachments of France ! "

And friends and acquaintances greeted each other with radiant eyes and glowing cheeks ; neighbors, entirely unknown to each other, shook hands and said, smilingly : " Now at length we shall have war ! At length we shall remove from our German honor the stains with which France has sullied it. At length we shall have war, and God will grant us—"

The ringing notes of the orchestra interrupted the animated conversation of the excited audience. Salieri had taken his seat again, he raised his baton, and the second part of " The Creation " commenced.

CHAPTER VI.

ANDREAS HOFER.

THE streets of Vienna were silent and deserted ; all houses were dark ; everywhere the note of life had died away, and only here and there a hackney-coach was heard to drive slowly through the lonely streets, or a belated wanderer was seen to return home with a weary step.

Vienna slept and dreamed of the welcome news which, despite the late hour, had spread like wild-fire from the concert-hall through the city—of the joyful ¡intelligence that war against France was resolved on, and that the time was at length at hand when the wrongs perpetrated by Napoleon were to be avenged.

Vienna slept and dreamed ; only in the wing of the imperial palace where lay the rooms occupied by the Archduke John, the lights had not yet been extinguished, and at times dark figures were seen moving to and fro behind the windows.

The Archduke John did not sleep yet, but he had already dismissed Conrad, his valet de chambre; he had permitted the other footmen to retire from the anteroom to their bedchambers, and had then himself locked the door of the outer anteroom.

"I do not trust Conrad, my valet de chambre," he said to Count Nugent, who was with him in his cabinet; "it is he, doubtless, who has been placed as a 'guardian angel' by my side, and is to report regularly all I am doing."

"Your highness ought to discharge the fellow forthwith," exclaimed Count Nugent, indignantly.

"I shall take good care not to do so," said John, smiling; "on the contrary, I shall try to keep Conrad as long as possible in my service, for I know him, and shall be able to mystify him. I shall always have to suffer a spy by my side, for the love and solicitude of my imperial brother will never leave me for a single moment without close surveillance; and Conrad is less distasteful to me than another spy probably would be. Still, I did not want him to report any thing about the visitors who will be here to-night, and therefore I dismissed him for the night."

"But he will probably stand in the street to watch his master's windows," said Nugent, with a shrug; "and the shadows which he will see he may distort into all sorts of spectres which will be mentioned in the emperor's police report to-morrow morning."

"Oh, I am not afraid of that at this hour," exclaimed John. "The emperor knows that I am to receive the delegates of the Tyrolese; I myself told him so to-day, and he approves of it. But harm might befall my Tyrolese at their homes, if their plans were discovered previous to their deliverance from the Bavarian yoke. But hush, did you not hear a rustling sound in the corridor ?"

"Yes, I did; it is drawing near—it is at the door now, and —somebody raps already."

"Our friends are there," exclaimed John, hastening to the door, and drawing back the bolt.

The archduke was not mistaken; his friends were there, and entered his cabinet now by the secret door. They were headed by Baron von Hormayr in his brilliant gold-embroidered uniform, which rendered doubly conspicuous the beauty of his slender yet firmly-knit form, and the noble expression of his prepossessing, youthful face. He was followed by three Tyrolese, clad in their national costume, and holding their rifles in their arms.

The first of them was a man about forty years old. His frame was Herculean, his shoulders broad, his strength immense ; his head was covered with dense black hair, his bronzed face was radiant with kind-heartedness and good-humor. His dress was the common habit of the country, with some trifling variations: a large black hat, with a broad brim, black ribbons, and a dark curling feather ; a green jacket, red waistcoat, broad green braces crossed on the breast; a black leathern girdle, adorned, according to the Tyrolese custom, with all sorts of ivory and other ornaments; black breeches, red stockings, and black shoes with buckles. About his neck was always to be seen a silver crucifix fastened to a heavy gold chain, and over it, down to the girdle, flowed his large black beard, which imparted a strange, fantastic air to his whole appearance. This man was Andreas Hofer, the innkeeper of Passeyr, to whom the Italian Tyrolese, on account of his long beard, had given the name of "Barbone."

The second of the Tyrolese who entered the archduke's cabinet was a man of no less imposing appearance, dressed entirely like Andreas Hofer; only the long beard was wanting to him, and, instead of a black hat, he wore the pointed green Tyrolese hat, adorned with hunting ornaments. His face, less good-natured and serene than that of his friend, was expressive of energy and resolution; courage and shrewdness beamed from his black eyes, and a peculiar expression of defiance and scorn played around his full lips. This was Joseph Speckbacher, known by every inhabitant of the northern Tyrol as "the bold chamois-hunter."

He was followed by a third Tyrolese, as proud and strong, as robust and fine-looking, as his two companions. It was Anthony Wallner, the innkeeper of Windisch-Matrey, and, like Speckbacher, Hofer's intimate friend.

The archduke advanced to meet the Tyrolese, and shook hands with each of them.

"Welcome, my Tyrolese, welcome !" he said, in a deeply-moved voice ; "may God and the Holy Virgin grant that no harm result from your visit to me ! You know that I have never ceased to love you, and that when, in the year 1805, I had to bid farewell to Andreas Hofer and the dear Tyrol, my heart almost broke with grief and despair."

"Look, look !" exclaimed Andreas Hofer, turning with a radiant smile to his two friends; "he is indeed the same man who bade us farewell at that time in Brunecken, and was not ashamed of embracing Andreas Hofer and shedding tears on his shoulder for the poor sacrificed Tyrol."

"And who is glad to-day to be able to embrace Andreas Hofer again," said the archduke, encircling the Herculean form of the Tyrolese innkeeper with his arms. "But I will shed no tears to-day, Andreas, for I hope the time of tears is over, and you have come to tell me so, to bring me love-greetings from the Tyrolese, and the hope of better times. Say, you three brave men from the Tyrol, Andreas Hofer, Joseph Speckbacher, Anthony Wallner, is it not so? Have you not come to tell me that the Tyrol is longing for her emperor and desirous of getting rid of the Bavarians?"

"Yes, we have come to say this to our dear John," exclaimed Andreas Hofer.

"We have come to ask if Austria does not intend to call upon her Tyrol to rise and fight under her banners," said Joseph Speckbacher.

"We have come to ask our Archduke John if he will help us with his troops and cannon in case we Tyrolese should rise now to expel the Bavarians from the country," said Anthony Wallner, with flashing eyes.

"We have come to ask our John, Is it time?" exclaimed Andreas Hofer.

The archduke held out his hand to him with a firm and resolute glance. "Yes," he said, "yes, Andreas Hofer, it is time! Yes, Anthony Wallner, Austria will assist the Tyrolese with her troops and cannon in expelling the Bavarians and French from their country. Yes, Joseph Speckbacher, Austria intends to call upon her faithful Tyrol to rise and fight under her banners; she will engage in a mortal contest for you and with you!"

"God grant success to our united efforts!" said Andreas Hofer, folding his hands over the crucifix on his breast. "During all these years I have prayed every day to the Holy Virgin to let me live and see the day when the Austrian eagle shall once more adorn our boundary-posts, and when we may again fondly and faithfully love our Emperor Francis as our legitimate sovereign. The good God in heaven, I hope, will forgive me for having been a very bad and obstinate subject of the King of Bavaria. I would never submit to the new laws, and could not discover in my old Austrian heart a bit of loyalty or love for the ruler who was forced upon us."

"No, you were a stubborn disloyalist, Andy," said Hormayr, "and, as spokesman of your whole district, you raised your voice against every new law which the Bavarian government promulgated in your country. But, it is true, the Tyrolese love their Andy for this, and say that he is the most honest, faithful, and reliable man in the whole valley of the Adige."

"To be courageous is not so difficult if the cause which you fight for is a good one," said Andreas Hofer, calmly. "God Himself engraved on my heart the commandment to be loyal to my emperor, my country, and its laws; and if you call me reliable, dear friend, you merely say that I do my duty as a Christian, for the Bible says, 'Let your communication be Yea, yea; nay, nay; for whatsoever is more than these cometh of sin.' Therefore, do not praise me for that which is only my duty, and which Speckbacher and Wallner, and all our dear friends in the valley of the Adige, do just as well as I. For the rest, I must tell you, gentlemen, it is not so strange that we should be attached to the emperor; for the Bavarians are governing our country in such a manner as if they were intent only on making us love our emperor every day more and more, and long for him more intensely."

"It is true, Andy is right," exclaimed Anthony Wallner; "the Bavarians oppress us fearfully, and we will not stand it any longer; we will become Austrians again, as our fathers were, and will fight for our liberty and our old privileges which Bavaria solemnly guaranteed, and which her authorities basely intend to overthrow."

"Which they have already overthrown," cried Joseph Speckbacher, his eyes flashing with anger. "The court of Munich seems intent only on making the utmost of their new acquisition. Our old constitution has been overthrown by a royal edict; the representative estates have been suppressed, and the provincial funds seized. No less than eight new and oppressive taxes have been imposed and are being levied with the utmost rigor; the very name of our country has been abolished; the royal property has all been brought into the market; new imports are daily exacted without any consultation with the estates of the people; specie has become scarce, from the quantity of it which is being drawn off to the Bavarian treasury; the Austrian notes have been reduced to half their value; and, to crown all these wrongs, compulsory levies are held among our young men, who are to serve in the ranks of our oppressors! No, we must break the yoke weighing us

down—we will become freemen again—as freemen we will
live and die—as freemen we will belong again to our beloved
Emperor Francis, whose ancestors have ruled over us for so
many centuries past."

"If all the Tyrolese think and feel as you three do," said
the Archduke John, with sparkling eyes, "you will recover
your liberty and your emperor, despite the Bavarians and
French."

"All feel and think as we do," said Hofer, thoughtfully;
"we have all vowed to God and the Holy Virgin that we will
deliver the Tyrol from the enemy; and every man, every lad
in our mountains and valleys, is ready to take up his rifle and
fight for his dear Emperor Francis."

"We are here as delegates of the whole Tyrol," said Anthony Wallner, "to ascertain the wishes and intentions of the
emperor and his government, prefer our bitter complaints,
and declare the firm resolution of the Tyrolese to shrink from
no sacrifice in order to be reunited with Austria and to reconquer our ancient rights and liberties."

"But we need assistance for this purpose," added Joseph
Speckbacher, "speedy and vigorous assistance ; above all, we
need troops, money, ammunition, and supplies. Will Austria
give them to us ? "

"She will," said the archduke. "She will send you a *corps
d'armée*, money, ammunition, and supplies. Only you must
be ready and prepared to rise as one man when we give you
the signal of insurrection."

"We are ready!" exclaimed Andreas Hofer, nodding joyously. "But you must not delay the signal very long, for
delays are highly dangerous under the present circumstances.
We and our friends have prepared the insurrection, and it is
as if a large torrent of fire were flowing secretly under the
surface of the Tyrol ; if some shrewd Bavarian should scratch
away some of the earth, he would discover the fire, fetch
water, and extinguish the flames, before the Austrians reach
the country and prevent him from so doing. A secret known
to a great many is seldom well kept ; it is, as it were, a ripe
fruit which must fall from the tree, even though it should hit
and crush the head of the owner of the tree."

"Yes, what is to be done must be done soon," said Anthony Wallner. "The men of Passeyr, Meran, Mays, and Algund, are ready, and have entered into a secret league with the whole valley of the Inn. The district of the Adige, too, has joined us, and the German and Italian Tyrolese, who formerly never liked each other, have now agreed to stand shoulder to shoulder and rise on one day and as one man, in order to drive the Bavarians and French from their mountains."

"We are waiting only for Austria to give the signal; pray do not keep us waiting too long, for we men of the Lower Inn-thal, too, are all ready and armed. An enormous worm of insurrection, as it were, is creeping through the Lower Inn valley, and the worm has four heads, which look toward all quarters of the world. One head is Rupert Wintersteller, of Kirchdorf; the second is Jacob Sieberer, of Thiersen; the third is Antony Aschbacher, of Achenthal ; and the fourth is I, Joseph Speckbacher, of Kufstein."

"In the Puster valley, too, a storm is brewing, and all are ready and impatient to rise in insurrection," said Hofer. "Therefore, dear brother of our emperor, give us good news, that we may take it home to the men of the Tyrol, for their hearts are longing and crying for their sovereign the emperor."

"And the emperor, on his part, is longing for his Tyro-lese," said the archduke. "The time has come when that which belongs together is to be reunited. Let us consult and deliberate, then, my friends, what we should do in order to attain our great object, and reunite the Tyrolese with their emperor."

"Yes, let us consult," said Hofer, solemnly ; "and let us pray God and the Holy Virgin to enlighten our minds."

He raised the crucifix from his breast to his face and bent over it, muttering a prayer.

"Now I am ready," he said, slowly dropping the crucifix ; "let us deliberate. But I tell you beforehand, I am no mili-tary hero, nor a wise man in council. I am resolved to do all that is necessary to deliver my dear Tyrol from the enemy, and to strike and fire at the Bavarians and French until they run away terror-stricken, and restore us to our dear Emperor Francis. But I am unversed in negotiations and devising shrewd tricks and stratagems. I am only a plain peasant, who has a great deal of love and fidelity in his heart, but only few thoughts in his head. Baron von Hormayr and the archduke may do the thinking for me. They shall be the head, and I the arm and heart. Speckbacher and Wallner yonder have good heads too, though I do not wish to say that their hearts are not also in the right place ; on the contrary, I know that they are. Let us consult, then, and bear in mind that God hears us, and that the Tyrolese are waiting for us."

"You are an excellent man, Andy," exclaimed John, holding out his hand to Hofer with a tender glance—"a childlike soul, full of love, fidelity, and tenderness ; and, in gazing at you, it seems as if the whole dear Tyrol, with its mountains and valleys, its Alpine huts and chapels, its merry singers and pious prayers, were present before me. Come, then, Andy, and you other dear friends, come, let us be seated and hold a council of war."

They seated themselves around the table standing in the middle of the room.

Day was already dawning, the candles had burned down very low, the streets began to become lively, and still the Tyrolese remained in the archduke's cabinet, their faces glowing with defiance and resolution, and their eyes flashing with boldness and enthusiasm. For every thing was settled and decided now ; each of them had received his instructions and been informed of the part which he was to play in the struggle. War with the Bavarians and French, and liberty for the Tyrol, was the battle-cry and goal.

"The plan is settled, then," said the Archduke John, nodding kindly to the Tyrolese. "Eleven points, especially, have been agreed upon, after mature deliberation ; and it would be good for us to repeat them briefly."

"Let us do so," said Andreas Hofer. "First, then : The Tyrolese will rise against the Bavarians, in order to be reunited with Austria. We shall enlist as many soldiers for the insurgent army as possible, and try to make all Tyrolese our fellow-conspirators. They will meet on Sundays at the taverns, and the innkeepers in the valleys and mountains are the leaders of the conspiracy ; they will call the meetings and

facilitate the intercourse of the conspirators with each other.
If it please God, the insurrection will break out on the 9th of
April, when the Austrian troops will cross the frontier of the
Tyrol and hasten to our assistance. This is the best point,
and God grant that it may be well executed!"

"The second point," said Joseph Speckbacher, "is as follows : No written communication whatever shall be permitted among the conspirators, and those who violate this
order shall be severely punished. The secret messages will be
carried by reliable and well-tried messengers from court-house
to court-house and village to village. To this the third point
adds the following : The oldest men in the villages will
establish secret tribunals to try and punish those whom fear,
self-interest, or bribes may induce to turn traitors. The families of suspicious persons, and those who betray our secrets
from weakness or in a state of intoxication, must be closely
watched, and they themselves will be sent to distant Alpine
huts and into the mountain fastnesses, where they will be
kept in close confinement."

"Fourth," said Anthony Wallner : "Every innkeeper
must strive to amass provisions, forage, wine, and ammunition ; for the inns in the mountains are, as it were, small
fortresses for the Tyrolese, and the enemy can reach them
only slowly and after surmounting a great many difficulties.
Besides, the innkeepers must arrange target-shootings every
Sunday, that the men from the neighborhood may assemble
at their houses and join the great league of the defenders of
the country. The innkeepers at very important places will
receive for these purposes bills of exchange on Salzburg, Klagenfurth, and Trieste; and each of us three, Hofer, Speckbacher, and I, will take home with us one hundred and twenty
ducats to be distributed among the innkeepers. Fifth : The
intercourse between the mountain districts, on one side, and
the plains and towns, on the other, must henceforth become
rarer and rarer till the hour of the outbreak. But the mountaineers must send out, at intervals of four days, spies to ascertain the state of affairs in other parts of the country."

"Sixth," exclaimed the Archduke John, with beaming eyes :
"On the day when the insurrection is to break out, Field-

Marshal Jellachich will arrive in front of Innspruck, and the vanguard of Field-Marshal Chasteler will march through the Puster valley to the heights of Schwabs and Elbach toward Brixen, and advance the head of his column beyond the Brenner as far as Botzen. Seventh : All the forces of the enemy moving toward Germany must be chased between these two columns of the Austrians and pursued and fired at incessantly by the mountaineers; they must be prevented night and day from obtaining rest and food ; the best marksmen must pick off their officers and blow up their ammunition-wagons. The Tyrolese should chase the Bavarians and the French in this manner from Botzen to Brixen, up the Brenner, and thence down to Trent. Now, friend Hormayr, repeat the remaining four points."

"The eighth point is : The removal of the Bavarian treasure must be prevented by all means. Ninth: The Tyrolese living on the rivers must prevent the enemy by all means from destroying the bridges and roads, so that the Austrians may be able to succor them more rapidly ; but they must also hold men and tools in readiness, that, after the Austrians have arrived, they may destroy the bridges in the rear of the enemy, and render the roads impassable, by obstructing them with piles of wood and rocks. Tenth : The Tyrolese will try cautiously to bring about an understanding with Switzerland, and establish connections with the Lower and Upper Engadine, Chur, Appenzell, and St. Gall ; for thence will come the English agents who will convey arms and money to the Tyrolese. Eleventh—"

"Ah, let me state the eleventh point," exclaimed Joseph Speckbacher, with flashing eyes. "I intend to take part in carrying out this point of the programme. It is, to take the fortress of Kufstein on the frontier by a nocturnal *coup de main*. Field-Marshal Jellachich will move several companies of riflemen as close up to the fortress as possible, and Jacob Sieberer and Joseph Speckbacher, who will beforehand enlist assistants in the town and spy out every thing, will join them. The capture of Kufstein is to commence the glorious struggle ; it is to be the first hymn of liberty which the Tyrolese will send up to heaven like a lark in spring, and by which they

will bless and praise the good God. The eleventh and last
point is Kufstein. God protect us in carrying out these eleven
points !" *

"Amen !" exclaimed Andreas Hofer, raising his crucifix
and pressing it to his lips. "We have, then, resolved here in
council with our Archduke John, and I hope also in council
with the good God above, that the Tyrol is to be restored to
its beloved imperial house. The work is to begin on the 9th
of April, and we must be ready to rise on that day. On the
9th of April the Austrians are to cross the frontier, and on the
previous evening they will inform us by firing off three rock-
ets that they are at hand. At the same time bale-fires will be
lighted on a hundred hills, and on the following morning we
shall throw large quantities of blood, flour, or charcoal, into
our mountain-torrents, that their blood-red, flour-white, or
coal-black waters, flowing into and out of the country, may
proclaim to the people that the time has come when all must
rise, rifle in hand, to conquer or die for the dear Tyrol and the
good Emperor Francis."

" And I, too, am ready to conquer or die for the Tyrol and
the emperor, and so is the corps whose commander I am," exclaimed the archduke enthusiastically. "The emperor, my
gracious master, intends to intrust me with the command of
the army which is to fight with and for the Tyrol, which will
check the advance of the enemy approaching the Tyrol from
the Italian frontier, and will second and strengthen the insurrection of the Tyrolese. Now, then, my friends and comrades
let us prepare the great work bravely, prudently, and carefully.
Collect your forces, as I shall collect mine ; make all your
dispositions, and exhort all to behave as true sons of the Tyrol.
Above all things, be cautious. Keep in check not only your
tongues but your faces, especially here in Vienna. For if the
Bavarian spies here ferret out that Andreas Hofer, Speckbacher, and Wallner are in Vienna, and that I have had an
interview with them, their keen noses will scent at once what

---

* These eleven points were settled in this manner at Vienna by the delegates of the Tyrolese, the Archduke John, and Baron von Hormayr, and
noted down by the latter.—See Hormayr, "Geschichte Andreas Hofer's," vol.
i., p. 193 et seq.

is going on, and they will send, even before we reach the
Tyrol, so many Bavarian and French soldiers into your country, that you will be tied hand and foot, and cannot raise your
arms on the 9th of April to seize your rifles. Therefore, I
repeat it, keep your faces in check, and do not allow yourselves to be seen in the streets of Vienna in the daytime.
Your beard, Andy, especially is a treacherous thing, and it
would really be best for the Barbone to shave off his long
mourning-flag."

Andreas Hofer seized his beard with both his hands, almost
in terror, and drew it caressingly through his fingers.

"No," he said, "my friends and countrymen know me by
my beard, and the Barbone is a welcome guest in the Italian
Tyrol. They would not recognize me if I should appear
among them with a smooth chin ; and they would doubt if it
was Andreas Hofer who talked with them about the great
conspiracy and insurrection in case they did not see his black
beard."

"No, archduke," said Speckbacher, smiling and winking,
"you must not object to our Andy's beard, for it is the flag
round which the Tyrolese will rally, and with which the Tyrol
will adorn itself on the day of insurrection, as they put on
their best clothes on the day of Assumption. Moreover, Andreas Hofer must not be ungrateful ; and he would be ungrateful if he should cut off his beard and throw it away, for
his beard gained him one day a couple of fat oxen."

"Is that true, Andy ?" asked John, laughing.

"It is," said Andreas Hofer. gravely. "My beard did gain
me two oxen. It happened as follows, archduke : I was quite
a young man yet, and had married my wife, Anna Gertrude
Ladurner, only a year before. I was very fond of my little
wife, and did not like to sit for hours in the tavern, as I had
done heretofore. I stayed at home often enough instead of
attending to my business, and going down to Italy or Germany
to carry on my traffic in corn, wine, horses, and oxen, by which
I had made a great deal of money. My friends sneered at my
staying so much at home, and said : ' Andy Hofer, the Sandwirth, is a henpecked husband, and his wife is master of the
house.' This was very disagreeable to me, for, although I love

my Anna Gertrude from the bottom of my heart, I have always
been the master ; and she has been obedient to me, as the Bible
says it should be between husband and wife. Well, one day I
sat at home with a few friends; we were drinking wine in the
bar-room. Suddenly there entered the room an old beggar
with a tremendous beard reaching down to his girdle. I
laugh at the beard and rejoice over its enormous length. One
of my friends, Anthony Waidlinger, the rich Amselwirth, asks
me : ' Well, Andy, would you like to wear as long a beard as
that ?' 'Why not ?' I reply merrily. 'Ah,' exclaims Anthony, laughing, 'you must not talk so saucily. You must not
wear so long a beard. Your wife will not permit it, Andy !'
This makes me very angry ; I start up, and hardly know what
I am doing. 'What !' I cry, 'my wife ? She must obey *me*
whether she likes it or not. What will you bet I will not
shave my beard for a whole year ?' 'I will bet you two oxen,'
says Anthony ; 'but let me warn you, Andy, you will lose the
oxen ; for I stick to it, your wife will never permit you to become the laughing-stock of the children by appearing in the
streets with such a lion's mane. Therefore consider the matter well, Andy, for there is time yet. Admit that you will not
win the bet, for two oxen are at stake !' 'I have already considered everything,' I say ; 'and as for the two oxen, they will
be just what I want. A year hence you will bring them to
me, Anthony Waidlinger.' And this prediction was fulfilled.
I did not shave my beard, and Anna Gertrude, my wife, re-
joiced at her Andy's beard instead of being angry at it, and
thought it made her husband look a great deal better. When
the year was up, Anthony Waidlinger drove his two oxen
with a sullen air into my stable, and said : 'Now you may cut
off your fur and have a pillow made from it for your wife.'
'I need not cut off my beard for that purpose,' I replied ; 'it
may be my wife's pillow even while it hangs down on my
breast. For she is a good and dutiful wife, and I am fondly
attached to her.' That, archduke, is the story of my beard,
which I have worn ever since, and which has often been a pillow when my little boy and my three girls fell asleep on my
lap, and under which they have often concealed their little
heads when their mother was looking for them. You will

ask me no more to cut off my beard—the pillow and plaything of my children."

"No, Andreas," said the archduke, kindly, "I will not. Wear your fine beard as you have done hitherto; may it be, notwithstanding its black color, the victorious flag round which the royal Tyrolese shall rally on rising for their lord and emperor! And now, farewell, my friends; it is dawning, and it is time for us to repose a little. Go home, therefore, and what remains to be settled you may talk over to-morrow with Baron von Hormayr, who will give you money for travelling expenses, and for distribution among the innkeepers. Day after to-morrow you will set out for home, and bring to all loyal Tyrolese the joyful news that war will break out."

"Yes, yes, war will break out!" exclaimed the three Tyrolese, exultingly.

"Hush, for God's sake, hush!" said John, laughing. "You must keep quiet, and, instead of doing so, you shout as jubilantly as though you were standing on a crest of the Brenner, and had just discovered the hiding-place of a chamois. Let me therefore tell you once more it is necessary that the people of Vienna should not find out that you are in the city. Pledge me your word, then, that you will not go into the street to-morrow in the daytime, nor allow any one to see you."

"We pledge you our word!" exclaimed the Tyrolese, with one accord; "we will not appear in the street to-morrow in the daytime, and day after to-morrow we shall set out."

"Yes, we shall set out then," repeated Andreas Hofer, "and return to our mountains and friends, and wait patiently and faithfully until the day when we shall see rising to the sky the signal which is to tell us that our dear Archduke John sends us his soldiers to assist us in delivering our country from the enemy, and restoring it, with our mountains, our love, and our loyalty, to our dear Emperor Francis. God grant that we may succeed in so doing, and may the Holy Virgin pray for us all, and restore the Tyrol to the emperor!"

CHAPTER VII.

ANDREAS HOFER AT THE THEATRE.

COUNT STADION, the minister of foreign affairs, was pacing his cabinet with a quick step and an anxious expression of countenance. At times he stood still, and, bending his head toward the door, seemed to listen intently for some sound; all remaining silent outside, he commenced again striding up and down, and whenever he approached the clock on the mantel-piece he cast an anxious glance on it.

"I am afraid Hormayr was not at home," he murmured moodily to himself; "his servants did not know where he was, and therefore the mischief cannot be stopped."

He drew a golden snuff-box from his pocket and took a large pinch from it. "I said at the very outset," he murmured, "that we ought to keep aloof from these stupid peasants, who will only involve us in trouble and mischief. But those gentlemen would not listen to me, and— Really, I believe I hear footsteps in the anteroom. Yes, yes, somebody is coming!"

Count Stadion was not mistaken. The door opened, and a footman announced, in a loud voice, "Baron von Hormayr!"

"Let him come in, let him come in, quick!" said Count Stadion, waving his hand impatiently; and when Hormayr appeared on the threshold of the door, he hastily went to meet him.

"In truth, it took my servants a good while to find you!" exclaimed the minister, angrily. "I have been waiting for you half an hour."

"I was at the Archduke John's rooms, with whom I had business of importance, your excellency," said Hormayr, emphasizing his last words. "Moreover, I could not guess that your excellency would wish to grant me an audience at so unusual an hour, and without my asking for it."

"At so unusual an hour!" cried Count Stadion, putting one pinch of snuff after another into his nose. "Yes, yes, at so unusual an hour! It would have been more agreeable to me, too, if it had been unnecessary for me to trouble you and myself. But it is your own fault. You do not keep your word."

"Your excellency!" cried Hormayr, indignantly.

"Bah! it is true. You do not keep your word. You promised me that your Tyrolese should not show themselves, lest we might be charged with fomenting an insurrection; and it was necessary, also, to prevent the Bavarians from learning prematurely our plans. Can you deny that you promised this to me?"

"No, your excellency, I do not deny it at all."

"Well, your Tyrolese are running around everywhere."

"Pardon me, your excellency, that cannot be true. You must have been misinformed."

"What! misinformed? How dare you say so to my face, sir? Your beardman, or bushman, or Sandwirth Hofer is at the Kärnthnerthor Theatre, and is the observed of all observers. I saw him with my own eyes; and that was the reason why I left the theatre and sent for you." *

"Your excellency saw him with your own eyes! Then, of course, it must be true, and I would beg leave of your excellency to go immediately to the theatre and take him to his hotel."

"That was just what I wished to ask you to do, Baron von Hormayr. Make haste and induce this bushman to leave Vienna immediately."

"He will leave the capital early in the morning. Your excellency will permit me now to withdraw."

Baron von Hormayr hastened down stairs, left the chancery of state, and crossed the Joseph's Place. On reaching the Kärnthnerthor Theatre, he bought a ticket at the office and entered the pit.

"The Marriage of Figaro," by Mozart, was performed at the Kärnthnerthor Theatre to-night, and this favorite opera of the Viennese had attracted so large an audience that not a seat was vacant, and the baron had to elbow his way with no little difficulty through the crowd filling the pit, in order to reach a

---

* Count Stadion's own words.—See Hormayr's "Andreas Hofer," vol i., p. 209.

point where he might be able to see every part of the house, and discover him for whose sake he had come.

At length he had succeeded in advancing so far that, leaning against one of the pillars supporting the upper tiers of boxes, he was able to survey the lower part of the house. But all faces were averted from it, all eyes were fixed on the stage. The opera had just reached the scene where Count Almaviva lifts the carpet from the chair and finds Cherubino under it. A loud outburst of laughter resounded from the pit to the upper gallery. But in the midst of the din, a loud and angry voice exclaimed : "Ah, you young good-for-nothing, if I had you here I would show you how to behave !" And a threatening fist and vigorous arm was raised in the midst of the orchestra-stalls.

"Good heavens ! that is really Andreas Hofer," murmured Baron von Hormayr, concealing himself anxiously behind the pillar. A renewed shout of laughter greeted Hofer's words, and all eyes turned toward the side where they had been uttered. And there sat the good Andreas Hofer, in his handsome national costume, with his long black beard, and his florid, kind-hearted face. There he sat, quite regardless of the gaze which the audience fixed upon him, utterly unaware of the fact that he was the observed of all observers, and quite engrossed in looking at the stage, where proceeded the well-known scene between Cherubino, the count, and Figaro. He followed the progress of the action with rapt attention, and when Cherubino tried to prove his innocence by all sorts of plausible and improbable falsehoods, Hofer's brow became clouded. He averted his eyes from the stage, and turned to his neighbor. "Why," he said, loudly and indignantly, "that boy is as great a liar as though he were Bonaparte himself !"

Now the merriment of the audience knew no longer any bounds. They applauded, they shouted, "Bravo ! bravo !" They forgot the scene on the stage entirely, and devoted their exclusive attention to the queer, bearded stranger in the orchestra-stall, on whom all eyes and opera-glasses were fixed.

Baron von Hormayr behind his pillar wiped the perspiration from his forehead, and cast furious glances on Andreas

Hofer, who, however, was utterly unaware of his presence, and from whose breast, protected as it was by his beard and crucifix, rebounded all such glances like blunted arrows.

The actors, who, interrupted by the unexpected cheers and the incident in the audience, had paused a few minutes, and had themselves hardly been able to refrain from bursting into laughter, now continued their scene, and the charms of the music and the interesting character of the action soon succeeded again in riveting the attention of the audience.

Andreas Hofer, who had in the mean time relapsed into his silent astonishment, gazed fixedly upon the stage. Baron von Hormayr left his place quietly and walked to the entrance. He slipped a florin into the hand of the doorkeeper, who was leaning against the wall. "Say," he whispered to him hastily, "as soon as the curtain drops, go to the giant with the long beard, who sits in the orchestra-stall yonder, and whose words amused the audience just now. He is a cattle-dealer from Hungary, and I must see him at once. Just whisper in his ear that his countryman with the wine and horses has arrived, and it is necessary he should come and see him right away.—Thank God, the curtain falls ! Now make haste. If you bring the cattle-dealer with you into the corridor, I will give you another florin."

The doorkeeper's face beamed with satisfaction ; he elbowed himself courageously through the crowd, and succeeded in reaching the "cattle-dealer from Hungary," who sat absorbed in his reflections, with his head bent on his breast. He touched his shoulder softly and whispered his message into his ear.

Andreas Hofer gave a start and stared at the doorkeeper. "What countrymen ? " he asked ; "and how can he bring to me wine and horses here as—"

"I do not know anything about it," whispered the doorkeeper ; "I know only that your countryman with the wine and the horses is waiting for you, and that he says he must see you right away."

"Well, then, come, conduct me to him," said Andreas, rising from his chair, and drawing up his colossal form to its full height. "I should like to know who this countryman is. Lead the way, sir ; I will follow you."

The doorkeeper retraced his steps through the crowd ; Andreas Hofer followed him, greeting kindly and pleasantly in all directions, and pushing aside the men like flies whenever they stood in his way.

At length they reached the door, and stepped into the corridor. Baron von Hormayr, like a tiger pouncing upon his prey, rushed upon Andreas Hofer, seized his arm, and drew him down the corridor into the outer hall, which was so deserted and silent that there was no danger of their conversation being overheard by an eavesdropper.

Here at length Hormayr stood still and dropped the arm of Andreas Hofer, who had followed him, dumfounded with astonishment, and glancing around as if looking for somebody else.

"Andy," exclaimed Hormayr, vehemently, "what am I to think of you ? The Tyrolese always keep their promises, and to think that our honest Sandwirth alone should not do so ! You pledged me your word that you would conceal your presence here in Vienna as much as possible, and now you are running about the city in your national costume and with your bearded face to hear the opera-trills and see how the ballet-dancers stretch their legs !" *

"Andreas Hofer never breaks his word," said Hofer, gravely. "I promised not to appear in the streets in the daytime, and I have faithfully kept my word. I stayed at home all day, and it was only after nightfall that we three went together into the street. Speckbacher and Wallner went to the Archduke John's gunsmith, Anthony Steger, to take leave of him, and I intended to go to St. Stephen's Cathedral to attend vespers. But I am a stranger in the city, and happened to lose my way. All at once I got into a dense crowd, and thought I had arrived at St. Stephen's Cathedral, and that the crowd consisted of pious Christians going to vespers ; hence, I allowed myself to be drawn along into the door, because I thought it was the church."

* Hormayr's own words.—See Hormayr's "Andreas Hofer," vol. i., p. 209.

"And on buying a ticket, Andy, you supposed you purchased indulgence, did you not ?"

"No, I did not," said Andreas in a tone of embarrassment.
"But, on seeing all those persons step to the office and get
tickets, I thought there were Christian passion-plays performed there, as at Innspruck in Lent ; and on hearing the
man standing before me shouting, 'Ticket for an orchestra-
stall,' I shouted, also, 'Ticket for an orchestra-stall,' and threw
a florin on the table. Thereupon they handed me a ticket,
and I followed the others into the hall. The performance
commenced almost at the same moment, the curtain rose, and
the actors began to sing. It is true, it is not a passion-play,
and there is nothing from the Bible in it ; but then it is a nice
play. I believe the curtain will rise again immediately, and
it is time for me to return to my seat. But I should like to
know where my countryman with the horses and wine is. He
insisted on seeing me, sent for me, and does not come now."

"But, Andy, do you not yet know that it was I who sent
for you ?" asked Hormayr. "Why, it was only a stratagem of
mine to get the Barbone out of the theatre and take him away
from here."

"But why do you want to take me away from here ? I
tell you I like the play very well, and have never seen any
thing like it. It is true, Cherubino, the boy, is an arrant liar,
but he is a jolly fellow, and I do not want him to come to
grief. And Figaro is a sly fox, and withal a brave man. I
should like to make his acquaintance and ask him if he really
promised old Marielle to marry her ; for it would be wrong if
he did not keep his word now, and refused to make her his
wife because he likes the young woman better than her. If I
knew where he lives, I would go to him this very night and
tell him what he ought to do."

"Oh, you foolish old child of Nature ! what you saw on
the stage was nothing but a play. Figaro never existed ; and
even though he did, you would not go to him, but accompany
me and take supper with me."

"I am sorry," said Andreas, gravely, "I cannot do so ; for,
in the first place, I must stay here and wait for the countryman who has arrived here with the horses and wine."

"Jesus Maria ! what do you say ? The countryman ? Did I not tell you that it is I, Andy ?"

"Oh, yes, I had already forgotten it. But, second, I cannot go because I must see the remainder of the play. Let me, therefore, return to my seat, for I paid for the whole performance ; I believe I have already missed a great deal ; but they will assuredly not return to me at the office a penny for what I did not hear." *

"They will not, and shall not either," cried Hormayr, angrily. "You will not return to your seat, Andy, but go and take supper with me. For you know, my dear fellow, that you have come to Vienna, not to go to the theatre, but to ask the dear Archduke John's assistance and succor for the beloved Tyrol, and inquire of the emperor if he will not aid his loyal Tyrolese in their attempt to become his subjects once more. And the emperor and the archduke will help you ; they promise to send soldiers and guns in time to the Tyrol. But, in return, you must do what the archduke asked you to do ; you must carefully conceal yourself, Andy, in order to prevent the Bavarians from learning of your trip to Vienna ; otherwise they would arrest you and your friends after your return to the Tyrol. Hence you must not return to your seat, where so many persons would see you, and unfortunately have seen you already."

"Well, if it must be so, let us go, sir," sighed Andreas. "But just listen how they are singing, shouting, and cheering inside ! Jesus Maria ! Figaro, I believe, will have to marry old Marielle after all, and give up pretty little Susanne. Ah, my God ! she will die heart-broken, for she loves him so dearly. Pray, sir, let me go in once more, that I may see whether or not he must marry old Marielle."

"No, Andy," said Hormayr, smiling, "you need not be uneasy ; Figaro will not marry old Marielle, for she is his own mother."

"What !" cried Andreas, in dismay ; "she his mother, and he has promised to marry her ? That is most sinful and infamous ! No good Christian should listen to such things. Come along, sir. I do not want to hear another word of it.

* Hofer's own words.—See Hormayr, " Andreas Hofer," vol. i., p. 310.

Good heavens ! what will Anna Gertrude say when I tell her what I have seen here, and that there are here in Vienna men infamous enough to promise to marry their mothers ? "

"But they never do so in reality, Andy, but only on the stage. Otherwise the police would be after them at once. For the emperor is a very pious and virtuous gentleman, and he does not permit any infractions of the sacred laws of God and the Church in his dominions."

"Yes, the emperor is a very pious and virtuous gentleman," exclaimed Andreas Hofer, enthusiastically, "and that is the reason why the Tyrolese love him and wish to be again his subjects and children. Come, I will go home with you. I do not want to hear any more of the theatrical nonsense. Let us speak of our emperor and our dear Archduke John. God grant that we may soon be able to say he is our emperor again, and the archduke is our John, and his Tyrolese are again his subjects, because they fought well for their liberty, and because God blessed their efforts and crowned them with victory. Come, we will go home, and to-morrow I shall re-turn to the Tyrol, to my wife and children, and mountain and valley shall know that the time has come, and that we shall become Austrians again. May the Holy Virgin protect us and grant us a safe return ; may she prevent the Bavarians from waylaying us and frustrating our great and noble pur-pose ! " *

CHAPTER VIII.

CONSECRATION OF THE FLAGS, AND FAREWELL.

THE die was cast, then. The war with France was to break out again. There was to be no more procrastination and hesi-tation. The time for action was at hand.

* The delegates of the Tyrolese left Vienna on the following morning; their presence there, however, had been reported to the Bavarian officers, who, during their homeward journey, almost succeeded in arresting them. John von Graff, a banker of Botzen, was apprised of their arrival in Vienna by his correspondent in that city and informed the commissary-general at Brixen

Already the French ambassador, Andréossi, had left Vienna, and all the members of the legation had followed him. Already Clement Count Metternich had arrived at Vienna; but he had not left Paris as Count Andréossi had left Vienna, quietly and unmolested, but Napoleon had caused him to be escorted to the French frontier by a detachment of *gens d'armes.*

And to-day, on the 9th of March, Austria was to proclaim to all Germany, by means of a public festival, that she was resolved to renew the struggle with France and risk once more the blood of her people and the existence of her imperial dynasty in order to deliver Germany from the usurper who was intent on crushing in his iron hands the liberty and independence of the German nation.

A solemn ceremony was to take place to-day on the Glacis of Vienna. The flags of the militia were to be consecrated by the Archbishop of Vienna, and the whole imperial family was to be present at the solemnity. Hence, all Vienna presented a festive appearance; all stores were closed, and no one was seen following his every-day avocations. The Viennese had made a holiday; no one would toil for his daily bread; all wished to refresh themselves only with mental food, and greet with their glances and acclamations the noble men who were to take the field for the salvation of the fatherland.

The people were surging in dense masses toward the glacis, rushing with irresistible impetuosity into the empty ditches, and climbing the trees on their edges, or gaining some other standpoint whence they could survey the solemnity which was to take place on the broad promenade of the glacis. On the large rondel of the glacis had been erected a tribune whose golden-broidered velvet canopy was surmounted by a very large imperial crown; four golden double-headed eagles adorned the four corners of the canopy, and held in their beaks the colors of Austria and Hungary. Under the canopy stood gilt arm-chairs, with cushions of purple velvet. This was the tribune destined for the emperor and his family;

of what he had learned. A warrant for the arrest of the three delegates was issued, but they escaped in time into the mountains.—Hormayr, vol. i., p. 191.

all eyes were riveted upon it, and all hearts longed to greet the sovereign, and thank him for the proud happiness of this hour.

Further on rose other and no less splendidly decorated tribunes, the seats of which had been sold at enormous rates to the aristocracy and wealthy citizens of Vienna for the benefit of the militia ; and thousands had found seats on the trees surrounding the broad promenade and the rondel, and paid for their airy perches only with some pains and bruises.

Since early dawn this pilgrimage to the glacis had been going on ; by ten o'clock all seats, roads, tribunes, trees, ditches, and bridges, were occupied by a dense crowd ; and, in order to prevent accidents, the authorities had already ordered all approaches to the glacis to be closed.

On the broad promenade, too, matters assumed a very lively aspect. The militia marched up with banners unfurled and drums beating. They drew up in line on both sides of the road, and their officers and standard-bearers repaired to the large rondel where another had been constructed in face of the imperial tribune. They ranged themselves around the altar, on whose steps priests in full vestments were kneeling, and which was surmounted by a gigantic crucifix, visible to all spectators far and near, and waving to all its blessings and love-greetings.

And now all the church-steeples commenced ringing their peals ; the iron tongues of their bells proclaimed to the inhabitants of Vienna, and to the many thousands of strangers who had come to witness the solemnity, that the emperor with his consort and his children had left the Hofburg, and was approaching the glacis, followed by his suite. The militia assumed a stiff military attitude, the drums rolled, the cannon boomed, the bugles sounded merry notes, and the emperor, leading his consort by the hand, entered the tribune. He looked pale ; his form was bent, and trembling as if shaken by an inward fever ; and even more singular appeared his down-hanging under-lip and the gloomy, morose expression of his lustreless blue eyes. But the people did not see this ; they saw only that their emperor had arrived—their emperor, who had resolved to deliver Austria from the ignominious foreign yoke ;

who would die with his subjects rather than longer bear the arrogance of France; and who boldly and courageously staked all in order to win all, to restore at length a lasting peace to Austria and Germany, and vindicate their honor and independence. For this reason all hearts greeted the Emperor Francis with love and exultation, and he was received with deafening and constantly-renewed cheers.

The emperor received with a forced smile the flattering homage which was rendered to him, but more radiant was the smile of his consort; in her dark and glowing eyes glistened tears of joyful emotion, when she glanced at this jubilant mass of spectators and the enthusiastic regiments of the militia. She was also full of exultation; she did not, however, give vent to her feelings, but pent them up in her heart, owing to the moroseness of her imperial husband.

In the midst of a fresh outburst of popular enthusiasm, Francis bent over the empress. "I suppose you are well satisfied now, empress?" he asked. "You have attained your object; all of you have fanned the flame until war is ready to break out, and every thing will go again topsy-turvy. But I tell you, empress, we shall fail again; I do not believe that we shall conquer."

"Well, your majesty, then we shall succumb and die, but it will be an honorable defeat. It is better to perish in a just and honorable struggle than submit patiently to foreign usurpation."

"A very nice phrase, but the practical execution of such ideas is sometimes by far more unpleasant than the theory which they express. I am afraid you will have good reason to regret this day, and—but what fearful noise is this again? The people are cheering as though they were welcoming God Almighty Himself. What is it?"

"Your majesty," said Ludovica, gazing timidly into her husband's face, "I believe the people are cheering the Archdukes Charles and John, for they are just walking along the ranks of the militia."

"Ah, my brothers!" murmured the emperor, with an angry expression, which, however, disappeared again immediately; "the people are cheering my brothers as though they were two divinities from whom alone they expect salvation and prosperity."

"Your majesty, the people cheer the archdukes because they are the brothers of the emperor, and because the confidence of your majesty has placed them at the head of the Austrian armies to lead them to battle, and, if it please God, to victory. It is your majesty alone that appointed the Archduke Charles generalissimo of all your forces, and the Archduke John commander of the army of Lower Austria."

"Yes, I did so, for, blessed as I am with brothers so heroic and spirited, I must of course distinguish and employ them in accordance with their merits ; otherwise they might believe I was jealous of their glory and splendor. This would be entirely false, for, so far from being jealous of them, I love them dearly, and give them now again another opportunity to gain laurels, as they did in 1805. It is true, my brother the generalissimo, was not victorious at Austerlitz, and my brother John has likewise sustained many a defeat ; but that does not prevent them from being heroes and great men. Just listen to the roars with which the people greet them ! Jesus Maria ! I hope the generalissimo will not have his fits from excessive joy."

Ludovica cast a quick, mournful glance on the maliciously smiling face of her husband. "Your majesty need not be alarmed," she said ; "your tender apprehensions will fortunately not be fulfilled. You see that the archduke is quite well ; he is just addressing his troops."

"Yes, yes, I know his speech. M. von Gentz wrote it for him, and I permitted him to deliver it. Ah, it abounds with fine phrases, and my dear Austrians will be astonished on hearing what liberal men we have become all of a sudden, and what grand ideas of liberty, equality, and popular sovereignty we have adopted. Just listen to him ! the conclusion is very fine, and sounds just as though the Marseillaise had been translated into the language of the Austrians."

"Soldiers," shouted the archduke, at this moment, in a loud, ringing voice, "the liberty of Europe has taken refuge under the flag of Austria ; the rights, freedom, and honor of all Germany expect their salvation only of our armies. Never shall

they, instruments of oppression, carry on in foreign countries
the endless wars of a destructive ambition, annihilate innocent
nations, and with their own corpses pave for foreign conquer-
ors the road leading to usurped thrones. Soldiers, we take up
arms only for the liberty, honor, and rights of all Germany ;
it is these sacred boons that we have to defend ! " *

A long-continued, deafening outburst of applause both of
the soldiers and the people was the reply to the stirring address of the generalissimo ; but suddenly every sound was
hushed, for at the altar, yonder by the side of the tall crucifix,
appeared now the archbishop, accompanied by the whole body
of the high clergy.

The emperor rose from his seat and bowed humbly and devoutly to the prelate who had been the teacher of his youth,
and had afterward married him three times, the last time only
a few months ago.

And now the archdukes marched the troops into the middle of the place, and the consecration of the flags commenced
amid the peals of all the church-bells and the booming of artillery.

The emperor looked on, standing, bareheaded, and with
hands clasped in prayer. Ludovica turned her eyes heaven-
ward, and her lips moved in a low, fervent prayer. Behind
them stood the young archdukes and archduchesses, muttering
prayers, and yet glancing around curiously ; and the cavaliers
of the imperial couple, looking gloomy, and plainly showing
in their sombre faces the rage that filled their hearts.

The ceremony being finished, the archbishop lifted up his
hands and stretched them out toward the soldiers. " Adieu,
until we meet again," he exclaimed with a radiant air, and in
a voice of joyful enthusiasm ; " adieu, until we meet again at
the hour of danger ! "

"Adieu, until we meet again at the hour of danger !"
echoed the soldiers with enthusiasm. Seeing then that the
archbishop bent his knees, they knelt likewise and bowed their
heads in prayer. Hushed was every sound on the vast place.
Only the church-bells were pealing and the artillery was booming in the distance, and the murmur of the devout prayers

---

* Hormayr, " Allgemeine Geschichte," vol. iii., p. 219.

which rose to God from so many pious hearts broke the silence.

In the fervent enthusiasm of this hour no one felt the least timidity, no one looked anxiously into the future.   Even the mothers did not shed tears for their sons who were about to take the field ; the affianced brides allowed their lovers to depart without uttering complaints or weeping at the thought of their impending departure ; wives took leave of their husbands with joyous courage, pressing their infants to their breasts and commending them trustingly to God's protection.   The patriotic enthusiasm had seized all, and carried away even the coldest and most selfish hearts.   The rich contributed their money with unwonted liberality ; those who were in less favorable circumstances laid down their plate and valuables on the altar of the country ; the mechanics offered to work gratuitously for the army ; the women scraped lint and organized associations for the relief of the wounded ; the young men offered their life-blood to the fatherland, and considered it as a favor that their services were not rejected.

The long-concealed hatred against France burst forth in bright flames throughout Austria and Germany ; the war was hailed with rapturous enthusiasm, and every heart longed to take part in this struggle, which seemed to all a war of holy vengeance and retribution.   For the first time in long years Austria felt again thoroughly identified with Germany, while the other Germans were looking upon Austria as a German state and holding out their hands to their Austrian brethren, telling them that they sympathized most vividly with the ends which they were trying to attain.

But while the utmost exultation was reigning among the people and the soldiers on this joyful day, a gloomy silence prevailed in the imperial palace.   The joyous mask with which the generalissimo, the Archduke Charles, had covered his face while on the glacis, had disappeared from it so soon as he had returned to his rooms.   Pale and faint, he rested in an easy-chair, and, fixing his sombre eyes on his quartermaster-general, Count Grünne, he said : " My friend, listen to that which I am going to say to you now, and which you will remember one day.   I have objected three times in the most emphatic manner to this declaration of war, for I know that our preparations are not sufficiently matured, and I know also that I have here in Austria powerful enemies who are intent on impeding all my efforts, and who will shrink from nothing in order to ruin me, and with me you too, my poor friend. The whole aristocracy is hostile to me, and will never allow the emperor's brothers to set bounds to its oligarchy by their merits and influence; it will always oppose us, even though it should endanger thereby the power and honor of the fatherland. I know all the perils and intrigues surrounding me, and because I know them I tried to avoid them, opposed the war, and strove to get rid at least of the command-in-chief. But the emperor would not allow me to do so; he ordered me to accept the arduous position of generalissimo of his forces, and, as his subject, I had to obey him. But I repeat it, this will be a disastrous war for Austria, and I look with gloomy forebodings into the future."

And as gloomy as the generalissimo's face was that of his brother, the Emperor Francis. He had retired into his cabinet, and strode growlingly up and down, holding the fly-flap in his hand, and striking savagely at the flies which his searching eyes discovered here and there on the wall.

Suddenly the door opened, and the footman announced the Archduke John. The emperor's face became even more morose. He cast the fly-flap aside, and murmured to himself, "My brothers never leave me any rest." He then said in a loud voice, "Let him come in."

A minute afterward the archduke entered the cabinet. His face was still joyously lit up by the soul-stirring solemnity in which he had participated in the morning; his eye was yet radiant with noble enthusiasm and exultation, and a serene smile played around his lips. Thus he appeared before his brother, whose face seemed doubly gloomy in the presence of his own.

"I come to take leave of your majesty and bid farewell to my brother Francis," he said, in a mild, tender voice. "I intend to set out to-night for Gratz, and organize my staff there."

"God bless you, commander of the Southern army!" said

the emperor, dryly ; "God bless you, brother. You were all eager for war ; now you have it ! "

"And your majesty has witnessed the enthusiasm with which the Austrian people hailed the declaration of war. And not only the people of Austria, but all Germany, looks now with joy, hope, and pride toward Austria, and participates most cordially in our warlike enthusiasm."

"I do not care for that," said the emperor, dryly. "Thank God, I cast off the crown of Germany three years ago, and am no longer Emperor of Germany."

"But one day, when your armies have conquered France and delivered the world from the insatiable usurper, Germany will gratefully lie down at your majesty's feet and beseech you to accept the imperial crown again at her hands."

"Much obliged, sir, but I would not take it," exclaimed the emperor, with a shrug. "But say, brother, are you really convinced that we can and shall conquer Bonaparte ? "

"I am. We shall conquer, if—"

"Well, if—" asked the emperor, when the archduke hesitated.

"If we are really determined to do so," said John, looking the emperor full in the face ; "if we act harmoniously, if we do not impede each other, if no petty jealousies favor the efforts of one and frustrate those of the other. Oh, brother, permit me at this farewell hour to utter a few frank and truthful words, and I beg your majesty to forgive me if my heart opens to you in unreserved confidence. Brother, I confess frankly all is not as it should be here. Where concord should reign, there is discord ; where all should have their eyes fixed only on the great goal, and avail themselves of all means and forces, they are split up into factions bitterly hostile to each other. Oh, my gracious emperor, I beseech you, do not listen to these factions, do not confide in those who would like to arouse your suspicion against your brothers. Believe me, you have no more loyal, devoted, and obedient subject than I am ; therefore, confide in me, who wish only to contribute to the greatness, honor, and glory of my country and my emperor, to the best of my power, however insignificant it may be. My brother, there has long been a gulf between us ; God knows that I did not dig it. But let us fill it up forever at this farewell hour. I implore you, believe in my love, my devoted loyalty ; take me by the hand and say, ' John, I trust you ! I believe in you ! ' See, I am waiting for these words as for the blessing which is to accompany me into battle, and rest on my heart like a talisman. Brother, speak these words of love and confidence ! Give me your hand—open your arms to your brother ! "

" Why should we enact here a sentimental scene ? " asked the emperor, harshly. " I do not like such things, and want to see family dramas only performed on the stage. Thank God, I am not a theatrical emperor, but a real one, and will have nothing to do with scenes from plays. Nor do I know of any gulfs existing between you and me. I never perceived them, and was never disturbed thereby. But why do you protest your love and loyalty in so passionate a manner to me ? Who tells you, then, that I suspect them ? That would be equivalent to considering my brother a traitor, and it would be very unfortunate for him ; for toward traitors I shall always be inexorable, whosover they may be, and whether they be persons of high or low rank. Let us speak no longer of it. But, besides, you have again advised me, without being requested to do so, and demand that I should not listen to any factions. I never do, brother. I never listen to any factions, neither to yours, nor to that of the others. I listen only to myself, and require submissiveness and obedience of my servants. You are one of the latter ; go, then, and obey me. I have resolved on war ; go, then, to your corps and fight, as you are in duty bound, for your emperor and for Austria. Defeat Napoleon if you can. You are playing a game which may easily become dangerous to ourselves. You have stirred up an insurrection in the Tyrol ; you will have to bear the responsibility if this insurrection shall be unsuccessful."

" I will bear it, and God will forgive what I have done ! " said John, solemnly. " Your majesty, you would not listen to the brother who offered you his love frankly and honestly. I have nothing to add to what I have said, nor shall I ever make another attempt to gain your confidence."

" Is that intended as a threat ? " asked the emperor, angrily.

"No," said John, mournfully, "I do not threaten you. I shall always bear in mind that I loved you, and that you are not only my lord and emperor, but also the son of my mother."

"And I," cried the emperor, vehemently, "shall always bear in mind that you were the head of the faction which, by its insensate clamor for war, first aroused Napoleon's anger, brought about demonstrations and armaments on our part, and finally obliged me to resolve on war, although I know full well that this resolution will inevitably involve Austria in great disaster. Let me likewise speak a farewell word to you, brother. We shall succumb again, although my wise and learned brothers are at the head of the army. I consulted the most experienced and sagacious men. I myself paid a visit to Count Cobenzl, who is lying at the point of death, and asked his opinion. He hates Napoleon as ardently as any one, and yet he is in favor of peace. I consulted the Prince de Ligne and Minister Thugut ; one is an ambitious captain, the other a vindictive diplomatist, who would like to overthrow Napoleon ; and yet both were for peace with France, and I will tell you the reason why : because they know that among all my captains and generals there is not one determined and able enough to cope with Napoleon and his marshals : because they knew that even my brother Charles, the generalissimo, is vacillating and irresolute ; and because they do not know what an eminent captain the Archduke John would be, if he only had a chance to show his military talents. If, despite all this, I resolved on war, it was because circumstances, and not my convictions, obliged me to do it—circumstances which were mostly brought about by you and your friends."

"Your majesty," said John, in a grave and dignified manner, "permit me to say a few words in reply to what you have just said. You allude to my military talents, which you say I have not had a chance to show. Well, give me such a chance ; deliver me from the surveillance tying my hands ; let me pursue my path as your general freely and without restrictions, and I pledge you my word that I will reconquer the Tyrol and your Italian provinces."

"See, see, what a nice plan !" exclaimed the emperor,

laughing. "You wish to be another generalissimo, and independent of any other commander's will ?"

"No, your majesty ; I wish to obtain only equal rights and
authority to deliberate and decide jointly with my brother
Charles."

"It is very bold in you, sir, thus to oppose your generalissimo," said the emperor, sternly. "To-day you will no longer
obey the generalissimo—to-morrow you will perhaps refuse to
obey the emperor. Not another word about it ! Go and do
your duty. The Archduke Charles is generalissimo, and you
will submit to his orders and instructions. Farewell, brother ;
may God and the Holy Virgin bless you and your army !"

"Farewell, your majesty," said the archduke, bowing ceremoniously to the emperor. He then turned hastily and left
the room.

The emperor looked after him with an angry air. "I believe the two archdukes will thwart each other on all occasions," he said, in a low voice. "There will not only be war
with France, but also war between the factions in Austria, and
the consequence will be, that my brothers will gain but very
few laurels."

The Archduke John returned slowly to his rooms. After
entering his cabinet, he sank on the divan, as if crushed and
heart-broken. He sat a long time in silence, his head bent
on his breast, and uttering from time to time heart-rending
groans. After a long pause, he slowly lifted his tearful eyes
to heaven.

"Thou knowest, my God," he said, in a low voice, "that
my intentions are good and pure, and that I desire nothing
but to serve my country and deliver it from the disgrace
which it has had to submit to for so many years past. Thou
knowest that I wish nothing for myself, but all for the fatherland. Help me, my God, help our poor, unfortunate Austria !
Let us not succumb and perish ! Grant victory to our arms !
O Austria, O Germany, why can I not purchase liberty and
independence for you with my blood ? But I can at least
fight and die .for you ! I shall welcome death, if my dying
eyes can behold liberty dawning upon Germany !"

CHAPTER IX.

'TIS TIME !

IT was late in the afternoon of the 8th of April. The setting sun was shedding his last red rays on the distant moun-
tain-crests of the Janfen and the Timbler Toch, whose blood-
red summits contrasted wonderfully with the deep azure of
the clear sky. On the lower slopes of the mountains twilight
had set in ; the pines, the daring chamois of the vegetable
kingdom, which had climbed up to the highest parts of the
mountains, cast the gray veil of dusk over these lower slopes.
Below, in the Passeyr valley, however, night already prevailed, for the mountains looming up on both sides of the
valley filled it with darkness even before sundown ; and only
the wild, roaring Passeyr, which rushes from the mountain
through the valley, glistened like a silver belt in the gloom.
The church-bells of the villages of St. Leonard and St. Martin,
lying on both sides of the valley, tolled a solemn curfew,
awakening here and there a low, sleepy echo ; and from time
to time was heard from a mountain-peak a loud, joyous *Jodler*,
by which a Tyrolese hunter, perhaps, announced his speedy
return to his family in the valley. The gloom in the narrow
Passeyrthal became deeper and deeper, and, like bright glow-
worms, the lights in the houses of St. Leonard and St. Martin
glistened now in the darkness.

Lights appeared not only in the valley below, but also here
and there on the mountain-slopes ; and especially in the solitary house on the knoll situated half-way between the two
villages, was seen the bright glare of many candles, and the
persons passing on the road in the valley looked up and whispered to each other : "Andreas Hofer is at home, and, it seems,
has a great many guests at his house, for all the windows of
his handsome inn are illuminated."

The solitary house on the knoll, then, belonged to Andreas
Hofer. It was the *Gasthaus zum Sand*, far famed throughout the Tyrol. And the passers-by were not mistaken. Andreas Hofer was at home, and had a great many guests at his

house. On the benches of the large bar-room sat his guests, handsome Tyrolese, with flashing eyes and animated faces, which were all turned toward the Sandwirth,* who was sitting on the small table yonder, and conversing in a low tone with his friends Eisenstecken and Sieberer. All the guests seemed excited and anxious ; no one opened his mouth to utter merry jests ; none of the gay songs so popular among the Tyrolese resounded ; and the guests did not even venture to address playful remarks to Hofer's pretty daughters, who were gliding noiselessly through the room to fill the empty beer-glasses.

"It seems," murmured Anthony Sieberer, "that the Austrian government has again postponed the matter, and we shall vainly look for the arrival of the message. This new delay puts an end to the whole movement."

"I do not think so," said Hofer, gravely, and loud enough to be heard by all. "Do not despond, my dear friends! The Austrian government will assuredly keep its word, for the dear brave Archduke John promised me in the emperor's name that Austria would succor the Tyrolese, and send troops into our country, if we would be in readiness on the 9th of April to rise against the Bavarians. My dear friends, do you put no confidence, then, in the word of our excellent emperor and the good archduke, who has always loved us so dearly ?"

"No, no, we put implicit confidence in their word !" shouted the Tyrolese, with one accord.

"The messenger will surely come, just have a little patience," added Hofer, with a pleasant nod ; "the day is not yet at an end, and until midnight we may smoke yet many a pipe and drink many a glass of beer.—Anna Gertrude, see to it that the glasses of the guests are always well filled."

Anna Gertrude, a fine-looking matron of thirty-six, with florid cheeks and flashing hazel eyes, had just placed before her husband another jug, filled with foaming beer, and she nodded now to her Andy with a smile, showing two rows of faultless white teeth.

"I and the girls will attend to the guests," she said, "but

* The name usually given to Hofer—Sandwirth, landlord of the inn "Zum Sand."

the men do not drink any thing. The glasses and jugs are all filled, but they do not empty them, and— Look! who comes there ?"

Andreas Hofer turned his head toward the door ; then suddenly he uttered a cry of surprise and jumped up.

"Halloo!" he exclaimed, "I believe this is the messenger whom we are looking for." And he pointed his outstretched arm at the small, dark form entering the room at this moment.

"It is Major Teimer," he continued, joyfully ; "I suppose you know yet our dear major of 1805 ? "

"Hurrah! Martin Teimer is there," shouted the Tyrolese, rising from their seats, and hastening to the new-comer to shake hands with him and bid him heartily welcome.

Martin Teimer thanked them warmly for this kind reception, and a flash of sincere gratification burst from his shrewd blue eyes.

"I thought I should meet all the brave men of the Passeyr valley at Andy's house to-night," he said, "and I therefore greet you all at once, my dear comrades of 1805. That year was disastrous to us, but I think the year 1809 will be a better one, and we shall regain to-day what we lost at that time."

"Yes, we shall, as sure as there is a God," shouted the Tyrolese ; and Andreas Hofer laid his arm on Teimer's shoulder and gazed deeply into his eyes.

"Say, Martin Teimer, are all things in readiness, and do you bring us word to rise ? "

"I do, all things are in readiness," said Teimer, solemnly. " Our countryman, Baron von Hormayr, whom the Austrian government appointed governor and intendant of the Austrian forces which are to co-operate with us, sends me to Andreas Hofer, whom I am to inform that the Austrian troops, commanded by Marquis von Chasteler and General Hiller, will cross the Tyrolese frontier to-night."

"Hurrah, hurrah ! the Austrians are coming !" shouted the Tyrolese, jubilantly, swinging their pointed hats in the air. "The war has broken out, the Austrians are coming, and we will expel the Bavarians from the country !"

Andreas Hofer's face, too, was radiant with joy ; but, instead of singing and shouting, he was silent, lifted his eyes slowly to heaven, and seized with both his hands the crucifix resting on his breast.

"Let us pray, my friends," he said in a loud and solemn voice ; "let us thank our Lord God and our patron saint in the stillness of our hearts."

The men paused ; like Andreas Hofer, they clasped their hands, bent their heads, and muttered fervent prayers.

After a long pause Hofer raised his head again. "And now, men, listen to what I have to say to you," he exclaimed, cheerfully. "I have invited you all because you are the most influential and respectable men in this part of the country, and because the fatherland has need of you and counts upon you and me. The sharpshooters of the Passeyrthal told me, if war should break out, I must be their captain ; and I accepted the position because I think that every one is in duty bound to risk his limbs and life for the sake of the fatherland, and place himself just where he can serve it best. But if I am to be your captain, you must all assist me to the best of your power. We must act harmoniously, and strain every nerve to deliver the fatherland and restore the Tyrol to our beloved emperor."

"We are resolved to do so," shouted the men, with one accord.

"I know it full well," said Andreas Hofer, joyously. "Let us go to work, then, and circulate throughout the Tyrol the message that the Austrians are coming, and that it is time. Say, Teimer, did you not bring a written message with you ?"

"Here is a letter from Hormayr," said Martin Teimer, drawing a large sealed paper from his bosom.

Andreas took it and opened it quickly. But while he was reading it, a slight cloud overspread his countenance, and for a moment he cast a rapid, searching glance on Martin Teimer's bright, keen face ; however, no sooner had he met Teimer's stealthy, inquiring glance, than he quickly turned his eyes again to the paper.

"Well," he said then, striking the paper with his right hand, "the statements contained in this letter are entirely in accordance with our wishes. We are to rise at once, for already to-morrow the Austrians will have crossed our frontiers. Marquis von Chasteler will march from Carinthia into the Puster valley ; General Hiller is moving from Salzburg toward the Lower Inn valley ; the former thinks he will reach Brixen in the course of four days; the latter says he will be at Innspruck within the same time. I and Martin Teimer here, who no longer keeps a tobacco-shop at Klagenfurth, but is again *Major* Teimer as he was four years ago—we are to direct and manage every thing in the Tyrol, and are intrusted with the duty of seeing to it that the flames of the insurrection burst forth now as speedily as possible from one end of the Tyrol to the other, and that it shall become a conflagration that will burn up all Frenchmen and Bavarians, or compel them to escape from the country. Assist us, then, my men, in spreading the news over the mountains and through the valleys, that all may rise and participate in the great work of deliverance. Every able-bodied man is to shoulder his rifle, and the women and children are to carry, from house to house, little balls of paper on which are written the words : ' 'Tis time ! ' as we have agreed at our meetings. And now, in compliance with the promise I gave Hormayr in Vienna, I will issue a circular to all our friends that they may know what to do under these circumstances. Is there among you any one who can write well and correctly, and to whom I may dictate? for my own handwriting is none of the best, and although what I write may be thought correctly, it is not spelled as learned men tell us it should be. If there is among you one who can write nicely and correctly what I wish to dictate, let him come forward."

"I can do it," said a young man, stepping forward.

"It is Joseph Ennemoser, son of John Ennemoser, the Seewirth," said Andreas Hofer, smiling. "Yes, I believe you are a good scribe ; you have become quite a scholar and an aristocratic gentleman, and are studying medicine at the University of Innspruck."

"For all that, I have remained an honest mountaineer ; and as for my studies, I will not think of them until we have delivered the Tyrol from the Bavarian yoke. I shall keep

only my pen, and act as Andreas Hofer's obedient secretary." *

"Sit down, then, my boy, and write. You will find pen
and ink in the drawer of yonder table. Take them, and I
will dictate to you."

And amidst the respectful silence of the men, walking up
and down slowly, and stroking his long beard with his right
hand, Andreas Hofer commenced dictating his "open order,"
which was as follows :

"Early in the morning of the 9th of April General Hiller
will march from Salzburg to the Lower Inn valley, and
General von Chasteler from Carinthia to the Puster valley.
On the 11th or 12th of April the former will arrive at Innspruck, and the latter at Brixen. The Archduke John orders
that the Mühlbach pass be occupied by peasants from the
Puster valley, and the Kuntersweg by mounted men. They
are to allow all forces of the enemy marching from Botzen
to Brixen to pass, and will cut off all communications only so
soon as they discover that the Bavarian civilians and soldiers
are trying to escape from Brixen to Botzen. Not a man must
be allowed to pass then."

While Andreas Hofer was dictating his "open order"
with a firm and thoughtful air, the peasants stood dumfounded with admiration, staring at him with a feeling of
awe, and delighted with his sagacity and understanding.
That Hofer cast from time to time a searching glance at Hormayr's letter did not disturb the admiration they felt for their
chosen leader, and they were silent and stared at him long
after he was through.

"So," said Andreas when the writing was finished, "now
Martin Teimer and I will affix our names to this open order ;
Ennemoser will then copy it half a dozen times, and six of
you will carry the copies to the other leaders who are already
waiting for them, and who will give the signal to their friends

---

* Joseph Ennemoser, son of John Ennemoser, the tailor and Seewirth
of the Passeyrthal, was a shepherd in his boyhood. His father sent him to
the gymnasium of Innspruck, and afterward to the university of the same
city, where he studied medicine. In 1809 he was Hofer's secretary. Afterward he became a celebrated professor of medicine at the University of Bonn.

in the lower valley. You, George Lanthaler, will carry the order to Joseph Speckbacher at Kufstein ; you, Joseph Gufler, will take it to the farmer at the Schildhof ; you, George Stein-hauferle, will go to Anthony Wallner, the Aichberger at Win-disch-Matrey. Quick, quick, my friends, we have no time to lose ; you must walk night and day ; you cannot rest on the road, for we must strike the blow with lightning speed, and it must be done at the same time all over the country."

"And I will likewise set out again to spread the news throughout the country," said Martin Teimer. "For two weeks past I have been in all parts of the Tyrol, and have worked everywhere for our cause, and know now that we may count upon all our countrymen. They are waiting for the signal, and we must give it to them. Here, take this package ; it contains a large number of those little paper balls upon which are written the words ' 'Tis time !' Each of you can take a handful of them and give them to your wives and children, that they may carry them to the neighbors and distribute them everywhere. Speckbacher and Wallner, too, have packages of such paper balls, and so soon as our faithful messengers bring them our 'open order,' they will likewise send around their wives and children through the neighborhood ; and everywhere the cry will be, ' 'Tis time !' We must expel the Bavarians ! I will go now, for I must concentrate my men in order to prevent the Bavarians from crossing the bridge of Laditch. Farewell, then, and God grant that we may all meet again before long as free and happy men at our good city of Innspruck ! "

"We must go too," exclaimed the Tyrolese when Martin Teimer had left the house as quickly as he had entered it. "We must go into the mountains and inform our friends that it is time."

"But go through the kitchen, my dear messengers," said Andreas Hofer ; "there is a bag of flour for each of you ; take it on your back, and on passing during your march a rivulet or a mountain torrent, throw some of the flour into it ; and wherever you find dry brushwood on the road, pile it up and kindle it, that the bale-fires may proclaim to the country, ' 'Tis time !' "

Half an hour afterward the large bar-room was deserted, and profound silence reigned in the inn *Zum Sand*. The servants and children of the Sandwirth had gone to bed ; only he himself and his faithful wife, Anna Gertrude, were yet up. Both had retired into the small sitting-room adjoining the bar-room. Andreas Hofer was walking up and down there silently and thoughtfully, his hands folded on his back ; Gertrude sat in the leather-covered arm-chair at the stove, and looked at her husband. Every thing was still around them ; only the slow, regular ticking of the clock broke the profound silence, and outside was to be heard the wild roaring of the Passeyr, which hurled its furious foaming waters not far from the inn over pebbles and fragments of rocks.

Finally, after a long pause, Andreas stood still in front of his wife, and gazed at her with a long, searching, and tender look. Gertrude, as if lifted up by this glance, rose, encircled his neck quickly with her arms, and looked with an expression of terror and anxiety into his face.

"Andy," she exclaimed, mournfully, "my own, dearest Andy, I am afraid harm will befall you !"

"That is what I expect," he said, sighing, "and I am sorry for you, my dearest wife. I was just speaking with God and my conscience, and asking them so fervently if it was not wrong in me not to think above all things of my dear wife and my beloved children, and if I ought not to live and die only for them. For I tell you, and I know, what I am going to do is dangerous, and may easily cost my life. I do not blind my eyes to it ; I may lose my life in either of two ways. A bullet may strike me in battle ; or, if my life should be spared in the struggle, and if we should be defeated, the Bavarians would treat me as a traitor ; and then a bullet would strike me also, for they would shoot me."

"Oh, Jesus Maria ! my Andy," cried Gertrude, taking Hofer's head in her hands, as if to protect it from the murderous bullets.

"I do not say that this *will* occur ; I say only that it *may* occur," said Andreas, with a gentle smile. "I wish to tell you only that I am fully alive to the dangers threatening me when I step to-morrow morning out of my street-door, and enter upon the duties of the position which they have conferred on me ; for I am to command the peasants of the Passeyr valley and direct the insurrection in all this part of the country. Therefore, I asked God and my conscience whether or not I did right in taking upon myself so responsible a task, and plunging my family, perhaps, into grief and distress. But do you know what both of them replied to me ? They said : ' It is your duty to love your wife and your children ; but you must also love your emperor and your country ; and when the latter call you and say, "Come, we need your arm and assistance," you must, as an honest man, obey the call, go to them, and leave your family ; for to love the fatherland is every man's highest honor, and to be loyal and devoted to the emperor is the first duty of every Tyrolese.' God and my conscience spoke to me thus in my breast, and now I ask you too, dear wife—I ask you before God and your conscience— would you like your husband not to obey the emperor's call, but stay at home, while his brave brethren and friends are taking the field to defend the country and expel the Bavarians ? "

"No, indeed, Andy, I would not," cried Gertrude, in dis- may ; "I should never dare again to lift my eyes before any- body ; I should not even venture to pray to the Holy Virgin and to God, for, as both gave up their divine Son, so an honest woman must give up her husband for the sake of the father- land."

Andreas laid his hand on his wife's head as if to bless her. "It is as you say, Gertrude," he said, solemnly. "For the sake of the fatherland and the emperor you must give up your hus- band, and your children their father ; and we are not allowed to shut our ears in order not to hear that the dear Tyrol and the good Emperor Francis have called me. I have heard the call, and must obey it. I shall do so joyously and readily, and yet my heart grieves, and there is in my breast here something telling me that our happiness is at an end, that our sun has set, and—Gertrude, I am not ashamed of it—I weep ! "

He leaned his head against his wife's shoulder, and, folding her to his heart, sobbed aloud. But this lasted only a short time ; then he raised himself again, and drew his hand quickly across his eyes.

"There," he said, "it is all over now. I wept as a good Christian is surely allowed to do when he takes leave of his wife and his children, and gives them up for the sake of his country. Did not Abraham weep too, and beg God for mercy, when he was to sacrifice his son to the Almighty? But he nevertheless was ready to make the sacrifice. And, like Abraham, I have wept and lamented now, but I shall make the sacrifice.—Here I am, my God," he added, lifting his eyes and hands to Heaven; "here I am, for Thou hast called me. Do with me as thou deemest best. I am nothing but Thy faithful servant; but if Thou wishest to use me for Thy great purposes, do so! I offer Thee my arms, my body, and my life! Take them!"

"But thou, Holy Virgin," murmured Gertrude, "and thou Saint George, our patron saint, stretch out your arms over him graciously and protect my Andy. Bear in mind that he is my most precious treasure on earth! Preserve my dear husband to me, and to my children the father whom they love so ardently!"

"Amen!" exclaimed Andreas. "And now, dearest wife, come and give me a kiss, a parting kiss!"

"You do not intend to set out this very night?" asked Gertrude, anxiously.

"No, Gertrude, but still it is a parting kiss. For henceforth I must become another man—a hard man, who will no longer think of his family, but only of the fatherland and the emperor. I wept a few minutes ago as a good father and husband, but now I must become as hard as a good soldier ought to be. Until the Bavarians have been expelled from the country, I shall no longer think of you and the children, but shall be only a brave and intrepid soldier of my lord and emperor, and the commander of the Passeyr militia. Kiss me, therefore, a last time, Anna Gertrude! There! Give me another kiss! Who knows but it may be the last time you will ever kiss me, dear Gertrude? And here is still another kiss for our girls. Now it is enough. Go to bed now, Gertrude, and pray for me."

"You will not go to bed, Andy?" asked Gertrude, anxiously.

" No, I will not, Anna Gertrude. I have business to attend
to in the yard with Joe, our laborer. We will kill the brin-
dled cow."

" What ? This very night ? "

" This very night. We need the blood and meat. We
shall pour the blood into the Passeyr, and you will see to-morrow that we need the meat, for I believe we shall have a great
many guests in the morning."

Andreas Hofer's prophecy was fulfilled. Already early in
the morning a great many men assembled in front of the inn
Zum Sand. They were the sharpshooters of the Passeyr valley, who were flocking from all parts of the district to Hofer's
house to report to the beloved commander of Passeyr. They
came down from the mountains and up from the valleys.
They wore their holiday dresses, and their yellow Sunday hats
were decorated with bouquets of rosemary and handsome ribbons. They were merry and in the best of spirits, as if they
were going to the dance ; only instead of their rosy-cheeked
girls, they held their trusty rifles in their arms. Nevertheless,
they smacked their lips, uttered loud exclamations of joy, and
shouted as merrily as larks—" 'Tis time ! The Bavarians
must leave the country ! Long live the emperor ! Long live
the Archduke John ! "

And echo seemed to answer, " The Bavarians must leave
the country ! " But it was not echo that had repeated these
words. They proceeded from the throats of merry men, and
a gay procession descended now from the mountain-path. It
consisted of the sharpshooters and peasants of Meran and
Algund, who were marching up in the beautiful costumes of
the Adige valley. Oh, how their eyes flashed, and the rifles in
their arms also. And with what jubilant *Jodlers* the men of
Passeyr received their dear friends from Algund and Meran.

All at once every sound was hushed, for in the door of the
inn appeared Andreas Hofer, looking like a king in his handsome holiday attire ; his good-natured, honest face gleamed
with joy, and his glance was mild and clear, and yet so firm
and commanding. His whole bearing breathed calm dignity,
and it seemed to the men of Passeyr as though the morning
sun which illuminated his face surrounded his head with a

golden halo. They stood aside with timid reverence and awe. Hofer advanced into the middle of the circle which the men of Passeyr, Meran, and Algund formed around him. He then looked around and greeted the men on all sides with a smile, a pleasant nod, and a wave of his hand.

"My friends," he exclaimed in a loud voice, "the day has come when we must expel the Bavarians from the country and restore the Tyrol to the Austrians. 'Tis time! The Bavarians have amply deserved such treatment at our hands, for they have sorely oppressed us. When you had finished a wooden image, could you carry it to Vienna and sell it? No, you could not! Is that freedom? You are Tyrolese; at least your fathers called themselves so; now you are to call yourselves Bavarians. And, moreover, our ancient castle of Tyrol in the Passeyr valley was not spared! Are you satisfied with this? If you harvest three blades of corn, the government claims two of them; is that happiness and prosperity? But there is a Providence and there are angels; and it was revealed to me that if we resolved to avenge our wrongs, God and St. George, our patron saint, would help us. Up, then, against the Bavarians! Tear the villains with your teeth while they stand; but when they kneel down and pray, give them quarter. Up against the Bavarians! 'Tis time!"

"Up against the Bavarians! 'tis time!" shouted all the brave men, enthusiastically; and the mountain echoes answered: "Up against the Bavarians! 'tis time!"

And the blood-red waters of the Passeyr carried down into the valley the message: "Up against the Bavarians! 'tis time!"

CHAPTER X.

ANTHONY WALLNER OF WINDISCH-MATREY.

AN unusual commotion reigned in the market-place of Windisch-Matrey on the afternoon of the 9th of April. The men and youths of Windisch-Matrey and its environs were assembled there in dense groups, and thronged in constantly-

increasing masses round the house of the innkeeper Anthony
Aichberger, called Wallner. The women, too, had left their
houses and huts, and hastened to the market-place. Their
faces were as threatening as those of the men; their eyes shot
fire, and their whole bearing betokened unusual excitement.
Everywhere loud and vehement words were uttered, clinched
fists were raised menacingly, and glances of secret understanding were exchanged.

The liveliest scene, however, took place in the large bar-
room of the inn. The foremost men of the whole district,
strong, well-built forms, with defiant faces and courageous
bearing, had assembled there around Anthony Wallner-Aichberger. They spoke but little, but sat on the benches against
the walls of the room, and stared into their glasses, which
Eliza, Wallner's eldest daughter, filled again and again with
beer. Even the young girl, who was usually so gay and
spirited, seemed to-day sad and dejected. Formerly her merry
laughter and clear, ringing voice were heard everywhere; to-
day she was moody and taciturn. Formerly her cheeks glowed
like purple roses, a charming arch expression played around
her beautiful small mouth, and the fire and spirit of youth
beamed from her large black eyes ; to-day, only a faint crimson tinged Eliza's cheeks, her lips were firmly compressed, and
her eyes were dim and lustreless. From time to time, while
waiting on the guests, she cast an anxious, searching glance
through the windows over the market-place, and seemed to
listen to the hum of voices, which often became as deafening
as the wild roar of the storm, and shook the window-panes.

Anthony Wallner, her father, was likewise grave and
anxious, and in walking to the groups of guests seated on the
benches here and there, he glanced uneasily toward the windows.

"It may be that they will not come, after all, Tony, and
that the Viennese have fooled you," whispered old Thurn-
walden from Meran to him.

"I cannot comprehend it," sighed Anthony Wallner. "The
insurrection was to break out on the 9th of April, and the Austrian troops were to cross the frontier on that day; and this
was the reason why we have hitherto resisted the conscription

and refused to pay the new taxes. But the 9th of April has come now, and we have received no message from Hofer or the Austrians."

"And to-day the time which the Bavarians have given us is up," growled George Hinnthal; "if our young lads do not report voluntarily to the enrolling officers by this evening, they will be arrested to-morrow."

"They shall not be arrested," exclaimed one of the Tyrolese, striking the table with his powerful fist.

"No, they shall not be arrested," echoed all, in loud, defiant tones.

"But you will not be able to prevent them," said old Thurn-walden, when all were silent again and had drunk a long draught from their glasses as if to confirm their words. "You know there is a whole company of soldiers at Castle Weissen-stein, and Ulrich von Hohenberg, the castellan's nephew, is their captain. He is a Bavarian, body and soul, and, if we resist the authorities, he will lead his men with muskets and field-pieces against us."

"Why, you have become greatly discouraged, Caspar Thurn-walden," said Anthony Wallner, sneeringly, "and one would almost think you had turned a friend of the Bavarians. We have got as good muskets as the Bavarians, and if they shoot we shall shoot back. And as for the field-pieces, why, we have got wheels and may roll down cannon from Castle Weissen-stein to Windisch-Matrey. But come, my dear friends, I see the Bavarian tax-collectors walking across the market-place yonder. They look very grim and stern, as if they meant to devour us all. Let us go out and see what is going on."

The men rose as if obeying a military order, and followed Anthony Wallner from the room to the market-place. Eliza Wallner was for a moment alone in the room; and now that she had no longer to fear the eyes of the guests, she sank quite exhausted on a chair and buried her face in her trembling hands.

"What am I to do?" she murmured in a low voice. "Oh, God in heaven, would I could die this very hour!"

"Why do you weep, Lizzie?" asked a gentle voice by her side, and, on looking up, Eliza beheld the grave, sympathetic face of her mother, who had just entered the room without being heard by her. Eliza sprang up and embraced her mother with passionate tenderness. "Dearest mamma," she whispered, "I am afraid."

"Afraid of what?" asked her mother, in a low voice. "Are you afraid the Austrians may not come, and the Bavarians may then imprison your dear father, because they have found out that he has instigated the people to disobey their behests?"

"No," said Eliza, blushing with shame, "no, that is not what I am afraid of. They will not dare to arrest my dear father, for they know full well that the people of the whole district are greatly attached to him, and that the men of the whole Puster valley would rise to deliver Anthony Wallner. It is something else, dearest mother; come with me into the chamber; there I will tell you all."

She drew her mother hastily into the chamber adjoining the bar-room and closed the door after her.

"Mother," she said, tremblingly and breathlessly, "listen to me now. I am sure the Austrians are coming, and if the men outside hear of it, they will kill all the Bavarians."

"Let them do it," said her mother composedly; "the mean, sneaking Bavarians have certainly deserved to be killed after the infamous treatment we have endured at their hands."

"But, mother, there are also good men among them," exclaimed Eliza. "You know very well I am a loyal Tyrolese girl, and love my emperor dearly, for you have taught me from my earliest youth that it was incumbent on me to do so. But, mother, there are also good men among the Bavarians. There is, for instance, Ulrich von Hohenberg up at Castle Weissenstein. You know his cousin has always treated me as a sister; we have grown up together, and I was allowed to participate in her lessons and learn what she learned. We were always together, and even now I have not ceased going to Castle Weissenstein, although it is garrisoned by a detachment of Bavarian soldiers. Father himself wished me to go to the young lady as heretofore, for he said it would look suspicious if I should stay away all of a sudden. Therefore I went to see my dear friend Eliza von Hohenberg every day,

and I always met there her cousin, the captain of the Bavarian
soldiers. He is a very kind-hearted and merry gentleman,
mother, and it is no fault of his that he is a Bavarian. His
father, our castellan's brother, has lived for thirty years past
down at Munich, and his son entered the Bavarian service
long before he knew that we people of Windisch-Matrey desire to become Austrian subjects again. Now his general sent
him hither with his soldiers for the purpose of helping the
officers to collect the taxes and enroll the names of our young
men. Is he to blame for the necessity he is under of obeying
the orders of his general ? "

"No, he is not," said her mother, gravely.

"But when the Austrians come now, and my father and
the other men rise, and expel and kill all the Bavarians, they will
kill Ulrich von Hohenberg too, although it is not his fault
that he is a Bavarian. Oh, dearest mamma, he is such a good,
kind-hearted young man ! he is my dear Eliza's cousin and
our castellan's nephew, and you know how well Eliza and her
father have treated me, and that they take care of me, whenever I am at the castle, as though I were the castellan's own
child. Dearest mamma, shall we permit our men to kill the
nephew of our excellent castellan ? "

"No, we will not, Lizzie," said her mother, resolutely.
"Quick, run up the footpath leading to the castle. Tell the
young officer that the Tyrolese are going to deliver themselves
from the Bavarian yoke, and that he had better effect his escape while there is time."

"Mother, he will not do it, for he is a brave young man !"
sighed Eliza ; "and then—I cannot betray father's secret to
him. If the Austrians did not come after all, and I had told
Ulrich von Hohenberg what father and the other Tyrolese
intend to do, would I not be a traitress, and would not father
curse me ? "

"True, true, that will not do," said her mother musingly ;
"your father would never forgive you. But I know what you
must do. Just run up to the castle and act as though you
wished only to pay a visit to your friend Eliza ; no one knows
as yet what is going to occur. None of your friends have dis-
closed the secret ; and the castellan too, though I think he is

a good Austrian at heart, does not yet know any thing about it. Your father told me so this very morning. You will remain at the castle, and so soon as you hear the report of a rifle on the market-place here, you will know that the insurrection is breaking out. There is father's rifle ; when it is time, I will step out of the back gate with it and shoot. You will hear the report, and tell the young officer that the Tyrolese are going to rise, and that he had better conceal himself until the first rage of the insurgents has blown over."

"Yes, I will do so," exclaimed Eliza ; "I will run up to the castle now. Good-by, dearest mamma."

She imprinted a kiss on the hand of her mother, and then sped away as gracefully as a young roe.

"She is a very good girl," said her mother, looking after her smilingly, "and has a soft and compassionate heart. She wishes to save the castellan's nephew merely because she pities the young man who is exposed to such imminent danger. It is very kind of her ! It— But, Holy Virgin ! what is the matter outside ? Is the outbreak to commence already ？ I believe it is my Tony who is talking outside in so loud a voice. I must go and hear what is the matter."

She hastened through the bar-room to the street-door opening upon the market place.

Yes, it was Anthony Wallner-Aichberger who was gesticulating so violently yonder. Round him stood the men of Windisch-Matrey, looking with gloomy faces at the three Bavarian revenue officers who were standing in front of Wallner.

"I repeat it, sir," exclaimed Anthony Wallner at this moment with an air of mock gravity, "that we are all very loyal and obedient subjects, and that it is wrong in you, Mr. Taxcollector, to call us stubborn, seditious fellows. If we were such, would we not, being so numerous here, punish you and your two officers for speaking of us so contemptuously and disrespectfully ? "

"You know full well that, at a wave of my hand, the company of soldiers will rush down from Castle Weissenstein and shoot you all as traitors and rebels," said the tax-collector haughtily.

"Well, Mr. Tax-collector," exclaimed Wallner, smilingly, "as for the shooting, we are likewise well versed in that. We are first-rate marksmen, we Tyrolese !"

"What !" cried the tax-collector, furiously, "do you speak again of Tyrolese ? Did I not forbid you to call yourselves so ? You are no Tyrolese, but inhabitants of South-Bavaria, do you hear ? His majesty the King of Bavaria does not want any Tyrolese as subjects, but only Southern Bavarians, as I have told you twice already." *

"Very well ; if his majesty does not want any Tyrolese as subjects, you need not tell us so more than once," exclaimed Anthony Wallner. "He prefers Southern Bavarians, does he ? Bear that in mind, Tyrolese ; the King of Bavaria wants only Southern Bavarians."

"We will bear that in mind," shouted the Tyrolese ; and loud, scornful laughter rolled like threatening thunder across the market-place.

"You laugh," exclaimed the tax-collector, endeavoring to stifle his rage ; "I am glad you are so merry. To-morrow, perhaps, you will laugh no longer ; for I tell you, if you do not pay to-day the fine imposed on you, I shall have it forcibly collected by the soldiers at daybreak to-morrow morning."

"We must really pay the fine, then ?" asked Anthony Wallner, with feigned timidity. "You will not relent, then, Mr. Tax-collector ? We really must pay the heavy fine, because we had a little fun the other day ? For you must say yourself, sir, we really did no wrong."

"You did no wrong ? You were in open insurrection. On the birthday of your gracious master the king, instead of hanging out Bavarian flags, as you had been ordered, you hung out Austrian flags everywhere."

"No, Mr. Tax-collector, you did not see right ; we hung out none but Bavarian flags."

"That is false ! I myself walked through the whole place, and saw every thing with my own eyes. Your flags did not contain the Bavarian colors, blue and white, but black and yellow, the Austrian colors."

"Possibly they may have looked so," exclaimed Anthony

* See "Gallery of Heroes : Life of Andreas Hofer," p. 15.

Wallner, "but that was not our fault. The flags were our old Bavarian flags : but they were already somewhat old, the blue was faded and looked like yellow, and the white had become quite dirty and looked like black."

"Thunder and lightning ! Wallner is right," exclaimed the Tyrolese, bursting into loud laughter. "The flags were our old Bavarian flags, but they were faded and dirty."

The young lads, who had hitherto stood in groups around the outer edge of the market-place, now mingled with the crowd to listen to the speakers ; and a young Tyrolese, with his rifle on his arm, and his pointed hat over his dark curly hair, approached with such impetuous curiosity that he suddenly stood close to the tax-collector. However, he took no notice of the officer, but looked with eager attention at Wallner, and listened to his words.

But the grim eyes of one of the two bailiffs noticed with dismay that this impudent fellow dared to place himself close by the side of the tax-collector without taking off his hat. Striking with his fist on the young fellow's hat, he drove it deep over his forehead.

"Villain !" he shouted, in a threatening voice, "do you not see the tax-collector ?"

The young fellow drew the hat with an air of embarrassment from his forehead, and crimsoning with rage, but in silence, stepped back into the circle of the murmuring men.

"That is just what you deserve, Joe," said Anthony Wallner. "Why did a smart Tyrolese boy like you come near us Southern Bavarians when we were talking about public affairs ?"

At this moment a lad elbowed himself hastily through the crowd. His dress was dusty, his face was flushed and heated, and it seemed as though he had travelled many miles on foot. To those who stood in his way he said in a breathless, panting voice : "Please stand aside. I have to deliver something to Anthony Wallner-Aichberger ; I must speak with him."

The men willingly stood aside. Now he was close behind Wallner, and, interrupting him in his speech, he whispered to him : "I come from Andreas Hofer ; he sends you his greetings and this paper. I have run all night to bring it to you."

He handed a folded paper to Wallner, who opened it with
hands trembling with impatience.

It was Andreas Hofer's "open order."

Wallner's face brightened up, he cast a fiery glance around
the place filled with his friends, and fixed his flashing eyes
then on the hat of the bailiff who had rebuked the young
Tyrolese in so overbearing a manner.   At a bound he was by
his side, drove the bailiff's round official hat with one blow of
his fist over his head, so that his whole face disappeared in the
crown, and exclaimed in a loud, ringing voice :

"Villain ! do you not see the Tyrolese ?"

A loud outburst of exultation greeted Wallner's bold deed,
and all the men crowded around him, ready to protect Anthony Wallner, and looking at the tax-collector with flashing,
threatening eyes.

The latter seemed as if stunned by the sudden change in
Wallner's demeanor, and he looked in dismay at the audacious
innkeeper who was standing close in front of him and staring
at him with a laughing face.

"What does this mean ?" he asked at length, in a tremulous voice.

"It means that we want to be Tyrolese again," shouted
Anthony Wallner, exultingly.   "It means that we will no
longer submit to brutal treatment at the hands of your Bavarian bailiffs, and that _we_ will treat you now as you _Boafoks_ *
have treated us for five years past."

"For God's sake, how have we treated you, then ?" asked
the tax-collector, drawing back from the threatening face of
Anthony Wallner toward his bailiffs.

"Listen to me, Tyrolese," shouted Anthony Wallner, scornfully, "he asks me how the Bavarians have treated us ! Shall
I tell it to him once more ?"

"Yes, yes, Tony, do so," replied the Tyrolese on all sides.
"Tell it to him, and if he refuses to listen, we will tie him
hand and foot, and compel him to hear what you say."

"Well, Mr. Tax-collector," said Wallner, with mock polite-
ness, "I will tell you, then, how you Bavarians have treated

* _Boafoks_, the nickname which the Tyrolese gave to the Bavarians at that
time. It signifies " Bavarian pigs."

us for four years past, and only when you know all our grievances will we settle our accounts. Listen, then, to what you
have done to us, and what we complain of. You have behaved toward us as perjured liars and scoundrels, and I will
prove it to you. In the first place, then, in 1805, when, to our
intense grief and regret, our emperor was obliged to cede the
Tyrol to Bavaria, the King of Bavaria, in a letter which he
wrote to us, solemnly guaranteed our constitution and our
ancient privileges and liberties. That is what your king promised in 1805. To be sure, we did not put much confidence in
what he said, for we well knew that when the big cat wants
to devour the little mouse, it treats the victim at first with
great kindness and throws a small bit of bacon to it ; but
no sooner does the mouse take it than the cat pounces upon its
unsuspecting victim and devours it. And such was our fate
too ; the cat Bavaria wanted to swallow the little mouse Tyrol ;
not even our name was to be left to us, and we were to be
called Southern Bavarians instead of Tyrolese. Besides, our
ancient Castle of Tyrol, the sacred symbol of our country, was
dismantled and destroyed. You thought probably we would
forget the past and the history of the Tyrol, and all that we
are, if we no longer saw the Castle of Tyrol, where the dear
Margaret Maultasch solemnly guaranteed to her Tyrolese their
liberties, great privileges, and independence, for all time to
come. But all was written in our hearts, and your infamous
conduct engraved it only the more lastingly thereon. You
took from us not only our name, but also our constitution,
which all Tyrolese love as their most precious treasure. The
representative estates were suppressed, and the provincial
funds seized. No less than eight new and oppressive taxes
were imposed, and levied with the utmost rigor ; the very
name of the country, as I said before, was abolished ; and,
after the model of revolutionary France, the Tyrol was divided
into the departments of the Inn, the Adige, and the Eisach ;
the passion plays, which formed so large a part of the amuse-
ments of our people, were prohibited ; all pilgrimages to chapels or places of extraordinary sanctity were forbidden. The
convents and monasteries were confiscated, and their estates
sold ; the church plate and holy vessels were melted down and

disposed of ; the royal property was all brought into the market. New imposts were daily exacted without any consultation with the estates of our people ; specie became scarce from the quantity of it which was drawn off to the royal treasury; the Austrian notes were reduced to half their value, and the feelings of our people irritated almost to madness by the compulsory levy of our young men to serve in the ranks of your army. In this manner you tried to crush us to earth. But I tell you, we shall rise again, the whole Tyrol will rise and no longer allow itself to be trampled under foot. You say the king does not want any Tyrolese as subjects. He shall not have any, for the Tyrolese want to become again subjects of their dear Emperor Francis of Austria. Men of the Tyrol, from Pusterthal, Teffereck, and Virgenthal, you wish to become again subjects of the Emperor Francis, do you not ? "

"We do, we do !" shouted the men, uttering deafening cheers. "Our dear Francis is to become again our lord and emperor ! Long live the Emperor Francis !"

"Silence !" cried the tax-collector, pale with rage and dismay ; "silence, or I shall send for the soldiers and have every one of you arrested, and—"

"Be silent yourself !" said Anthony Wallner, seizing him violently by the arm. "Sir, you are our prisoner, and so are the two bailiffs yonder. Seize them, my friends, and if they shout or resist, shoot them down. And if you utter a cry or a word, Mr. Tax-collector, so help me God if I do not kill you for a *Boafok*, as you are ! Keep quiet, therefore, be a sensible man, and deliver your funds to us. Come, men, we will accompany this gentleman to the tax-collector's office ; and now let us sing a good Tyrolese song :

> " D'Schörgen und d'Schreiber und d'Richter allsammt,
> Sind'n Teufel auskomma, druck'n überall auf's Land,
> Und schinden Bauern, es is kam zum sog'n,
> Es wär ja koan Wunder, wir thäten's allsammt erschlog n." *

* Song of the Tyrolese in 1809.—See Mayr, " Joseph Speckbacher," p. 29.
> " The pushing—the writers, and magistrates all,
> Possessed by the devil, our country enthrall,
> And grind the poor peasants ; alas, 'tis a shame !
> No wonder if we too share ruin the same."

He concluded with a long and joyous *Jodler*, and shouted triumphantly : " Dear brethren, Andreas Hofer sends you his greetings, and informs you that the Austrians have invaded the Tyrol. Hurrah, 'tis time ! "

" Yes, 'tis time," murmured Anna Maria, Anthony Wallner's wife, to herself ; " 'tis time for me to give Lizzie the signal, for the insurrection has broken out."

She hastened into the house, took her husband's old rifle from the chamber, ran with it out of the back-door of the house, and fired the signal for her daughter.

" There," she said, returning quietly into the house, " she will have heard the report, and there is time yet to save him. I will do now what Tony asked me to do. When he sings the song, I shall take the paper-balls from the table-drawer in the back-room, give a package to each of the two boys and two servant-girls, and tell them to go with it into the mountains and circulate the paper-balls everywhere, that the inhabitants of the whole Pusterthal, from one end to the other, from the Gross-Glockner to the Venediger and Krimler Tauern, may learn this very day that it is time, and that the *Boafoks* are to be expelled from the country. Halloo, boys, come here ! Halloo, girls, your mistress wants to speak to you ! "

CHAPTER XI.

THE DECLARATION OF LOVE.

Eliza Wallner, after leaving her mother, had sped with the utmost rapidity through the back-door, across the yard, through the garden, out of the small gate leading to the meadow, down the foot-path, up the mountain-road, jumping from stone to stone, courageous and intrepid as a true daughter of the Tyrol. Now she stood at the portal of the castle, in front of which some of the Bavarian soldiers were lying in idle repose on a bench, while others in the side-wing of the castle allotted to them were looking out of the windows, and dreamily humming a Bavarian song, frequently interrupted by loud yawns.

Eliza walked past them with a slight greeting and entered the house. The old footman sitting in the hall received her kindly, and told her, in reply to her inquiry, that the castellan, old Baron von Hohenberg, had set out early in the morning for Salzburg to attend court, but that his daughter and her cousin, Captain Ulrich von Hohenberg, were lunching in the small dining-room up-stairs.

This was all the information Eliza needed; she nodded to the footman, and ascended the staircase quickly. The old footman did not follow her; he knew that it was unnecessary for him to announce beautiful Lizzie to his mistress, but that she always was welcome to her. He therefore sat down again quietly, and took up the wood-work with which he had been occupied before.

Eliza reached the dining-room and threw open the door with a hasty hand; a blissful smile then overspread her flushed face, for on the balcony yonder, behind the open glass door, she beheld the tall slender form of Captain Ulrich von Hohenberg. She heard him chatting and laughing gayly; and through the door she also saw her friend Elza von Hohenberg, who was listening to her cousin's words in smiling repose. Scarcely touching the floor with her feet, she hastened through the room.

"I assure you, cousin," said Elza at this moment, in her clear, distinct voice, "I believe at times that she is the resuscitated Maid of Orleans, and that she will perform heroic deeds one day. Oh, I know my dear beautiful Eliza Wallner, and—"

"Do not speak of me, for I am listening to you," exclaimed Eliza, entering the balcony.

"Ah, my Lizzie," exclaimed Elza, rising and tenderly embracing her friend. "Have you come at length, my merry, beautiful lark?"

"Yes, I have, and I am glad that I am here," said Eliza; and her large hazel eyes turned for a moment smilingly to the young officer, who, like his cousin, had risen on beholding Eliza Wallner. He did not utter a word of salutation; nevertheless, Eliza blushed on meeting his glance, and averted her eyes timidly from him, turning them toward the distant summits of the glaciers which were glittering around the horizon yonder in wonderful majesty.

"You are glad that you are here, my sweet child? Why did you not come at an earlier hour?" asked Elza. "You are always expected. My dear silent cousin, she is always expected, is she not?"

"Most assuredly she is," said the young captain, with a smile; "and she is as welcome as the first rose of May."

"How impudent you are!" exclaimed Miss Elza, laughing; "you bid my Lizzie welcome as the first rose of May, and yet I was here before her!"

"He means only the wild hedge-rose, Elza," said Eliza, smiling archly, "for you know very well that the beautiful and aristocratic roses do not yet bloom in May."

"Well, tell me, cousin, did you really intend to compare my darling here with a wild hedge-rose?" asked Elza.

"Do not answer, sir," exclaimed Eliza, eagerly. "You have blundered in trying to flatter me, and that is good. You will see at length that fine phrases amount to nothing, and that they are colors that fade in the sunshine. You had better speak frankly and honestly to me, for I have often told you I am a stupid daughter of the Tyrol, and do not know what to reply to such fine city phrases."

"But for all that you are not stupid, my beautiful Eliza," said Ulrich von Hohenberg. "In truth, I who compare you with a rose am not a liar, but he would be who should charge you with stupidity."

"But if I should, nevertheless, assert that I am stupid, whom would it concern?" asked Eliza, defiantly.

"Ah, there they are quarrelling again," exclaimed Elza, laughing. "Come to me, sweet Lizzie; sit down by my side on this bench and give me your hand. I am so glad that you are here, for it always seems to me as though I were a lonely orphan when my dearest Lizzie, with her pretty face and her merry laughter, is absent from me. But here, Lizzie, you must look upon me with due awe to-day, for to-day I am not only your friend and sister, but I am the castellan! My father will be absent four days, and I represent him here. He delegated his whole power to me, and intrusted me with all the keys. Treat me, therefore, with great respect, Lizzie."

"That is what I always do, Elza," said Lizzie, tenderly, pressing the slender white hand of her friend to her lips. "You are always my better self, and I obey you because I love you, and I love you because I obey you so gladly!"

"Well, then, I command you, Lizzie, to be our guest all day and stay with us until nightfall. Oh, no objections, Lizzie; if you love me, you must obey!"

"And I obey you willingly, Elza; only when my father sends for me, I must go, for you know we must not violate the fourth commandment; our worthy priest would never forgive us."

"When your father sends for you, Eliza, I shall myself go down to him and beg him to leave you here. Well, then, you belong to us for the whole day, and we will consider now how we shall spend this day. Cousin, do not stand there in silence all the time, staring at the glaciers, but look at us and propose quickly some excursion for us to make to-day."

"What could I propose?" asked the young officer, shrugging his shoulders.

"I submit rather silently and obediently to your proposals, for Miss Eliza would certainly reject all my proposals merely because I make them."

Eliza burst into merry laughter. "Elza, dearest Elza," she exclaimed, "he calls me 'Miss Eliza!' No, sir, let me tell you, a poor Tyrolese girl like me is no 'miss,' no aristocratic lady; people call me Lizzie, only Lizzie; do not forget that!"

"People here call her 'beautiful Lizzie,'" said the officer, in a low voice, casting an admiring glance on the young girl.

"That does not concern you, sir," she replied, blushing like a crimson rose; "you do not belong to the people here, and you must not call me anything but Lizzie, do you hear? I think the notions which city folks entertain about beauty are different from those of peasants like us. We consider the daisy and the Alpine rose beautiful; though they are but small flowers, yet they suit us. However, the city folks laugh at our taste, and step recklessly on our flowers. They consider only the proud white lilies and the large gorgeous roses beautiful flowers. I do not belong to them, I am only a daisy ; but my Elza likes this daisy and fastens me to her bosom, and I rest there so soft and sweetly."

She encircled Elza's neck with her arms, leaned her head against her breast, and looked tenderly up to her with her hazel gazelle eyes.

Elza bent over her and kissed her eyes and white forehead. Ulrich von Hohenberg looked at them both with a tender, ardent glance ; then he averted his head to conceal the crimson glow suffusing his cheeks.

At this moment the door opened, and the castellan's overseer entered with an air of hurry and self-importance.

" Miss Elza," he said, " the wood-cutters have brought wood and are waiting for a receipt. Besides, the head dairy-woman wishes to see you about the butter which she is to send to town ; and the cattle-dealer has arrived, and—"

" I am coming, I am coming," exclaimed the young lady, laughing. "Do you see, Lizzie, what an important person I am ? But for me the whole machine would stand still and sink in ruins. Fortunately, I am equal to the occasion ; and set the wheels in motion, and the machine can go on. You may stay here and consider how we are to amuse ourselves to-day. In the mean time I shall regulate our domestic affairs a little, and when I come back, you will inform me what pleasure you have devised for us to-day."

" No, Elza, let me go with you," begged Eliza, almost anxiously, " I shall assist you—"

" You cannot help me outside, Lizzie," said Elza, laughing ; "but here you can take my place and be my cousin Ulrich's companion. Be merry, my dear children, until I come back ! "

She nodded pleasantly to them, took the large bunch of keys from the table, and swinging it noisily in her hand, skipped through the room and out of the door.

Lizzie had followed her a few steps ; then, as if arrested by a sudden thought, she paused and returned slowly to the balcony. She cast a quick glance on the officer, who was leaning against the wall on one side of the balcony, and, with his arms folded on his breast, did not avert his eyes from her.

Eliza gave a start and withdrew to the other side of the balcony. There she sat down on the bench like a timid little bird, and allowed her eyes to wander dreamily and thoughtfully over the landscape. And, indeed, the view which they enjoyed from the balcony was wondrously beautiful. On one side extended the splendid valley, with its meadows clad in the freshest verdure of spring, its foaming white mountain-torrents, its houses and huts, which disappeared gradually in the violet mists bordering the horizon. On both sides of the valley rose the green wooded heights, interspersed here and there with small verdant pastures and clearings, on which handsome red cows were grazing or lying in majestic repose. Behind the clearings black pines and firs dotted the slopes, which, however, in their more elevated portions became more and more bare ; where the trees ceased, appeared here and there again green pastures, and on them, gray and small, like birds' nests, the huts of the mountain cow-keepers, who, the most advanced sentinels, as it were, were guarding the frontiers where the war between nature and man commences, the frontiers of the snowy region and the world of glaciers. Behind the cow-keepers' huts flashed already masses of snow from several mountain-gorges ; farther above, the snow had spread its white silver veils far and wide over all the mountain-peaks, so that they glittered and sparkled with indescribable beauty in the bright morning sun, and loomed like swans' necks up to the azure sky.

Below, in the foreground of the valley, at the foot of Castle Weissenstein, lay the village of Windisch-Matrey, with its scattering groups of handsome houses, from whose midst arose the church, with its tall, pointed steeple. From the standpoint which she occupied, Eliza was able to distinctly survey the market-place and its crowds of men, which, in the distance, resembled busy black ant-hills. She gazed upon them fixedly, and the small specks seemed to her practised eye like human forms ; she thought she could distinguish several of them, and, among others, the tall and powerful form of her father ; she thought—

" Eliza," said all at once a low voice by her side—" Eliza, you do not want to see me, then ? You are still angry with me ? "

She gave a start, and crimsoned, when, on looking up, she saw young Ulrich von Hohenberg standing close in front of her, and gazing at her with ardent and beseeching eyes.

"No, sir," she said, "I really did not see you."

"That is to say, Eliza, you are still angry with me ?" he asked, eagerly. "You are silent, you avert your head. My God ! Eliza, what did I do, then, to incur your anger ? "

"Not much, perhaps, for city folks, but by far too much for a poor peasant-girl," she said, with eyes flashing proudly. "You told me you loved me, you tried forcibly to embrace and kiss me, and begged me to go up early in the morning to the yellow grotto, where you would wait for me. You told me further not to say a word about it to anybody ; it should remain a secret between you and me, and I should not even mention it to the priest at the confessional. That was not honest of you, sir ; nay, it was bad of you to try and persuade me to such mean things. It showed me that you cannot be a good man, and that your friendship for me is prompted by evil intentions."

"I do not feel any friendship for you, none whatever," said the young man ardently, seating himself by her side, seizing her hand in spite of her resistance, and pressing it to his heart. "I do not want to be your friend, my sweet, beautiful, wild Alpine rose ; no, not your friend, but your lover. And I commence by loving you with intense ardor, by desiring and longing for nothing, and thinking of nothing but you alone. Oh, Eliza, believe me, I love you intensely—by far more than Elza, more than your parents, more than all your friends together."

"More, perhaps, but not better," she said, shaking her head, and gently withdrawing her hand from him.

"No, let me keep your hand !" he exclaimed hastily, seizing it again ; "let me keep it, Eliza, for I tell you I love you better too than all the others ; I love you with my soul, with my heart, with my blood, with my life ! Oh, believe me, sweet, lovely child ; believe me and give me your heart ; follow me, and be mine—mine forevermore ! I will give you a happy, brilliant, and beautiful existence ; I will lay at your feet all the pleasures, enjoyments, and charms of this world—"

"Sir," interrupted Eliza, hastily, jumping up, and fixing her eyes upon him with a strange, ardent expression, "I hope I understand you right, and my ears do not deceive me ? You offer me your hand ? You want to marry me and make me your wife ?"

The young man gave a slight start and dropped his eyes. Eliza saw it, and a sarcastic smile played round her lips. "Why do you not speak ?" she said. "Reply to me. Did I understand you ? Did you make serious proposals of marriage to me ? Will you go down to my father this very day and say to him : "Listen, sir. I, the aristocratic gentleman, I, Captain Ulrich von Hohenberg, want to marry your daughter Lizzie. I think this country girl, with her manners, her language, and bearing, is well fitted to associate with my aristocratic and distinguished family, and my parents in Munich would be overjoyed if I should bring to them this Tyrolese girl as their daughter-in-law, and a brown cow and a white goat as her dower.' Tell me, sir, will you go down to my dear father, the innkeeper of Windisch-Matrey, and say that to him ?"

"But, Eliza," sighed the young man, mournfully, "if you loved me only a little, you would not immediately think of marriage, but would forget every thing else, allow your whole past to sink into oblivion behind you, and think of nothing but the fact that I love you intensely, and that you return my love."

"But I do not admit at all that I love you," said Eliza, proudly ; "on the contrary, you alone say and swear that you love me, and I reply that I do not believe you."

"And why do you not believe me, cruel, beautiful girl ?"

"Because you utter so many fine phrases which amount to nothing at all. You tell me that you are very fond of me, but I think if you love any body with all your heart, you must be anxious to preserve him from misfortune, and do all you can to make him happy, even though it were at the expense of your own happiness. But you, sir, do not intend to make me happy ; on the contrary, you are bent on plunging me into misery and disgrace, and that is the reason why I contend that you do not love me."

"Then you have a heart of stone," cried Ulrich von Hohenberg, despairingly ; "you will not see what I am suffering, nor how intensely I love you."

"Sir," said she, smiling, "if I cannot comprehend it, pray explain to me how you love me."

"I love you as the most beautiful, lovely, and charming creature I have ever known and admired. I love you as a girl whose innocence, naturalness, and goodness, fill my heart with ecstasy and profound emotion ; by whose side I should like to spend my whole life, and united with whom I should wish to seek for a lonely island of happiness to dream there—remote from the world, its prejudices and follies—a sweet, blissful love-life, from which only death would arouse us."

"Sir, if you really love me in this manner, you need not run away with me to seek elsewhere in foreign lands the 'lonely island of happiness,' as you call it, for in that case you would have it round you wherever we might be, and, above all things, here in our mountains. But, look, it is just as I said ; you are desirous to find a 'lonely island of happiness'—that is to say, nobody is to find out that the aristocratic gentleman loves the poor Tyrolese girl, and that is the reason why you want us to hide in the mountains or elsewhere, and see if we can be happy without the blessing of the priest, our dear parents, and all other good men."

"Oh, Eliza, have mercy on me. I swear to you that I love you intensely ; that I would be the happiest of men if I could marry you publicly and make you my wife in the face of the whole world, that—"

Eliza interrupted him by singing with a smiling air, and in a merry, ringing voice :

> " Und a Bisserle Lieb' und a Bisserle Treu'
> Und a Bisserle Falschheit ist all'zeit dabei ! " *

"No, no falsehood," cried Ulrich, "only the irksome, terrible necessity, the—"

The loud crash of a rifle, finding an oft-repeated echo in

---

* " And a bit of love, and a bit of truth,
  And a bit of falsehood, make life, forsooth ! "

the mountains, interrupted him. Eliza uttered a cry of dismay and jumped up.

"Jesus Maria!" she murmured in a low voice, "it is the
signal. It has commenced!"

"What! What has commenced?" asked the young man,
in surprise.

Eliza looked at him with confused and anxious eyes.
"Nothing, oh, nothing at all," she said, in a tremulous voice.
"Only—I mean"—she paused and looked with fixed attention
down on the large place. She distinctly saw the groups moving rapidly to and fro, and then pouring with furious haste
through the streets.

"They are coming up here," she murmured ; and her eyes
turned toward the wing of the castle on the side of the balcony, where the Bavarian soldiers had their quarters. The
latter, however, apparently did not suspect the imminent
danger. They were sitting at the windows and smoking or
cleaning their muskets and uniforms. Eliza could hear them
chatting and laughing in perfect tranquillity.

"Well, Eliza, beautiful, cruel girl," asked Ulrich von Hohenberg, "will you tell me what has suddenly excited you so
strangely?"

"Nothing, sir, oh, nothing," she said ; but then she leaned
far over the railing of the balcony and stared down ; she beheld four young Tyrolese sharpshooters running up the castle-
hill at a furious rate, and the host of their comrades following
them. The four who led the way now entered the court-yard,
and reached with wild bounds the large door forming the entrance of the wing of the building occupied by the soldiers.
With thundering noise they shut it, turned the large key
which was in the lock, and drew it immediately out.

Two sharpshooters now ran up from the opposite side.

"We have locked the back-gate," they shouted exultingly.

"That door is locked too," replied the others, jubilantly.
"They are all prisoners in the castle!"

"Sir," cried Eliza, drawing Ulrich von Hohenberg back
from the balcony, "you may come with me into the dining-
room ; I must tell you something."

"No," he said, "I shall stay here and see what is the matter. What does this mean? More than fifty Tyrolese are entering the court-yard; and why did those mad young fellows lock the door upon my soldiers?"

"I suppose it is some mad freak of theirs, that is all, "said Eliza, trembling. "Come, dear sir, leave the balcony and follow me into the room. I wish to tell you something— quite secretly, sir,—oh, come! I do not want heaven and God and the snow-clad mountains yonder to hear a word of it."

"Eliza," he exclaimed, transported, "how you smile, how you blush! Oh, my God, what do you wish to say to me?"

She encircled his arm with her hands and drew him into the room. "Listen," she said, looking at him with imploring eyes, "if it is true that you love me give me, a proof of it and swear that you will do what I shall request of you!"

"I love you, Eliza, and will prove it to you. I swear, therefore, to do what you shall request of me."

"Thank you, thank you," she exclaimed, joyfully. "Now come with me; I will conduct you under the roof; I know of a hiding-place there where no one will find you, and you will swear to me to stay there until I come to you with a suit of clothes which you will put on. Thereupon I shall conduct you in the dead of night into the mountains, and thus you will escape."

"Escape? Never! And why, then?"

"Sir, because the peasants will assassinate you if you remain."

The young officer burst into loud laughter. "They will assassinate me? Ah, I have my soldiers and my own arms, and am not afraid of the peasants. My soldiers would soon put down the insurgents if they should really rebel to-morrow."

"Sir, they will not wait until to-morrow; they have already risen; the insurrection has commenced this very hour. Oh, thank God, you did not find out what was going on; you felt so secure in your pride and despised the Tyrolese so much that you did not fear them.* But I tell you now, the

* The Tyrolese kept the secret of their intended insurrection so well, and the Bavarians were so overbearing and careless, that they did not know any

insurrection has broken out; the whole Tyrol is rising; all
our people are in commotion from Innspruck down to Salzburg. You can no longer prevent or stifle it. You must
submit. Save yourself, then, sir; you have sworn to grant
my request, and you must keep your word."

"No, I cannot and will not! I must do my duty. Let me
go, Eliza! I must go! I must go to my soldiers!"

"You can no longer reach them, for they have locked them
up. Come, you must save yourself!"

She seized his arm with superhuman strength, and tried to
draw him away, but he disengaged himself and rushed toward
the door. But Eliza was quicker than he; she bounded forward like an angry lioness, and just as Ulrich was about to
seize the knob, she stood before the door and pushed him
back.

"I shall not permit you to leave the room," she cried.
"You must kill me first; then you may go."

"Eliza, I cannot stay. I implore you, let me go out. My
honor, my good name, are at stake. You say the peasants
have risen in insurrection, my soldiers are locked up, and you
think I could be cowardly and miserable enough to conceal
myself and surrender my name to well-deserved disgrace?
Let me go out, Eliza; have mercy upon me! Do not compel
me to remove you forcibly from the door!"

"Ah," cried Eliza, with scornful laughter, "you think I
will step back from the door and let you go to kill my father
and my brothers? Listen, sir; you said you loved me. Give
me a proof of it. Let me go out first, let me speak with my
father—only three words! Perhaps I may persuade him to
release your soldiers and go home with his friends."

"Very well, I will prove to you that I love you. Go down,
Eliza, speak with your father. I give you ten minutes' time;
that is to say, I sacrifice to you ten minutes of my honor."

Eliza uttered a cry of joy; she encircled Ulrich's neck impetuously with her arms and imprinted a glowing kiss on his
forehead.

thing about the plans of the insurgents until the day of the rising, and on
that day they tried to levy contributions by force of arms.—See " Gallery of
Heroes: Andreas Hofer," p. 50.

"Farewell, sir," she whispered, "farewell, and God bless you!"

Then she pushed him back, hastened to the door, threw it open, and sprang out. She closed the door carefully behind her, locked it with a firm and quick hand, drew the key from the lock, and concealed it in her bosom.

"Holy Virgin, I thank Thee!" she exclaimed, joyfully. "He is saved, for the room has no other outlet, and the balcony is too high for him to jump down."

CHAPTER XII.

FAREWELL!

SHE sped as gracefully and quickly as a gazelle down the corridor. In the large hall into which it led stood Elza, surrounded by more than twenty Tyrolese sharpshooters, with whom she was talking in a loud, animated voice. Her cheeks were very pale, her lips were quivering, but her eyes flashed courageously, and, notwithstanding the paleness of her face, it did not betray the least anxiety or terror.

"Have you considered well what you are going to do, men of the Puster valley?" she asked, in a clear, full voice. "Do you know that you are about to rebel against your government and your king, and that the rebels will be judged and punished with the full rigor of the law?"

"But the Bavarians will not judge us, for we shall drive them from the country," shouted the Tyrolese. "We do not want a king nor a Bavarian government; we want to get back our Emperor Francis and our old constitution."

"But you will not succeed," said Elza; "you are too weak against them. There are too many of them and too few of you; they have cannon, and you have nothing but your rifles, and there are many of you who have not even a rifle."

"But we have our God and our emperor, and those two will help us. The Austrians, as Andreas Hofer has written to us, are already in the country, and all the people are rising to drive the French and Bavarians from the country."

"It is so, Elza," said Eliza, encircling her friend's neck with her arm. "I know you—I know that you are a loyal daughter of the Tyrol, and you will be glad to see our dear country delivered from the foreign yoke and restored to the good Emperor Francis."

"But, Lizzie, think of my poor cousin Ulrich," whispered Elza to her. "He will defend himself to the last drop of his blood."

"He is unable to do so," whispered Lizzie, with a cheerful smile. "I have locked him up in the dining-room, and the key is here in my bosom. Ulrich cannot get out, therefore, and though he is furious and grim, he must remain in the room like a mouse in a trap."

"That reassures me," said Elza, smiling, "and I understand now, too, why my father acted in the manner he did. He doubtless suspected what would occur here, and got rid of all responsibility, leaving me entirely free to choose between my Bavarian relative and my Tyrolese countrymen. Here is my hand, Anthony Wallner; I am a loyal daughter of the Tyrol, and shout with you, 'Long live our Emperor Francis!'"

"Hurrah, long live our Emperor Francis!" shouted the Tyrolese. "Long live Miss Elza, the loyal daughter of the Tyrol!"

"Thank you," said Elza, smiling. "I think I shall prove my loyalty when dangers and war beset us. I shall establish here in the castle a hospital for our wounded, and the women of Windisch-Matrey will assist me, scrape lint, and help me to nurse the wounded. For without wounds and bloodshed we shall not recover our independence, and the Bavarians will not suffer themselves to be driven from the country without offering the most obstinate resistance. Have you considered that well, my friends?"

"We have; we are prepared for every thing," said Anthony, joyously. "We will suffer death rather than give up our emperor and our dear Tyrol. We do not want to become Southern Bavarians, but we will remain Tyrolese, and defend our constitution and our liberty to the last drop of our blood. Will we not, my friends ?"

"Yes, we will," shouted the Tyrolese.

"And as for the Bavarians, we are not afraid of them," said Wallner, firmly. "All the functionaries have already humbly submitted to the freemen of the Tyrol. They have surrendered with their wives and children, delivered their funds at our demand, and are now guarded in their official dwellings by our men. And as for the Bavarian soldiers at the castle here, we need not be afraid of them either, for we have locked them up, like badgers in their holes, and they cannot get out of the door."

"But if they cannot get out of the door, they will jump out of the windows," said Elza, "and offer the most determined resistance."

"We shall see if they can," exclaimed Wallner, energetically. "We must get through with them right away. Come, men, we must see to the *Boafoks*."

And Anthony Wallner, followed by his sharpshooters, hastened out into the court-yard. Large numbers of armed men had assembled there in the mean time ; even married women and young girls, carried away by the universal enthusiasm, had armed themselves and came to take an active part in the struggle for the fatherland and the emperor. All shouted and cheered in wild confusion, all swore to remain true to the fatherland and the emperor to their last breath. The soldiers looked on wonderingly, and watched in breathless irresolution for their captain from the windows.

At this moment, Anthony Wallner and a number of courageous sharpshooters took position in front of the windows.

"Soldiers," he shouted, in a thundering voice, "surrender ! you are our prisoners ! Surrender, throw your muskets and fire-arms out of the windows, and we will open the door of your prison and allow you to return to Bavaria."

The soldiers made no reply, but leaned far out of the windows and shouted : "Captain ! Where is our captain ?"

"Here I am !" shouted a powerful voice above the heads of the Tyrolese ; and, looking up in great surprise, they beheld on the balcony young Captain Ulrich von Hohenberg, with a

pale face, his features distorted with rage and grief, and
stretching out his right arm, with his flashing sword menacingly toward the Tyrolese.

"Great God!" murmured Eliza, clinging anxiously to Elza's arm, "if he resists, he is lost."

"Here I am, my brave soldiers!" shouted Ulrich von Hohenberg a second time. "Come to me, my brave lads! I
have been locked up here; hence, I cannot come to you.
Come up to me, then. Knock the doors in, and deliver your
captain."

"First, let them deliver themselves, sir," shouted Wallner
up to him. He then turned once more to the soldiers. "Listen to what I am going to say to you in the name of my countrymen, in the name of the whole Tyrol," he shouted. "For
four long years you have oppressed and maltreated us: you
have insulted, humiliated, and mortified us every day. But
we are Christians, and will not revenge ourselves; we want
only our rights, our liberty, and our emperor. Therefore, if
you submit willingly and with good grace to what cannot be
helped, we will let you depart without punishing or injuring
you in any way, and allow you to return to your accursed
Bavaria. But first you will have to do two things, to wit:
throw all your muskets out of the windows, and swear a solemn oath that you will no longer bear arms against the Tyrolese."

"You will never swear that oath, soldiers," shouted Ulrich
von Hohenberg from his balcony. "You will keep the oath
which you swore to your king and commander-in-chief. You
will not incur the disgrace of surrendering to a crowd of rebellious peasants!"

"No, no, we will not," shouted the soldiers to him; and
thereupon they disappeared from the upper floor, and soon re-
appeared in dense groups at the windows of the lower story.
These windows were only five feet above the ground, and they
were therefore able to jump out of them.

"Shoot down the first soldier who jumps out of the window!" cried Anthony Wallner to his sharpshooters.

The soldiers took no notice of his threats; a soldier appeared in each of the windows ready to risk the leap. One of

them, more agile and intrepid than the others, was the first to jump down. Scarcely had his feet touched the ground, when a rifle crashed and a cloud of white smoke enveloped every thing for a moment. When it disappeared, the Bavarian soldier was seen to writhe on the ground in the agony of death, while one of the Tyrolese sharpshooters was quietly reloading his rifle.

But now crashed another shot, and the Tyrolese rifleman, pierced through the heart, reeled back into the arms of his friends with the last groan of death.

"Soldiers," cried Ulrich von Hohenberg, raising his discharged gun triumphantly, "I have avenged the death of your comrade. Now forward, jump down! Forward for your honor and your king!"

"Yes, forward for our honor and our king!" shouted the soldiers, and one of them jumped out of each of the windows.

Another shot was fired from the balcony, and wounded one of the Tyrolese sharpshooters.

Wild cries of rage filled the court-yard, all eyes turned menacingly to the balcony. But Ulrich von Hohenberg had stepped back into the room, and nobody saw that he was reloading his fowling-piece, which, with his hunting-pouch and powder-horn, had hung in the dining-room.

"I shall defend myself until my soldiers come to deliver me," he said courageously to himself. Thereupon he moved the large table from the room to the balcony, placed it on its side, and leaned it against the railing; on the other side of the balcony he placed the bench in the same manner, and, protected behind this three-cornered barricade from the bullets of the Tyrolese, he pushed his gun into the aperture between the bench and the table, and fired again.

Furious cries again filled the court-yard, for the captain's shot had disabled another Tyrolese. The women wailed and lamented loudly, the men uttered fierce imprecations, and lifted their clinched fists menacingly toward the balcony. The soldiers had withdrawn from the windows, and were deliberating with their officers as to the course which they were to adopt. A defence was almost impossible, for, although they had their side-arms and carbines, they could not do any thing

with the former before reaching the ground and engaging in
a hand-to-hand fight with the peasants ; and the carbines were
utterly useless, as no ammunition had been distributed among
them, the cartridges being in the captain's room in the main
part of the castle.

"Ten of you will enter the castle," commanded Anthony
Wallner now. "You will take the captain prisoner, and if he
refuses to surrender, shoot him down as he has shot three of
our brethren."

Ten of the most courageous sharpshooters stepped from the
ranks and rushed into the castle.

"He is lost !" murmured Eliza Wallner, with pale lips,
and she sank on her knees by the side of her friend Elza.

Now were heard resounding in the castle the thundering
blows which the Tyrolese struck with the butt-ends of their
rifles against the door of the room where Ulrich von Hohenberg was locked up.

"The door is old and worm-eaten, it will give way," sighed
Elza, and she hastened resolutely toward Anthony Wallner,
who was just calling again on the soldiers with cool intrepidity to surrender to him.

"Anthony Wallner," she said, in a soft, suppliant voice,
"you will not stain your great and sacred cause by cowardly
murder. You will never think of killing in my father's own
house his relative and guest ?"

"Let him surrender ; no harm will befall him then," cried
Anthony Wallner, in a harsh, stern voice. "He has shed the
blood of our men, and if he is killed, it will be done in a fair
fight. Leave us now, miss ; the struggle between the Tyrolese
and the *Boafoks* has commenced ; look at the corpses yonder,
and say for yourself whether we can retrace our steps, and—"

A loud, thundering crash, followed by triumphant cheers,
resounded in the castle.

"They have opened the door," murmured Eliza, still on her
knees. "Holy Virgin, protect him, or he is lost !"

A shot crashed in the dining-room, a cloud of white smoke
issued from the open balcony doors, and a loud cry, accompanied by wild imprecations, was heard.

"He has shot another Tyrolese, you will see that he has ! "

shouted Wallner, raising his clinched fists menacingly toward the balcony.

The cries drew nearer and nearer, and now Captain Ulrich von Hohenberg, his features pale and distorted with rage, rushed out on the balcony.

"Surrender !" shouted the Tyrolese, pursuing him.

"Never !" he cried. "I will die sooner than surrender to a rabble of peasants like you."

And forgetful of the dangers besetting him, and in the despair of his rage and grief, the captain jumped from the balcony into the midst of the crowd in the court-yard.

CHAPTER XIII.

THE BRIDEGROOM.

WILD shouts were heard now, and a great commotion arose among the Tyrolese. The bold deed of the Bavarian had surprised and confused them ; they had forgot the soldiers for a moment, and riveted their whole attention on the captain.

He was uninjured, for, in jumping down, he had fallen on the backs of two Tyrolese, dragged them down with him, and thus broke the violence of the fall.

Before the two men, stunned by their sudden fall, had recovered from their surprise, Ulrich was again on his feet, and, drawing his sword, cleared himself a passage through the quickly-receding crowd.

"Come to me, my soldiers, come to me !" he shouted, in a panting voice.

"Here we are, captain," cried twenty soldiers, driving the crowd back with powerful strokes. They had profited by the favorable moment when the windows had not been watched, and had jumped to the ground.

Now followed a hand-to-hand struggle of indescribable fury. Nothing was heard but the wild imprecations and shouts of the fighting, the shrieks and groans of the wounded and the screams of the women and children.

But amidst the struggle and the general confusion Anthony Wallner did not lose his presence of mind. He had posted twenty sharpshooters in front of the windows, behind which the soldiers were standing, and, with rifles raised, they threatened death to all who should dare to approach the windows. Hence, the soldiers had retired into the back part of the rooms, and were deliberating on the course which they were to pursue. But their faces were anxious and irresolute, and they whispered to each other : " If our captain should fall, nothing remains for us but to surrender."

But their captain had not yet fallen ; he still lived and defended himself courageously, surrounded by his soldiers, against the Tyrolese, who attacked him furiously and parried the sabre-strokes with the butt-ends of their rifles, but had no room, and did not dare to shoot at him, for fear of hitting in the wild *mêlée* one of their own men instead of their enemy.

But the odds were too great ; six of the soldiers had already been knocked down by the butt-ends of the Tyrolese rifles. The Tyrolese had wrested the sabres from the hands of the fallen soldiers, and had rushed with them upon their comrades. Then followed a furious hand-to-hand struggle. The fumes of the blood flowing on the ground, the shouts of the combatants, the hatred and fury with which the enemies stood face to face, had filled their hearts with boundless ferocity. Nobody gave, nobody asked quarter. Under the butt-end blows of the Tyrolese, the Bavarians sank to the ground with a glance of hatred ; pierced by the swords of the Bavarians, the Tyrolese fell, with an imprecation on their lips.

Ulrich von Hohenberg was still holding his ground ; his sword had spread destruction and death around him ; he was still encouraging his soldiers with loud shouts, but his voice was beginning to grow faint, and his blood was running from a terrible wound in his shoulder.

"To the rescue, soldiers ! " he shouted now with a last effort ; " do not suffer your captain to be slain by miserable peasants. To the rescue ! help me or shoot me, that I may die an honorable death, and not be assassinated by the traitors."

"I will comply with your wishes," cried Anthony Wallner, rushing into the midst of the bloody *mêlée* close up to the captain ; "yes, you shall die ; I will put an end to your life !"

And his arm, brandishing the sword of a fallen Bavarian, rose threateningly above Ulrich's head, while two other Tyrolese rushed upon him from behind with furious shouts.

At this moment two hands clutched Wallner's arm convulsively, and a loud, anxious voice exclaimed :

"Father, do not kill him ! He is my bridegroom !"

"Her bridegroom !" echoed the Tyrolese, starting back in surprise.

"Your bridegroom ?" asked Anthony Wallner, casting a look of dismay on his daughter Eliza, who was standing in front of her father, pale, with flashing eyes, encircling Ulrich's neck with one arm, lifting up the other menacingly, and staring at her father with a resolute and defiant expression.

"Away from him, Lizzie !" cried Wallner, furiously ; " I cannot believe that my child will inflict on me the disgrace of loving a Bavarian."

"Yes, I love him," exclaimed Eliza, with glowing cheeks. "If you wish to kill him, you must kill me first, for we have sworn to live and die together. He is my bridegroom, father, and shall become my husband, so help me God !"

"No, never !" cried Ulrich von Hohenberg, trying to disengage himself from Eliza. "Never can the peasant-girl become my wife ! Begone, Eliza, I have nothing further to do with you."

"And still you swore a few minutes ago that you loved nothing on earth more dearly than me alone," said Eliza, in a loud voice, "and you implored me to go with you and remain always by your side ?"

"But never did I say that I would marry you," exclaimed Ulrich, pale with rage, and still trying to disengage himself from Eliza's arm.

"You would not marry her !" cried Anthony Wallner ; "you intended only to dishonor her, my proud Bavarian gentleman ? You thought a Tyrolese peasant-girl's honor an excellent pastime, but you would not marry her ?"

"Father, father," cried Eliza, beseechingly, clinging firmly to Ulrich's side, "father, I love him and cannot live without him. He is my bridegroom!"

"No, no!" shouted Ulrich, and a wild imprecation against Eliza burst from his lips.

The Tyrolese in the mean time had long since overpowered the few soldiers, and, attracted by the strange scene, crowded around the curious group; only the twenty sharpshooters were still standing with rifles raised in front of the windows of the imprisoned soldiers, and watching them with threatening eyes.

Anthony Wallner had dropped his arm and looked down musingly; on hearing the captain's insulting words, he gave a shout and lifted up his face flushed with pride and indignation.

"Just listen to the traitor, brethren!" he said in the cold, quiet tone which only the most profound exasperation imparts to the human voice. "First he turned the girl's head and heart by the protestations of his love, causing her even to forget her father and her Tyrol; and now he insults her and refuses to marry her!"

"He said it only in his rage, father, but he loves me after all," exclaimed Eliza, clinging to the captain notwithstanding his resistance, and trying to wrest his sword from him.

"Begone, Eliza!" cried Ulrich, "or ——" He pushed her violently from him, and quickly raised his sword against her. But two Tyrolese prevented him from carrying out his fell design by rushing upon him, seizing his arm with Herculean strength, wresting the sword from his hand, throwing the weapon far away, and exclaiming triumphantly: "Now surrender, Bavarian! You are our prisoner."

"Then shoot me at least," shouted Ulrich, beside himself with rage; "shoot me, I say; death is preferable to the disgrace of being a prisoner of such miserable rabble."

"Hush, beloved, for God's sake, hush!" said Eliza, clinging to him tenderly.

He pushed her violently from his side. "Begone, hypocritical wench!" he shouted in a paroxysm of fury; "I do not want to have any thing to do with you!"

"But you shall have something to do with her," said Anthony Wallner, with proud calmness. "The girl says that she loves you, and that you promised to marry her. It was bad in you to persuade her behind the backs of her parents and infatuate her poor heart, and you shall be punished now for your infamy. You shall marry Lizzie. The proud and wealthy baron who despises the Tyrolese peasants so much shall now marry the Tyrolese peasant-girl."

"Yes, yes, that is right," exclaimed the Tyrolese exultingly; "the proud baron shall marry the Tyrolese peasant-girl."

"Let us go down to the village, then," said Anthony Wallner; "our curate shall marry them immediately at the church; and then let the two leave the place as quickly as possible, and beware of ever returning to Windisch-Matrey; for never shall the wife of the Bavarian Captain Ulrich von Hohenberg dare to say that she is Eliza Wallner, daughter of the Tyrolese Anthony Wallner-Aichberger, the innkeeper of Windisch-Matrey. I have no longer a daughter—I tear her from my heart, as she tore honor, righteousness, and faith from hers."

Eliza called two Tyrolese with an impetuous wave of her hand to her side. "Hold him," she said, pointing to Ulrich, who, pale and tottering, exhausted from his superhuman efforts and loss of blood, was scarcely able to stand on his feet; "hold him, I must speak to my father."

She hastened to him, seized both his hands despite his resistance, and drew his face so close to hers that his hot, panting breath touched her cheek; but he averted his eyes with a gloomy expression and avoided meeting her fiery glances.

"You do not want to know me, father!" she asked mournfully. "You avert your eyes from your Lizzie, whom you called only yesterday your dear, brave Tyrolese girl?"

"You are no child of mine, you are no Tyrolese girl," exclaimed her father, angrily and mournfully. "You want to marry the Bavarian, and become an aristocratic lady."

"It is all the same to me whether Ulrich yonder is an aristocratic gentleman or not," said Eliza, shaking her head proudly; "I love him only because he pleases me so well, and because he loves me so fondly and ardently. But, father, you must not say that I am no true daughter of the Tyrol, and do not love the fatherland. I will prove to all of you that I do love it; and to Ulrich yonder, who wished to persuade me to run away with him secretly, and who must marry me now to atone-for it, I will prove likewise that I am no baroness although I love him, and that I do not love his king and his brilliant uniform, but that I will remain loyal to my emperor alone. Listen to me, therefore, father, and all of you: Ulrich von Hohenberg is my bridegroom, and therefore you shall not kill him, nor do him any harm, but convey him as a prisoner to my father's house, not for the purpose of being married to me, but to be kept and nursed as a wounded prisoner. I swear by the Lord God and the Holy Virgin, I will not marry him till we have conquered, till all Bavarians have been driven from the country, and the Emperor Francis is once more sovereign of the Tyrol. Nor shall I stay at home to nurse my bridegroom and speak with him of love and marriage, but I will go and fight with you for our Tyrol and our emperor. I will fight with my father and my countrymen, and prove that I am a true daughter of the Tyrol. When you have nothing to eat, I will cook for you ; and when you go to fight the Bavarians, I will fight with you. My father's lame porter, our faithful Schröpfel, shall have my bridegroom in his custody, and protect him until we return to our homes. But we shall not return before our dear Tyrol is free and restored to the Emperor Francis, and then, father, when your Lizzie has bravely fought for our dear Tyrol, you will permit her to marry the man whom she loves, and you will no longer say that she is not your daughter, will you ?"

"No, Lizzie, then I shall no longer say or think so," cried Wallner, folding his daughter to his heart, overcome by his emotion. "Yes, you are a brave child of the Tyrol ; you shall march to the field with us, and when we return to our homes, you shall marry your Bavarian. Say, my dear friends, shall it be so ?"

"Yes, it shall," shouted the Tyrolese. "Her wedding shall take place when we return to our homes, and when the Tyrol is free."

"No, no," cried Ulrich, raising himself up with a last effort;

"never will my father's son dishonor himself so deeply as to marry a peasant-girl—"

He said no more ; a stream of blood rushed from his mouth, a mortal pallor overspread his cheeks, his eyes closed, and he sank to the ground with a groan of pain.

"He is dying ! he is dying !" cried Eliza, despairingly. She rushed to him, knelt down by his side, and encircled him firmly with both her arms, so that his head reposed on her breast.

A cry, a loud, painful cry, resounded above her in the air ; all eyes turned toward the balcony, but no one was there ; only for a moment it seemed to them as though a female form glided through the dining-room.

"Elza, it was Elza !" murmured Eliza. "Why does she not come to me ? why—" At this moment Ulrich opened his eyes again, and fixed a look of proud hatred full upon Eliza's face, which was tenderly bent over him.

"I do not love you, I detest you !" he hissed, between his firmly-compressed teeth.

"He lives, thank God, he lives !" cried Eliza ; "now all is well, and I am no longer afraid of anything. Schröpfel, come here ; take him on your shoulders, dear Schröpfel, or let John help you to carry him to my chamber, where you will lay him on my bed. You swear to me by the Holy Virgin that you will watch over him faithfully ? "

"I swear by the Holy Virgin," said Schröpfel, lifting his heavy fists to heaven, and then fixing his small, flashing eyes on Ulrich; as a watch-dog eyes the bone he fears may be taken from him.

"And now let us settle that affair with the soldiers yonder," said Anthony Wallner, going to the windows, in front of which the sharpshooters were still drawn up in line.

"Soldiers in the rooms," he shouted in a powerful voice, "surrender ! The fight is at an end ; your captain is our prisoner. Surrender, or you are lost ; we will set fire to the house, and shoot down whosoever jumps out of the windows. If you wish to save your lives, surrender."

One of the sergeants appeared at the window.

"We are locked up and surrounded," he said ; "we have

no ammunition, and our captain is a prisoner. Therefore, we will surrender if you will allow us to evacuate the castle."

"Yes, but without arms," said Anthony Wallner, imperatively. "You will all come in squads of four to the windows and hand out your carbines and side-arms. There are yet a hundred of you in the rooms. As soon as we have got a hundred carbines and a hundred sabres we shall open the portal and let you out. You may return then to Bavaria, and tell your government that no Southern Bavarians, but true Tyrolese, live in the Pusterthal, the Vintschgau, and the Passeyrthal."

"We accept your terms," replied the sergeant; "come, therefore, and receive our arms."

The Tyrolese stepped up to the windows, at each of which squads of four soldiers made their appearance, and silently and sullenly handed out their arms, which the Tyrolese took and stacked in the middle of the court-yard.

"Now I will go and see where my Elza has concealed herself," murmured Eliza to herself; and she glided hastily through the ranks of the Tyrolese into the castle.

No one was to be seen in the large hall, and, unnoticed by anybody, Eliza ascended the staircase, hastened down the corridor, and entered the dining-room.

The instinct of her heart had guided her rightly; yonder, in the most remote corner of the room, sat Elza, groaning aloud in bitter woe, her hands clasped on her knees, her head bent on her breast, and not perceiving in her agony that Eliza came in, that she hastened rapidly, yet noiselessly and on tiptoe through the room, and stood still now close in front of her.

"Why do you weep, dearest Elza?" asked Eliza, kneeling down before her friend.

Elza gave a start, and quickly raised her face, over which were rolling rivers of scalding tears. "I do not weep at all, Eliza," she said, in a low voice.

"Eliza?" she asked, wonderingly. "You call me Eliza? Then I am no longer your darling, your Lizzie? You did not assist me when I had to save your cousin Ulrich below in the court-yard? You uttered a loud cry when he lay more dead than alive in my lap, and you did not come to help him and me ? And now you call me Eliza ? "

"What should I have done there ? " asked Elza, in a bitter, mournful tone. "He reposed well on your breast ; he did not need me. I am only his cousin, but you, you are his affianced bride."

"But formerly, I suppose, Elza, he was to be your affianced bridegroom ? " asked Eliza, in a low, tremulous voice. "Oh, I always thought so ; I knew it all the time, although you never told me so. I always thought Elza and Ulrich would be a good match ; they are suited to each other, and will love each other and be happy. Elza, Ulrich was to be your bridegroom, was he not ? "

"What is the use of talking about it now ? " asked Elza, vehemently. "He is *your* bridegroom, he has sworn eternal fidelity to you, and I shall not dispute him with you. Marry him and be happy."

"And would your Lizzie be happy if her Elza were not content with her ? " asked Eliza, tenderly. "Tell me only this : your father and his parents thought you were a good match—did they not ? "

"Yes, they did," whispered Elza, bursting again into tears. "My father told me yesterday that it was his wish, as well as that of Ulrich's parents."

"And Ulrich told you, too, that he loved you and would marry you ? Tell me the truth, Elza. Never mind what I said in the court-yard about Ulrich being my bridegroom. Remember only that I am your Lizzie, who loves you better than she can tell you, but who will prove it to you if the good God will permit her to do so. Tell me therefore, my darling, Ulrich said to you he loved you and wished to marry you ? "

"No, he did not say so, Lizzie, but—but I thought so, I believe, and he thought so, too ; and, O God ! I believe I love him. It seemed to me as though a dagger pierced my heart when you said that he was your bridegroom. I could not bear it, and hastened into the house in order not to see and hear any thing further. I meant to seat myself quietly in the dining-room here and submit to all that might happen ; and yet I was drawn irresistibly toward the balcony, and on rush-

ing out I saw you holding him in your lap and pressing his dear
pale head to your bosom. I felt as though the heavens were
falling down on me ; I had to cry out aloud in my anguish
and despair. I hurried back into the room, fell on my knees,
and prayed that death might deliver me from my pains. O
God, God ! it did not ; I must carry on life's dreary burden
and cannot die ! "

She buried her face in her hands and sobbed aloud.

While Elza was speaking, Eliza had turned paler and
paler ; a slight tremor passed through her whole frame, and
she compressed her lips firmly, as if to restrain the cry oppress-
ing her bosom.

Now she laid her hand gently on Elza's head. "You love
him, Elza," she said mildly. "I understand your heart, dearest Elza, you love him. And now dry your tears and listen to
what I have to say to you. But first you must look at me,
Elza, and you must show me your dear face ; otherwise I
won't tell you the good news I have got for you."

Elza dropped her hands from her face, and looked, smiling
amid her tears, into Eliza's countenance, which seemed now
again entirely calm and serene.

"Now listen, Elza," she whispered, hurriedly ; "Ulrich is
not my bridegroom, and he never told me that he loved me."

Elza uttered a cry of joy, and a sunbeam seemed to illumi-
nate her face.

"I merely said so in order to save him," added Lizzie ;
"that was the reason why I uttered that impudent lie, which
God Almighty, I hope, will forgive me. I saw that my father
was just about to kill him, and my heart told me I ought to
save him at all hazards. I hastened to my father, and the
words escaped my lips, I myself do not know how. I said I
loved him, he would marry me, and was my affianced bridegroom ; and this saved him, for he was intent on dying rather
than fall alive, as he said, into the hands of the peasant-rabble.
That was the reason why he was so bold, abused the Tyrolese
so violently, and would not cease resisting them. Therefore,
I had to save him, not only from my father, but from his own
rage ; and I did it."

"But do you not love him ?" asked Elza, smiling.

"Do you not know that Joseph Thurmwalder has been courting me for a year past? My father will be glad to have me marry him; for he is the son of rich parents and the most skillful and handsome hunter in the whole Puster valley."

"But you have often told me that you did not love him?"

"Have you not often told me likewise that you did not love Ulrich, Elza? We girls are queer beings, and never say whom we love!"

"But Ulrich! He loves you! Yes, yes, I know he loves you. I have suspected it a long time, and always teased him with his attachment to you."

"And he always denied it, did he not?"

"Yes, he did, and yet—"

"And he denied it to-day too, when the lie would have saved him at once. He would die rather than be a peasant-girl's bridegroom! You see, therefore, that he does not love me, Elza. But my lie saved his life, and no one must find out that Ulrich is not my bridegroom. For if my father and his friends should discover it, they would kill him, because he insulted them too deeply to be forgiven. He must remain my bridegroom until tranquillity is re-established in the country."

"Yes, my Lizzie, my darling!" exclaimed Elza, encircling Eliza's neck with her arms; "yes, let him remain your bride-groom, my sagacious, brave Tyrolese girl. I always said and knew that you would be a heroine if you should have to meet a great danger, and to-day you *were* a heroine."

"Not yet, Elza, but I shall be one. I am going to prove to my father and all his friends that I am a true daughter of the Tyrol, even though the Bavarian captain is my bridegroom. And now, farewell, dearest Elza; I must go down again to my father. But listen, I have to tell you something else yet. I shall leave our village with my father to-day. We shall march with our friends to Andreas Hofer, for the Tyrolese must concentrate their whole forces in order to be strong enough when they have to meet the enemy. Hence, it was resolved at the very outset, that, so soon as it was time for the people to rise against the Bavarians, Speckbacher and his friends, and my father with the peasants of the Puster valley, should join the men of the Passeyr valley under Hofer's com-

mand. I know that father will set out to-day, and I shall accompany him, Elza. I am not afraid of death and the enemy ; I know that our cause is just, and that the good God
will be on our side."

" But, nevertheless, many noble hearts will be pierced for
this just cause, and yours, dearest Lizzie, may be among
them," exclaimed Elza, tenderly folding her friend to her
heart. " Oh, stay here, my darling, let the men fight it out
alone ; stay here !"

" No, Elza, I must go with them. My honor requires it,
and forbids me to stay at our house with Ulrich von Hohenberg, for whose sake my father called me publicly to-day a recreant daughter of the Tyrol, and threatened to disown me
forever. I must prove to all the world that I am a loyal
daughter of the Tyrol ; and I feel, Elza, that it will do me
good to contribute my mite to the deliverance of the fatherland. I am not gentle and patient enough to sit quietly at
home and wait until dear Liberty looks into my door and says
to me, ' God bless you, Lizzie ! I am here now, and you also
may profit by the happiness which will be caused by my arrival.' No, Elza, I must go with my father, I must help him to
find this dear Liberty on the mountains and in the valleys,
and must say to her, ' God bless thee, Liberty ! I am here now,
and thou mayst profit by my strength, and I will help thee
that thou mayst rule again over the mountains and valleys of
our dear Tyrol.' "

" Oh, Lizzie, you are a genuine heroine !" exclaimed Elza ;
"I blush to think that I shall not accompany you and fight by
your side for Liberty."

" You cannot," said Lizzie, gravely. " You have an aged
father who will stay at home, and whom you must take care
of ; and the poor and sick count upon you, for they know
that Elza will always be their good angel. Stay at home and
pray for me. But never go down to my father's house, do not
inquire for Ulrich, and do not try to have him brought to the
castle here. He is under Schröpfel's surveillance, and Schröpfel would shoot him if he should suspect that all is not as it
should be. But if God should decree my death, Elza, Ulrich
would be free at once, and my father would not injure him,

inasmuch as he was his Lizzie's affianced bridegroom. He would set him free. Ulrich would then come to you, and, Elza, you will tell him not to think that Lizzie Wallner was a bad girl, and that she was intent only on getting an aristocratic husband. You will tell him that my sole object was to save his life, and that I never thought of marrying him. You will tell him also that I forgave him the injury which he did me to-day, and that I shall pray to God Almighty for him. And when you stand before God's altar, and the priest joins your hands, think of me, and do not forget that I loved you, dearest Elza, better than any once else on earth. And now, farewell, Elza ; I shall not kiss you again, for it makes my heart heavy."

"Lizzie, Lizzie !" shouted a powerful voice outside at this moment ; "Lizzie, where are you ? 'Tis time to set out !"

"Here I am, dear father !" exclaimed Lizzie, stepping quickly out on the balcony. "I shall come down to you now. I was only taking leave of Elza. Now I am ready to set out and fight for the dear Tyrol and the dear Emperor Francis !"

"Hurrah, we will do so !" cried the Tyrolese. "We will fight for the dear Tyrol and the dear Emperor Francis ! Hurrah ! We will expel the Bavarians ! Hurrah ! the Austrians are coming ! Hurrah ! the Tyrol will be free again !"

CHAPTER XIV.

THE BRIDGE OF ST. LAWRENCE.

ANTHONY WALLNER and his men marched all day and all night through the Puster valley, along the road to the Mühlbach pass. His daughter Eliza, and young John Panzl, his friend and sympathizer, walked by his side ; and behind him marched the brave Tyrolese, whose force gained strength at every step as it advanced, and who, amidst the most enthusiastic acclamations, appointed Anthony Wallner commander-in-chief of the men of the Puster valley, and John Panzl his lieutenant and assistant.

"I accept the position, my friends," said Wallner, taking

off his hat and kindly greeting the men; "yes, I accept the position, and will be your commander, and will always lead you faithfully and honestly against the enemy. But will you always follow me? Will you not be afraid of the enemy's fire, and take to your heels before his artillery?"

"No, we will not," shouted the brave men; "we will stand by you faithfully, and fight with you for the fatherland and the emperor!"

"That is right, men," cried John Panzl, making a leap which drew loud exclamations of admiration from the Tyrolese. "I tell you it is right in you to think so, and therefore I will likewise joyfully accept the honor which you have offered to me; I will be your second commander, will always obey the orders of our brave commander-in-chief, and assist him and you in driving the enemy from our country, for the glory of God and our emperor. Ah, my dear Tyrolese, I would we could catch the French and the *Boafoks* at length, take them by the neck, and hurl them out of the country. I tell you, after we have done it, I shall dance so merrily with Eliza Wallner, my dear cousin, that the snowy heads of the Gross-Glockner and Venediger will become warm and melt with delight. Lizzie, we two, the most celebrated dancers of the whole Puster valley, will perform a dance in honor of our victory, will we not?"

"We will, Cousin Panzl," said Eliza, smiling. "But before dancing, we must march on and never run back."

"No, never run back," shouted the merry and courageous Tyrolese.

"Forward, then, forward!" commanded Anthony Wallner, and the whole force set out again and marched rapidly across the mountains and through the valleys; it was received everywhere with deafening cheers, and gained at every step fresh accessions of men, who rushed enthusiastically out of their huts, armed with their rifles, or other weapons, even though they had only wooden clubs, and bravely joined the defenders of the country.

Already they approached their destination; in the expansive valley below, yonder, lay the town of Brunecken, surmounted by Castle Bruneck and other ancient and decaying feudal castles; and behind it, on the way down toward Brixen, in the narrower gorge, bordered on both sides by precipitous mountains, through which the Rienz hurls its foaming waters, they beheld already the small town of St. Lawrence. After reaching St. Lawrence they had only an hour's march to the Mühlbach pass, which, in accordance with Andreas Hofer's orders, the brave men of the Puster valley were to occupy and defend against the enemy moving up from Botzen.

But all at once, right in the midst of the march, Anthony Wallner stood still, and, turning to Panzl, who was walking by the side of the column, gave him a sign to halt. The whole column stopped and listened.

Yes, there was no doubt about it, that was the rattle of musketry at a distance! And now they heard also the loud booming of artillery, and the ringing of the tocsin at Bruneck-en and St. Lawrence.

"Now forward, Tyrolese, forward!" shouted Anthony Wallner. "At the double-quick down to Brunecken!"

"Forward!" shouted the men; and their exclamations were echoed joyously by the women who had courageously accompanied their husbands, and who were ready, like them, to fight for their country and their emperor.

They marched with great speed down the Brunecken. The whole town was in the utmost commotion. Young and old men, women, children—all were hurrying toward the gate leading to St. Lawrence.

"What is the matter?" shouted Anthony Wallner, grasping the arm of an old man, who, armed with a pitchfork, was speeding along at a furious rate.

"What is the matter?" echoed the old man, endeavoring to disengage his arm from Wallner's powerful grasp. "The matter is, that the insurrection has broken out at length. The Bavarians are bent on destroying the bridge of St. Lawrence, in order to prevent the Austrians from crossing it. The whole military detachment left our place some time ago for the bridge, and sappers and miners, who are to blow it up, have arrived this morning from Brixen. But we will not allow them to do it. They must shoot us all before we permit them to destroy the bridge."

"No, we will not!" cried Anthony Wallner. "Forward, men of the Puster valley, forward to the bridge of St. Lawrence!"

They continued their march through the valley at the double-quick. They heard the rattle of musketry and the booming of artillery more and more distinctly, and now, at a bend in the valley, the most wonderful and striking spectacle presented itself to their eyes.

Yonder at a distance lay the well-known bridge, composed of a single arch, between tremendous rocks; by its side stood two battalions of Bavarian infantry in serried ranks, and on a knoll, close to the bank of the river Rienz, had been planted three cannon pointed menacingly both against the bridge and the people who were moving up to it in denser and denser masses. Captains and other officers were galloping up and down in front of the Bavarians, and encouraging their men to attack these insurgents who were coming up behind, in front, and on both sides of them. The courageous sons of the Tyrol rushed down from all the heights; the tocsin of Brunecken and St. Lawrence had not called them in vain. They came down the mountains and up the valley; they came, men and women, old men and children; and all were armed: he who did not possess a gun had a flail, a pitchfork, or a club. Like a broad, motley river, the crowd was surging up from all sides, and at the head and in the midst of the warlike groups were to be seen priests in holy vestments, holding aloft the crucifix, blessing the defenders of the country with fervent, pious words, and uttering scathing imprecations against the enemy.

And amidst this commotion thundered the field-pieces, whose balls crashed again and again against the bridge; the bells were tolled in the church-steeples, and the musketry of the Bavarians rattled incessantly. But few of their bullets hit their aim. The Tyrolese were too remote from them, and only occasionally a loud scream indicated that a half-spent bullet had found its way into the breast of a Tyrolese. More fatal and unerring were the bullets of the Tyrolese sharpshooters, who had concealed themselves on the heights on both sides of the valley, and fired from their hiding-places at the Bavarians, never missing their aim and picking off a soldier by every shot they discharged.

Anthony Wallner comprehended the whole situation at a glance. "Boys!" he shouted, in a ringing voice, "we must take the cannon. We must not permit the enemy to destroy the bridge which the Austrians are to cross. Let us attack the Bavarians! We must take the cannon!"

"Yes!" shouted the men, "we must take the cannon!"

And the shouts reached another troop of armed peasants, who repeated it with tumultuous enthusiasm, and soon the men on the heights and in the valley cried, "We must take the cannon!"

Anthony Wallner gave the signal to his sharpshooters, and moved with them into a small forest extending up the mountain near the cannon. The courageous men disappeared soon in the thicket, and, as if in accordance with a general agreement, the other Tyrolese likewise entered the forest. Below, in the valley, knelt the women and children, and before them stood the priests with their crucifixes, protecting them therewith, as it were, from the enemy who was posted on the other side of the valley, and whose ranks were thinned more and more by the bullets of the Tyrolese.

All at once, on the height above the cannon, where there was a clearing, and where the rocks were moss-grown and bare, the Tyrolese were seen rushing in dense masses from the forest. They were headed by Anthony Wallner and John Panzl. Each of them jumped on a projection of the rocks and raised his rifle. They fired, and two gunners fell mortally wounded near the cannon.

The Tyrolese greeted this exploit of their leaders with loud cheers; but up from the Bavarians resounded the commands of the officers; a whole volley crashed, the bullets whistled round the ears of Wallner and Panzl, but none hit them; and when the smoke cleared away, John Panzl was seen to make a triumphant leap in the air, which he accompanied with a shout of victory, while Anthony Wallner calmly raised his

rifle again. He fired, and the gunner at the third field-piece
fell dead.

"Now, boys, at them ; we must take the cannon !" shouted
Wallner, jumping forward, and the Tyrolese followed him
down the slope with furious shouts.

"Forward, forward !" shouted the lieutenant-colonel in the
valley to his Bavarians ; "forward ! the cannon must not fall
into the hands of the peasants ; we must defend them to the
last man. Therefore, forward at the double-quick !"

And the Bavarians rushed forward up the slope.

But the Tyrolese had already succeeded in shooting or
knocking down all the gunners, and taken possession of the
cannon. While Anthony Wallner, at the head of a furious
detachment of his men, hastened to meet the approaching Bavarians, and hurled death and destruction into their ranks,
John Panzl remained with the others to defend the guns.

A furious hand-to-hand fight now arose ; the Bavarians
were repulsed again and again by the Tyrolese, and the sharpshooters, posted behind the trees and rocks, assisted their fighting brethren with their rifles, which, aimed steadily, never
missed their man. But the Bavarians, who were drawn up
farther down in the valley, likewise endeavored to assist their
struggling comrades : but the bullets which they fired up the
hill frequently struck into the ranks of their countrymen, and
not into those of the Tyrolese. Often, on the other hand,
these bullets did not miss their aim, but carried wounds and
death into the midst of the insurgents. Whenever this occurred a young woman was seen to rush amidst the deadliest
shower of bullets into the ranks of the fighting men, lift up
the fallen brave, and carry him in her strong arms out of the
thickest of the fight to the quiet spot on the edge of the forest,
which a protruding rock protected from the bullets of the
enemy.

This young woman was Eliza Wallner. Behind the rock
she had established a sort of field hospital ; a few women and
girls had assembled around her there, and taken upon themselves the sacred care for the wounded, while two priests had
joined them to administer extreme unction to the dying. But
Eliza Wallner had reserved the most difficult and dangerous

part of this work of love for herself. She alone was courageous enough to plunge into the thickest of the fight to remove the fallen brethren; she alone was strong enough to carry them to the quiet asylum, and it was only the joyous enthusiasm inspired by the consciousness of doing good that imparted this strength to her. Her eyes were radiant, her cheeks were flushed, and the face of the young girl, formerly so rosy and serene, exhibited now the transparent paleness, and grave, proud calmness which only great resolves and sublime moments impart to the human countenance.

And the women followed her example with joyous zeal; they washed the wounds of the brave Tyrolese with water fetched from the neighboring spring, tore their handkerchiefs and dresses to make the necessary bandages of them, and closed, with tears of devout compassion, the eyes of those who gave up the ghost amid the blessings of the priests.

From these pious works of charity the women were suddenly aroused by the loud cheers of the Tyrolese. Eliza sprang forth from behind the rock to see what was the matter. Renewed and still louder cheers resounded, for the victory was gained. Anthony Wallner and his men had attained their object. They had succeeded in hurling the three field-pieces from the height into the Rienz, which was rolling along far below in its rocky bed. The earth was shaking yet from the terrific crash, and echo was resounding still with the thundering noise with which the field-pieces had fallen into the Rienz, whose waters had hurled their foaming spray into the air, and were rolling now with an angry roar over the sunken cannon.

This exploit, which excited the transports of the Tyrolese, exerted a contrary effect upon the Bavarians. They had lost their artillery, and with it the means of blowing up the bridge; and now they stood before the enemy uncovered and almost defenceless. In obedience to a loud command uttered by Anthony Wallner, the Tyrolese returned quickly into the forest, and, hidden behind trees and rocks, hit a Bavarian with every bullet, while the Bavarians vainly fired at the well-concealed enemy.

The commander of the Bavarians, Lieutenant-Colonel

Wreden, perceiving the danger and uselessness of a continuance of the struggle, ordered his troops to retreat ; and no
sooner had the Bavarians received this longed-for order, than
they fell back at the double-quick from the bridge and took
the road to Sterzing.

This retreat of the enemy was greeted by the renewed
cheers which Eliza Wallner had heard ; and, both laughing
and weeping for joy, she hastened to fold her father to her
heart, and thank God that no bullet had hit him.

Wallner embraced her tenderly, and imprinted a kiss on
her forehead.

"You have behaved very bravely, Lizzie," he said ; "I saw
how you carried our poor brethren out of the thickest of the
fight. My heart was proud of you, and I should not have
wept to-day even though you had fallen in the sacred service
of the fatherland. But I thank God that nothing has happened to you, and I beseech you, dearest Lizzie, do not accompany us any farther. I now believe again in you, and I know
that you are a true daughter of the Tyrol, although you unfortunately love a Bavarian. Therefore go home ; for it is no
woman's work that is in store for us ; we have a hard struggle
before us, and a great deal of blood will be shed before we
have driven the mean Bavarians and the accursed French
from our beloved country."

"No, father, I shall stay with you," exclaimed Eliza, with
eager determination. "I am not able to sit at home and spin
and pray when my father is fighting for the country. Mother
can attend alone to our household affairs, and Shröpfel
will assist her ; but you cannot attend alone to the hard work
here, and I will help you, dearest father. I will be the doctor
and surgeon of your men until you have found a better and
more skilful physician. You must not reject me, dearest
father, for you would commit wrong against the poor wounded
who have no other assistance than what they receive at my
hands and at those of the women whom I beg and persuade to
help me."

"You are right, Lizzie ; it would be wrong in me to send
you home and not permit you to assist and nurse the wounded," said her father, gravely. "May God and the Holy Vir-

gin help and protect you ! I devote you to the fatherland to which I devote myself."

He kissed her once more, and then turned to the Tyrolese, who, encamped in groups on the edge of the forest, and reposing from the struggle, were partaking of the bread and meat which they had brought along in their haversacks.

"Brethren," exclaimed Anthony Wallner, in a powerful voice, "now let us be up and doing ! We must cut off the enemy's retreat to Sterzing. We must also occupy the Mühlbach pass, as Andreas Hofer ordered us to do in the Archduke John's name. The enemy has set out thither, and if he gets before us through the gap of Brixen and reaches the bridge of Laditch, we shall be unable to prevent him from passing through the Mühlbach pass and marching to Sterzing. Hence, we are not at liberty to repose now, but must advance rapidly. One detachment of our men, commanded by my Lieutenant Panzl, will push on quickly on the mountain-road to the Mühlbach pass. The rest of us will follow you, but we must previously detain the enemy at the gap of Brixen ; and while we are doing duty, another detachment of our men will go farther down to the bridge of Laditch and destroy it in order to prevent the enemy from crossing the Eisach. Forward, my friends ! Forward to the gap of Brixen ! We must roll down trees, detach large fragments from the rocks, and hurl them down on the enemy ; we must fire at them from the heights with deadly certainty, and every bullet must hit its man. Forward ! forward ! To the bridge of Laditch !"

"Yes, yes !" exclaimed the Tyrolese, with enthusiastic courage. "Forward to the bridge of Laditch !"

CHAPTER XV.

THE BRIDGE OF LADITCH.

NIGHT had at length brought some repose to the exhausted Bavarians. At no great distance from the gap of Brixen they had halted late in the evening, and encamped on the bare ground in the valley below. The green turf was their bed, a stone their pillow ; nevertheless, they had been able to enjoy a few hours of peaceful slumber, for they were familiar with the habits of the Tyrolese ; they knew that they never undertook any thing, not even a hunting-excursion, in the dead of night, and that they had nothing to fear from them until sunrise.

But now the first streaks of dawn illuminated the sky ; it was time, therefore, to continue the march. Lieutenant-Colonel von Wreden rose from the couch which the soldiers had prepared for him of moss and branches, and reviewed, accompanied by his officers, his small force, which began sullenly and silently to form in line. A cloud darkened Wreden's face when, marching through the ranks, he counted the number of his soldiers. He had arrived yesterday at the bridge of St. Lawrence with nearly four hundred men ; scarcely one-half of them were left now ; the other half lay slain at the bridge of St. Lawrence, or, exhausted by the loss of blood and by the pains of gaping wounds, had sunk down on the road and been unable to continue the march.

"And these poor men will likewise be killed to-day unless speedy succor comes," murmured the lieutenant-colonel to himself ; "we are all lost if the miserable rabble of peasants reach the gap of Brixen before us. We are all lost, for we shall be entirely cut off from our friends and surrounded by our enemies, who are able to avail themselves of their mountain fastnesses and hiding-places, while we must march through the valley and across the open plain. But all these complaints are useless. We must do our duty ! The soldier's life belongs to his oath and his king ; and if he falls in the service, he has done his duty."

And with strong determination and bold courage the lieutenant-colonel threw back his head, and fixed his eye steadfastly on his soldiers.

"Forward," he shouted, "forward, boys ! Forward against these miserable peasants, who have violated the faith they plighted to our king. Forward ! forward !"

The column, headed by Lieutenant-Colonel von Wreden, commenced moving. His eyes glanced anxiously over the plain now opening before them. Suddenly they are riveted on a point yonder on the mountain-road leading southward to Italy. What is that? Does it not flash there like a mass of bayonets? Does it not look as though a brilliant serpent, glittering in blue, red, and gold, were moving along the road? It draws nearer and nearer, and the lieutenant-colonel is able to distinguish its parts. Yes, these parts are soldiers; this serpent consists of regiments marching along in serried ranks.

Lieutenant-Colonel von Wreden uttered a cry of joy and galloped forward. Already he discerned distinctly the uniforms of the staff-officers riding at the head of the column. They were friends; they were French soldiers headed by General Bisson.

Wreden galloped forward to salute the general and communicate to him in brief, winged words his own disaster and his apprehensions regarding the immediate future.

"Well, you have nothing to fear now," said General Bisson, with a pleasant and proud smile. "It was no accident, but a decree of Fate, that caused us to meet here. I was ordered by my emperor to march with a column of four thousand men from Mantua to Ratisbon, and I am now on the road to the latter place. Hence, our route leads us through the gap of Brixen, and as a matter of course you will join us with your troops. I hope our united forces will succeed in routing these miserable peasants!"

"Yes, if we could meet them in the open plain," sighed Lieutenant-Colonel von Wreden. "But in their mountains and gorges our thousands will vainly struggle against their hundreds. The bulwarks of their mountains protect them."

"We shall drive them from these bulwarks," said General Bisson, haughtily. "But I believe the rabble will not even wait for this, but take to their heels as soon as they see the head of my column. Therefore, join my regiments, lieutenant-colonel, and let us march fearlessly through the gap of Brixen."

Half an hour afterward they had reached the dark and awe-inspiring gap of Brixen, and the united Bavarian and French troops marched with a measured step along the narrow road, on both sides of which rose steep gray rocks, covered here and there with small pine forests, and then again exhibiting their naked, moss-grown walls, crowned above with their snowy summits glistening like burnished silver in the morning sun.

The column under General Bisson penetrated deeper and deeper into the gorge. Enormous rocks now closed the road in their front and rear. A profound, awful stillness surrounded them ; only here and there they heard the rustling of a cascade falling down from the mountains with silvery spray, and flowing finally as a murmuring rivulet through the valley ; now and then they heard also the hoarse croaking of some bird of prey soaring in the air ; otherwise, all was still.

General Bisson, who was riding in the middle of his column, turned smilingly to Lieutenant-Colonel Wreden : " Did I not tell you, my dear lieutenant-colonel," he said, " that these miserable peasants would take to their heels so soon as our column came in sight ? They were, perhaps, able to cope with your few hundred men, but my four thousand men—"

The loud crash of a rifle interrupted his sentence ; a second, third, and fourth report followed in rapid succession. The heights seemed all at once to bristle with enemies. Like an enormous man-of-war, lying at first calm and peaceful, and then opening her port-holes, these gray rocks seemed suddenly to open all their port-holes and pour out death and destruction.

From the rock in front yonder, from the steep mountains on both sides, from the precipitous hill jutting out in their rear and closing the gloomy gorge, rifle-shots rattled down with unerring aim ; every bullet hit its man, every bullet struck down a soldier in the ranks of the Bavarians and French ; then were heard the triumphant cheers of the Tyrolese, who, for a moment, stepped forth from their safe hiding-places, danced on the rocks, jeered at the enemy with loud, scornful words, and disappeared again so quickly, that the bullets which the soldiers fired at them glanced harmlessly from the flanks of the rocks.

But the Tyrolese fought not with their rifles alone against the enemy marching through the deep and awful gorge. Nature had prepared other means of defence for them; it had given them trees and rocks. They hurled the trees, which the storms had felled years ago, and which fragments of rock had held on the brink of the precipice, into the depth of the gorge ; they detached large fragments from the rocks, and rolled them down on the soldiers, many of whom were crushed by these terrible missiles. And when these trees and rocks fell into the depth, and spread death and confusion in the ranks of the soldiers, the Tyrolese profited by this moment to aim and strike down additional victims by their rifle-bullets.

And there was no escape for these poor soldiers, who, exposed to the fury of their enemies, did not even enjoy the consolation of wreaking vengeance upon them. In silent despair, and shedding tears of rage, the French and Bavarians continued their march ; the corpses of their brethren, which the rear-guard met on the horrible road, could not detain them ; they had to pass over them, and abstain even from coming to the assistance of their dying friends ; crushed under their feet, the latter had to give up the ghost.

At length the gorge widens before them ; the rocks in front recede on both sides, and a bright, expansive plain opens to their view. The soldiers greet this prospect with loud cheers of delight, which their officers dare not repress in the name of discipline ; for, on emerging from an open grave, a soldier feels like a human being, and thanks God for the preservation of his life. Hundreds had fallen, but several thousands were left, and their ardent rage, their fiery revengefulness longed for the struggle in which they might avenge their fallen comrades. And Fate seemed intent on fulfilling their wishes. Yonder, at the extremity of the plain through which the soldiers were now marching ; yonder, on the bank of the Eisach, was seen a motley crowd ascending the slopes of the mountains on both sides of the river.

"Yes, there are the Tyrolese, there are our enemies," cried the Bavarians and French, with grim satisfaction ; and they marched at the double-quick toward the bank of the river.

"The peasants, I believe, intend to prevent us from crossing the river," said General Bisson, with a contemptuous shrug.

"They have taken position in front of the bridge of Laditch, and so closely that I can see nothing of it," replied

Lieutenant-Colonel von Wreden. Suddenly he uttered a cry
of surprise, and looked steadfastly toward the extremity of
the valley, where the rocks jutted out again into it, and where
the furious Eisach makes a sudden bend from one side of the
valley to the other. Formerly there had risen here, between
tremendous rocks, the majestic arch of the bridge of Laditch.
For many centuries past this wonderful arch had spanned the
abyss ; it was a monument dating from the era of the ancient
Romans, and Cæsar himself, perhaps, had crossed this bridge
on his march against the free nations of the North. But now
this arch had disappeared, or rather its central part had been
removed, and between its two extremities yawned a terrible
abyss, through which the Eisach rushed with thundering
noise.

"The Tyrolese 'have destroyed the bridge !" exclaimed
Von Wreden, in dismay.

"Ah, the brigands !" said Bisson, contemptuously. "It
will, therefore, be necessary for us to construct a temporary
bridge in order to get over to the other side."

Yes, the Tyrolese had destroyed the bridge of Laditch ; and
while a small division of their men had quickly moved on to
occupy the Mühlbach pass, the others, under the command of
Anthony Wallner, had taken position on the opposite bank of
the Eisach, in order to prevent the enemy from crossing the
river. All the men from the neighboring village of Laditch
had joined the forces of Anthony Wallner, and on the mountains stood the sharpshooters from the villages far and near,
called out by the tocsin, and ready to dispute every inch of the
beloved soil with the enemy.

The columns of the Bavarians and French approached, and
shots were exchanged on both sides. "Forward !" shouted
Anthony Wallner, and he advanced with his brave men to the
Puster valley, close to the bridge upon which the enemy was
moving up.

The bullets whistled around him, but he paid no attention
to them ; he saw only the enemy, and not the dangers menacing him. But the other Tyrolese saw them only too well.
Up in the mountains they were brave and resolute ; but in
the plain, where they were on equal ground with the enemy,

they felt ill at ease and anxious. Moreover, the odds of the enemy were truly formidable, not only in numbers but also in arms. Only a part of the Tyrolese were provided with rifles and muskets; more than half of them were armed only with flails, pitchforks, and clubs. The soldiers had not only their muskets, but also field-pieces, whose balls thundered now across the plain and carried death into the ranks of the Tyrolese.

Terror and dismay seized the sharpshooters; they turned and began to flee into the mountains. But an unexpected obstacle obstructed their path. A number of intrepid women, who had flocked to the scene from the neighboring villages, met them at this moment. They received the fugitives with threatening invectives; they drove them back with uplifted arms, with flaming eyes, with imprecations, and scornful laughter, down the slope, regardless of the bullets whistling around them, and of the enemy moving up closer and closer to them. The fugitives are obliged to turn and plunge once more into the struggle, which becomes more and more furious. Yonder, close to the fragments of the bridge, stand the Tyrolese; here, near the fragments on this side of the river, are the soldiers and the French engineers advancing to construct a temporary bridge across the chasm, and thereby unite again the disrupted ends of the ancient Roman structure.

The fire of the Tyrolese becomes weaker; loud lamentations burst from their ranks. They are exhausted and weary, owing to the heavy exertions of the day; hunger and thirst torment them, and their strength is gone.

"Give us something to eat! Give us something to drink!" they shout to the women occupying the mountain-path in their rear up to the solitary house, the inn *Zur Eisach*, which has already been hit by many a ball from the enemy's guns.

"Courage, brethren, courage!" shouted Eliza Wallner. "I will bring you refreshments."

And, like a gazelle, she hastens up the hillside, skipping from rock to rock until she reaches the battered house. The bullets whistle around her, but she laughs at them, and does not even turn to vouchsafe a glance at the danger. She leaps on courageously; now she reaches the house, she disappears through the door, and no sooner has she entered than a cannon-ball strikes the wall right above the door. After a very brief space of time, Eliza Wallner reappears in the door. On her head she carries a keg, which she supports with both her uplifted arms. With a serene glance, with rosy cheeks and smiling lips, a charming picture of grace, loveliness, and courageous innocence, she descends the mountain-path again, and even the bullets of the enemy respect her ; they whistle past her on both sides, but do not hit her. Eliza hastens down the slope, and now she reaches the bridge, and arrives where are posted the Tyrolese, who receive the courageous girl with deafening cheers.

All at once she feels a jerk in the keg on her head, and immediately after its contents pour in a clear cold stream down on her face and neck. A bullet had struck the keg and passed clear through it. Eliza bursts into merry laughter, lifts the keg with her plump, beautiful arms from her head, and stops the two holes with both her hands, so that the wine can no longer run out.

"Now come, boys," she shouts, in a loud, merry voice ; "come and drink, else the wine will run out. The enemy has tapped the keg ; he wished to save us the trouble. Come and drink."

"Stand back, Lizzie," shouts Panzl to her; "step behind the rock yonder, that the bullets may not hit you."

"I shall not do it," said Eliza, with a flushed face ; "I shall not conceal myself. I am a true daughter of the Tyrol, and God will protect me here as well as there.—Come, boys, and drink. Bring your glasses, or rather apply your mouth to the keg and drink."

Two young Tyrolese sharpshooters hastened to her. Eliza held up the keg ; the two young men knelt before her and applied their mouths to the holes made by the bullet, and sucked out the wine, looking with enamoured glances up to the heroic girl who looked down on them smilingly.

"Now you have drunk enough, go and fight again for the fatherland," she said, and signed to two other sharpshooters to refresh themselves from the keg. The two young men hastened back to their comrades, not knowing whether it was the wine or the sight of the lovely Tyrolese girl that filled them with renewed courage and enthusiasm.

The two other Tyrolese had drunk likewise. Suddenly another bullet whistles along and darts past close to Eliza's cheeks, causing her to reel for a moment. A cry of dismay burst from the lips of those who saw it; but Eliza already smiled again, and she exclaimed, in a merry voice: "Make haste, boys! else another bullet will come and pierce the keg again, when the wine will run into the grass. Therefore, make haste!"

Two other Tyrolese hastened up to drink; then two more, and so on, until the keg was empty.

"Now you have refreshed yourselves," cried Eliza, "and you must bravely return to the struggle."

And the Tyrolese took position on the river-bank, with re-doubled courage and enthusiasm, to prevent the French from finishing the temporary bridge.

But the fire of the enemy thinned the ranks of the Tyrolese fearfully; their shots became few and far between, and gradually a regular panic seized them. They began to give way; even the scornful cries of the women, who tried to obstruct their path, were powerless to keep them back. They pushed the women aside, and rushed resistlessly up the mountain-path.

At this moment loud cheers burst from the lips of the enemy. The Tyrolese started. They looked back, and saw to their dismay that the engineers had succeeded in finishing the temporary bridge across the Eisach, and that nothing prevented the enemy now from passing over to their side of the river.

"Surrender! Lay down your arms!" shouted Lieutenant-Colonel von Wreden, on the other bank.

The Tyrolese were silent, and gazed with mute dismay upon the bridge. All at once they heard a voice resounding on the hills above them as it were from the clouds. This voice shouted: "The imperialists are coming! The Austrians, our saviours, are coming!"

And at the same time a detachment of light-horse appeared on the heights of Schaps. They galloped down the slope, and were followed by several companies of chasseurs and infantry, who rushed down at the double-quick.

Loud, exulting cheers burst from the lips of the Tyrolese, and found thundering echoes in the mountains and gorges.

The French and Bavarians started, for this sudden apparition took them completely by surprise; they had not even suspected that the Austrians had already invaded the Tyrol. They hesitated, and did not venture to cross the river.

This hesitation of the enemy and the arrival of the Austrians filled the Tyrolese with transports. Some threw down their rifles to embrace each other and swing their hats merrily, while others were dancing with their rifles as though they were their sweethearts; and others again sang and warbled ringing Tyrolese *Jodlers.* Finally, some of them, filled with profound emotion and fervent gratitude, sank down on their knees to thank God for this wonderful rescue and the long-wished-for sight of the dear Austrian uniforms.

The French and Bavarians, in the mean time, thunderstruck at the sudden arrival of the Austrians, whose numbers they were as yet unable to ascertain, had made a retrograde movement in their first terror. But this did not last long. "If we do not want to perish here to the last man, we must try to force a passage," said General Bisson. "Forward, therefore, forward!"

The troops moved, and began to march across the bridge.

But now the Austrians had come close up to them. The Tyrolese received them with deafening shouts of "Long live the Emperor Francis! Long live Austria!"

Then they turned once more with fervent enthusiasm toward the enemy. "Down with the base Bavarians! Forward! forward! Down with them!" they shouted on all sides; and the Tyrolese rushed with furious impetuosity upon the enemy. Their scythes and flails mowed down whole ranks, and many soldiers were soon laid prostrate by the unerring aim of the mountain sharpshooters. Mountains of corpses were piled up, rivers of blood flowed down into the waters of the Eisach, and the crimson-colored waves carried down through the Tyrol the intelligence that the struggle for the fatherland had commenced.

Nevertheless, the forces of the enemy were too numerous for the Tyrolese and the small advanced guard of the Austrians to annihilate them entirely. The Bavarians and French forced a passage through the ranks of their enthusiastic enemies with the courage and wrath of despair ; hundreds of them remained dead on the bloody field, but nearly two thousand ascended the Eisach toward Sterzing.

Anthony Wallner beckoned to his daughter, and stepped with her behind a jutting rock. " First, Lizzie, my heroic girl, give me a kiss," he said, encircling her with one of his arms, and pressing her fondly to his broad breast. " You have been your father's joy and pride to-day, and I saw that the dear little angels were protecting you, and that the bullets for this reason whistled harmlessly around you. Hence, you are now to render an important service to the fatherland. I must send a messenger to Andreas Hofer, but I need the men for fighting here ; and, moreover, the enemy might easily catch my messenger. But he will allow a Tyrolese girl like you to pass through his lines, and will not suspect any thing wrong about her. Now will you take my message to Andreas Hofer ? "

" I will, father."

" Run, then, my daughter, run along the mountain-paths ; you can climb and leap like a chamois, and will easily get the start of the enemy, who is marching on the long roads in the valley. Hasten toward Sterzing. If all has passed off as agreed upon, you will find Andreas Hofer there. Tell him now in my name that the Austrians are coming up from Salzburg and that I have done my duty and redeemed my pledge. Tell him further that the whole Puster valley is in insurrection, and that we are bravely at work, and driving the Bavarians and French from the country. But tell him also to be on his guard, for we have not been able to annihilate the enemy entirely, and they will soon make their appearance at Sterzing. Let him be ready to receive the enemy there as they deserve it."

" Is that all, dearest father ? "

age, as you seem to think, brother Sieberer. I know full well
that we owe it to our good emperor and the fatherland to defend it to the last breath, and I do not tremble for myself. I
have dedicated my life to the dear fatherland; I have taken
leave of my wife and my children, and belong now only to
the Tyrol and the emperor. If my blood were sufficient to
deliver our country, I should joyously and with a grateful
prayer throw myself down from this peak and shatter my
bones; and dying, I should thank God for vouchsafing such
an honor to me, and allowing me to purchase the liberty of
the country with my blood. But I am but a poor and humble
servant and soldier of the Lord, and my blood will not be sufficient; but many will have to spill theirs and die, that the rest
may be free and belong again to our dear emperor. And this is
the reason why, on contemplating the brave men and courageous lads who have followed my call, I feel pity, and ask myself
again and again, Had I a right to call them away from their
homes, their wives and children, and lead them, perhaps, into
the jaws of death? Will not the Lord curse me for preach-
ing insurrection and war instead of submissiveness and humility?"

"Well, you are a pious man, Andy," said Sieberer, with a
reproachful glance, "and yet you have forgotten what our Redeemer said to the Pharisees."

"What do you mean, Anthony? Tell me, if it will comfort me."

"He said, ' Render unto Cæsar the things which are Cæsar's,
and unto God the things that are God's.' Now, I think that
our Tyrol is the emperor's, and that the Bavarians and French
have nothing to do with it, but have merely stolen it from the
emperor. Therefore, we act only in accordance with the precepts of our Lord Jesus Christ, if we stake our lives and fortunes to restore to the emperor that which is the emperor's.
And I think, too, that the churches and convents are the
houses of the Lord and belong to Him alone. Now, the Bavarians have stolen the houses of the Lord in the Tyrol, and
have ignominiously driven out His servants. Hence we act
again in accordance with the precepts of our Lord Jesus Christ,
if we stake our lives and fortunes to restore to God that which

is God's ; and if, in doing so, we should all lose our lives, we should die in the holy service of God and the emperor !"

"You are right, brother Sieberer," exclaimed Hofer, joyfully, "and I thank you for comforting and strengthening my heart. Yes, we are in the service of God, our emperor, and the beloved Tyrol."

"And God and the emperor have imposed on Andreas Hofer the duty of acting at the same time as prophet of the Lord and as captain of the emperor. Go, then, Andreas, and do your duty !" said Sieberer, solemnly.

"I shall do my duty bravely and faithfully to the last !" exclaimed Hofer, enthusiastically. Then he raised the small crucifix from his breast, kissed it devoutly, and prayed in a low voice.

A sarcastic smile overspread Anthony Sieberer's face, but it disappeared quickly when he happened to turn his eyes to the neighboring mountains. He looked keenly and searchingly toward the mountain-path leading to Mittewald. He saw there a small black speck which was advancing with great rapidity. Was it a bird ? No, the speck had already become larger ; he saw it was a human being—a woman speeding along the mountain-path. Now she was so close to them that he could distinguish her face ; it was that of a young girl ; her cheeks flushed, her eyes radiant ; bold and intrepid as a chamois, she hastened forward ; her long, black tresses were waving round her head, and her bosom heaved violently under the folds of her white corset.

Now, she stood still for a moment, and seemed to listen ; then she bent far over the precipice, on the brink of which she was standing, and below which the Tyrolese were encamped. No sooner had she perceived them than she uttered a loud cry of exultation, and bounding forward, she exclaimed joyously : "There are the men of the Passeyr valley ! Now I shall find their leader, Andreas Hofer, too !—Andreas Hofer ! where are you, Andreas Hofer ?"

"Here I am !" shouted Andreas Hofer, starting up from his fervent prayer, and advancing a few steps.

The young girl gave a start on discovering the two men, who had hitherto been concealed from her by a large rock ;

shall be a cry of woe and lamentation, and shall resound throughout
all Europe ; it shall reach every throne, and every one shall hear my
voice calling out : ' Woe ! woe ! woe to us all ; our thrones are tottering, they will surely fall if we do not ruin this evil-doer who
threatens us all !' "

With a fearful groan, the queen fell fainting into the arms of
Countess Ogliva. But the sorrows and humiliations of this day
were not the only ones experienced by Maria Josephine from her
victorious enemy.

It is true her cry for help resounded throughout Europe. Preparations for war were made in many places, but her allies were not
able to prevent the fearful blow that was to be the ruin of Saxony.
Though the Dauphine of France, daughter of the wretched Maria
Josephine, and the mother of the unfortunate King of France, Louis
XVI., threw herself at the feet of Louis XV., imploring for help
for her mother's tottering kingdom, the French troops came too late
to prevent this disaster. Even though Maria Theresa, Empress of
Austria, and niece to the Queen of Saxony, as her army were in
want of horses, gave up all her own to carry the cannon. The Austrian cannon was of as little help to Saxony as the French troops.

Starvation was a more powerful ally to Prussia than Austria,
France, Russia, and Sweden were to Saxony, for in the Saxon camp
also a cry of woe resounded.

It was hunger that compelled the brave Saxon General Rutrosky
to capitulate. It was the same cause that forced the King of Saxony
to bind himself to the fearful stipulations which the victorious
King of Prussia, after having tried in vain for many years to gain
an ally in Saxony, made.

In the valley of Lilienstein the first of that great drama, whose
scenes are engraved in blood in the book of history, was performed,
and for whose further developments many sad, long years were
necessary.

In the valley of Lilienstein the Saxon army, compelled to it by
actual starvation, gave up their arms ; and as these true, brave soldiers, weeping over their humiliation, with one hand laid down
their weapons, the other was extended toward their enemies for
bread.

Lamentation and despair reigned in the camp at Lilienstein, and
there, at a window of the catstle of Königstein, stood the Prince-
Elector of Saxony, with his favorite Count Brühl, witnesses to their
misery.

After these fearful humiliations, by which Frederick punished
the Saxons for their many intrigues, by which he revenged himself
for their obstinate enmity, their proud superiority—after these

humiliations, after their complete defeat, the King of Prussia was no longer opposed to the King of Saxony's journey. He sent him the desired passports; he even extended their number, and not only sent one to the king and to Count Brühl, but also to the Countess Brühl, with the express command to accompany her husband. He also sent a pass to Countess Ogliva, compelling this bigoted woman to leave her mistress.

And when the queen again raised her cry of woe, to call her allies to her aid, the King of Prussia answered her with the victorious thunder of the battle of Losovitz, the first battle fought in this war, and in which the Prussians, led by their king, performed wonders of bravery, and defeated for the third time the tremendous Austrian army, under the command of General Brown.

"Never," says Frederick, "since I have had the honor to command the Prussian troops, have they performed such deeds of daring as to-day."

The Austrians, in viewing these deeds, cried out:

"We have found again the old Prussians!"

And still they fought so bravely, that the Prussians remarked in amazement:

"These cannot be the same Austrians!"

This was the first act of that great drama enacted by the European nations, and of which King Frederick II. was the hero.

had occupied the bridge of Laditch, he deemed it prudent to evacuate Sterzing and await our men in the open plain. I saw his troops marching through the valley while I was walking on the heights ; and I think it will not be long until we can see them below in the plain."

"See, there they are already !" exclaimed Anthony Sieberer, who, while Eliza was speaking, had spied with his keen eyes far into the plain called the Sterzinger Moos.

In fact, a large, motley mass was to be seen moving up in the distance yonder ; yes, they were Bavarian soldiers, and they were drawing nearer and nearer.

" Hurrah ! the Bavarians are coming, the struggle begins," exclaimed Anthony Sieberer, joyously ; and the Tyrolese encamped below echoed his shout with loud exultation : "The Bavarians are coming ! The struggle begins !"

"The struggle begins," said Hofer, "and God grant, in His mercy, that not too much blood may be shed, and that we may be victorious ! Come, dear girl, I will take you under my protection, for you cannot immediately set out for home, but must stay here with me. I shall see to it that no harm befalls you, and, while we are fighting, we will try to find a cave or nook in the rocks where we may conceal you."

" I do not want to conceal myself, Andreas Hofer," said Eliza, proudly. " The priests and women have likewise to perform their parts in war-times : they must carry the wounded out of the range of the enemy's bullets and dress their wounds ; they must pray with the dying, and nurse those whose lives are spared."

"You are a brave daughter of the Tyrol ; I like to listen to your soul-stirring words," exclaimed Andreas Hofer. "Now come, we will speak with our men."

He grasped Eliza's hand, beckoned to his adjutant Sieberer, and descended with them the path toward the Tyrolese.

They were no longer reposing, but all had risen and were looking with rapt attention in the direction of the enemy. On beholding Hofer, they burst into loud cheers, and asked him enthusiastically to lead them against the enemy.

" Let us ascertain first where he is going, and what his intentions are," said Hofer, thoughtfully. " Perhaps he does not know that we are here, and intends to continue his march. In that case we will let him pass us, follow him, and attack him only after he has entered the Mühlbach pass."

"No, he does not intend to continue his march," exclaimed Sieberer. "Look, he takes position in the plain and forms in squares as he has learned to do from Bonaparte. Oh, brethren, let us attack him now. Never fear. I know such squares, for, in 1805, I often attacked them with our men, and we broke them. Forward, then, my friends, forward! Now let us fight for God and our emperor!"

"For God and our emperor!" shouted the Tyrolese; and all seized their arms and prepared for the struggle.

"Hold on!" cried Hofer, in a powerful voice. "As you have elected me commander, you must be obedient to me and comply with my orders."

"We will, we will!" shouted the Tyrolese. "Just tell us, commander, what we are to do, and we shall obey."

"You shall not descend into the plain, nor attack the enemy on all sides. For you see, the squares are ready to shoot in all directions, and if you attack them on all sides in the open plain, you will be exposed to their most destructive fire; moreover, as they are by far better armed than we, and have cannon, many of our men would be uselessly sacrificed in such an attack."

"What the commander says is true," growled the Tyrolese. "It is by far better for us to attack the enemy from a covered position, and have our rear protected by the mountains."

"And I will show you now such a covered position from which you are to attack the enemy," said Andreas Hofer, with impressive calmness. "Look there, to the left. Do you see the ravine leading into the mountains yonder? Well, we will now ascend the mountain-path rapidly, descend into the ravine, and thence rush upon the enemy."

"Yes, yes, that is right! We will do so. Andreas Hofer is a good captain!" said the Tyrolese to each other.

Hofer waved his hand imperatively toward them. "Now keep very quiet," he said, "that we may not attract the attention of the enemy prematurely, and thereby cause him to occupy the ravine before we have reached it. Forward, then,

quickly through the forest, and then descend noiselessly into
the valley. But before setting out, we will pray two rosaries.
If we long for success in battle, we must invoke God's assistance."

He took his rosary and prayed ; and the Tyrolese bent their
heads devoutly, and prayed like their commander. Then they
glided quickly and noiselessly through the thick forest, headed
by Andreas Hofer, who led Eliza Wallner with tender solicitude by the hand. At length they reached the gorge, and
Andreas Hofer was just about entering it with the others,
when Anthony Sieberer, Jacob Eisenstocken, and a few other
prominent Tyrolese, stepped to him and kept him back with
tender violence.

"A general does not accompany his soldiers into the thickest of the fight," said Eisenstocken. "That is not his province.
He has to direct the battle with his head, but not to fight it
out with his arm."

"But bear in mind that Bonaparte does not leave his soldiers even in battle," said Andreas Hofer, trying to push them
aside and advance.

"No, dearest commander," exclaimed Anthony Sieberer,
"you must not go down with the men. Think of it, what
would become of us and our cause if an accident befell our
commander and a bullet shattered his beloved head ! Our
friends and sharpshooters would feel as though that bullet
had shattered all their heads ; they would be discouraged and
give up our cause as lost. No, no, Andreas Hofer, you owe it
to your fatherland, your emperor, and your Tyrolese, not to
expose yourself to too great dangers ; for your life is necessary
to us, and you are the standard which the Tyrolese are following. If our standard sinks to the ground, our Tyrolese will be
panic-stricken and run away. Consequently you must not go
into battle, either to-day or at any time hereafter."

"You are right, I see it," said Hofer, mournfully. "They
would be thunderstruck if a bullet should hit their commander ; hence I submit, and shall stay here. You will stay
with me, Lizzie Wallner, and Ennemoser, my secretary, shall
do so too. Now go, all of you, and God grant that we may
all meet again. I shall stay at this very spot, and he who

wants to see me must come hither. I can survey from here
the whole plain of the Sterzinger Moos. Now, my dear
friends and brethren," he shouted in a loud, ringing voice,
"for God, the fatherland, and your emperor !"

"For God, the fatherland, and our emperor !" shouted the
Tyrolese, rushing down the mountain-path into the ravine
whence they were to attack the enemy.

But the Bavarians had been on their guard, and their commander, Colonel Bärenklau, divining the tactics of the Tyrolese, had ordered his two guns to be pointed against the
ravine.

Now the first shots thundered from their mouths, and volleys of musketry were discharged from all the squares at the
same time, at the advancing column of the Tyrolese. The
Tyrolese, not prepared for so sudden and violent an attack,
dismayed at the havoc produced in their ranks by the balls
and bullets of the Bavarians, gave way and ran over the
corpses of their brethren back to the ravine. But there stood
the crowd of women who had accompanied the column, who
had hastened up from Sterzing, and the whole neighborhood,
and had advanced with the Tyrolese out of the ravine almost
close to the squares of the enemy. They received the fugitives with invectives and angry glances ; they strove to kindle
their courage ; they went and begged them with clasped hands
and tearful eyes not to desert the cause of the fatherland, become discouraged in so disgraceful a manner in the very first
battle, and thereby make themselves the laughing-stock of the
hateful Bavarians and French.

And the men listened to these voices ; they drank courage
from the wine which the women handed to them, and rushed
forward a second time. Their rifles crashed and mowed down
the front ranks of the Bavarians, but behind the corpses stood
the rear ranks, and their volleys responded to the Tyrolese,
and the cannon thundered across the plain reeking with gore
and powder.

The Tyrolese gave way a second time, for the murderous
fire of the Bavarians filled them with stupor and dismay

"In this manner we shall never gain a victory, and our
men will be uselessly slaughtered," said Andreas Hofer, who

was watching the struggle with breathless suspense. "But we
must not incur the disgrace of losing the first battle, for that
would discourage our men for all time to come. Come, Ennemoser, run down to them and tell them to try a third time.
If they do not, Andreas Hofer will rush all alone upon the
enemy and wait for a bullet to shatter his head."

Young Ennemoser, the secretary, sped down the ravine;
Hofer pressed his crucifix to his lips and prayed; Eliza Wallner advanced close to the edge of the precipice, and peered
down into the plain. Her eyes filled with tears when she perceived the many corpses piled up on both sides of the ravine,
but the squares of the enemy likewise had been considerably
thinned, and death had made fearful havoc in their ranks.

"Andreas Hofer," she cried, exultingly, "your message
was successful. Our men are rushing forward. Do you not
hear their cheers?"

"I do, and may the good God grant them success!" sighed
Andreas Hofer, stepping close up to Eliza.

They saw the Tyrolese emerging again at the double-quick
from the ravine, and rushing upon the enemy, who received
them with volleys of musketry and artillery-fire. But, alas!
they saw the Tyrolese give way again and retreat, though
more slowly than before, to the ravine.

"This will never do," cried Hofer, despairingly. "Our men
are slaughtered in this way, and cannot reach the enemy,
whose cannon are mowing them down like scythes. O God,
show me a way to help our men!"

His eyes glanced despairingly over the plain, as if searching for relief. All at once a bright flash of joy lit up his
features.

"I have found a way! I thank Thee, my God!" he exclaimed, aloud. "See, Lizzie, look there! What do you see
in the plain yonder behind the ravine?"

"I see there four large wagons filled with hay," said Lizzie;
"yes, four wagons filled with hay, nothing else."

"And these wagons filled with hay will save us. They
must be driven toward the ravine directly toward the enemy;
our sharpshooters will conceal themselves behind them, and
will safely advance; and when close enough to the enemy,

they will discharge their rifles, and first pick off the gunners, in order to silence the guns which have made such havoc among our men. Come, Lizzie, we will go down to Sieberer and the other captains, and give them my orders. I hope there will be four lads intrepid enough to drive the hay-wagons toward the enemy."

"There will be!" exclaimed Eliza, enthusiastically.

"It is only necessary for one to risk his life, and drive the first wagon. The other wagons will be covered by the first. But the driver of the first wagon will doubtless be killed, and I shall be responsible for his death."

"He will die for the fatherland," exclaimed Eliza. "Go, Andreas Hofer, descend and tell our men what is to be done, for it is high time for the hay-wagons to come up and cover our men."

"Come, let us go, Lizzie; give me your hand."

"No, lead the way; I will follow you immediately."

CHAPTER XVII.

THE HAY-WAGONS.

ANDREAS HOFER had already descended half the mountain-path with a rapid step, and he did not once look behind him, for he was sure that Wallner's daughter was following him, and he kept his eyes steadfastly fixed on his friends and brethren.

But Eliza did not follow him. She looked after him until the dense shrubbery below concealed her from his eyes; then she knelt down, and, lifting both her hands to heaven, exclaimed, in a loud, beseeching voice: "Holy Virgin, protect me! Grant success to my enterprise for the beloved father-land!"

She then jumped up, and, quick as a chamois, scarcely touching the ground with her feet, she hastened toward the point where the hay-wagons were standing.

Meanwhile, Andreas Hofer had descended into the ravine

whence constantly new crowds of Tyrolese were rushing forward, although they were driven back again and again by the murderous fire of the enemy. On beholding Hofer's erect and imposing form, and his fine head, with the splendid long beard, the Tyrolese burst into loud cheers, and his presence seemed to inspire them with fresh courage. They advanced with the most intrepid impetuosity. Andreas Hofer called the brave captains of his sharpshooters to his side, and communicated to them briefly the stratagem he had devised.

"That is a splendid and very shrewd idea," said Anthony Sieberer.

"The hay-wagon is your Trojan horse with which, like Ulysses, you will conquer your Troy," exclaimed the learned Ennemoser, Hofer's young secretary.

"I do not know where Troy is situated," said Andreas Hofer, quietly, "but I know where the Sterzinger Moos lies, and what should be done there. For the rest, there are no horses before the hay-wagons, but oxen, and it is all-important that the gunners should not immediately hit the driver of the first wagon."

"But his last hour has surely come, and he may rely on going to paradise to-day!" exclaimed Ennemoser. "But look, what throng is yonder in the ravine, and what causes the women to shout so vociferously? Their shouts sound like triumphant cheers. And the lads now join in the acclamations too, and all are rushing forward so impetuously."

Indeed, the whole mass of men and women assembled in the rear of the ravine rushed forward with loud shouts, like a single immense wave, surging with extraordinary impetuosity up to Andreas Hofer and the captains standing by his side.

All at once this wave parted, and in the midst of all this eager, shouting throng, which took position on both sides of the ravine, appeared two of those broad-horned, brown-red oxen, of a beauty, majesty, and strength such as can be found only in the Tyrol and in Switzerland. Behind these two oxen came the wagon filled up with hay.

But who drove the hay-wagon? Was it really the lovely young girl hanging on the back of the ox—the beautiful creature whose face was radiant with enthusiasm, whose cheeks were glowing like the morning sun, and whose eyes flashed like stars ?

Yes, it was she—it was Eliza Wallner, who, with sublime courage, had mounted the back of the ox, and who now was driving forward with loud shouts and lashes of the whip the two animals, frightened by the crowd and the shots crashing incessantly.

"Eliza Wallner !" cried Andreas Hofer, with an air of dismay, as the heavily-laden wagon rolled more rapidly forward.

She turned her head toward him, and a wondrous smile illuminated her face. "Send greetings to my dear father !" she exclaimed. "Send greetings to him in my name, if I should die."

"I cannot allow her to do it—it is certain death !" cried Andreas Hofer, anxiously. "Let me go and lift her from the ox."

"No, no, Andreas," said Anthony Sieberer. "Let her proceed. The intrepidity of this young girl will fire the courage of the lads; and, for the rest, if lives have to be sacrificed, the life of a girl is not worth any more than that of a lad. We are all in God's hand."

"May God and His heavenly host protect her !" said Andreas Hofer, laying his hand on the image of St. George, which adorned his breast.

"Now, boys," shouted Anthony Sieberer, "do not allow the girl to make you blush. Quick, march behind the hay-wagon, and when you are close enough to the enemy, step forward and shoot down the gunners."

Ten young lads hastened forward, amid loud cheers, and took position in pairs behind the wagon, which advanced heavily and slowly, like an enormous avalanche.

There was a breathless silence. All eyes followed the wagon, all hearts throbbed and addressed to heaven prayers in behalf of the courageous girl who was driving it.

Suddenly a cry of horror burst from all lips. A cannon-ball had struck the hay-wagon, which was shaking violently from the tremendous shock.

But now a ringing cheer was heard in front of the wagon,

By this cheer Eliza Wallner announced to the Tyrolese that the ball had not hit her, and that she was uninjured.

The cannon boomed again, and Eliza's ringing voice announced once more that the balls had penetrated harmlessly into the closely compressed hay.

Meanwhile the wagon rolled out farther and farther into the plain of the Sterzinger Moos. Even the oxen seemed to be infected with the heroism of their fair driver, and trotted more rapidly toward the enemy, whose balls whistled round them without hitting them.

Suddenly Eliza stopped their courageous trot, and, turning back her head, she shouted : " Forward now, boys ! Do not be afraid of the Bavarian dumplings. They do not hit us, and we do not swallow them as hot as the Bavarians send them to us ! "

The young sharpshooters concealed behind the wagon replied to Eliza, amid merry laughter : " No, we are not afraid of the Bavarian dumplings, but we are going to pick off the cooks that send them to us."

And with their rifles lifted to their cheeks, five sharp-shooters rushed forward on either side of their green bulwark. Before the Bavarians had time to aim at the ten daring sharpshooters, the latter raised their rifles and fired, and the gunners fell dead by the sides of their guns.

The Bavarians uttered loud shouts of fury, and aimed at the sharpshooters ; but the Tyrolese had already disappeared again, whistling and cheering, behind the wagon, which was still advancing toward the enemy.

The other hay-wagons now rolled likewise from the ravine. The first of them was driven by another young girl. Imitating the heroic example set by Eliza Wallner, Anna Gamper, daughter of a tailor of Sterzing, had courageously mounted the back of an ox, and drove forward the wagon, filled with an enormous quantity of hay. Twenty young sharpshooters, encouraged by the success of their comrades, followed this second wagon. Behind them came the third and fourth wagons, followed by twenty or thirty more sharpshooters, who were well protected by the broad bulwark which the wagons formed in front of them.

The gunners had fallen ; hence the cannon no longer thundered or carried destruction and death into the ranks of the Tyrolese ; only the musketry of the Bavarians was still rattling, but they only hit the hay, and not the brave girls driving the oxen, nor the sharpshooters, who, concealed behind the hay, rushed from their covert whenever the enemy had fired a volley, raised their rifles triumphantly, and struck down a Bavarian at every shot.

All four hay-wagons had now driven up close enough, and the Tyrolese, who were nearly one hundred strong, burst with cheers from behind them, and rushing forward in loose array, but with desperate resolution, using the butt-ends of their rifles, fell with savage impetuosity upon the Bavarians, who were thunderstruck at this unexpected and sudden attack.

Loud cheers also resounded from the ravine. The whole force of the Tyrolese advanced at the double-quick to assist their brethren in annihilating the enemy.

A violent struggle, a fierce hand-to-hand fight now ensued. The Bavarians, overwhelmed by the terrible onset of the peasants, gave way ; the squares dissolved ; and the soldiers, as if paralyzed with terror, had neither courage nor strength left to avoid the furious butt-end blows of the peasants.

Vainly did Colonel von Bärenklau strive to reform his lines ; vainly did those who had rallied round him at his command, make a desperate effort to force their way through the ranks of the infuriated Tyrolese. The fierce bravery of the latter overcame all resistance, and rendered their escape impossible.

"Surrender !" thundered Andreas Hofer to the Bavarians. "Lay down your arms, and surrender at discretion !"

A cry of rage burst from the pale lips of Colonel von Bärenklau, and he would have rushed upon the impudent peasants who dared to fasten such a disgrace upon him. But his own men kept him back.

"We do not want to be slaughtered," they cried, perfectly beside themselves with terror ; "we will surrender, we will lay down our arms !"

A deathly pallor overspread the cheeks of the unfortunate officer.

"Do so, then," he cried. "Surrender yourselves and me to utter dishonor! I am no longer able to restrain you from it."

And with a sigh resembling the groan of a dying man, Colonel von Bärenklau fainted away, exhausted by the terrible exertion and the loss of blood which was rushing from a gunshot wound on his neck.

"We surrender!" We are ready to lay down our arms!" shouted the Bavarians to the Tyrolese, who were still thinning their ranks by the deadly fire of their rifles and their terrible butt-end blows.

"Very well, lay down your arms," cried Andreas Hofer, in a powerful voice. "Stop, Tyrolese! If they surrender, nobody shall hurt a hair of their heads, for then they are no longer our enemies, but our brethren.—Lay down your arms, Bavarians!"

The Tyrolese, obedient to the orders of their commander, stopped the furious slaughter, and gazed with gloomy eyes at their hated enemies.

There was a moment of breathless silence, and then the Bavarian officers were heard to command in tremulous voices, "Lay down your arms!"

And their men obeyed readily. Three hundred and eighty soldiers, and nine officers, laid down their arms here on the plain of the Sterzinger Moos, and surrendered at discretion to the Tyrolese.*

On seeing this, the Tyrolese burst into loud cheers, and Andreas Hofer lifted his beaming eyes to heaven. "I thank Thee, Lord God," he said; "with Thy assistance we have achieved a victory. It is the first love-offering which we present to fatherland and our Emperor Francis."

"Long live the Tyrol and our Emperor Francis!" shouted the Tyrolese, enthusiastically.

The Bavarians stood silent, with downcast eyes and pale faces, while the active Tyrolese lads hastily collected the arms they had laid down and placed them on one of the wagons, from which they had quickly removed the hay.

"What is to be done with our prisoners, the Bavarians?"

* "Gallery of Heroes: Andreas Hofer," p. 31.

said Anthony Sieberer to Andreas Hofer. "We cannot take them with us."

"No, we cannot, nor will the enemy give us time for doing so," replied Hofer. "Anthony Wallner has informed me that a strong corps of Bavarians and French is approaching in the direction of the Mühlbacher Klause. They must not meet us here on the plain, for a fight under such circumstances would manifestly be to our disadvantage. They would be a great deal stronger here than we. But in the mountains we are able to overcome them. They are the fortresses which the good God built for our country ; and when the enemy passes, we shall attack and defeat him."

"And shall we take the prisoners with us into the mountains, commander ? "

"No, we will not, for we cannot guard them well up there, and they would escape. We will not take the prisoners with us, but convey them to the Baroness von Sternberg at Castle Steinach. She is ardently devoted to our cause, and loves the Tyrol and the emperor. She will take care of the prisoners, and they will be unable to escape from the large tower, the Wolfsthurm, on the crest yonder, which you can see from here."

"But who is to convey the prisoners to Castle Steinach ? Are we all to march thither and deliver them before advancing farther ? "

"No, no, Anthony Sieberer ; we have not time for that. We must bury the corpses here quickly, and remove every trace of the contest, in order that the French, on arriving here, may not discover what has occurred, and that we are close by. Only thirty of our men shall escort the prisoners to Castle Steinach."

"Only thirty, commander ? Will that be sufficient for three hundred and eighty prisoners ? If they should attack our men on the road, they would beat them, for they would be twelve to one."

"That is true," said Andreas Hofer in confusion ; "what are we to do to get a stronger escort for the prisoners ? "

He stroked his beard nervously, as was his wont in moments of great excitement, and he glanced uneasily,

now here, now there.   All at once a smile illuminated his
face. .

"I have got it," he said merrily.   "Look there, Sieberer,
look there.   What do you see there ?"

"The women who have accompanied us, and who are
kissing Eliza Wallner and Anna Gamper for their heroic conduct."

"The women shall help our thirty sharpshooters to escort
the prisoners to Castle Steinach.   Our women have brave
hearts and strong arms, and they know how to use the rifle
for the fatherland and the emperor.   Let them, then, take
some of the arms which we have conquered, and, jointly
with thirty of our men, escort the prisoners to the good
Baroness von Sternberg.   Oh, Lizzie Wallner, Lizzie Wallner !"

"Here I am, commander," cried Eliza, hastening to Andreas Hofer with flushed cheeks and beaming eyes.

He patted her cheeks smilingly.   "You are a brave, noble
girl," he said, "and none of us will ever forget what you
have done to-day ; and the whole Tyrol shall learn what a
splendid and intrepid girl you are.   But I wish to confer a
special reward on you, Lizzie ; I wish to appoint you captain
of a company, and your company is to consist of all those
women."

"And what does the commander-in-chief order me to do
with my company of women ?" asked Eliza Wallner.

"Captain Lizzie, you are to escort with your company and
thirty Tyrolese sharpshooters the three hundred and eighty
Bavarians to Castle Steinach.   Your arms you will take from
the wagon yonder, which Captain Lizzie drove so heroically
toward the enemy.   Will you undertake to escort the prisoners safely to Steinach ?"

"I will, commander.   But after that I should like to return
to my father.   He must be uneasy about me by this time, and
he would like also to know how the Tyrolese have succeeded
on this side.   Oh ! he will be exceedingly glad when I bring
him greetings from his beloved Andreas Hofer."

"Go, then, my dear child," said Andreas Hofer, nodding to
her tenderly, and laying his hand on her beautiful head.

"Go, with God's blessing, and greet your father in my name. Tell him that God and the Holy Virgin are with us and have blessed our cause ; therefore we will never despond, but always fight bravely and cheerfully for our liberty and our dear emperor. Go, Lizzie ; escort the prisoners to Steinach, and then return to your father."

Eliza kissed his hand ; then left him and communicated Andreas Hofer's order to the women. They received it joyously, and hastened to the wagon to get the arms.

Half an hour afterward a strange procession was seen moving along the road leading to Castle Steinach. A long column of soldiers, without arms, with heads bent down and gloomy faces, marched on the road. On both sides of them walked the women, with heads erect, and proud, triumphant faces, each shouldering a musket or a sword. Here and there marched two Tyrolese sharpshooters, who were watching with the keen and distrustful eyes of shepherds' dogs the soldiers marching in their midst.

CHAPTER XVIII.

CAPTURE OF INNSPRUCK.

GENERAL KINKEL, governor of Innspruck, had just finished his dinner, and repaired to his cabinet, whither he had summoned some of the superior officers to give them fresh instructions. To-day, the 11th of April, all sorts of news had arrived from the Tyrol ; and although this news did not alarm the Bavarian general, he thought it nevertheless somewhat strange and unusual. He had learned that Lieutenant-Colonel von Wreden, despite General Kinkel's express orders, had rashly evacuated his position at Brunecken and destroyed the bridge of Laditch. Besides, vague rumors had reached him about an insurrection among the peasants in the neighborhood of Innspruck ; and even on the surrounding mountains, it was said, bands of armed insurgents had been seen.

" We have treated these miserable peasants by far too leniently and kindly," said General Kinkel, with a shrug, when his officer communicated this intelligence to him. "We shall adopt a more rigorous course, make examples of a few, and all will be quiet and submissive again. What do these peasants want? Are they already so arrogant as to think themselves capable of coping with our brave regular troops?"

"They count upon the assistance of Austria," replied Colonel Dittfurt; "and General von Chasteler is said to have promised the peasants that he will invade the Tyrol one of these days."

"It is a miserable lie!" cried the general, with a disdainful smile. "The Austrians will not be so bold as to take the offensive, for they know full well that the great Emperor Napoleon will consider every invasion of Bavarian territory an attack upon France herself, and that we ourselves should drive the impudent invaders from our mountains."

"That is to say, so long as the mountains are still ours, and not yet occupied by the peasants, your excellency," said Major Beim, who entered the room at this moment.

"What do you mean?" asked the general.

"I mean that larger and larger bands of peasants are advancing upon Innspruck, that they have already attacked and driven in our pickets, and that the latter have just escaped from them into the city."

"Then it is time for us to resort to energetic and severe steps," cried General Kinkel, angrily. "Colonel Dittfurt, send immediately a dispatch to Lieutenant-Colonel von Wreden, who is stationed at Brixen. Write to him in my name that I am highly indignant at his evacuating his position at Brunecken and destroying the bridge of Laditch. Tell him I order him to act with the utmost energy; every peasant arrested with arms in his hands is to be shot; every village participating in the insurrection is to be burned down; and he is to advance his patrols again to and beyond Brunecken. These patrols are to ascertain if Austrian troops are really following the insurgent peasants. Bring this dispatch to me that I may sign it, and then immediately send off a courier with it to Lieutenant-Colonel von Wreden." *

* General Kinkel sent off this dispatch a day after Wreden had been defeated by the Tyrolese, and after the Austrians had invaded the Tyrol. The

Colonel Dittfurt went to the desk and commenced writing the dispatch. "Miserable peasants!" he murmured, on handing the dispatch to the general; "it is already a humiliation that we must devote attention to them and occupy ourselves with them."

"Yes, you are right," sighed the general, signing the dispatch; "these people, who know only how to handle the flail, become every day more impudent and intolerable; and I am really glad that I shall now at length have an opportunity to humiliate them and reduce them to obedience. Henceforth we will no longer spare them. No quarter! He who is taken sword in hand, will be executed on the spot. We must nip this insurrection in the bud, and chastise the traitors with inexorable rigor. Well, what is it?" he asked vehemently, turning to the orderly who entered the room at this moment.

"Your excellency, I have to inform you that all our pickets have been driven into the city. The peasants have assembled in large masses on the neighboring mountains and opened thence a most murderous fire upon our pickets. Only a few men of each picket have returned; the others lie dead outside the city."

"Matters seem to become serious," murmured General Kinkel. "All our pickets driven in! That is to say, then, the peasants are in the immediate neighborhood of the city?"

"All the environs of Innspruck are in full insurrection, your excellency, and the citizens of Innspruck seem likewise strongly inclined to join the insurrection. There are riotous groups in the streets, and on my way hither I heard all sorts of menacing phrases, and met everywhere with sullen, defiant faces."

"Ah, I will silence this seditious rabble and make their faces mild and modest!" cried the general, in a threatening voice. "Let all the public places in the city be occupied by troops, and field-pieces be placed on the bridges of the Inn. Let patrols march through the streets all night, and every citizen who is found in the street after nine o'clock, or keeps his house lighted up after that hour, shall be shot. Make

Bavarian authorities at Innspruck were in complete ignorance of all these events.

haste, gentlemen, and carry my orders literally into execution. Have the patrols call upon all citizens to keep quiet and not appear in the streets after nine o'clock. Sentence of death will be passed upon those who violate this order."

Owing to these orders issued by the general, a profound stillness reigned at night in the streets of Innspruck ; no one was to be seen in the streets, and on marching through them the patrols did not find a single offender whom they might have subjected to the inexorable rigor of martial law. But no sooner had the patrols turned round a corner than dark forms emerged here and there from behind the pillars of the houses, the wells, and the crucifixes, glided with the noiseless agility of cats along the houses, and knocked here and there at the window-panes. The windows opened softly, whispers were heard and the rustling of paper, and the forms glided on to commence the same working and whispering at the next house.

The Bavarian patrols had no inkling of these dark ravens flitting everywhere behind them, as if scenting in them already the prey of death ; but the citizens of Innspruck considered these birds of the night, who knocked at their windows, auspicious doves, even though, instead of the olive-branch, they brought only a sheet of paper with them. But this sheet of paper contained words that thrilled all hearts with joy and happiness ; it announced that the Austrians had already invaded the Tyrol ; that General von Chasteler was already advancing upon Innspruck ; that the Emperor Francis sent the Tyrolese the greetings of his love ; and that the Archduke John was preventing the French troops in Italy from succoring the Bavarians in the Tyrol ; nay, that he and his army would deliver and protect the Tyrol. Some of the brave sharpshooters of the Passeyr valley had been bold enough to steal into the city of Innspruck despite the presence of the Bavarian troops, and the patrols could not prevent the citizens from receiving the joyful tidings of the approach of the Austrians, nor the Tyrolese sharpshooters from whispering to them : "Be ready early to-morrow morning. To-morrow we shall attack the city ; assist us then, hurl down from the roofs of your houses on the Bavarians stones, jars, and whatever you may have at hand ; keep your doors open, that we may get in, and hold food and refreshments in readiness. We shall come to-morrow. Innspruck must be delivered from the Bavarians to-morrow ! "

The morrow came at last. The 12th of April dawned upon the city of Innspruck.

The Bavarians had carried out the orders of General Kinkel ; they had occupied all the public places, and planted batteries on the bridges of the Inn.

But so ardent was the enthusiasm of the Tyrolese, that these batteries did not deter them. They rushed forward with loud shouts ; using their spears, halberds, and the butt-ends of their muskets, they fell with resistless impetuosity upon the Bavarians, drove them back, shot the gunners at the guns, and carried the important bridge of Mühlau.

Tremendous cheers announced this first victory to the inhabitants of Innspruck. The Tyrolese then rushed forward over the bridge and penetrated into the streets of the Höttinger suburb. The street-doors of the houses opened to them ; they entered them, or took position behind the pillars, and fired from the windows and their hiding-places, at the Bavarians who were stationed on the upper bridge of the Inn, and were firing thence at the Tyrolese. The Bavarian bullets, however, whistled harmlessly through the streets, the alert Tyrolese concealing themselves, before every volley, in the houses or behind the walls. But no sooner had the bullets dropped than they stepped forward, sang, and laughed, and discharged their rifles, until the exasperated Bavarians fired at them again, when the singing Tyrolese disappeared once more in their hiding-places.

All at once loud cheers and hurrahs resounded on the conquered bridge of Mühlau, and a tall, heroic form, surrounded by a detachment of armed Tyrolese, appeared on the bridge.

It was Joseph Speckbacher, who, after capturing Hall by a daring *coup de main*, had now arrived with his brave men to assist the Tyrolese in delivering Innspruck from the Bavarians.

The Tyrolese thronged exultingly around him, informing him of the struggle that had already taken place, and telling

him that the Bavarians had been driven from the bridge and
hurled back into the city.

"And now you stand still here, instead of advancing?"
asked Speckbacher, casting fiery glances toward the enemy.
"What are you waiting for, my friends? Why do you not
attack the enemy?"

Without waiting for a reply, Speckbacher took off his hat,
swung it in the air, and shouted in a loud, enthusiastic voice:
"Long live the Emperor Francis! Down with the Bavarians!"

All repeated this shout amid the most tumultuous cheers.
All cried, "Long live the Emperor Francis! Down with the
Bavarians!"

"Now forward! forward! We must take the bridge!"
shouted Speckbacher. "Those who love the Tyrol will follow
me!"

And he rushed forward, like an angry bear, toward the
bridge of the Inn.

The Tyrolese, carried away by their enthusiasm, followed
him at the double-quick toward the bridge, where the mouths
of the cannon were staring at them menacingly. But the
Tyrolese were not afraid of the cannon; death had no longer
any terrors for them! their courage imparted to them resistless power and impetuosity. They rushed up to the cannon,
slew the gunners with the butt-ends of their rifles, or lifted
them up by the hair and hurled them over the railing of the
bridge into the foaming waters of the Inn. Then they turned
the cannon, and some students from Innspruck, who had
joined the Tyrolese, undertook to man them.

A dense column of Bavarians advanced upon them; the
peasants uttered loud cheers, the cannon thundered and
mowed down whole ranks of them. They gave way, and the
Tyrolese, who saw it, advanced with triumphant shouts into
the city and took street after street. And wherever they
came, they met with willing assistance at the hands of the
citizens; in every street which they entered, the windows
opened, and shots were fired from them at the Bavarian
troops; every house became a fortress, every tower a citadel.
A frightful scene ensued: the Bavarians in some places sur-

rendered and begged for quarter ; in others they continued the combat with undaunted resolution ; and in the *mêlée* several bloody deeds were committed, which, in their cooler moments, the Tyrolese would have been the first to condemn.

All at once loud cheers burst forth in the streets, and the Tyrolese repeated again and again the joyful news : "Major Teimer has arrived ; he has several companies of the militia under his command, and with these brave men he has already penetrated into the heart of the city, up to the principal guardhouse ! He has already surrounded the *Engelhaus*, General Kinkel's headquarters, and is negotiating a capitulation with the general." This almost incredible intelligence raised the enthusiasm of the Tyrolese to the highest pitch. They rushed forward with irresistible impetuosity toward the barracks and disarmed all the soldiers who had remained there in order to relieve their exhausted comrades. Then they rushed again into the street, toward the principal guard-house, where an obstinate struggle was going on. There, at the head of his regiment, stood Colonel Dittfurt, firmly determined to die rather than surrender to the peasants.

But the peasants came up in overwhelming numbers, and a detachment of sharpshooters, headed by Major Teimer, had already penetrated into the general's house, and entered his sitting-room. From the houses all around, the Tyrolese were firing at the soldiers, who, gnashing their teeth with rage and grief, did not even enjoy the satisfaction of wreaking vengeance on them ; for their enemies were concealed behind the walls and pillars, while the soldiers were defenceless, and had to allow themselves to be laid prostrate by the unerring aim of the sharpshooters.

Angry, scolding, imperious voices were now heard at General Kinkel's window, and a strange sight was presented to the eyes of the dismayed soldiers. Teimer's face, flushed with anger and excitement, appeared at the window. He was seen approaching it hastily and thrusting General Kinkel's head and shoulders forcibly out of it.

"Surrender !" threatened Teimer ; "surrender, or I shall hurl you out of the window !"

* Hormayr's " History of Andreas Hofer," vol. i., p. 249.

"Colonel Dittfurt," cried General Kinkel, in a doleful voice, "you see that further resistance is useless. We must surrender !"

"No !" shouted the colonel, pale with rage ; "no, we shall not surrender; no, we shall not incur the disgrace of laying down our arms before this ragged mob. We can die, but shall not surrender ! Forward, my brave soldiers, forward !"

And Dittfurt rushed furiously, followed by his soldiers, upon the Tyrolese who were approaching at this moment. Suddenly he reeled back. Two bullets had hit him at the same time, and the blood streamed from two wounds. But these wounds, instead of paralyzing his courage, inflamed it still more. He overcame his pain and weakness, and, brandishing his sword, rushed forward.

A third bullet whistled up and penetrated his breast. He sank down ; blood streamed from his mouth and his nose. The Tyrolese burst into deafening cheers, and approached the fallen officer to take his sword from him. But he sprang once more to his feet ; he would not fall alive into the hands of the peasants ; he felt that he had to die, but he would die like a soldier on the field of honor, and not as a prisoner of the peasants. Livid as a corpse, his face covered with gore, his uniform saturated with blood, Dittfurt reeled forward, and drove his soldiers, with wild imprecations, entreaties, and threats toward the hospital, whence the Tyrolese poured their murderous fire into the ranks of the Bavarians. But scarcely had he advanced a few steps when a fourth bullet struck him and laid him prostrate.

His regiment, seized with dismay, shouted out that it would surrender, and, in proof of this intention, the soldiers laid down their arms.

The Bavarian cavalry, to avoid the disgrace of such a capitulation, galloped in wild disorder toward the gate and the Hofgarten. But there Speckbacher had taken position with the peasants, who, mostly armed only with pitchforks, had hurried to the scene of the combat from the immediate environs of Inspruck. But these pitchforks seemed to the panic-stricken cavalry to be terrible, murderous weapons ; cannon would have appeared to them less dreadful than the glittering pitchforks, with which the shouting peasants rushed upon them, and which startled not only the soldiers but their horses also. The soldiers thought the wounds made by pitchforks more horrible and ignominious than utter defeat, and even death. Thunderstruck at their desperate position, hardly knowing what befell them, unable to offer further resistance, they allowed themselves to be torn from their horses by the peasants, to whom they handed their arms in silence. The Tyrolese then mounted the horses, and in a triumphant procession, headed by Joseph Speckbacher, they conducted their prisoners back to Innspruck.*

There the enemy had likewise surrendered in the mean time, and the barracks which, until yesterday, had been the quarters of the oppressors of the Tyrolese, the Bavarian soldiers, became now the prisons of the defeated. Escorted by the peasants, the disarmed and defenceless Bavarians were hurried into the barracks, whose doors closed noisily behind them.

Innspruck was now free ; not an armed Bavarian soldier remained in the city, but the Tyrolese, to the number of upward of fifteen thousand, poured into the streets, and the citizens joined them exultingly, and thanked the courageous peasants for delivering them from the foreign yoke. The city, which for three hours had been a wild scene of terror, havoc, bloodshed, and death, resounded now at the hour of mid-day with cheers and exultation ; nothing was heard but hurrahs, songs, and cheers for the Emperor Francis and the beloved Tyrol.

Every minute added to the universal joy. The victorious Tyrolese, mounted on the horses of the Bavarian cavalry, and headed by the proud and triumphant Speckbacher and a rural band of music, appeared with their prisoners. Two badly-tuned violins, two shrill fifes, two iron pot-lids, and several jews'-harps, were the instruments of this band. But the musicians tried to make as much noise with them as possible, and the citizens considered their music sweeter and finer than the splendid tunes which the bands of the Bavarian regiments had played to them up to this time.

* Hormayr's " History of Andreas Hofer," vol. i., p. 250.

New cheers rent the air at this moment. A squad of peasants brought the great imperial eagle, which they had taken
down from the tomb of Maximilian in the High Church of
Innspruck. They had decorated it with red ribbons, and
carried it amid deafening acclamations through the streets.
On beholding the eagle of Austria, the excited masses set no
bounds to their rejoicings ; they flocked in crowds to gaze at
it ; citizens and peasants vied in manifesting their devotion to
the precious emblem ; they blessed it and kissed it. No one
was permitted to stay a long while near it, for the impatience
of his successor compelled him to pass on. But an aged man,
with silvery hair, but with a form still vigorous and unbent,
would not allow himself to be pushed on in this manner. An
hour ago he had fought like a lion in the ranks of the Tyrolese, and anger and rage had flashed from his face ; but now,
at the sight of the Austrian eagle, he was as mild and gentle
as a lamb, and only love and blissful emotion beamed from
his face. He encircled the eagle with both his arms, kissed
the two heads and gilded crowns, and, stroking the carved
plumes tenderly, exclaimed : "Well, old eagle, have your
plumes really grown again ? Have you returned to the loyal
Tyrol to stay here for all time to come ? Will—"

Loud cheers interrupted him at this moment. Another
crowd of Tyrolese came up the street, preceded by four peasants, who were carrying two portraits in fine golden frames.
Deafening acclamations rent the air as soon as the people beheld these two portraits. Everybody recognized them as those
of the Emperor Francis and the Archduke John. The peasants had found them in the old imperial palace.

"Long live the Emperor Francis ! Long live our Archduke
John !" shouted the people in the streets, and in the houses
which the procession passed on its march through the city.
Even the Austrian eagle, which had been greeted so tenderly,
was forgotten at the sight of the two portraits, and all accompanied this solemn procession of love and loyalty.

This procession moved through the whole city until it
finally reached the triumphal arch which Maria Theresa had
ordered to be erected in honor of the wedding of her son Leopold. The Tyrolese placed the portraits of Leopold's two sons

on this triumphal arch, and surrounded them by candles kept constantly burning; every one then bent his knee, and exclaimed: "Long live the Emperor Francis! Long live our dear Archduke John!" Woe unto him who should have dared to pass these portraits without taking off his hat! the Tyrolese would have compelled him to do it, and to bend his knee.

"Well," they exclaimed, "there is our Francis, and there is our John. Look, does it not seem as though he were smiling at us, and were glad of being here again and able to gaze at us? Long live our dear Archduke John!"

And they again burst into cheers which, if the Archduke John had been able to hear them, would have filled his heart with delight and his eyes with tears.

These rejoicings around the eagle and the portraits lasted all day. The whole city presented a festive spectacle, and the overjoyed Tyrolese scarcely thought to-day of eating and drinking, much less of the dangers which might menace them. They sang, and shouted, and laughed; and when night came they sank down exhausted by the efforts of the fight, and still more by their boundless rejoicings, to the ground where they were standing, in the streets, in the gardens, in the fields, and fell asleep.

Profound silence reigned now in the streets of Innspruck. It was dark everywhere; bright lights beamed only from the portraits of the emperor and the Archduke John; and the stars of heaven looked down upon the careless and happy sleepers, the victors of Innspruck.

They slept, dreaming of victory and happiness. Woe to them if they sleep too long and awake too late, for the enemy does not sleep! He is awake and approaching, while the victors are sleeping.

CHAPTER XIX.

THE CAPITULATION OF WILTAU.

THE Tyrolese were were still asleep, and profound stillness reigned yet in the streets of Innspruck, although it was already after daybreak, and the first rays of the rising sun shed a crimson lustre on the summits of the mountains. All at once this silence was broken by a strange, loud, and plaintive note which seemed to resound in the air; it was followed by a second and third note; and, as if responding to these distant calls, the large bell of the High Church of Innspruck aroused with its ringing voice the weary sleepers to renewed efforts.

They raised themselves from the ground; they listened, still drowsy, to these strange notes in the air. Suddenly two horsemen galloped through the streets, and their clarion voices struck the ears of the Tyrolese.

"Up, sleepers!" cried Joseph Speckbacher; "do you not hear the tocsin? Rise, rise, take your rifles! the French and Bavarians are at the gates of the city, and we must meet them again."

"Rise, Tyrolese!" shouted Major Teimer; "the French and Bavarians are coming. We must prevent them from penetrating into Innspruck. We must barricade the gates, and erect barricades in the streets."

The Tyrolese jumped up, fresh, lively, and ready for the fray. Their sleep had strengthened them, and yesterday's victory had steeled their courage. The enemy was there, and they were ready to defeat him a second time.

The bells of all the churches of Innspruck were now rung, and those of the neighboring village steeples responded to them. They called upon the able-bodied men to take up arms against the enemy, whose advanced guard could be seen already on the crests yonder. Yes, there was no mistake about it: those men were the French and Bavarians, who were descending the slope and approaching in strong columns.

A Tyrolese rushed into the city. "The French are coming!" he exclaimed, panting and breathless. "I have hurried across the mountains to bring you the news. It is General Bisson with several thousand French troops, and Lieutenant-Colonel Wreden with a few hundred Bavarians. We had a hard fight with them yesterday at the bridge of Laditch and in the Mühlbacher Klause ; but they were too strong, and were joined yesterday by another French column ; therefore, we were unable to capture them, and had to let them march on. We killed hundreds of their soldiers ; but several thousands of them escaped, and are coming now to Innspruck."

"They will not come to Innspruck, for we are much stronger than they are, and we will not let them enter the city," exclaimed Speckbacher, courageously.

"No, we will not, except in the same manner in which you brought the cavalry into the city yesterday, that is, to imprison them in the barracks," said Major Teimer.

"Yes, yes, we will do so," shouted the Tyrolese ; "we will let the French come to Innspruck, but only as our prisoners."

"Well, let us be up and doing now, my friends," exclaimed Speckbacher. "We must fortify the city against the enemy. Having gone thus far yesterday, we cannot retrace our steps to-day. But we do not want to retrace them, do we ?"

"No, we do not !" cried the Tyrolese.

"We have raised the Austrian eagle again," said Major Teimer, "and the portraits of the emperor and our dear Archduke John are looking down upon us from the triumphal arch. They shall see that we are good soldiers and loyal sons of our country. Forward, men, let us be up and doing ! Barricade the city, the streets, and the houses ; make bullets, and put your arms in readiness. The French are coming ! Hurrah ! Long live the emperor Francis and the Archduke John !"

Deafening cheers responded to him, and then the Tyrolese rushed through the streets to barricade the city in accordance with Teimer's orders.

The gates were immediately barricaded with casks, wagons, carts, and every thing that could be found for that purpose ; and the approaches to the city were filled with armed men, ready to give the enemy a warm reception. The doors of the houses were locked and bolted, and frantic women within them boiled oil and water which they intended to pour on the heads of the soldiers in case they should succeed in forcing their way into the city ; bullets were made and stones were carried to the roofs, whence they were to be hurled on the enemy. Meanwhile the tocsin resounded incessantly, as if to invite the Tyrolese to redoubled efforts and increased vigilance.

The tocsin, however, had aroused not only the Tyrolese, but also the Bavarians who were locked up in the barracks ; the prisoners understood full well what the bells were proclaiming. To the Tyrolese they said : " The enemy, your enemy, is approaching. He will attack you. Be on your guard !" To the prisoners they proclaimed : " Your friends are approaching. They will deliver you. Be ready for them ! " And now the Bavarians began to become excited, their eyes flashed again, the clouds disappeared from their humiliated brows; and with loud, scornful cheers and fists clinched menacingly, they stepped before their Tyrolese guards and cried : " Our friends are coming. They will deliver us and punish you, and we shall wreak bloody vengeance on you for the disgrace you have heaped upon us. Hurrah, our friends are coming ! We shall soon be free again ! "

" No, you will not," shouted a loud, thundering voice ; and in the middle of the large dormitory occupied by the Bavarians appeared suddenly the tall, herculean form of Joseph Speckbacher. On passing the barracks, he happened to hear the cheers of the prisoners and had entered in order to learn what was the matter. " No," he said once more, " you will not ; you must not suppose that we shall be so stupid as to allow you to escape. Do not rejoice therefore at the approach of the French and your countrymen ; for I tell you, and I swear by the Holy Mother of God, if the French should enter the city victoriously, our last step before evacuating it would be to kill every one of you. Do you hear, Tyrolese guards ? If the prisoners do not keep quiet, if they make any noise, or even threaten you, shoot down the ringleaders ! But if the enemy penetrates into the city, then shoot them all, and do not spare a single one of them.* We will not incur the dis-

* Hormayr's " History of Andreas Hofer," vol. i., p. 253.

grace of re-enforcing the enemy by several thousand men. The guards at all doors here must be quadrupled, and at the first symptom of mischief among the prisoners, you will fire at them. Now you know, Bavarians, what is going to be done. Beware, therefore ! "

And Joseph Speckbacher left the hall with a proud nod of the head. The listening Bavarians heard him repeating his rigorous instructions to the sentinels outside ; they heard also the acclamations with which the Tyrolese responded to him. The prisoners, therefore, became silent ; they forced back their hopes and wishes into the depths of their hearts, and only prayed inwardly for their approaching friends, and cursed in the same manner their enemies, the ragged mob of the peasants.

The tocsin was still ringing, and its sinister notes penetrated likewise into the large guard-house, and spoke to the prisoners confined there. One of these prisoners was a gloomy, broken-down old man, General Kinkel; the other was a youth, mortally wounded and violently delirious. It was Colonel Dittfurt. The bullet of the Tyrolese had not killed him ; he still lived, a prisoner of the peasants, and, amidst his delirium and his agony, he was fully conscious of his disgrace. This consciousness rendered him raving mad ; it brought words of wild imprecation to his cold, bloodless lips ; he howled with rage and pain ; he called down the vengeance of Heaven upon "the ragged mob," the peasants, who had dared to lay hands upon him, the proud, aristocratic colonel, and rob him not only of his life, but also of his honor. All the night long he had raved in this manner ; and it was truly horrible to hear these words, full of contempt, hatred, and fury, in the mouth of a dying man ; it was dreadful to see this scarred form on the bloody couch, writhing in the convulsions of death, and yet unable to die, because anger and rage revived it again and again. At daybreak Major Teimer had entered the guard-house with a detachment of Tyrolese; and while he repaired with some of them to General Kinkel, the other Tyrolese had entered Colonel Dittfurt's room, to see the miracle of a man whose head had been pierced by a bullet having vi-

tality enough left to rave, swear, and curse, for twenty-four
hours.

Gradually the whole room became crowded with Tyrolese,
who yesterday had been the mortal foes of the colonel, but
who gazed to-day with profound compassion and conciliated
hearts at the poor, mutilated being that disdained even on the
brink of the grave to consider a peasant as entitled to equal
rights and as a brother of the nobleman.

Colonel Dittfurt lay on his couch with his eyes distended
to their utmost, and stared at the Tyrolese assembled round
him.   For some minutes the curses and invectives had
died away on his lips, and he seemed to listen attentively to
the sinister notes of the alarm-bells which were calling incessantly upon the Tyrolese to prepare for the struggle.

"Is that my death-knell?" he asked wearily. "Have I,
then, died already, and is it death that is lying so heavily on
my breast?"

"No, sir, you still live," said one of the Tyrolese, in a low,
gentle voice. "You still live; the bells you hear are ringing
the tocsin; they aroused us because the French and Bavarians are advancing upon the city."

"The Bavarians are coming! Our men are coming!"
cried Dittfurt exultingly, and he lifted his head as if to rise
from his couch.   But the iron hand of death had already
touched him and kept him enthralled. His head sank heavily
back upon the pillow, and his eyes became more lustreless
and fixed.

"They vanquished me," he said, after a pause; "I know I
am a prisoner of the peasants, and it is they who keep me
chained to this couch and prevent me from going out to participate in the contest. Oh, oh, how it grieves me! A prisoner of the peasants! But they fought like men, and their leader must be an able and brave officer. Who was the leader of
the peasants?"

"No one, sir," said the Tyrolese, on whom the dying officer
fixed his eyes. "We had no leader; we fought equally for
God, the emperor, and our native country."

"No, no," said Dittfurt, "that is false; I know better, for I
saw the leader of the peasants pass me often. He was mounted

on a white horse ; his face was as radiant as heaven, his eyes twinkled like stars, and in his hand he held a sword flashing like a sunbeam. I saw the leader of the peasants, he always rode at their head, he led them into battle, I—"

He paused, the expression of his eyes became more fixed, the shades of death descended deeper and deeper on his forehead, which was covered with cold perspiration.

The Tyrolese minded him no longer. They looked at each other with exultant and enthusiastic glances. "He saw a leader at our head ?" they asked each other. "A leader mounted on a white horse, and holding in his hand a sword flashing like a sunbeam ? It must have been St. James, the patron of the city of Innspruck. He was our leader yesterday. Yes, yes, that is it ! St. James combated at our head, unknown to us ; but he showed himself to the enemy and defeated him. Did you not hear, brethren, what the pious priests told us of the Spaniards who have likewise risen to fight against Bonaparte, the enemy of the Pope and all good Christians ? St. James placed himself in Spain likewise at the head of the pious peasants ; he led them against Bonaparte and the French, and made them victorious over the enemy, who was bent upon stealing their country and their liberties. And since St. James got through with the Spaniards in Spain, he has come to the Tyrol to lend us his assistance. St. James, our patron saint, is our leader ! He assists us and combats at our head !"

And the Tyrolese, regardless of the colonel, who at this moment was writhing in the last convulsions of death, rushed out of the room to communicate the miracle to their brethren outside. The news spread like wildfire from house to house, from street to street ; all shouted joyously : "St. James, our patron saint, is our leader. He assists us and combats at our head !" *

And this belief enhanced the enthusiasm of the Tyrolese, and with the most intrepid courage they looked upon the enemy, who had by this time come close up to the city, and was forming in line of battle on the plain adjoining the village of Wiltau. From the houses in the neighborhood of

* " Gallery of Heroes: Andreas Hofer," p. 41.

the triumphal arch the Tyrolese were able to survey the whole position of the enemy ; they could discern even the various uniforms of the French and Bavarian soldiers. Up yonder, on the roof of a house, stood Speckbacher and Teimer, and with their eyes, which were as keen and flashing as those of the eagle, they gazed searchingly upon the position of the enemy and that of their own forces. The line from the village of Wiltau down to the river Sill was occupied by the French troops under General Bisson ; on the right side of Wiltau to the Inn stood Lieutenant-Colonel Wreden with the Bavarians, his front turned toward the city.

"Now we must surround them as in a mouse-trap, and leave them no outlet for escape," said Major Teimer, with a shrewd wink. "Is not that your opinion too, Speckbacher ?"

"Certainly it is," replied Speckbacher. "Mount Isel yonder, in the rear of the Bavarians, must be occupied by several thousands of our best sharpshooters, and a cloud of our peasants must constantly harass their rear and drive them toward Innspruck. Here we will receive them in fine style, and chase them until they are all dead or lay down their arms. The only important thing for us is to cut off their retreat and keep them between two fires."

"You are right, Speckbacher ; you are a skilful soldier, and are better able to be a general than many an officer—for instance, General Kinkel. Kinkel is an old woman ; he wept and swore in one breath when I was with him just now ; he says all the time that he will commit suicide, and yet he is not courageous enough to do it, but preferred to comply with my demands."

"And what were your demands, Teimer ?"

"I demanded that he should give me an open letter to General Bisson, urging him to send some confidential person into the town who might report the state of affairs, and convince him of the immense superiority and enthusiasm of the Tyrolese, and of the impossibility of defeating us or forcing his way through our ranks."

"And did old General Kinkel give you such a letter ? "

"He did, and I will send it out now to the French camp. We must make all necessary dispositions, that when the general sends a confidential envoy into the town he may become fully alive to the fact that it is impossible for him to defeat us. Above all things, we must send several thousand sharp-shooters to Mount Isel and the adjoining heights, in order to cut off the enemy's retreat."

The letter which Major Teimer had extorted from General Kinkel had really the effect which he had expected from it. General Bisson sent to Innspruck one of his staff-officers, accompanied by Lieutenant-Colonel von Wreden, the commander of the Bavarians. A few other officers followed these two, and repaired with them to Major Teimer, who received them at the principal guard-house in the presence of the most prominent Tyrolese.

Meanwhile General Bisson awaited with painful impatience the return of the two ambassadors whom he had sent into the town ; and, his eyes constantly fixed on Innspruck, he walked uneasily up and down. But already upward of an hour had elapsed, and the ambassadors had not yet made their appearance. He had good reason to be uneasy and anxious, for the situation of the French and Bavarians was now almost desperate. He had found out at the bridge of the Eisach, on the plain of the Sterzinger Moos, and at the Mühlbacher Klause, that the French had to deal with an enemy who was terribly in earnest ; that the whole Tyrol was in insurrection ; that Chasteler, with a body of armed peasants, as well as a few regular troops, was descending the Brenner, and already menacing his rear ; while the rocks and thickets in his front and flanks were bristling with the peasants of the Innthal, who, in great strength, obstructed his advance.

"We shall die here, for we are hemmed in on all sides," said General Bisson, gloomily, to himself. "There is no hope left, and in the end we may be obliged to submit to the disgrace of surrendering to the mob of peasants. But what on earth prevents the officers from returning to me ?"

And Bisson turned his searching eyes again toward Innspruck. Now he perceived two men approaching at a run. He recognized them ; they were the companions of his staff-officer and lieutenant-colonel, Von Wreden, and their pale, dismayed faces told him that they were bearers of bad tidings.

"Where are the two gentlemen whom I sent to Inn-spruck ?" he asked, advancing rapidly toward them.

"They were taken into custody at Innspruck," faltered out one of them.

"Major Teimer said he had taken upon himself no obliga-tion in regard to these officers, and would retain them as hostages," panted the other. "He then caused us to be con-ducted through the whole city, that we might satisfy ourselves of the tremendous strength of the Tyrolese and their for-midable preparations. Oh, your excellency, the peasants are much superior to us in strength, for there are at least twenty thousand able-bodied men in their ranks ; they are well armed, and the most celebrated marksmen and the most dar-ing leaders of the Tyrol are among them."

"Bah ! it would make no difference, even though they were ten to one!" cried General Bisson ; "for ten peasants cannot have as much courage as one soldier of the grand army of my glorious emperor. We will prove to them that we are not afraid of them. We will attack them. A detachment of Tyrolese yonder has ventured to leave the city. Fire at them! Shoot them down until not one of them is left !"

The shots crashed, the artillery boomed, but not a Tyrolese had fallen ; they had thrown themselves on the ground, so that the bullets and balls had whistled harmlessly over their heads. But now they jumped up and responded to the shots of the enemy ; and not one of their bullets missed its aim, but all carried death into the ranks of the French. At the same time the sharpshooters posted on Mount Isel, in the rear of the French and Bavarians, commenced firing, and mowed down whole ranks of the soldiers.

General Bisson turned in dismay toward this new enemy, covered by the thicket, which, rising almost to the summit of Mount Isel, made the Tyrolese invisible, and protected them from the missiles of the soldiers.

"We are between two fires," he murmured to himself, in dismay. "We are caught, as it were, in a net, and will be annihilated to the last man."

And this conviction seized all the soldiers, as was plainly to be seen from their pale faces and terror-stricken looks.

There was a sudden lull in the fire of the Tyrolese, which had already struck down several hundred French soldiers, and from the triumphal arch of Innspruck issued several men, waving white handkerchiefs, and advancing directly toward the French. It was Major Teimer, accompanied by some officers and citizens of Innspruck. He sent one of them to General Bisson to invite him to an interview to be held on the public square of the village of Wiltau.

General Bisson accepted the invitation, and repaired with his staff and some Bavarian officers to the designated place.

Major Teimer and his companions were already there. Teimer received the general and his distinguished companions with a proud, condescending nod.

" General," he said, without waiting for the eminent officer. to address him, " I have come here to ask you to surrender, and order your soldiers to lay down their arms."

General Bisson looked with a smile of amazement at the peasant who dared to address to him so unheard-of a demand with so much calmness and composure.

" My dear sir," he said, " I am convinced that you are not in earnest, but know full well that we never can or will comply with such a demand.   Moreover, our situation does not by any means compel us to allow conditions to be dictated to us. Nevertheless, I am ready to make some concessions to you. Hence, I will pledge you my word of honor that I will neither attack you, nor injure the city of Innspruck in the least.   But in return I demand that you allow us to pass without molestatation through Innspruck, that we may march to Augsburg in obedience to the orders of my emperor."

" And you believe we can be so stupid as to grant this demand, general ?" asked Teimer, shrugging his shoulders.   " I do not want to be beaten down, but stick to my first demand. Either you order your troops to lay down their arms, or you will all be put to the sword."

" No, so help me God ! never will I accept so arrogant a demand," cried the general, indignantly ; " never will I incur the disgrace of signing so ignominious a capitulation."

" Then, general, you will appear this very day before the throne of God to account for the lives of the thousands whom you devote to an unnecessary death. For all of you will and must die ; there is no escape for you. You know it full well, general, for otherwise you, the proud general of Monsieur Bonaparte, and commander of several thousand splendid French soldiers, would not have come to negotiate here with the leader of the peasants, who knows nothing of tactics and strategy. You know that there are enemies both in your front and rear. Our men occupy Mount Isel, and the whole country back of Mount Isel is in insurrection. You cannot retrace your steps, nor can you advance, for you will never get to Innspruck, and there is no other road to Augsburg. We have barricaded the city, and have nearly twenty thousand men in and around Innspruck."

" But I pledged you my word that I would not attack you, nor take any hostile steps whatever. All I want is to march peaceably through the city ; and, in order to convince you of my pacific intentions, I promise to continue my march with flints unscrewed from our muskets, and without ammunition."

" I do not accept your promises, they are not sufficient," said Teimer, coldly.

" Well, then," cried General Bisson, in a tremulous voice, " hear my last words. I will march on with my troops without arms ; our arms and ammunition may be sent after us on wagons."

" If that is your last word, general, our negotiations are at an end," replied Teimer, with perfect *sang-froid.* " You have rejected my well-meaning solicitude for your safety ; nothing remains for me now but to surrender you and your troops to the tender mercies of our infuriated · people. Farewell, general."

He turned his back on him and advanced several steps toward Innspruck. At the same time he waved his arm three times. Immediately, as had been agreed upon, the Tyrolese on Mount Isel, and in front of Innspruck, commenced firing, and their close discharges, admirably directed, thinned the ranks of the French grenadiers, while the shouts with which the mountains resounded on all sides were so tremendous that they were completely panic-struck.

General Bisson saw it, and a deadly pallor overspread his

face. Teimer stood still and gazed sneeringly at the disheartened and terrified soldiers, and then glanced at their general.

Bisson caught this glance. "Sir," he cried, and his cry resembled almost an outburst of despair, "pray return to me.
Let us negotiate !"

Teimer did not approach him, he only stood still. "Come
to me, if you have any thing to say to me," he shouted ;
"come, and—"

The rattle of musketry, and the furious shouts of the Tyrolese, now pouring down from all the mountains, and advancing upon the French, drowned his voice.

To render his words intelligible to Teimer, and to hear his
replies, General Bisson was obliged to approach him, and he
stepped up to him with his staff-officers in greater haste perhaps than was compatible with his dignity.

"What else do you demand ?" he asked, in a tremulous
voice.

"What I demanded at the outset," said Teimer, firmly. "I
want your troops to lay down their arms and surrender to the
Tyrolese. I have already drawn up a capitulation ; it is only
necessary for you and your officers to sign it. The capitulation is brief and to the point, general. It consists only of
four paragraphs. But just listen to the shouts and cheers
of my dear Tyrolese, and see what excellent marksmen they
are !"

Indeed, the bullets of the Tyrolese whistled again at this
moment through the ranks of the enemy, and every bullet hit
its man. Loud shouts of despair burst from the ranks of the
French and Bavarians, who were in the wildest confusion, and
did not even dare to flee, because they knew full well that
they were hemmed in on all sides."

General Bisson perceived the despair of his troops, and a
groan escaped from his breast. "Read the capitulation to me,
sir," he said, drying the cold perspiration on his forehead.

Teimer drew a paper from his bosom and unfolded it. He
then commenced reading, in a loud, ringing voice, which
drowned even the rattle of musketry :

"In the name of his majesty the Emperor Francis I. of Austria, a capitulation is entered into at this moment with the

French and Bavarian troops which advanced to-day from Steinach to Wiltau ; the following terms were accepted :

"*First.* The French and Bavarian soldiers lay down their arms on the spot now occupied by them.

"*Secondly.* The members of the whole eighth corps are prisoners of war ; and will be delivered as such to the Austrian troops at Schwatz, whither they will be conveyed immediately.

Thirdly. The Tyrolese patriots in the custody of these troops will be released on the spot.

Fourthly. The field and staff-officers of the French and Bavarian troops will retain their baggage, horses, and side-arms, and their property will be respected."

"You see, sir, it is impossible for me to sign this," cried General Bisson. "You cannot expect me to subscribe my own disgrace."

"If you refuse to subscribe the capitulation, you sign thereby not only your own death-warrant, but that of all your soldiers," said Teimer calmly. "See, general, here is fortunately a table, for this is the place where the people of Wiltau assemble on Sundays, and dance and drink. Fate placed this table here for us that we might use it for signing the capitulation. There is the capitulation ; I have already affixed to it my name and title as commissioner of the Emperor Francis. I have also brought pen and ink with me, that you might have no trouble in signing the document. Subscribe it, therefore, general, and let your staff-officers do so too. Spare the lives of your poor soldiers, for you see every minute's delay costs you additional losses."

"I cannot sign it, I cannot !" cried Bisson, despairingly. He burst into tears, and in his boundless grief he struck his forehead with his fist and tore out his thin gray hair with his trembling hands. * "I cannot sign it," he wailed loudly.

"Sign it," cried his officers, thronging round the table. "You must refuse no longer, for the lives of all our soldiers are at stake."

"But my honor and good name are likewise at stake,"

* Hormayr's " Andreas Hofer," vol. i., p. 257.

groaned Bisson, "and if I sign the capitulation, I shall lose both forever."

"But you will thereby preserve to the emperor the lives of upward of three thousand of his soldiers," exclaimed the officers, urgently.

"Never will the emperor believe that this disaster might not have been averted," wailed General Bisson. "Even were I merely unfortunate, he would impute it to me as a crime. He will forgive me no more than Villeneuve and Dupont. His anger is inexorable, and it will crush me."

"Then let it crush you, general," said Teimer, calmly. "It is better that you should be crushed than that several thousand men should now be crushed by the Tyrolese."

"Sign, sign!" cried the French officers, stepping close up to the table, taking up the pen, and presenting it to the general.

"Then you are all determined to sign the capitulation after I have done so?" asked General Bisson, still hesitating.

"We are," cried the officers.

"We are ready to do so," said Major Armance, "and in proof hereof I affix my name to the capitulation before you have signed it, general."

He subscribed the paper with a quick but steady hand. Another staff-officer stepped up, took the pen, and also wrote his name, "Varin."

"Now, general," he said, presenting the pen to Bisson.

The general took the pen, cast a last despairing glance toward heaven and then toward his soldiers, bent over the paper, and signed it.

The pen dropped from his hand, and he had to lean against the table in order not to sink to the ground. Major Teimer drew a white handkerchief from his pocket and waved it in the air. The Tyrolese ceased firing immediately, and deafening cheers burst forth on all sides.

"You see, general, you have saved the lives of your soldiers," said Teimer.

Bisson only sighed, and turned to his officers. "Now, gentlemen," he faltered out, "give orders to the troops to lay down their arms on the spot now occupied by them."

place, at a slight distance from the king, broke into a loud hurrah,
and shouted, "Long live our king!"

The king turned slowly toward them, but when he saw all that
remained of his noble army, he became pale, and pressed his lips
tightly together, as if to suppress a cry of horror. Then advancing,
followed by his generals, to where his weary, wounded soldiers
were lying, he said :

"Children, is this all that is left of you?"

"Yes, father, we are the last," said an old gray-headed officer,
standing before the king.   "There were many thousands of us, now
there are two hundred and fifty."

"Two hundred and fifty!" repeated the king, with a bitter smile.

"And it was not our fault," continued the old officer, "that we
did not fall with the rest. We fought as bravely as they ; but Death
did not want us. Perhaps he thought it best to leave a few of us, to
guard our king. We all think so! Some were left to repay those
abominable Saxons for their to-day's work."

"And why alone the Saxons?" asked the king.

"Because it was those infamous Saxon troops that hewed down
our regiment. They fell upon us like devils, and striking their
cursed swords into us, cried out, 'This is for Striegau!'"

"Ah! you see," cried the king, "that while beating you, they
could but think of the many times you had conquered them."

"They shall think of this again, father," said another soldier,
raising himself with great pain from the ground.   "Wait until our
wounds have healed, and we will repay them with interest."

"You are wounded, Henry?" said the king.

"Yes, your majesty, in the arm."

"And old Klaus?"

"Is dead!"

"And Fritz Verder?"

"Dead! He lies with the others upon the battle-field. There
are seven hundred and fifty of us in heaven, and only two hundred
and fifty on earth. But those above, as well as below, still cry—
'Long live our king!'"

"Long live our king," cried they all, rising.

The king made no reply ; his eye passed from one to the other
pale, exhausted countenance, and an inexpressible sorrow overcame
him.

"Dead!" murmured he, "my faithful guards dead! seven hundred and fifty of my choice men have fallen." And overpowered by
his emotion, the king did not force back the tears welling to his
eyes. They stole softly down his cheek, and Frederick was not
ashamed. He did not blush, because his warriors had seen him weep·

"Children," cried the old officer, after a pause, and wiping the tears from his weary eyes, "from now on it will be glorious to die; for when we are dead, our king weeps for us."

CHAPTER VIII.

THE INIMICAL BROTHERS.

"THE king comes! The king is entering Bautzen!"

This announcement brought pale terror to the hearts of the Prince of Prussia and his generals. They who had heretofore sprang joy-fully to meet the call of their king, now trembled at his glance. They must now present to him the sad and despoiled remnant of that great army which, under the command of the Prince Augustus William of Prussia, had made the retreat from Lausitz.

It had, indeed, been the most fearful retreat ever attempted by the Prussian troops. It had cost them more than the bloodiest battle, and they had suffered more from hardships during the last few days than ever before during a whole campaign. They had marched over narrow, stony, rugged mountain-paths, between hills and horrible abysses, sometimes climbing upward, sometimes de-scending. Thousands died from exhaustion; thousands pressed backward, crushed by those in the front; thousands, forced onward by those in the rear, had stumbled and fallen into fathomless cav-erns, which lay at the foot of these mountain passes, yawning like open graves. If a wheel broke, the wagon was burned; there was no time for repairs, and if left in the path, it interrupted the pas-sage of the flying army. At last, in order to facilitate the flight, the provision-wagons were burned, and the bread divided amongst the soldiers; the equipages and pontoon-wagons were also burned. Exhausted by their unusual exertions, beside themselves from pain and unheard-of suffering the whole army was seized with a death-panic.

The soldiers had lost not only all faith in their good fortune, but all faith in their leaders. Thousands deserted; thousands fled to escape death, which seemed to mock at and beckon to them from every pointed rock and every dark cavern.*

While one part of the army deserted or died of hunger or exhaus-tion, another part fought with an intrenched enemy, for three long days, in the narrow pass of Gabel, under the command of General von Puttkammer. They fought like heroes, but were at last obliged to surrender, with two thousand men and seven cannon. Utterly

* Warner's " Campaigns of Frederick the Great."

forces, as he had concerted at Vienna with the Archduke
John and Hormayr, in order to bring to the Italian Tyrolese
the liberty which the German Tyrolese had already conquered.

Hence Andreas Hofer, though his heart yearned for it, had
refrained from making his solemn entrance into Innspruck,
and had gone on the 17th of April to Meran, where he was to
review the *Landsturm* of that town and its environs, the
brave men who were to accompany him on his expedition to
the Italian Tyrol.

The Tyrolese were drawn up in four lines; at their head
was to be seen Hormayr, surrounded by the priests and civil
officers who had been exiled by the Bavarians, and who were
returning now with him and the Austrian army.

A cloud of dust arose from the neighboring gorges of the
Passeyr valley, and a joyous murmur ran through the ranks
of the Tyrolese. Deafening cheers rent the air then, for Andreas Hofer galloped up on a fine charger, followed by the
men of the Passeyr valley. His face glowed, his eyes beamed
with delight, and his whole bearing breathed unbounded satisfaction and happiness.

He shook hands with Hormayr, laughing merrily. "We
have kept," he exclaimed, "the promises we made at Vienna,
have we not? And our dear Archduke John, I suppose, will
be content with us?"

"He sends the best greetings of his love to his dear Andreas Hofer," said Hormayr, "and thanks him for all he has
done here."

"He thanks me?" asked Hofer, in surprise. "We have
done only what our hearts longed for, and fulfilled our own
wishes. We wished to become Austrians again, for Austrians
means Germans; we wanted no longer to be Bavarians, for
Bavarians meant French; hence, we were anxious to rid our
mountains of the disgrace and make our country again free
and a province of Germany. We have succeeded in doing so,
for the good God blessed our efforts and helped us in our sore
distress. Now we are once more the faithful children of our
dear emperor, and the dear Archduke John will come to us
and stay with us as governor of the Tyrol."

"He certainly will, and I know that he longs to live again in the midst of his faithful Tyrolese. But for this reason, Andy, we must help him that he may soon come to us, and aid him in delivering the Southern Tyrol. I have great news for you, Andy, from the Archduke John. I wished to communicate it to you first of all. No one was to hear of it previous to you."

"I hope it is good news, Baron von Hormayr, said Andreas Hofer, anxiously. "The dear archduke, I trust, has not met with a disaster? Tell me quick, for my heart throbs as though one of my dear children were in imminent peril."

"You yourself are a child, Andy. Do you suppose I should look so cheerful if our dear archduke had met with a disaster? And even though such were the case, would I then be so stupid as to inform you of it now, at this joyful hour, when it is all-important that we should be in high spirits? No, Andy, I bring splendid news. The Archduke John achieved yesterday a glorious victory at Sacile over the Viceroy of Italy, Eugene Beauharnais; it was a great triumph, for he took eight thousand prisoners, and captured a great many guns. But amidst this triumph he thought of his dear Tyrolese, and dispatched from the battle-field a courier who was to bring to me the news and his order to tell his dear Tyrolese that he defeated the French yesterday."

Andreas Hofer, overjoyed and with his countenance full of sunshine and happiness, galloped down the long line of his sharpshooters.

"Hurrah! my dear friends and brethren," he shouted, "the Archduke John sends his greetings to you, and informs you that he defeated the French yesterday at Sacile and took eight thousand prisoners and a great many guns. Hurrah! long live the Archduke John, the future governor of the Tyrol!"

And the Tyrolese repeated, with deafening cheers: "Hurrah! long live the Archduke John, the future governor of the Tyrol!"

"And I have to bring you still another greeting from the Archduke John," shouted Baron von Hormayr. "But you shall not hear it here in the plain, but up at the ancient castle

of Tyrol. It is true, the Bavarians and the miserable French
have destroyed the fine castle, but the ruins of the ancient
seat of our princes remain to us. We will now ascend to
those ruins, and up there you shall hear the message which
the Archduke John sends to you."

The whole force of the Tyrolese thereupon moved up the
mountain-path leading to the castle of Tyrol, headed by Andreas Hofer and Baron von Hormayr.

On reaching the crest of the hill, Hofer stopped and
alighted from his horse. He knelt down amidst the ruins of
the castle with a solemn, deeply-moved face, and holding the
crucifix on his breast between his hands, and lifting his eyes
to heaven, he exclaimed with fervent devotion : "Thanks,
Lord God, thanks for the aid that thou hast hitherto vouchsafed to us ! Thanks for delivering the country and permitting us to be Austrians again ! O God, grant now stability to
our work—and preserve it from falling to ruin ! If Thou art
content with me, let me further serve and be useful to my native country ! I am but a weak instrument in Thy hand, my
God, but Thou hast used it, and I pray Thee not to cast it aside
now, but impart to it strength and durability, that it may
last until the enemy has been driven from the country, and
the whole Tyrol is free again for evermore ! I kiss the dear
soil where our princes walked in former times, and where they
swore to their Tyrolese that they should be freemen, and
that their free constitution should be sacred for all time to
come !"

He bent down, kissed the moss-grown stones, and encircled
them tenderly with his arms as though they were an altar
before which he was uttering devout vows and prayers. The
Tyrolese, who had gradually reached the summit, had silently knelt down behind Andreas Hofer, and were praying
like him.

One sentiment animated them all and illuminated their
faces with the radiant lustre of joy : the Tyrol was delivered
from the foreign yoke, and they, the sons of the country, had
alone liberated their beloved fatherland.

"Now, men of the Tyrol," shouted Hormayr, "listen to the
message which the Archduke John sends to you."

And amid the solemn silence of the Tyrolese, and the peals of the Meran church-bells penetrating up to them, Hormayr read to them a document drawn up by the Archduke John, by virtue of which he resumed possession of the Tyrol in the name of the emperor, declared it to be incorporated with the imperial states, and solemnly vowed that, as a reward of its loyalty, it should remain united with Austria for all future time. At the same time, the ancient constitution and the former privileges were restored to the Tyrolese, and Baron von Hormayr was appointed governor of the Tyrol.

CHAPTER XX.

ELIZA WALLNER'S RETURN.

ALL Windisch-Matrey was again in joyful commotion to-day, for a twofold festival was to be celebrated : the return of the men of Windisch-Matrey, who had so bravely fought for the country and so aided in delivering it ; and then, as had been resolved previous to their departure, Eliza Wallner's wedding was to come off to-day.

She had redeemed her pledge, she had proved that she was a true and brave daughter of the Tyrol, and Anthony Wallner, her father, was no longer angry with her ; he wished to reward her for her courage and intrepidity, and make her happy. Therefore, he had sent a messenger secretly and without her knowledge to Windisch-Matrey, and had ordered his wife to decorate the house festively, and request the curate to repair to the church and perform the marriage rites. The returning Tyrolese were to march to the church, and, after thanking God for the deliverance of the Tyrol, the curate was to marry Eliza Wallner and her lover in presence of the whole congregation.

Since early dawn, therefore, all the married women and girls of Windisch-Matrey, dressed in their handsome holiday attire, had been in the street, and had decorated the route which the returning men were to take, and adorned the church with wreaths and garlands of flowers.

Wallner's wife alone had remained at home, for she had to
attend to the preparations for the wedding-banquet, with
which she and her servant-girls had been occupied during the
whole of the previous day. There were a great many things
to be done yet; the table had to be set in the large bar-
room for the wedding-guests; the roasts had to be looked
after in the kitchen; and the whole house had to be decorated, and festoons of flowers to be suspended round its entrance.

"Schröpfel might render me good service now," said
Wallner's wife, eagerly. "I have so many things to attend
to, and he does not move his hands, but sits like a log at
the door of dear Ulrich von Hohenberg, and cares for nothing else. Oh, Schröpfel, Schröpfel, come here! I want to
see you!"

At the staircase leading down into the hall appeared the
sunburnt, furrowed face of old Schröpfel.

"If you want to see me, you must come up here," he
shouted. "I have been told to stand guard here, and I will
not desert my post, even for the sake of Mrs. Wallner, until I
am relieved."

"He is a queer fellow," said Mrs. Wallner, laughing, "but
I must do what he says."

She hastened up-stairs. At the door of the room where
the prisoner was confined stood the servant, pressing his face
to the brown panels of the door.

"Now, Schröpfel," asked Mrs. Wallner, laughing, "can
you see through the boards? For you put your eyes to the
door as though it were a window."

"It is a window," said Schröpfel, in a low voice, limping
up a few steps to his mistress. "I have bored four small
holes in the door, and through them I am able to see the
whole room and all that the prisoner is doing. Look, Mrs.
Wallner! the hole below there is my window when he is in
bed and asleep; I can see his face through it. The hole a
little above it enables me to watch him while he is seated at
the table, and writing or reading; and through the hole up
here I can see his face when he is pacing the room."

"You are a strange fellow," said Mrs. Wallner, shaking

her head. "You watch the poor sick prisoner as though he were an eagle, always ready to fly from the nest."

"He is about what you say," said Schröpfel, thoughtfully. "He is no longer sick, and his wings have grown a great deal during the week since he was here. I believe he would like to fly from here."

"Oh, no," said Mrs. Wallner, with a shrug. "He loves my Lizzie, and I do not believe that he who loves that girl will wish to fly away before she flies with him."

"I do not know about that ; I have my own notions about it," said Schröpfel. "He is a Bavarian for all that, and the Bavarians are all faithless and dishonest. I swore to watch him and not lose sight of him, and I must keep my oath ; hence, I shall not leave the door until I am relieved."

"Then you will not come down-stairs and help me fix the wreaths and garlands, set the table, and clean the knives ? "

"No, dear Mrs. Wallner, I am not allowed to do so, much as I would like to assist you. A sentinel must never leave his post, or he will be called a deserter, and Mr. Wallner always told me that that was a great disgrace for an honest fellow. Now, as I am an honest fellow, and, owing to my lame leg, cannot serve the country in any other way than watching this prisoner, I shall stay here as a sentinel and take good care not to desert."

"Well, do so, then," exclaimed Mrs. Wallner, half angrily, half laughingly. "But you may go in to the gentleman and tell him to be of good cheer, for Eliza will come back to-day, and the wedding will take place immediately after her return, when he will be free. Tell him to prepare for the ceremony ; for, when the bells commence ringing, the returning defenders of the country will have reached the village, and we are to go with him to the church, where the curate will await us."

"Of course, I shall tell him all this," growled Schröpfel, and Mrs. Wallner hastened down-stairs again.

"Yes, I shall tell him," murmured Schröpfel to himself, "but I wonder if it will gladden his heart ? During the first few days, when he had the wound-fever, he talked strange things in his delirium, and derided and scorned our beautiful

Lizzie, who, he said, was bent upon becoming an aristocratic
lady. Since he is well again, he abuses her no longer, but he
looks very sombre, and during the whole week he has not
once inquired after his betrothed. God blast the accursed
Boafok if he should love the girl no longer, and if he did not
honestly intend to make her his wife ! I will go in to him
and see how he receives the news."

Ulrich von Hohenberg was seated in his armchair, and
gazing musingly out of the window. He did not turn when
the old servant entered his room ; he seemed not to have
noticed his arrival, but continued staring at the sky even
when Schröpfel stood close to him. The face of the young
man was still pale and wan, and under his eyes, formerly so
clear and cheerful, were to be seen those bluish circles indica-
tive of internal sufferings of the body or the soul. However,
since the wound-fever had left him, he had never uttered a
complaint, and the wound, which was not very severe, had
already closed and was healing rapidly. Hence, it was doubtless grief that imparted so gloomy and sickly an appearance
to Captain Ulrich von Hohenberg, and it was this very suspicion that rendered Schröpfel distrustful, and caused him to
watch his prisoner night and day with sombre vigilance.

He stood a few minutes patiently, and waited for the captain to address him; but Hohenberg continuing to take no
notice of him, he resolutely laid his hand on his shoulder.

"Sir, awake !" he exclaimed sullenly.

The captain gave a slight start, and pushed the servant's
hand with an angry gesture from his shoulder.

"I am awake," he said ; "it is therefore quite unnecessary
for you to lay hands on me. What is it ? What do you want
of me ? "

"I want to tell you only that our men will return this
morning, and that this will be a great holiday in Windisch-
Matrey. For our men are victorious, and the country is delivered from the enemy. Mr. Wallner has written to us that
the brave Tyrolese delivered the whole country in three days,
that they have taken prisoners eight thousand infantry and
one thousand cavalry, and captured eight guns, two stands of
colors, and two French eagles. Besides, several thousand

French and Bavarians have perished in the gorges and on the battle-fields. Very few of our own men have been killed, and not one of them made prisoner. Now the whole country is free, and our victorious men are coming home."

Not a muscle in the captain's face had betrayed that he had heard Schröpfel's report. He still stared quietly at the sky, and his features expressed neither grief nor surprise at the astounding news.

"You do not ask at all, sir, if Eliza Wallner will return with the men ?" asked Schröpfel, angrily. "I should think you ought to take some interest in that, for Lizzie is your be-trothed."

"She is not !" cried the captain, starting up indignantly, with flushed cheeks and flashing eyes.

"Yes, she is," said Schröpfel, composedly. "I myself heard the girl say to her father and the men of Windisch-Matrey: 'He is my bridegroom ; I love him, and you must not kill him.' And because she said so, the men spared your life, although Anthony Wallner-Aichberger was very angry, and would not forgive his daughter for having given her heart to an enemy of her country, a Bavarian, and, moreover, a nobleman, and not to an honest peasant. But Lizzie begged and wailed so much that her father could not but yield, and promised her to forgive all if she proved that she was no trait-oress to her country, but a true and brave daughter of the Tyr-ol ; after doing so, he would permit her to marry her Bava-rian betrothed. And now she has proved that she is a true and brave daughter of the Tyrol, and the whole country is full of the heroic deeds performed by Lizzie Wallner, and of the intrepidity which she displayed under the most trying cir-cumstances. And to-day, captain, you will meet again your betrothed, who saved your life, and who went with the men only to perform heroic deeds that would induce her father to consent to her union with you. I tell you, sir, beautiful Lizzie Wallner, your betrothed, will return in an hour or two."

The young man's face crimsoned for a moment, and when the color disappeared from his cheeks, their pallor was even more striking and ghastly than before.

" Eliza Wallner fought, then, very bravely against—against my countrymen ? " he asked, pantingly.

"No, she did not fight, sir, but she went into the thickest shower of bullets to carry away the wounded Tyrolese, and attend to their injuries; and she drove a hay-wagon directly toward the enemy, and our men were concealed behind the hay, and she brought a keg of wine to our men while the bullets were whistling round her ; and, finally, she and the other women escorted the Bavarian prisoners to Castle Stein-ach."

The young man uttered a cry, and buried his face in his hands.

"What a disgrace, oh, what a disgrace ! " he groaned, de-spairingly; and in his grief he seemed to have entirely for-gotten the presence of the servant, for he wept, wept so bit-terly that large scalding tears trickled down between his fingers.   " Our brave soldiers were defeated by miserable peasants," he wailed.   "The Bavarian prisoners were marched off under an escort of women ! "

Schröpfel stood as if petrified, and this outburst of the grief of the usually haughty and laconic young man filled him with the utmost surprise and confusion.

However, the captain suddenly dried his tears and dropped his hands from his face.

" And Eliza Wallner, you say, led the women who escorted the Bavarian prisoners ? " he asked, in a firm, almost menac-ing voice.

" Yes, sir, she did," said Schröpfel.   "And now her father is reconciled with her, and, to prove it, he will marry his daughter to you to-day."

The captain said nothing ; only a proud, scornful smile played around his lips for a moment.

" Yes," added Schröpfel, " the wedding will come off to-day. Immediately after their return the procession will move to the church, where a thanksgiving service will be held ; it will be followed by the marriage ceremony.   Mr. Wallner wrote to his wife to send you to the church as soon as the bells commenced ringing; and to keep you in the vestry until you were sent for.   Remember, therefore, as soon as the bells commence ringing, I shall call for you and take you to the vestry."

The young man was silent, and gazed thoughtfully before him; he then threw back his head with an air of bold resolution.

"All right," he said, "I shall accompany you. Did you not say that my baggage had been sent hither from the castle?"

"Yes, yes, Miss Elza sent every thing hither by her servants, and she herself came with them. And during the first days, when you had the wound-fever, she came here at least three times a day and asked how you were, and cried and lamented, and entreated me for God's sake to admit her to your room only for a brief moment. But I had sworn not to admit any one to my prisoner, nor to permit him to speak with any one; hence, I could not make an exception even in favor of the kind-hearted young lady. She comes nevertheless every day and inquires about you; and she begged hard and long until Mrs. Wallner permitted her to send your dinner always from the castle. As you will be free to-day, I may tell you all this, for it will no longer do any harm."

"No, it will no longer do any harm," said the captain, with a peculiar smile. "Listen, I wish to dress up for to-day's ceremony, and don my gala uniform. Therefore be so kind as to fetch it."

"I will, captain, I will fetch the uniform and be back directly," said Schröpfel, cheerfully, limping hastily toward the door. But outside he stood still and pressed his finger thoughtfully to his nose. "I do not know exactly what to think of it," he murmured to himself. "At first he uttered a loud cry and said Lizzie Wallner was not his betrothed; afterward he lamented piteously because Lizzie Wallner escorted the Bavarian prisoners; and finally he asked for his gala uniform in order to dress up for the ceremony. Well, we shall see very soon if he has honest intentions toward Lizzie and really loves her. If he thinks he can play her a trick, he had better beware, for I shall never lose sight of him; I shall always be behind him, and if he does not treat the girl as he ought to, I will strike him down with my fists like a mad bull! I will do it, so help me God!"

CHAPTER XXI.

THE CATASTROPHE.

THE bells were ringing, the men were rejoicing, and the girls of Windisch-Matrey and its environs took position with baskets of flowers on both sides of the street. For the victorious defenders of the country were approaching ; their cheers were already heard at a distance ; and they already saw the merry boys who had gone out to meet them, and who now headed the procession amid manifestations of the liveliest delight. Yes, they were coming, they were coming ! Yonder, down the mountain-slope, moved the motley procession of the Tyrolese, resembling a glittering serpent of gigantic proportions. How their rifles flashed in the sun ! How beautifully the bouquets adorned their pointed green hats ! And now they were already able to distinguish the faces and the individual forms. Immediately behind the boys, at the head of the procession, walked Anthony Wallner-Aichberger. How splendid the commander-in-chief looked ; and how beautiful was Lizzie, walking by his side, handsomely dressed, and wearing a beautiful bouquet in her bosom ! Her attentive father had despatched a special messenger to his wife for Lizzie's holiday dress and her trinkets, so that Lizzie, the pride and joy of his heart, might make her entrance in a becoming manner into Windisch-Matrey.

Lizzie looked really splendid in her holiday attire. Her raven hair, flowing down in heavy tresses on her neck, was interwoven with dark-red ribbons, and large rosettes of the same color were fastened with silver pins to her head. Her low-necked corset, adorned with silver trimmings, was fastened on the breast with silver chains ; and above it rose a white chemisette trimmed with laces, and veiling chastely her faultless bust and beautifully-shaped shoulders. Large white sleeves covered her arms and were fastened to her wrists with dark-red rosettes. An ample skirt of fine dark-red wool, trimmed with black velvet, fell from her slender waist down to her ankles, and her small feet were encased in handsome stockings and shoes adorned with large silver buckles. The boys had brought to her the splendid bouquet which she wore in her bosom, and had told her, amid laughter and cheers, that her betrothed sent her the bouquet as a wedding-present.

But these words had rendered Lizzie silent and sad. The smile had disappeared from her lips, and the color had faded from her cheeks ; she looked anxiously at her father, but he nodded to her and said laughingly : "Do not ask me any questions to-day, Lizzie, for I will not tell you any thing. Await quietly the events that will take place, and bear in mind that your father loves you dearly, and is anxious to make his little daughter happy and contented."

Eliza tried to divine what these words of her father meant, and a gloomy foreboding, a terror which she was unable to explain to herself, filled her heart.

She listened no longer to the joyous shouts of the boys, and ceased singing with Panzl the fine songs of the Tyrolese mountains, but walked along, pale, silent, and hanging her head.

Now they reached Windisch-Matrey, and stood still at the entrance of the street, where the clergy, municipal authorities, and the beautifully-dressed girls, bade them welcome. Oh, it was a soul-stirring moment, a sacred festival of welcome ! The brave men had gone out to fight for their native country, their emperor, and the liberties of the Tyrol ; and God had granted them victory. He had assisted them in all contests, the country was free, the emperor was again master of the Tyrol, and the men of Windisch-Matrey returned victoriously to their homes. All seemed to greet them with glowing looks of love ; the whole earth seemed to shout "Welcome!" to them. Even the glistening snow-clad summits of the Gross-Glockner seemed to look at them over the other mountains with an air of curiosity and solemn kindness ; and on the green mountain-pastures stood the red cows so proud and handsome, as if they had placed themselves there for the purpose of adorning the landscape for the returning heroes. And the wild Iselbach murmured merrily at the roadside and sent its silvery spray into the air, and the boys laughed and sang ; the bells pealed so loudly and solemnly, and received

ringing responses from the villages farther down in the valley ; the priests stood with solemn, devout faces at the entrance of the place, blessing the heroes with uplifted hands,
and eyes turned to heaven ; and the girls and matrons, strew-
ing flowers to the returning men, stood on both sides of the
street, and greeted them with beaming smiles.

Oh, this sweet, sublime moment silenced all cares and
doubts. The smile returned to Eliza's lips, her cheeks crimsoned, and her eyes beamed with the purest joy. With a loud
cry of delight she throw herself into the arms of her mother,
and kissed her a thousand times, and scarcely listened to the
address of the curate, who returned thanks to her in the name
of the whole parish for her courage and the assistance she had
rendered to her countrymen wounded in battle.

But now Eliza heard a dear familiar voice, which caused
her to raise herself from her mother's arms and look up.

Yes, it was the old, kind-hearted Baron von Hohenberg
who was standing before her, and held out his hand to her
with his sunniest and kindest smile. " My brave daughter,"
he said, feelingly, " give me your hand. You know that I
love you as though you were my own child ; and now I am
proud of you, for you have become a heroine, and have done
honor to our Tyrol. Elza was right after all in always calling you another Maid of Orleans, and saying you were a born
heroine."

" But where is Elza ?" said Lizzie, anxiously, to the old
castellan.

" Here I am, dearest Eliza," said the young lady, who had
hitherto kept herself behind her father and the clergyman.

" Oh, my Elza, my dear, dear Elza !" exclaimed Eliza, rapturously ; and she encircled her friend's neck with her arms,
and imprinted a glowing kiss on her lips.

But she felt that Elza's lips quivered, that she did not return the kiss, nor press the friend to her heart ; and it seemed
to Eliza as though a cold hand suddenly touched her heart and
pressed it rudely and cruelly. She raised her head from Elza's
shoulder, and looked her full in the face. It was not until
now that she saw how pale Elza was, how red her eyes with
weeping, and how forced her smile.

"You are sick, Elza," she said, anxiously.

"No," whispered Elza, "I am not."

"Then you love your Lizzie no longer?" asked Eliza, pressingly.

"Yes, I do," said Elza, in a hollow voice, and with a wondrously mournful smile. "I do love you, and, to prove it, I present you with this wreath. God bless you, dear Lizzie; may He grant you happiness!"

"Elza," cried Eliza, anxiously, "Elza, pray come to me and tell me what it means, what—"

"Hush, Lizzie, hush," said her father, seizing her hand and drawing her forward. "Do you not see that the procession is moving on, and that we must go with it? See, the curate and the castellan are already far ahead, and we must go too."

"But where, father, where?"

"To the church, you dear little goose!"

"To the church? What are we to do there? Why do we not go home?"

"Have you become so impious during your campaign, Lizzie, as not to know that we must always render homage to God first and above all things? We are going to church to return thanks; come with me, and ask no more questions."

"But I will take off the myrtle-wreath!" exclaimed Lizzie, lifting her hand anxiously to the wreath. But her father drew back her hand.

"No, Lizzie," he said, "do not remove the wreath. It fits well on your head."

"But I am no bride going to church on her wedding-day."

"Really, Lizzie, are you not?" asked her father, laughing. "But hush now, my child, we are already at the church-door, and do you not hear the glorious swelling notes of the organ? Let us enter the church, dear Lizzie."

He drew her forward, and Eliza followed him: but indescribable anguish oppressed her soul; she did not know why, and she felt as though something dreadful were about to happen here, and as though she ought to flee, flee far into the mountains, into solitude.

But her father held her by the hand, and walked with her up the main aisle to the large altar. Rows of chairs, decorated with flowers, had been placed here, and Eliza had to seat herself on one of these chairs ; by her side sat her father ; opposite her, the castellan and her friend Elza ; then came the municipality, and John Panzl, lieutenant-commander of the men of Windisch-Matrey, and behind them stood the dense crowd of the sharpshooters of the Pusterthal.

Eliza cast a searching glance on the dense crowd ; she looked at all the pews, and yet she did not know what she was looking for, nor what alarmed her heart so much.

All at once she started in sudden terror, and her cheek turned deadly pale. Yonder, behind the windows of the vestry, she beheld a young man in a handsome uniform ; it was he, he whom she had looked for without knowing it herself ; he from whose sight her heart had shrunk with anxiety and dismay. And yet Eliza had longed to see him, for she had been uneasy on his account ; she had feared lest he should still suffer gravely from the consequences of his wound. But she had not dared to ask any one about him ; hence, she was glad to see that he was well, and showed her gladness in her gaze at him. Their eyes met, but he looked upon her with an expression of hatred and contempt ; a haughty, disdainful smile played round his lips, and he threw back his head superciliously, instead of nodding pleasantly to her.

Eliza felt a terrible pain in her heart ; she wished to jump up, she— All at once she heard her name drop from the lips of the curate, who was standing before the altar, and who had just concluded the thanksgiving prayer. What did he say— why did he mention her ? She held her breath to listen to him. Great heavens ! another name fell from the curate's lips. He uttered the name of Ulrich von Hohenberg ; he proclaimed him the bridegroom of Eliza Wallner, who was present ; he called upon Captain Ulrich von Hohenberg to appear before the altar, and receive the consecration of his union with his betrothed in the presence of all these witnesses.

With a hollow groan, crushed, and as if broken-hearted, Eliza sank back into her chair, and her pale lips murmured : "Now I am lost, and so is he !"

"Ulrich von Hohenberg," shouted the priest at the altar, "come hither and take your bride by the hand."

The door of the vestry opened, and Ulrich von Hohenberg stepped in. His tall, slender form presented a very fine appearance in the brilliant gala uniform; a flashing cross adorned his breast; in his hand he held his gold-laced hat, with the waving white plume; only the sword was wanting to his side, and this alone betokened his humiliating position, and showed that he was a prisoner amidst all these armed men. But the consciousness of this fact seemed not to humiliate him, for he walked up, his head proudly raised, and his stern, cold eyes gazing scornfully upon the assembly.

He stepped close up to the altar. "Reverend father," he said, in a clear, loud voice to the priest, "you have called me. Here I am. What do you want of me?"

"I have called you, Ulrich von Hohenberg, to marry you to your betrothed. Eliza Wallner, step to the side of your bridegroom."

But Eliza Wallner did not rise from her chair; she leaned her head, almost in a swoon, against the back of her chair, and stared, as if unconscious of what was going on around her, at the priest and the young man, who fixed his eyes on her at this moment with an air of cold contempt.

"Eliza Wallner," he cried aloud, "do not come hither, for I am not your betrothed, and never shall you become my wife!"

A deafening cry of rage burst from all lips: the eyes of all the brave men in the church flashed with anger, and they laid their hands menacingly on their rifles.

But Anthony Wallner sprang to his feet, pale with rage, his eyes shooting fire, like those of an angry tiger, rushed toward the captain, and seized his arm.

"What!" he cried, furiously, "you infamous, perjured scoundrel, refuse to marry my daughter? First you stole her love, you promised to marry her, and now that I would give her to you, you refuse to take her!"

"Yes, I do," cried Ulrich von Hohenberg, almost joyously. "Never will Eliza Wallner, the peasant-girl, become my wife; never will I stoop so low as to allow a wife to be forced upon me, merely to save my life, and least of all her who has fought against my countrymen and brethren; who participated in the studied insult inflicted upon the brave soldiers of my king, and in the infamous treason you have all committed against your king and lord.   Yes, I tell you, you are infamous rebels and traitors, and you think I, Captain Ulrich von Hohenberg, a soldier who took the oath of allegiance to his king, could act so dishonorably and meanly as to join the rebels ! No, never ! Never will the daughter of the rebel Anthony Wallner become my wife ! Kill me now if you want to do so. You may take my life, but you cannot dishonor me ! "

Eliza sat still motionless, and as if petrified. She had heard, as if in a dream, the captain's words ; and, as if in a dream, she saw that Schröpfel rushed forward and raised his powerful arm against him, and that all the men crowded up to him with menacing gestures ; as if in a dream, she heard wild shouts and imprecations.

All at once two ice-cold, trembling hands seized Eliza's arms, and a beloved voice penetrated her ear with the vehemence of mortal anguish and terror.

" Eliza ! " cried this voice—" Eliza, will you allow them to kill him ? "

" Elza ! " murmured Eliza, as if starting up from a trance, " Elza, what is the matter ? "

" They will assassinate him, Eliza ! " wailed Elza. " They have tied and gagged him, and say that they will take him out and shoot him. Eliza, you alone can save him ! Have mercy, forget what he said in his rage and grief. Have mercy upon him, upon me ! For I tell you, they will assassinate him. Oh, see, they are forming a circle round him, and dragging him down the aisle ! They are taking him out to the public place ! They intend to shoot him ! Save him, Eliza, save him ! "

Eliza made no reply ; she sprang up from her seat and hastened down the aisle after the men, who were just issuing from the church-door, and in whose midst was walking Captain Ulrich von Hohenberg, conducted by Anthony Wallner, and his servant, lame old Schröpfel, his hands tied on his back, and a gag in his mouth.

But the sharpshooters surrounded the prisoner like a thick, impenetrable wall. Vainly did Eliza beg and implore the men to let her pass ; vainly did she try with the strength of despair to elbow her way through the ranks. The men pushed her back impetuously.

"You shall not intercede in behalf of the infamous villain," they said ; "you shall not save the life of the mean Bavarian who calls us rebels and traitors, and yet did not keep his own word. He shall and must die, he has forfeited his life." And their strong arms pushed her from the circle which they now formed on the large place in front of the church. In its middle stood the captain, by his side Anthony Wallner, and behind him Schröpfel, like a watch-dog ready at any moment to tear his enemy.

Anthony lifted his arm with slow, solemn tranquillity, and dropped it heavily on the captain's shoulder.

"Ulrich von Hohenberg," he said, "you are an infamous villain, for you pledged your word to my daughter that you would marry her, and now you repudiate her. You are a liar and a slanderer, for you call us infamous rebels and traitors merely because we fought for our country and our emperor. Therefore, you have sinned against God, man, and honor. Ulrich von Hohenberg, you must die!"

"Yes, you must die!" shouted the men ; and they took the rifles from their shoulders and loaded them.

Anthony Wallner and Schröpfel stepped back from the prisoner, and the men who had stood behind him moved out of the way. Hence the circle, which had hitherto been impenetrable, now opened. Eliza saw it, and sprang forward, regardless of the sharpshooters, who were just raising their muskets, regardless of the danger menacing herself. Pale, with panting breath, her hands lifted to heaven, she sped across the open space toward the captain, and, placing herself before him, exclaimed, with flashing eyes, and in an exulting voice : "Now shoot, men, shoot! For I tell you he shall not die alone, and if you shoot him, you shall kill me too."

"Eliza!" cried her father, beseechingly, and withal angrily, "Eliza, stand back! He is a traitor, and must die."

"He is no traitor, nor must he die ; and if you assassinate him you shall assassinate me too," cried Eliza.

"But, Lizzie, did you not hear, then, how he repudiated and abused you, the faithless Bavarian?" asked her father.

"I did, and I forgive him," she said gently, "for I know full well that he does not mean what he says. Are you so stupid, men, as not to comprehend that he cannot act otherwise, and that he must speak thus and not otherwise? Father, you said I was a true daughter of the Tyrol, and that you loved me and were content with me. I pray you, then, dearest father, spare the life of my betrothed until to-morrow morning, and have him taken back as a prisoner to our house until then. Schröpfel may watch him, and not take his eyes from him. Oh, dear, kind friends, brave men, have mercy upon me! Bear in mind that we fought together for our beloved country, and that you told me you would never forget me, and would comply with my wishes whenever you could. I wish now that you spare the life of my betrothed only until to-morrow morning."

"He says he is not your betrothed, Lizzie, and will never marry you!" exclaimed the men, with irresolute faces, and already half softened by the beseeching, touching expression of Eliza's countenance.

"He says so," she said, casting a fiery glance on the captain, who stood pale and motionless, heard every word, and was unable to make a reply; "he says so, but I know that he loves me, and will be joyously ready to-morrow morning to do what I ask of him. Father," she added, in a low voice, seizing Anthony Wallner's arm, and drawing him aside quickly, "do you not comprehend, then, that Ulrich cannot speak differently? Would not his king, after his return to Bavaria, pronounce him a traitor, and charge him with having joined us and the Austrians, and with having convicted himself by marrying a Tyrolese girl? Be wise, dearest father, and see how shrewdly Ulrich manages every thing, and that he acts precisely as I told him. It must look as though he did not marry me of his own accord, but compelled by you; otherwise his king and his father, who is a very proud man, would never forgive him. But when they hear what has occurred here, and that you threatened to shoot Ulrich because he would not marry me, the gentlemen at Munich will understand that Ulrich had to take me in order to save his life."

"And are you satisfied to have it look as though he married you only under compulsion ?" asked her father, gloomily.

"I am, father," she said, "for I love my betrothed ; and he shall not become unhappy for my sake and forfeit the good graces of his king and his father. State all this to your friends, dear father, and tell them to let Ulrich and me alone for to-day; but ask them all to come to our house to-morrow morning and accompany the bride and bridegroom to the church, for Ulrich will marry me at nine to-morrow morning."

"But, Lizzie, why not to-day ?" asked her father. "Why not at this hour ?"

"It will not do, father. If you had told me beforehand what was to be done here, I should have told you at once what I am telling you now : it will not do for a young girl to appear before God's altar without due preparation, and as though she were going to a dance. What I am going to do is something very serious, and I will do it seriously. I will pray to God to-day, go to confession, and have a great many things to talk over with Ulrich, for I know he wants me to set out with him immediately after we have been married, and that it may not look as though he had stayed voluntarily with you in our valley. I must, therefore, pack up my things and prepare for departing as soon as we have been married. Let us alone, then, dear father, to-day, and invite the men to come to-morrow morning and attend my marriage with Captain Ulrich von Hohenberg."

"Well, then, Lizzie, I will comply with your wishes," said Wallner, after a short reflection. "I will give you and him time until to-morrow morning ; but I tell you, my daughter, if he continues the same game to-morrow, and talks then in the same strain as to-day, I shall take the jest in dead earnest, and will not believe a word of all you say to excuse him: and then his life is forfeited, and he must die.—No, Schröpfel, come here ; take the prisoner back to my house, and confine him where you have kept him for a week past. But I tell

you, watch him well, and admit no one to him except Lizzie,
and prevent him from talking with anybody but his betrothed."

"I will do so, and watch him as I have done up to this
time," said Schröpfel, gloomily. "He shall not talk with
anybody, and I should like it best if he were not permitted
either to speak with Lizzie, for I do not believe at all that she
is his betrothed."

"We shall see to-morrow morning, when the marriage is
to take place," said Anthony Wallner.—"Take the prisoner
away."

"You let him go?" exclaimed the men. "You spare his
life?"

"Only until to-morrow morning, because Lizzie begged
me to do so," said Anthony Wallner. "The wedding will
take place at nine to-morrow morning; I invite you all to
attend it, men, and we shall see then. To-morrow morning
there will be a wedding or an execution. Now let us speak
no more of it to-day; let us forget what has happened to
Anthony Wallner and his daughter; and let us bear in mind
only that we have returned after delivering our dear Tyrol
from the French and Bavarians. Let us go now to my house,
where my wife awaits us with a keg of excellent wine. Come,
we will drink to the welfare of our fatherland, and to the
health of our dear Emperor Francis!"

CHAPTER XXII.

ELIZA AND ULRICH.

Schröpfel, the faithful servant, had taken Ulrich von
Hohenberg, in obedience to Anthony Wallner's order, back
to the small room where he had passed the last eight days as
a prisoner. Since he had him again in his custody, no additional precautions were necessary, for Schröpfel knew that
he could rely on his own vigilance, and that the prisoner
surely would never escape from him. Hence, he loosened

the cords with which he had been tied, and removed the handkerchief with which he had been gagged.

"If it affords you pleasure," said Schröpfel, "you may use your mouth and inveigh against Lizzie Wallner, who has saved your life to-day a second time, and whom you rewarded, like a genuine Bavarian, that is to say, with black ingratitude and treachery. But I advise you not to abuse her loud enough for me to hear you outside, for I am not as patient as Lizzie, and I shall never permit you to abuse and treat so contemptuously the noblest and best girl in the whole country. She acted toward you to-day as a good Christian and a brave girl, for you insulted her, and she not only forgave you, but protected you, and saved your life. And now, sir, abuse her if you cannot help it ; but I tell you once more, do not speak too loud, lest I should hear you."

And Schröpfel turned with a last threatening glance and left the room. Outside he sat down on the cane-settee which, for the past eight days, had been his seat by day and his couch by night ; and he pressed his eye to the middle hole which he had bored in the door. He could distinctly see and watch the captain through it. Ulrich had sunk down on a chair and leaned his head on his hand ; he lifted his sombre eyes to heaven, and there was a strange expression of emotion and grief upon his face. But he seemed not to intend availing himself of the permission which Schröpfel had given him to abuse Lizzie Wallner, for his lips were firmly compressed, and not a sound fell from them. Or could Schröpfel, perhaps, not hear him, because the men down in the bar-room were laughing and shouting so merrily, and speaking so loudly and enthusiastically of the Tyrol, and drinking the health of the emperor and the Archduke John, who had again taken possession of their country and solemnly proclaimed that he would restore the ancient and liberal constitution of the Tyrolese ?

"How merry they are down-stairs !" growled Schröpfel. "I might be there too ; I have amply deserved to have a little exercise and pleasure. Instead of that I must sit here with a dry mouth ; and if this goes on much longer, I shall surely grow fast to my settee. And all that for the sake of the mean, perfidious Bavarian, who is so utterly dishonest, and

who treated our beautiful, noble Lizzie in so infamous a manner ! Well, if I were in the girl's place, I would not take the
perfidious wretch who has denied her twice already. Oh,
how merry they are down-stairs ! No one thinks of me and
gives me a drop of wine that I may likewise drink to the welfare of the fatherland."

But Schröpfel was mistaken for once, for quick footsteps
ascended the staircase at this moment, and now appeared the
lovely head of Eliza Wallner above the railing, then her whole
form, and a second afterward she stood in the passage close
before Schröpfel. In her hands she held a plate with a large
piece of the fine cake which her mother herself had baked, and
a large glass of excellent red wine.

"There, good, faithful Schröpfel," she said in her gentle
voice, nodding to him pleasantly, and handing the plate to
him, "eat and drink, and let me in the mean time go and see
your prisoner."

"What do you want of him ?" asked Schröpfel, moodily.

"I want to see him about our wedding to-morrow," said
Eliza calmly ; "and you know father has given me permission
to go to him and speak with him."

"Yes, he did, and I cannot prevent you from entering
which I would do otherwise," growled Schröpfel. "Go in,
then, but do not stay too long ; and if he should abuse you
again, pray call me, and I will assist you."

"Thank you, dear Schröpfel," said Eliza, "but pray admit
me now."

Schröpfel withdrew his settee from the door and allowed
Eliza to open it, and, entering to the prisoner, closed it again
behind her.

Ulrich von Hohenberg still sat, as Schröpfel had seen
him, at the table, leaning his head on his hand ; only he
had now covered his eyes with his hands, and long sighs
issued from his breast. He seemed not to know that the
door had opened and some one had entered, or rather perhaps
he thought it was only Schröpfel, and he did not wish to take
any notice of him.

Eliza Wallner stood leaning against the wall, and gazed at
him a long time with a wondrous expression of love and grief ;

for a moment she laid her hand on her bosom, as if to stifle the cry which her lips were already about to utter ; then she cast a beseeching glance toward heaven, and, as if strengthened by this mute invocation, she stepped forward.

"Captain Ulrich von Hohenberg !" she said, in her sweet, melodious voice.

He gave a start, dropped his hand from his face, and jumped up.

"Eliza Wallner !" he said, breathlessly and in great confusion.

She only nodded her head, and fixed her clear, piercing eyes with a proud, reproachful expression on his face ; he dropped his eyes before her gaze. On seeing this, Eliza smiled, and, crossing the room with a rapid step, went to the window.

"Come here, sir, and look at that. What do you see yonder ?"

Ulrich stepped to her and looked out. "I see the mountains and the summits of the glaciers," he said ; "and in the direction in which you are pointing your finger, I see also my uncle's castle."

"Do you see also the balcony, Ulrich von Hohenberg ?" she asked, somewhat sarcastically.

"I do," he replied, almost timidly.

She looked at him with the proud and lofty air of a queen.

"When we met last and spoke with each other, we stood on yonder balcony," added Eliza. "Do you remember what we said at the time, sir ?"

"Eliza," he murmured—

"You remember it no longer," she interrupted him, "but I do. On yonder balcony you swore to me that you loved me boundlessly ; and when I laughed at you, you invoked heaven and earth to bear witness of your love. Now, sir, heaven and earth gave you an opportunity to prove your ardent love for Eliza Wallner. Did you profit by that opportunity ?"

"No," he said, in a low voice ; "it is true, I acted harshly and cruelly toward you, I occasioned you bitter grief, I—"

"I do not complain," she exclaimed, proudly. "I do not

speak of myself, but only of you. You swore eternal love to me at that time, but you did so as a mendacious Bavarian; I did not believe you, and knew full well that you had no honest intentions toward me. For this reason I laughed at you, and said the peasant-girl was no suitable match for you, and rejected all your oaths and protestations of passionate love."

"But afterwards, to punish me for venturing to speak of love to you," he exclaimed, impetuously, "you feigned to have believed my protestations and oaths; and although you had previously laughed at me, you wished now to become my wife."

"No," she said, with a fiery glance of disdain; "no, afterwards I only wished to save your life. You have utterly mistaken Eliza Wallner's character, Ulrich von Hohenberg. You thought Lizzie Wallner would deem herself exceedingly fortunate to become the wife of an aristocratic gentleman, even though he took her only by compulsion: you thought she would be content to leave the Tyrol by the side of the nobleman who disdained her, and go to the large foreign city of Munich, where the aristocracy would scorn and mock the poor Tyrolese girl. No, sir, I tell you, you have utterly mistaken my character. I attach no value whatever to your aristocratic name, nor to the distinguished position of your family; when I marry, I shall choose a husband who loves me with all his heart, and who does not wish to live without me, and takes me of his own accord, and with the full enthusiasm of a noble heart. But he would have to remain in the mountains and be a son of the Tyrol; for my heart is attached to the mountains, and never would I or could I leave them to remove to a large city. You see, therefore, Ulrich, that a marriage with you would by no means appear to me a very fortunate thing; and, moreover, if you had allowed yourself to be compelled to marry me, had you not refused to do so, I should have despised you all my life long as a miserable coward. I thank you, therefore, for resisting the men so bravely, for I should have been sorry to be obliged to despise you; you are my dear Elza's cousin, and I myself have always liked you so well."

"Eliza," he exclaimed, impetuously, "you are an angel of goodness and lenity, and I stand before you filled with shame and grief. You say you always liked me so well, and I treated you with so much ingratitude and disdain ! Oh, let me press this dear hand to my lips, let me thank you for all that you have done for me !"

He tried to seize her hand, but she withdrew it from him quickly.

"Captain von Hohenberg," she said, "we are no longer on the balcony yonder ; nor is it necessary that you should kiss my hand. That may be suitable when you have fair ladies from the city before you, but not when you are speaking with a Tyrolese girl. Besides, I did not tell you all this to obtain praise and admiration from you, but to prevent you from taking me for a mean-spirited girl, respecting herself so little as to try to get a husband in so dishonorable a manner. No, by the Holy Virgin, I would rather die and be buried under an avalanche than act so meanly and disgracefully. But when the peasants were going to kill you, there was no other way for me to save your life than that of saying that you were my betrothed, and that was the only reason why I said so. However, I had no idea that the wedding was to take place to-day, for my dear father had concealed it from me, and wished to surprise me, because he really believed that I loved you. If I had known beforehand what father had in view, I should have devised some way of preventing him from carrying his plan into effect. But I swear to you, I had no inkling of it. Therefore, I beg your pardon, sir, for the harsh treatment you received at their hands for my sake."

"Eliza," he said, mournfully, "your words rend my heart. Oh, do not be so gentle and generous ! Be angry with me, call me an infamous villain, who, in his blindness, did not penetrate your magnanimity and heroic self-sacrifice ; do not treat me with this charming mildness which crushes me ! You acted like an angel toward me, and I treated you like a heartless barbarian."

"I forgive you with all my heart, and therefore you may forgive yourself," she said, with a gentle smile. "But let us speak no longer of the past ; let us think only of the future.

You heard what father said : ' To-morrow morning there will
be a wedding or an execution.' "

" Well, then, there will be a wedding to-morrow morning,"
exclaimed Ulrich, casting an ardent glance on the young
girl ; " yes, there will be a wedding to-morrow morning.
Pray, Eliza, save my life a third time to-morrow ; become my
wife ! "

" I will save your life," she said, throwing back her head,
proudly ; " but fortunately it is unnecessary for me tó become
your wife for that purpose. I have come here only to save
you. Sir, you must escape to-night."

" Escape," he said, shrugging his shoulders ; " escape, when
Schröpfel is guarding my door ? "

" Hush ! do not speak so loud, sir ; he might hear you, and
he must know nothing about it. Bend your head closer to
me and listen : Go to bed early this evening, but extinguish
your light beforehand, lest Schröpfel should see any thing.
My mother told me Schröpfel had bored holes in the door,
and was watching you all the time. Therefore, go to bed
early, and leave your window open. When the church-clock
strikes two, listen for any noise, and hold yourself in readiness. That is all I have to say to you, and now good-by."

She nodded to him, and turned to the door.

" But I, Eliza—I have to tell you many things yet," said
Ulrich, detaining her. " Pray, stay yet awhile and listen to
me ! "

" No, sir, it is time for me to go ; my mother is waiting for
me," replied Eliza, withdrawing her hand from his. " Good-
by, and if you can pray, pray to God to protect you to-
night ! "

She opened the door hastily and stepped out, and smiled
at Schröpfel, but the old servant looked at her gloomily.

" You stayed a long while with the Bavarian," he growled.

" And yet you did not eat your cake nor empty your glass
in the mean time," said Eliza, with a smile. " You looked
again through the hole in the door, did you not ? You saw,
then, Schröpfel, that we stood together like a pair of sensible
lovers."

" I did not see any thing," exclaimed Schröpfel, angrily,

"for you placed yourself close to the window, and my hole
does not enable me to look around the corner ; nor did I hear
any thing, for you whispered as softly as though you were a
couple of sparrows which understand each other when billing
and cooing."

"Fie, Schröpfel ! do not talk such nonsense," cried Eliza,
blushing deeply. "Behave yourself, Schröpfel, and I will
bring you another bottle of wine to-day, and beg father to let
you come down to supper to-night, and permit you to sleep in
your bedchamber."

"I shall take good care to do no such thing," growled
Schröpfel. "I am a sentinel here, and must not desert my
post."

"But you may take your sentry-box with you," said Eliza,
pointing to his settee. "When a soldier remains close to his
sentry-box, he does not desert his post. Well, good-by,
Schröpfel ; the sentinel will be relieved to-night."

Eliza's words were fulfilled. Toward nightfall she informed Schröpfel that her father permitted him to take his
supper at the table down-stairs, and afterward go to bed in
his own chamber.

"Well, and who is to watch the prisoner in the mean
time ?" asked Schröpfel.

"You yourself ! Look, you will lock the door and put the
key in your pocket. In addition, you may put that heavy box
yonder against the door ; then you will be sure that your prisoner cannot get out, for I think his chamber has no other outlet."

"Yes, it has—the window !"

"Do you think the Bavarian has wings and will fly out of
the window to-night ?"

"It is true he cannot fly out, nor can he jump out, for he
would simply break his neck. But, nevertheless, I do not like
this arrangement at all. Something tells me that it will turn
out wrong. I shall, at least, unchain the watch-dog, who will
prevent the Bavarian from escaping through the window.
For the rest, I feel that all my limbs are stiff, and that I have
at length deserved some repose. As it is your father's will, I
will go down-stairs, take supper, and afterward go to bed in

my chamber. If any thing happens, I shall wash my hands of it."

"Wash them as much as you please, Schröpfel, but come down to supper," cried Eliza, hastening down-stairs with the agility of a bird.

Schröpfel looked after her, shaking his head; he then locked the door, put the key in his pocket, and placed the heavy iron-bound box against the door.

"And before going to bed I shall unchain Phylax," he said, as if to console himself, while he was going slowly and stiffly down-stairs.

Schröpfel kept his word. Weary and exhausted as he was, he waited until all the inmates of the house had gone to bed, and until all noise had died away. He then went into the yard and unchained the formidable and ill-humored watch-dog. Phylax howled and trembled with joy and delight at being released; but Schröpfel seized his ear and pointed his other hand at the prisoner's window, which was brightly illuminated by the moon.

"Watch that window well, Phylax," he said, "watch it well; and if you see anything suspicious, call me at once. I shall not sleep so fast as not to hear your barking. Watch it well, Phylax."

The dog looked up to the window as if he had understood the order; he then fixed his clear, lustrous eyes on Schröpfel, and uttered a threatening growl.

"Very well," said Schröpfel, "you have understood me. You will watch him, and I may go to bed."

He dropped the ear of the dog, who thereupon bounded wildly through the yard, while Schröpfel limped back into the house. He was heard slowly ascending the staircase and opening the creaking door of his bed-chamber, and then all became silent.

Night spread its pall over the weary, the sleepers, and the weeping; the moon stood with silvery lustre high in the heavens, and illuminated the snow-clad summits of the mountains rising in the rear of the outbuildings in Wallner's yard. Hour after hour passed by, and all remained silent; not a sound broke the holy stillness of night.

Hour after hour passed by; nothing stirred in the yard; the dog sat, as if he had really understood Schröpfel's words, in the middle of the yard, and stared steadfastly at the prisoner's window. Phylax watched, as Schröpfel had gone to bed; Phylax watched, and did not avert his eyes from the window on which his whole attention seemed to be concentrated, for he did not stir, he did not even disturb the flies buzzing round his ears; he was all attention and vigilance. All at once something occurred that had never happened to him during his nocturnal service; a wondrous, appetizing scent was wafted to him on the wings of the night-breeze. Phylax averted his eyes for a moment from the window and glanced searchingly round the yard. Nothing stirred in it, but this wonderful scent of a roast sausage still impregnated the air, and seemed to grow even stronger and more tempting; for Phylax pricked up his ears, raised his nose, snuffing eagerly to inhale the scent, and rose from the ground. He glanced again round the yard, and then advanced a few steps toward the window yonder on the side of the house. This window was open, and the keen nose of the dog told him that the appetizing scent had come from it. All at once, however, Phylax stood still, as if remembering his master's orders, and looked again toward the prisoner's window.

At this moment a low voice called him: "Phylax! come here, Phylax!"

The dog hesitated no longer; he had recognized the voice of his friend and playmate, Eliza Wallner. With two tremendous bounds he was at the window, and, raising himself up, laid his forepaws on the window-sill, and stretched out his head, waiting longingly for the appetizing sausage.

"Come, Phylax, come," whispered Eliza; and she stepped back with the sausage into the interior of the room. "Come to me, Phylax, come to me."

The temptation was too strong. Phylax hesitated no longer; he moved back a step, and leaped through the window into the room.

The window was closed behind him immediately, and the four-footed custodian of the prisoner was now a prisoner himself.

The yard was empty now. Schröpfel slept soundly in his bed-chamber up-stairs, and Phylax was revelling in epicurean joys in the larder.

The yard was empty now, but not long, for the door of the house opened noiselessly, and a human form stepped out. For a moment it stood still near the door, and two voices were heard whispering in a low tone.

"Good-by, dearest mother," said one voice. "It is time now, I must go."

"God and the Holy Virgin will protect you, dear Lizzie," said the other voice : "for that which you are going to do is right and noble ; and father himself will see before long that you did right. Go, Lizzie, and return safely."

"I shall be back at eight in the morning," whispered Lizzie. "Until then, you must say nothing about it, dear mother, but tell father I wished to be alone in my chamber till the wedding-hour. Good-by until then."

She imprinted a kiss on her mother's lips, and hastened into the yard. The door was closed softly. At this moment the church-clock struck two.

Eliza glided noiselessly across the yard toward the large ladder leaning against the stable. She lifted it up with vigorous hands, carried it across the yard, and placed it against the dwelling-house, so that its top reached the open window of the prisoner. She examined if the ladder stood firm, laid a few stones at its foot, to prevent it from sliding, and then ascended it with cat-like agility, carrying a small bundle on her arm, while she had put down another in the yard.

Now she had reached the captain's window.

"Are you awake, sir ?" she asked, in a low voice.

"I am, Eliza," whispered a voice inside. "I have been awake and waiting for you an hour."

"Take this, sir," she said, handing the bundle into the window. "It is a suit of clothes which you must put on. It is my father's holiday dress, for you must not wear the Bavarian uniform now. You must put up for a few days with being disguised as a Tyrolese. Put it on quickly, and then wrap up your uniform in the blanket in which I brought the suit of clothes. But make haste, and when you are ready,

descend the ladder, and come down into the yard, where I
shall await you. Bring the package with the uniform with
you, and, above all things, make haste."

She gave the captain no time for reply, but glided rapidly
and noiselessly down the ladder. On arriving in the yard,
she took the haversack which she had left there, hung it over
her shoulder, and took up the rifle. Then she seated herself
quietly on a large log close to the ladder, and looked up to
the moon, which illuminated her face and her whole form.
Her face wore a wonderfully calm expression ; only round
her crimson lips quivered at times something like hidden
grief, and a tear glistened in her large, dark eyes. But when
this tear rolled down her cheek slowly, Eliza shook her head
indignantly, and brushed it away with her hand.

"Foolish girl ! " she murmured, "how can you weep now ?
You must bravely take your heart in your hands now, and
hold it so firmly that it can neither cry nor tremble. You
must be proud and stiff, and never forget what is due to your
honor, and what you owe to your friend Elza. Therefore, do
not weep, but be a brave Tyrolese girl. To-morrow night you
may weep in your chamber, for nobody will see you there ;
but not to-night—no, no, not to-night ! "

She shook her head violently, forced herself to smile, and
gazed pleasantly up to the moon. "God bless thee, golden,
rapid wanderer ! " she said. "Thou shalt accompany us to-
night, and pray, dear moon, send all clouds home, and remain
as bright and clear as now ; for our route is a dangerous one,
and if thou dost not help us, we may easily fall into an abyss,
and— Hush, hush, he is coming."

She rose and looked up to the window, whence the captain
emerged at this moment, and appeared on the ladder.

"Throw down your package, sir—I will catch it," whispered Eliza.

"Thank you, I can carry it myself," said Ulrich, in a low
voice ; and he was soon at the foot of the ladder, and standing
in the yard close to Eliza.

"Now come," she said ; "tread lightly, and do not speak,
but go softly behind me."

She left him no time for reply, but walked across, opened

the door of the small shed, which was ajar, went quickly through it, and passed through the opposite door into the orchard lying behind it. She stood still in front of the door of the shed, and when Ulrich had emerged from it, she locked it, and put the key into her pocket.

"Now let us walk as fast as possible, sir," she whispered. "We must walk for three hours. Keep your eyes on me, and follow me wherever I go."

"I will follow you, Eliza," said the captain, earnestly, "wherever you go. You see I have implicit confidence in you, for I do not even ask whither you intend to conduct me, or what you wish to do with me. I place my life and my future in your hands, and shall do whatever you want me to."

"It will be the best for you," she said, nodding her head slightly. "Now come."

And with the quick, firm step peculiar to the Tyrolese, she advanced through the garden, out of the gate, and into the narrow path leading through the valley and up to the mountains rising on the opposite side. The moon still shone brightly upon the valley, and illuminated the two forms rapidly walking behind each other, casting their long, dark shadows on the side of the road.

Ulrich von Hohenberg saw in the moonlight that Eliza was carrying the haversack and rifle; he therefore advanced quickly until he stood by her side, and laid his hand on her arm.

"Eliza," he said, vehemently, "pray let me carry the rifle and the haversack; let me take your burden upon myself."

She looked at him with a singular expression. "Every one has to carry his own burden," she said; "you have yours, and I have mine."

"But what are the arms for, Eliza? You have armed yourself against me?"

She shrugged her shoulders carelessly. "Were I afraid of you, I would not allow you to walk behind me. But grant me one request, will you?"

"Speak, Eliza, and whatever it may be, I will comply with it."

"Well, then, sir, be so kind as not to speak with me.

Speaking exhausts us and makes us absent-minded. We have a long march before us, and must save our breath, and devote our whole attention to the route ; for it will lead us over the narrow paths of the chamois-hunters, and a single false step may hurl us into an abyss. Therefore, sir, pray do not address me until I speak to you."

"I will obey," said Ulrich, humbly. "Lead the way; I will follow."

She nodded to him, and advanced through the narrow valley. The road soon became steeper, and led them past precipices, from one rock to another, all of which were spanned by narrow planks, under which unfathomable chasms yawned. Then it led through thickets of shrubbery and pine-forests, or down precipitous slopes, and over small fragments of rock, which gave way at every step, and rolled into the depth. Eliza suddenly stood still and broke the silence for the first time.

"You must not go behind me here, sir," she said, "for the loose stones would not permit you to advance. Come to me, and give me your hand. We must walk side by side."

He was immediately by her side, and took her hand. "May I speak now, Eliza ?" he asked.

"No," she said, imperatively, "we have no time for chatting. Forward!"

And they continued ascending the mountain. The valley, and even the mountain-forest, lay already deep under them. Only scattered and stunted trees stood here and there, and finally even these disappeared entirely. The moon commenced paling in the heavens, and yet it did not become darker, for the gray twilight was lit up at times with a purp'e lustre ; the small, scudding clouds began to turn red ; the pale, foggy mountain-peaks colored, and a strange whispering passed through the air.

Now they had reached the summit, and the peak on which they were standing afforded them a strikingly beautiful view.

"This is the place where we may rest," said Eliza, drawing a deep breath.

"And may I speak now, Eliza ?" asked Ulrich.

"No," she said ; "do you not see that God is speaking now ? "

And she pointed to the part of the horizon which, radiant in its crimson lustre, lay at the end of the lovely valley opening before them. Gazing at it, Eliza sank noiselessly down on the fragment of a rock, and clasping her hands on her knees, she contemplated the glorious spectacle by which God speaks to man every morning.

The valley was still wrapped in the gloom of twilight, but behind the flat and gently-rounded mountains yonder rose the flaming glow of radiant crimson, and sent a few purple clouds as heralds of the approaching majesty into the azure sky. A rosy hue covered the glaciers of the Venediger and Gross-Glockner, which looked down in proud majesty on the mountains bordering the valley, and which had hitherto wrapped their summits in veils of glistening silver. On beholding the divine majesty of the sun, they dropped their veils, their summits crimsoned and loomed up to the sky in dazzling splendor. The rays gilding them shed a lustre on the lower wooded mountains, greeted the spires of the churches rising amidst the villages, dissipated the mist which had hitherto filled the valley, and converted the waters of the foaming Isel, meandering through the valley, into liquid gold. The gloom entirely disappeared, and the whole landscape was radiant in its morning beauty. God had willed that there should be light, and the earth lay smiling and surpassingly beautiful under the first glowing rays of the sun.

Eliza gazed with a rapt smile upon the sublime scene ; the clouds had disappeared from her brow also, and the gloom had vanished from her eyes.

"Oh, how beautiful is the world ! how beautiful is my dear Tyrol ! " she exclaimed, fervently. "I greet you, beloved mountains guarding our frontiers ! I greet you, Gross-Glockner and Venediger ! Yes, gaze upon the Tyrol, for now you may rejoice over it ! The enemy is no longer in the country, and I am bringing you the last Bavarian who is still here, that you may send him across the border. Sir," she added, turning her face, illuminated by the sun, slowly to the young man, who had not contemplated the sun, but only her face,

" we must part here. I only intended to conduct you hither, to the Kalser Thörl. You will now descend to the village of Kals, which you see in the valley yonder. Look, back there, its red roofs are rising out of the green shrubbery. You will go to the inn there, and give this letter to Lebrecht Panzl, the innkeeper. He is my mother's brother, and she writes him in this letter to give you a reliable guide, who is to conduct you over the Pruschler Thörl and the Katzenstein to Heiligenblut. You will reach Heiligenblut in seven hours. Its inhabitants speak Bavarian German ; your Bavarian dialect will not be suspicious to them, and you will easily find there a guide to conduct you wherever you wish to go. You will find some food for to-day in the haversack here, and also some money, and powder and lead. Take it, sir ; here is the rifle, and here the haversack. Unless you have them with you, no one will take you for a genuine Tyrolese. There. Put your clothes into the sack, you can carry them better that way ; hang the rifle round your shoulder, and then adieu ! "

"And you think, Eliza, I can accept all this kindness and magnanimity ? " cried Ulrich, vehemently; " you think I can accept at your hands food, money—nay, more, my life, my honor, and leave you with a cold 'thank you,' after denying and insulting you in the despair of my wounded military honor ? No, Eliza, you have mistaken my character. I will not go, I will not leave you. I followed you here to see how far your magnanimity and noble self-abnegation would go ; but now I shall return with you to Windisch-Matrey. Your father invited to the wedding the men who wished to kill me yesterday; they will await us at the church at nine this morning, and they shall not wait in vain. Come, Eliza, let us return to Windisch-Matrey; for all your kindness and magnanimity I shall give you the only thing I have to give, my name. You will, you shall become my wife ! Come, your father and your friends await us at the church ; I will conduct you thither and to the altar."

" I will not do it," she exclaimed proudly; " for, as sure as there is a God in heaven, I should say ' no ' before the altar, and reject your hand."

"Well, then, do that," he said, gently ; "I have deserved this humiliation ; I owe you an opportunity to wreak your vengeance on me."

"I do not want to avenge myself. I have sworn to myself and to my dear Elza to save you, and I will. Go, sir ; time is fleeting, and you have a march of seven hours before you."

"No, I will not go," cried Ulrich, vehemently; "I cannot go, for I love you, Eliza. Oh, I have loved you a long while, but my haughty heart revolted at this love, and would not yield to it ; and yet I was deeply, passionately enamoured of you. But my heart did not know itself, it believed at last that it might hate you, when all at once your generosity, lenity, and magnanimity dissipated all mists concealing my heart from my eyes, and I perceived how passionately I loved you. Oh, Eliza, beloved girl, do not turn from me ! Give me your hand ; let us go home ; accept my hand, become my wife ! Love beseeches of you now what pride refused to you before : accept my hand, my name ! Let us descend into the valley, go to the church, and be married."

She shook her head slowly. "I have already told you," she said, "that I should say ' no ' before the altar. We do not belong together. You are a nobleman, and I, as you have often called me in your anger, am a peasant girl ; you are a Bavarian, and I, thank God, am again an Austrian. We do not belong together, and I believe it would not behoove you to appear with me now before the altar and marry me. For every one would think you took me only to save your life, and your honor would be lost, not only in Bavaria, but also here among us. The brave men would despise you, and contempt—I felt it when you looked at me so disdainfully yesterday—is worse than death. Go, therefore, my dear sir ; your honor requires it."

"Well, then, you are right ; I will go. I see that I must not apply for your hand at this juncture. But I shall return so soon as peace is restored to the country, and when all these troubles are over. Promise me, Eliza, that you will wait for me and not forget me. For I swear to you, I shall return and marry you, in spite of the whole world."

" You will not," she said, shaking her head, " for I shall not take you. I do not love you."

" Eliza," he cried, seizing her hand impetuously, and gazing deep into her eyes, " you are just as much mistaken as I was myself. I loved you a long time without knowing it, and thus, sweet one, you love me too ! "

" No," she exclaimed, vehemently, and turning very pale, " no, I do not love you ! "

" Yes, you do," he said, tenderly. " I felt it, and knew it by the tone in which, stepping before me, and shielding me with your body, you exclaimed yesterday, ' If you shoot him, you shall kill me too.' Pity and compassion do not speak thus ; only love has such tones of anguish, despair, and hero-ism. I felt it at that moment, and the blissful delight which filled my heart on recognizing it, made me at length conscious of my own love. I confessed to myself that I never should be able to love any other woman on earth, and never would marry any other woman than you. Oh, Eliza, let us no longer resist the happiness that is in store for us. Let the whole past be buried behind us. Let the future be ours, and with it love and happiness ! "

She shook her head slowly. " You have read badly in my heart," she said ; " you do not understand the letters written in it, and what you spell from it is false. I do not love you, and would never consent to become your wife. Let us drop the subject. We two can never be husband and wife, but we may remember each other as good friends. And so, sir, I will always remember you, and shall be glad to hear that you are well and happy. But let us say no more about it, and go. You have a march of seven hours before you ; I must be at home again by eight o'clock, in order not to keep the men waiting. Let us part, therefore."

" Well, then," sighed Ulrich, " it is your will, and we must part, but not forever. I swear, by God Almighty and my love, I shall return when the war is over, and when the quar-rels of the nations are settled. I shall return to ask you if you will be mine, my beloved wife, and if you will at last crown my love with happiness. Hush, do not contradict me, and do not tell me again that you do not love me. I hope in the future, and we shall see whether it will bring me happiness or doom me to despair. Farewell, then, Eliza ; and if you will yet give to the poor wanderer, to whom you have given life, food, money, and clothes, a priceless treasure, a talisman that will shield him from all temptations of the world, then give me a kiss ! "

" No, sir ; an honest Tyrolese girl never kisses any man but the one whose wife she is to be. You see, therefore, that I cannot give you a kiss. Go, sir. But have you no commissions to give me for your uncle and my dear Elza ? "

" Greet them both ; tell them that I love you, Eliza, and that you rejected my proposals."

" That does not concern anybody, and only we two and the good God shall know it, but no one else. But, sir, give me a souvenir for Elza ; it will gladden her heart."

" I have nothing to give her," he said, shrugging his shoulders.

She pointed to the crimson Alpine roses blooming at their feet amidst the grass and moss.

" Gather some of these flowers, and give them to me," she said ; " I will take them to Elza, and tell her that you gathered the flowers for her."

He knelt down, gathered a handful of Alpine roses, and tied them together with a few blades of grass. " I would," he said, still kneeling in the grass, " they were myrtles that I was gathering for you, Eliza, for you, my affianced bride, and that you would accept them at my hands as the sacred gift of love. There, take the bouquet for Elza, and give it to her with my greetings."

She stretched out her hand to take it ; but Ulrich, instead of giving it to her, pressed the bouquet to his lips, and imprinted an ardent kiss on the flowers ; then only did he hand it to Eliza.—" Now, Eliza," he said, " take it. You refused me a kiss, but you will carry my glowing kiss home with you, and with it also my heart. I shall come back one day to demand of you your heart and my kiss. Farewell ! It is your will, and so I must go. I do not say, forget me not ; but I shall return, and ask you then : ' Have you forgotten me ? Will you become my wife ? ' Until then, farewell ! "

He gazed at her with a long look of love and tenderness; she avoided meeting his look, and when he saw this, a smile, radiant as sunshine and bliss, illuminated his features.

"Go, sir," she said, in a low voice, averting her face.

"I am going, Eliza," he exclaimed. "Farewell!"

He seized her hand impetuously, imprinted on it a burning kiss before she was able to prevent him, dropped it, and turned to descend the slope with a slow step.

Eliza stood motionless, and as if fascinated; she gazed after him, and followed with an absorbed look his tall, noble form, descending the mountain, surrounded by a halo of sunshine.

All at once Ulrich stood still and turned to her. "Eliza," he shouted, "did you call me? Shall I return to you?"

She shook her head and made a violent gesture indicating that he should not return, but said nothing; the words choked in her breast.

He waved his hand to her, turned again, and continued descending the slope.

Eliza looked after him; her face turned paler and paler, and her lips quivered more painfully. Once they opened as if to call him back with a cry of anguish and love; but Eliza, pressing her hand violently upon her mouth, forced the cry back into her heart, and gazed down on Ulrich's receding form.

Already he had descended half the slope; now he reached the edge of the forest, and alas! disappeared in the thicket.

Eliza, uttering a loud cry, knelt down, and tears, her long-restrained, scalding tears, streamed like rivers down her cheeks. She lifted her arms, her clasped hands, to heaven, and murmured with quivering lips: "Protect him, my God, for Thou knowest how intensely I love him!"

She remained a long time on her knees, weeping, praying, struggling with her grief and her love. But then all at once she sprang to her feet, brushed the tears from her eyes, and drew a deep breath.

"I must and will no longer weep," she said to herself in a loud, imperative voice. "Otherwise they would see that I had been weeping, and no one must know that. I must descend in order to be at home in time, and then I will tell father and the other men that Ulrich never was my betrothed, and that I said so only to save his life. They will forgive me for helping him to escape when I tell them that I never loved him nor would have taken him, because he is a Bavarian, but that I saved him because he is a near relative of my dear Elza. And after telling and explaining all this to the men, I shall go to Elza, give her the flowers, and tell her that Ulrich sent them to her, and that his last word was a love-greeting for her. God, forgive me this falsehood! But Elza loves him, and it will gladden her heart. She will preserve this bouquet to her wedding-day, and she will not notice that I kept one flower from it for myself. It is the flower which he kissed; it shall be mine. I suppose, good God, that I may take it, and that it is no theft for me to do so?"

She looked up to heaven with a beseeching glance; then she softly drew one of the flowers from the bouquet, pressed it to her lips, and concealed it in her bosom.

"I will preserve this flower while I live," she exclaimed. "God strengthened my heart so that I was able to reject him; but I shall love him forever, and this flower is my wedding-bouquet. I shall never wear another!"

She extended her arms in the direction where Ulrich had disappeared. "Farewell!" she cried. "I greet you a thousand times, and my heart goes with you!"

Then she turned and hastily descended the path which she had ascended with Ulrich von Hohenberg.

CHAPTER XXIII.

THE TRIUMPH OF DEATH.

IT was a wondrously beautiful morning in May; the sun shone clear and bright; the birds sang in all the shrubs and trees, and the gay spring flowers exhaled their fragrant odors in all the gardens. Nature had donned its holiday attire, and yet humanity was in mourning; the sun shone clear and bright, and yet the eyes of men were sombre and lustreless, and instead of rejoicing over the fresh verdure and the blossoms of spring, they grieved, and their hearts were frozen with care and pain.

For the Emperor Napoleon had raised his proud hand again against Germany ; he had defeated the Austrians at Ratisbon and Landshut, and made his triumphant entrance into Vienna on the 12th of May, 1809.

For the second time the imperial family, fleeing from the victorious Napoleon, had been compelled to leave the capital ; for the second time the foreign emperor occupied the palace of Schönbrunn, and Vienna had to bow again to the will of the all-powerful conqueror. The Emperor Francis had escaped with his wife and children to Hungary, and Vienna, whose inhabitants had at first sworn enthusiastically to defend their city to the last man, and lay it in ashes rather than surrender it to the French, had nevertheless opened its gates already on the 12th of May to the Emperor Napoleon and his army. It had to bow to stern necessity, for during the previous night the Archduke Maximilian, with the weak forces with which he had been ordered to defend Vienna, had evacuated the city, had burned the great bridge of Thabor to prevent Napoleon from pursuing him, and had succeeded in escaping, leaving it to the Viennese to make terms with the conqueror and invoke his clemency and generosity. They had thus been obliged to conceal their rage and exasperation in their hearts, and surrender to the tender mercies of the French emperor ; they had opened their gates to the enemy, but not their hearts. Their hearts were filled with boundless rage and shame, which brought wild imprecations to the lips of the men, and tears to the eyes of the women.

Joseph Haydn, the silver-haired octogenarian, had still the heart of a fiery man in his bosom, and his trembling lips cursed the conqueror, the relentless foe of Austria, and called down the wrath of Heaven on the French emperor, who always spoke of peace and conciliation, and always stirred up quarrels and enmities. The latest reverses of Austria had produced a most painful impression upon the aged *maestro*, and the ravishing joy which had illuminated Joseph Haydn's face at the performance of "The Creation," had long since disap-

peared from his careworn and mournful countenance. His
eyes were gloomy and dim, and often veiled with tears ; and
when he played his imperial hymn, as he did every morning,
he could not sing to it, for tears choked his voice, and the
words, so full of confidence and triumphant hope, seemed to
him a bitter mockery.

He led now a very quiet and lonely life at his small house
in the Mariahilf suburb, and he did not even leave it, as he
had formerly always done, on Sundays, in order to go to mass.
The sight of the French uniforms wounded his heart, and
he grieved on seeing his beloved Viennese oppressed and humiliated.

"God is every where," said Haydn to his faithful servant
Conrad, "and He will hear my prayer even though I should
utter it in my quiet closet, and not at church. But to-day,
my friend, I will pray to God in the open air. See how gloriously the sun shines, and how blue the sky is ! To-day is
Sunday. Let us, therefore, put on our Sunday clothes. Conrad, give me the fine ring which the great King of Prussia
presented to me, and then come to hear mass in my little
garden."

Conrad fetched quickly the Sunday clothes of his master ;
he helped him to put on the silken and silver-embroidered
coat, and put the large diamond-ring, which Frederick the
Great had one day sent to the great master of harmony, on
his finger. Then he handed him his hat and his strong cane,
which was adorned with a golden cross-piece, that the tottering octogenarian might lean on it. Joseph Haydn now left
the room slowly, his right hand leaning on his cane, his left
arm resting on the shoulder of his servant. Behind him
walked with a grave step the old cat, an heirloom from
Haydn's lamented wife, and hence highly prized and honored by the aged *maestro*. Purring softly, now raising
its beautiful long tail, now rolling it up, the cat followed close
in the footsteps of its master, through the hall and across the
yard to the small garden.

"How beautiful it is here !" said Haydn, standing still in
the door of the garden, and slowly looking around at the
flowers and shrubbery, the humming bees and flitting butter-

flies. "Oh, how gloriously beautiful is God's creation, and how radiant—"

"How radiant is nature," interrupted Conrad; "how brilliantly the sun shines, and how splendid the lawn looks!"

"You are a fool, old Conrad, to repeat these words from *my* 'Creation,'" said Haydn, with a gentle smile. "I was not thinking of *my* 'Creation' at this moment, but of God's creation. And He certainly knew more about the music of the creation than I did, and—just listen how the nightingale sings in the elder-bush yonder! It is an air such as is to be found only in God's Creation, and, as Joseph Haydn, with all his talents and enthusiasm, never was able to compose. Oh, how sweetly this *prima donna assoluta* of the good God sings, and what divine melodies, modulations, and harmonies she warbles forth, and—But what is that?"

"That is the parrot singing an air from Joseph Haydn's 'Creation,'" exclaimed Conrad, bursting into triumphant laughter. "And just listen, doctor, the *prima donna assoluta* of the good God has become entirely silent, and listens with delight to the divine melodies, modulations, and harmonies of my dear master Joseph Haydn."

"You are a fool, Conrad, despite your seventy years," said Haydn, "to call old Paperl my *prima donna assoluta*, and compare him with the nightingale. But tell me, for God's sake, where did the bird hear that melody? Why, Paperl whistles the great base-air from 'The Creation' as though he were the first singer. Where did he learn it?"

"I taught him the melody, doctor," said Conrad, proudly; "I gave him lessons for three months, and he took pains to learn the melody, for he knew full well that we two were preparing a little surprise and joy for our dear master, the great Joseph Haydn."

"And that is the reason why I have not seen Paperl for so long," said Haydn, nodding his head gently. "I did not wish to inquire after him, for I was afraid the answer would be that the bird was dead and had gone home to my dear old wife."

"Well, I am sure Paperl would never go to her," said Conrad, laughing; "the two could never get along with each other, and were always quarrelling. Whenever Paperl could catch one of your wife's fingers, he bit it with his thick beak, and she hated the bird cordially for it, and would have preferred sending him to the grave than descending into it herself. But Paperl did not die, and you need not be anxious on his account, doctor. Such parrots live a thousand years. Therefore, I locked him up in my chamber for three months, and taught him the beautiful air, that the bird might whistle it to mankind a thousand years hence, and remind all of the great composer, Joseph Haydn."

"Ah, my dear old Conrad," sighed Haydn, sinking into the easy-chair which Conrad had placed for him under the fragrant elder-bush, "a thousand years hence no one will know any thing about us, and we shall be nothing but dust returned to dust. But God will remain, and His sun will shine a thousand years hence as gloriously as it does to-day ; and His nightingales will sing the same wonderful melodies from His creation long after my 'Creation' has been forgotten."

He paused, and clasping his hands devoutly, lifted his eyes to heaven. By his side, on the high pole, its right leg fastened to it with a small silver chain, the parrot sat, and fixed its piercing, sagacious eyes upon him ; the cat lay at Haydn's feet, and gazed with philosophical equanimity at the flies which were buzzing from flower to flower, and pricked up its ears attentively whenever a small bird rustled in the shrubbery, or skipped merrily from branch to branch in the fragrant walnut tree. Beside the easy-chair stood Conrad, the old servant, his faithful, honest face turned toward his master with an expression of infinite tenderness, and quite absorbed in contemplating this mild, smiling, and calm octogenarian, whose eyes were looking around slowly, and seemingly greeting God and Nature. In the distance bells were ringing and calling devout worshipers to divine service ; their notes resounded tremulously through the air like a solemn accompaniment to the voices of Nature.

"Oh, how beautiful, how beautiful !" murmured Haydn. "Why can I not exhale with this sigh of joy my old life, which is no longer good for any thing ? Why can I not die with this prayer of gratitude toward God on my lips, and waft my soul up to heaven, as that bird yonder is at this moment soaring toward the sun !"

"Oh, sir, why do you talk already of dying?" cried Conrad, anxiously ; "you must live yet a long while, a joy to mankind, and honored and esteemed by the whole world."

"And a burden to myself," sighed Haydn. "I am exhausted, Conrad ; I have no longer strength enough to live. This unfortunate war crushed to the ground and broke my poor heart.* When Napoleon made his second entrance into Vienna, and our good Emperor Francis had to escape again from the capital, I felt as though my heart were rent asunder, and this rent will never heal again. The misfortunes of my fatherland will cause me to bleed to death ! Ah, how dreadful it is that Austria and my emperor were humiliated so profoundly, and that they had to bow to the Emperor of the French ! I cannot comprehend why the Lord permits it, and why He does not hurl down His thunderbolts upon the head of this hypocritical French emperor, who throws the firebrand of war into all parts of Europe, who always has pharisaical words of peace in his mouth, and gives himself the appearance of wishing to reconcile all, when he is intent only on setting all at variance. Oh, Conrad, when I think of this Emperor Napoleon, of the innocent blood which he has already shed, and of the many thousand victims which have already fallen to his ambition, my heart swells up in boundless exasperation, and I begin to doubt even the goodness and justice of God !— But hush, hush, my wild heart," he interrupted himself, lifting his eyes with a beseeching glance to heaven. "God will manage everything for the best. He will one day, with a beck of His hand, hurl the French usurper from his throne, and cause Austria to rise great and powerful from her humiliating position. He will protect Germany from the wrongs inflicted upon her by France, and avenge the disgrace which every German has to suffer at the hands of the French. That is the hope which I shall take with me into my grave ; that is the confidence I have in Thee, O my God !"

He lifted both his hands toward heaven, and prayed in a

* Haydn's own words.—"Zeitgenossen," vol. iv., p. 36.

low voice. Then he rose slowly from his chair, and turned
his head with smiling greetings on all sides.

"Conrad," he said, gently, "I take leave of Nature to-day,
for it seems to me as if I never should see again my dear little
garden, the flowers and birds, the sun and the sky. Oh, farewell, then, great and holy Nature! I have loved thee passionately all my life, and glorified thee in my works to the
best of the power which God imparted to me. · Farewell,
Nature! farewell, sunshine and fragrant flowers! Joseph
Haydn takes leave of you, for his task is fulfilled, and his
soul is weary. Come, my old Conrad, conduct me back to the
house. I will return to my room. I am tired, ah, so exceedingly tired!"

He passed his arm around Conrad's neck, and, leaning his
other hand on his cane, walked slowly and pantingly up the
narrow path.

At this moment the nightingale in the elder-bush recommenced its jubilant song, and at the same time the parrot
raised its shrill voice, and began to whistle the sweet notes of
the air from Haydn's· "Creation."

Haydn stood still and listened. "Conrad," he said, in a
low voice, "we will now consult an oracle as to my life and
death. If the parrot pauses first, I shall die soon; if the
nightingale pauses, God will permit me to live a while
longer."

He lifted his eyes devoutly to the sky, over whose azure
plain white cloudlets were scudding like silver swans, and his
lips muttered a low prayer.

The nightingale still sang its wonderful love-songs, and
the parrot tried to drown its notes with Haydn's beautiful
melody.

Conrad smiled blissfully. "My Paperl has a long breath,"
he said, "and the nightingale will be unable to cope with
him; Rupert will outsing it."

But the nightingale, as if irritated by this rivalry, now
seemed to put forth its whole art and strength. The ringing
trills were followed by long, sweet, flute-notes, which filled
the air like a joyous hymn of tenderness, drowning the
voices of all other birds, and the sighing breeze, and seemed

to arouse the flowers from their sweet slumber, till they trembled with blissful transports, and softly raised their flowery crowns toward the blooming elder, in whose dark foliage was concealed the nightingale, Nature's great and yet modest *artiste*.

Yes, all Nature seemed to listen with blissful attention to this wonderful song of the nightingale, and even the parrot could no longer resist the charm. Paperl hesitated, then commenced again, hesitated a second time, and was silent.

Haydn dropped his clasped hands slowly, and turned his eyes from heaven to earth. "I knew it full well," he murmured ; "the oracle has decided my fate, and Joseph Haydn's 'Creation' is silenced by God's creation. Come into the house, Conrad ; I am cold and tired. But first give me a few of my fragrant friends, my dear flowers. They shall speak to me in my room of the splendor and beauty of the world."

Conrad gathered hastily a full bouquet of roses, pinks, and elder-flowers, dried the tears filling his eyes, and conducted his master carefully back into the house.

He had just seated him in his easy-chair, and placed the embroidered cushion under his feet, when the shrill street-bell resounded in the hall.

"Go and see who is there," said Haydn, holding the bouquet in both his hands, and contemplating it with loving eyes.

Conrad slipped out of the room and returned in a few minutes.

"There is a stranger from Berlin," he said, "who begged me urgently to admit him to Dr. Haydn. Mr. Schmid, the manager of the theatre, is with him, and requests you to see the stranger, who, he says, is a celebrated poet."

"If Schmid is with him, let them come in," said Haydn, mildly ; "it will doubtless be the last time I shall see my dear old friend on earth."

Conrad threw open the door, and beckoned the gentlemen, who were standing outside, to come in. The two crossed the threshold softly on tiptoe, and with faces expressive of profound reverence ; as if seized with compassion or pious awe, they stood still at the door, and gazed with eyes full of tenderness upon Haydn, who, at this moment, overcome perhaps by the spring air, had closed his eyes, and not heard the entrance of the visitors.

"That is he," whispered one of the two, a man of a tall, erect form, with a face radiant with understanding and sagacity. "That is he !" he repeated, fixing his ardent eyes on the composer.

"Yes, that is Joseph Haydn," said the other, in a low voice, and an expression of profound grief overspread his broad, good-natured face. "But hush ! he opens his eyes."

And he approached Haydn, who held out both his hands to him, and greeted him with a gentle smile.

"Do you come to bid farewell to your old friend once more previous to his death ?" he asked, mildly. "Do you wish to take leave of me, my dear friend Schmid ?"

"No, I do not come to bid you farewell, but wish you good-day," said Schmid, warmly, "and pray you to receive this gentleman here kindly. It is Iffland, the celebrated actor and poet from Berlin. He had come to Vienna before the French took the city, and after its capture he could no longer get out: they detained him, and it was not until now that, by dint of the most pressing solicitations, he received permission to return to Berlin."

"But I could not leave Vienna without seeing the great Haydn," exclaimed Iffland, in his fine, sonorous voice. "What would the people of Berlin think of me if I had not seen the most illustrious genius of our time ?"

"Sir," said Haydn, with a sigh, "look at me, and learn from my weakness how fragile man is with all his glory."

"Man alone is fragile, but genius is immortal," exclaimed Iffland, "and Joseph Haydn is a genius whose glory will never die."

"Let my footman tell you the glory of the nightingale and the parrot," said Haydn, with a faint smile. "The works of man are perishable, but the works of God last forever."

"But the works of man come likewise from God, for it was He who gave him the strength to create them," replied Iffland, warmly. "Did not the great and glorious creations of your genius come just as much from God as the flowers which you hold in your hand, and the perfumes of which delight you so visibly?"

"Yes, these flowers are beautiful," said Haydn, musingly.

"The bouquet is doubtless a gift from one of the many fair admirers of our *maestro*?" asked Schmid, laughing.

Haydn looked up to him smilingly and shook his head gently. "No," he said, "it is the last souvenir of Nature, to which I have bidden farewell. I worshipped to-day in the open air, and this is the rosary with which I will pray. Ah, I love Nature so passionately!"

"And you have taught those whose eyes and ears were closed against the holy charms of Nature, how to see and hear," said Iffland. "Your 'Seasons' is the most glorious hymn on God's splendid world."

"Yes, the 'Seasons,'" cried Haydn, almost vehemently, "gave me the death-blow. It was so difficult for me to derive enthusiasm from the words of the text. The words said so little, really so very little! Frequently a single passage caused me a great deal of trouble for several days, and I did not succeed after all in expressing the idea I wished to convey to the hearers. The words were a dead weight on my music. Well, it is all over now. Yes, you see, it is all over now. The 'Seasons' is to blame for it, for it exhausted my last strength. I have had to work hard all my lifetime; I had to suffer hunger, thirst, and cold in my wretched attic, whence I had to descend a hundred and thirty steps before reaching the street. Privations, hard work, hunger, in short, all that I suffered in my youth, are now exerting their effects on me and prostrating me. But it is an honorable defeat—it is hard work to which I am succumbing. However, God assisted me. I never felt it more strikingly than this very day, and therefore I am so happy, oh! so happy, that I must shed tears of blissful emotion. Do not laugh at me on this account. I am a weak old man, and when any thing affects me profoundly, I must weep. It was otherwise in former years. Ah, in former years!" He turned his tearful eyes toward the window, and gazed into vacancy. "In former years my mind was strong and vigorous," he sighed, "and when I wrote my 'Creation,' a manly fire filled my heart."

"Your enthusiasm is imprinted on your great work, and it will never disappear from it," said Iffland. "Joseph Haydn's 'Creation' is immortal and full of eternal youth. The Viennese proved it to you on hearing your sublime music the other day."

"But I proved to them that I had become so feeble that I could no longer bear listening to my own music. I had to leave the room long before the performance was at an end."

"You ought not to have gone to the concert at all," said Schmid. The excitement might have been injurious to your health."

"It was injurious to me," said Haydn, "but considerations of health had no right to prevent me from being present. It was not the first time that homage had been rendered to Haydn, and I wished to show that I was able to bear it this time too. Ah, it was a glorious evening, and never did I hear a better performance of my ' Creation.' "

"It was the great composer's apotheosis which the musicians and singers were celebrating," said Iffland, deeply moved.

"It is true the Viennese have done a great deal for me. They are so good, and they love me dearly."

"Oh, the Viennese are not ahead of the people of Berlin in this respect," exclaimed Iffland. "In Berlin, too, every one knows and loves the great Joseph Haydn, and his ' Creation' is likewise recognized there as a masterpiece. It was performed in Berlin quite recently at a charity concert, the receipts of which amounted to over two thousand dollars."

"Over two thousand dollars for the poor," said Joseph Haydn, with beaming eyes; "oh, my work, then, gave the poor a good day. That is splendid, that is the most beautiful reward for a life of toils and privations. But," he added, after a brief pause, "it is all over now. I can no longer do any thing. I am a leafless tree, which will break down to-day or to-morrow."

"The fall of this tree will move the whole of Germany as a great calamity befalling every lover of his country."

"Yes, it is true, much love has been manifested for me,

much homage has been rendered to me," said Haydn, musingly.

"All nations and all princes have rendered homage to you,"
exclaimed Iffland. "The laurel-wreath, for which we other
poets and artists are struggling all our lifetime, and which is
generally bestowed upon us only after we are in the grave,
was long since granted to you in the most flattering and gratifying manner. Europe has presented you, not with one, but
with many laurel-wreaths, and you may look back on your
life like a victorious hero, for each of your exploits was a
triumph for which you received laurel-wreaths and trophies."

"Yes, I have many souvenirs of my past," said Haydn,
smilingly. "I will show them to you.—Conrad, give me my
treasures."

Conrad opened the drawer of the large writing-table which
was standing close to Haydn, and which contained a great
many large and small *étuis*, caskets and boxes.

"You shall see my treasures now," exclaimed Haydn,
cheerfully. In the first place, he showed them a beautiful
casket made of ebony and gold. It was a gift with which the
young Princess Esterhazy had presented the beloved and
adored friend of her house only a few weeks ago, and on
whose lid was painted a splendid miniature representing the
scene at the last performance of "The Creation," when Haydn
received the enthusiastic homage of the audience. He then
showed them the large gold medal sent him, in 1800, from
Paris, by the two hundred and fifty musicians who, on Christ-
mas evening in that year, had performed "The Creation," and
thereby delighted all Paris. Then followed many other med-
als from musical societies and conservatories, and valuable
diamond rings, snuff-boxes, and breastpins from kings and
emperors. Last, Haydn showed them, with peculiar emotion,
the diploma of citizenship which the city of Vienna had conferred on him. It was contained in a silver case, and its
sight caused his eyes even now to flash with the most intense
satisfaction.

He had placed on the table before him every piece, after
showing it to them and explaining its meaning; and now
that all the treasures were spread out before him, he con-

templated them with a blissful smile, and nodded to them as
if to dear old friends.

"Do not laugh at me," he said, lifting his eyes to Iffland,
almost beseechingly. "I am fondly attached to these things,
and hence it delighted me to look at them from time to time
with my friends. You will say they are the playthings of an
old man. But they are more than that to me ; on beholding
them, I think of my past life, and my recollections render me
young again for a few moments. After my death all these
things will pass into dear hands, and I hope that, when I am
slumbering in my grave, my souvenirs will be carefully preserved and honored if only for my sake." *

"I hope the day is distant when Germany will have to
lament the death of her favorite, Joseph Haydn," exclaimed
Iffland.

"That day is close at hand," said Haydn, calmly ; "I feel
to-day more distinctly than ever before that my end is drawing nigh. My strength is exhausted."

"Let us go," whispered Schmid, pointing to Haydn, who
had feebly sunk back into his easy-chair, and was leaning his
pale head against the cushions.

Iffland fixed his eyes for a long time with an expression of
heart-felt grief on the groaning, broken form reposing in the
easy-chair.

"And that is all that is left of a great composer, of a genius
who delighted the whole world !" he sighed. "Ah, what a
fragile shell our body is, a miserable dwelling for the soul
living in it ! Come, my friend, let us softly leave the room.
Only I would like to take a souvenir with me, a flower from
the bouquet which Haydn held in his hands. May I venture
to take one ? "

At this moment Haydn opened his eyes again, and fixed
them with a gentle expression on Iffland. "I heard all you
said," he remarked ; "but I was too feeble to speak. You
wish to get one of my flowers ? No, you shall have them
all."

He took the bouquet, looked at it tenderly, and buried his

* Haydn bequeathed all his trinkets and manuscripts to the Esterhazy
family, who had honored him so highly during his whole life.

whole face for a moment in the flowers, and then handed it to Iffland with a gentle smile.

"Farewell," he said ; "remember me on looking at these flowers. I would I had known you in happier days, when I should have been able to enjoy your genius and admire your art. You must be a great actor, for you have a wonderfully sonorous and pliable voice. I should like to hear you declaim, even though you should recite but a few verses."

"Permit me, then, to recite the lines in which Wieland celebrated your 'Creation,'" said Iffland ; and, advancing a few steps, holding the bouquet in his hand, and fixing his gleaming eyes on Haydn, who gazed at him with a gentle smile, Iffland recited in his full sonorous voice Wieland's beautiful lines :

"Wie ström't dein wogender Gesang
In uns're Herzen ein! Wir sehen
Der Schöpfung mächt'gen Gang,
Den Hauch des Herrn auf dem Gewässer wehen ;
Jetzt durch ein blitzend Wort das erste Licht entstehen,
Und die Gestirne sich durch ihre Bahnen drehen ;
Wie Baum und Pflanze wird, wie sich der Berg erhebt,
Und froh des Lebens sich die jungen Thiere regen.
Der Donner rollet uns entgegen ;
Der Regen säuselt, jedes Wesen strebt
In's Dasein ; und bestimmt, des Schöpfers Werk zu krönen
Sehn wir das erste Paar, geführt von Deinen Tönen.
Oh, jedes Hochgefühl, das in dem Herzen schlief,
Ist wach! Wer rufet nicht : wie schön ist diese Erde!
Und schöner, nun ihr Herr auch dich in's Dasein rief,
Auf dass sein Werk vollendet werde!" *

* "Thy wondrous song in melting strains
    To our mute hearts swift entrance gains ;
    By magical yet unfelt force,
    We see creation's mighty course :
    The firmament appears in space—
    God breathes upon the water's face.
    One flashing word bids primal light appear,
    Revolving stars begin their vast career ;
    Upheaving mountains now are seen,
    Tall trees and tender herbage green ;

After concluding his recitation, Iffland approached the old man quickly, knelt down before him and imprinted a kiss on his clasped hands. Then, without adding another word, he rose, and, walking backward as if before a king, approached the door, opened it softly, and went out, followed by Schmid.*

"Farewell!" exclaimed Haydn, in a deeply-moved voice, and sank back in the easy-chair. Profound silence now reigned around him; but all at once this silence was broken by a thundering crash, which caused the windows to rattle and shook the walls. The deafening noise was repeated again and again, and rolled through the air like the angry voice of God.

And now the door opened, and Conrad and Kate, the aged servant-woman, rushed into the room. "Ah, master, master, it is all up now, and we are all lost! The Austrians and the French are in force close to Vienna, and the battle has already commenced."

"The battle has commenced!" exclaimed Joseph Haydn, rising from his easy-chair, and lifting his hand to heaven. "The battle has commenced! Good and great God in heaven, protect our fatherland, and grant Austria a glorious victory over her arrogant foe! Do not allow Austria and Germany to succumb; help us to defeat the proud enemy who has humiliated and oppressed us so long! O Lord my God,

> Young animals to being rise,
> And animate by living cries;
> We hear the mighty thunder roar,
> And rains in gushing torrents pour.
> All creatures struggle into life; and stand
> Before our eyes, fresh from their Maker's hand,
> The first pair, led by thy sweet tones.
> Now waked by inspiration's art,
> Enthusiasm stirs our heart.
> Who cries not, ' Earth is passing fair!'
> Yet far more fair her Maker is,
> How perfect every work of his!"

* The whole account of this interview between Joseph Haydn and Iffland is in strict accordance with Iffland's own report of it in his "Theatre-Almanac," pp. 181-207.

shield the honor of Germany and Austria ! Protect the emperor !"

And Joseph Haydn walked through the room with the vigor and alacrity of a youth, dropped his hands on the keys of the piano, and began to play in full concords the melody of his imperial hymn, " *Gott erhalte Franz den Kaiser !* "

Conrad and Kate stood behind him, singing in a low, tremulous tone ; but outside, the booming of artillery continued incessantly, and they heard also the cries of the people who were hurrying in dismay through the streets, and the tolling of all the church-bells, which called upon the Viennese to pray to God.

All at once Haydn paused in the middle of the tune ; his hands dropped from the keys, a long sigh burst from his lips, and he sank fainting into the arms of his faithful Conrad. His servants carried him to his couch, and soon succeeded in restoring him to consciousness. He opened his eyes slowly, and his first glance fell upon Conrad, who stood weeping at his bedside.

" The nightingale was right ; my end is drawing nigh," he said, with a faint smile. " But I will not die before learning that the Austrians have defeated the enemy, and that my emperor has gained a battle."

And in truth Joseph Haydn's strong will once more overpowered death, which had already touched him with its finger. He raised himself upon his couch ; he would not die while Austria was struggling on the reeking, gory field of battle for the regeneration or her end.

Two days followed, two dreadful days of uncertainty and terror ; they heard incessantly the booming of artillery ; but although the Viennese gazed down from their church-steeples all day, they were unable to discern any thing. Tremendous clouds of smoke covered the country all around, and wrapped the villages of Aspern and Essling and the island of Lobau in an impenetrable veil of mist.

Joseph Haydn passed these days, the 21st and 22d of May, in silent grief and gentle resignation ; he prayed often, and played his imperial hymn three times a day.

Thus the morning of the 22d of May had come. Conrad

had gone into the street to ask for news, for the booming of artillery had ceased, and the battle was over. "Which side was victorious?" That was the question which caused all to tremble, and which filled all hearts with intense anxiety.

Haydn's heart, too, was full of grave anxiety, and, to overcome his impatience till Conrad's return, he had caused Kate to conduct him to his piano.

"I will play my imperial hymn," he said, hastily; "I have often derived comfort and relief from it in the days of uneasiness and anxiety; and when I play it my heart is always so much at ease. Its strength will not fail me to-day either." *

He commenced playing; a blissful smile illuminated his features; he lifted his radiant eyes to heaven, and his music grew louder and fierier, and his fingers glided more powerfully over the keys of the piano. Suddenly the door was thrown open, and Conrad rushed in, panting from the rapid run, flushed with excitement, but with a joyful face.

"Victory!" he shouted. "Victory!" And he sank down at Haydn's feet.

"Which side was victorious?" asked Haydn, anxiously.

"The Austrians were victorious," said Conrad, pantingly. "Our Archduke Charles has defeated the Emperor Napoleon at Aspern; the whole French army retreated to the island of Lobau, whence it can no longer escape. Thousands of French corpses are floating down the Danube, and proclaiming to the world that Austria has conquered the French! Hurrah! hurrah! Our hero, the Archduke Charles, has defeated the villainous Bonaparte! Hurrah!"

"Hurrah! hurrah!" repeated the parrot on its pole; and the cat raised its head from the cushion on which it had lain, and gazed with keen, searching eyes at the parrot, as if it had understood Paperl's jubilant notes.

Joseph Haydn said nothing, but clasped his hands and looked rapturously upward. After a pause he exclaimed, in a loud and joyous voice: "Lord God, I thank Thee for not disappointing my firm trust, but protecting Austria and helping her to vanquish her foe. I knew full well that the just cause would triumph, and the just cause is that of Austria; for

* Haydn's own words.—See "Zeitgenosson," vol. iv., third series, p. 36.

France, hypocritical France alone provoked this war, and Austria drew the sword only to defend her honor and her frontiers. The just cause could not but triumph, and hence Austria had to conquer, and France, had to succumb in this struggle. God protect the Emperor Francis! I may lay down now and die. Austria is victorious! That is the last joyful greeting which the world sends to me. With this greeting I will die—ay, die! Death is already drawing nigh. But Death wears a laurel-wreath on its head, and its eye is radiant with triumphant joy. Glory to Austria! Glory to the German fatherland!"

These were Joseph Haydn's last words. He fainted away. It is true the physicians succeeded in restoring him to life, and he breathed yet for six days; but his life resembled only the last feeble flicker of the dying flame, and in the night of the 30th of May death came to extinguish this flickering flame.

CHAPTER XXIV.

THE ARCHDUKE JOHN AT COMORN.

THE unheard-of event, then, had taken place. Napoleon had been defeated by the Austrians. The Archduke Charles had gained a brilliant victory; Napoleon had transferred his whole army to the island of Lobau; he himself passed his time in moody broodings at the castle of Ebersberg, and the unexpected disaster which had befallen him, and which at the same time had brought about the death of one of his favorites, Marshal Lannes, seemed to have suddenly deprived the emperor of all his energy. He did not speak, he did not eat; he sat for whole days in his cabinet, staring at the maps spread out before him on his table, and yet forgetting to cover them, as he used to do on conceiving the plans of his campaigns, with the colored pins which represented the different armies. Victory had no longer been able to soften this marble Cæsarean face, but defeat caused his features now to wear an expression of profound anger and grief. Nevertheless, he did not complain,

and never did he confess even to his confidants that he was
suffering. Only once, for a brief moment, he lifted the veil
concealing his feelings, and permitted his marshals to see into
the innermost recesses of his soul. Marmont had dared to
pray the emperor, in the name of all the marshals, to yield no
longer to his grief at what had occurred, but bear in mind that
it was incumbent on him to preserve himself for the welfare
of his subjects and the glory of his future. Napoleon had answered with a faint smile : " You think I am sitting here to
brood over my misfortune ? It is true, I am burying my dead,
and, as there are unfortunately a great many of them, it takes
me a long time to do it. But over the tomb of the dead of
Essling I am going to erect a monument which will be radiant
with the splendor of victory, and on its frontispiece shall be
read the word ' Vengeance ! ' The Emperor of Austria is lost.
Had I defeated him in this battle, I should, perhaps, have forgiven his arrogance and perfidy ; but as he defeated me,
I must and shall annihilate him and his army."

While Napoleon was thus burying his dead, and reflecting
on his " monument of vengeance," the utmost rejoicings
reigned at the headquarters of the Archduke Charles, the victor of Aspern ; and all Austria, all Germany joined in these
rejoicings, and blessed the glorious day of Bonaparte's first
humiliation.

And this victory was soon followed by the news of a triumph hardly less glorious than the battle of Aspern. The Tyrolese, those despised peasants, had gained a brilliant victory
over the French veterans, and their Bavarian auxiliaries, on
the 21st of May, on Mount Isel, near the city of Innspruck.
Andreas Hofer, commander-in-chief of the united forces of
the Tyrolese, jointly with Speckbacher, Wallner, and the Capuchin Haspinger, had again defeated the Bavarians and
French, who had re-entered the Tyrol, and delivered the province a second time from the enemy.

Count Nugent, quartermaster-general of the Archduke
John, had entered the latter's room with this joyful news, and
told him with sparkling eyes of the heroic deeds of the Tyrolese ; of Hofer's pious zeal ; of the bold exploits of Wallner
and Speckbacher, whose deeds recalled the ancient heroes of

Homer ; of the intrepid Capuchin friar, Haspinger, who, with
a huge wooden cross in his hand, led on the attack, and animated his followers not less by his example than the assurances
of Divine protection which he held forth. Count Nugent had
related all these heroic deeds with fervid eloquence to the
archduke, and yet, to his utter astonishment, the latter's
face had remained gloomy, and not a ray of joy had illuminated it.

"Your imperial highness, then, does not share my exultation ?" he asked, mournfully. "You receive the news quite
coldly and indifferently, and yet I am speaking of your beloved Tyrolese, of your heroes, Andreas Hofer, Joseph Speckbacher, and Anthony Wallner ! They and their heroic men
have delivered the Tyrol a second time from the enemy, and
your imperial highness does not rejoice at it ? "

"No, my dear Count," said the archduke, sighing, "for
they will lose it again. All this blood will have been shed in
vain, and my poor Tyrol will be lost in spite of it."

"You believe so ?—you who called upon the Tyrolese to
take up arms, who invited its heroes and champions to such
daring efforts, who are ready yourself to fight for the courageous mountaineers to the last extremity ? "

"Yes, I am always ready to do so," cried John, laughing
bitterly, "but what good will it do ? They will wind cunning shackles enough round my feet to make me fall to the
ground ; they will manacle my hands again, and put my will
into the strait-jacket of loyalty and obedience. I cannot
do what I want to ; I am only a tool in the hands of others,
and this will cause both my ruin and that of the Tyrol. I am
willing to sacrifice my life for the Tyrol, and yet I shall be
unable to save it. For the rest, my friend, I knew already
all these particulars of the battle on Mount Isel. A courier
from Hormayr had just reached me and brought me full
details. I was able to send back by the courier a fine reward
for the brave Tyrolese, a letter from the emperor, my august
brother, which I received this morning with the order to
forward it to them. I kept a copy of the imperial letter, for
there may be a day when it will be necessary for me to remind the emperor of this letter. Here is the copy. Read it

aloud, that I may hear, too, how fine the imperial words
sound."

The archduke handed a paper to Count Nugent, who read
as follows :

" After our arms had suffered heavy reverses, and after the
enemy had captured even the capital of the empire, my army
succeeded in defeating the French army under Napoleon on
the 21st and 22d of May, on the Marshfield, and driving it in
disorder across the Danube. The army and people of Austria
are animated with greater enthusiasm than ever ; every thing
justifies the most sanguine hopes. Trusting in God and my
just cause, I declare to my loyal provinces of the Tyrol and
Vorarlberg, that they shall never again be separated from the
Austrian empire, and that I will sign no peace but one which
will indissolubly incorporate these provinces with my other
states. Your noble conduct has sunk deep into my heart ; I
will never abandon you. My beloved brother, the Archduke
John, will speedily be among you, and put himself at your
head.   FRANCIS." *

" And your imperial highness doubts, even after this solemn promise given to the Tyrolese by his majesty the emperor ? "

"My friend," said the archduke, casting a long, searching
look round the room, " we are alone ; no one watches, and, I
trust, no one hears us. Let me, therefore, for once, speak
frankly with you ; let me unbosom to you, my friend, what I
have hitherto said to God alone ; let me forget for a quarter of
an hour that I am a subject of the emperor, and that his
majesty is my brother ; permit me to examine the situation
with the eyes of an impartial observer, and to judge of men as
a man. Well, then, I must confess to you that I cannot share
the universal joy at the recent events, and—may God forgive
me !—I do not believe even in the promises which the emperor
makes to the Tyrolese. He himself may at the present hour
be firmly resolved to fulfil them ; he may have made up his
mind never to sign any peace but one which will indissolubly
incorporate the Tyrol with his empire ; but the events, and

* Hormayr, " Das Heer von Inner-Oesterreich unter den Befehlen des
Erzherzogs Johann," p. 189.

especially men, will assuredly compel him to consent to another treaty of peace. You know full well that there are two parties about the emperor, and that there is a constant feud between these two parties. One wants war, the other wants peace ; and the peace-party is unfortunately headed by the Archduke Charles, the generalissimo of our army. You know the fawning and submissive letter which the generalissimo addressed to Napoleon after the defeat of Ratisbon, and which Napoleon disdained to answer.* The war-party is headed by the empress and Count Stadion. But the empress has unfortunately little influence over her husband, and Count Stadion is no more influential than her majesty. His generous enthusiasm and fiery impetuosity are repugnant to the emperor, who will remove him so soon as he has discovered a more submissive and obsequious successor who has as much work in him as Stadion. But there is one point as to which these incessantly quarrelling parties are agreed and join hands, and that is their common hostility against the archdukes, the emperor's brothers ; so virulent is this hatred, that the peace-party deserts its leader in order to operate with the war-party against him and his interests. The Austrian nobility has always claimed the privilege of filling all superior offices, and it is furious at seeing the archdukes animated with the desire of dedicating their abilities to their fatherland and their emperor. Hence, the nobility is decidedly opposed to the success of the archdukes, which might set bounds to its

* The Archduke Charles wrote to Napoleon on the 30th of April, 1809: " Your Majesty announced your arrival by a salvo of artillery ; I had no time to reply to it. But, though hardly informed of your presence, I speedily discovered it by the losses which I experienced. You have taken many prisoners from me, sire, and I have taken some thousands from you in quarters where you were not personally present. I propose to your majesty to exchange them, man for man, rank for rank ; and, if that proposal proves agreeable to you, point out the place where it may be possible to carry it into effect. I feel flattered, sire, in combating the greatest captain of the age ; but I should esteem myself much happier if Heaven had chosen me to be the instrument of procuring for my country a durable peace. Whatever may be the events of war, or the chances of an accommodation, I pray your majesty to believe that my desires will always outstrip your wishes, and that I am equally honored by meeting your majesty either with the sword or the olive-branch in your hand."

oligarchy. It opposes me as well as the other archdukes, whether this opposition may endanger the interests of the fatherland, and even the emperor, or not. Things would be even more prosperous in this campaign, if the generals serving under the archdukes had carried out the orders of their superiors with greater zeal, promptness, and willingness. But they have been intentionally slow; they have often hesitated, misunderstood, or purposely forgotten their orders. They are intent on proving the incapacity of the archdukes in order to overthrow them; and they well know that they are rendering a service to the emperor by doing so, for they are aware that the emperor does not love his brothers."

"No, your imperial highness," exclaimed Nugent, when the archduke paused with a sigh. "I hope that this is going too far, and that you are likewise mistaken about it. It is impossible that the emperor should not love his brothers, who are doing so much honor to the imperial house by their surpassing accomplishments, virtues, and talents."

"My friend, you speak like a courtier," said John, shaking his head, "and you exaggerate as a friend. But even though you were right, those qualities would not be calculated to render the emperor's heart more attached to us. He wants the emperor alone to shed lustre on, and do honor to the imperial house, and not the archdukes, his father's younger sons, whom he hates."

"No, no, your imperial highness, it is impossible that the emperor should hate his brothers!"

"And why impossible?" asked John, shrugging his shoulders. "Do not his brothers, the archdukes, hate each other? Or do you believe, perhaps, that the Archduke Charles, our generalissimo, loves me, or even wishes me well? I was so unfortunate as to be twice victorious during the present campaign, while he was twice defeated; I beat the French at Sacile and St. Boniface, while he lost the battles of Landshut and Ratisbon. This is a crime which the archduke will never forgive me, and for which he will revenge himself."

"Perhaps he thinks that he took a noble and glorious revenge at the battle of Aspern?"

"Oh, my friend, you forgot that our mother was a daughter

of Italy, and that we, therefore, do not care for a noble and glorious revenge, but long for an Italian *vendetta*. The generalissimo will not content himself with having obtained glory, but I must suffer a defeat, a disgrace, which will neutralize what few laurels I gathered at Sacile and St. Boniface. Oh, I know my brother the generalissimo ; I see all the little threads which he is spinning around me, and which, as soon as they are strong enough, he will convert into a net, in which he will catch me, in order to exhibit me to the world as an ignoramus and dreamer, destitute both of ability and luck as a general. Do not tell me that I am mistaken, my friend ; I have hitherto observed every thing with close attention, and my observations unfortunately do not deceive me. The generalissimo is desirous of punishing me for my victories at Sacile and St. Boniface, and for advocating a declaration of war when he pronounced three times against it. He has already several times told the emperor that I am self-willed, disobedient, and always inclined to oppose his orders by words or even deeds ; and the emperor always takes pleasure in informing me of the generalissimo's complaints."

"It is true," sighed Count Nugent ; "this aversion of the generalissimo to your imperial highness unfortunately cannot be denied, and you yourself have to suffer by it."

"Oh," cried John, impetuously, "if that were all, I should not complain ; I should add it to the many other pin-pricks of my fate, and strive to bear it without murmuring. But my soldiers and the glory of the Austrian arms suffer by it, and it will destroy the liberty of the Tyrol. It is well known that this is my most vulnerable point ; that I love the Tyrol, and am determined to leave nothing undone in order to redeem the emperor's pledges to preserve the Tyrol to the imperial house, and restore its ancient privileges and liberties. It is known, too, that I long intensely to live in the future days of peace as the emperor's lieutenant in the Tyrol ; to live, far from the noisy bustle of the capital, in the peaceful seclusion of the mountain country, for myself, my studies, and the men whom I love, and who love me. Oh, my poor, unfortunate Tyrol will grievously suffer for the love which I bear it ; Austria will lose it a second time, and now, perhaps, forever."

"Does your imperial highness believe so ?" cried Nugent, in dismay. "You believe so, even after communicating to me the letter in which the emperor promises to the Tyrolese never to sign a peace that will not indissolubly incorporate the Tyrol and Vorarlberg with his monarchy, and in which he announces the speedy arrival of his beloved brother John, who is to put himself at the head of the Tyrolese ?"

"My friend, these numerous and liberal promises are the very things that make me distrustful, and convince me that they are not meant seriously. If the emperor had the preservation of the Tyrol really at heart, and intended earnestly that my army should succor and save the Tyrolese, would he not have left me at liberty to operate according to the dictates of my own judgment and in full harmony with the Tyrolese, instead of tying my hands, and regarding and employing my force only as a secondary and entirely dependent corps of the generalissimo's army ? Look into the past, Nugent, bear in mind all that has happened since we took the field, and tell me then whether I am right or not ?"

"Unfortunately you are," sighed Nugent; "I can no longer contradict your imperial highness, I cannot deny that many a wrong has been inflicted on you and us; that you have have always been prevented from taking the initiative in a vigorous manner; that you and your army have constantly been kept in a secondary and dependent position; that your plans have incessantly been frustrated; and that your superiors have often done the reverse of what you wished and deemed prudent and advisable."

"And yet they will hereafter say that I was alone to blame for the failure of my plans," cried the archduke, with a mournful smile; "they will charge me with having been unable to carry out the grandiloquent promises which I made to the emperor and the Tyrolese, and the emperor will exult at the discomfiture of the boastful archduke who took it upon himself to call out the whole people of the Tyrol, put himself at their head, and successfully defend against all enemies this fortress which God and Nature erected for Austria. The faithful Tyrolese have taken up arms ; I am ready to put myself at their head, but already I

have been removed from the Tyrol, and my arm is paralyzed
so that I can no longer stretch it out to take the hand which
the Tyrol is holding out to me beseechingly. If I had been
permitted to advance after the victories which my army
gained over the Viceroy of Italy and Marmont, I should probably now already have expelled the enemy from Upper Italy
and the Southern Tyrol. But I was not allowed to follow up
my successes ; I was stopped in the midst of my victorious
career. Because the generalissimo's army had been defeated
at Ratisbon, I was compelled, instead of pursuing the enemy
energetically and obliging him to keep on the defensive, to retreat myself, and, instead of being the pursuer, be pursued by
the forces of the viceroy. Instead of going to the Tyrol, I was
ordered by the generalissimo to turn toward Hungary and
unite with the volunteers in that country. No sooner had I
done so, than I was ordered to advance again toward the
Southern Tyrol, march upon Villach and Salzburg, unite with
Jellachich, form a connection with Field-Marshal Giulay,
and operate with them in the rear of the enemy, who was
already in the immediate neighborhood of Vienna. And he
who gave me these orders did not know that Jellachich had
in the meantime been beaten at Würzl ; that Villach had
been occupied by the French ; that I was not in the rear of
the enemy, but that the enemy was in my rear ; he did not or
would not know that the Viceroy of Italy was in my rear
with thirty-six thousand men, and that the Duke of Dantzic
was in front of my position at Salzburg. Since then we
have been moving about amidst incessant skirmishes and incessant losses ; and scarcely had we reached Comorn to re-
organize and re-enforce my little army, when we received
orders to march to the island of Schütt and toward Presburg.
I vainly tried to remonstrate and point to the weakness and
exhaustion of my troops ; I vainly asked for time to reorgan-
ize my forces, when I would attack Macdonald and prevent
him from uniting with Napoleon. I vainly proved that this
was his intention, and that no one could hinder him from
carrying it into effect, so soon as I had to turn toward Presburg and open to Macdonald the road to Vienna. My remonstrances were disregarded ; pains were taken to prove to me

that I was but a tool, a wheel in the great machine of state,
and the orders were renewed for me to march into Hungary.
Well, I will submit again—I will obey again ; but I will not do
so in silence ; I will, at least, tell the emperor that I do it in
spite of myself, and will march to Presburg and Raab only if
he approves of the generalissmo's orders."

"That is to say, your imperial highness is going to declare
openly against the generalissimo ? "

"No ; it is to say that I am going to inform my sovereign
of my doubts and fears, and unbosom to him my wishes and
convictions. You smile, my friend. It is true, I am yet a
poor dreamer, speculating on the heart, and believing that
the truth must triumph in the end. I shall, however, at least
be able to say that I have done my duty, and had the courage
to inform the emperor of the true state of affairs. I shall repair this very day to his majesty's headquarters at Wolkersdorf. I will dare once more to speak frankly and fearlessly
to him. I will oppose my enemies at least with open visor,
and show to them that I am not afraid of them. God knows,
if only my own personal honor and safety were at stake, I
should withdraw in silence, and shut up my grief and my apprehensions in my bosom ; but my fatherland is at stake, and
so is the poor Tyrol, so enthusiastic in its love, so unwavering
in its fidelity; and so are the honor and glory of our arms.
Hence, I will dare once more to speak the truth, and may God
impart strength to my words ! "

CHAPTER XXV.

THE EMPEROR FRANCIS AT WOLKERSDORF.

THE Emperor of Austria was still at his headquarters at
Wolkersdorf. The news of the victory at Aspern had illuminated the Emperor's face with the first rays of hope, and
greatly lessened the influence of the peace-party over him.
The war-party became more confident ; the beautiful, pale
face of the Empress Ludovica became radiant as it had never

been seen before ; and Count Stadion told the emperor he would soon be able to return to Vienna.

But the Emperor Francis shook his head with an incredulous smile. " You do not know Bonaparte," he said, " if you think he will, because he has suffered a defeat, be immediately ready to make peace and return to France. Now he will not rest before he gains a victory and repairs the blunders he has committed. .There is wild and insidious blood circulating in Bonaparte's veins, and the battle of Aspern has envenomed it more than ever. Did you not hear, Stadion, of what Bonaparte is reported to have said ? He declared that there was no longer a dynasty of the Hapsburgs, but only the petty princes of Lorraine. And do you not know that he has addressed to the Hungarians a proclamation advising them to depose me without further ceremony, and elect another king, of course one of the new-fangled French princes ? Do you not know that he has sent to Hungary emissaries who are calling upon the people to rise against me and conquer their liberty, which he, Bonaparte, would protect ? In truth, it is laughable to hear Bonaparte still prating about liberty as though it were a piece of sugar which he has only to put into the mouth of the nations, when they are crying like babies, in order to silence them, and thereupon pull the wool quietly over their eyes. But it is true, the nations really are like babies ; they do not become reasonable and wise, and the accursed word 'liberty,' which Bonaparte puts as a flea into their ears, maddens them still as though a tarantula had bitten them. They have seen in Italy and France what sort of liberty Napoleon brings to them, and what a yoke he intends to lay on their necks while telling them that he wishes to make freemen of them. But they do not become wise, and who knows if the Magyars will not likewise allow themselves to be fooled and believe in the liberty which Bonaparte promises to them ? "

" No, your majesty," said Count Stadion, " the Magyars are no children ; they are men who know full well what to think of Bonaparte's insidious flatteries, and will not permit him to mislead them by his deceptive promises. They received the Archduke John with genuine enthusiasm, and every day volunteers are flocking to his standards to fight against the des-

pot who, like a demon of terror, tramples the peace and prosperity of all Europe under his bloody feet. No, Bonaparte
can no longer count upon the sympathies of the nations; they
are all ready to rise against him, and in the end hatred will
accomplish that which love and reason were unable to bring
about. The hatred of the nations will crush Bonaparte and
hurl him from his throne."

"Provided the princes of the Rhenish Confederation do
not support him, or provided the Emperor Alexander of Russia does not catch him in his arms," said Francis, shrugging
his shoulders. "I have no great confidence in what you call
the nations ; they are really reckless and childish people. If
Bonaparte is lucky again, even the Germans will idolize him
before long ; but if he is unlucky, they will stone him. Just
look at my illustrious brother, the generalissimo. After the
defeats of Landshut and Ratisbon, and the humble letter which
he wrote to Bonaparte, you, Count Stadion, thought it would
be good for the Archduke Charles if we gave him a successor,
and if we removed him, tormented as he is by a painful disease, from the command-in-chief of the army. We, therefore, suggested to the archduke quietly to present his resignation, which would be promptly accepted. But the generalissimo would not hear of it, and thought he would have first to
make amends for the defeats which he had sustained at Landshut and Ratisbon. Now he has done so ; he has avenged his
former defeats and achieved a victory at Aspern ; and after
this brilliant victory he comes and offers his resignation, stat-
ing that his feeble health compels him to lay down the command and surrender it to some one else. But all at once my
minister of foreign affairs has changed his mind : the victory
of Aspern has converted him, and he thinks now that the generalissimo must remain at the head of the army. If so sagacious and eminent a man as Count Stadion allows success to
mould his opinion, am I not right in not believing that the
frivolous fellows whom you call 'the nations' have no well-
settled opinions at all ?"

"Pardon me, sire," said Count Stadion, smiling ; "your
majesty commits a slight error. Your majesty confounds
principles with opinions. An honorable man and an honor-

able nation may change their opinions, but never will they change their principles. Now the firmer and more immovable their principles are, the more easily they may come to change their opinions ; for they seek for instruments to carry out their principles ; they profit to-day by the services of a tool which seems to them sufficiently sharp to perform its task, and they cast it aside to-morrow because it has become blunt, and must be replaced by another. This is what happens to the nations and to myself at this juncture. The nations are bitterly opposed to France ; the whole German people, both north and south, is unanimous in its intense hatred against Napoleon. The nations do not allow him to deceive them; they see through the Cæsarean mask, and perceive the face of the tyrant, despot, and intriguer, lurking behind it. They do not believe a word of his pacific protestations and promises of freedom and liberal reforms ; for they see that he always means war when he prates about peace, that he means tyranny when he promises liberty, and that he gives Draconic laws instead of establishing liberal institutions. The nations hate Napoleon and abhor his despotic system. They seek for means to annihilate him and deliver at length the bloody and trembling world from him. If the princes were as unanimous in their hatred as the nations are, Germany would stand as one man, sword in hand; and this sublime and imposing spectacle would cause Napoleon to retreat with his host beyond the Rhine, the German Rhine, whose banks would be guarded by the united people of Germany."

"You speak like a Utopian, my dear count," said the emperor, with a shrug. "If the united people of Germany are alone able to defeat and expel Bonaparte, he will never be defeated and expelled, for Germany will never be united ; she will never stand up as one man, but always resemble a number of rats grown together by their tails, and striving to move in opposite directions. Let us speak no more of a united Germany ; it was the phantom that ruined my uncle, the Emperor Joseph, whom enthusiasts call the Great Joseph. But I do not want to be ruined, and therefore I do not want to hear any thing of a united Germany. Thank God, since 1806, I am no longer Emperor of Germany, but only Emperor of Austria, and that is enough for me. I do not care what the princes of the Confederation of the Rhine are doing, nor what intrigues Prussia is entering into in order to rise from its humiliating prostration; I fix my eyes only on Austria, and think only whether Austria will be able to cope with Bonaparte, or whether she may not ultimately fare as badly as Prussia did. We have unfortunately experienced already one Austerlitz; if we should suffer another defeat like it, we would be lost; hence we must be cautious, and I ask you, therefore, why you do not want me now to accept the resignation of the generalissimo, when, only a fortnight ago, you advocated his removal from the command-in-chief of the army?"

"Your majesty, because a fortnight ago he had been repeatedly defeated, and because he has now gained a brilliant victory. This shows your majesty again the difference between opinions and principles. Opinions change and are influenced by success. After the battle of Ratisbon, the generalissimo was looked upon with distrust and anxiety by his army, nay, by the whole people of Austria, who turned their eyes to the Archduke John, the victor of Sacile and St. Boniface, and wanted to see at the head of the army a victorious general, instead of the defeated Archduke Charles; but the latter has acted the hero, and been victorious at Aspern, and the love and confidence of the army and people are restored to him; all look upon him as the liberator of the fatherland, and will stand by him until—"

"Until he loses another battle," interrupted the emperor, sneeringly. "My dear count, one swallow does not make a summer, and— Well, what is it, Leonard?" said the emperor, turning quickly to his footman, who entered the room at this moment.

"Your majesty, his imperial highness the Archduke John has just arrived, and requests an audience."

"Let the archduke come in," said the emperor; and when the footman had withdrawn, Francis turned again to the minister. "He is the second swallow in which the childish people here are hoping," he said. "But two swallows do not make a summer either; there may still be a frost under which

John's young laurels of Sacile and St. Boniface will wither.—
Ah, here is my brother."

The emperor advanced a few steps to meet the Archduke
John, who had just crossed the threshold, and stood still at
the door to bow deeply and reverentially to his imperial
brother.

"No ceremonies, brother, no ceremonies," said the emperor, smiling ; "we are here not in the imperial palace, but
in the camp ; my crown is in Vienna, and my head is therefore bare, while yours is wreathed with laurels."

The emperor said this in so sarcastic a tone that the archduke gave a start, and his cheeks crimsoned with indignation.
But he restrained his anger, and fixed his eyes calmly on the
sneering face of the emperor.

"Your majesty condescends to jest," he said, composedly,
"and I am glad to see from this that my brother, the victor of
Aspern, has gladdened your majesty's heart."

"Your majesty," said Count Stadion, in a low, pressing
tone, "will you not graciously permit me to withdraw ?"

"Ah, you think your presence would be inconvenient during our interview, and might hinder the free exchange of our
confidential communications ? But I do not believe that I
and my brother have any special secrets to communicate to
each other, so that the presence of my minister would be inconvenient to us. However, let the archduke decide this
point. Tell me therefore, brother, is it necessary that you
should see me alone and without witnesses ?"

"On the contrary, your majesty," said John, calmly, "it
will be agreeable to me if the minister of foreign affairs is
present at our interview ; for, as your majesty deigned to observe, we never have confidential communications to make to
each other, and as we shall speak only of business affairs, the
minister may take part in the conversation."

"Stay, then, count. And now, my esteemed brother, may
I take the liberty of asking what induced the commanding-
general of my army of Upper Austria, now stationed at Comorn, to leave his post and pay me a friendly visit here at
Wolkersdorf ?"

"Your majesty, I come to implore my sovereign to gra-

ciously fulfil the promise which your majesty vouchsafed to
me at Vienna. Your majesty promised me that I should succor with the forces intrusted to me the Tyrolese in their heroic
struggle for deliverance from the foreign yoke, and that I
might devote all my efforts to aiding this noble and heroic
people, which has risen as one man in order to be incorporated
again with Austria. It was I who organized the insurrection
of the Tyrol, who appointed the leaders of the peasants, and
fixed the day and hour when the insurrection was to break
out."

"Yes, yes, it is true," interrupted the emperor; "you
proved that you were a skilful and shrewd revolutionist, and
it was really fortunate for me that you availed yourself of
your revolutionary talents, not *against* me, but *for* me. If I
shall ever recover full possession of the Tyrol, I shall be indebted for it only to the revolutionary skill of my brother
John; and I shall always look upon it as an act of great dis-
interestedness on your part to leave me the Tyrol, and not
keep it for yourself; for it is in your hands, and it is you
whom the Tyrolese in their hearts call their real emperor."

"Your majesty is distrustful of the love of the faithful Tyrolese," said John, mournfully, "and yet they have sealed it
with their blood since the insurrection broke out; it was always the name of their Emperor Francis with which they
went into battle, the name of the Emperor Francis with which
they exulted triumphantly when God and their intrepidity
made them victorious."

"No, archduke, I know better!" exclaimed the Emperor,
vehemently. "They did not confine themselves to rendering
homage to me, but when the peasants had taken Innspruck,
they placed the Archduke John's picture on the triumphal
arch by the side of my own portrait, surrounded it with
candles, and rendered the same homage to it as to that of the
emperor."

"It is true, the honest peasants know nothing of etiquette,"
said John, sadly. "They believed in their simplicity that
they might love a little their emperor's brother, who had been
sent to their assistance by his majesty, and that they might
place his picture without further ceremony by the side of that

of the emperor. But that they nevertheless knew very well
how to distinguish the emperor from the archduke, and that
they granted to the emperor the first place in their hearts, and
deemed him the sole object of their loyalty, is proved by the
song which the Tyrolese sang with enthusiastic unanimity on
fastening the Austrian eagle to the imperial palace at Innspruck. As such full particulars of the events in the Tyrol
were sent to your majesty, I am sure this beautiful song was
likewise communicated to you."

"No, it was not," said the emperor, carelessly. "What
song is it ?"

"Your majesty, it is a hymn of joy and triumph which, ever
since that day, is sung by all Tyrolese, not only by the men,
but also by the women and children, and which resounds
now as the spring-hymn of the new era both in the valleys
and on the summits of the mountains. I am sorry that I do
not know the words by hearts, but I shall have the honor of
sending them to your majesty. I remember only the refrain
of every verse, which is as follows :

> "'Ueberall lebt'st sch treu und bieder,
> Wo der Adler uns angeschaut,
> Und nu' haben wir unsern Franzel wieder,
> Weil wir halt auf Gott und ihn vertraut.'"*

"That is quite pretty," said the emperor, smiling. "And
is that the song they are singing now in the Tyrol ?"

"Your majesty, they not only sing it, but they believe in it
too. Yes, the Tyrolese confide in your majesty ; they believe
implicitly in the promises which your majesty has made to
them, and they would punish as a traitor any one who should
dare to tell them that these promises would not be fulfilled."

"And who asserts that they will not be fulfilled ?" asked
the emperor.

"Your majesty, the facts will unfortunately soon convince
the Tyrolese that they must not look for the fulfilment of these

---

* "Far reaching as the eagle's view,
  Are beating loyal hearts and true ;
  Once more our Francis can we claim,
  Because we trust in God's great name !"

promises," said the archduke, sighing. " At the very moment when the Tyrol is being threatened by two hostile armies, those of the Viceroy of Italy and the Duke of Dantzic, and when the Tyrol, therefore, if it is not to succumb again to such enormous odds, urgently needs assistance and succor, I receive orders to leave the Tyrol and march to Hungary. That is to say, I am to give up Salzburg, which is occupied by the French ; I am not to succor Innspruck, which is men-aced by Baraguay d'Hilliers. Not only am I not to lend any assistance to the Tyrolese, but I am to break their moral courage and paralyze their energy, by showing to them by my retreat that the emperor's promises will not be fulfilled, and that the army of Upper Austria abandons the Tyrol to succor Hungary."

" Well, the Tyrol is not yet abandoned, even though the Archduke John is no longer there," said the emperor, shrug-ging his shoulders. " We have two generals with corps there, have we not ? Are not the Marquis of Chasteler and Count Buol there ? "

" They are, your majesty ; but the Marquis of Chasteler is morally paralyzed by the sentence of outlawry which Napo-leon has issued against him, and Count Buol has too few troops to oppose the enemy's operations, which are not checked by any corps outside the Tyrol."

" Ah, you wish to give me another proof of the fraternal love reigning between you and the Archduke Charles ? " asked the emperor sarcastically. " You wish to oppose the orders of your generalissimo ? "

" I wish to ask the emperor, my sovereign, whether I am to give up the Tyrol or not ; I wish to ask him if he orders me to march my army to Presburg, unite with the insurgent forces, and operate there against the enemy."

" Are these the generalissimo's orders ? "

"They are, your majesty."

" And what else does he command ? "

" He commands me, further, to make myself master of the two islands of Schütt in front of Presburg, take Altenburg by a *coup de main*, and garrison, supply, and provision the two fortresses of Raab and Comorn for six months."

A sarcastic expression overspread the emperor's face. "Well, these are excellent and most energetic orders," he said. "Carry them out, therefore."

"But, your majesty, it is not in my power to do so. These orders look very fine on paper, but they cannot be carried into effect. I have neither troops nor supplies enough to garrison, supply, and provision Raab and Comorn, and hold Presburg, even after effecting a junction with the troops of the Archduke Palatine and the Hungarian volunteers. And the generalissimo is well aware of it, for I have always acquainted him with what occurred in my army; he knows that my forces and those of the Archduke Palatine together are scarcely twenty-five thousand strong, and that one-half of these troops consists of undisciplined recruits. He knows that the enemy is threatening us on all sides with forty thousand veteran troops. The generalissimo is so well aware of this, that he spoke of the weakness of the remnants of my army in the dispatches which he addressed to me only a few days ago. But the victory of Aspern seems suddenly to have made the generalissimo believe that, inasmuch as he himself has performed extraordinary things, he may demand of me what is impossible."

"What is impossible!" said the emperor, with mischievous joy. "So brave and heroic a soldier as you, archduke, will not deem impossible what his chief orders him to do. The Archduke Charles is your chief, and you have to obey him. He orders you to hold Raab and Presburg. Go, then, and carry out the orders of your commander-in-chief."

"As your majesty commands me to do so, I shall obey," said John, calmly; "only I call your majesty's attention to the fact that, if the enemy accelerates his operations and compels me soon to give battle, I shall be unable to hold Raab, for which so little has been done hitherto, and that I shall lose the battle unless the generalissimo sends a strong corps to my assistance."

"It is your business to come to an understanding with the generalissimo as to that point. He possesses my full confidence, for he showed excellent generalship at Aspern. There is no reason why I should distrust him."

"And God forbid that I should wish to render you distrustful of him!" exclaimed John, vehemently. "I hope my brother Charles will remain yet a long while at the head of the army, and give many successors to the victory of Aspern."

"But you doubt if he will, do you not?" asked the emperor, fixing his small light-blue eyes with a searching expression on John's face. "You do not rejoice much at the brilliant victory of Aspern? You do not think that Bonaparte is entirely crushed and will hasten to offer us peace?"

"Your majesty, you yourself do not believe it," said John, with a smile. "Napoleon is not the man to be deterred by a defeat from following up his plans ; he will pursue them only the more energetically, and he will attain his ends, though, perhaps, somewhat less rapidly, unless we adopt more decisive measures."

"Look, Stadion," exclaimed the emperor, smiling, "I am glad that the Archduke John agrees with me. He repeats only what I said to you about Bonaparte."

"But, your majesty, the archduke added something to it," said Count Stadion, quickly ; "he said Austria ought to adopt more decisive measures."

"Ah, and now you hope that the archduke will say to me what you have already said so often, and that he will make the same proposals in regard to more decisive measures as you did, minister?"

"Yes, I do hope it, your majesty."

"Well, let us see," exclaimed the emperor, with great vivacity. "Tell me, therefore, archduke, what more decisive measures you referred to."

"Your majesty," replied John, quickly, "I meant that we should strive to get rid of our isolated position, and look around for allies who will aid us not only with money, as England does, but also with troops."

"And what allies would be most desirable for Austria, according to your opinion, archduke?"

The archduke cast a rapid, searching glance on the face of the minister, who responded to it by a scarcely perceptible nod of his head.

" Your majesty," said Archduke John, quickly, " Prussia would be the most desirable ally for Austria."

The emperor started back, and then turned almost angrily to Stadion. " In truth," he said, " it is just as I thought ; the archduke repeats your own proposals. It seems, then, that the formerly so courageous war-party at my court suddenly droops its wings, and thinks no longer that we are able to cope single-handed with Bonaparte. Hence, its members have agreed to urge me to conclude an alliance with Prussia, and now come the besieging forces which are to overcome my repugnance. The minister himself was the first to break the subject to me ; now he calls the Archduke John to his assistance, and takes pains to be present at the very hour when the archduke arrives here to second his efforts in attacking me. Half an hour later, and the empress will make her appearance to assist you, and convince me that we ought to secure, above all things, the alliance of Prussia."

" Pardon me, your majesty," said Count Stadion, earnestly ; "I have, unfortunately, not the honor of being one of the archduke's confidants, and I pledge you my word of honor that I did not know at all that his royal highness was coming hither."

" And I pledge your majesty my word of honor that neither the empress nor Count Stadion ever intimated to me, directly or indirectly, that they share my views, and have advocated them already before your majesty."

" Then you have come quite independently, and of your own accord, to the conclusion that we ought to form an alliance with Prussia ? "

" Yes, your majesty ; I believe that this has now become a necessity for us."

" But Prussia is a humiliated and exhausted state, which exists only by Bonaparte's grace and the intercession of the Emperor of Russia."

" Your majesty speaks of Prussia as it was in 1807," said Count Stadion, "after the defeats of Jena, Eylau, and Friedland. But since then two years have elapsed, and Prussia has risen again from her prostration ; she has armed secretly, rendered her resources available, and found sagacious and energetic men, who are at work silently, but with unflagging zeal, upon the reorganization of the army, and preparing every thing for the day of vengeance."

"Let us ally ourselves with regenerated Prussia, which is longing for vengeance!" cried John, ardently; "let us unite with her in the struggle against our common foe. Prussia and Austria should be harmonious, and jointly protect Germany."

"No," said the emperor, almost angrily, "Prussia and Austria are natural enemies; they have been enemies ever since Prussia existed, for Prussia, instead of contenting herself with her inferior position, dared to be Austria's rival; and, moreover, Austria can never forgive her the rapacious conquest of Silesia."

"Oh, your majesty," exclaimed John, impetuously, "let us forget the past, and fix our eyes on the present and future! France is the common enemy of all Europe; all Europe ought to unite in subduing her, and we will not even solicit the co-operation of our neighbor! But an alliance between Austria and Prussia will render all Germany united, and Germany will then be, as it were, a threatening rock, and France will shrink from her impregnable bulwarks, and retire within her natural borders."

"Words, words!" said the emperor, shrugging his shoulders. "You enthusiasts always *talk* of a united Germany, but in reality it has never existed yet."

"But it will exist when Prussia and Austria are allied; only this alliance must be concluded soon, for we have no time to lose, and every delay is fraught with great danger. France is intent on establishing a universal monarchy; Napoleon does not conceal it any longer. If France really succeeds in keeping the German powers at variance and enmity, and uniting with Russia against them, our last hour will strike; for these two powers, if united, will easily come to an understanding as to the division of Europe; and even though Russia did not entertain such an intention, France would communicate it to her.* Hence, Russia should likewise be gained, and its alli-

* The archduke's own words.—See "Letters from the Archduke John to Johannes von Müller," p. 81.

ance, by Russia's intercession, be secured, so that Germany, in days of adversity, might count upon her."

"You believe then, archduke, that days of adversity are yet in store for us ?" asked the emperor.

"Your majesty, I am afraid they are, if we stand alone. All is at stake now, and all must be risked. We are no longer fighting for provinces, but for our future existence. We shall fight well ; but even the best strength is exhausted in the long run, and he who holds out longest remains victorious. Which side has better chances ? Austria, so long as she opposes France single-handed, has not ; but Austria and Prussia, if united, assuredly have. If Austria falls now, the best adversary of France falls, and with her falls Prussia, and Germany is lost."

"And what would you do, archduke, if Austria, as you say, were lost ?"

"Your majesty, if Austria should sink into ruin, I should know how to die ! "

"You would, like Brutus of old, throw yourself upon your sword, would you not ? Well, I hope we shall not fare so badly as that, for you have pointed out to me a way of saving the country. You have proved to me that Austria can be saved by an alliance with Prussia. Fortunately, I have sometimes ideas of my own, and even a head of my own: I had this morning a long interview with the Prince of Orange, who has just arrived from Königsberg, where he saw the King of Prussia. He laid before me a detailed report of what he had seen there, and I made up my mind before I had heard your advice.—Count Stadion, be so kind as to take the paper lying on the desk. Do you know the handwriting ? "

"I believe it is your majesty's handwriting," said Count Stadion, who, in accordance with the emperor's order, had taken the paper from the desk.

"Yes, it is my handwriting ; for, though not as learned as my brother John, I am at least able, if need be, to write a letter. Be so kind, minister, as to read my letter aloud."

Count Stadion bowed, and read as follows :

"To his majesty, King Frederick William of Prussia :

" HEADQUARTERS, WOLKERSDORF, *June 8, 1809.*

"SIR, MY BROTHER : The Prince of Orange, who has arrived at my headquarters here, has told me unreservedly, and with full confidence, of the repeated conversations he had with your majesty during his recent sojourn at Königsberg. You left no doubt in his mind as to your firm conviction that the existence of our two monarchies can be protected from the rapacious system of the Emperor Napoleon only by an active and cordial alliance. For a long time past, aware of the opinions and wisdom of your majesty, I could foresee that your majesty would not refuse to take a step, justified not less by the logic of events than the loyalty of the nations which Providence has confided to our care.

"The bearer, Colonel Baron Steigentesch, a distinguished staff-officer of my army, will confer with your majesty's government as to the questions which may arise in regard to an alliance between the two countries : he is authorized to regulate the proportions of the forces to be employed on both sides, and the other arrangements not less salutary than indispensable for the security of the two states. For the same reasons I shall speedily send instructions to my ambassador at Berlin in conformity with the overtures made by Count von der Goltz.

"Your majesty will permit me to assure you that I remain as ever,   Your most obedient,

"FRANCIS, Emperor of Austria." *

While Count Stadion was reading the letter, the emperor closely watched the effect it produced upon the archduke. He saw that John was at first surprised, that his eyes gradually brightened, that his face crimsoned with joy, and that a smile played round his lips.   •

When Count Stadion was through, the archduke stepped up to the emperor with an expression of profound emotion and intense gratitude.·

"Your Majesty," he cried, "you have filled me both with shame and ecstasy. Oh, give me your hand, let me press it **to**

* "Lebensbilder," vol. iii., p. 266.

my lips ; let me thank you for this gracious punishment ! I am grateful, too, for the gracious confidence with which you initiate me into your plans."

"That is unnecessary," said the emperor, without giving him his hand ; "you need not thank me. Nor was it my intention to give you a special proof of my confidence. I did not cause the letter to be read to you in order to have you participate in my plans, but only to prove to you that I can make up my mind without your advice, and to request you not to molest me henceforth with any such suggestions. Now, brother, we have nothing further to say to each other. Return to Comorn, and carry out the generalissimo's order, as behooves a good officer, promptly, carefully, and without grumbling. Fortify and hold Raab, defend Presburg, take Altenburg by a *coup de main;* in short, do all that the generalissimo wants you to do. If I should need your advice and wisdom, I shall send for you ; and when Baron Steigentesch returns from his mission to Prussia, you shall be informed of the results. Farewell, brother, and let me soon hear of new victories ! "

CHAPTER XXVI.

THE REPLY OF THE KING OF PRUSSIA.

Two weeks after this interview between the Archduke John and the emperor, the archduke, at the request of the emperor, repaired again to the imperial headquarters at Wolkersdorf, and sent in his name to his brother.

"You come just in time, brother," said the emperor, when John entered his cabinet. "I knew that Baron Steigentesch would arrive here to-day, hence I sent for you, for I promised to let you hear the reply of the King of Prussia to my proposal. The colonel did arrive a few minutes ago, and waits in the anteroom for an audience."

"Before admitting him, your majesty, pray listen to me," said John, in a grave, tremulous voice.

"I hope you do not intend to reveal a secret to me ?" asked the emperor.

"No, your majesty ; unfortunately that which I have to say to you will soon be known to everybody, and our enemies will take care to let their triumphant bulletins circulate the news throughout Europe."

"It is a defeat, then, that you have to announce to me ?" asked the emperor, gloomily.

"Yes, your majesty, a defeat. I met the enemy yesterday at Raab [June 14, 1809]. Our men fought bravely ; some performed the most heroic exploits ; but the odds of the enemy were too overwhelming. The Viceroy of Italy attacked us with his well-disciplined veteran troops, thirty-nine thousand strong. In the outset, we, that is, the Archduke Palatine and I, were about as strong, including the Hungarian volunteers. But the very first attack of the enemy, the first volleys of musketry, caused the volunteers to fall back ; they fled panic-struck, abandoned the hill where I had posted them, and rushed in wild disorder from the field of battle. The enemy then occupied the hill, and this decided the fate of the day against us, shortly after the commencement of the battle. However, we might have held out and gained a victory, if all had carried out my orders promptly and carefully, and if, as usually during this campaign, no obstacles had been placed in my way."

"Ah, archduke, to avoid charges being preferred against yourself, you intend to prefer charges against others !" exclaimed the emperor, shrugging his shoulders.

"Yes, your majesty ; I charge Ignatius Giulay, Ban of Croatia, with violation of my orders, disobedience, and intentional delays in making the movements I had prescribed. I had ordered the Ban in time to join me at Comorn on the 13th of June, and he had positively assured me, by letter and verbally, that he would promptly be on hand on the stated day. I counted upon his arrival, and made my dispositions accordingly. The generalissimo had instructed me to keep open my communications with the main army on the right bank of the Danube by way of Raab ; and I, therefore, started on the morning of the 13th from Comorn, firmly convinced that

Giulay's troops would join me in time and follow me. But I waited for him in vain ; he failed me at the critical moment, despite my orders and his promises, and this was the principal reason why we lost the battle." *

"You prefer a grave charge against a man whom I have always found to be faithful, brave, and honorable," said the emperor, with cutting coldness.

"Your majesty, I beg you to be so gracious as to call the Ban of Croatia to a strict account," exclaimed John, vehemently. "I beg you to be so gracious as to send for the orders which I gave him, and ask him why he did not obey them."

"I shall do so," replied the emperor, "and it is my conviction that he will be able to justify himself completely."

The Archduke John gave a start, a deathly pallor overspread his cheeks, his eyes shot fire, his lips opened to utter an impetuous word, but he restrained it forcibly ; compressing his lips, pale and panting, he hastily moved back a few steps and approached the door.

"Stay !" ordered the emperor, in a harsh voice. "I have yet some questions to put to you. You are responsible for this battle of Raab, and you owe me some explanations concerning it. How was the retreat effected ? Where are your forces now ?"

"The retreat was effected in good order," said John, in a low, tremulous voice. "I marched with four battalions of grenadiers and two battalions of Gratz militia slowly along the heights to Als, where we arrived at midnight ; and to-day we went back to Comorn. There our forces are now."

"And Raab ? Have the enemy taken it already ?"

"No, your majesty, it still holds out : but it will fall, as I told your majesty two weeks ago, for the generalissimo has sent me neither amunition nor re-enforcements, despite my most pressing requests."

"Is that to be another charge ?" asked the emperor, sternly.

"No," said John, mournfully ; "it is only to be my defence, for unfortunately it is always necessary for me to defend myself."

* See Schlosser's " History of the Eighteenth Century," vol. vii., p. 540.

"Ah, archduke, you always consider yourself the victim of
cabals," exclaimed the emperor ; "you believe yourself always persecuted and calumniated ; you suspect invariably
that you are slighted and placed in false positions by those
who are jealous of your exalted qualities, and envious of your
talents.   You think that your greatness excites apprehensions, and your genius and learning create misgivings, and
that you are therefore persecuted ; that intrigues are entered
upon against you, and that not sufficent elbow-room is given
to your abilities.   But you are mistaken, archduke. I am not
afraid of you, and although I admire you, and think, like
you, that you are the greatest captain of the age—"

"Your majesty," interrupted John, in a loud, vehement
voice, "your majesty, I—"

"Well, what is it ?" cried the emperor, hastily advancing
a few steps toward his brother, and staring at him with defiant eyes.   "What have you got to say to me ?"

"Nothing, your majesty," said John, in a hollow voice ;
"you are the emperor ! I am silent, and submit."

"And you are very prudent in doing so, for, as you say, I
am the emperor, and I will remain the emperor, despite all
my great and august brothers.   If your imperial highness
does not like this, if you think you are treated unjustly, if
you consider yourself a martyr, why do you not imitate what
the generalissimo has done already three times during the
present campaign—why do you not offer your resignation ?
Why do you not request your emperor to dismiss you from
his service ?"

"Will your majesty permit me to make a frank and honest reply to this question ?" asked John, looking at the emperor firmly and gravely.

"I will."

"Well, then, your majesty, I do not offer my resignation
because I am not an invalid ; because I am young, strong,
and able to work.   I request the emperor not to dismiss me
from the service, because I serve not only him, but the fatherland, and because I owe to it my services and strength. I
know well that many would like me to retire into privacy
and withdraw entirely from public affairs ; but I cannot fulfil

their wishes, and never shall I withdraw voluntarily from the service. No matter what wrongs and slights may be inflicted upon me, they will be fruitless, for they will never shake my purpose. All the disagreeable things that happen to me in my career, I think proceed from individuals, and not from the fatherland ; why should I, then, avenge myself on the fatherland by resigning and depriving it of my services when it has done me no wrong ?* I serve the fatherland in serving your majesty ; should I resign, I should be unfaithful to both my masters, and only then would your majesty have a right to despise me."

"Listen," said the emperor ; " the word fatherland is a dangerous and two-edged one, and I do not think much of it. The insurgents and revolutionists have it always in their mouths ; and when rising against their prince and refusing him obedience, they likewise say that they do so in the service of the fatherland, and devote their strength and fidelity to it. The soldier, above all, has nothing to do with the fatherland, but only with his sovereign ; it is to him alone that he has sworn allegiance, and to him alone he must remain faithful. Now, as you are a soldier and wish to remain in the service, pray bear in mind that you have sworn allegiance to your emperor, and let me hear no longer any of your subtle distinctions between your emperor and your fatherland. And now that you have reported to me the result of the disastrous battle of Raab, Baron Steigentesch may come in and report the results of his mission to Königsberg. Stay, therefore, and listen to him."

The emperor rang the bell, and ordered the footman who entered the room to admit immediately Minister Count Stadion and Colonel Baron Steigentesch. A few minutes later the two gentlemen entered the cabinet.

" Now, colonel," said the emperor to him, " you are to report the results of your mission to Königsberg, and I confess I am quite anxious to hear them. But before you commence, I wish to say a few words to your minister of foreign affairs. On the same day that I dispatched Colonel Steigentesch to

* The archduke's own words.—See his " Letters to Johannes von Müller," p. 92.

Königsberg, I handed you a sealed paper and ordered you to preserve it till my ambassador's return. Have you done so?"

"I have, your majesty."

"And have you brought it with you now?"

"Here it is, your majesty," said Count Stadion, drawing a sealed envelope from his bosom, and presenting it to the emperor, with a low bow. Francis took it, and examined the seal with close attention, then held it to his nose and smelled it.

"Indeed," he exclaimed joyfully, "it has retained its perfume, and is as fresh and brilliant as though it had been put on only at the present moment. And what a beautiful crimson it is! I have, then, at length, found the right receipt for good sealing-wax, and this, which I made myself, may vie with that made at the best Spanish factories. Oh, I see, this sealing-wax will drive my black cabinet to despair, for it will be impossible to open a letter sealed with it; even the finest knife will be unable to do it. Do you not think so too, minister?"

"I am no judge of sealing-wax," said Count Stadion, coldly, "and I confess that I did not even look at the seal of this envelope; your majesty ordered me to keep it and return it to you after Baron Steigentesch's return. I complied with your majesty's orders, that is all."

The emperor smiled, and laid the sealed paper with a slight nod on the table by his side; then he sank into an easy-chair, and beckoned to the gentlemen to take seats on the chairs on the other side of the table.

"Now, Colonel Steigentesch, let me hear the results of your mission. In the first place, tell me, has King Frederick William sent no letter to me in reply to mine?"

"No, your majesty," replied Colonel Steigentesch, with a significant smile; "I am only the bearer of a verbal reply. I believe the king thought a written answer too dangerous, or he was afraid lest he should thereby compromise himself. But after every interview I had with the king or the queen, I noted down every word their majesties spoke to me; and if your majesty permits, I shall avail myself of my diary in replying to you."

"Do so," said Francis, "let us hear what you noted down in your diary."

Colonel Steigentesch drew a memorandum-book from his bosom and opened it.

"Well, then, how did the king receive you?" inquired Francis, after a pause.

"The king received me rather coldly and stiffly," read Colonel Steigentesch from his diary; "he asked me what was the object of my mission. I replied that my emperor's letter stated this in a sufficiently lucid manner. The king was silent for a while; then he said rather morosely: 'The emperor asks for succor now; but hereafter he will, perhaps, conclude a separate peace and sacrifice me.' I replied, 'The Emperor Francis, my august master, does not ask for succor. The battle of Aspern has proved that means of defence are not wanting to Austria. But as it is the avowed object of this war that the powers should recover their former possessions, it is but just and equitable that they should take an active part in the contest, whose only object can be attained by seizing the favorable moment. I have not been sent to you to argue a question which should be settled already, but to make the arrangements necessary for carrying it into effect.'"

"An expedient reply," exclaimed the emperor, nodding his head eagerly. "And what did the King of Prussia answer to you?"

"The king was silent a while, and paced his room repeatedly, his hands clasped on his back. Then he stood still in front of me, and said in a loud, firm voice: 'Despite the fear which I might have of being deserted by Austria, I am determined to ally myself *one day* with your court; but it is not yet time. Continue the war; in the mean time I will gradually strengthen my forces; only then shall I be able to take a usefu. part in the contest. I lack powder, muskets, and money   my artillerists are all young and inexperienced soldiers. It is painful to me to avow the whole wretchedness of my position to an Austrian officer; but I must do so to prove to your master what it is that keeps me back at this juncture. You will easily convince yourself that I am striving to be useful to you by all means. Your sick soldiers are nursed at my hospitals and sent to their homes ; I give leave of absence to all my officers who wish to serve in your army. But to ask me to declare now in your favor, is to call upon me to sign my own ruin. Deal the enemy another blow, and I will send an officer out of uniform to your emperor's headquarters to make all necessary arrangements.' * After these words the king bowed to me and dismissed me."

"Ah, indeed, the King of Prussia gives very wise advice," exclaimed the emperor ; "we are to deal Bonaparte another blow, and then Prussia will negotiate with us. After we have gained another victory, the cautious King of Prussia will enter into secret negotiations with me, and send to my headquarters an officer, but, do you hear, out of uniform, in order not to compromise himself. Did you not wear your uniform, then, colonel ?"

"Pardon me, your majesty, I did. But this seemed to be disagreeable to the king, and he asked me to doff my uniform at Königsberg ; but I replied, that I was, since the battle of Aspern, so proud of my uniform that I could not doff it. † The king thereupon requested me to state publicly that I had come to Prussia only for the purpose of asking of the king permission to buy corn in Silesia and horses in Prussia."

"And you complied with this request, colonel !"

"I did not, your majesty. I replied that I could not even state this, for it was repugnant to my sense of honor ; however, I would not contradict such a rumor if it were circulated."

"Very well, colonel," said the emperor, smiling ; "you have acted in a manner worthy of a true Austrian. And now tell me, did you see the queen also ?"

"I did, your majesty. Her majesty sent for me on the day of my arrival. The queen looked pale and feeble, but she seemed to take pains to conceal her sufferings under a smile which illuminated her face like a sunbeam."

"See, see," exclaimed the emperor, sarcastically ; "our colo-

* The king's own words.—See " Lebensbilder," vol. iii., p. 262.
† Ibid.

nel talks in the enthusiastic strain of a poet now that he re-
fers to the queen. Is she so very beautiful, then ?"

"Your majesty, she is more than beautiful ; she is at the
same time a noble, high-spirited woman, and an august
queen. Her misfortunes and humiliations have not bent her
neck, but this noble lady seems even more august and majestic in the days of adversity than in those of splendor and
prosperity."

"And what did the queen say to you ? Was she of her
husband's opinion that Austria should not be succored at
this juncture, and that Prussia, before declaring in our favor,
ought to wait and see if Austria can defeat France single-
handed ?"

"Your majesty, the queen was more unreserved and frank
in her utterances than the king. She openly avowed her
hatred against Napoleon, and it is her opinion that Prussia
should take a decided stand against France. 'For,' she said,
'I am convinced that the hatred of the French emperor
against Austria, and his intention to overthrow all dynasties,
leave no hope of peace. I am the mother of nine children, to
whom I am anxious to preserve their inheritance ; you may,
therefore, judge of the wishes which I entertain.'"*

"If such were the queen's sentiments, I suppose she profited
by the great influence which she is said to have over her husband, to prevail upon him to take a bold stand, and you bring
me the news of it as the final result of your mission, do you
not ?"

"Pardon me, your majesty, I do not. It seems the influence of the queen does not go far enough to induce the king
to change his mind after he has once made it up. Now, the
king has resolved not to ally himself with Austria at this
juncture, but to wait until Austria, as he says, 'has dealt the
Emperor of the French another blow.' All my interviews
with the king were, as it were, only variations of this theme.
In the last interview which I had with the king, he did not
express any thing but what he had already told me in the
first. He repeated that he would, as soon as Austria had
dealt France another decisive blow, send an officer out of uni-

* The queen's own words.—See "Lebensbilder," vol. iii., p. 260.

form to the headquarters of your majesty ; but then, he
added, 'I hope to come myself, and not alone. ' When I took
leave of the queen, she was even sadder than usual, and her
voice was tremulous, and her eyes filled with tears, when she
said to me she hoped to meet me soon again under more favorable circumstances."

"And what did the other persons at the Prussian court
say ? How did the princes, the generals, and ministers express themselves ? "

"Prince William, the king's brother, said to me with a
shrug : 'You will not find the spirit reigning here much to
your taste. The king's irresolution will ruin him again.'
The princess, his wife, apologized for not inviting me to dinner, the king having positively forbidden her to do so. The
king's generals and ministers unreservedly gave vent to their
impatience and indignation. Grand-chancellor von Beyme
said to me : 'The king would like to unite with you, but he
cannot make up his mind to do so. However, as everybody
about him is earnestly in favor of an alliance with Austria, I
hope that the king will be carried away.'* General Blücher
wrote to the king in his impetuous, frank manner, that ' he
would not witness the downfall of the throne, and would prefer serving in a foreign army, provided it were at war with
the French.' Scharnhorst, the minister of war, spoke as violently, and with as undisguised hostility against France.
He presented to the king a memoir, in which he said : 'I will
not go dishonored into my grave ; I should be dishonored did
I not advise the king to profit by the present moment, and declare war against France. Can your majesty wish that Austria
should return your states to you as alms, if she were still generous enough to do so ; or that Napoleon, if victorious, should
disarm your soldiers like the militia of a free city ? ' But all
these remonstrances, these supplications, nay, even the tears
of the queen, were in vain. The king repeated that he would
unite with Austria one day, but it was not yet time. Austria
ought first to deal France another blow, and gain a decisive
victory ; then would have come for Prussia the moment to
declare openly against France. This, your majesty, is the

* "Lebensbilder," vol. iii., p. 262.

only reply which I bring with me from my mission to
Prussia."

"Well, I must confess that this reply is decidedly cautious
and wise !" exclaimed the emperor, laughing. "After we
have drawn the chestnuts out of the fire, Prussia will be kind
enough to sit down with Austria and help her to eat them.
Well, what do you think of it, brother John ?"

"I think that this hesitating policy of Prussia is a misfortune not only for Austria and Prussia, but for Germany. For
if France and Russia join hands now against our disunited
country, Germany will be lost. The welfare of Europe is now
inseparably bound up with an alliance between Austria and
Prussia, which can alone prevent the outbreak of a European
war. But this alliance must be concluded openly, unreservedly, and with mutual confidence. No private interests,
no secondary interests calculated to frustrate the enterprise,
but the great ends of saving the states, and restoring peace
and prosperity to humanity, should be kept constantly in
view ; then, and then only, success will crown the great undertaking."*

"And Prussia seems little inclined to keep such ends in
view," said the emperor. "Well, minister, you do not say a
word. You were so eloquent in trying to gain me over to this
alliance with Prussia ; you assured me so often that Prussia
was waiting only for me to call upon her, when she would ally
herself with me ; and now—"

"Now, your majesty," said Count Stadion, mournfully, "I
see, to my profound sorrow, that Prussia prefers her separate
interests, to the interests of Germany ; and I confess that I
was mistaken in Prussia."

"And you tried to convince me that I was wrong in enter-
taining a different opinion ; and my esteemed brother yonder
spoke so wisely and loftily of our Prussian brethren, and the
united Germany which we would form together ! Well, you
shall see at least that, although I yielded, and, to get rid of all
you wise men, applied to Prussia, I did not believe in the success of the mission. Minister, be kind enough now to take

* The archduke's own words.—See his " Letters to Johannes von Müller,"
p. 91.

the letter which you have kept for me so long. There! Now break the nice seal, open the letter, and read to us what I wrote on the day when I dispatched Colonel Steigentesch to the King of Prussia. Read!"

Stadion unfolded the letter and read :

"Colonel Steigentesch will return from his mission without accomplishing any thing. Prussia and Austria are rivals in Germany, and will never join hands in a common undertaking. Austria can never forgive Prussia for taking Silesia from her, and Prussia will always secretly suspect that Austria is intent upon weakening her rising power and humbling her ambition. Hence, Prussia will hesitate and temporize even at this juncture, although it is all-important now for Germany to take a bold stand against her common enemy, rapacious and insatiable France ; she will hesitate because she secretly wishes that Austria should be humiliated ; and she will not bear in mind that the weakening of Austria is fraught with danger for Prussia, nay, the whole of Germany."

"Now, gentlemen," said the emperor, when Count Stadion was through, "you see that my opinion was right, and that I well knew what I had to expect from Prussia. We must now carry on the struggle against France single-handed; but, after dealing her another blow, for which the King of Prussia longs, we shall take good care not to invite Prussia to our victorious repast. It would be just in us even to compel her to give us the sweet morsel of Silesia for our dessert. Well, we shall see what time will bring about. Our first blow against France was successful.—Archduke, go and help us to succeed in dealing her another ; and, after defeating France single-handed, we shall also be masters of Germany."

CHAPTER XXVII.

THE BATTLE OF WAGRAM.

"AT length!" exclaimed the Archduke John, joyously, holding up the letter which a courier of the generalissimo had just brought him from the headquarters of Wagram. "At length a decisive blow is to be struck.—Count Nugent, General Frimont, come in here! A courier from the generalissimo!"

So saying, the archduke had opened the door of his cabinet, and called the gentlemen who were in the anteroom.

"A courier from the generalissimo," he repeated once more, when the two generals came in.

"Your highness's wish is fulfilled now, is it not?" asked Nugent. "The generalissimo accepts the assistance which you offered to him. He permits you to leave this position with your troops and those of the Archduke Palatine and reenforce his own army?"

"No, he does not reply to my offer. It seems the generalissimo thinks that he does not need us to beat the French. But he writes to me that he is about to advance with his whole army, and that a decisive battle may be looked for. He says the enemy is still on the island of Lobau, busily engaged in erecting a *tête-de-pont*, and building a bridge across the Danube."

"And our troops do not try to prevent this by all means!" cried General Frimont, vehemently. "They allow the enemy to build bridges? They look on quietly while the enemy is preparing to leave the island, and do not prevent him from so doing?"

"My friend," said the archduke, gently, "let us never forget that it does not behoove us to criticise the actions of the generalissimo, and that our sole duty is to obey. Do as I do; let us be silent and submit. But let us rejoice that something will be done at length. Just bear in mind how long this inactivity and suspense have lasted already. The battle of Aspern was fought on the 22d of May, to-day is the 3d of July; and in the mean time nothing has been done. The enemy remained quietly on the island of Lobau, nursing his wounded, reorganizing his troops, erecting *têtes-de-pont*, and building bridges; and the generalissimo stood with his whole army on the bank of the Danube, and took great pains to watch in idleness the busy enemy. Let us thank God, therefore, that at last the enemy is tired of this situation, that he at length takes the initiative again, and brings about a decision.

The generalissimo informs me that the enemy's artillery dislodged our outposts yesterday, and that some French infantry crossed over to the Mühlau. The generalissimo, as I told you before, advanced with his troops, and hopes for a decisive battle within a few days."

" And yet the generalissimo does not accept the assistance which your imperial highness offered to him ?" asked Count Nugent, shaking his head.

" No, he does not. The generalissimo orders me, on the contrary, to stay here at Presburg and operate in such a manner against the corps stationed here, that it may not be able to join Napoleon's main army. Well, then, gentlemen, let us comply with this order, and perform at least our humble part of the generalissimo's grand plan. Let us help him to gain a victory, for the victory will be useful to the fatherland. We will, therefore, form a pontoon-bridge to-day, and make a sortie from the *tête-de-pont*. You, General Frimont, will order up the batteries from Comorn. You, General Nugent, will inform the Archduke Palatine of the generalissimo's orders. Write him also that it is positive that the enemy is moving all his troops to Vienna, and that all his columns are already on the march thither. Tell him that it is all-important for us to detain him, and that I, therefore, have resolved to make a sortie from the *tête-de-pont*, and request the Archduke Palatine to co-operate with me on the right bank of the Danube. Let us go to work, gentlemen, to work ! We have no time to lose. The order is to keep the enemy here by all means ; let us strive to do it ! "

And they went to work with joyous zeal and untiring energy ; all necessary dispositions were made for forming a pontoon-bridge, and preventing the enemy from joining Napoleon's main army. The Archduke John superintended every thing in person ; he was present wherever difficulties were to be surmounted, or obstacles to be removed. In his ardent zeal, he did not hesitate to take part in the toils of his men, and the soldiers cheered enthusiastically on seeing him work so hard in the midst of their ranks.

Early in the morning of the 5th of July the bridge was completed, the *tête-de-pont* was fully armed, and every thing was in readiness for the sortie. The Archduke, who had not slept all the night long, was just returning from an inspection of the preparations, when a courier galloped up to him in the middle of the bridge. On beholding the archduke, he jumped from his horse, and handed him, panting and in trembling haste, a letter from the generalissimo.

"You have ridden very rapidly? You were instructed then to make great haste?" asked John.

"I rode hither from Wagram in ten hours, your imperial highness," said the courier, breathlessly; "I was instructed to ride as rapidly as possible."

"You have done your duty faithfully. Go and rest."

He nodded kindly to the courier, and repaired to his head-quarters to read the letter he had just received from his brother.

This letter revoked all orders which had been sent to him up to this time. The archduke had vainly offered his co-operation and that of the Archduke Palatine four days ago. At that time not even a reply had been made to his offer; now, at the last moment, the generalissimo called impetuously upon his brother to hasten to his assistance. He demanded that the Archduke John should set out at once, leave only troops enough to hold the *tête-de-pont*, and hasten up with the remainder of his forces to the scene of action.

When the archduke read this order, a bitter smile played round his lips. "See," he said, mournfully, to General Frimont, "now I am needed all at once, and it seems as if the battle cannot be gained without us. It is all-important for us to arrive in time at the point to which we are called so late, perhaps too late. Ah, what is that? What do you bring to me, Nugent?"

"Another courier from the generalissimo has arrived; he brought this letter."

"You see, much deference is paid to us all of a sudden; we are treated as highly important assistants," sighed the arch-duke. He then unfolded the paper quickly and read it.

"The generalissimo," he said, "informs me now that he has changed his plan, and will not give battle on the bank of the Danube, but take position in the rear of Wagram. He instructs me to make a forced march to Marchegg, advance, after resting there for three hours, to Siebenbrunn, and take position there. Very well, gentlemen, let us carry the generalissimo's orders into effect. At one o'clock to-night, all must be in readiness for setting out. We need the time between now and then to concentrate the extended lines of our troops. If we are ready at an earlier hour, we shall set out at once. Make haste! Let that be the password to-night!"

Thanks to this password, all the troops had been concentrated by midnight, and the march was just about to begin when another courier arrived from the generalissimo, and informed the archduke that the enemy was advancing, and that it was now the generalissimo's intention to attack him and force him to give battle. The Archduke John was ordered to march as rapidly as possible to Siebenbrunn, whither a strong corps of the enemy had set out.

The Archduke John now advanced with his ten thousand men with the utmost rapidity toward Marchegg. The troops were exhausted by the toils and fatigues of the last days; they had not eaten any thing for twenty-four hours; but the archduke and his generals and staff-officers always knew how to stir them up and induce them to continue their march with unflagging energy. Thus they at length reached Marchegg, where they were to rest for three hours.

But no sooner had they arrived there than Count Reuss, the generalissimo's aide-de-camp, galloped up on a charger covered all over with foam. The count had ridden in seven hours from Wagram to Marchegg, for it was all-important that the archduke should accelerate his march. The battle was raging already with great fury. The generalissimo was in urgent need of the archduke's assistance. Hence, the latter was not to rest with his troops at Marchegg, but continue his march and advance with the utmost speed by Siebenbrunn to Loibersdorf. At Siebenbrunn he would find Field-Marshal Rosenberg; he should then, jointly with him, attack the enemy.

"Let us set out, then, for Loibersdorf," said John, sighing; "we will do all we can, and thus avoid being charged with tardiness. Up, up, my braves ! The fatherland calls us ; we must obey it ! "

But the soldiers obeyed this order only with low murmurs, and many remained at Marchegg, exhausted to death.

The troops continued their march with restless speed, and mute resignation. The archduke's face was pale, his flashing eyes were constantly prying into the distance, his breast was panting, his heart was filled with indescribable anxiety, and he exhorted his troops incessantly to accelerate their steps. Now they heard the dull roar of artillery at a distance ; and the farther they advanced, the louder and more terrific resounded the cannon. The battle, therefore, was going on, and the utmost rapidity was necessary on their part. Forward, therefore, forward ! At five o'clock in the afternoon they at last reached Siebenbrunn. But where was Field-Marshal Rosenberg ? What did it mean that the roar of artillery had almost entirely died away ? And what dreadful signs surrounded the horizon on all sides ? Tremendous clouds of smoke, burning villages everywhere, and added to them now the stillness of death, which was even more horrible after the booming of artillery which had shaken the earth up to this time. Where was Field-Marshal Rosenberg ?

An officer galloped up at full speed. It was a messenger from Field-Marshal Rosenberg, who informed the archduke that he had been repulsed, that all was over, and that the day was irretrievably lost.

"I have been ordered to march to Loibersdorf," said the archduke, resolutely ; "I must comply with my instructions."

And he continued his march toward Loibersdorf. Patrols were sent out and approached Wagram. The fields were covered with the dead and wounded, and the latter stated amid moans and lamentations that a dreadful battle had been fought, and that the Austrians had been defeated.

The archduke listened to these reports with a pale face and quivering lips. But he was still in hopes that he would receive a message from the generalissimo ; hence, he remained at Loibersdorf and waited for news from his brother. Night came ; profound stillness reigned all around, broken only now and then by dull reports of cannon and musketry fired at a distance ; and there was no news yet from the generalissimo !

One of the patrols now brought in a French officer who had got separated from his men, and whom the Austrians had taken prisoner. The archduke sent for him, and asked him for information regarding the important events of the day.

The officer gave him the required information with sparkling eyes and in a jubilant voice. A great battle had been fought during the previous two days. The French army had left the Island of Lobau on four bridges, which Napoleon had caused to be built in a single night by two hundred carpenters, and had given battle to the Archduke Charles at Wagram. A furious combat had raged on the 5th and 6th of July. Both armies had fought with equal boldness, bravery, and exasperation ; but finally the Archduke Charles had been compelled to evacuate the field of battle and retreat. The Emperor Napoleon had remained in possession of the field ; he had gained the battle of Wagram.

Large drops of sweat stood on the archduke's forehead while he was listening to this report ; his eyes filled with tears of indignation and anger ; his lips quivered, and he lifted his eyes reproachfully to heaven. Then he turned slowly to General Frimont, who was halting by his side, and behind whom were to be seen the gloomy, mournful faces of the other officers.

"The generalissimo has lost a battle," he said, with a sigh. "This is a twofold calamity for us. You know that we could not come sooner. We arrived even at an earlier hour than I had promised. You will see that the whole blame for the loss of the battle will be laid at our door, and we shall be charged with undue tardiness. This pretended tardiness will be welcome to many a one. A scapegoat is needed, and I shall have to be this scapegoat !" *

The Archduke John was not mistaken ; he had predicted his fate. He was really to be the scapegoat for the loss of the battle. In the proclamation which the Archduke Charles issued to his army a few days afterward at Znaym, and in

* The archduke's own words.—See Hormayr's work on " The Campaign of 1809," p. 236.

which he informed it that he had concluded an armistice with the Emperor Napoleon, he deplored that, owing to the too late arrival of the Archduke John, the battle had not been won, despite the admirable bravery which the troops had displayed at Wagram, and that the generalissimo had been compelled thereby to retreat.

The Archduke John did not defend himself. He lifted his tearful eyes to heaven and sighed : "Another battle lost, and this battle decides the fate of Austria ! Now Prussia will not ally herself with us, for we did not strike the second blow which the king demanded, and she will look on quietly while Austria is being humiliated ! O God, God, protect Austria ! Protect Germany ! save us from utter ruin !"

CHAPTER XXVIII.

THE ARMISTICE OF ZNAYM.

THE guests of Anthony Steeger, the innkeeper of Lienz, had been greatly excited to-day; they had talked, debated, lamented, and sworn a great deal. In accordance with the request of Andreas Hofer, the most influential leaders of the Tyrolese had met there and drawn up, as Hofer proposed, a petition to the Emperor Francis, who was now in Hungary at one of the palaces belonging to the Prince of Lichtenstein. The disastrous tidings of the battle of Wagram had been followed a few days afterward by news fully as disheartening. The Archduke Charles had concluded an armistice with the Emperor Napoleon at Znaym, on the 12th of July, 1809. By this armistice hostilities were to be suspended till the 20th of August ; but in the mean time the Austrians were to evacuate the Tyrol, Styria, and Carinthia entirely, and restore to the Bavarians and French the fortified cities which they had occupied.

These calamitous terms of the armistice had induced Andreas Hofer to summon some of his friends to Lienz, and draw up with them a petition to the emperor, in which they implored him with touching humility to have mercy upon them in their distress, and not to forsake his faithful Tyrol. They

stated that they had been told that the Austrian troops, in
accordance with the stipulations of the armistice, were to
evacute the Tyrol, but this did not confer upon the French
and Bavarians the right of occupying the Tyrol. They besought the emperor to prevent this, and not to permit the
enemy to occupy the country.

Such were the contents of the petition which Andreas
Hofer and the other leaders of the Tyrolese had signed to-day
at the inn of Anthony Steeger, at Lienz, and which Jacob
Sieberer was to convey as the last cry of the despairing Tyrol
to the headquarters of the emperor at Totis, while Eisenstecken was to deliver a copy of the petition to General Buol,
commander-in-chief of the Austrian troops.

Night had now come ; the friends and comrades had long
since left Anthony Steeger's house, and Andreas Hofer alone
remained with him to talk with his faithful friend about the
disastrous change in their affairs, and the gloomy prospects of
the future.

"I cannot believe that all is as they say," said Andreas
Hofer, with a sigh. "The emperor promised us solemnly
never to give up or forsake again his faithful Tyrol, and it
would be high-treason to suppose that the emperor will not
honestly redeem his pledges. No, no ; I tell you, Anthony,
the emperor and our dear Archduke John certainly do not
intend to abandon us ; only the Austrian generals are opposed to the continuance of the war, and long to get away
from our mountains, because they are afraid of Bonaparte,
and think he would punish them if they should stay here any
longer and refuse to deliver the province to his tender mercies."

"I am likewise loth to believe that the Emperor Francis
would forsake us," said Anthony Steeger, nodding his head
approvingly. "For the emperor loves us, and will not allow
us to fall into the hands of the infidel Bonaparte, who has
just committed another outrage by arresting the Holy Father
in Rome and dragging him away from his capital."

"Well, the Holy Father excommunicated him for this
outrage," cried Andreas Hofer, with flashing eyes; "he called
down the wrath of God and man on the head of the Anti-

christ, and rendered it incumbent on every pious Christian to
wage war against the criminal who laid his ruthless hands even
upon the holy Church, and trampled under foot him whom the
Almighty has anointed. Anthony Steeger, let me tell you, I
will not allow the French to return to our country, and never
will I permit the Austrians to evacuate the Tyrol."

"And how will you prevent them from so doing ? " asked
Anthony Steeger, shrugging his shoulders.

" I said to-day how I and all of us are going to prevent it.
We shall not suffer the Austrians to depart ; we shall keep
them here by prayers, stratagems, or force. I have given instructions to all the commanders to do so ; I have given
them written orders which they are to communicate to our
other friends, and in which I command them not to permit
the departure of the Austrians. I believe I am commander-
in-chief as yet, and they will obey my bidding."

" If they can do it, Andy, they certainly will ; but what if
they cannot ? What if the Austrians cannot be kept here by
prayers or stratagem ? "

" In that case we must resort to force," cried Hofer, im-
petuously. " We must compel them to stay here ; the whole
Tyrol must rise as one man and with its strong arms keep the
Austrians in the country. Yes, yes, Anthony, we must do it ;
it will be best for us all. It must look as though we detain the Austrians by force, and this will be most agreeable
to the Emperor Francis ; for what fault of his is it that the
Tyrolese prevent him from carrying out what he promised to
Bonaparte in the armistice ? It is not his fault, then, if the
Austrians stay here, and if we prevent them from leaving our
mountains. We must detain them, we must. And I will
write immediately to old Red-beard, Father Haspinger, Joseph Speckbacher, and Anthony Wallner. I will summon
them to a conference with me, and we will concert measures
for a renewed rising of the Tyrol. Give me pen and ink,
Tony; I will write in the first place to old Red-beard, and
your Joe shall take the letter this very night to his convent."

Anthony Steeger hastened to bring him what he wanted,
and while Hofer scrawled the letter, his friend stood behind

him, and followed with attentive eyes every word which Andreas finished with considerable difficulty.

Both were so much absorbed in the letter that they did not perceive that the door opened behind them, and that Baron von Hormayr, in a dusty travelling-dress, entered the room. For a moment he stood still at the door and cast a searching glance on the two men ; he then advanced quickly toward Andreas Hofer, and, laying his hand on his shoulder, he said : " Well, Andy, what are you writing there ? "

Andreas looked up, but the unexpected arrival of the baron did not seem to excite his surprise. " I am writing to old Red-beard," he said ; " I am writing to him that he is to come to me immediately. And after finishing the letter to old Red-beard, I will write the same thing to Speckbacher and Anthony Wallner, Mr. Intendant of the Tyrol."

" Do not apply that title to me any longer, Andy," said Hormayr, with a slight frown. " I am no longer intendant of the Tyrol, for you know that we must leave the Tyrol and restore it to the French and Bavarians."

" I for one do not know it, Mr. Intendant of the Tyrol," cried Andreas, with an angry glance. " I know only that the Archduke John appointed you military intendant of the Tyrol, and that you took a solemn oath to aid us in becoming once more, and remaining, Austrians."

" I think, Andy, I have honestly redeemed my pledges," said Hormayr. " I assisted you everywhere to the best of my power, was always in your midst, encouraging, organizing, fighting, and mediating ; and I think you will admit that I had likewise my little share in the deliverance of the Tyrol, and proved myself one of its good and faithful sons."

" Well, yes, it is true," murmured Hofer ; " you did a great deal of good, and, above all things, you gained over to our side the Austrian generals, who would not have anything to do with us peasants, and refused to make common cause with us ; for you possess a very eloquent tongue, and what can be accomplished by means of the tongue you do accomplish. But now, sir, the tongue will no longer suffice, and we must fight also with the sword."

" God forbid, Andy ! " exclaimed Hormayr ; " you know

that the emperor has concluded an armistice with Bonaparte, and while it lasts we are not allowed to fight with the
sword."

"The emperor has concluded an armistice ? Well, then,
let there be an armistice. But you will not confine yourself
to an armistice—you intend to evacuate the Tyrol. That
seems to me no fair armistice, and therefore I shall summon
old Red-beard, and my other faithful friends, and concert
with them measures to prevent you from concluding such an
unfair armistice, and forsaking us."

"And Andy is right in doing so !" exclaimed Anthony
Steeger. "We must not permit the Austrians to leave the
province, and we are firmly resolved that we will not."

"You are fools, both of you," said Hormayr, shrugging his
shoulders. "The Emperor Francis agreed positively that the
Austrian troops should evacuate the Tyrol during the armistice ; hence, the troops must leave, lest the emperor should
break his word."

"But if they do, the emperor breaks the word he pledged
to us," cried Anthony Steeger, vehemently.

"Anthony Steeger," said Hormayr, sternly, "I have come
hither to have an interview with Andreas Hofer, to whom I
wish to communicate something of great importance. Therefore, be so kind as to withdraw, and leave me alone with
him."

"I believe Andy does not want to keep any thing secret
from me, and I might, therefore, just as well stay here. Say,
Andy, is it not so ? "

"It is. Speak, Mr. Intendant ; Tony may hear it all."

"No, Andy, I shall not speak unless I am alone with you ;
and what I have to say to you is highly important to the
Tyrol. But no one but yourself must hear it."

"If that is the case. go out and leave me alone with the intendant," said Hofer, shaking hands with his friend.

Anthony Steeger cast an angry glance on Hormayr, and
left the room. "I know very well why he wanted to get rid
of me," he growled, as soon as he was out in the hall. "He
intends to persuade Andreas Hofer to leave with the Austrians
and abandon the Tyrol. He thinks when he is alone with

Hofer, he will yield sooner because he is a weak and good-hearted man, who would like to comply with every one's wishes. He thinks if I were present I should tell Andy the truth, and not permit him to desert our cause, and set a bad example to the others. Well, I will keep a sharp lookout, and if the intendant really tries to take him away with him, I will endeavor to detain him forcibly."

When the door had closed after Anthony Steeger, Hormayr nodded kindly to Andreas Hofer and shook hands with him.

"Now we are alone, Andy," he said, "and will speak confidentially a word which no one is to hear save us two."

"But you should always bear in mind that God Almighty is present, and listens to us," said Hofer, lifting his eyes devoutly to heaven.

"We shall speak nothing that can offend the good God!" exclaimed Hormayr, laughing. "We shall speak of you, Andy, and the Tyrol. I wish to pray you, Andy, in the name of the Archduke John, who sent me to you, and who sent his kindest greetings with me, not to close your ears against good and well-meant advice."

"What did the archduke say? What does he want of me?" asked Andreas, quickly.

"He wishes Andreas Hofer, like himself, to submit to the emperor's orders quietly and patiently; he wishes Andreas Hofer to yield to stern necessity, and no longer sow the seeds of hatred and discord, but obey the will of his master with Christian humility and resignation. He wishes Andreas Hofer to set a good example to all the Tyrolese, and undertake nothing in opposition to the stipulations of the armistice; and the Archduke John finally wishes his beloved Andreas Hofer to secure his life and liberty by leaving the Tyrol with the Austrian troops, and remaining for some time under the protection of the imperial army."

"Never, never will I do that!" cried Andreas, vehemently; "never will I leave my beloved country! I swore to the priest, and in my own heart, that, while I lived, I would be faithful to my God, my emperor, and my country, and that I would spill the last drop of blood for our liberty, our constitution, and our emperor ; and never will I break my oath, never will I desert my flag like a faithless soldier ! "

"But, Andy, you are not to desert it, but only convey it to a place of safety for a short time. Listen to me, Andy, and let me tell you all about it. You think all may be changed yet, and you may prevent the Austrians from leaving your mountains. But unfortunately it is already too late. Already the Austrian general-in-chief, Baron von Buol, has concentrated his scattered forces, and marched them to-night from Brixen to Schabs. There you can do nothing against him ; his artillery and ammunition are safe there, and you cannot hinder him from marching with his troops this very day into Carinthia."

" But we can prevent General Schmidt from surrendering the fortress of Sachsenburg to General Rusca," cried Andreas, triumphantly.

" Do you think Commander Joseph Türk, in Upper Carinthia, surprised and occupied the fortress of Sachsenburg immediately, because you wrote to him to do so previous to Rusca's arrival ? You look at me so wonderingly, you big child ? See, here is your letter to Joseph Türk ! Our men intercepted it ; hence, Joseph Türk did not occupy the fortress, and General Rusca has arrived there already."

" It is my letter, indeed," sighed Andreas Hofer, staring at the paper which Hormayr had handed to him. " They did not allow it to reach Joseph Türk ; they no longer respect what I say and do."

" They cannot, Andy, for your and their superior, the emperor, has ordered the soldiers to evacuate the Tyrol. It was surely most repugnant to the emperor to do so, and I know that the Archduke John shed tears of grief and rage on being obliged to instruct General Buol to evacuate the Tyrol. But he submitted to stern necessity, and you will do so too, Andy."

" What am I to do, then ? What do you want of me ? " asked Andreas, with tears in his eyes.

" The Archduke John wants you to preserve yourself for better times, Andy. He implores you to repair to a place of safety, not only for the sake of your wife and children, but also for that of your fatherland. Believe me, Andreas, a gloomy time is dawning upon the Tyrol. The enemy is approaching on all sides, and the French and Bavarians have already crossed the frontiers of the Tyrol in order to occupy it again."

" And all our blood has been shed in vain ! " cried Hofer, bursting into tears. " All the faithful Tyrolese who have fallen in battle gave up their lives for nothing. We fought bravely ; the good God helped us in battle ; but men deserted us, and even the emperor, for whom we fought, will not redeem the pledges he gave us, nor help us in our sore distress."

" The emperor will never abandon his faithful Tyrolese," said Hormayr ; "only you must be patient. He cannot do any thing now ; he can not endanger his whole empire to serve the small province of the Tyrol. For the time being, further resistance is out of the question, but the emperor profits by the armistice to concentrate a new army ; and when hostilities are resumed, he will first think of the Tyrol, and deliver it from the enemy."

" But until then the Tyrol itself ought to maintain its liberty ! " exclaimed Andreas Hofer, with flashing eyes. " Listen to what I wish to say to you, Mr. Intendant, and what God Himself prompts me to tell you. I see full well that the emperor himself is unable to speak for the Tyrol, and cannot order his troops to remain in the country ; I see full well that the emperor, sorely pressed as he is by Bonaparte, cannot do any thing for us. But until he is ready again, some one ought to be courageous enough to take his place, and, as the emperor's lieutenant, defend the Tyrol against the enemy. You, Mr. Intendant, are the man to do it. You have often assured us that you were a brave and patriotic son of the Tyrol ; prove now that you told us the truth. Instead of leaving the Tyrol at this hour of its greatest peril, and surrendering it to the enemy, place yourself at its head, protect it against the enemy, and preserve it to the emperor. * Become Duke of Tyrol, take charge of the government and defence of the country. As provisional duke, call upon the faithful people to take up arms, and they will rise as one man and defend its frontiers against every enemy. Rule over the Tyrol in the emperor's place, until he himself is able again to do so and fold us again to his heart."

"What you say is nonsense, Andy," exclaimed Hormayr, shrugging his shoulders. "You want me to become provisional Duke of Tyrol ? Why, the whole world would laugh at me, and the emperor would punish me as a rebel !"

"Well, then," cried Andreas Hofer, in a powerful voice, "if you will not do it, I will ! I shall take charge of the government and call myself 'Andreas Hofer, Sandwirth of Passeyr and Duke of Tyrol,' as long as it pleases God !" *

"No, you will not, Andy," said Hormayr, gravely ; "you will be sensible, on the contrary, and not, from worldly pride, endanger your country, your friends, and yourself. Bear in mind, Andy, that you would be responsible for the blood that would be shed, if you should incite the people to rebellion, and that you would be the murderer of all those who should fall in the struggle provoked by you so recklessly and in open opposition to the orders of your emperor. Bow your head, Andy, and submit as we all do. Intrust your and our cause to God ; as it is good and just, He will not forsake it, but render it victorious when it is time."

"I believe you," sighed Andreas; "but how can I keep quiet when, as you have often told me, I am God's instrument and destined by Him to deliver the dear Tyrol from the enemy ? And what would my brave lieutenants say if their commander-in-chief, Andreas Hofer, were to leave the country in its sore distress, after he had taken an oath to defend it while he lived ? Would they not point their fingers at me, and call me a traitor, a Judas Iscariot who sold his country for the sake of his own safety ?"

"You are mistaken, Andy. You think your friends, the captains and other commanders, with whom you fought for the deliverance of the Tyrol, would despise you if you followed the Austrians now and saved your life ? Now listen to me, my friend. Your best friends, the brave Tyrolese captains, in whom you repose the greatest confidence, will leave

* Andreas Hofer's own words.—See Hormayr's " Andreas Hofer," vol. ii., p. 361.

the Tyrol this very day of their own accord and accompany
our Austrian troops to Carinthia."

"That is false, that is impossible!" cried Andreas, vehemently. "Speckbacher will never do so."

"Yes, he will, Andy. I saw him this morning. He resisted and fought as long as he could; but since the armistice
compels him to lay down the sword, and since, moreover, the
French and Bavarians are entering the country once more, he
feels that it is better for him to save his life than be caught
and hung here by the vindictive enemy. Hence, Speckbacher accepted the offer of the Austrian officers, and will accompany them."

"Joseph Speckbacher will leave the Tyrol?" murmured
Andreas Hofer, mournfully.

"And he is not the only one, Andreas: Aschbacher, Püch-
ler, Sieberer, and many other brave captains of the Tyrolese,
will likewise leave with the Austrians. All have asked me to
implore you to follow their example, and flee from the perils
menacing you all. Oh, believe them, believe me, Andreas!
If you stay here, the Bavarians will not rest until they have
taken you prisoner—until their hated enemy, the formidable
Barbone, has fallen into their hands. Dear Andy, think of
your wife at home, the faithful Anna Gertrude, who prays for
you morning and evening, and beseeches the Almighty to
spare the life of her dear husband; think of your dear children, whose only protector and supporter you are; do not
make your dear wife a widow, nor your sweet children or-
phans! Andreas Hofer, you cannot now be useful to the
fatherland; save yourself, then, for your wife and children!"

"My good wife, my dear children!" sighed Andreas, profoundly moved; "it is true, they love me dearly, and would
be very lonely on earth if their father should be taken from
them!"

"Preserve their father to them, then, and preserve yourself
also to the fatherland! Follow the example of your brave
friends Speckbacher, Aschbacher, Sieberer, and all the others;
accompany us, leave the Tyrol for a while, and when the time
has come, return with them and fight once more for the deliverance of the country."

"Speckbacher will leave, and so will all the others," murmured Andreas to himself. "The Tyrol will fall again into the enemy's hands, and all has been in vain!"

He hung his head and heaved a deep sigh.

"Come, Andreas, be sensible; think of yourself and your family," said Hormayr, beseechingly. "I have come hither for the sole purpose of taking you with me; let me not have travelled in vain from Brixen to Lienz. Come, Andreas, come! My carriage is in readiness at the door; let us ride together to Matrey. Speckbacher, the other friends, and the Austrians are waiting for us there; we shall cross the Tyrolese frontier with them this very day, and you and all your friends will be safe. Therefore, do not hesitate any longer, but come!"

"I cannot make up my mind so suddenly," said Hofer, disengaging himself gently from the hand of Hormayr, who was trying to draw him up from his chair. "It is a grave, momentous step which you ask me to take, and before I can do so I must consult God and pray to him fervently. Therefore, pray leave me alone a little while, that I may speak to the good God and consult him and my conscience."

"Very well, Andy, I give you a quarter of an hour to make up your mind," exclaimed Hormayr, approaching the door.

"A quarter of an hour is not enough," said Andreas, shaking his head. "It is late at night, and night is the time for repose and prayer. Therefore, stay here, Mr. Intendant; sleep a few hours, and to-morrow morning, at sunrise, come to my chamber and awaken me. I will tell you then what God in heaven has told me to do."

"You pledge me your word, Andreas, that you will not leave during the present night?"

"I do. I shall stay here. And now good-night. My heart is profoundly moved, and I long for repose. This is my chamber; I begged Anthony Steeger to let me have it; he has fine rooms for aristocratic guests up-stairs, and he will give you one of them. "Now good-night, sir!"

He bowed kindly to the baron, shook hands with him, and conducted him to the door.

CHAPTER XXIX.

HOFER AND SPECKBACHER.

SCARCELY had the sun risen next morning when Baron von Hormayr arose and quickly prepared every thing for their departure. After seeing that his carriage was at the street door, he descended the staircase in order to go to Andreas Hofer.

Anthony Steeger followed him with a gloomy face, and watched his every movement attentively. "If he tries to take Andy with him," he said to himself, "I will strangle him. It is true, he has told me already that Hofer will accompany him, but I do not believe it, and he shall not coax him away. This time I shall be present, and see what he is after."

They stood now in front of Hofer's door, and Hormayr put his hand on the knob to open it, but it was locked on the inside.

"Andreas Hofer, Andreas Hofer!" he shouted out almost imperatively. "The time is up; come to me, Andreas Hofer!"

The door opened, and the tall, powerful form of the Sandwirth appeared in it.

"Here I am," he said, smiling calmly, "and you see I am ready to set out."

"You will accompany me then, Andy?" asked Hormayr, joyfully.

"You will leave us?" cried Anthony Steeger, indignantly.

"I was waiting for you, sir," said Andreas, quietly; "and if you had not come of your own accord, Tony, I should have called you, for you shall hear what I have got to say to the intendant. Come in, then, both of you, and let us speak a last word with each other. Anthony Steeger, Baron von Hormayr, our countryman, came hither to persuade me to accompany him and leave the Tyrol. Our friends will do the same thing, for the Bavarians and French are already entering the country. Speckbacher, Sieberer, and others, will save their lives for this reason, and go with the Austrians; and the intendant thinks I ought to do the same, for the sake of my wife and children. However, I wished first to consult the good God. I did so all night long. I prayed and reflected a great deal, and it seemed to me as though the Lord spoke to me and enlightened my soul to find the true path. Listen then, Mr. Intendant of the Tyrol, and you, too, friend Anthony Steeger, to what I have resolved to do with God's assistance. I took an oath to serve the fatherland as long as I lived ; as an honest man, I must keep my word, and stay in the Tyrol."

Anthony Steeger uttered a loud cry of joy, but Hormayr's face grew very sombre. " You do not see, then, that you are rushing upon your own destruction ?" he asked. " You are intent on rendering your wife and children unhappy ? You are bent on incurring the most imminent peril ? "

" I will incur it courageously," said Hofer, kindly. " I know very well that what I am about to do is not prudent, but it is right. When the tempter took Jesus up into an exceeding high mountain, showed him all the kingdoms of the world and their glory, and said, ' All these things will I give Thee, if thou wilt fall down and worship me,' the Saviour did not accept the offer, but remained true to Himself, and sealed His teachings with his death. I will follow the Saviour's ex-ample, and never, while I live, prove recreant to the love which I vowed to the dear Tyrol ; never will I leave it, but I will stand by it and serve it to the last. Depart, then, Baron von Hormayr ; I cannot accompany you, for the country keeps me here, and never will I abandon it whatever may happen ! " *

" Is that your last word, Andreas ? " asked Hormayr, gloomily.

" It is," said Hofer, gently. " But pray, sir, do not be angry with me for it. Were I more prudent and sagacious, I should certainly follow your advice ; but I am only a plain peasant, and cannot but obey the promptings of my heart. Let the Austrians leave the Tyrol. Andreas Hofer cannot accompany them, nor can he look on quietly while the enemy is re-entering the country. Many brave men, many excellent sharpshooters will remain in the Tyrol, and I shall call upon

* " Gallery of Heroes: Andreas Hofer," vol. iii., p. 104.

them to rally round me. We have twice delivered the country from the enemy without any outside assistance, and we shall, perhaps, succeed a third time."

"But if you should fail," cried Hormayr, "if the seduced Tyrolese should curse you, if the tears and lamentations of your family should accuse you, if you ruin yourself and your country, then remember this hour, and the warning I gave you in order to save you!"

"I will, Mr. Intendant," said Andreas, calmly. "Every one must do his duty after his own fashion. You think you are doing yours by leaving the Tyrol; I think I do mine by staying in the country. God will decide which did right. And now, God bless you, sir! Greet Speckbacher and all the others; and when you see the Archduke John, tell him that my heart has not lost faith in him, and that I know full well he would never have given up the poor Tyrol if he could have helped it. And now, sir, do not look at me so indignantly; shake hands with me, and let us part in peace."

He held out his hand, but Hormayr, overcome by his emotion, spread out his arms and threw them around Hofer's neck with an air of impassioned tenderness.

"Farewell, Andy, farewell," he said, in a low voice. "I cannot approve of what you are doing, but I must love and admire you for all that. Farewell, farewell!"

He disengaged himself quickly, hastened out of the room, and walked hurriedly through the hall. A few minutes afterward his carriage rolled away with thundering noise.

"He is gone!" cried Anthony Steeger, joyously; "the tempter has left us, and you have remained firm, Andy; you did not allow yourself to be seduced by his blandishments. The Tyrol will reward you and love you for it for evermore!"

"If you speak the truth, it is well; if you do not, it is well too," said Andreas, calmly. "I remain because it is my duty, and because I feel that the Tyrol needs me. Anthony, the enemy is re-entering the country; we must drive him out a third time; that is my opinion."

"It is mine, too," replied Anthony Steeger, exultingly. "After succeeding twice in so doing, we shall expel him a third time also."

"It is true, it is a bad and mournful thing that Speck-bacher is going to desert us," said Andreas, musingly; but Anthony Wallner and the Capuchin will surely stand by us, and Peter Mayer will not leave us either. Besides, you are here, and so am I, and we five men will raise our voices and call upon the people to rise and expel the enemy once more. I believe the brave men will listen to our voices, and not one of them will stay at home; all will come to us, bring their rifles with them, and fight the French and Bava-rians."

"I think so too, Andy. When the brave Tyrolese hear your voice, they will come to a man, and we will achieve another Innspruck triumph, and gain another victory on Mount Isel."

"God grant it in His mercy!" exclaimed Andreas, touch-ing the crucifix on his breast. "But I must set out now, my friend. So long as we are unable to cope with the enemy, we must avoid meeting him, conceal our forces, and prepare actively for the struggle. Hence, I shall not tell you where I am going, and no one shall learn of my whereabouts until the time has come for me to appear once more at the head of a strong and brave army. Do your duty here, Tony, and en-list courageous sharpshooters for the fatherland. Inform all the patriots secretly of my plan, and tell them that we must not heed the armistice concluded by Austria, but must fight on for our liberty and our emperor. Have my horse brought to the door, my friend; the sun is already over the moun-tains, and it is time for me to start."

Anthony Steeger hastened away; he saddled his friend's horse with his own hands and brought him to the door. Andreas vaulted with the agility of a youth into the saddle, and shook hands with his friend.

"Farewell, Anthony Steeger," he said; "you shall hear from me soon."

He then spurred his horse and galloped along the high-way leading through the Puster valley. His horse knew the way very well; it was unnecessary for Andreas Hofer to guide him; he could let him trot along quietly, and absorb himself in his plans and thoughts. He was animated only

by one idea, that his beloved country was in danger, and that
it needed him.

"I do not know if I shall be able to save it," he murmured
to himself, "but I do know that I must not run away. I shall
hide as long as it is necessary, and prepare myself by prayer
and devotion. Forward, my horse, forward !"

And he rode on through the valley and across the heights.
Profound silence reigned everywhere. It was yet early in the
morning, the road was quite deserted, and Andreas could
brood uninterruptedly over his thoughts and conceive his
plans. All at once his musings were interrupted by the roll of
a wagon approaching on the road. It was a large wagon
with racks, drawn by four horses, and many men sat in it.
Andreas Hofer was as yet unable to see who they were, but
the red and white colours of their gold-and-silver-embroidered
coats showed him that they were soldiers. When the wagon
came closer up to him, he recognized them ; they were Austrian officers and soldiers. But who was he that occupied
one of the front seats among them ? Who was that tall,
slender man in the dress of the Tyrolese, his head covered
with a pointed green hat ? The wagon came nearer and
nearer. Andreas Hofer halted his horse and looked steadfastly at the Tyrolese seated in the midst of the Austrian
officers. "Good heavens," he murmured, giving a start, "I
believe it is Joseph Speckbacher ! Yes, yes, it is."

Now the wagon was close by his side, and it was really
he, it was Joseph Speckbacher ; and it was plainly to be seen
that he had likewise recognized Andreas Hofer, for he uttered
a cry, and a deep blush suffused his cheeks. But the Austrian officers had also recognized the brave Sandwirth, the universally beloved Barbone, and they shouted to the coachman
to drive quicker and whip his horses into a full gallop. The
coachman did so, and the carriage sped away at a furious rate.
Andreas Hofer halted at the roadside ; his tearful eyes gazed
upon his friend, and when Speckbacher was whirled past him,
Andreas exclaimed in a loud, mournful voice, "Speckbacher,
are you too going to desert the country ? They are driving
you to your own disgrace, Joe !" *

* Andreas Hofer's own words.—See Mayr's "Joseph Speckbacher," p. 143.

The wagon passed him noisily, and Joseph Speckbacher's horse, which was tied behind, galloped rapidly after it. Andreas Hofer looked after his friend until a cloud of dust enveloped the disappearing wagon, and he heard only the sound of the wheels at a distance. He then heaved a deep sigh, wiped a tear from his eye, and rode on. But his heart was heavy and melancholy, and his thoughts returned again and again during his ride on the lonely road to Joseph Speckbacher, who had turned his back on the Tyrol and was about to leave it in the hour of its sorest distress. Suddenly he thought he heard his own name uttered behind; the call was repeated louder and more urgently.

Andreas Hofer halted his horse and turned. A cloud of dust came up the road like a whirlwind; now it opened, and the head and neck of a horse and the slender rider mounted on him came in view. The cloud veils his face as yet, but he comes nearer and nearer; his horse is now by Andreas Hofer's side, the rider stretches out his arms toward him and exclaims exultingly: "Andy, here I am! I heard what you said, and jumped from the wagon, untied my horse, vaulted into the saddle, and sped after you, my Andy. I had to overtake you and tell you that I do not want to be disgraced; that I will not leave the Tyrol unless you do too."

"I never will, Joe, unless I should die," said Andreas Hofer, solemnly. "But God be praised that I have got you back, for a piece of my heart would have left the country with you. But you are back, and I am so glad of it! And I must give you a kiss in the name of God, the country, and the Emperor Francis. Welcome home, good and faithful son of the fatherland!"

He encircled Speckbacher's neck with his arms and imprinted a kiss on his forehead. They remained locked in a long embrace, keeping their horses side by side, and gazing at each other with proud, smiling joy.

"And now tell me, Andy, what are you going to do?" asked Speckbacher, after a long pause. "I hope you will not look on quietly and peaceably while the Bavarians and French are re-entering the country? I could not bear it, and this was the very reason why I did not want to stay in the country;

for the Austrian officers told me, if I wished to remain in the
Tyrol, I should have to keep very quiet and allow the enemy
to take possession of the province, in accordance with the
stipulations of the armistice. And you see, Andy, my heart
revolted at that ; therefore I wished to get away and remain
abroad until the armistice had expired, when we would be
once more allowed to fight bravely for our country and our
emperor."

"No one shall prevent us from doing so now," said Andreas, calmly. "What do we care for the armistice ? The
emperor concluded it ; we did not, and I believe the emperor
will not blame us for disregarding it and continuing the war
as we commenced it."

"You are right, we will do so," exclaimed Speckbacher,
joyfully. "And now I will communicate to you some important news which the Austrian officers received only this morning. Anthony Wallner, of Windisch-Matrey is also of your
opinion ; he refuses likewise to acknowledge the armistice
and make peace with the enemy. When the Bavarians, four
days ago, intended to cross the frontier near Windisch-Matrey, Anthony Wallner and John Panzl went to meet them
with four hundred sharpshooters whom they had gathered in
great haste. They took position at the bridge of Taxenbach
and tried to prevent the Bavarians from crossing it. The Bavarians were seven thousand strong, and Wallner had only
four hundred men ; but our friends, nevertheless, defended
the bridge for seven hours, killed and wounded over three
hundred Bavarians, and retreated into the mountains only because the odds were too great." *

"I know Anthony Wallner, and was convinced that he
would not submit quietly," said Andreas, joyfully. "And we
will follow his example, Joseph. The good God has imposed
on us the task of defending the Tyrol, and we will fulfil it
faithfully."

"Yes, we will, and we will begin this very hour. We
must find out, above all things, if all of our countrymen
are of our opinion, and if they are courageous enough

* Peternader, "Die Tyroler Landesvertheidigung im Jahre 1809," vol. ii.,
p. 84.

to continue the struggle, even after the Austrians have left us."

"What good did the Austrians do us while they were here?" asked Andreas, indignantly. "Let me tell you, Joe, on the whole I am glad that the Austrians are evacuating the province. It is better for us to fight alone, and trust only our own strength. Regular troops and insurgents never fight well together in the end, for there are always jealousies between them; they mutually charge each other with the blunders committed during the campaign, and grudge each other the glory obtained in the battles. Hence, it is better for us to be alone and have no other allies than the good God, the Holy Virgin, and her blessed Son." *

"You are right, always right, Andy," said Speckbacher. "We will go courageously to work, then; and you shall see, my Andy, that Speckbacher is still what he always was, and that he will henceforth never think of leaving the country, but will stand faithfully by it and fight until the enemy has been expelled once more, and we are free again. I will ride now through the whole Puster valley, and then from Brunecken through the Dux valley to my home, the Rinn; and I will stir up the people everywhere, and call upon the men to follow me and fight once more for liberty and the fatherland."

"Do so, Joe, and I will follow your example. I will return to the Passeyr valley; you shall all hear from me before long, and then my voice shall resound throughout the Tyrol. God will make it strong enough to penetrate to every ear, and fill every heart with enthusiastic devotion to the country and the emperor. Farewell, then, Joseph! The Tyrol and I have recovered you, and my heart thanks God fervently for it. Farewell, you shall hear from me before long!"

He nodded once more kindly to Joseph Speckbacher and galloped down the valley, while Speckbacher trotted up the mountain-path.

Andreas Hofer rode all day long through the country. He

* Andreas Hofer's own words.—See Mayr's " Joseph Speckbacher," p. 145.

saw the people everywhere in commotion and uproar; they greeted him with jubilant cheers, and the men swore everywhere that they would not allow the enemy to re-enter the country without resistance; that they did not believe in the pacific assurances of the proclamations with which the Bavarians had flooded the country; that they were satisfied, on the contrary, that the enemy would revenge himself as cruelly as he had done after his return in May; and that they were, therefore, firmly resolved to fight and expel the enemy once more.

"Get your rifles and ammunition, then, and prepare for the struggle," said Andreas Hofer everywhere to the men who were so full of ardor. "You shall hear from me soon, and learn what God wants us to do."

Andreas Hofer did not rest even at night. The great task which was imposed upon him urged him on incessantly. He therefore profited by the clear moonlight to ride across the Janfen, and at daybreak his horse neighed joyously and stopped at the bank of the foaming Passeyr, at no great distance from the white house of the Sandwirth, the home which contained his greatest treasures on earth, his wife and children.

But Andreas Hofer did not intend to return to them now; he did not want to have his heart softened by the sight of his wife, who would certainly weep and lament on learning of his resolve to renew the war against the Bavarians and French. And for the same reason he wished to avoid meeting his children, whose dear faces might remind him that he was about to endanger the life of their father, and that their bright eyes might soon fill with tears of bitter grief. He would speak only to God, and solitude was to be his sole adviser. Andreas Hofer greeted his house and its beloved inmates with a long, tearful look; he then dried his eyes and alighted. The horse neighed joyously and sped merrily down the hill toward his stable. But Andreas Hofer took a by-path and ascended the mountain through the forest and shrubbery to the Kellerlahn, a cave known only to him and some of his intimate friends, where his faithful servant had prepared him a couch, and kept always in readiness for him, in a secret cupboard fixed in the rock, wine and food, some prayer-books, and writing-materials.

In this cave Andreas Hofer intended to pass a few days in prayer and solitude.

———

CHAPTER XXX.

THE CAPUCHIN'S OATH.

A GREAT festival was to be celebrated at Brixen to-day. It was the 2d of August, the day of St. Cassian, and not only were the bones of this saint, which reposed in the cathedral adorned with two splendid towers, to be exhibited, as they were every year, to the devout pilgrims, but the pious bishop had resolved that these sacred relics should be carried in solemn procession through the whole city, that all might have an opportunity to see the saint's remains and implore the assistance of God in the sore distress which had befallen the Tyrol again. Since early morning, therefore, the peasantry had been flocking from all sides toward the gates of Brixen ; women and children, young and old men, came from all parts of the country to take part in the solemn procession and the devout prayers for the welfare of the country.

Among those who were wandering along the road to Brixen, was a monk of strikingly bold and martial appearance. His tall, broad-shouldered form was remarkable for its military bearing ; his long, well-kept red whiskers and mustache did not correspond to the tonsure on his head, which was covered with thin reddish ringlets ; and in striking contrast with it were likewise the broad red scar on his healthy sunburnt countenance, and the bright, defiant glance of his eyes, which indicated boldness and intrepidity rather than piety and humility. He had tucked up his brown robe, and thus exhibited his stout legs, which seemed to mock the soft sandals encasing his broad, powerful feet. In his hand he held a long brown staff, terminating at its upper end in a carved image of St. Francis ; and the Capuchin did not carry this staff in order to lean upon it, but he brandished it in the air like a sword, or held it up triumphantly as though it were a victorious banner.

But however strange and unusual the Capuchin's appearance might be, no one laughed at him, but he was greeted everywhere with demonstrations of love and reverence ; and when he passed some slow wanderers with his rapid step, they looked after him with joyful surprise, and said to each other, "Look at old Red-beard, look at brave Father Haspinger ! He has fought often enough for the fatherland. Now he is going to pray for the Tyrol."

" Pray, and fight again, if need be," said the friar, turning to the speakers.

" You think, then, reverend father, that there will be war again ? " asked many voices ; and dense groups surrounded the friar, and asked him anxiously if he advised them to allow the enemy to re-enter the country ; if it would not be better to drive him back forcibly, or if he thought it would be preferable for them to keep quiet and submit to stern necessity ?

" I think there is a time for every thing—for keeping quiet as well as for fighting, for praying as well as for politics," said Father Haspinger, shrugging his shoulders. " If you wish to pray and confess your sins, come to me. I am ready to teach you how to pray, and exhort you with true earnestness. But if you want to fight and expel the enemy from the country, why do you not apply to your commanders, and consult, above all, the brave and pious Andreas Hofer ? "

" We cannot find him anywhere," shouted several voices. " He is not at home, and even his wife does not know where he has concealed himself."

" Do you, impious wretches, think that the most pious man in the whole Tyrol, Andreas Hofer, has concealed himself because he is afraid of the Bavarians who are re-entering the country ? " asked the friar, in a thundering voice.

" No, your reverence, we do not. We know well that Andreas Hofer will not act like Ashbacher, Sieberer, Teimer, Eisenstecken, and Speckbacher, and abandon us in our sore distress."

" He who does not extricate himself from his sore distress will not be saved by others," cried the friar, indignantly.

"Do you not know the eleventh commandment you white-livered cowards, who think you are lost when there is no leader to put himself at your head? Do you not know the eleventh commandment, saying that he who trusts in God and fights well will overpower his enemies? But you will never overpower your enemies; you do not trust in God, and hence you can not fight well."

"But we will fight well, your reverence," replied the men, with bold, defiant glances; "only our leaders do not stand by us. Every one cannot fight alone and at random, but there must be some one at the lead to lead the whole movement. Since Andreas Hofer cannot be found, pray put yourself at our head, your reverence, and become our leader!"

"That request is not so stupid," said the Capuchin, smiling, and stroking his red beard. "You know very well that old Red-beard does not stay at home when an effort is to be made to save the fatherland, and perhaps I may soon be able to accept your offer and call upon you to defend the Tyrol."

"Do so, do call upon us," shouted the men enthusiastically. "We will not permit the French and Bavarians to murder our people and burn our houses as they did last May; we will fight rather until we have driven them from the country or perished to a man!"

"These are brave and pious sentiments," said Father Haspinger, his eyes flashing for joy; "and we will speak further about them. Come up to the church of Latzfons to-morrow, and hear me preach; and after the sermon we will confer as to the state of the country. But now keep quiet, for you see we are at the gate of Brixen; turn your souls, therefore, to God, and pray St. Cassian to have mercy upon you, and intercede for you with God and the Redeemer."

And Father Haspinger's face became suddenly very grave and devout; he lifted the rosary hanging at his belt, and, while entering the city by the gate, he commenced praying a *Pater-noster* in an undertone.

The city meanwhile was already in great commotion. The bells had begun to ring their solemn peals, and all devout worshippers, consisting on this occasion of the whole population of the city, were flocking to the cathedral. All at once the doors of the cathedral were thrown open, and under a gold-embroidered baldachin borne by four priests appeared the pious bishop, carrying in his uplifted right hand the casket containing the bones of Saint Cassian. Behind the bishop came the priests bearing wax-lights, and singing soul-stirring hymns. Next followed the long line of acolytes with smoking censers ; and pious worshippers, carrying torches, and repeating the hymns intoned by the priests, closed the procession. This procession gained strength at every step as it advanced, and soon it had been joined by the whole population of the city and the hundreds of pious pilgrims who had flocked to Brixen to take part in the holy festival.

Haspinger, the Capuchin friar, was likewise in the procession ; he walked in the midst of the brave peasants with whom he had conversed, singing with head erect and in a tone of solemn earnestness the hymns with which the holy relics were being invoked. Only it seemed to the peasants who heard his powerful voice as though he somewhat changed the passage imploring Saint Cassian to grant the Tyrolese peace, protection, and tranquillity, and prayed for the very reverse. The passage was as follows : " Have mercy upon our weakness, and grant us peace and tranquillity." But Father Haspinger, brandishing his staff with the image of Saint Francis, sang in a tone of fervent piety : " Have mercy upon our valor, and grant us war ! " To those who looked at him wonderingly on account of this change of the text, he nodded with a shrewd twinkle of his eyes, and murmured : " Come to-morrow to the church of Latzfons. We will hold a council of war there ! "

The procession had not yet finished one-half of its route, and had just reached the market-place when a horseman galloped up the street leading from the gate to the market-place. It was probably a belated worshipper, who intended to take part in the procession. He alighted hurriedly from his horse, and tied it to the brass knob of a street-door, and then walked close up to the procession. However, he did not join it, but stood still and contemplated every passer-by with prying eyes. Now he seemed to have found him whom he sought, for a smile illuminated his sunburnt face, and he advanced directly toward Father Haspinger, who was singing again :

"Have mercy upon our valor, and grant us war!" But on perceiving the young lad who was approaching him, he paused, and a bright gleam of joy overspread his features.

"It is Andreas Hofer's servant, Anthony Wild," murmured Father Haspinger, joyfully, holding out his hand to the lad. "Say, Tony, do you come to bring me a message from brother Andreas?"

"I do, reverend sir. The Sandwirth sends me to you, and as I did not meet you at your convent of Seeben near Klausen, I followed you to Brixen; for my master instructed me to deliver my message as quickly as possible into your hands and return with your answer."

"What message do you bring me, Tony?"

"This letter, reverend sir."

The friar took it and put it quickly into his belt. "Where is brother Andreas?" he asked.

"In the cave which is known only to him, to you, and to myself," whispered Anthony Wild, into the friar's ear. "He awaits your reply there, reverend sir."

"And you shall have it this very day, Tony. Now, however, we will not forget our divine service, but worship God with sincere piety. Take the place behind me in the procession; and when we return to the cathedral, follow me wherever I may go."

And the friar commenced singing again; his hand, however, no longer held the rosary, but he put it firmly on the letter which was concealed in his belt, and whose contents engrossed his thoughts.

At length the procession had returned to the portals of the cathedral. Father Haspinger signed to the Sandwirth's servant, who was walking behind him, and instead of accompanying the other worshippers into the church, he walked along the procession until he reached a tall, slender young man, with whom he had already exchanged many a glance.

"Martin Schenk," said the friar to him, "will you go home now?"

"I will, and I request you, reverend sir, to accompany me," said the young man, hastily. "I believe you will find a number of friends at my house. Peter Kemnater, the innkeeper of

Schabs, and Peter Mayer, the innkeeper of Mahr, will be there. I invited them, and had I known that you would be here, I should have invited you too."

" You see that I come without being invited, for I think the fatherland has invited us all ; and I believe we will not partake of an epicurean breakfast at your tavern to-day, but confer as to the terrible calamities of our country. We are the cooks that will prepare a very spicy and unhealthy breakfast for the French and Bavarians, and I believe I am the bearer of some salt and pepper from Andreas Hofer for this purpose. See, Martin Schenck, in my belt here, by the side of the rosary, is a letter from our dear brother Andreas Hofer."

"And what does he write to you ? I hope he does not want us to keep quiet and permit the enemy to re-enter the country, as all prudent and cautious people advise us to do ?"

" Hush, hush, Martin ! do not insult our commander-in-chief by such a supposition. I have not read the letter yet, but I believe I know its contents, and could tell you beforehand every word that the good and faithful Andreas has written to us. Ah, here is your tavern, and let me ask a favor of you now. The lad who is following us is Andreas Hofer's faithful servant, Anthony Wild, who brought me the letter from his master, and who must wait for my answer. Give him a place where he may rest, and a good breakfast, for he must set out for home this very day."

"Come in, Anthony Wild ; you are welcome," said the young innkeeper, shaking hands with Hofer's servant.

"Thank you, but I must first fetch my horse, which I tied to a pole somewhere down the street. I rode very fast, and must first attend to the horse ; afterward I will request you to let me have some breakfast."

And Hofer's servant hastened down the street. The innkeeper and the friar entered the house and stepped into the large bar-room. Two men came to meet them there.

One of them, a man about forty-five years old, dressed in the simple costume of the Tyrolese, and of a tall, powerful form, was Peter Mayer, known throughout the Tyrol as one of the most ardent and faithful patriots, and a man of extraordinary intrepidity, firmness, and energy.

The other, a young man of scarcely twenty-two, slender yet well built, and far-famed for his fine appearance, boldness, and wealth, was Peter Kemnater, the most faithful and devoted friend of the fine-looking and patriotic young innkeeper, Martin Schenk.

The two men shook hands with the new-comers and bowed to them, but their faces were gloomy, and not the faintest gleam of a smile illuminated them.

"Have you come hither, Father Joachim Haspinger, only to join in the peace-prayers?" asked Peter Mayer in his laconic style, fixing his dark, piercing eyes on the friar's face.

"No, Peter Mayer," said the Capuchin, gravely; "I have come hither because I wanted to see you three, and because I have to say many things to you. But previously let me read what our pious and patriotic brother Andreas Hofer has written to me."

"You have a letter from Andreas Hofer!" exclaimed Mayer and Kemnater, joyfully.

"Here it is," said the friar, drawing it from his belt. "Now give me a moment's time to read the letter, and then we will confer upon the matter that brought us here."

He stepped to the window and unfolded the letter. While he was reading it, the three men looked at him with rapt suspense, seeking to read in his features the impression produced by Andreas Hofer's words on the heart of the brave Capuchin. Indeed, the friar's features brightened more and more, his forehead and face colored, and a smile illuminated his hard features.

"Listen, men," he exclaimed triumphantly, waving the paper as though it were a flag; "listen to what Andreas writes to me!" And the friar read in a clarion voice:

"Dear brother Red-beard! Beloved Father Joachim Haspinger: You know, brother, that all has been in vain; the Austrians are evacuating the country, and the emperor, or rather not the emperor, but his ministers and secretaries, stipulated in the armistice concluded with Bonaparte, that the French and Bavarians should re-enter the Tyrol and recommence the infamous old system. But I think, even though the emperor has abandoned us, God Almighty will not do so;

and even though the Austrian soldiers are crossing our frontiers, our mountains and glaciers remain to us ; God placed
them there to protect our frontiers, and He gave us strong
arms and good rifles and keen eyes to discern the enemy and
hit him. We are the inhabitants of the Tyrol, and the Austrian soldiers are not, hence it is incumbent on us to protect
our frontiers, and prevent the enemy from invading our territory. If you are of my opinion, gather about you as many
brave sharpshooters as you can, call out the *Landsturm* where
it is possible, tell the other commanders to do the same, and
advance, if possible, at once toward the Brenner, where I hope
you will meet me or hear further news from me. Joseph
Speckbacher did not leave the country either ; he is enlisting
sharpshooters and calling out the *Landsturm* in his district.
It is the Lord's will that the Tyrol be henceforth protected
only by the Tyrolese. Bear this in mind, and go to work.—
Your faithful Andreas Hofer, at present not knowing where
he is." *

"Well," asked the friar, exultingly, "do you think that
Andreas Hofer is right, and that we ought not to allow the
enemy to re-enter the country ?"

"I think he is," said Peter Kemnater, joyously. "I think
it will be glorious for us to expel the French and Bavarians
once more from our frontiers."

"Or, if they have already crossed them, drive them ignominiously from the country," added Peter Mayer.

"I have passed, during the last few days, through the
whole of Puster valley," said Martin Schenk. "Everywhere
I found the men determined to die, rifle in hand, on the field
of battle, rather than stay peaceably at home and bend their
necks before the enemy. 'It is a misfortune,' said the men,
'that the Austrians are abandoning us at this critical juncture ;
but it would be a greater misfortune still for us to abandon
ourselves and consent to surrender at discretion.'"

"And I say it is no misfortune at all that the Austrians
have left us," cried the Capuchin, vehemently. "The cause
of the fatherland has not suffered much by the retreat of the

* Andreas Hofer signed all his letters and orders in this strange manner
while he was concealed in his cave.

Austrians. Who assisted us at the battle of Mount Isel?
Who helped us to drive the enemy twice from the country?
Not an Austrian did! We accomplished all that was great
and glorious in the short and decisive struggle. Let us not
complain, then, that no one stands by us now, and that we
know that no one will help us but God and we ourselves.
But we must not plunge blindly and furiously into the struggle; on the contrary, we must consider whether we are able
to defeat the enemy. The French and Bavarians are sending
large forces on all sides to the poor Tyrol. I cannot conceal
from you that the enterprise which we are going to undertake,
and to which Andreas Hofer invites us, is a dangerous one.
Let me tell you that that miserable assassin and ruffian Lefebre,
whom they call the Duke of Dantsic, is approaching from the
north with twenty-five thousand men, and is already close to
Innspruck. General Deroi, too, is coming; he intends to
march through the whole Vintschgau, and force his way over
the Gerlos Mountains to the district of Innspruck. Rusca's
wild legions are already near Lienz; General Pery is moving
up from the south with his Italian troops; and the exasperated
Bavarians, under Generals Wreden and Arco, are already at
Salzburg. In short, more than fifty thousand men are coming up from all sides to trample the poor Tyrol under foot.
They are veteran soldiers; they have got artillery and better
arms than we, and are superior to us in numbers, equipments,
and strength. Consider, therefore, whether you are willing
to undertake the heavy task nevertheless; consider that you
risk your property, your blood, and your lives, and that, if you
should be so unfortunate as to fall into the enemy's hands, he
would perhaps punish you as criminals and rebels. It is true,
you are ready to risk your property, your blood, and your
lives, for the fatherland and the liberty of the Tyrol; but then
you have also duties to your families, your parents, your
brides; you have a duty to yourselves—that of not endangering your lives recklessly. It is true, even though the enemy
should punish you as rebels, you would die the beautiful death
of martyrs for your fatherland, and the halo of your virtue
and love of country will immortalize your names; but you
must consider, also, whether your death will be useful to the

country, and whether you will not shed your blood in vain.
Ask your hearts, my friends, whether they will be courageous
and strong enough to brave cheerfully whatever reverses and
calamities may befall us, and whether they really will risk
death, imprisonment, and the scaffold, without flinching
and trembling ?   That is what I wished to say to you
before concerting measures with you and sending an answer to Andreas Hofer.   Consider it all, my friends, and then
speak."

"We are to ask our hearts if they will not flinch and tremble ?" said Peter Mayer, almost contemptuously.   "When the
enemy returned to the Tyrol last May, he burned down eight
houses which belonged to me, and for some time I did not
know but that my wife and children had perished in the
conflagration.   Did you see me tremble—did you hear me
complain at that time ?   Did I not stand up cheerfully in the
battle on Mount Isel, without weeping or murmuring, and
bearing in mind only that I was fighting for liberty, the
fatherland, and the emperor ?   It was not until we had gained
the victory, and obtained our freedom, that I went home to
mourn and weep on the smoking ruins of my houses.   But I
found my wife and my children alive and well ; a friend had
concealed them and taken care of them ; and after thanking
God for our victory, I thanked Him for preserving my wife
and children ; and only now, when we were happy and free,
did I shed tears.   But since the enemy is re-entering the
country, and fresh misfortunes are to befall us, my tears are
dried again ; my heart is full of courage and constancy ; and
I believe we must risk all, because otherwise every thing that
we have done hitherto will be in vain.   I love my wife dearly;
but, if she came now to dissuade me from taking part in the
struggle, and if I felt that my heart was giving way to her
persuasion, I would strangle her with my own hands, lest she
should prevent me from serving the great cause of the fatherland.   It is true, our task is difficult, but it is not impossible;
and that which is not impossible should be tried for the fatherland !   I have given you my opinion; it is your turn now, my
young friends.   Peter Kemnater, speak !   Tell Father Red-
beard whether your heart is trembling and flinching, and

whether you think we had better keep quiet, because the enemy is so powerful and superior to us."

"I have an affianced bride of whom I am very fond," said Peter Kemnater, with flushed cheeks and flashing eyes; "a girl whom I love better than my parents, than anything in the world, and whom I intended to marry a fortnight hence; but I swear to God and the Holy Virgin that my wedding shall not take place until the Tyrol is free again, and we have expelled the enemy once more from the country. And if my bride should be angry at this, and demand that I should think more of her than of the fatherland, and prefer living for her alone to dying perhaps for the fatherland, I should break with her, and never look at her again, never speak another word with her. I have many houses and lands; but even though I knew that my fields and meadows were to be devastated, and my houses burned down, like those of Peter Mayer, I should say, nevertheless, we will fight for the fatherland! We will defeat the enemy, even though we should all become beggars, and even though I knew that I should die before seeing my affianced bride again, and that she would curse me in my grave. That is what I have got to say. Now you may speak, Martin Schenk; tell the father whether your heart is flinching and trembling."

"Yes, it is," cried Martin Schenk, "but only when I think the men of the Tyrol could be so cowardly and mean-spirited as to keep quiet and submit to their oppressors, because the latter are powerful and superior to us in numbers. I have a young wife whom I married only a year ago, and who gave birth to a little boy a week since, and I assure you that I love her and her child with all my heart. But if I knew that their death would be useful to the fatherland, and would contribute to its salvation, I would shoot them with my own rifle, and should not weep on seeing their corpses at my feet; but I should rejoice and exclaim, 'I did it for the sake of the fatherland; I sacrificed my most precious treasures for the beloved Tyrol.' Even though the enemy is very strong and numerous, even though the emperor has abandoned us, God stands by us. The mountains stand firm yet; they are our fortresses, and we will fight in them until we are all dead, or until we

have defeated the enemy, and delivered the Tyrol a third time.
Now you know my opinion, Father Joachim Haspinger."

The Capuchin made no reply. He stood with hands
clasped in prayer and eyes lifted to heaven, and two large
tears rolled down his bronzed cheeks into his red beard.

"Great God in heaven," he murmured in a voice tremulous with emotion, "I thank Thee for letting me see this hour,
and hear the soul-stirring words of these patriotic men. What
can I say now, what have I to sacrifice to the fatherland? I
have no wife, no children, no property; I am but a poor Capuchin! I have nothing but my blood and my life. But I will
give it to the country, even though the bishop and the abbot
should excommunicate me for it and condemn my soul to
burn in everlasting fire. It is better that a poor Capuchin's
soul should burn in hell than that the fatherland should
groan with pain and wear the brand of disgrace and slavery
on its forehead. It is better to be a faithless son of the bishop
and abbot, than a faithless son of the fatherland. It is better
to be a bad Christian than a bad patriot. Therefore, whatever may happen, I shall share every thing with you, danger
or victory, triumph or death. Henceforth I am no longer a
Capuchin, but old Red-beard Joachim Haspinger, the de-
fender of his country; and I swear that I will no more lay
down my head and repose before we have delivered the country from the enemy and concluded an honorable peace. If
that is your sentiment also, swear here before God that you
will fight henceforth for the country, devote your whole
strength to it, and perish rather than give up the struggle,
make peace with the enemy, and submit to the Bavarian
yoke."

And the three men lifted their hands and eyes to heaven,
and exclaimed with one accord, in a loud and solemn tone:
"We swear by God Almighty, and by all that is sacred and
dear to us on earth, that we will fight henceforth for the
country, devote our whole strength to it, and perish rather
than give up the struggle, make peace with the enemy, and
submit to the Bavarian yoke!"

"*Benedictus! benedictus!*" cried Father Haspinger, laying
his hands on those which the three men had joined on taking

the oath. "The Lord has heard and accepted your oath ; the Lord will bless you, the Holy Virgin will protect you ! Amen !"

"And now let us concert measures for the struggle, and consider what we ought to do," said the friar, after a pause. "In the first place, we will inform Andreas Hofer that his wishes shall be complied with, and that we will call out the *Landsturm* and all our forces. Let me write to him, therefore, and then we will hold a council of war."

The council of war lasted until midnight ; and while all Europe was truckling to the " invincible Emperor Napoleon," while all Germany was lying humbly prostrate at his feet, and while all the princes were basking in the sunshine of his favor, four poor men, neither learned nor even well educated, three peasants and a monk, were concerting measures to bid defiance to " Bonaparte, the robber of crowns," and expel his powerful armies from their mountains ! All Germany was subjugated, and had given up all further resistance to the all-powerful conqueror ; only the small Tyrol would not suffer herself to be subjugated ; only the brave sons of the German mountains were still intent on braving the tyrant, and upholding their liberty and independence, despite the formidable efforts he was making to crush them.

Already on the following morning the tocsin sounded in all the valleys and on all the heights, and called upon the men to fight for the fatherland. After midnight the three brave men had left Brixen ; each had set out in a different direction to incite the men to insurrection, inform them of Andreas Hofer's order, and implore them in the name of the fatherland to take up their rifles again and risk once more their lives for the deliverance of the Tyrol.

Father Haspinger had walked all night to Latzfons, and on the following morning he preached to the people at the church of that place an enthusiastic sermon, in which he called upon them to make one more effort in behalf of their beloved country, and promised entire absolution for one year to every one who should kill a dozen French soldiers, and absolution for five years to any who should kill twice as many.*

* Mayer's " Speckbacher," p. 151.

Carried away by the soul-stirring words and promises of the Capuchin, full of ardor to serve the fatherland, and desirous of obtaining absolution, the men took up arms, and even a company of women was formed for the holy service of the fatherland.

At night on the same day three hundred sharpshooters had rallied around the martial friar, and with them he marched toward Unterau, constantly receiving re-enforcements on the road ; for the inhabitants everywhere rose again as one man, and with their redoubted rifles on their shoulders descended every lateral glen and ravine, and joined his command to conquer or die under him.

And joyful news arrived from all sides, announcing that the inhabitants were rising throughout the Tyrol. Already Peter Mayer and Peter Kemnater had gathered around them all the sharpshooters of the neighboring towns and villages, and their four companies now united with the friar's troops. News also came from Andreas Hofer : he had emerged again from the cave, and at his call all the sharpshooters of the Passeyr valley had rallied around him, and companies had flocked to him from all parts of the country to fight again under their beloved commander-in-chief. Andreas Hofer had marched with them across the crest of the precipitous Janfen, and his army gathering strength like a mountain-torrent from every tributary stream which crossed its course, soon embraced all the able-bodied men of Passeyr, Meran, and Algund.

The Tyrolese had risen a third time to defend the independence of their country.

CHAPTER XXXI.

THE FIRST BATTLE.

WHAT the four men had sworn at the inn of Brixen, and what Andreas Hofer had agreed upon with his friend Speckbacher, had succeeded. The whole Tyrol had risen and was eager for the fray. A small army, commanded by Father

Haspinger, was encamped near Brixen, and received hourly fresh accessions. Peter Kemnater and Peter Mayer were still traversing the country, and calling upon the peasants to repair to Father Red-beard's camp near Brixen, and their appeals were readily complied with. The brave peasants of Rodeneck, Weitenthal, and Schoneck, led by their courageous pastor, George Schoneck, came into camp ; and so did Anthony Wallner with the four hundred men who had followed him from the Puster valley.

Father Haspinger received these brave men exultingly, and folded their leader, Anthony Wallner, tenderly to his heart.

" You have fought again like a hero," he exclaimed, patting his cheeks affectionately ; "the whole Tyrol is extolling your exploits at the murderous battle of Taxenbach, and they are telling wonderful stories about the surpassing heroism and bravery you displayed on that occasion."

"It is true, we fought bravely," said Anthony Wallner, sighing ; " but it did not do much good, for the enemy was ten to one, and we were finally unable to check his advance. But we followed him, and will now unite with you, reverend father, in order to expel him once more from the country. I believe there will be another battle on Mount Isel, for the enemy is always intent on forcing his way to Innspruck, believing that the whole Tyrol is subjugated so soon as the capital has fallen into his hands. We must strive, therefore, to meet him there once more ; for you know the old prophecy, saying that Mount Isel will be a lucky place for the Tyrolese."

" I do know it," said the friar ; ." and if it please God we will verify it. The freedom of the Tyrol is buried on Mount Isel near Innspruck, and we will disinter the golden treasure there and cause it to shed its lustre once more on our mountains and valleys. You shall help me to do it, Anthony Wallner, you and your famous sharpshooters of Windisch-Matrey. But previously I think, my friend, we shall have something to do here ; for our scouts have returned with the news that the enemy is approaching. His column is headed by Saxon and Bavarian troops under the French general, Royer ; his forces are followed by the main army under the commander-

in-chief, Marshal Lefebvre, or as he proudly call himself, the
Duke of Dantsic. General Royer has got already as far as
Sterzing, and if we do not interfere the Saxons will soon reach
Brixen."

"But we will interfere," cried Anthony Wallner ; "we
will not allow them to advance to Brixen, and I will occupy
immediately with my sharpshooters the mountain-passes on
the route of the enemy. We will receive the Duke of Dantsic
with fireworks which will sadden his heart."

"Do so, dear Anthony," exclaimed Haspinger, joyfully.
"I myself will first go to Brixen and teach the members of
the municipality better manners. Their terror and anguish
have rendered them quite eloquent, and they have dissuaded
many hundred peasants, who were passing through Brixen to
join my command, from so doing, and induced them to return
to their homes. I shall speak a serious word with those gentlemen, and teach them a little patriotism."

Haspinger nodded kindly to Anthony Wallner, and calling
ten of his best sharpshooters to him repaired to the city hall
of Brixen, where the members of the municipality were assembled. He made them a furious speech, which, however,
did not impress the gentlemen as forcibly as the threats which
he added to it. He swore that, if the members of the municipality would not have the tocsin sounded immediately and
send out mounted messengers to call out the peasants and
send them to him, he would cause every one of them to be
hanged or shot in the morning ! And this oath was effectual
enough, for the terrified gentlemen knew full well that Father
Haspinger had the power and the will to fulfil his oaths.
Hence, the tocsin was sounded, mounted messengers were sent
out in all directions, and on the following morning upward
of two thousand able-bodied men arrived at Haspinger's
camp.*

"All right," said the friar ; "if Andreas Hofer and Speckbacher join us with their forces, I believe we shall succeed,
and St. Cassian will have understood our prayers."

While Anthony Wallner and his sharpshooters occupied
the mountain-gorges this side of Brixen on the road to Mitte-

* "Gallery of Heroes : Andreas Hofer," p. 110.

wald, Joseph Speckbacher and his men had penetrated far beyond Mittewald toward Sterzing, and had learned that the Saxons, under General Royer, were resting at Sterzing with the intention of advancing in the morning through the wild valley of the Eisach toward Brixen.

"Well, if the Saxons are resting we must work in order to prepare eternal repose for them," said Joseph Speckbacher, gayly. "Now come, my brave lads, we must take the Saxons between two fires. They are miserable scoundrels and traitors. Ah, they do not shrink from serving the rapacious conqueror Bonaparte, and turning their arms against their German countrymen, merely because the French emperor orders them to do so, and because we refuse to submit to the foreign yoke and are determined to preserve our German tongue and our German rights ! How disgraceful it is that Germans should attack Germans at the bidding of the foreign oppressor ! Therefore, we will punish the Saxons and Bavarians in the name of God and the Holy Virgin. We will let them advance down the defile, and attack them only after they are in it. They cannot retrace their steps, for we are behind them ; nor can they advance very far, for Father Red-beard will meet them in front. Now come and let us make festive preparations, as it behooves those who are expecting distinguished guests. We will erect a few triumphal arches to them, and show them how avalanches roll down our mountains. Ah, we will build up for them artificial ruins which will excite their sincere admiration ! "

"Yes, yes, we will ! " shouted the peasants, who went to work, singing and laughing. In the first place, they erected "triumphal arches" to the enemy ; that is to say, they obstructed the road by raising a number of abatis, besmeared with pitch the wooden railing of the bridge built across the Eisach near the village of Pleis, loosened the planks of the bridge, and began to build "avalanches." They felled a considerable number of tall larches, tied ropes to both ends of them, lowered them half-way down the precipitous side of the mountain, and fastened the ropes above to the strong branches of trees firmly rooted in the soil of the crest. Then they threw huge masses of rock and heaps of rubbish on these hanging scaffolds ; and after the "avalanches" had thus been completed, they withdrew cautiously and rapidly into the mountain-gorges. Only Zoppel, Joseph Speckbacher's servant, and an old peasant remained near the "avalanches." They stood on both sides of the ropes, hatchet in hand, casting fiery glances into the defile on the bank of the Eisach, and between overhanging wood-clad precipices.

Profound silence reigned all around ; only from time to time a rustling noise was heard in the shrubbery ; the flashing barrel of a rifle was then seen, and it seemed as though the fleet-footed chamois appeared on the heights above. But they were Tyrolese sharpshooters who had climbed up to the watch-towers of their natural fortresses to espy the enemy and on his appearance to welcome him with the bullets of their rifles.

Profound silence reigned all around, and the two men were still standing, hatchet in hand, by the side of the ropes holding the artificial avalanches.

All at once a loud, shrill whistle resounded in front of the entrance to the defile ; it was repeated all around the gloomy gorge.

"That is the signal that the enemy has passed the inn *am Sack* and is entering the defile of the Eisach," murmured Zoppel, examining once more the edge of his hatchet with his hand. Then he looked down attentively into the depth, where only a footpath meandered close along the bank of the foaming Eisach.

A few soldiers were now seen entering the defile yonder, where the road projected between two jutting rocks forming the background of the gorge.

The form of a Tyrolese sharpshooter appeared at the same moment on the top of the precipitous rock. He stepped close to the edge of the rock, allowed the soldiers, who looked around slowly and distrustfully, to advance a few steps, and then raised his rifle. He fired ; one of the soldiers fell immediately to the ground, and the Tyrolese sharpshooter reloaded his rifle. He fired again, and laid another soldier prostrate.

The two reports had accelerated the march of the enemy.

The soldiers entered the defile with a hasty step ; in order to advance, they had to remove the two soldiers who were writhing in the agony of death and obstructing the narrow path, and throw them into the waters of the Eisach, which received with a wild roar the two corpses, the first victims of the reopening struggle.

Meanwhile the Tyrolese sharpshooter on the height above had reloaded his rifle and shot another soldier. On seeing this, he uttered a loud *Jodler*, made a leap of joy, and nodded laughingly to the enemy, who cast threatening glances on him. But he did not see that one of the officers below called four soldiers to him, pointed his hand at the top of the rock, and gave them a quick order. The four soldiers sprang at once from the ranks and disappeared in the shrubbery covering the base of the rock.

The sharpshooter was reloading his rifle, when the shrubbery behind him rustled, and, on turning hastily, he saw one of the soldiers rushing toward him. A cry of rage burst from the lips of the sharpshooter. He then raised his rifle and fired. The soldier fell, but at the same moment one of his comrades hastened from the thicket toward the top of the rock. Another cry burst from the sharpshooter's lips, but this time it sounded like a death-cry. He saw that he was lost, for already the uniforms of the other two soldiers were glittering among the trees, and the second soldier was only a few steps from the edge of the rock where the sharpshooter was standing. The Tyrolese cast a last despairing glance around him, as if to take leave of heaven and earth, and of the mountains and valleys of his beloved Tyrol. Then he threw down his rifle and seized the soldier furiously. His arms encircled the body of his enemy like iron clasps, and he forced him with irresistible impetuosity toward the edge of the rock.

"In God's name, then," he shouted in a loud voice echoed by the rocks all around. "In God's name, then !"

With a last effort he threw himself with the soldier into the depth, and both disappeared in the waters of the Eisach.

Speckbacher's servant the faithful Zoppel, had seen and

understood everything; and when the two sank into the foaming torrent, he wiped a tear from his eyes.

"He died like a brave son of the Tyrol," he murmured, "and the Holy Virgin will assuredly bid him kindly welcome. But we, Hisel, will avenge his death on the accursed enemy below."

"Yes, we will," cried the peasant grimly; and he raised his hatchet with a furious gesture.

"It is not yet time," said Zoppel thoughtfully. "Just wait until a larger body of troops has entered the defile. See, Hisel, how splendid they look in their gorgeous uniform, and how proudly they are marching on!"

The Saxons did march on proudly, but not with drums beating. They advanced in silence, filled with misgivings by the profound stillness which surrounded them all at once, listening attentively to every sound, and examining anxiously the top of every projecting rock.

The head of the serried column had arrived now directly under the hanging "avalanche" in the middle of the gloomy defile. The silence was suddenly broken by a loud angry voice, which seemed to resound in the air like the croaking of the death-angel.

This voice asked, "Zoppel, shall I cut the rope now?"

"Not yet! not yet!" replied another voice; and the precipitous rocks all around echoed "Not yet! not yet!"

The Saxons gave a start and looked up. Whence came these voices? What meant that huge black mass suspended on the precipitous side of the mountain right over their heads?

Thus they asked each other shudderingly and stood still, fixing their eyes on the black mass of rock and rubbish, which filled their hearts with wonder and dismay.

"Let us retrace our steps! Let us not penetrate farther into the defile," murmured the soldiers with trembling lips, but in so low a tone that the officers marching by their sides could not hear them.

But the officers, too, were filled with strange misgivings; they ordered the soldiers to halt, and hastened back to General Royer to report to him the mysterious words which they had

heard, and to ask him whether they were to halt or retrace
their steps.

"Advance at the double-quick !" commanded the general,
sternly.

"Advance at the double-quick !" they repeated to their soldiers along the whole line ; the latter, in obedience to this order, hurried on under the black mass which still hung threateningly over their heads.

All at once a powerful voice above shouted out : "Now,
Hisel, in the name of the Holy Trinity, cut the ropes !"
Thereupon they heard the strokes of two hatchets.

The soldiers, who were rushing forward in serried ranks,
looked up again, and indescribable horror seized them. The
black mass of rock and rubbish which had hitherto hung over
them, commenced moving and rolling down with a terrible
crash. A cloud of dust rose and filled the gloomy defile as
with the smoke of powder. At the same time a heavy fire
burst forth on all sides, and from amid the leafy screen the
deadly bullets of the sharpshooters brought death with every
discharge into the allied ranks. A death-like silence then ensued for a moment, for out of the depths rose the wails and
lamentations of the hundreds of soldiers who had been crushed
and mutilated by the "avalanche." The Tyrolese, filled with
curiosity and compassion, looked down into the defile. The
smoke and dust had disappeared, and they could distinctly
survey the scene of horror, devastation, and death, in the
gorge.

Happy those whom the falling "avalanche" had hurled
from the narrow footpath into the foaming torrent ! It is
true, death had been in store for them there, but it had quickly
put an end to their sufferings. But what was the agony of
those who lay buried under the fragments of the rocks, their
limbs fearfully mutilated ! What were the sufferings of the
hundreds of soldiers lying on the road, on this narrow, gory
path, upon which the "avalanche" had thundered down !

It was a horrible sight ; even the Tyrolese trembled on beholding this rubbish, these fragments, whence large numbers
of bloody corpses protruded, and amidst which torn, mutilated
limbs were moving, while here and there soldiers, covered all

over with dust, and bleeding from fearful wounds, tried painfully to raise themselves from the ground.

Those of the Saxons who had not been struck by the terrible avalanche, fell back shuddering. When the Tyrolese saw this, their compassion at the cruel fate of the dead gave way, and with deafening shouts they burst forth from their concealment, and, mingling with the enemy, a frightful slaughter took place.

The Saxons rallied, however ; courageous discipline presided over unskilled valor, and the column advanced slowly and painfully in the direction of the bridge, through a murderous fire, and surmounting the ruins which obstructed the road and covered the bodies of their comrades.

All at once exultant shouts and cheers resounded at the entrance of the defile, and the clarion-notes of martial music joined in these stirring acclamations. Fresh troops, re-enforcements of the Saxons, were coming up from the rear. The Bavarians had arrived with their artillery, which they had placed in a very favorable position ; they had already taken the two farm-houses at the entrance of the gorge where the Tyrolese had taken position, and were now rushing into the defile. The Tyrolese, dismayed at this impetuous advance, retreated into the mountains.

For two days the struggle was continued in these gorges near Mittewald. For two days Saxons and Tyrolese opposed each other in this fratricidal contest, in which Germans fought against Germans in obedience to the behests of the tyrant who had subjugated all Germany, and to whom only the undaunted Tyrol still offered a stubborn resistance.

The victory was long undecided. Once the forces of the Duke of Dantsic succeeded at one extremity of the defile in driving back the sharpshooters under Joachim Haspinger, the Capuchin, and clearing a passage for the Saxons struggling in the gorge. But the Capuchin had retreated only to bring up fresh forces, dispatch messengers to Speckbacher, Peter Mayer, Andreas Hofer, and Anthony Wallner, sound the tocsin, and concentrate more armed peasants. And Speckbacher came up with his brave sharpshooters in the rear of the Saxons ; Anthony Wallner and his men made their appearance likewise ; Peter Mayer brought up fresh forces ; and Andreas Hofer sent word that he would be on hand speedily.   But the Saxons were likewise re-enforced, both by the French, who moved up from Brixen, and the Bavarians, who approached from Sterzing.

The contest was continued with unabated violence, and both sides struggled obstinately for the victory.   But the Tyrolese fought for their rights, their liberty, their German country ; the Saxons and Bavarians fought for tyranny, for the foreign oppressor, and the subjugation of their country-men.   God granted victory to the Tyrolese, and in the defile of Mittewald upward of a thousand Saxons had to atone by their death for having fought at the bidding of the French conqueror on German soil against their German countrymen.

The Tyrolese fought for their rights, their liberty, their German country ; and the Duke of Dantsic, the proud mar-shal of France, was defeated by the despised peasants ; he had to flee from their wrath, and arrived without his cloak and hat, trembling and deathly pale, on his foaming horse at Ster-zing, which he had left a few hours previously with the firm conviction that he would inflict a crushing defeat upon the "haughty peasant-rabble."   Now this " haughty peasant-rab-ble " had defeated him.

God is with those who fight for the rights and liberty of Germany.   God is with those who rise boldly against French tyranny and French arrogance !

CHAPTER XXXII.

THE FIFTEENTH OF AUGUST AT INNSPRUCK.

GOD is with those who fight for the rights and liberty of Germany. He had granted another victory to the Tyrolese.

Animated by their brilliant successes, the patriots no longer stood on the defensive, but, flocking from all quarters to the standard of Hofer, assembled in great multitudes on Mount Isel, the scene of their former triumphs, and destined to be immortalized by a still more extraordinary victory. Lefebvre had collected his whole force, consisting of twenty-six thousand men, of whom two thousand were horse, with forty pieces of cannon, on the little plain which lies between Innspruck and the foot of the mountains on the southern side of the Inn. They were far from being animated, however, by their wonted spirit ; the repeated defeats they had experienced had inspired them with that mysterious dread of the mountaineers with which regular troops are so often seized, when, contrary to expectation, they have been worsted by undisciplined bodies of men ; and a secret feeling of the injustice of their cause, and the heroism with which they had been resisted, paralyzed many an arm which had never trembled before a regular army.

The Tyrolese consisted of eighteen thousand men, three hundred of whom were Austrian soldiers who had refused to follow their officers, and remained to share the fate of the inhabitants. They were tolerably supplied with ammunition, but had little provisions, in consequence of which several hundred peasants had already gone back to their homes.

Joseph Speckbacher commanded the right wing, whose line extended from the heights of Passberg to the bridges of Hall and Volders ; Hofer was with the centre, and had his headquarters at the inn of Spade, on the Schönberg ; Haspinger directed the left, and advanced by Mutters.

At four in the morning, the brave Capuchin roused Hofer from sleep, and, having first united with him in fervent prayer, hurried out to communicate his orders to the outposts.

The battle commenced at six, and continued without intermission till midnight, the Bavarians constantly endeavoring to drive the Tyrolese from their position on Mount Isel, and they, in their turn, to force the enemy back into the town of Innspruck.

For a long time the contest was undecided, the superior discipline and admirable artillery of the enemy prevailing over the impetuous but disorderly assaults and deadly aim of the mountaineers ; but toward nightfall the bridge of the Sill was carried after a desperate struggle, and their left flank being thus turned, the French and Bavarians gave way on all

sides, and were pursued with great slaughter into the city.
They lost six thousand men, of whom seventeen hundred
wounded fell into the hands of the Tyrolese, while on the side
of the latter not more than nine hundred had fallen.   Lefebvre had to retreat hastily toward Salzburg, where his whole
army was collected on the 20th.

This great victory was immediately followed by the libera-
tion of the whole Tyrol ; and when, on the morning of the
15th of August, the sun rose over Innspruck, Andreas Hofer
and his victorious host stood on Mount Isel, gazing with profound emotion on the reeking, gory battle-field, on which,
two days ago, war had raged with all its horrors, and on the
city of Innspruck, whose smoking and burning houses betokened the last outburst of the rage of the fugitive French marshal.*

"See how much blood it has cost, and how many wrongs
had to be committed, that we might obtain our rights !"
sighed Andreas Hofer, pointing to the battle-field.   "My heart
overflows with pity on seeing these horrors, and I implore
you all to be merciful with the wounded and to treat the prisoners leniently.   Among these prisoners are about one thousand Bavarians and Saxons.   See, they are standing down
yonder in dense groups, and our men surround them, mock-
ing and abusing them.   Go down to them, dear Secretary
Döninger ; tell them to be merciful and compassionate, and
to bear always in mind that the prisoners are no longer their
enemies, but their German brethren ; that they are Saxons
and Bavarians, speak one and the same language with us, and
are our countrymen.   Repeat this to our men, Döninger, and
say to them in my name, ' Do not injure the prisoners ; they
are Saxons and Bavarians, and good and brave men ! ' " †

"They are not exactly good men," said Speckbacher, who
was standing on the right side of Andreas Hofer ; "no, they
are not exactly good men, Andy ; otherwise they would not
have fought against us, who are assuredly good men and have
done nothing but defend our dear country."

Instead of replying to him, Andreas Hofer turned smil-

* "Gallery of Heroes : Andreas Hofer," p. 126.
† Andreas Hofer's own words.—Ibid., p. 125.

ingly to the Capuchin, who was standing on his left side.
"Brother Joachim," he said gently, "you ought to exhort our
Joseph here a little, that he may comply with the Redeemer's
precept and forgive his enemies. He is a very good, but very
stubborn fellow ; a brave and excellent soldier, but it would
do him no harm if he were a better Christian."

"If we had been good Christians latterly we should never
have defeated the enemy," growled the Capuchin, shaking his
head. "If we were good Christians, we should have to love our
enemies, do good to them that hate us, and pray for those who
despitefully use us and persecute us. So long as we are soldiers, Andy, we cannot be good Christians ; and I thank God
for it that we fought like downright brave heathens. But
after the enemy has been expelled from the country, and peace
prevails again everywhere, and I have returned to my tedious
convent at Seeben, I will become again a pious Capuchin, and
exhort our dear brave Joseph Speckbacher to become as good
a Christian as our Andreas Hofer."

"No, no, brother Joachim, we will not wait until then to
show to the world that we are good Christians," exclaimed
Andreas. "God stood by us in the battle of Mount Isel and
made us victorious over our enemies. Let us thank Him,
therefore, for His surpassing goodness and mercy ; let us pray
Him to bless our victory and grant a glorious resurrection to
those who had to sacrifice their lives for it."

He drew his large rosary from his bosom, and, lifting his
eyes devoutly to heaven, sank down on his knees.

"Yes, let us pray God to bless our victory," said Father
Haspinger, bending his knees like Andreas Hofer ; and Joseph
Speckbacher followed his example.

And the pious Tyrolese, seeing their leaders kneeling on the
height above, were filled with devout emotion ; they knelt
likewise ; their cheers and *Jodlers*, their shouts and laughter
died away ; only prayers were heard from their lips, and, as
an accompaniment to them, the melodious peals of the bells,
with which the people of Innspruck were celebrating the departure of the French marshals, and the approach of the defenders of the country.

At this moment the sun burst forth from the clouds, and

shed a radiant lustre on this whole sublime scene—the three kneeling heroes on the height above, and all around the Tyrolese, clad in their picturesque national costume, kneeling and thanking God, with tears in their eyes, for the victory He had vouchsafed to them.

The Bavarian and Saxon prisoners, carried away by this spectacle, knelt down like the Tyrolese, and prayed to God, like their enemies—not thanking Him, as the latter did, for the victory, but for having made them prisoners, of good and pious victors.*

All at once this pious scene was interrupted by loud cheers, shouts, and *Jodlers*, and a long, imposing procession of singing, jubilant men ascended the mountain. The new-comers were the students of Innspruck, who came to congratulate Andreas Hofer on his brilliant victory, and accompany him on his triumphal entry into the city. Many persons followed them, and all shouted exultingly, "Where is Andreas Hofer, the savior of the country ? Where is Andreas Hofer, the liberator ?"

The band heading the procession of the students, struck up a ringing flourish on beholding Andreas, who had risen from his knees at their approach. But he raised his arm imperatively ; the band ceased playing immediately, and the cheers died away on the lips of the students, who bowed respectfully to the tall, imposing form of the Barbone.

"Hush, hush," said Andreas, gravely ; "pray ! No cheers, no music ! Neither I nor any of us did it ; all the glory is due to Him above !" †

"But you helped the good God a little," said the speaker of the students, "and therefore you must submit to accept the thanks of the whole Tyrol, and to being called the savior and liberator of the country. We come to you as messengers of the capital of the Tyrol, and are instructed to request you to tarry no longer, but make your triumphal entry into the city."

"Yes, I will come," exclaimed Andreas, joyfully ; "what I implored of the Lord as the highest boon has been realized

* Mayer's " Joseph Speckbacher," p. 196.
† Andreas Hofer's own words.—Ibid., p. 197.

now : we shall make our triumphal entry into the city, where the mean enemy behaved so shamefully. Return to Innspruck, my friends, and say to the inhabitants that we shall be in the city in the course of an hour—old Red-beard, Speckbacher, and I—and that we shall be glad to meet all our excellent friends there again."

And an hour afterward Andreas Hofer and his friends made their entry into Innspruck. He sat in a gorgeous carriage, drawn by four splendid white horses, which he himself had taken from a French colonel during his flight across the Brenner. By the side of the Sandwirth sat Joachim Haspinger, the Capuchin, and beside the carriage rode Joseph Speckbacher, with a radiant face, and his dark, fiery eyes beaming with triumphant joy ; he was mounted on the proud magnificently-caparisoned charger that had borne the haughty Duke of Dantsic two days ago.

The carriage was preceded by a crowd of rejoicing peasants, and a band of fifers and fiddlers ; carpets and banners hung from all the windows and balconies ; ladies in beautiful attire greeted the conquering hero with waving handkerchiefs ; and the people in the streets, the ladies on the balconies, and the boys on the roofs and in the trees, shouted enthusiastically, "Long live Andreas Hofer ! Long live the commander-in-chief of the Tyrol !" And the bells pealed, the cannon posted on the market-place thundered, and the fifers and fiddlers made as much noise as possible.

"Listen, brother Haspinger," said Andreas Hofer, turning to the Capuchin, while the carriage was moving on slowly, "I should really dislike to enter the city always amid such fuss and noise ; and I believe it is heavy work for princes always to look well pleased and cheerful when they are so much molested by the enthusiasm of the people. I looked forward with a great deal of joy to the day when we should make our entry into the city, and I thought it would be much more beautiful ; but now I am greatly tired of the whole thing ; I should be glad if they would cease fiddling, and clear a passage for the carriage to move on more rapidly. I am hungry, and I would I were already at the tavern of my dear friend Niederkircher."

"Well, you must learn to put on a pleasant face when the people cheer you," said Haspinger, laughing. "You have now become a prince too, and I think your people will love you dearly."

"What nonsense is that, brother ?" asked Hofer, angrily.

"It is no nonsense at all, Andy ; on the contrary, it is quite true. Just listen to their acclamations."

"Long live Andreas Hofer !" shouted the crowd, which was dancing and singing around the carriage. "Long live the commander-in-chief of the Tyrol !"

"They call me commander-in-chief of the Tyrol," said Andreas, musingly. "Tell me, Joachim, is it necessary for me to assume that title ?"

"Yes, it is. There must be a head of the state, a man to whom the people may look up as its star, and to whom it may apply as its comfort, support, and judge. And as the people have confidence in you and love you, you must be the man to hold the whole together, lest it should fall asunder. You shall be the head, and we others will be your hands and thoughts, and will work and fight, and think for you and the Tyrol. We must have a leader, a commander-in-chief of the Tyrol, and you are the man, Andy."

"If you say so, it must be so," said Andreas, nodding his head gently. "Well, then, I shall be commander-in-chief of the Tyrol until order and peace are restored, and until the enemy has been expelled from the country for evermore. But see, we have arrived in front of Niederkircher's tavern, and there is Niederkircher himself with his dear round face. God bless you, Niederkircher, why do you look at me so solemnly, and why have you dressed up so nicely ? Why, you wear your holiday clothes, and yet I think this is neither Sunday nor a holiday."

"It is a great holiday," exclaimed Niederkircher, "the commander-in-chief of the Tyrol, the great Andreas Hofer, is making his triumphal entry into the city. That is why I have put on my Sunday clothes and look so solemn ; for it would not be becoming for me to embrace the distinguished commander-in-chief of the Tyrol, as I should like to do under other circumstances."

"You are a fool, old fellow !" said Andreas, encircling his friend's neck with his arm ; "if I am commander-in-chief before the world, I am, before my friends, always Andreas Hofer, the Sandwirth and humble peasant. Let us go into the house, my dear friend ; and you Joachim, come with us. There ! Take me to the small back room which I always occupy during my stay in the city."

"God forbid !" exclaimed the innkeeper ; "you never must occupy the back room again ; that would not be becoming for the commander-in-chief of the Tyrol. You must take my best room with the balcony opening on the street ; besides, all is there in readiness for your reception."

"Must I take it, Joachim ?" said Andreas to the Capuchin, almost anxiously.

"Yes, Andy, you must," replied the friar. "You must do honor to your new dignity, and to us all."

"It is a pity that I must do so," sighed Andreas. "I was so glad that I should soon be in the old back room, where it is so cozy and quiet, and where you do not hear any thing of the noise and shouting outside. But, if it cannot be helped, let us go to the best room ; but pray, if it is possible, give us something to eat there. Some sound dumplings and a glass of native wine, friend Niederkircher."

"No, no, Andreas Hofer, that will not do to-day," replied the innkeeper ; "I have had all my servants at work in the kitchen ever since sunrise, and you will have a dinner suitable for the commander-in-chief of the Tyrol."

"I should have preferred dumplings and native wine in the small back room," said Andreas Hofer, dolefully, while he ascended with the innkeeper and the Capuchin to the best room on the first floor.

This was a very fine room indeed, and even though it was not as cozy as the back room for which Hofer had longed, it was at all events very agreeable to him to be once more under a hospitable roof, and enjoy a little rest and tranquillity. In the middle of the room stood a table handsomely festooned with flowers, and covered with bottles of wine, cake, and all sorts of fruit.

"Now, my distinguished friends, make yourselves as comfortable as possible," said Niederkircher, cheerfully ; "lie down awhile on the silken divan and repose. Meanwhile I will go to the kitchen and order dinner to be served to the commander-in-chief and his two generals, Haspinger and Speckbacher."

"I shall comply with your request," growled the Capuchin, "and make myself as comfortable as possible."

He hurled his heavy, dusty leathern shoes quickly from his feet into a corner of the room ; he then lay down on the carpet in front of the divan, and stretching his limbs, exclaimed, "Forsooth, I have not been able for a long while to make myself as comfortable as to-day !"

"But you, commander-in-chief," said Niederkircher, beseechingly, "I hope, will not disdain my divan ? Rest there a little, Andy, until the waiters bring you your dinner."

"God forbid ! I must first attend to my horses," exclaimed Andreas. "I suppose, Niederkircher, you saw my four splendid white horses ? They are honest war-spoils ; I will keep them forever and never sell them, although I could get a round sum for them, for they are fine animals ; only the first horse on the right-hand side, I believe, is a little weak in the chest, and ought not to be overworked. Before going to dinner and making myself comfortable, I must go and feed the horses and see if they are comfortable. You know, Niederkircher, I have always fed my horses myself, and will do so to-day also."

And he hastened toward the door ; but Niederkircher ran after him and kept him back.

"For God's sake, Hofer," he cried in dismay, "what are you going to do ? Why, you are not a horse-trader nor the Sandwirth to-day, but commander-in-chief of the Tyrol."

"It is true, I forgot it," sighed Andreas. "Go, then, dear friend, get us our dinner, and have a large bundle of hay put into the manger of the horses.—But, great God ! what dreadful noise is that in the street ? Why, those men are shouting so loudly that the walls are shaking and the windows rattling ! What do they want ? Why do they always repeat my name ? Look out, Niederkircher, and see what is the matter."

Niederkircher hastened to the window and drew the cur-

tain aside in order to look out into the street. A dense crowd
was assembled in front of the tavern ; it was incessantly
cheering and shouting : "Andreas Hofer ! Come out ! Long
live the commander-in-chief of the Tyrol, the liberator ! We
want to see him, we must thank him for delivering us from
the enemy. Andreas Hofer ! Andreas Hofer ! "

"You cannot get around it, Andy ; you must step out on
the balcony," said Niederkircher, stepping back from the window. "The people are perfectly beside themselves with love
and enthusiasm, and will not keep quiet until you come out
and make a speech to them. Do, my friend, step out on the
balcony ! "

"Must I do it ? " asked Andreas, dolefully, turning to the
Capuchin, who was stretching himself comfortably on the
carpet.

"You must, brother," said Haspinger, gravely. "The people wish to see their beloved leader, and it would be ungrateful not to accept their love."

Andreas Hofer sighed, but he yielded and approached the
balcony, the doors of which were thrown open by the innkeeper.

No sooner had the thousands assembled in front of the
house beheld the tall form of their favorite leader, than thundering cheers rent the air ; all waved their hats and shouted,
"Long live Andreas Hofer ! Long live the commander-in-
chief of the Tyrol ! "

And now a feeling of profound emotion overcame the tender, grateful heart of Andreas Hofer ; joy and ecstasy filled
his soul in the face of so much love and enthusiasm, and tears
of the most unalloyed bliss glistened in his eyes, which greeted
the jubilant people with tender, loving glances. He was
anxious to thank these kind people and give utterance to his
love ; and he lifted up his arm, asking them to be quiet that
he might address them.

The cheers and acclamations ceased immediately, and
Hofer spoke amidst the breathless silence of the crowd in a
loud, ringing voice :

"God bless you, dear people of Innspruck ! As you
wanted me to become your commander-in-chief, I am now in

your midst. But there are many other Tyrolese who are not inhabitants of Innspruck. All who wish to be my comrades must fight as brave and honest Tyrolese for God, the emperor, and our fatherland. Those who are unwilling to do so must go back to their homes. Those who wish to become my comrades must never desert me. I shall not desert you either, as sure as my name is Andreas Hofer! You have seen me now, and heard what I had to say to you; therefore good-by!" *

When Hofer had concluded his speech, thundering cheers rent again the air; they continued even after he had left the balcony, closed the door after him, and stepped back into the room.

"That was a very fine speech, Andy," said Niederkircher, shaking hands with him, and gazing tenderly into his flushed face. "It was evident that your words were not learned by rote, but came from your heart, and hence they could not but make a profound impression. But now, commander-in-chief of the Tyrol, dinner is ready. The soup is already on the table, and I myself shall have the honor of waiting on you."

"But Speckbacher is not yet here," said Andreas Hofer, "and we cannot dine without him. We fought and worked together; now we will also rest and attend to our comforts together. Do you not think so too, brother Red-beard?"

But the Capuchin made no reply, or rather he responded only by a loud and long snore.

"By the Holy Virgin! Haspinger has fallen asleep on the floor yonder," exclaimed Andreas, smiling.

"Let us waken him, then," said Niederkircher, turning to the sleeper.

"No, my friend, no, we will not do so," whispered Andreas, drawing him back. "Our faithful and brave brother Red-beard has been so long awake and at work that we must let him rest, and it would be very wrong in us to arouse him from his sleep. Let us defer dinner, therefore, until Speckbacher is here, and until Haspinger has slept enough."

"But you said you were hungry, Andreas. Why do you want to wait, then? Why do you not dine now and let the

* Hofer's own words.—See "Gallery of Heroes: Andreas Hofer," p. 126.

other two dine afterward? You are commander-in-chief, the
highest officer of all, and they must do as it suits you, and you
must not do as it suits them."

"Do not repeat such nonsense," cried Andreas, vehemently.
"I am commander-in-chief only because it is necessary that
there should be one to hold the whole together lest it should
fall asunder. That is what Father Haspinger said, and it is
true. But even though I am commander-in-chief of the Tyrol,
I am not commander-in-chief of my friends in my intimate intercourse with them. All three of us have worked to the best
of our power for the fatherland, and I have not done more-
than Speckbacher or the Capuchin. It is true, I am hungry,
but I shall not go to dinner without my friends ; moreover, it
is good that they are not here yet, and that I have a little time
left. The cravings of my stomach made me almost forget
my duty to God, and by the absence of my friends He reminds
me that I owe Him something and must come to Him. Keep
your fine soup, therefore, a little while, Niederkircher ; I will,
in the mean time, go to the church of the Franciscans to report there to the Lord as His faithful servant and soldier."

He took his black Tyrolese hat, descended hastily the staircase, and went into the street. He had not noticed the dissatisfied air of Niederkircher, and the fact that the innkeeper had
not even thanked him for his greeting ; for all his thoughts
were now fixed upon God, and he reproached himself contritely with almost forgetting God, owing to the cravings of
his stomach.

"Forgive me, my Lord and God," he murmured, on entering the gloomy nave of the church, "for not coming to
Thee at once !"

He walked up the aisle with a noiseless, hurried step, in
order not to disturb the worshippers, to one of the small altars,
before which he knelt down devoutly.

"Here I am, my Lord and God," he murmured, clasping
his hands, "to render homage to Thee and thank Thee for delivering us from the enemy and granting victory to us. I
thank Thee for it from the bottom of my heart, for Thy mercy
was with us, and Thou didst lead us as a true general. Guide
us henceforth likewise, my Lord and God, and stand by Thy

faithful servant, that he may not fail in the difficult task which
he has now taken upon himself.   Lord, Thou knowest that
vanity and pride do not prompt me to become more than I
ought to be ; Thou knowest that I would rather be quietly at
home with my wife and children, than play the distinguished
gentleman here and assume an aristocratic title.   But the
Capuchin, who is wiser than I, says it must be so, and I must
be commander-in-chief.   Hence, I submit patiently, and consent to play the ruler here until Thou, my Lord and God, al-
lowest me again to be Thy humble and simple servant, and to
return to my beloved Anna Gertrude, my three little daughters, and my dear little boy.   O Holy Virgin, watch with ma-
ternal care over my dear ones at home ; protect them, and
grant peace to their hearts, that they may not tremble for my
safety.   Grant peace to us all, Holy Mother of God, and—"

"Look, look, there he is !" shouted a loud voice behind
him, interrupting him in his prayer.   "See, there is the great
hero !   How humbly he is kneeling before the altar !   Look
at Andreas Hofer."

Andreas Hofer turned, indignant at the interruption and
the words so loudly uttered in that sacred place.   He saw several hundred persons thronging the aisle and fixing their eyes
upon him.   All crowded forward and raised their heads to see
Andreas Hofer, admire his fine beard, and examine his whole
appearance.   They had followed him quietly, and as the news
that Andreas Hofer, commander-in-chief of the Tyrol, had
gone to the church of the Franciscans, spread rapidly, all had
hastened thither to see him and render him homage.

But Andreas Hofer thought this homage decidedly irksome, and he was angry that the spectators had disturbed
his prayer.   He, therefore, made a bitter-sweet face in re-
sponse to the enthusiastic demonstrations and affectionate
greetings of the people, and elbowed his way hastily toward
the door.

"I thank you for your attachment," he said to those who
were close to him, "but I should have been better pleased if
you had allowed me quietly to pursue my way, and had not
interrupted my prayer.   But now pray let me go home alone,
and do not follow me.   It may be becoming for aristocratic

gentlemen to have a large suite behind them, but I am only a simple Tyrolese like you all, and do not want to be any thing else. Moreover, I am a very ordinary-looking man, and there is no reason whatever why you should stare at me in this manner. Pray, therefore, do not go with me, but let me return quietly to Niederkircher's tavern, where I am going to dine."

They obeyed, of course, and opened a passage for him to step out of the church door. But thereupon they rushed out to look after him and shout, " Long live Andreas Hofer, the pious commander-in-chief of the Tyrol ! " But no one ventured to follow him ; all gazed affectionately and reverentially after his tall form, as he walked with a slow and dignified step down the street.

"There are strange people in these cities," murmured Hofer to himself, while walking along ; " they do not even let me pray quietly, and are as curious as swallows. They follow me everywhere, and stare at me as though I were a wild beast. If that is being a famous man, I do not care for fame ; and for the whole world I would not be an aristocratic or famous man all my lifetime. When peace has been restored to the country, and there is no longer an enemy to fight, they will forget my humble services, and I shall live again quietly at my inn in the Passeyr valley. No one will then run after the Sandwirth when he comes to Innspruck to sell horses ; and I shall sit again in Niederkircher's back room, eat dumplings, and drink native wine. Ah, Holy Virgin, let it soon be so again, that the commander-in-chief may be again Sandwirth Andreas Hofer."

" Hurrah, long live the commander-in-chief of the Tyrol ! " shouted at this moment some men who had recognized him, and stood still to do homage to him as though he were a sovereign prince.

Andreas Hofer accelerated his step, and was very glad on reaching the tavern soon afterward.

CHAPTER XXXIII.

ANDREAS HOFER, THE EMPEROR'S LIEUTENANT.

ANDREAS ascended the staircase hastily, and entered the balcony-room.

The Capuchin had now risen from the carpet ; Joseph Speckbacher was with him, and both hastened to meet Andreas Hofer.

"You have kept us waiting a long while, brother," said the Capuchin, indignantly ; " you ought to have borne in mind that we have not eaten any thing, and are, therefore, very hungry."

"Yes, Father Andy," exclaimed Speckbacher, smiling, " you hung our bread-basket very high ; we are quite weak from waiting and hunger."

"Now they blame *me* for keeping *them* waiting," said Andreas mildly. "And yet I think they kept me waiting, and hunger drove me to the church. Well, never mind, my dear friends and comrades ; we are together now, and I am very glad of it. Look at Niederkircher and his large dish ! How splendidly it smokes and smells, and how good it will be to eat ! Well, Niederkircher, put the dish on the table here, and sit down and dine with us."

"No, no, commander-in-chief, it is my duty to-day to wait on you, for you are now a highly distinguished gentleman, and so are the other two ; hence, it would not behoove me to dine with you."

"If you refuse to do so, I shall not eat at all," cried Andreas Hofer.

"And I shall run away," said Speckbacher, jumping up from his chair.

"I shall sit still," growled the Capuchin, "but I shall henceforth turn my back upon Neiderkircher if he allows our soup to become cold instead of sitting down at once and dining with us."

"I will do so," cried Niederkircher, moving a chair to the table, and seating himself on it. " But now my friends, permit me at least to fill your plates."

"We will not object to that !" exclaimed the three friends, laughing ; "and pray fill them well, Niederkircher."

There was a long pause now ; nothing was heard but the rattling of the spoons on the plates. All at once this comfortable silence was broken by deafening cheers and shouts uttered on the street.

Hofer dropped his spoon, frowned, and listened. "I believe they are calling me again," he sighed, dolefully.

He was not mistaken. Hundreds of youthful voices were heard shouting Andreas Hofer's name, and their cheers were followed by a loud, ringing flourish of violins, fifes, bugles, and trumpets.

"They have musicians with them," exclaimed Hofer, anxiously. "Holy Virgin, just listen how they are roaring ! It seems as if they were intent on upsetting the house."

"They are calling you, they want to see you," said Niederkircher, who had stepped to the window. "They are the students of the university ; they have come in their holiday attire to serenade you."

"And why do they want to serenade *me* ?" asked Andreas Hofer, almost indignantly. "Why not Speckbacher, or the Capuchin, or Peter Mayer, or Anthony Wallner ? They all did just as much as I did, and perhaps even more."

"But you are the people's favorite, brother," said the Capuchin, smiling ; "the people believe in you, and it would be cruel and short-sighted in us to shake their faith in you. Every thing must come from you ; you must have done and accomplished every thing."

"And what we others did, we did only in your name, Father Andy !" exclaimed Speckbacher ; "the people and the sharpshooters would not have obeyed us so well, had they not believed that you had issued all the orders and instructions which we gave them. On hearing your name they obeyed, fought well, and were confident that we should succeed. And for this reason they are justified in coupling your name with the celebration of the victory. Just listen how they are shouting your name ! It is true, the dear boys have tremendous lungs, and if you do not comply with their wishes, and show yourself on the balcony, I am afraid they will make us deaf and themselves quite hoarse."

"Well, I do not care," sighed Andreas ; " open the door again, Niederkircher, I must step out on the balcony."

"And make another fine speech as before," said the innkeeper, throwing open the folding-doors.

Andreas made no reply, but went to the balcony with a grave and almost angry face. Deafening cheers greeted him, and the dense crowd assembled in the street shouted : " Long live Andreas Hofer, the commander-in-chief ! Long live Andreas Hofer, the liberator ! "

" My brave son, Joseph Speckbacher," said the Capuchin, filling his glass, " you see every one gets his due in the end. Day before yesterday, while we were fighting in the sweat of our brows on Mount Isel, my dear brother Andreas Hofer sat up at his friend Etschmann's tavern. A bottle of wine stood before him, and his rosary lay on the table ; and while we were fighting, he prayed and drank, and sent us from time to time his orders, which sounded like oracles, which no one understood, and which every one interpreted as he deemed prudent. Now he must toil in his turn and fight with his tongue, while we are sitting here snugly and drinking our wine. There is another flourish outside ! Trara ! trara ! "

And the Capuchin waved his glass and emptied it at one draught.

Suddenly the crowd in the street became silent ; a student came forward and advanced several steps toward the balcony.

" Andreas Hofer, beloved commander-in-chief of the Tyrol," he said, in a loud, solemn voice, " our hearts are full of love for you and praise of your heroic deeds, and our lips, too, would like to overflow. Permit us, therefore, noble hero, beloved liberator, to sing before you a song glorifying your exploits ; a song praising your struggles and victories ; a song which will henceforth be sung by every man, woman, and child, throughout the Tyrol. We students wrote the song, for your heroic deeds filled our hearts with enthusiasm, and our attachment to you taught us the finest music for it. Permit us, therefore, to sing before you the song of the victorious hero Andreas Hofer."

"No, no, my dear friends, do not sing," exclaimed Hofer, gravely and almost angrily. "Do not sing, and do not play any longer on your fifes and violins. We did not take the field to sing and dance, and I did not leave my wife and children at home with a light heart, but with tears and anxiety. But I did it because it was the Lord's will; and as He accompanied me into battle we succeeded in defeating the enemy. But it was a hard and mournful task; many brave and excellent men lost their limbs or even their lives, and many wounded patriots are yet imploring God to relieve them of their terrible agony. And while they are groaning and wailing, can you wish to sing? While so many fathers and mothers are lamenting their fallen sons, can you wish to exult here and make music? No, my dear friends, that would not be becoming for a Christian and charitable people. You had better lay your violins aside and take up your rosaries. Do not sing, but pray. Pray aloud and fervently for our beloved emperor, and, if you like, you may add a low prayer for poor Andreas Hofer. But you shall not sing any songs in his honor, for God alone accomplished it all, and homage should be rendered to none but Him. Therefore, do not sing, but pray. Pray in my name, too, for I have not much time now, and cannot pray as much as I should like to do. Say to the good God that we toiled honestly and bravely; say to Him that we suffered privations, watched, fought, and conquered, for the fatherland; and pray to Him for the brave men who accompanied us to the holy struggle, and who will never return, but have succumbed to their mortal wounds. Do not sing, but pray for their poor souls. Play your merry melodies no longer, but go home quietly and pray God to protect us henceforth as He has heretofore. That is what I wish to tell you, my dear friends. And now God bless you, and accept my heart-felt thanks for your love and attachment." *

The students, seized with profound emotion, and deeply impressed by the simple yet soul-stirring words of Andreas Hofer, complied quietly and willingly with his request. Their

* "Gallery of Heroes: Andreas Hofer," p. 130.

fifes, violins, and bugles became silent, and the crowd dispersed noiselessly, without uttering any more cheers and acclamations.

"They are fine, dear lads," said Andreas Hofer, looking after them with beaming eyes ; " strong and hearty lads, full of spirits and impetuosity, but on the other hand so gentle and submissive !—Well, now," he exclaimed joyfully, stepping back into the room, " I hope we shall have some rest, and shall be able to finish our dinner in peace."

This hope, however, was not to be fulfilled. The dinner was not yet over by any means, when cheers and loud noise resounded once more in the street, and another solemn procession approached the tavern. This time, however, the members of the procession did not remain in the street, but entered the house, and the landlord, who had just gone downstairs to fetch some more bottles of wine from the cellar, hastened back to the balcony-room and announced that all the commanders of the *Landsturm* and the municipal officers had arrived to pay their respects to the commander-in-chief of the Tyrol and communicate a request to him.

"Well, then," sighed Hofer, rising, "let them come in here. I see that our dinner is spoiled anyhow. Let them come in here, Niederkircher."

"God forbid ! there are so many of them that they would not have room here ; besides, it would not be becoming for you to receive all these gentlemen here where there is a dinner-table. I have conducted them all to the large ballroom ; they await you there, Andreas Hofer."

"I would I knew what they want of me," sighed Hofer, stroking his long beard.

"I know what they want, Father Andy," said Speckbacher, smiling. "I myself suggested to the commanders of the *Landsturm* the plan of asking of you what they are going to communicate to you now. And you must not refuse to comply with their request, Father Andy ; for the good of the country demands that you should yield, and the emperor himself will thank you for so doing."

"I know likewise what these gentlemen want of you, brother Andy," exclaimed the Capuchin, filling his glass. "I

was yesterday already in Innspruck, where I conferred with
the mayor and the members of the city council, and they will
tell you now what we resolved then.   You must not resist,
brother ; you must, on the contrary, comply with their request ; for it is God's will that you should, and therefore you
must.   Now go to the ballroom, dear Andy."

"I shall not, unless you two accompany me thither," answered Andreas Hofer, emphatically.   "They will finally believe I wish to monopolize all honors, and will charge me with
forgetting that Haspinger and Speckbacher, day before yesterday, did a great deal more than myself at the battle of Mount
Isel, and that we should never have gained a victory there
without them.   Therefore, you must walk side by side with
me, one on my right, the other on my left hand ; and we will
enter the ballroom just as we fought in battle."

On entering the ballroom, where the commanders of the
Landsturm in their uniforms and the officers of the municipality had ranged themselves along the walls, the three heroes
were received with three deafening cheers ; and this time Andreas Hofer was not bold enough to tell the enthusiastic gentlemen to be silent, but he looked quite respectfully at the
mayor in his long black robe, who was approaching him with
a grave step between two members of the city council.

"We come," he said, solemnly, "not only to thank you for
the heroic deeds which you have performed, but to pray you to
do still more for us and the fatherland.   You have delivered
the country from the enemy, but there is lacking to it a head,
a crown.   The Bavarian government commission, and Count
Rechberg, the king's lieutenant, have escaped from Innspruck
with the French forces.   We are free from the Bavarian yoke ;
we are no longer governed by the king's lieutenant, and in his
place we want a lieutenant of the emperor.   There must be
one in whose hands all power is concentrated, and who rules
over the country in the emperor's name.   You must fill this
position, Andreas Hofer.   The authorities and the people of
Innspruck elect you the emperor's lieutenant.   You shall
govern the country in his name, and we will all swear to you
obedience, fidelity, and love."

After he had concluded his address, Anthony Wallner

stepped forth from the ranks of the commanders of the *Land-sturm.* "Yes," he exclaimed, "you shall be the emperor's lieutenant. We will all swear to you obedience, fidelity, and love. We commanders of the *Landsturm* wished to say this to our commander-in-chief, and this was the reason why we came hither. We want to pray you to govern the Tyrol in the emperor's name. Your consent would give us the greatest satisfaction."

"We want to pray you," said one of the members of the city council, coming forward from the midst of his colleagues, "to take up your residence as the emperor's lieutenant in the imperial palace on the Remplatz."

"That will never do," cried Andreas Hofer, in dismay. "How could I be so impudent as to reside in the palace of his majesty the emperor ? No, no, that will never do ; I cannot consent to it."

"It will do very well, and you must consent to it," said Haspinger, solemnly. "You shall reside in the imperial palace, not to gratify your own vanity, but to reassure the people, and show them that they are not entirely destitute of a ruler and protector. You shall govern the country for God and the emperor until all our enemies are worsted and the war is at an end. The emperor has not time at this juncture to take care of us : he must devote his whole attention to the reorganization of his army and prepare for the resumption of hostilities. The armistice expires at the end of this month, and war will then, of course, break out once more, for the French emperor will not keep quiet and submit before he is worsted and crushed entirely ; and we have still a great deal to do, a great deal to fight, and much more blood will have to be shed, before we have delivered the whole Southern Tyrol, Carinthia, and Carniola, from the yoke of the tyrant. In order to do so, Speckbacher, Wallner, and I, will lead the brave Tyrolese against the enemy. Now, if the country is to be governed properly while we are fighting, a man in whom both the people and the authorities have confidence must be at the head of the government. You are this man, Andreas Hofer. The people, the authorities, and the defenders of the country, pray you to

consent to it; but God commands you through my mouth
to accept the position."

"Well, then," exclaimed Andreas, enthusiastically, lifting
his eyes devoutly to heaven, "I will do joyfully what God
commands, and what you request me to do. I will take upon
myself this arduous duty; I will comply with your wishes.
You say it is necessary for the good of the country and the
emperor that there should be a lieutenant of the emperor;
and if there is no other and better man than I, and if you
have confidence in me, I will accept the position. I am nothing but an instrument in the hand of God my Lord, and I do
what He wants me to do, even though it should cost my life.
My life is in His hand, and what I am, and have, and can be,
belongs to my emperor and my country. I will be, then, the
emperor's lieutenant in the Tyrol until the emperor issues orders to the contrary, or until peace is restored to the country,
and the emperor is able again to take charge of the govern-
·ment. Let us pray God and the Holy Virgin that that day
may soon dawn upon us!"

"Long live the emperor's lieutenant!" shouted the whole
assembly, joyously.

"Now," exclaimed the mayor, "give me your hand, Andreas Hofer, lieutenant of the emperor, and commander-in-
chief of the Tyrol. We will conduct you in solemn procession to the imperial palace, for the lieutenant must take up his
residence there."

"Yes, yes, let us accompany Andreas Hofer to the imperial
palace," exclaimed all, in joyful excitement.

"Well, if it please God, I will take up my residence in the
imperial palace," exclaimed Andreas Hofer, solemnly, giving
his hand to the mayor and stepping with him to the door of
the ballroom.

He was followed by the Capuchin, Joseph Speckbacher,
Anthony Wallner, the other commanders of the *Landsturm*,
and the municipal authorities. On stepping into the street,
they were received with thundering cheers by the people who
thronged the street and the neighboring place; and amid
singing and deafening acclamations, and the ringing of all
the church-bells, the emperor's lieutenant and commander-in-

chief of the Tyrol, Andreas Hofer, was conducted to the magnificent imperial palace, where the Sandwirth was to take up his residence.

CHAPTER XXXIV.

THE FIFTEENTH OF AUGUST AT COMORN.

WHILE the people of Innspruck set no bounds to their rejoicings on the 15th of August, and accompanied Andreas Hofer, the emperor's lieutenant, amid the most rapturous manifestations of enthusiasm, to the imperial palace ; while the Emperor Napoleon was celebrating the 15th of August, his birthday, by a great parade at Schönbrunn, and the bestowal of orders and rewards on many distinguished persons, the Emperor Francis was at the fortress of Comorn. Only a few of his faithful adherents had followed him thither ; only his servants and officers surrounded him at his mournful court there.   The Empress Ludovica and the archduchesses had already repaired to Totis, a country-seat of Prince Lichtenstein, in Hungary, whither the emperor intended to follow her in the course of a few days.

" I should set out this very day," he said, pacing his cabinet, to his confidential agent Hudelist, the Aulic councillor, "but I should like to see previously Count Bubna, whom I have sent to Bonaparte."

"I hope, your majesty, that the count will yet return to-day," replied Hudelist, in his humble bland voice.

"God grant it !" sighed the emperor. "It is very tedious here, and I hope our sojourn at Totis will not be so mournful and wearisome. Prince Lichtenstein told me there were excellent fishing-ponds there, and he added that he had caused to be built a laboratory where I might manufacture sealing-wax. I think, Hudelist, we shall be very industrious there, and manufacture new and beautiful styles."

"I received to-day a new receipt for making carmine sealing-wax, perfumed à la rose," said Hudelist, smiling.

"Ah, that is nice," exclaimed the emperor ; "give it to me —let me read it."

The Aulic councillor drew a paper from his bosom **and**
handed it with a low bow to the emperor. Francis took it
quickly, and fixed his eyes smilingly on it.

His features, however, suddenly became very gloomy,
and he threw the paper indignantly on the table. "What
do you give me this for ?" he asked, angrily. "In speaking
of the receipt, I had forgotten the abominable political
situation for a moment, but you must at once remind me
of it."

"My God !" faltered out Hudelist, "what did I do, then, to
excite your majesty's indignation ?"

The emperor took the paper from the table and handed it
to him. "See," he said, already half pacified, "is that a receipt
for making sealing-wax ?"

"Good heavens !" groaned Hudelist, in dismay, "I made a
mistake. In place of the receipt, I handed to your majesty the
draft of the proclamation to your subjects, which your majesty ordered me to write. Oh, I humbly beg your majesty's
pardon for having made so lamentable a blunder ; I—"

"Well, never mind," interrupted the emperor ; "there is
no harm done. You handed me one receipt, in place of another ; and it is true, the sealing-wax receipt may remain in
your pocket until we arrive at Totis, but the other receipt is
needed immediately, for it is destined to reduce the people to
submissiveness and tranquillity. Well, read the proclamation you have drawn up."

"Your majesty, I have carried out carefully the orders of
your majesty, and the instructions of your minister, Count
Metternich, and written only what your majesty had agreed
upon with the minister."

"Read it," said the emperor, taking the fly-flap from the
table ; and, while he was slowly gliding along the walls, and
killing now and then a fly, Hudelist read as follows :

"To my people and my army !—My beloved subjects, and
even my enemies know that, in entering upon the present
war, I was induced to take up arms neither by thirst for conquest nor by mortified personal feelings.

"Self-preservation and independence, a peace which would
be compatible with the honor of my crown, and which would

give security and tranquillity to my people, were the lofty and only objects which I strove to attain.

"The fickle fortunes of war have not fulfilled my expectations ; the enemy penetrated into the heart of my states, and exposed them to the devastations of a war carried on with the most relentless exasperation and barbarity ; but, at the same time, he became acquainted with the patriotic spirit of my people and the bravery of my army.

"This experience, which he purchased after fearful bloodshed, and my unvarying solicitude for the happiness of my subjects, brought about mutual advances for peace negotiations. My plenipotentiaries met with those of the French emperor.

"I am desirous of concluding an honorable peace, the terms of which offer the possibility and prospect of its duration. The bravery of my army, its unwavering courage, its ardent patriotism, its emphatic wish not to lay down its arms prior to the conclusion of an honorable peace, prevent me from submitting to terms which would shake the foundations of the empire, and dishonor us after such great and generous sacrifices and so much bloodshed.

"The noble spirit animating the army is a sufficient guaranty that, if the enemy should after all mistake our intentions and strength, we shall certainly obtain the reward of constancy in the end."*

"There," cried the emperor at this moment, striking with the fly-flap at the wall, "that will at length put an end to your humming, with which you have dinned my ears for a quarter of an hour. Come here, Hudelist, and look at this bluebottle fly. The whole time while you were reading I was chasing it, and have only just got it. Did you ever see so large a fly ?"

"It is a very large fly indeed," said Hudelist, with a grin.

"I do not believe that it is a bluebottle fly," exclaimed the emperor. "It is Bonaparte, who has transformed himself into a bluebottle fly, as Jove once transformed himself into an ox ; and he came hither to annoy me and din my ears until I am quite sick. Yes, yes, Hudelist, believe me, Bonaparte is a huge bluebottle fly, which drives all Europe mad. Ah, would

* See Hormayr's " Andreas Hofer," vol. ii., p. 440.

I could treat him as I treat this abominable bluebottle fly now, and crush him under my foot !"

And the emperor crushed the writhing insect under his heel.

"Your majesty will surely enjoy one day the pleasure of crushing Bonaparte, the huge bluebottle fly, under your heel," said Hudelist. "Only your majesty must be gracious enough to have patience, and not now try to attain what you will surely accomplish at a later time. At this juncture Bonaparte is strong and superior to us ; but let us wait until there is a moment when he is weak ; your majesty will profit by this moment, and crush him."

"See, see how kind you are !" exclaimed the emperor, with a sardonic smile ; "you are so obliging as to give me advice which I did not ask for. I thank you, Mr. Aulic Councillor, but I believe it will be better for me to follow my own understanding. As God Almighty has placed me at the head of Austria and made me emperor, He must confide in my ability to discharge the duties of my imperial office. Well, you need not look so dismayed ; I know that your intentions are good, and I confide in you."

"Your majesty knows that I am ready to die for you, and that I should shed my blood for you unhesitatingly and joyously," exclaimed Hudelist, enthusiastically. "It was, therefore, only my intense love and veneration which made me venture to communicate my views freely and openly to your majesty ; but I shall never do so again, for I was unfortunate enough to displease your majesty thereby."

"On the contrary, you shall always do so, you shall always tell me your opinion freely and openly," cried the emperor, vehemently. "You shall tell me all that you believe, all that you know, and all that you hear and learn from others. Your ears, eyes, and tongue, shall belong to me."

"And my heart, above all things, belongs to my adored emperor, your majesty."

"Have you really got a heart ?" asked the emperor, smiling. "I do not believe it, Hudelist ; you are a clever, sagacious man, but you had better say nothing about your heart, for I think you have used it up in your countless love-affairs.

Moreover, I do not care for it. I do not think a great deal of men who have too much heart, and who always allow their rash heart to influence their actions. My distinguished brother, the Archduke John, for instance, has this fault and weakness ; his heart frequently runs away with his head, and his legs finally run after it."

"But he is a very brave general," said Hudelist, gently ; "a courageous captain, and a most defiant and foolhardy enemy of France. How unwavering were the courage and intrepidity with which he met the Viceroy of Italy everywhere, and attacked him, even though he knew beforehand that he would be unable to worst the superior enemy ! How great was the magnanimity with which he risked all, and did not shrink from sacrificing the lives of thousands in attempting to carry out an insignificant *coup* against the enemy ! And how sublime was the heroism with which he has often dared to brave the orders of the commander-in-chief and pursue his own way, on finding that these orders were dangerous and pernicious to his army ! "

"Yes," cried the emperor, bursting into scornful laughter, "it was owing to this disobedience and stubbornness that we lost the battle of Wagram. If the Archduke John had been more obedient, and arrived with his troops in time, we should have gained the battle, I should not be in this miserable hole, and it would not be necessary for me to sue Bonaparte so humbly and contritely for generous terms of peace. The good heart of my distinguished brother subjected me to this unpleasant necessity, and I shall one day manifest to him my gratitude for it."

"Oh, your majesty," said Hudelist, in his blandest voice, "if the archduke should have unwittingly committed a blunder on this occasion, he has made a thousand amends for it. Your majesty should bear in mind all that the noble Archduke John accomplished in the Tyrol. Your majesty owes it only to the archduke that the Tyrol rose as one man, that it fought, and is fighting still, with the utmost heroism. He arranged it all ; he organized a conspiracy in the Tyrol while the country was yet under the Bavarian yoke—a vast, gigantic conspiracy ; owing to his secret instigation, the revolution

broke out simultaneously in all parts of the Tyrol, and it is
the name of the Archduke John which fills this people of
heroes with the sublime courage which it displays in the most
murderous battles."

"It is bad enough that it is so," exclaimed the emperor,
striding uneasily up and down the room. "The Archduke
John sowed the seeds of pernicious weeds, and played a very
dangerous game."

"It is true, it is dangerous to preach rebellion to a people,
and teach it how to rise in insurrection," said Hudelist,
thoughtfully. "And it cannot be denied that the insurrection
of the Tyrolese sets a deplorable example in some respects. It
is true, the archduke organized the conspiracy only for the
good of Austria and her emperor; but what the Tyrolese are
doing to-day *for* the emperor, they might another time do
against him; and if the archduke were not so exceedingly
loyal and entirely above suspicion, one might think he had
stirred up the insurrection for his own purposes and benefit.
At all events, it only depends on him to have himself proclaimed King of the Tyrol, for his influence is all-powerful in
that province."

The emperor uttered a cry of rage. His eyes shot fire, his
lips quivered and muttered incoherent threats, his cheeks had
turned livid, and he paced his room in indescribable agitation.
Then, as if to give vent to the rage filling his breast, he took
up the fly-flap and struck violently at the flies seated here and
there on the wall.

Hudelist followed his every motion with his cold, stealthy
eyes, and an expression of scorn and malicious joy illuminated his sombre face for a moment.

"It was effectual," he murmured to himself; "jealousy
and suspicion have struck roots in his heart, and we shall succeed in neutralizing the influence of the archduke, who constantly preaches war, and war at any cost."

Suddenly the emperor cast his fly-flap aside, and turned
to Hudelist, whose face had quickly resumed its quiet, humble,
and impenetrable expression.

"Hudelist," said the emperor, in a low and mysterious tone,
"always tell me all you know about the archduke, and do not

conceal any thing from me. I must know all, and count upon your sincerity and talent of observation."

"Your majesty," cried Hudelist, ardently, " I swear that I will faithfully carry out the orders of my emperor. Not a word, not a step, not a manifestation of public opinion shall be concealed from your majesty ; for, as your majesty was gracious enough to observe, my ears, eyes, and tongue, belong to your majesty."

At this moment the door of the anteroom opened, and a footman announced Count Bubna.

" Let him come in," said the emperor ; and he dismissed, with a quick wave of his hand, Hudelist, who, bowing respectfully, and walking backward, left the emperor's cabinet at the same moment that Count Bubna appeared on the threshold of the opposite door.

The emperor hastened to meet him. " Now speak, count !" he exclaimed, eagerly ; " did you see Bonaparte ? Did he admit you ? "

"Yes, your majesty," said Count Bubna, with gloomy gravity, " the Emperor Napoleon did admit me. I had a long interview with him."

The emperor nodded his head. " Did he offer you terms of peace ? "

" He did, but I cannot conceal from your majesty that the Emperor Napoleon will impose very harsh and oppressive conditions. He is exceedingly irritated, and the heroic resistance which our army offered to him, our brilliant victory at Aspern, and the fact that his victory at Wagram was after all little better than a drawn battle, seem to have exasperated him in the extreme. For this reason he is resolved to impose rigorous terms of peace on us, because, if Austria should submit to them, she would thereby admit that the Emperor of the French gained a great victory at Wagram."

"Well, I am glad that he is irritated," said the emperor, shrugging his shoulders ; " so am I, and I shall not accept any peace which would impose humiliating terms on Austria. That is what I have promised this very day to my people in the proclamation lying on the table yonder ; and I owe it, moreover, to myself. Either an honorable peace, or a deci-

sion by the fortune of war. If need be, I will call upon my
whole people to take up arms ; I will place myself at the head
of this grand army, and either defeat Bonaparte, or succumb
honorably."

"Ah, if your people could see your majesty in your generous excitement, with how much enthusiasm they would follow
their emperor and expel the enemy !" exclaimed Count Bubna.
"And yet even the most intense enthusiasm might fail, for
circumstances are more powerful than your majesty's heroism.
The Emperor Napoleon is determined to follow up his success
to its most extreme consequences, and we are at this juncture
unable to cope with him in the long run. All the gaps in his
army have been filled up, and his soldiers are flushed with
victory, and eager to meet our own forces. Our army is
greatly weakened, disorganized, and disheartened ; and, moreover, it has no commander-in-chief, inasmuch as your majesty
has accepted the resignation of the generalissimo. To continue the war would be equivalent to endangering the existence of Austria and the imperial dynasty itself."

"Ah, you mean that Bonaparte would be pleased to say of
my dynasty what he said of Naples and Spain : 'The Bourbons
have ceased to reign' ? "

"Your majesty, although the Emperor Napoleon did not
dare to use such unmeasured language, he did not fail to hint
at such an event. Having admitted me after repeated refusals
and hearing my first words, 'My august master, the Emperor
of Austria,' the Emperor Napoleon interrupted me, and cried
vehemently, 'There is no longer an Emperor of Austria, but
only a Prince of Lorraine !'"

"Ah, indeed, he permits me at least to retain the title of a
Prince of Lorraine ! And what else did he say ? Do not conceal any thing from me, Count Bubna, but bear in mind that
I must know all, in order to take my resolutions accordingly."

"Your majesty, if I did not bear this in mind, I should
never venture to repeat what the Emperor Napoleon permitted
himself to say to me. He seemed to speak quite unreservedly
in my presence ; lying on the floor by the side of his maps, or
sitting on the table and placing his feet on a chair, or stand-

ing before me with folded arms, he spoke to me with a frankness which almost frightened me, and which at times seemed to me quite involuntary."

"There you were mistaken, at all events," said Francis, shrugging his shoulders. "Bonaparte never does any thing unintentionally, and not a word escapes him but what he wants to utter. I know him better than you all, though I have seen him only once in my life; and God knows that, after my interview with him subsequent to the battle of Austerlitz, my heart was filled with intense hatred against him. Now, my heart is more constant in hatred than in love; and if it is said that love makes us blind, hatred, on the other hand, renders us keen-sighted, and that is the reason why I am able to see through Bonaparte and know him better than you all. Tell me, therefore, what he said so frankly to you, and I shall know what to think of his statements which seem to you unintentional expressions of his real sentiments. What does he think of the armistice? Is he really intent on drawing the sword once more, or is he inclined to conclude peace?"

"Inclined, your majesty, is not the right word. He intends to *grant* peace to your majesty in return for heavy sacrifices. Your majesty will have to sacrifice much territory, many fortresses, and finally a great deal of money, in order to obtain peace."

"And what if I should not do so?" cried Francis, impetuously. "What if I should prefer to resume hostilities and die honorably on the ruins of my empire rather than purchase a dishonorable peace? What would he say then?"

"Then he would resume hostilities with his strong and enthusiastic army; he would, as he told me more than once in his thundering voice, be inexorable, and no considerations of generosity would prevent him from wreaking vengeance on his personal enemy; for as such he would regard your majesty in that event."

"But the people of Nuremberg do not hang any one before they have got him," said the emperor, calmly. "Bonaparte has not got me yet, and I think he will not catch me soon. Despite all his braggadocio, he will be obliged to allow the continued existence of the Austrian Empire, for all Europe would rise against him ; even Russia herself would become his enemy, and draw the sword against him, if he should be daring enough to appropriate the Austrian Empire and swallow it as he swallowed Italy."

"Your majesty, I also do not believe that he would menace Austria in case he should be driven again to hostilities ; he threatens only the Emperor of Austria."

"What do you mean, Bubna ? " asked the emperor, vehemently.

"Your majesty," said Count Bubna, in a low, timid voice, "the Emperor Napoleon thinks you are his personal and inexorable enemy, and he believes if a monarch more favorable to him were seated on the throne of Austria, he would not only soon conclude peace with Austria, but also have a faithful ally in her hereafter. If hostilities should be resumed, and if the fortune of war should decide in favor of the Emperor Napoleon—"

"Proceed, proceed," cried the emperor, impatiently, when Count Bubna hesitated ; "I must know all, and am not so cowardly as to be frightened by mere words."

"But I, your majesty, am afraid of uttering words whose meaning fills me with loathing and horror—words which, thank God, will never become deeds ! "

"No preamble, count, but speak out," cried the emperor, impatiently. "What would Bonaparte do in case he should defeat us again ? "

"Your majesty, he would place another emperor on the Austrian throne."

"Ah, always the same old strain," exclaimed the emperor, contemptuously. "One of his brothers or brothers-in-law is to become Emperor of Austria, I suppose ? 'The Hapsburg dynasty has ceased to reign '—that is it, is it not ? "

"No, another prince of the Hapsburg dynasty is to be placed on the throne, one of the brothers of the Emperor Francis."

"Ah, ah ! he thinks of my brothers," murmured the emperor, whose cheeks turned very pale. "Well, which of my brothers did he designate as future Emperor of Austria ? "

"He thought it would be best for France if the throne were ceded to the Grand-duke of Würtzburg, the Archduke Ferdinand. He said he had had confidence in the grand-duke ever since he had been in Tuscany, and he believed that the grand-duke was likewise friendly to him. He would make him Emperor of Austria, and add the grand duchy of Würtzburg to the kingdom of Bavaria."

"And the Tyrol?" asked the Emperor Francis. "Will Bonaparte, in his liberality, give that also to Bavaria, or will he leave it to my brother Ferdinand, the future Emperor of Austria?"

"No, your majesty. The Emperor Napoleon seems to have entirely new and rather singular plans in regard to the Tyrol. According to these plans, Bavaria is not to keep it, for Napoleon said angrily that Bavaria had not at all known how to deal with the simple and honest Tyrolese. He added that profound tranquillity should reign in the mountains ; hence, he could not restore the Tyrol to Bavaria, against which the Tyrolese were animated by intense hatred. As the Tyrolese had manifested their attachment and fidelity to Austria in so admirable a manner, it would be best to make the Tyrol an independent principality, and give it also to one of the archdukes, the brothers of the emperor." *

"By the Eternal! my brothers seem to be the special favorites of the Emperor Napoleon," exclaimed the emperor. "Which of the archdukes is to receive the new principality of the Tyrol at Bonaparte's hands?"

"Your majesty, he said the Tyrol should be given to that archduke for whom the Tyrolese had always manifested the greatest love and enthusiasm, the Archduke John."

"John!" cried the emperor, giving a start ; "John is to become sovereign of the Tyrol? Ah, my sagacious and learned brother has speculated correctly, then! He first stirred up a rebellion in the Tyrol in the shrewdest manner, and he will now quiet the beloved Tyrol, by becoming its sovereign and ruler."

"Your majesty," exclaimed the count, in dismay, "it is not

* Napoleon's own words.—See "Lebensbilder," vol. v., p. 217.

the noble Archduke John who conceived such plans, but the Emperor Napoleon."

" He seems at least to keep up a touching understanding with my brothers. I should like to know whether his generosity will not provide crowns and states for the other archdukes too. And then, you have not told me yet what he intends to do with me after hurling me from the throne. Does he want to keep me confined like the King of Spain and Pope Pius, or will he permit me to live as a refugee in foreign lands, like the King of Naples ? "

"Your majesty, Napoleon only dreamed of the future, and dreams never are logical and consistent. I myself listened to his dreams in silence, and they amused me as the merry fairy-stories of my childhood did—fairy-stories invented only for the purpose of making us laugh."

" Yes, let us laugh at them," exclaimed the emperor, bursting into loud laughter, which, however, sounded so unnatural that Count Bubna did not join in it. "And now," said the emperor, whose face suddenly became very gloomy, "having spoken enough about Bonaparte's funny dreams, let us turn to more serious matters. What are the terms on which the Emperor of the French would make peace with me ? What does he demand ? "

"Your majesty, his demands are so exorbitant that I scarcely dare to repeat them."

"Never mind," said the emperor, dryly. "If I could listen quietly to the plan regarding my brothers, I believe I shall be able to bear the rest. Speak, therefore. What are the terms on which Napoleon would conclude peace ? "

" He demands the cession of all the provinces actually occupied by the French armies ; the surrender of the fortresses still occupied by our troops in these provinces, with their magazines, arsenals, stores, and supplies ; the surrender of the fortresses of Gratz and Brunn ; and large contributions in kind, to be collected by M. Daru, the French intendant-general."

" He intends to spoliate Austria as mercilessly as he formerly plundered Hamburg and the whole of Northern Germany," said the emperor, shrugging his shoulders. "And does not Bonaparte demand any money this time? Will he content himself with provinces, fortresses, and contributions in kind? Will he extort no money from us?"

"Your majesty, he demands an enormous sum. He demands the immediate payment of two hundred and thirty-seven millions of francs." *

"Well, well, he will take less than that," exclaimed the emperor.

"Then your majesty will graciously negotiate with him on his terms of peace?" asked Count Bubna, joyously. "Bearing in mind only the welfare of your monarchy, you will not reject his rigorous demands entirely, and not allow the armistice to lead to a resumption of hostilities, which, under the present circumstances, could not but involve Austria in utter ruin?"

"I shall think of it," said the emperor; "at all events, I have already shown my desire for peace by sending my ministers, Counts Stadion and Metternich, to Altenburg, to negotiate there with Bonaparte's minister Champagny. I shall not recall them, but allow them to continue the negotiations. They are skilled diplomatists, and men of great sagacity. The labors of diplomatists generally make slow headway; hence, it will be good for us to lend them a little secret assistance. While the plenipotentiaries are negotiating publicly at Altenburg in Hungary, I will secretly begin to negotiate with the emperor himself; and you, Count Bubna, shall be my agent for this purpose."

"Your majesty," exclaimed Count Bubna, in a tone of surprise rather than joy, "your majesty reposes in me so much confidence—"

"Which, I hope, you will appreciate, and strive to render yourself worthy of," interrupted the emperor. "I count on your skill, your zeal, and, above all, your discretion. You will take new proposals of peace to-morrow, on my part, to the headquarters of the Emperor Napoleon, at Schönbrunn. But no one must learn of your mission, and, least of all, my two ministers who are negotiating at Altenburg."

"Sire, I shall keep as silent as the grave."

* See Schlosser's "History of the Nineteenth Century," vol. viii., p. 113.

"A bad comparison, Bubna, for new life is to blossom for Austria from your secret negotiations. Well, go now and repose ; we will afterward confer again in regard to this matter, and I will explain my views to you. But say, Bubna, do you really think that Bonaparte was in earnest about his dreams, and that, in case he should defeat us again, he would seriously think of carrying into effect his plans regarding the Archdukes Ferdinand and John ?"

"I am afraid, your majesty, he was in earnest."

"The Emperor Napoleon, then, hates me intensely ?'"

"He believes that your majesty hates him intensely. He told me once frankly that only your majesty's personal hatred had brought about this war, and that he was afraid this hatred would frustrate all peace negotiations. I ventured to contradict him, but he shook his head vehemently and exclaimed, ' The Emperor Francis hates me so intensely, that I believe he would lose his crown and empire sooner than ally himself with me in a cordial manner, even though he should derive the greatest advantages therefrom. Do you think, for instance, that the Emperor Francis, if I wished to become his son-in-law, would give me the hand of his daughter, even though I should relinquish half the war contribution, and restore to him all the provinces occupied by my armies ?"

"What ? Did Napoleon really say that ?" asked the emperor, with unusual, almost joyful vivacity. "But," he added, gloomily, "this is nothing but one of Napoleon's dreams. He has a wife, and the Empress Josephine is so young and gay yet that she does not think of dying."

"But the Emperor Napoleon, I have been told, thinks a great deal of getting a divorce from her."

"The pope, whom he keeps imprisoned, will never grant it to him," exclaimed the emperor.

"I think he will not even apply to him for it, your majesty. The Emperor Napoleon never had his union with the Empress Josephine consecrated by the Church, and the dissolution of a civil marriage does not require the pope's consent. The emperor can dissolve it by virtue of his own authority."

"That is a very convenient arrangement for M. Bonaparte," said Francis, smiling. "Well, go now, count, and repose. I am very content with your services, and I think I shall be so hereafter also.   Adieu.   I shall send for you again."

He nodded kindly to the count, and stood still smilingly at his writing-table in the middle of the cabinet, until the door of the anteroom closed behind Count Bubna.   But thereupon his face assumed a gloomy, bitter expression, and he lifted up his clinched fist with a menacing gesture.

"My brothers !" he cried, in an angry voice ; "always my brothers !   They are always eager to push me aside.   *I* am always to be kept in the shade, that *their* light may shine more brightly.   Ah, we shall see who is Emperor of Austria, and to whom the Tyrol belongs ; we shall see who is the master, and who has to obey.   As yet I am emperor, as yet *I* have to decide on war and peace.   And I will decide.   I will humiliate them and compel them to be obedient, these boastful archdukes, who always preach war and are worsted in every battle !   Oh, they are stirring up rebellion, and stretching out their hands for my property !   But one stroke of my pen will shatter their crowns, stifle their rebellion, and reduce them to submissiveness.   I will make peace with Napoleon, and the seditious Tyrol shall be quieted without being bestowed upon the Archduke John.   I would rather have it restored to Bavaria than that it should be conferred on my brother.   That would be a just retribution for the seditious peasants ; they have set a bad example, and should be punished for it.   I do not want any conspirators among my subjects.   Let Bavaria see how she will get along with the rebellious Tyrolese !   I shall withdraw my hand from them.   I want peace.   I will remain Emperor of Austria despite all my brothers !"

CHAPTER XXXV.

A DAY OF THE EMPEROR'S LIEUTENANT.

THE imperial palace at Innspruck was still the residence of
Sandwirth Andreas Hofer, commander-in-chief of the Tyrol,
and lieutenant of the Emperor Francis. He had lived there
since the 15th of August ; but as simply, quietly, and modestly
as he had lived when he was a horse-dealer and innkeeper, so
he lived now when he was ruler of the Tyrol, and the emperor's
lieutenant. Instead of occupying the large state apartments
of the imperial palace, as his friends had often asked him to do,
Andreas had selected the plainest and humblest rooms for his
quarters, and his style of living was as simple and modest as
his dwelling-place. Vainly his suite tried to persuade him to
hold levees and receive guests at his festive table. Andreas
rejected all such suggestions with proud and withal humble
indignation.

"Do you think I took this arduous task upon myself to
play the aristocratic gentleman, and revel in luxury ? " he replied to those who asked him to adopt such a course. "I did
not become the emperor's lieutenant to display vain and empty
splendor, but to serve my dear Tyrol and preserve it to the
emperor. I am only a simple peasant, and do not want to
live like a prince. I am accustomed to have bread, butter, and
cheese for breakfast, and I do not know why I should change
this now, merely because I am no longer at home with my
dear wife, but here at Innspruck at the emperor's palace. I
am also accustomed to dine very plainly, and am therefore
opposed to any expensive repasts being got up for me here. I
do not like the meats prepared by the cooks of the aristocracy ;
and while I do not want anything but bread, butter, cheese,
and wine, I shall send to Niederkircher's tavern for my dinner.
But it must never cost more than half a florin. I will invite
guests, for I like to have merry people about me ; but the
guests must not come for the sake of the repast, but for that
of our pleasant conversation. I shall send to Niederkircher
for the dinner of all my guests, and he must send enough,

lest any of them should remain hungry. But there must
never be more than six guests, for it would be too bad if I,
who intend to preserve the Tyrol to the emperor, were to cost
him a great deal of money here. In order to prevent mistake, Niederkircher must send in his bill every morning for
me to examine ; the financial secretary shall pay it every
week, and send me the receipt." *

Andreas Hofer remained in these days of his splendor as
active, industrious, and simple as he always had been. The
welfare of his beloved country engrossed all his thoughts, and
he was desirous of devoting his whole strength to it. He issued a number of useful and liberal decrees, which, it is true,
Ennemoser, Döninger, Kolb, or other friends of his had drawn
up, but which he had approved and signed.

Andreas Hofer gave public audiences every morning like a
real prince, and the sentinels placed in front of the imperial
palace and at the door of the commander-in-chief had received
stringent orders not to refuse admittance to the audience-room
to any one, but allow all to come in, how poorly soever they
might be dressed. Andreas listened to every one with kind
patience and cordial sympathy, and always took care to help
console the distressed, make peace, and conciliate ; and every
one who needed comfort and assistance hastened to apply to
the always helpful commander-in-chief.

To-day again many persons were in the audience-room,
waiting impatiently for the moment when the door should
open, and when Andreas Hofer should make his appearance on
the threshold, greet all with a pleasant nod of his head, and
then beckon to him who was nearest to the door to enter his
cabinet.

But the hour fixed for the audience had struck long ago,
and the commander-in-chief, who was usually so punctual and
conscientious, had not yet opened the door of his audience-
room. He had already been half an hour in his cabinet, and
Döninger sat at the desk, ready to write down the names of all
applicants for audience, and add a brief statement of their

---

* The expenses of Hofer and his whole suite, during their six weeks'
sojourn in the city of Innspruck, cost the public exchequer only five hundred
florins.

wishes and petitions. But Andreas was still pacing the room, his hands behind his back ; and although he had already laid his hand twice on the door-knob, he had stepped back as if in terror, and continued striding up and down.

"Commander-in-chief," said Döninger, after a long pause, during which he had watched Hofer's irresolute bearing smilingly, "there is something that disquiets you, is there not ?"

"Yes, Cajetan," sighed Andreas. "As you have found it out, I will no longer deny that there is something that disquiets me."

"And what is it, commander-in-chief ? Will you not communicate it to your faithful and discreet Cajetan ?"

"Yes, I will, my dear Cajetan," said Hofer. "I am afraid I did something very stupid yesterday, and I am ashamed of it."

"Ah, you allude to the lawsuit which you decided yesterday," exclaimed Döninger.

"You see, no sooner did I say that I did something very stupid, than you at once knew what I meant ; what I did must, therefore, have been very stupid indeed. Yes, I alluded to the lawsuit, Cajetan, for I am afraid I did not decide it, but made it only more complicated."

"On the whole, there was nothing to be decided," said Döninger, dryly. "The lawsuit was already decided ; the supreme-court had given judgment in favor of the plaintiff and awarded to him the sum of one thousand florins, which was at issue, and sentenced the defendant to pay that sum and the costs. But the defendant—"

"It was no man, Cajetan," interrupted Andreas ; "it was a woman, and that was the worst of it. I cannot bear to see women weep. They know so well how to touch my heart by their tears and lamentations, that I long to help them. Lord Jesus, how that woman, the defendant in the lawsuit, wept ! And was it the poor woman's fault, Cajetan, that her deceased husband was head over ears in debt, that he borrowed one thousand florins from a friend, and meanly affixed his wife's name without her knowledge to the note which he gave for it ?"

"But that is just the trouble, commander-in-chief ; not only did she know it, but she herself put her name under the note. I myself asked the judges about it yesterday. They say that the woman is known to be avaricious, greedy, and mean, and they would not have given judgment against her if there had not been sworn evidence to the effect that she herself signed the note. They add that she is rich enough to pay back the thousand florins which her husband certainly borrowed from his friend."

" I cannot believe it," exclaimed Andreas. " She wept and lamented so very unaffectedly ; during my whole wedded life I have not seen my wife weep so much as the woman wept during that quarter of an hour yesterday ; and I think one that can weep so much must be innocent. Hence, I did what I had a perfect right to do ; I wrote to the judges and reversed their decision."

" Well, commander-in-chief, if you think you were justified in what you did, why does it disquiet you ? "

" It does," said Andreas Hofer, " because I think now that the plaintiff, who lost his suit, may feel very sore over it, and blame me for depriving him of what he thought was due to him ; and I shudder to think he may be in the other room, and intend to reproach me with ruining him and taking from him what the judges had already awarded to him."

" And, Andy, because you would not like to see one man, you keep the others waiting outside."

" You are right, Cajetan. I ought not to do that ; I am a selfish, cowardly fellow," cried Andreas, contritely. " I will no longer keep them waiting, but admit them at once."

And he went with a hasty step to the door of the audience-room, threw it open, and stepped upon the threshold. The large room was crowded with persons of every age and rank ; all thronged toward the door, and every one was desirous of being the first to greet the commander-in-chief, and to be invited by him into his cabinet.

Andreas Hofer bowed kindly to all; his eyes fell on an old man with silver-white hair, who was striving to penetrate to him, and cast beseeching glances on him.

" My old friend," said Andreas, mildly, " it is true you are not nearest to the door, but you are the oldest person in the room, and therefore it is right for me to listen to you first. Come in, then, and tell me what you want of me."

The old man, leaning on his cane, hastened forward and entered the cabinet, the door of which Andreas Hofer himself closed behind him.

"Now tell me, my aged friend, who are you, and what I can do for you."

"Much, very much, commander-in-chief," replied the old man, in a tremulous voice. "You can grant me justice. My name is Friedel Hofmeier, and I am the unfortunate man who gained his lawsuit yesterday, and who was to get his thousand florins back, but from whom you took them again by virtue of your supreme authority."

"Cajetan, it is as I said," sighed Andreas, turning with a doleful air to Döninger, who sat at the desk, pen in hand, and bowed to the commander-in-chief with a shrug.

"I come to you, the emperor's lieutenant, to demand justice," added the old man. "Your decree was unjust and contrary to law. The judges had decided in my favor, and by reversing their judgment, you treat with harshness and cruelty an old man who stands on the brink of the grave, and deprive my poor grandchild of its whole inheritance."

"May God and the Holy Virgin preserve me from committing such a crime," murmured Andreas Hofer, crossing himself devoutly. "Ah, my friend, why did you not come to me ere this, and tell me all about it? I should have gladly assisted you in recovering what was due to you."

"And yet it is your fault that I cannot recover what is due to me," cried the old man, mournfully. "Why should I have come hither ere this, and robbed you of your precious time? I confided in my good and just cause; I knew that the good God would not abandon me, and that He would not take from me, after losing innocently most of my property by the cruelty of the enemy, who burned down my house and outbuildings, the last remnant of my little fortune, the thousand florins which I lent to my friend, and which his rich wife engaged in her own handwriting to pay back ten years after date. The ten years had expired; the good God did not abandon me, for

He caused the judges to grant me justice and adjudge the thousand florins to me."

"And I took them from him again," murmured Andreas Hofer, with tears in his eyes ; "and it is my fault that he will die with a grief-stricken heart. Cajetan, I have ruined the old man ; tell me, advise me how to make amends for it."

"You reversed the decision of the judges," said Döninger, slowly ; "you possess the power of reversing all decisions."

Andreas Hofer was silent for a moment, and gazed thoughtfully into vacancy, as if to fathom the meaning of an obscure oracle ; all at once his face brightened, and a joyous smile played round his lips.

"I know it now, Cajetan," he exclaimed. "I have the power to reverse all decisions, and therefore my own also."

Cajetan Döninger nodded with silent satisfaction. The old man clasped his hands and gazed at Hofer with an expression of ardent gratitude.

"Will you really do so, Andreas Hofer ?" he asked tremblingly. "Will you reverse your own decree for the sake of justice ?"

"Yes, I will," exclaimed Hofer, joyfully; "and I will do it immediately. Cajetan, take up your pen and write what I am going to dictate to you. There ! now write as follows : ' I, the undersigned, confess by these presents that I committed a mistake yesterday, and violated the laws. To confess mistakes and avow faults is no disgrace; hence, I do so now, and beg pardon of the good God and the judges for doing wrong. I hereby reverse the decision which I made yesterday. Friedel Hofmeier is to receive the thousand florins which the supreme court adjudged to him, and the decision of the judges is to be valid, notwithstanding my decree issued yesterday.' Now give me the pen and let me sign the document."

"Oh, dear commander-in-chief," exclaimed the delighted old man, "what a noble and kind-hearted man you are, and—"

"Hush !" interrupted Andreas, looking up from the paper; "if I make a mistake now, the whole document will be invalid, and we must commence anew. Now I tell you it is hard work to write one's name with such a pointed pen on the paper, and my name, moreover, has such a long-tailed title. Therefore, keep quiet and let me write. There, it is done now —'Andreas Hofer, commander-in-chief of the Tyrol.' Now, my dear old friend, your document is valid. Take it to the city hall, and permit me to congratulate you on having recovered your thousand florins. Say nothing about it now, but hasten to the city hall. There are outside a great many persons who wish to see me."

He handed the paper to the old man, and conducted him to the door, which he himself opened for him. He was about to follow him, when he suddenly drew back and closed the door after him.

"Cajetan," he whispered, anxiously, "I saw something dreadful!"

"What was it, commander-in-chief?"

"Cajetan, I saw the woman whom Friedel Hofmeier sued, and to whom I gave the decree yesterday. Cajetan, I was not afraid when we were on Mount Isel and at Brixen, but I am afraid of that woman and her dreadful lamentations. I do not know what to do, Döninger, if she should have found out what I have done, and come in here to reproach me with it."

"We shall not admit her, commander-in-chief," said Döninger, laughing.

"But, Cajetan, I made a vow never to refuse admittance to any one, and not, as many princes do, to allow distressed persons to wait in my anteroom and send them away without listening to them and comforting them."

"But you heard, Andreas, that the woman is not in distress, for she is rich and very avaricious. She told you the most impudent falsehoods; hence, she must not be admitted; for, if you allow her to come in again, she would lie as she did yesterday."

"You are right, Cajetan, she must not come in; and now, my friend, pray go and admit the next applicant, but not that bad woman."

Döninger went to the door, and, opening it, beckoned to the person standing nearest to it.

A young woman, dressed plainly, but very neatly,

came in, and remained at the door, in visible confusion and
grief.

"Well, madame," said Andeas to her, "do you come to tell
me that all is right, and that your husband and you, his pretty
young wife, live together in happiness and content ? Well, it
was heavy work to reconcile you two, and persuade you to remain together and love each other, as it behooves a Christian
couple. It cost me a whole forenoon, but I do not regret it,
for I accomplished my task, and reconciled you, and all was
right again between you. And I made you promise to return
in two weeks and tell me how you got along with each other.
The two weeks are up to-day, and here comes the pretty
young wife to tell me that Andreas Hofer did his work well,
and that her husband is now faithful, tender, and good. Is he
not ? "

"Alas, he is not ! " 'sobbed the young wife, bursting into
tears. "Tony, my husband, never stays at home in the evening ; he returns only late at night, scolds me for weeping and
upbraiding him with his bad conduct, and yesterday—yesterday he wanted even to beat me ! "

"What a bad man ! " cried Andreas, vehemently. "Why
did he want to beat you, then ? What had you done ? "

"I had locked the street-door, and would not let him have
the key when he wanted to leave the house."

"H'em ! that was a little too severe," said Hofer, hesitatingly. "Why should a young man be prevented from going
out a little ? He cannot always stay at home."

"But he shall not go out without me, and he would not
take me with him. I had requested him to do so, and he had
refused ; therefore, I locked the house and would not permit ·
him to leave it. He shall not go out without me, for he is
such a fine-looking man, that all the pretty women of Innspruck admire him in his handsome national dress, and ogle
him when he passes by."

"Well, let them admire and ogle him," exclaimed Andreas,
smiling. "What do you care for it, provided your husband
does not ogle them ? "

"But he does, commander-in-chief ; he runs after the pretty women ; he goes to the theatre and the concerts to see them,

and speak and flirt with them. Believe me, dearest commander-in-chief, he deserts me, he is faithless, and all your fine
and pious exhortations were in vain. He loves me no longer,
and I love him so dearly, and would like to be always with him
and never desert him. But he says it would be inconvenient
to him, and make him ridiculous, if he should always appear
together with his wife, like a convict with his jailer."

"What a bad, hard-hearted man!" cried Andreas, indignantly.

"He is hard-hearted, indeed," sobbed the young wife. "He
scolds me for my love, and when I like to be with him all the
time, he says my jealousy is disagreeable to him, and there is
nothing more abominable than a jealous wife!"

"Well, he may be right so far as that is concerned," said
Döninger, busily engaged in cutting his pen.

"What did you say, Cajetan?" asked Hofer, turning to
him.

"I did not say anything, but thought aloud," said Döninger, trying his pen.

Hofer was silent for a moment, and gazed into vacancy.
"Yes, my dear woman," he then said boldly, "your husband
may not be altogether wrong in complaining of your jealousy.
I really believe that you are a little jealous, and beg you to try
to overcome your jealousy ; for jealousy is a grievous fault,
and makes many husbands very wretched."

"But must I not be jealous?" she cried, vehemently, weeping bitterly. "Do I not see that the women are trying to se-
duce him and make him desert me? Do I not see him at the
theatre gazing at the finely-dressed ladies and admiring their
bare arms and shoulders?"

"What!" exclaimed Hofer. "Is it true, then, that the
women here appear in public with bare arms and shoulders?"

"Yes, sir, it is," sobbed the young wife. "You can see it
everywhere ; it is the new fashion which the French brought
here ; the women wear low-necked dresses with very short
sleeves, so that their shoulders and arms are entirely bare.
All the aristocratic ladies of Innspruck have already adopted
this new fashion ; and on seeing them in their boxes at the
theatre, you would believe they were in a bath, precisely as

the good God created them. And it is owing only to these
bare arms and shoulders that my dear husband deserts me and
loves me no longer. The aristocratic ladies, with their naked
charms, have seduced him ; and just think of it, he wants me
to adopt the new fashion too, and go as naked as the other
women ! "

"You must not do it," said Hofer in dismay ; "it is a
shameless, unchristian fashion, and no decent woman should
adopt it. This is not the first complaint that I have heard in
regard to the indecent dress of the women here. Some of my
neighbors were at the theatre yesterday, and were indignant
at the indecent appearance of the women there ; they told me
the women sat there dressed in the highest fashion, their busts
entirely bare and not covered with a handkerchief such as
every decent woman in the Passeyr valley wears, and their
arms adorned with all sorts of golden trinkets such as we see
only on those of strolling players who perform in barns. But
I will put an end to it ; I will preserve the good and virtuous
men from seduction, and will not suffer vice to dress up, and
shamelessness to stalk by the side of decency. Just wait, my
dear woman ; I will protect your husband and all other good
men from the seductive wiles of frivolous women, and issue a
decree which will tell all the beautiful women how to behave.
Sit down there and listen to the decree which I shall dictate to
Cajetan Döninger. Cajetan, take a large sheet of stamped
paper and write what I shall dictate to you."

And pacing the room, and slowly stroking his fine black
beard with his right hand, Andreas Hofer dictated as follows :

"Every one will perceive that we have good reason to
thank the kind and almighty God for helping us so signally
to deliver the fatherland from a powerful and cruel enemy ;
and every one will desire that we should henceforth remain
free from this scourge, with which the Lord, as He punished
His chosen people often in the Old and New Testament, visited
and chastised our fatherland, that we might turn to Him and
mend our ways. We will, therefore, turn to God with heart-
felt thanks for his great mercy, and with the sincere purpose
of improving our morals, and pray Him to protect us from
further persecution. We must try to gain His paternal love

by a devout, chaste, and virtuous life, and discard hatred,
envy, covetousness, and all vices, obey our superiors, lend as
much assistance as possible to our fellow-citizens, and avoid
everything that might give offence to God and man. Now,
many of my excellent comrades and defenders of the country
have been scandalized at the neglect of many women to cover
their arms and breasts, whereby they give rise to sinful desires
which must be highly offensive to God and all good Christians. It is to be hoped that they will repent, lest God should
punish them ; but if they do not, it will be their own fault
if they should be covered with mire in an unpleasant manner." *

"Shall I really write that ? " asked Döninger, looking up
from his paper.

"Yes, you shall ; and you shall not omit a word of it," exclaimed Andreas Hofer. "Give me the paper, Cajetan ; I
want to see if you have not scratched out the last words. No,
there it is : 'But if they do not, it will be their own fault if
they should be covered with mire in an unpleasant manner.'
That is right—now give me the pen, Cajetan, that I may sign
the document. Then seal it up and send it to the Official Jour-
nal and the Gazette ; they are to publish it at once, that all the
women of Innspruck may read it to-morrow and know what
to do. Now, my dear woman, I hope you will have some rest,
and need not be afraid of the seductive wiles of those ladies.
Go home, then ; and if you will permit me to give you good
advice, be very gentle and kind toward your husband ; and
for God's sake do not torment him with jealousy, for that is a
bitter herb which even the best husband cannot digest, and
which renders him morose and angry. Go, then, with God's
blessing, and come back a week hence, and tell me whether my
decree has been effectual, and whether your husband goes any
longer to the theatre and ogles the women there."

"May God and the Holy Virgin have mercy on us ! "
sighed the woman, going to the door ; "for I shall not bear it
if my dear husband ogles other women, and something dreadful will happen if he does not mend his ways."

* See "Gallery of Heroes: Andreas Hofer," p. 185 ; and Hormayr's "Hofer," vol. ii., p. 445.

"·God be praised ! " said Döninger, with a deep sigh, when the woman had left the room.

"Why do you say 'God be praised'?" asked Andreas, in surprise.

"God be praised that I am not the husband of this jealous woman. She will torment her husband to death, and leave him not a moment's repose before he dies."

"It is true, she does not seem to be very gentle," said Andreas, smiling. "But then, Cajetan, she loves her husband dearly, is doubtless a virtuous woman, and will never sin against the seventh commandment. Well, my friend, do not grumble so much, but go and admit another person."

CHAPTER XXXVI.

THE LOVERS.

DÖNINGER went to the door and opened it, and a beautiful young girl slipped immediately into the room. "Hush, hush," she whispered to Döninger; "do not say anything to him." And she hastened on tiptoe to Andreas Hofer, who was reading once more with close attention the proclamation which he had dictated to Döninger.

She bent down and kissed the hand in which Hofer held the paper. "God bless you, dear, great father and liberator of the people !" she said, in a silver voice.

"Lizzie Wallner !" exclaimed Andreas, joyfully, casting aside the paper. "Yes, by the Eternal, it is she ! It is Lizzie, the dearest child of my best friend—the most heroic girl in the Tyrol. Come, Lizzie, embrace your second father, Andy, and give me a kiss for father and mother, and one for yourself, my dear girl."

Eliza encircled Hofer's neck, and imprinted a tender kiss on his lips. "God bless you, dear father, for you are the father of the whole Tyrol," she whispered, "and must not scold me for calling you my father too."

"On the contrary, it gladdens my heart," exclaimed Andreas, folding her tenderly to his breast. "It seems to me as though I were holding one of my own girls in my arms, and as though I heard her dear voice calling me father. Lizzie, I can tell you I often long for my pretty daughters and their mother, Anna Gertrude, and sometimes I feel very lonely indeed."

"And why do you not send for your wife and children, father Andy, and have them brought here ? I am sure there is room enough for them in this large house."

"No, they shall stay at home," exclaimed Andreas, vehemently. "The mother must attend to household affairs, and keep every thing in good order, and the girls must help her do it. Otherwise all would go amiss, and when I should have no longer to work for the emperor here, and went back to my home, the inn in the Passeyr valley would be worthless ; we should be destitute, and become beggars. Besides, I do not want my girls to become proud, and think they are aristocratic young ladies now, because their father is commander-in-chief of the Tyrol, and the emperor's lieutenant. We are peasants, and will remain peasants. However, let us speak no more of myself, but of you, Lizzie. Where do you come from, what do you want here, and how did you get into the midst of the crowd in the audience-room ? "

"I came to see you, father Andreas. I asked the sentinel in the passage outside where I would find you, as I had to see you on important business. The sentinel told me to enter the audience-room. It was already crowded with persons who wished to see you, and who told me that one was admitted to you after another ; but, on hearing that I had come all the way from Windisch-Matrey, and had walked two days and two nights without intermission, they took pity on me, and would not let me wait until my turn came, but allowed me to advance close to the door, so as to be the first to enter your room."

"The people of Innspruck are very kind-hearted indeed," exclaimed Andreas, joyously. "Then you have come all the way from Windisch-Matrey, Lizzie ? And where is your father ? "

"He and his sharpshooters joined Joachim Haspinger and

Joseph Speckbacher, and the united forces of the three commanders marched against the Bavarians. Father and his seven hundred sharpshooters expelled the Bavarians from the Unken valley, and is now encamped near Berchtesgaden and Reichenhall. Speckbacher is stationed at Neuhäuser and Schwarzbach, and Haspinger is still at Werfen. They are going to reunite their forces and advance against the Bavarians, in order, if possible, to drive them from the pass of Lueg, which the enemy has occupied with a large force."

"And you are not with your father, Lizzie, nor with your friend the Capuchin, who speaks of you only as a heroine? You no longer carry the wounded out of the thickest of the fight, to dress their wounds and nurse them?"

"I have another duty to fulfil now, and my father has permitted me to come to you in regard to it, dear father Andreas Hofer. I am in great distress, and you alone, dear, all-powerful commander-in-chief of the Tyrol, are able to help me."

"Tell me quick, Lizzie, what can I do for you?" asked Andreas, eagerly. "I owe you yet a reward for your heroic deed on the day of the hay-wagons, and I should like to discharge this debt of the fatherland. Tell me, therefore, dear girl, what can I do for you?"

"You can restore to me the dearest friend I have on earth," said Eliza, beseechingly. "You can deliver a patriotic girl from Bavarian captivity, and an excellent nobleman, who has done no other wrong than that he possesses a loyal Tyrolese heart, from grief and despair."

"I will do so with all my heart," exclaimed Andreas; "only tell me, Lizzie, whom you refer to."

"I refer to Baron von Hohenberg, who lived at the castle of Windisch-Matrey, and his daughter, my dear and only friend Elza. The old baron was always a very pious and affable gentleman, a benefactor and father of the poor; and not a poor man, not a woman in distress applied to him, but whom he willingly relieved and assisted. He lived for twenty years in the Tyrol, at his castle at Windisch-Matrey, and became in this manner an ardent son of the Tyrol, although he is a native of Bavaria, and his whole aristocratic family lives in Munich. His daughter Elza is my dearest friend; we grew

the house, and asked if Camilla was at home—then hastened on to
the door of Camilla's room.

The young girl advanced to meet her with a joyous greeting.
"I am glad you have come, Marietta. Without you I should have
been condemned to pass the whole evening shut up in my room,
wearying myself with books. But I am resolved what I will do in
future. If mamma insists upon my being a child still, and banishes
me from the parlor when she has company, I will either run away,
or I will invite company to amuse me. My cousin, Lieutenant
Kienhause, is again in Berlin; his right arm is wounded, and the
king has given him a furlough, and sent him home. When mamma
is in the saloon, I will invite my cousin here." She laughed merrily,
and drew Marietta dancing forward. "Now I have company, we
will laugh and be happy."

"Who is in the saloon?" said Marietta, "and why are you ban-
ished to-day?"

"Well, because of this Italian count—this insufferable Ranuzi.
He has been here for an hour, and mamma commanded no one to be
admitted, as she had important business with the count."

"And you believe that he will remain the whole evening?" said
Marietta.

"I know it; he remains every evening."

Marietta felt a cold shudder pass over her, but she was outwardly
calm.

"Poor child!" said she, "you are indeed to be pitied, and, if you
really desire it, you shall have my society; but first, I have a commission to execute, and then I will bring some notes, and we will
sing together." She kissed Camilla upon the brow, and withdrew.

The last moment of respite had expired for Ranuzi; there was no
longer a ray of mercy in Marietta's heart. Rushing forward, she
soon reached the castle, and announced herself to the marquis. She
was introduced into his study, and the marquis advanced to meet
her, smiling, and with an open letter in his hand.

"You come at the right time, madame," said he; "an hour since I
received this letter from his majesty."

"Has the king named the person to whom I am to confide my
secret?" she said, hastily.

"Yes, madame, his majesty has been pleased to appoint me for
that purpose."

"Let me see the letter," said Marietta, extending her hand.

The marquis drew back. "Pardon me," said he, "I never allow the
king's letters to pass out of my own hands, and no one but myself
can see them. But I will read you what the king says in relation
to this affair, and you will surely believe my word of honor.

Listen, then : 'Soyez, marquis, le dépositaire de mes secrets, le confidant des mystères de Madame Taliazuchi, l'oreille du trône, et le sanctuaire où s'annonceront les complots de mes ennemis.'* Madame, you see that I am fully empowered by the king to receive your confidence, and I am ready to hear what you will have the goodness to relate." He led her to a divan, and seated himself opposite to her.

"Tell the king to be on his guard !" said Marietta, solemnly. "A great and wide-spread conspiracy threatens him. I have been made a tool by false pretences ; by lies and treachery my confidence was surreptitiously obtained. Oh, my God !" cried she, suddenly springing up; "now all is clear. I was nothing but an instrument of his intrigues ; only the weak means made use of to attain his object. He stole my love, and made of it a comfortable, convenient robe with which to conceal his politics. Alas ! alas ! I have been his *postillon de politique.*" With a loud, wild cry, she sank back upon the divan, and a torrent of tears gushed from her eyes.

The marquis sprang up in terror, and drew near the door ; he was now fully convinced that the woman was mad.

"Madame," said he, "allow me to call for assistance. You appear to be truly suffering, and in a state of great excitement. It will be best for you, without doubt, to forget all these political interests, and attend to your physical condition."

Marietta, however, had again recovered her presence of mind ; she glanced with a wan smile into the anxious countenance of the marquis.

"Fear nothing, sir, I am not mad ; return to your seat. I have no weapons, and will injure no one. The dagger which I carry is piercing my own heart, and from time to time the wound pains ; that is all. I promise you to make no sound, to be gentle and calm —come, then."

The marquis returned, but seated himself somewhat farther from the signora.

"I tell you," said Marietta, panting for breath, "that he made use of my credulity—made me a tool of his political intrigues—these

---

* "I will give the conclusion of this letter which the polite marquis did not read aloud: 'Pour quitter le style oriental, je vous avertis que vous aurez l'oreille rebattue de misères et de petites intrigues de prisonniers obscurs et qui ne vaudront pas le temps que vous perdrez a les entendre. Je connais ces espèces de personnes du genre de Madame Taliazuchi—elles envisagent les petites choses comme très-importantes; elles sont charmées de figurer en politique, de jouer un rôle, de faire les capables d'étaler avec faste le zèle de leur fidélité. J'ai vu souvent que ces beaux secrets révélés n'ont été que des intrigues pour nuire au tiers ou au quart à des gens auxquelles ces sortes de personnes veulent du mal. Ainsi, quoique cette femme vous puisse dire, gardez-vous bien d'y ajouter foi, et que votre cervelle provençal ne s'échauffe pas au premier bruit de ces récits.'"—Œuvres, vol xix., p. 92.

to tell him what he is to say in your name to your friend. — Go, therefore, Cajetan, take the papers to the captain, and conduct him to Lizzie. But do not bring him in here, for there are in the anteroom still a great many persons whom I must see before I can converse further with you. Take him, therefore, into the other room ; and when he is there, return to me, Cajetan. Lizzie may then go in there and see the captain ; and we shall speak with the poor people in the audience-room who have had to wait already so long to-day.—But I shall not let you go again, my Lizzie," added Hofer, after Döninger had left the room ; "no, I shall not let you go again. You must stay with me at the palace here, and be my dear little daughter until the captain returns from his mission, and until you know if he brings your friend and her father along with him. Will you do so, Lizzie ? "

"I will, dear father Andreas ; I will stay with you until then, and take care of you as a good daughter, until my dear Elza, if it please God, returns, when I will go back with her to Windisch-Matrey."

At this moment Döninger re-entered the room. "The captain is in the room yonder," he said, pointing to a side-door ; "he awaits you, and will set out after seeing you. The carriage is already at the door. Go, therefore, Eliza Wallner."

"I am going already," said Eliza. She nodded to Andreas with a sweet smile and opened the door of the adjoining room, while Döninger admitted another person from the audience-room into Hofer's cabinet.

The room which Eliza entered was one of the large state apartments of the palace, which Andreas did not occupy, and which he used only on rare occasions. It was a wide room with heavy silken hangings on the walls ; curtains of the same description covered the windows, so that only a dim twilight reigned in the large apartment. Magnificent gilt furniture lined the walls ; between the windows stood large Venetian mirrors in broad carved golden frames, and gorgeous lustres of rock-crystal were suspended from the ceiling.

Was it the splendor and magnificence surrounding her all at once that rendered Eliza so timid and anxious ? She leaned for a moment in great embarrassment against the door, as if she could not venture to advance on the glittering floor. Her large, bright eyes glancèd uneasily around the great room, and now she saw in the window-niche yonder the tall form of a gentleman ; his head was averted from her, and he seemed to be looking eagerly out of the window.

"I do not know him ; surely, I do not know him," said Eliza to herself. "It is foolish in me to think so ; be strong, therefore, my heart, strong and calm, and do not throb so very impetuously !"

And overcoming her bashfulness with a courageous effort, she advanced toward the officer, who was still turning his back upon her.

Now she was close behind him, and said in a low, bashful voice : "Captain, I—"

He turned quickly, and gazed at her with eyes radiant with joy and intense love.

Eliza uttered a cry ; she raised her hands involuntarily, made a step forward, and lay in his arms before knowing it ; she felt his burning kisses on her lips, in her heart, and thought and knew nothing but—"It is he ! It is he ! I see him again ! He still loves me !"

"See, dearest Eliza," whispered Ulrich, drawing her close to his heart, "I had to act thus in order to elicit your heavenly secret from you. I knew it was you who wished to see me ; I wanted to take you by surprise, and I succeeded. Your surprise betrayed what the timid and chaste lips of my Eliza would not confess to me. Yes, you love me ! Oh, deny it no longer, for your heart betrayed you when you recognized me, and when joy illuminated your face like a bright ray of sunshine. Now you are mine, Eliza, and nothing on earth must or shall separate us any longer. No, do not try to disengage yourself from my arms, my beautiful, sweet, affianced bride ! I shall not leave you ; even though the whole world should come to take you from me, I should not leave you—no, not for the whole world and all its treasures !"

"The whole world will not come," said Eliza, disengaging herself gently from his arms ; "the world does not concern itself in the affairs of a poor peasant-girl like me. But I myself intend to leave you, sir ; you must let me go, that we may converse in a sensible manner, as it behooves two decent young persons. Take your arms away, Captain von Hohenberg ; it is not right in you to embrace me here while we are all alone. You would certainly be ashamed of it if any one should see you folding the peasant-girl to your heart."

"No, Eliza, I would not ; I should fold you only the more tenderly to my heart, and exclaim proudly in the face of the whole world : 'Eliza Wallner, the peasant-girl, is my affianced bride ; I love and adore her as the most faithful, noble, and generous heart ; she is to become my wife, and I will love and cherish her all my life !'"

"And if you said so, the world would laugh at you ; but your parents and my dear Elza would weep for you. Now, my Elza shall never weep on my account, and never shall your aristocratic parents be obliged to blush for the daughter-in-law whom you bring into their house. As a daughter-in-law I can never be welcome to them ; hence, they could never be welcome to me as parents-in-law."

"Oh, Eliza, your beauty, your angelic purity and goodness would surmount their resistance, for no heart is able to withstand you ; and when my parents are once acquainted with you, when they have submitted to stern necessity, they will soon love you, and fold you as a daughter to their hearts."

"But first they would have to submit to stern necessity, and I should have to be forced upon them, that they might afterward learn to love me. Much obliged to you, sir; I am only a peasant-girl, but I have my pride too, and will never allow myself to be forced upon a family, but will only take a husband whose parents would come to meet me affection-ately, and give me their blessing on the threshold of my new home. And now let us drop the subject, and tell me what has happened to you during our separation."

"You see, Eliza, what has happened to me," said Ulrich, mournfully. "After your divine magnanimity had set me free, I succeeded in passing through the insurgent country to the Bavarian lines and re-entered the service. We fought and suffered a great deal, and at length, on the 14th of August, I was made prisoner by the Tyrolese at the battle of Mount Isel and taken to Innspruck. However, they do not know my real name here, for I did not want the news of my captivity to reach my parents ; I preferred that they should lament me as killed in battle, rather than as a prisoner in the hands of the insurgents. But fate decreed that it should be otherwise; I am no longer to be allowed to keep my mournful incognito ; I am to repair to Munich to negotiate there an exchange of the prisoners for the hostages whom our troops carried off."

"Your uncle and my Elza are among the hostages," exclaimed Eliza. "Oh, sir, if you really think that you are under obligations to me, if you have not forgotten that I saved your life, pray procure the release of your dear old uncle, and bring him back hither ; for he has indeed a hard time of it in Munich, where they charge him with treason, and where even his own relatives inveigh bitterly against him. This gnaws at his heart, and, unless released speedily, he will die of grief."

"I did not know that so sad a fate had befallen him," said Ulrich, gently; "Döninger was the first to tell me of it, on bringing me the papers, and conducting me hither. But, I confess, in my intense joy on meeting you, my dear, sweet Eliza, my ungrateful heart had forgotten my old uncle, who gave me so many proofs of his love and kindness, and treated me for months as a son at his house. I will try to reward his love by availing myself of my influential connections and my whole eloquence to bring about his release ; I will go myself to the king to intercede in his behalf."

"But you must bring my Elza with you too, sir," exclaimed Eliza. "Oh, I implore you, by all that is sacred and dear to you—"

"Then implore me by your name, by your sweet face," he interrupted her, enthusiastically.

"I implore you from the bottom of my heart," she continued, without taking any notice of his words, "bring my Elza back to me. She is the better half of my soul; we grew up together, we shared all joys and afflictions, and have sworn to shed our heart's blood and die for each other, if need be, and to stand by each other in faithful friendship to the last day of our lives. Now, I am only half alive when my Elza is not

with me. Therefore, dear Ulrich, restore my Elza to me, and
I will thank you, and bless you, and love you as a brother."

"As a brother!" he cried mournfully. "But I do not
want you to love me as a brother. I want your heart, your
whole heart, Eliza; and it is mine in spite of you—mine!
But you are vindictive, and cannot forget and forgive; and
because I denied and misunderstood you once in my blind
stubbornness, you wish to wreak vengeance on me, drive me
to despair, and make me unhappy for my whole life!"

"I!" she exclaimed, mournfully; "I wish to make you
unhappy?"

"Yes, you," he said bitterly; "you see my sufferings, and
gloat over them; you feel that I love you boundlessly, and
with cold, sneering pride you try to resent my former con-
temptible haughtiness. You oppose your peasant pride to my
insensate aristocratic pride; you want to make me go mad or
die heart-broken, and your coolness never leaves you for a
moment, and my grief makes no impression on you; for,
when I am dead, you will be able to exclaim: 'I fought for
my country as a brave daughter of the Tyrol! I killed a
Bavarian, I broke his heart laughingly!'"

"You lie, I shall never say so!" cried Eliza, in an outburst of generous indignation; "you lie if you think me
capable of so miserable a revenge; you lie if you believe
that I have a cold and cruel heart. I wish I had, for then I
should not suffer what I am suffering now, and I should at
least be able to forget you. You really charge me with having a cold heart, with hating and despising you? Do you not
see, do you not even suspect what I am suffering for your
sake? Look at me, then; see how pale my cheeks are; see
how dim my eyes are! I do not take any notice of it, I do
not look at myself in the mirror—why should I, and for
whom?—but mother tells me so every day, and weeps for me.
And why am I so pale and thin, and why are my eyes so
dim? Because my heart is full of grief; because I have no
rest day or night; because there is in my heart a voice which
I can never silence, not even when I am praying or kneeling
in the confessional. Do you think I am grieving for the
sake of the country or the bloody war? What does the

country concern me? I think no longer of it, and yet every battle makes me tremble; and on hearing the booming of artillery, I kneel down and pray with tears of anguish to the Holy Virgin. Oh, may God forgive me! I do not pray for my father, nor for our soldiers; I pray for a Bavarian, I pray for you!"

"Eliza!" exclaimed Ulrich, radiant with joy, and stretching out his arms toward her, "Eliza!"

"Hush!" she said, stepping back proudly, "do not speak. I have told you the truth, for I do not want you to accuse and curse me, when I am blessing you every day. But now go, sir; forget what I have said, but remember me always as one who never hated you, and never thought of revenging herself upon you."

"Eliza," said Ulrich, gravely, taking her hand, and gazing deeply into her eyes, "let us now be honest and frank toward each other. Our hearts have spoken with each other, and God has heard them. You love me, and I love you. Do you remember what I said to you when taking leave of you on the mountain?"

"I do not, sir," she whispered, dropping her eyes.

"But I do," he continued, gravely and firmly. "I said to you: 'I will go now, but I shall return and ask you: "Do you remember me? Will you become my wife?"' Now, Eliza, I have returned, and ask you as I asked you on the mountain, Eliza, will you become my wife?"

"And I reply as I replied to you on the mountain," she said solemnly. "We can never belong to each other as husband and wife, but we can remember each other as good friends. And so, sir, I will always remember you, and it will always gladden my heart to hear that you are well and happy."

"Is that your last word?" asked Ulrich, angrily.

"Yes, sir, it is my last word."

"Then you are intent on making us unhappy?" he cried, mournfully. "Oh, you crystal-heart, so transparent and clear, so hard, so hard! will you never, then, allow yourself to be softened by the sunbeams of love? Will they always only harden your heart?"

"I cannot act otherwise, sir, I assure you I cannot," she said, beseechingly.

"Well, then, I cannot act otherwise either," he cried. "I shall not accept this mission, I shall not go to Munich, I shall stay here."

"No, no, I implore you to go!" exclaimed Eliza. "Save my imprisoned countrymen; save, above all, my Elza and her father! Oh, she is unhappy, she longs for her home; she is weeping for me, for you, sir! Make haste, make haste; have mercy upon Elza and myself!"

"Why should I have mercy when you have none?" he asked, quickly. "Let the prisoners die of grief; I am a prisoner too, and shall know also how to die. I shall not leave Innspruck unless you promise me that you will become my wife on my return, and plight me your faith before the altar of God. I swear by all that is sacred to me, I will not leave this city unless I take with me your solemn pledge that you will overcome your pride and become my wife."

"Well, then," she said, blushing deeply, "go, then. Procure my Elza's release, bring her home, and then—"

"And then?" he asked, as she hesitated.

"Then you shall receive at the hands of the priest a bride who loves you, loves you with infinite tenderness," she said, in a low voice.

He uttered a cry of joy, and folded her to his heart. But she disengaged herself gently. "Make haste now," she said; "for the sooner you depart, the sooner you will return."

"I will set out immediately," he cried, radiant with joy. "But swear to me, Eliza, that I shall receive immediately on my return, even though it should be early in the morning, at the hands of the priest, my bride—the bride who loves me with infinite tenderness."

"I swear by the Holy Virgin," said Eliza, solemnly, "that if you bring my Elza to me here, you shall receive your bride at the hands of the priest on the day of your return, whether it be early in the morning or late at night."

"Captain Ulrich," shouted Cajetan Döninger, opening the door, "it is high time for you to set out. The carriage has been at the door for upward of an hour."

"I am ready," said Ulrich, holding out his hand to Eliza with a happy smile. "Farewell, Eliza ; I shall return with your Elza in two weeks."

CHAPTER XXXVII.

ELZA'S RETURN.

A SPLENDID festival was being celebrated at Innspruck on the 3d of October, and there were great rejoicings in the city. A message of love and joy had reached Innspruck from the headquarters of the Emperor Francis at Totis. Three of the former leaders of the Tyrolese insurrection, who had escaped to Austria at the time of the second invasion of the Bavarians —Sieberer, Frischmann, and Eisenstecken—had arrived at Innspruck as couriers of the emperor. They had succeeded in passing through Styria and Carinthia, although both these provinces were occupied by French troops, and had safely arrived at Innspruck amid the jubilant acclamations of the population. They brought cheering news from the Emperor Francis. He sent to the commander-in-chief of the Tyrol, his beloved and faithful Andreas Hofer, a large gold chain and medal containing the emperor's portrait ; and he sent also three thousand florins as a gift to the brave sharpshooters. But better than all this was an autograph letter from the emperor, who extolled in it the bravery of the Tyrolese, called upon them to persevere in their resistance, and promised that Austria would succor them vigorously with money and troops. The letter stated that the emperor would soon dispatch Baron von Reschmann with funds and full instructions to the Tyrol, where he would act as commissioner and intendant of the army, and that the Tyrolese might confidently look for the speedy resumption of hostilities.

These joyful tidings were received with unbounded enthusiasm, and Andreas Hofer's face beamed with delight when he was formally invested with the gold medal and chain in the great church of Innspruck, at the foot of the tomb of

Maximilian, by the Abbot of Wiltau, amid the tears and acclamations of a vast concourse of spectators, who afterward, preceded by the municipal authorities, accompanied him in solemn procession to the imperial palace. Andreas presented a
splendid appearance in the fine gold-embroidered uniform
which he wore to-day in honor of the celebration, in place of
his Tyrolese costume ; his heavy gold chain and the medal
with the emperor's portrait, glittered under his fine black
beard on his breast, and he wore a black hat with a plume and
inscription to him as the commander-in-chief of the Tyrol, the
gift of the holy sisterhood of Innspruck.

Andreas Hofer's face shone with happiness as he walked
along in this manner amid the acclamations of the whole
population and the ringing of all the bells ; but his heart was
nevertheless full of humility, and lifting his beaming eyes to
heaven, he murmured to himself, " O my Lord and God, Thou
hast accomplished every thing ; Thou hast protected us and
vouchsafed us victory ! Glory to Thee alone ! Preserve me,
O Lord, from pride and arrogance, and let me recognize always that I am nothing but Thy unworthy servant, and that
Thou alone vouchsafest us victory and blessest our cause ! "

The imperial palace was festively decorated to-day, and a
splendid banquet was to take place there in honor of the celebration. All the functionaries of Innspruck had been invited ;
a brilliant ball was to be given at night in the large throne-
hall, and the beautiful girls of Innspruck were to dance to the
inspiring notes of the orchestra in honor of the festive day.
For the first time Andreas Hofer had permitted music and
dancing, and all the beautiful girls of Innspruck were preparing to take part in the brilliant festival and enjoy the rare
amusement.

All faces were radiant ; even Eliza's sweet countenance
was lit up to-day with the sunshine of happiness. A great joy
had fallen to her share to-day, for Ulrich von Hohenberg had
arrived early in the morning, and with him his uncle, old
Baron von Hohenberg, and his daughter Elza. Ulrich had
redeemed his promise ; precisely two weeks had elapsed since
his departure, and now, after these terrible days of suspense,
which Eliza had passed in tears, in silence, and at the same

time in mysterious activity, Ulrich had returned, and with him Elza, Eliza's dearest friend.

Ulrich had looked on with an expression of quiet happiness when Eliza embraced her Elza again and again with tears of joy ; she knelt down repeatedly by the side of the couch on which had been laid the old baron, whose strength had been utterly exhausted by the journey, the excitement, and the sufferings he had endured in prison ; she pressed his hands to her lips tenderly, and withal humbly, and thanked God that her good old friend and her Elza, the better half of her life, had been restored to her.

But after this impetuous and joyous meeting, the old baron felt so very feeble that he urgently needed repose and silence, and Elza had to conduct him to the bedroom which had been prepared for him.

Eliza and Ulrich were alone now. She trembled, and, wishing to avoid this *tête-à-tête*, glided softly to the door ; but Ulrich hastened after her and seized her hand.

" Eliza," he said, solemnly, " I have fulfilled all your wishes. I have brought back with me my uncle and your friend Elza ; the King of Bavaria accepted the exchange which I offered ; he released the baron and his daughter, and Andreas Hofer sets me free in his turn. I am, therefore, no longer a prisoner, and as a free man I ask you now, do you remember the oath you swore to me on the day of my departure ? "

" I do," she whispered in a low voice.

" Repeat the oath to me," he said, imperatively.

" My oath was as follows : ' I swear by the Holy Virgin that, if you bring my Elza to me here, you shall receive your bride, who loves you with infinite tenderness, at the hands of the priest.' "

" You have not forgotten the words, Eliza. But will you fulfil them now ? "

" You insist on it ? " she asked, looking up to him timidly and mournfully.

" Yes, I do," he said, with a blissful smile.

" Well, then," she whispered, almost inaudibly, " I shall keep my oath."

He uttered a joyous cry, pressed her hand to his lips, and

gazed with an expression of infinite tenderness into her blushing, quivering face.

"Oh, do not tremble, love," he said ; "do not look anxiously into the future. I shall know how to protect my wife from
grief and humiliation. To make you happy shall be my sweet-
est joy ; to see you honored and recognized by society will be
my incessant effort, as it will be my bounden duty. You will
fulfil your oath, and you must do it this very day. Let me
go, then, and get a priest ; and you, my sweet girl, place a
myrtle-wreath on your head, for I shall call for you soon and
conduct you triumphantly to the great church of Innspruck ;
for our marriage shall take place publicly and in the face of
the whole population."

"No, sir," she said, shaking her head gently. "I will redeem my promise, but I beg, nay, I implore you, permit me to
make all necessary arrangements, and let me have for once
my own way."

"And what do you wish, then, beloved ?"

"I wish that no one should learn of our plan, and that you
should conceal it all day long from every one, and speak of it
to no one, neither with your uncle, nor with Elza, nor with
Andreas Hofer."

"But how am I to get a priest to marry us ?"

"Leave it all to me, sir. I will get a priest. I have confided only to my dear old friend Joachim Haspinger, the Capuchin, who was lately in Innspruck, what would take place
in case you should return with my Elza, and he promised that
he himself would marry us. Accordingly, on being informed
this morning by the courier of your speedy arrival, I sent at
once a mounted messenger to Father Haspinger, and I am sure
that he will come to Innspruck to-day."

"You intended, then, to redeem your promise of your own
accord !" exclaimed Ulrich, joyfully ; "you thought of it
without being reminded of it. Oh, I thank you, my Eliza, for
I see now that you really love me."

"Yes, sir, I really love you," said Eliza, solemnly. "You
will find it out this very day. Will you promise me now to
conceal our plan from every one, and let me make all necessary arrangements ?"

"I do, my sweet girl. Tell me what I am to do, and I will obey you silently and unconditionally."

" Well, then, dear Ulrich," she said, in a tremulous voice, "come to-night, at nine o'clock, to the chapel here in the imperial palace. As a witness, I hope you will find there our dear commander-in-chief, Andreas Hofer. Father Haspinger will stand before the altar, and your betrothed will kneel before the altar too, ready to become your wife, and love and serve you all her life."

"And I shall find there my betrothed, to whom I shall plight my faith before the altar, and whom I will love and cherish all my life !" exclaimed the captain, in profound emotion.

She bent her head gently, as if to accept his solemn vow. "Then you will come to the chapel at nine ? " she asked.

" I will," he said, smilingly, "and you may be sure that I shall be promptly on hand. I shall be as punctual as the digger after a hidden treasure, who must disinter it at the stated hour, if he does not want to lose it entirely. I shall be at the chapel at nine o'clock."

" Very well, at nine o'clock. And now farewell until then, sir. I have a great deal to attend to yet in getting up the bridal dress and ornaments, for I do not want you to be ashamed of me to-day, Ulrich. Your bride must not look like a peasant-girl. She must be dressed up beautifully, like an aristocratic lady—like Elza, for instance."

"Dress as you please," he said, smilingly, "but do not believe that I shall ever be ashamed of the peasant-girl, and try to conceal the descent of my sweet, lovely wife."

"And will you ride with me to-morrow to my father's house ? " she asked. "Will you present yourself to my father, Anthony Wallner, commander of the Puster valley, as his son-in-law ? Oh, you know full well, Anthony Wallner is a hero ; not only the Tyrol, but all Germany is familiar with the heroic deeds which he performed at the battle of Taxenbach against the Bavarians. He has taken the field again, and, after joining the forces under Joseph Speckbacher, and Father Haspinger, he will attack the Bavarians at the Pass of Lueg, and, if it please God, defeat them. I suppose, Ulrich, you

will accompany me to my father, Anthony Wallner, and ask
your father-in-law to give you his blessing ? "

"But you told me just now, Eliza, that he is not at
home ? "

"Well, then," she exclaimed, earnestly, "we will ride to the
Pass of Lueg."

Ulrich was silent, and looked down in evident confusion ;
he did not see that Eliza fixed her eyes on him with a searching, mournful expression.

"Eliza," he said, after a pause, lifting his head slowly,
"you possess a magnanimous heart and a delicate soul. Your
heart will forgive me, therefore, for not fulfilling your wish,
and your soul will understand that I cannot fulfil it. Your
father is the commander of the Tyrolese, who have risen in rebellion against Bavaria, and he is fighting against the Bavarians, my countrymen and comrades. I have recovered my
liberty, but I had to swear not to take up arms again during
the present war against the Tyrolese. The King of Bavaria
permitted me to take this oath, and ordered me to return to
Munich, where I am to remain till the end of the war. I must
set out for the Bavarian capital to-morrow, and my sweet, beloved wife will accompany me. After the war is over, and
when there is peace again in the beautiful Tyrol, I shall return
with my Eliza to her home, and ask my father-in-law, Anthony
Wallner, to give me his blessing. I shall be at liberty then to
praise his heroism loudly, and love and honor him as my wife's
father. Do you understand that I cannot act otherwise, beloved ? "

"I do," she replied ; "I do understand that the Bavarian
Captain Ulrich von Hohenberg cannot now go to the Tyrolese
commander, Anthony Wallner, ask him, while he is fighting
against the Bavarians, to bless him, and call him father-in-
law. Let us leave it to the future to grant us peace and happiness."

"You understand that I cannot act otherwise," he said,
anxiously. "But you are sad ? I see a cloud on your forehead, Eliza."

"No, not a cloud," she exclaimed, shaking her head.
"Every thing is clear in my mind, and I see distinctly what I

must do. Come, then, to the chapel at nine ; every thing will be in readiness there."

"You will be there, my lovely bride," exclaimed Ulrich, blissfully, opening his arms to her. "Oh, do not avoid me, Eliza ; you are mine now, your place is on my heart, do not avoid me ! See, I am submissive and obedient, and I will not take what you do not give me of your own accord. But give me now your bridal present, Eliza ; give me the first kiss of love ! "

"No, sir," she said, almost anxiously ; "on the wedding-day no pious bride must desecrate her lips by kissing or partaking of food before going to the altar. Only devout thoughts should fill her heart ; and she ought to pray and implore the saints to vouchsafe happiness to her. Let me go, therefore, and fulfil my sacred duties."

"Yes, my sweet, innocent dove, I will let you go," said Ulrich, gently. "Pray to God and the saints for you and me, but be punctual to-night."

"I shall, sir. Now, farewell. Go out by this door, for Elza is coming to me. I have to tell her a great many things yet."

"She will know your secret then ? You will confide to her what I am not to betray to any one ? "

"No, sir, I shall tell her nothing about it. No one but God must know my secret. For the last time, then, farewell, sir ! "

"Farewell, Eliza ! Oh, give me your hand ! " Let me press it once to my heart ! Oh, fear nothing, Eliza, my unholy lips shall not desecrate even your hand to-day. Now I will go, my child ; farewell until to-night, my sweet love ! "

He bowed to her with a blissful smile, and left the room quickly. Eliza looked after him, motionless, breathless, listening to his footsteps, and heaving a deep sigh when they died away in the distance. Then she laid both her hands convulsively on her heart.

"Oh, it is in great pain ! " she murmured. "It seemed at one time as though it would break, and as though I should die on the spot. But I must not die, nor even weep. And I feel that the good God helps me, and that he approves of what I am going to do. It was God Himself who prompted me to ask Ulrich if he would accompany me to my father. He was obliged to reply that he could not go to the enemy, though this enemy was to become his father-in-law. When he told me that, my heart bridled up, and was once more glad and strong. I knew all at once that I was doing right, and I will carry out my plan to the bitter end. But hush, hush! here comes Elza! I must put on a cheerful face now."

"Lizzie, my Lizzie, are you here?" asked Elza, opening the door.

"Yes, here I am, Elza," exclaimed Eliza, who hastened with a smiling face to her friend.

"And where is Ulrich? Why is he not here? Oh, I sat with such a throbbing heart at father's bedside; I longed so much for him to fall asleep! Oh, Lizzie, I have to tell you so many things! Ah, you do not know how happy I was during this splendid, charming journey! To be always by Ulrich's side, what a bliss! And how tenderly and attentively he took care of my dear old father, just like a good, grateful son, who would like to guess from his father's eyes every wish he might entertain. I often wept tears of joy on seeing him support my father, almost carrying him into the carriage, and arranging his seat for him, and on hearing him comfort the old man in gentle yet manly words. Ulrich did not speak of God and the saints, and yet what he said was pious, pious as a prayer of holy charity. Oh, how noble, good, brave, and gentle, Ulrich is!"

"And you love him, Elza, do you not?"

"Yes, I love him with all my heart, and shall for evermore. But where is he? Where is Ulrich? Was he not with you?"

"He was, Elza; he left me at the moment when you came."

"He was here so long? And what did you speak of? Oh, tell me, Eliza, what did you speak of?"

"Of you, Elza," said Eliza, with a wondrous, radiant expression.

"Ah, of me!" exclaimed Elza, joyfully. "Oh, tell me, Lizzie, do you think he loves me?"

"I do not believe it, Elza, I know it for certain. He intrusted me with an important commission for you, and asks of you a great proof of your love. Come, Elza, let us go to my room. We will be sure there not to be overheard by any one. I will tell you everything there."

CHAPTER XXXVIII.

THE WEDDING.

Night had come, and the people of Innspruck had not yet set bounds to their rejoicings. All the streets were brilliantly illuminated ; a festive performance was played at the theatre, and the apartments at the imperial palace began to fill with the guests who had been invited to the ball.

But while the palace was shining with splendid lustre for the first and last time during the reign of Andreas Hofer, one of its wings had remained gloomy and silent. It seemed as though the loud voices of the world shrank from penetrating hither. Even the sentinel pacing the long, deserted corridor, trod more softly and crossed himself every time he reached the end of the passage. For the imperial chapel lay at the end of the corridor in this wing of the palace, and through the high windows there one could look down upon the altar and the holy lamp.

The sentinel had just walked up the corridor once more slowly and dreamily, when he suddenly saw two men coming along. He stood still respectfully and presented arms. These two men were Andreas Hofer, the commander-in-chief, and Old Red-beard, Joachim Haspinger, who was walking by his side, in his brown cowl and his heavy leather shoes.

On approaching the sentinel, Andreas Hofer stood still and nodded kindly to him. "It is not necessary for you, Joe, to stand here all alone and present arms. I know you are one of the best dancers in the Passeyr valley, and as there is a ball at the palace, you had better go there and dance. I believe the good God Himself will watch over His chapel here."

"Much obliged to you, commander-in-chief—much obliged to you !" exclaimed the soldier, joyfully ; and he ran down the corridor as fast as his feet would carry him.

"How gay and high-spirited these young folks are !" sighed Hofer.

"And why are you not merry too, brother Andy ?" asked the Capuchin. "A great honor was conferred upon you to-day ; they paid you homage and cheered you as though you were the Messiah. The whole city is illuminated for your sake to-night ; at the theatre, the orchestra played flourishes three times, and the whole audience rose the moment the commander-in-chief entered the house. But scarcely had the morose hero been there a quarter of an hour when he sneaked off again. I followed him stealthily, and found him at last in his office ; and while the whole city is rejoicing, he sits at the table covered with papers, and weeps big tears into his beard !"

"But I told you, brother, that couriers had arrived from the valley of the Adige, and informed me that the prospects of our cause are very gloomy there. The people are split up into factions, which are engaged in bitter wranglings. How can I rejoice at the extraordinary honors paid to me, when there are such dark spots in the country ?"*

"Do not think of that now, Andy. The Lord has helped us hitherto, and He will help us henceforward ; for our cause is just, and no enemy is able to stand up against it."

"And do you think, brother, that what we are going to do now is also good and just ?" asked Hofer, hesitatingly.

"Yes, I do, Barbone. Lizzie Wallner is a noble, brave girl, and the good God and His angels love her."

"Well, if you say so, brother Capuchin, it must be all right ; for you are a priest of the Lord, and would certainly not consent to cheat God in so holy a place."

"God cannot be cheated," said the Capuchin, solemnly ; "only short-sighted man can. Now, Lizzie Wallner has keen eyes and a pure heart ; hence she looks into the future, and

* Andreas Hofer's own words.—See "Bilder und Erinnerungen aus Tyrols Freiheitskämpfen von 1809," by Loritza, p. 13.

sees what the short-sighted Bavarian cannot see, and helps
him and herself to escape from the abyss into which both of
them would otherwise fall. She is a genuine heroine, and I
am proud and fond of her. Otherwise I should not have
come to Innspruck to-day. I came only for her sake and at
her urgent request. We are exceedingly busy at the earth-
works near the Pass of Lueg, and look from day to day for
the Bavarians to attack us. Hence I must return there this
very night, that I may be with our men to-morrow in case
there should be a fight."

"God grant that you may be victorious!" sighed Andreas.
"But hark! the clock strikes nine, and the sexton is already
lighting the candles on the altar."

"But he has been instructed to light only two of them, lest
there should be too much light," said the Capuchin. "Let us
go down now, brother Andreas, and do not forget what you
have to do. When the bride enters by the small side-door,
you go to meet her, take her hand, and conduct her to the
altar. After they are married, you offer her your hand again
and beg of her permission to accompany her to the door of her
room."

"All right, I will do so," said Andreas. "Come, let us go
down to the chapel."

A dim twilight reigned in the small chapel. Only two of
the tall wax-lights burned on the altar, and shed their flickering rays on the vigorous form of the Capuchin, who was
standing in front of it, and praying in a low voice with
clasped hands. Close to him, near the steps of the altar, stood
Andreas Hofer, his head bent down, and his hands clasped on
the small crucifix which was to be seen about his neck by the
side of the gold medal and chain.

Footsteps were heard now in the aisle of the chapel, and a
tall man in dark civilian's dress approached the altar. Andreas Hofer drew himself up to his full height and went to
meet him.

"God bless you, Captain Ulrich!" he said, kindly; "I
hope you will accept me as witness of your marriage."

"I thank you, commander-in-chief, for consenting to be
our witness," said Ulrich, cordially; "and I thank you also,

Father Haspinger, for coming to Innspruck from such a distance to marry us."

"I come whenever Eliza Wallner calls me and needs me," said the Capuchin, solemnly.

A small side-door now opened, and a female form in a long white silk dress came in. Her head was covered and concealed with a white veil, which surrounded her whole form like a cloud, and flowed down to the ground. On her head, over the veil, she wore the diadem of the virgin and bride, a blooming myrtle-wreath.

While Andreas Hofer went to meet her and took her hand to conduct her to the altar, Ulrich contemplated her with a throbbing heart, and unutterable bliss filled his bosom.

"She has kept her word," he thought; "she has doffed the costume of the Tyrolese girls and thereby divested herself of her whole past. Oh, how splendid her form looks in this dress; she seems taller and prouder, and yet so lovely and sweet."

He gazed at her as she approached slowly with a light springing step, leaning on Andreas Hofer's arm; he saw only her! He did not hear a door opening softly yonder in the vestry, which contained several latticed windows ; he did not see the dark female form which approached the windows, and whose pale face looked out for a moment and then disappeared hastily. He saw only her, his beloved, his bride, who stood now by his side, whose hot, trembling hand now rested in his own, and who returned gently the tender pressure of his hand.

And now Father Haspinger raised his voice and spoke in devout and impressive words to the bride and bridegroom of the solemnity of this sacred hour, of the importance of the union which they were about to enter upon before God, and of the sacred duties the fulfilment of which they were to vow before the altar.

"And now I ask you, Captain Ulrich von Hohenberg," he said, in a loud voice, "will you take your betrothed here for your wife, and love and cherish her all your life long ?"

He replied in a loud, joyous voice, "Yes."

"And you, young maiden," added the Capuchin. "will you

take your betrothed here for your husband, and love and cherish him all your life long ?"

A low, timid "Yes" fell from her lips. Stifled sobs and groans resounded in the direction of the vestry.

"Join hands, then," said the Capuchin, solemnly, " and let me exchange your rings in token of your union. I marry you now in the name of God, and henceforth you are man and wife. What God hath joined together, let not man put asunder. Kneel down now and receive the benediction."

The bride and bridegroom knelt down hand-in-hand before the altar ; the concealed woman knelt down in the vestry alone, trembling and quivering with anguish.

When the benediction had been given and the bride and bridegroom rose, she rose likewise from her knees. "Holy Virgin," she prayed in a low voice, "give me strength now ! Thou beholdest my heart, and seest what I am suffering ! Oh, be with me in Thy mercy, and give me strength and constancy !"

The ceremony was over now, and Andreas Hofer approached the bride.

"As your father was prevented from being present," he said, " permit me to take his place and conduct you to your room. I suppose you do not object to it, Captain Ulrich !"

"On the contrary, I am obliged to you for taking the place of my sweet bride's father. Lead the way, I will follow you."

"No, sir, wait a moment," exclaimed Father Haspinger, solemnly. "I must speak a few words with you privately."

"And I have to thank you for your kindness in coming to our wedding," said Ulrich, standing still in front of the altar, and following only with his eyes his bride, who was just leaving the chapel with Andreas Hofer by the side-door.

"Captain Ulrich," said the Capuchin, after the door had closed behind the two, "I have complied with Eliza Wallner's request, and married you to your betrothed. You are now man and wife, and nothing but death can separate you from your wife. Do not forget this, sir. But will you also do what I am now about to ask of you ?"

"I promise to do it, if it be in my power."

"In the vestry yonder is one who wishes to see you. Go to

her. But promise me by all that is sacred to you that you will listen to her calmly ; that, whatever she may say to you, you will not inveigh against her ; and that you will overcome your heart and submit like a brave man to that which cannot be helped."

"I do not comprehend what you mean," said Ulrich, smilingly, "but I promise to submit like a brave man to that which cannot be helped."

"Go, then, to the vestry," said Father Haspinger ; "I will leave the chapel, for no one except God should hear what she has to say to you."

He bowed to Ulrich, and quickly walked down the passage to the large door of the chapel. Ulrich hastened to the vestry, and, opening the door, murmured to himself: "What a strange mystery ! Who can await me here ?"

"I await you here, sir," said a low, tremulous voice.

Ulrich looked up, and stared at her who stood before him with clasped hands and gazed at him with beseeching eyes.

"Eliza !" he exclaimed, starting back with a cry of horror; "Eliza, you are here ?"

"Yes, I am here," she said ; "I am here to implore your forgiveness."

"My forgiveness ?" he asked, trembling, and pressing both his hands to his temples. "My God! my head swims—I believe I shall go mad! Eliza is here, she stands before me in her peasant costume, and she left me only a few moments ago in a white bridal dress, and with a myrtle-wreath on her head. What does this quick transformation mean, and how was it possible ?"

"It is no transformation, sir," said Eliza, bashfully. "I am Eliza Wallner, the peasant-girl, and she who left you in the chapel is your wedded wife, the young Baroness von Hohenberg—"

"You are my wedded wife, you alone ?" he cried, impetuously.

"No, sir, I am not !"

"You are not ?" he cried, vehemently. "And who is she who went from me there ?"

"She is your wife, who loves you with all her heart," said

Eliza, solemnly; "she is the wife whom your parents selected for you from your earliest youth; she is Elza von Hohenberg."

Ulrich uttered a cry of rage and despair, and rushed upon Eliza with uplifted hand, pale as a corpse, and with flashing eyes.

She bent her head and whole form before him. "Strike me, I deserve your anger," she said, humbly.

Ulrich dropped his arm with a groan. "Then you have cheated me, wretched girl!" he cried, furiously. "You wished to revenge yourself on me, you lied to me, you betrayed me, you enmeshed me with hypocritical falsehoods, and played an infamous game with me! Well, why do you not laugh? Your efforts were successful, you have revenged yourself. Oh, I am in despair; my rage and grief will break my heart. Why do you not laugh?"

"I do not laugh, sir, because I see that you grieve, and because God knows that I would give up my heart's blood to spare you an hour of suffering."

He burst into scornful laughter. "And yet you have treated me so infamously? You have played a miserable comedy with me, and perjured yourself?"

"Sir, I have not perjured myself," cried Eliza. "I have fulfilled faithfully the oath I swore to you when you took leave of me and went to procure my Elza's release."

"You have fulfilled it? False girl! repeat your oath to me, that I may convict you of perjury."

"I said that if you would bring back Elza, you should receive your bride, who loved you with infinite tenderness, at the hands of the priest, whether it was early in the morning or late at night!"

"Well, then, have you fulfilled your oath? Have you not perjured yourself?"

"I have fulfilled my oath; I have not perjured myself. Elza loves you, sir; she loves you with infinite tenderness."

"Oh, what miserable, insidious sophistry!" cried Ulrich, sinking despairingly on a chair. "Your words were as full of duplicity as your heart is; and I, poor, short-sighted dupe, believed your words ! And not you alone, but Elza, too, has cheated me—she whom I loved as a sister, and whom I should have loved even better, if you had not stepped in between us, if I had not seen you. Elza has betrayed me too; she did not shrink from playing so unworthy a part ! Oh, it will break my heart, it will break my heart ; I lose in this hour all that I loved ! Nothing remains to me but contempt, scorn, and dreadful loneliness ! "

He buried his face in his hands and wept bitterly.

"Sir," exclaimed Eliza, with a cry of despair, kneeling down before him, " you weep ? "

" Yes, I weep," he sobbed ; " I weep for my fallen angels, my lost paradise ! I am a man; therefore I am not ashamed of my tears."

Eliza lifted her eyes and clasped hands to heaven. "Holy Virgin," she exclaimed, " give strength to my words, that he may hear and understand me ! "

She rose from her knees, stepped close up to Ulrich, and laid her hand on his shoulder. "Sir," she said, " do you remember yet what I said to you on taking leave of you on the mountain ? I reminded you of it the other day, but you forgot it again. I said to you : 'You are a nobleman, and I am a peasant-girl; you are a Bavarian, and I, thank God, am again an Austrian. We do not suit each other, and can never become husband and wife.' That is what I said to you, and I repeated it to you the other day, but you would not understand it."

"Because I loved you, Eliza; because I felt that my love would be strong enough to surmount all obstacles ! "

" Was your love strong enough to prevail on you, sir, to go to my father, Anthony Wallner, and ask him to bless you, his son-in-law ? See, I asked you to do so, because I knew that you would refuse, and because I thought it would convince you that we could never become man and wife and ought to part. For without the blessing of my parents I could never follow a husband into the world ; nor would you want a wife who did not bring with her either the blessing of her parents or that of your own, for you are a good and excellent man. That was the reason, sir, why we could not become man and wife, even though it should break our hearts."

"*Our* hearts?" he cried, impetuously. "Do not speak of your heart; it is cold and hard."

"What do you know about my heart?" she asked. "I do not bear it on my lips, nor in my eyes either. It rests deep in my bosom, and God alone sees and knows it. But I, sir, know another heart; I gazed deeply into it, and discovered in it the most fervent love for you, sir. This other heart is that of my Elza: Elza loves you! And you know that I love Elza, and therefore you must believe me, even though you distrust me in other respects. I shall love my Elza as long as I live, and I swore to her never to abandon her, never to deceive her. She confides in me, sir; she did not conceal from me a single fold of her heart. Should I have told her, 'Captain Ulrich, whom you love, and whom your father wants to become your husband, loves me; and I, whom you call your best friend, although she is but a peasant-girl, while you are the daughter of a nobleman, will take your lover from you and make him my husband?' No, sir, never could I have said so; never should I have been capable of breaking Elza's heart; I preferred to break my own!"

"She does not know that I love you? She ought to have known it, inasmuch as she consented to play this unworthy part and take your place before the altar."

"She did not know any thing about it; I deceived her. I told her you sent me as a love-messenger to her, and that I had taken it upon myself to obtain her consent to a clandestine marriage with you, because you were obliged to set out for Munich this very night, and because you wished to take with you the certainty that she would be yours forever, and that you might have the right of protecting her after God had taken her father from her and made her an orphan. Sir, Elza loves you, and therefore she consented, and became your wife."

"And her father? Did he, too, consent to the deception?"

"Her father, sir, is very sick, and I believe he is on his death-bed. Elza told him nothing of it, for the excitement,

the joy might have killed him. I told her it was your will
that she should be silent ; and because she loves you and
would comply with all your wishes, she was silent, obeyed
your call, and came all alone to the altar to become your
wife."

"My wife ! she is not my wife! The marriage is null and
void, and I shall never acknowledge it."

"Elza is your wife, sir, your wife before God and man. A
priest married you, and you swore before the altar to love
and cherish her. Oh, sir, I beseech you, do not repudiate my
Elza, for she loves you; and by repudiating Elza you will repudiate me, for Elza is the better half of my heart. In making her happy, think that you make me happy; and in loving
her, think I feel that you love *me!*"

"Oh, Eliza," cried Ulrich, gazing at her as she stood before him with a glowing countenance, "Eliza, you angel, why
can I not possess you ?"

"Because it is not God's will, sir ! 'The blessing of the
parents builds houses for the children,' says the proverb ;
hence we could not build a house, sir, for we had not the
blessing of our parents. Now you have it, Elza brings it to
you, and she brings you love, sir, and happiness. No, do not
shake your head; she brings you happiness. You do not believe it now, for your heart grieves, and he who has such a
wound thinks that it never will heal. But love is a good surgeon. Elza will dress your heart and heal it."

"And your heart, Eliza, will it heal, too ? For your heart
has likewise a wound, and, whatever you may say to the contrary, you loved me."

"I *loved* you!" she exclaimed. "No, say rather I still
love you ! If I had not loved you, should I have been strong
enough to withstand your supplications and resist my own
heart in order to secure *your* happiness ? Oh, be happy, then,
—be happy through me and for my sake ! Fold Elza to your
heart, love her and let her love you ; and when in future
days, happy in Elza's arms, and surrounded by her sweet
children, you remember the past and its grief smilingly, do
not forget me, but say, 'Lizzie was right after all! She loved
me faithfully!'"

"Faithfully ?" he asked, bursting into tears. "Your heart will heal likewise, Eliza ; you will forget me in the arms of another husband."

"No, sir ! My heart, I hope, will heal, but God alone will heal it, and no other husband. I am not able to love another man, and I believe, moreover, I have something else to do. The fatherland needs brave hands, and I belong to my fatherland and my father. We shall have war again, sir, war with the Bavarians. Thank God, you will not be among our enemies ! I shall carry our wounded out of the thickest of the fight, and nurse them ; and if a bullet hits me, well, then, I shall die for the fatherland, and it will gladden your heart, also, to hear that Lizzie Wallner died as a brave daughter of the Tyrol. I pray God to let me die in this manner. Amen ! But now, sir, go to your young bride. She will be wondering already at your long absence. Oh, go to her, sir, and be kind and loving to her ; let her never suspect what has taken place between us, and that you did not marry her of your own accord."

"I cannot dissemble, Eliza ; I cannot turn my heart like a glove."

"Do I ask you to do so ? Have you not always loved Elza ? Love her now, then; love her for my sake, love me in her ! Go, sir; Elza is waiting for you. I shall go too. Our good Haspinger is waiting for me, and I shall go with him to my father. We shall never meet again, and therefore I will give you now my wedding-present. You asked me for it this morning, and I refused; but now I will give it to you voluntarily. Close your eyes, sir, for you must not see what I give you; and do not open them until I tell you to."

"I will close my eyes, Eliza, but I shall see you nevertheless in my heart."

She glided up to him with a noiseless step. Faithful to his word, he had closed his eyes firmly. She gazed at him long and tenderly, as if to engrave his features deeply on her heart; then she bent over him and imprinted a kiss on his forehead.

"God bless you, Ulrich," she whispered, and kissed his forehead once more. " Farewell ! "

And before he was able to prevent it, or even know it, she glided to the small door leading from the vestry into the street.

Ulrich heard the jar of the door, and opened his eyes. Eliza stood in the open door, and cast a last, parting glance on him. Joachim Haspinger stood behind her.

"Eliza," cried Ulrich, hastening to her, "you will leave me?"

He would have seized her hand, but Haspinger stepped between them. "Go to your bride, sir," he said, imperatively. "Eliza will accompany me and go to her father!"

CHAPTER XXXIX.

THE TREATY OF PEACE.

THE Emperor Francis was still at Prince Lichtenstein's castle of Totis, in Hungary, but for some days past there had no longer reigned there the profound silence and calm monotony which had prevailed during the first days of the imperial sojourn. Couriers came and went, equipages rolled up, and conveyed to the castle some of the Austrian diplomatists, with whom the emperor conversed a long while in his cabinet, whereupon they departed again. Even Baron von Thugut, the all-powerful ex-minister, had been drawn from his tranquil retirement, and called to the headquarters of the Emperor Francis at Totis. Francis had locked himself up with him in his cabinet, and conversed with him in so low a tone that Hudelist, although he had applied his ear to the keyhole, had been unable to hear a single word of importance; and the emperor was so reticent as to the subject of his conversation with Thugut, that the Empress Ludovica, although, after Thugut's departure, she had sought frequently to fathom the meaning of his presence there in her interviews with the emperor, did not receive the slightest information from her husband.

Great commotion reigned at Castle Totis already early in

the morning of the 12th of October. Prince Lichtenstein had arrived in the first place, and Count Bubna had come soon afterward. The emperor had gone with the two diplomatists to his cabinet; they had left it several hours afterward, and departed immediately.

Count Metternich had likewise arrived at Totis, and re-paired at once to the emperor's rooms. The count ordered the footman in the anteroom to announce him to his majesty, but the servant shook his head with a polite smile.

"It is unnecessary for me to announce your excellency," he said. "His majesty ordered me to conduct your excellency at once to his cabinet. Be so gracious, therefore, as to follow me, your excellency."

And he hastened, with a noiseless step, through the apart-ments. Count Metternich followed him quickly, and an im-perceptible sneer played over his fine youthful face as he was walking through these sumptuous rooms, whose deserted ap-pearance was the best proof of the precarious situation of the emperor.

The footman stood now before the door of the imperial cab-inet; after waiting until his excellency had come close up to him, he opened this door, and said, in a loud voice, "His ex-cellency, Count Metternich!"

When the count entered the cabinet, the emperor was sit-ting at his writing-table, and holding in his hand a paper which he had read, but which he laid down now, to rise and greet the count. It did not escape Metternich's keen, prying eyes, that the emperor's face was more serene to-day than it had been for a long time past; and, on bowing deeply to his majesty, he asked himself what might be the cause of this unusual seren-ity, and who might have brought the glad tidings which had awakened so remarkable a change.

"Welcome, count, welcome!" said the emperor, in his sonorous voice, and with a graceful smile. "I sent for you because I am exceedingly anxious to learn the progress of your peace-negotiations at Altenburg. Is there no prospect yet of a speedy termination of this abominable war?"

"Your majesty, I regret to say that the negotiations are progressing very slowly," said Count Metternich, mournfully.

"The Emperor of the French persists with stubborn petulancy in all his demands, and refuses firmly to abate them."

"Indeed, is Bonaparte so stubborn?" asked the emperor, kindly. "How far have you advanced in your conferences with Minister Champagny?"

"Your majesty, we have not advanced yet beyond the difficult questions concerning the contributions in money, and the fortresses. France refuses obstinately to take less than two hundred and thirty-seven millions of francs, and insists on the cession of the fortresses of Gratz and Brünn, which her troops have not even occupied up to this time."

"That is to say, you have not advanced in your peace negotiations beyond what both sides were willing to concede at the outset?"

"Pardon me, your majesty. In the beginning of the negotiations we were entirely ignorant of the demands of France, while we are familiar with them now, and know what course to adopt in regard to them. After learning the adversary's intentions, one may more easily devise ways and means to frustrate them."

"But you have been devising them a long time already without obtaining any results," said the emperor, shrugging his shoulders. "Well, what do you think, my dear count, will be the upshot of your peace negotiations?"

"Will your majesty permit me to tell you the truth?" asked Count Metternich, with his most winning smile.

The emperor nodded his head.

"Well, then, your majesty, I believe that war will be the upshot of all these peace negotiations. The demands of France are so exorbitant that Austria cannot submit to them. Austria's *honor* will compel us to resume hostilities; for a government may, if need be, acquiesce in the loss of some of its territories, but it must never submit to a violation of its honor."

"But do you know that a resumption of hostilities will endanger not only some of our territories, but our existence? Our armies are disorganized, disheartened, and without a competent commander-in-chief; and my distinguished brothers, who are at the head of the different corps, are quarreling as though they were old women, and not princes. Besides, money, the best general in war times, is wanting to us."

"Only declare your determination to resume hostilities, your majesty, and money will not be wanting to you. Your people will gladly sacrifice all their property for this purpose, for your people hate Napoleon and desire vehemently that hostilities should be resumed."

"See here," exclaimed the emperor, almost menacingly, "let me advise you not to allude to my people, if you want me to remain on good terms with you. I have no people ; I have subjects, and want only subjects.* If I need money, I shall impose additional taxes on my subjects, and they will be compelled to pay them ; but they need not offer me any presents, for I think it would be incompatible with my imperial honor to accept them. An emperor must not accept any thing as a present at the hands of his subjects, not even their love, for it is the duty of the subjects to love their emperor. Bear this in mind, count, and do not repeat again this new-fashioned word ' people ;' I cannot bear it, it smells so much of the republic and guillotine. Well, I have told you that, if we resumed hostilities, we should be destitute of three very essential things, namely, a good army, a great captain, and money. There is no doubt whatever that we should lose the first battle again ; and if we were compelled then to sue for peace, Bonaparte would impose still more rigorous terms upon us : we should be obliged to accept them, and should lose both territories and honor. Now you know my views, count, and you shall know also the principal reason why I sent for you. Look at this paper. Do you know what it contains ? The treaty of peace !"

"The treaty of peace ?" cried Metternich, in dismay. "Your majesty does not mean to say—"

"I mean to say that I have made peace with the Emperor of the French. Here is the paper ; take it. The whole thing is done now."

"Your majesty," exclaimed Metternich, looking at the paper which the emperor had handed to him, "it is really true, then ? You have already signed the treaty without be-

* Schlosser's "History of the Eighteenth Century."

ing so gracious as to employ your ministers or even inform
them of it ?"

"Yes, I have, for I thought we needed peace ; hence, I
signed the treaty, and Prince Lichtenstein and Count Bubna
have taken a copy of it to the headquarters of the Emperor
Napoleon at Schönbrunn, and I believe he will sign it also.
Well, do not look so dumbfounded, count, and do not wonder
any longer that I succeeded in making peace without your
assistance. I allowed you and Stadion to go on with the negotiations, and did not prevent you from displaying your
whole diplomatic skill at Altenburg against Bonaparte's minister, Champagny; but all this could not prevent me either from
promoting the affair a little here at Totis, after my own fashion,
and now all is over. For the rest, my dear count, bear in mind
what I now say to you. I appointed you my minister, because
you are an able and clear-headed man, and an industrious and
reliable functionary. I shall let you act, decide, and govern,
and not complain if people say that you are all-powerful in
Austria, and that your will alone guides the ship of state. Let
people say and think so, but *you* shall not think so, count; you
shall know once for all what our mutual position is. I
allow you to govern so long as you govern in accordance
with my views ; but if I am not satisfied with the course
you are pursuing, I shall pursue my own course, and it will
only remain for you to follow me, or retire from public
affairs. Now decide, my dear count ; will you follow me,
or—"

"Sire, there is no 'or,'" interrupted Count Metternich.
"It is your majesty's incontestable right to lead the way, and
indicate to me the course I am to pursue."

"That is right; I like to hear that kind of language !" exclaimed the emperor, holding out his hand kindly to the count.
"You may depend upon it now that we two shall remain yet
a long while together, and that, since we are going to have
peace in the country, we shall rule together in tranquillity
and harmony. There, take the paper now to your room, and
read it attentively, that you may become thoroughly familiar
with it ; above all things, do not forget the secret articles, for
you know they are always the most important of all. Pray

return to me in an hour from now ; we will then work together."

"Sire, I shall be here punctually," said Count Metternich, bowing deeply, and walking backward to the door.

"I believe he *will* be here punctually," said the emperor, smiling, after Metternich had left the room. "He is afraid, if he should not be promptly at my door, it might never open to him again. I want them all to feel that I am their master and emperor—I alone! Now I am through with Metternich, and it is my brother's turn. I will give him to day a lesson which he will not forget all his life long."

The emperor rang the bell. "Has my brother, the Archduke John, not yet arrived ?" he asked the footman who entered the room.

"Your majesty, the archduke has just arrived, and is waiting for your orders."

"I request my brother to come to me immediately," said the emperor. After the footman had glided noiselessly out of the room, Francis walked repeatedly up and down, and his face assumed a gloomy expression. "He shall learn now that I am his master," he murmured ; "I will break his haughty spirit, and humiliate him so deeply that he will never think any more of plotting against me."

At this moment the door opened, and the Archduke John, whom the footman announced, entered the room. He looked pale and sad ; the last months, full of care and grief, had gnawed deeply into his soul, and deprived his eyes of their fire, and his form of its youthful fulness.

The emperor saw it, and a sardonic smile illuminated for a moment his features, which, however, quickly resumed their gloomy expression. "Ah, brother," exclaimed the emperor, greeting the archduke with a slight nod of his head, "we have not seen each other for a long time ; hence, I sent for you. I wish to communicate important news to you. The war is at an end. I have concluded peace with the Emperor of the French."

"Peace ?" asked John, incredulously. "Your majesty condescends to jest, and that is a good symptom of your majesty's excellent health."

"I never jest with you," said the emperor, dryly. "I tell you in dead earnest, I have concluded peace with Napoleon. Austria loses a great deal by this peace ; she cedes one-third of her territory, and pays, moreover, besides the contributions imposed heretofore, the sum of eighty-six millions of franc." *

"But what of the Tyrol ?" asked John. "I am sure your majesty will keep the faithful Tyrol ?"

"No," said Francis, looking his brother full in the face, "the Tyrol will be divided ; one part of it will be restored to Bavaria ; the other part will be given to the Viceroy of Italy, and become a province of French Italy."

"That is impossible ! " cried John, in dismay ; "that cannot be your will—"

"And why not ? Why is it impossible ?" asked the emperor, sternly.

"Your majesty," said John, facing his brother boldly, "you pledged your word to the Tyrolese solemnly, in the face of God and the whole world, that you would not conclude a peace which would separate the Tyrol from your monarchy."

"Ah, you dare to remind me of it ?" cried Francis, in a threatening tone.

"Yes, I do," said John, vehemently ; "and I have a right to do so, for it is I who pledged my honor that the imperial promise would be redeemed. It was I who stirred up the insurrection of the Tyrolese, who repeated the promises of their beloved emperor to them ; it was I who called upon them in the emperor's name to organize a conspiracy and rebellion, and who induced them to draw the sword and fight for their liberty. Your majesty, thousands of the noblest Tyrolese have lost their lives in this contest ; thousands lie wounded and in great pain ; the soil of the Tyrol, formerly so tranquil and peaceful, is reeking yet with gore ; the fields are not cultivated; where prosperity formerly reigned, there is now distress and starvation; where peace and tranquillity prevailed, there rages an insurrection; where merry and happy people used to live, and where nothing was heard formerly but the ringing notes of the *Ranz des Vaches* and the merry *Jodlers* of the herdsmen, there are to be seen now only pale, mournful

* Napoleon signed the treaty of Schönbrunn on the 14th of October, 1809.

invalids, tottering along painfully, and nothing is heard but
the booming of artillery and the lamentations of the impover-
ished and starving mountaineers. And yet, despite all their
disasters and privations, the faithful Tyrolese stand firm, for
their hearts are full of hope and love for their emperor. They
risked all in order to become Austrians again; and even now,
when the deplorable armistice has compelled your troops to
sheathe their swords, the faithful and confiding Tyrolese continue their struggle for their emperor and the liberty of their
beloved country. All Europe gazes with astonishment and
admiration upon this heroic people, which alone is yet courageous enough to resist the French despot, which alone does
not yet bow to his decrees, and still draws its sword against
him, while all Europe is crouching before him in the dust.
Oh, your majesty cannot and will not abandon this faithful
people, which loves you and believes in you. It would be
high treason to think your majesty capable of such a step, for
you pledged your word to the Tyrolese, and never will an Emperor of Austria break his word and incur the disgrace of perjuring himself."

The emperor uttered a cry of rage, and, entirely forgetful
of his assumed calmness, rushed upon the archduke with flashing eyes and uplifted arm.

"You dare to insult me !" he cried. "You are impudent
enough to charge me with perjury ! You—"

The archduke on seeing his brother so close before him,
furious and with clinched fist, started back a few steps. "Your
majesty," he said, "I am sure you do not intend to insult your
brother. Pray take your hand away, for if it should touch
my face, my forehead, I should be obliged to forget that you
are the emperor, that you are my brother, and should demand
satisfaction of you."

"The emperor would not give satisfaction to a rebel," said
Francis, dropping his arm slowly ; "he would crush the rebel
by a word, and deliver the traitor into the hands of his
judges."

"Well, then, do so," exclaimed John ; "punish me, let me
expiate with my blood the boldness with which I reminded you
of the sacred promise which you gave to the Tyrolese. But do

not forget your word ; do not abandon the faithful Tyrol ; do
not destroy the only hope of these honest, innocent children
of nature, who confide so touchingly in their emperor ! Oh,
your majesty, let us both forget the vehement words which
anger and grief caused us to utter just now ! I implore your
majesty's forgiveness—I confess that I sinned grievously
against my emperor. But now have mercy in your turn !
See, I bow to you, I kneel down before you, and implore you,
by your imperial honor and in the name of the Tyrol, do not
abandon the Tyrol and its commander-in-chief, Andreas Hofer, and do not forget your solemn promise that you would
never consent to a treaty of peace that would not forever incorporate the Tyrol with your states.   You want to make
peace with Napoleon ; but the treaty has not been proclaimed
yet, the world does not know of it yet, and it is still possible
for your majesty to break off the negotiations.   Oh, do so,
your majesty ; redeem the word you pledged to the Tyrol, and
do not conclude a peace which will not indissolubly unite the
Tyrol with your monarchy.   Permit the Tyrolese at least to
conquer their liberty once more, and, after they have done so,
protect it.   Send me to the Tyrol, permit me to place myself
at the head of the brave mountaineers, and you shall see that
the Tyrolese will rise as one man and fight with the courage
of lions.   Oh, your majesty, send me to the Tyrol, that the
Tyrolese and the whole world may learn that the emperor of
Austria keeps his word and does not abandon them, and that
he sends his own brother to tell them that he
will not consent to any peace which will not incorporate their
country with Austria ! "

The emperor burst into loud and scornful laughter. "Ah,
you are very shrewd, brother," he said ; "you think I myself
should give you permission to go to the Tyrol and play there,
with redoubled splendor, your part as savior and liberator of
the province.   You think I am ignorant of your nice little
plan, and do not know why you wish to go to the Tyrol, and
what intentions you entertain in regard to it.   Yes, sir, I know
all ! I am aware of your plans. I know that you are a revolutionist and rebel. You wanted to make yourself sovereign
of the Tyrol. That is the reason why you incited the people

to rebellion, and intrigued and plotted until the poor peaceable peasants became insurgents and rebels against their Bavarian king, and unfurled the banner of blood with frantic fanaticism. You say thousands have fallen in the Tyrol in the struggle for liberty ; you say thousands lie wounded on the gory soil of their native country ; that prosperity has disappeared, and poverty and starvation reign in the Tyrol ? Well, then, all this is your work ; it is your fault. You stirred up the insurrection, and committed the heavy crime of inciting a people to revolution. The Tyrol belonged to Bavaria ; the Tyrolese were subjects of the King of Bavaria ; nothing gave them the right to shake off the rule of their king and choose another sovereign. And you think I should be so weak as to approve of the bad example set by the Tyrolese, and encourage the crimes committed by the revolutionists ? You think I should sanction your work and consecrate your traitorous schemes by permitting you to go to the Tyrol in order to preach insurrection once more, make yourself sovereign of the Tyrol, come to an understanding with M. Bonaparte, and be recognized and confirmed by him as Duke of Tyrol ?"

"Brother," cried John, in dismay, "I—"

"Hush," interrupted the emperor, imperiously ; "no one has a right to say a word when I am speaking. I am not speaking to you as your brother, but as your emperor. And as your emperor, I tell you now, you will not go to the Tyrol, you will not dare to cross again the frontiers of the Tyrol without my permission ; and I promise you that you will have to wait a long while for this permission. And as your emperor I order you further to inform the Tyrolese that I have concluded peace with France, and to call upon them to lay down their arms and submit to their fate."

"Your majesty, never, never will I do that!" cried John.

"Oh, you think the good Tyrolese would then begin to doubt the honesty of their adored archduke, and withdraw from him their love, which was to erect a throne for him ?"

"No, your majesty," said John, looking him full in the face ; "I mean that I have pledged my word to protect the Tyrolese, and help and succor them in their struggle for liberty and for their emperor, and that I will not incur the disgrace of having cheated a whole people and abused their confidence and love in the most revolting manner."

"Oh, you want to intimate to me once more that I have done so—that I have abused the confidence and love of the Tyrolese in a revolting manner?" asked the emperor, with a freezing smile. "No matter, keep your opinion; but you shall surely obey me, and do it at once in my presence. Seat yourself at my writing-table yonder. You are a scholar, and know how to wield the pen quickly and skilfully. Write, therefore. Inform the faithful Tyrolese that peace has been concluded; order them to lay down their arms and submit obediently to their new master."

"I cannot, brother," cried John, mournfully. "Have mercy upon me! I cannot deliver a whole people to the executioner's axe. For, if you withdraw your hand from the Tyrol, if you surrender it to the tender mercies of the Bavarians and French, they will wreak a fearful revenge on the Tyrolese for all the defeats and humiliations which the heroic mountaineers have made them undergo."

"That will deter the mountaineers from entering into any more conspiracies and revolutions, and teach them to be patient and submissive; and they will thereby become an awful example to my own subjects. Do not disobey me any longer. Seat yourself and write, archduke!"

"No," cried John, vehemently, "your majesty may punish me as a rebel, take my life, or sentence me to everlasting imprisonment, but I cannot obey! I cannot write such a proclamation!"

"I shall not punish you as a rebel," said the emperor, shrugging his shoulders; "I shall not take your life, I shall not sentence you to everlasting imprisonment; but I will withdraw my hand entirely from the Tyrol. I will not, as I had resolved and stipulated expressly, give the fugitive Tyrolese, if they should succeed in crossing the frontier, an asylum here in Austria, and protect them to the best of my power; but I will deliver them as escaped criminals to their legitimate sovereigns, that they may punish them according to their deserts. Nor shall I, as I intended to do, stipulate in the treaty of peace that the ancient constitution shall be confirmed and guaranteed to the Tyrolese ; nor shall I, finally, as I had resolved to do, appoint a commission which will afford relief to the fugitives who escape with their families to Austria. It will be your fault if the poor Tyrolese are deprived of these boons, and you will expose the deserted people to the most fearful persecutions."

"No, your majesty ; no one shall ever be able to say that," cried John, profoundly moved. "I will obey your order and draw up the proclamation."

He hastened to the writing-table, and, throwing himself on a chair in front of it, uttered a deep groan and dropped his head on his breast as though he were dying.

"Well, do not reflect so long, brother," said Francis, "but write !"

John took up the pen, and, restraining the tears which filled his eyes, wrote quickly a few lines. He then rose as pale as a corpse, and, approaching the emperor slowly, handed the paper to him.

"Your majesty," he said, solemnly, "I have complied with your order. I inform the Tyrolese that peace has been concluded, and exhort them to submit. Will you now fulfil the conditions, on account of which I have written this to the Tyrolese ? Will you grant an asylum here in Austria to those who shall succeed in escaping their tormentors and executioners ? Will you appoint an imperial commission which will afford relief to the fugitives and their families? And last, will you see to it that the ancient constitution is guaranteed to the Tyrolese in the treaty of peace ?"

"I pledged you my word that I would do so, dear brother," said the emperor, smiling ; "and you yourself said a while ago, 'Never will an Emperor of Austria break his word and incur the disgrace of perjuring himself.' Well, read to me now what you have written. I should like to hear it from your own lips."

The archduke bowed and read in a tremulous voice:

"DEAR, BRAVE TYROLESE : The news that peace has been concluded will soon reach you. The emperor has ordered me to confirm this intelligence to you. The emperor would have done every thing to fulfil the wishes of the Tyrol, but, however great an interest the emperor takes in the fate of the honest and excellent inhabitants of that province, he has had to submit to the stern necessity of making peace. I inform you of this by order of his majesty, with the addition that it is his majesty's wish that the Tyrolese should keep quiet and not sacrifice themselves needlessly.

"The Archduke JOHN."

"H'm !" said the emperor, taking the paper from John's hand and contemplating it attentively, "it is written quite laconically indeed. But, no matter, you have complied with my order and done your duty."

"I thank your majesty for this acknowledgment. And now that I have done my duty, I request your majesty to be so gracious as to dismiss me from your service, and permit me to retire from the court into private life. I feel weak and exhausted, and need repose. Moreover, since we have peace now, my services are superfluous and may be easily dispensed with."

"And you wish me to dismiss you very speedily, do you not ?" asked the emperor, sarcastically. "You would like to retire as quickly as possible into private life, that the whole world, and, above all, the dear Tyrolese, may perceive that the noble and beloved Archduke John is dissatisfied with the treaty, and has therefore withdrawn in anger from the court and service of his emperor ? I am sorry that I cannot afford you this satisfaction. You will remain in the service ; I do not accept your resignation, I do not permit you to retire into private life. You should devote your abilities to the state ; you are not allowed to withhold your services from it at this juncture."

"Your majesty, I can no longer be useful to the state. I am exhausted to death. I repeat my request in the most urgent manner : dismiss me from the service, and permit me to retire into private life."

"What !" cried Francis, vehemently. "Your emperor has informed you of his will, and you dare to oppose it ? That is a violation of subordination, for which the emperor, as su-

preme commander of his army, would punish his rebellious
general rigorously, but for the fact that this general unfortunately is his brother. I repeat it, I do not accept your resignation. You remain in the service ; I demand it as your general-in-chief ; I remind you of the oath of allegiance which
you have sworn to me, your emperor and master."

"Your majesty does right in reminding me of the oath I
took," said the archduke, with freezing coldness. "It is true,
I swore that oath ; and as I am in the habit of keeping my
word, and as it is disgraceful for any one to break his word
and perjure himself, I shall fulfil my oath. Hence, I shall
obey my emperor and general-in-chief, and not leave the service. But now I ask leave of your majesty to withdraw for to-
day, if your majesty has nothing further to say to me."

"Yes, I have something else to say to you, my dear brother," said the emperor, smilingly. "I will give you a proof of
the great confidence which I repose in you, and with which I
count upon your discretion. I will communicate to you a
family secret which is known at present only to the Emperor
Napoleon, Baron von Thugut, who acted as my agent on this
occasion, and myself."

"What !" asked John, in surprise ; "the Emperor Napoleon is aware of a family secret of your majesty ?"

"As it concerns himself, he must be aware of it," said the
emperor. "Napoleon intends to marry a second time."

"A second time ? Has his first wife, the Empress Josephine,
then, died suddenly ?"

"No, she still lives, and is acting yet at this moment in
Paris as the emperor's legitimate consort. But Napoleon, immediately after his return from Germany, will annul this marriage, which was never consecrated by a priest ; he will divorce
himself solemnly from his wife, and have then the right of
marrying a second time. He requested my secret agent, Baron
von Thugut, to ask me if I would consent to a marriage between him and an archduchess of Austria. I replied in the
affirmative, and this agreement forms one of the secret articles
of the treaty of peace."

"An archduchess of Austria is to become the consort of
the French despot !" cried John, in dismay. "And who,

your majesty, is to be sacrificed to the Minotaur? Which of your sisters or cousins will you let him have?"

"None of my cousins or sisters," said Francis, calmly, "but my eldest daughter, Maria Louisa, is to become the consort of the Emperor Napoleon."

"Maria Louisa!" cried John, with an expression of dismay. "Maria Louisa!"

And John staggered back several steps, as pale as a corpse, and grasped the back of the chair in order not to sink to the floor.

Francis did not seem to perceive this. "Yes, Maria Louisa will be Napoleon's second consort," he said. "Every thing is settled already, and the marriage will take place next March. I think, brother, you may stand proxy for Napoleon on that occasion."

The archduke gave a start, and pressed his hands to his temples as if he were afraid lest this dreadful "family secret" would burst his head.

"Your majesty," he said, in a tremulous and almost inaudible voice, "I beg leave to withdraw."

Without waiting for a reply, the archduke turned and left the room with a tottering step, and leaning now and then against the wall in order not to sink to the floor.

The emperor looked after him, smilingly. "It seems Hudelist was not mistaken," he said. "My dear brother really loved Maria Louisa, and intended to become my son-in-law. What a nice idea! But he must give it up now. He—Holy Virgin! What noise is that in the anteroom? What fell to the floor there?"

The emperor stepped quickly to the door and opened it. "What is the matter here?" he asked.

"Your majesty," exclaimed the footman, who hastened to him, "the archduke fainted and fell to the floor, striking with his head against the corner of a chair, and wounding his forehead, which is bleeding copiously."

"Well, I hope it is only a slight scratch," said the emperor, composedly. "Carry the archduke to his bedchamber and send for my surgeon. I will afterward call on him myself."

Without taking any further notice of the archduke, the emperor returned into his cabinet and closed the door after him.

"He fainted," said Francis, triumphantly. "Henceforth he shall be entirely powerless. No one shall have any power here but myself. Ah, I have broken his pride, bent his will, and prostrated him at my feet. All my brothers shall bow to me, acknowledge me as their master, and obey me. Ah, I believe I have played a bad trick on my brothers. The Archduke John will not become Duke of Tyrol ; the Grand-duke Ferdinand of Würtzburg will not be Emperor of Austria, for Napoleon will become *my* son-in-law, and he will take good care not to deprive his father-in-law of his throne. I alone am, and shall remain, Emperor of Austria."

CHAPTER XL.

DREADFUL TIDINGS.

ALL the Tyrolese were in the highest excitement and terror. Pale faces were to be seen everywhere, and nothing was heard but the anxious query : "Is it true ? Has our emperor really made peace with Bonaparte ? Is it true that he has abandoned us entirely, and that we are to become again subjects of France and Bavaria ? "

And some of the timid and disheartened sighed : " It is true ! We read so yesterday in the *Innspruck Gazette*, and the Viceroy of Italy has sent two messengers through the Puster valley to proclaim that the Emperors of Austria and France concluded a treaty of peace on the 14th of October, and that the Tyrolese are to lay down their arms and become again subjects of France and Bavaria."

" It is not true ! " cried the bold and courageous. "The Emperor Francis has not made peace with Bonaparte ; and if he has, he has certainly not abandoned the Tyrol, but stipulated that we remain with Austria ; for he pledged us his word that we should, and the emperor will redeem his promise."

"It is not true ; there is no peace, and we are still at war
with the Bavarians and French," cried Joseph Speckbacher,
"and we will continue the war."

"Yes, we will," shouted his brave men.

And as Speckbacher said, so did Andreas Hofer, so did Joachim Haspinger, so did Anthony Wallner, Jacob Sieberer, and
all the intrepid commanders of the sharpshooters.

Led by these heroic men, the Tyrolese formed again a large
army, which took position on Mount Isel, and awaited there
the Bavarians who were marching upon Innspruck under the
command of the crown prince Louis.

This time, however, the Tyrolese were not victorious ; the
Bavarians expelled them from Innspruck, and, on the 29th of
October, the crown prince Louis of Bavaria made his triumphal entry into the city, after a bloody battle of four days'
duration on Mount Isel and near the Judenstein. A part of
the Tyrolese forces remained on Mount Isel, and another part
hastened with unbroken courage to other regions, to meet the
armies of the enemy and drive them beyond the frontiers of
the country.

Anthony Wallner returned with his sharpshooters to the
Puster valley, and advanced thence against General Rusca,
who was coming up from Carinthia with his corps ; he intended to defend the frontiers of his country, against him and
General Baraguay d'Hilliers, who was also approaching with
a strong force.

Joseph Speckbacher marched his intrepid men to the
Ziller valley and the Mühlbach Pass, where he united with
Joachim Haspinger, and advanced with him upon the enemy.

All were in good spirits, and no one believed in the dreadful tidings which at first had frightened them all so much : no
one believed that peace had been made.

Andreas Hofer himself thought the news was false. He
had remained courageous and undaunted in spite of the disastrous battle on Mount Isel, and he sent messengers throughout the country, calling upon all able-bodied men to take up
arms and attack the enemy, who had invaded the Tyrol once
more. He was still encamped with his army near Mount Isel,
and had established his headquarters at Steinach. The crown

prince of Bavaria had sent to him hither two plenipotentiaries, who informed him that peace had really been concluded, and that the Tyrolese had no course left but submission. But Andreas Hofer replied to these plenipotentiaries, shaking his head indignantly, "That is a mean lie ; the Emperor Francis, our beloved master, will never abandon his loyal Tyrolese. He pledged us his word, and he will keep it. Your intention is to deceive us, but you cannot catch us by such stratagems. We believe in the emperor and the good God, and neither of them will ever abandon us ! "

And Andreas Hofer returned to his room with a calm smile and went to bed.

In the dead of night, however, he was suddenly aroused from his sleep. Cajetan Döninger stood at his bedside and informed him that the intendant of the Puster valley, Baron von Wörndle, had arrived with an envoy of the Emperor Francis, Baron von Lichtenthurn, and both wished urgently to see the commander-in-chief.

"I will admit them," said Hofer, rising hastily ; "God grant that they are the bearers of good news ! "

He dressed himself quickly and followed Döninger into the room, where he found the two envoys and several members of his suite.

"Now tell me, gentlemen, what news do you bring to us ?" asked Hofer, shaking hands with the two envoys.

"No good news, commander-in-chief," sighed Baron von Wörndle, "but there is no use in complaining ; we must submit patiently to what cannot be helped. The Emperor Francis has made peace with France."

"Do you sing in that strain too, Mr. Intendant ?" asked Andreas, with a mournful smile. "I shall never believe it until I see it in black and white, and until the emperor or the dear Archduke John informs me of it."

"I bring it to you in black and white," exclaimed Baron von Lichtenthurn, drawing a paper from his bosom and handing it to Andreas. "Here is a letter from the Archduke John, which I am to deliver to you."

Hofer hastily seized the paper, which contained that proclamation which the Archduke John had written at Totis, and read it again and again slowly and attentively. While he was doing so, his cheeks turned pale, his breath issued heavily and painfully from his breast, and the paper rustled in his trembling hands.

"It is impossible! I cannot believe it!" he exclaimed, mournfully, gazing upon the paper. "The Archduke John did not write this. Just look at it, his seal is not affixed to the paper. Sir, how can you say that this letter is from the Archduke John? Where is the seal? Where is the address?"

"Well, it is no private letter," said Baron von Lichtenthurn; "it is an open letter, a proclamation, which I am instructed to show to everybody in the Tyrol. A proclamation cannot contain a seal and an address. But the Archduke John sent it; he himself wrote every word of it."

"I do not believe it!" cried Andreas, in a triumphant voice; "no, I do not believe it. You are a liar, and want to betray us. Look at him, my friends; see how pale he turns, and how he trembles! For I tell you he has a bad conscience. Bring me the Archduke John's seal, and then I will believe that the paper is from him. But, as it is, I look upon it as a cunning device got up by the enemy to entrap me. Arrest him; he must confess all. I will not allow myself to be caught by cunning and treachery!"[*]

He laid his heavy hand upon the shoulder of the baron, who sank to the floor, uttering a loud cry of distress, and fell into fearful convulsions.

"See!" cried Andreas, "that is the punishment of Heaven! The hand of God has struck him. He is a traitor, who intended to sell us to the French."

"No, he is an honorable man, and has told you the truth," said Baron von Wörndle, gravely. "Your violent accusation frightened him, and he fell into an epileptic fit. He is affected with that disease."[†]

He and some of the bystanders raised the unfortunate baron from the ground, and carried him into the adjoining

---

[*] Andreas Hofer's own words.—See Hormayr's "Andreas Hofer," vol. ii., p. 490.

[†] Ibid.

room. He then returned to Andreas, who was walking up and down with a hasty step, and murmuring to himself, "I cannot believe it! The Archduke John did not write it. His hand would have withered while writing it. He did not do it."

"Yes, Andreas, he did," said Wörndle, gravely ; "he was obliged to submit, as we all shall have to do. The Archduke John was obliged to yield to the will of his emperor as we shall have to do. The treaty of peace has been concluded. There is no doubt of it."

"Lord God ! the treaty of peace has been concluded, and the emperor abandons us ?" cried Andreas.

"The emperor, it seems, was unable to do any thing for the Tyrol," said Wörndle in a low voice. "He had to consent that the Tyrol should be restored to the French and Bavarians."

"But that is impossible !" cried Andreas, despairingly. "He pledged us his word, his sacred word, that he would never consent to a peace that would detach the Tyrol from Austria. How can you now insult the dear emperor by saying that he has broken his word ?"

"He has not broken his word, but he was unable to keep it. Look, commander-in-chief, I bring you another letter, to which, as you see, is affixed a large imperial seal, the seal of the Viceroy of Italy, who wrote the letter to you and all the Tyrolese."

"Read it," exclaimed Andreas, mournfully ; "I cannot, my eyes are filled with tears. Read it to me, sir."

Wörndle read as follows :

"To the people of the Tyrol : His majesty the Emperor of the French, King of Italy, Protector of the Confederation of the Rhine, my august father and sovereign, and his majesty, the Emperor of Austria, have made peace. Peace, therefore, reigns everywhere around you. You are the only people which does not enjoy its blessings. Seduced by foreign instigations, you took up arms against your government and overthrew it. The melancholy consequences of your seditious course have overtaken you. Terror reigns now in your towns, idleness and misery in your fields, and discord and disorder are to be found in all parts of the country. His majesty the emperor and king, profoundly moved by your wretched condition, and the proofs of repentance which some of you have manifested to him, has consented in the treaty to forgive your errors. I bring you peace and forgiveness, but I warn you of the fact, that you will be forgiven only if you return of your own accord to law and order, lay down your arms, and offer no longer any resistance whatever. As commander-in-chief of the armies surrounding you, I shall accept your submission or compel you to surrender. Commissioners will precede the armies; they have been instructed to listen to whatever complaints and grievances you may wish to prefer. But, do not forget that these commissioners are authorized to listen to you only after you have laid down your arms. Tyrolese! I promise that you shall obtain justice if your complaints and grievances are well-grounded. Headquarters at Villach, October 25, 1809.

" EUGENE NAPOLEON." *

Baron von Wörndle had long since ceased to read, and still Andreas Hofer stood motionless, his hands folded on his breast, his head thrown back, and his eyes turned toward heaven. All gazed in respectful silence upon that tall, imposing form which seemed frozen by grief, and at that pale, mournful face, and those pious eyes, which seemed to implore consolation and salvation from heaven.

At last Döninger ventured to put his hand softly on Hofer's arm. " Awake, dear commander-in-chief," he said in a low voice, "awake from your grief. These gentlemen here are waiting for an answer. Tell them what you think—"

" What I think ? " cried Hofer, giving a start and dropping his eyes slowly. " What I think ? I think that we are poor, unhappy men, who have vainly risked our property and our blood, our liberty and our lives. Tell me, then, my friends, is it possible that the Emperor Francis, whom we all loved so dearly, and who pledged us his word so solemnly and often, has abandoned us after all ? Cajetan, do you believe it ? "

" It is in black and white here," said Döninger, in his ha-

* Hormayr's " Andreas Hofer," vol. i., p. 490.

bitual laconic style, pointing to the proclamation of the Archduke John. "It is the archduke's handwriting; I am familiar with it. You need no longer question its authenticity.
Peace has been concluded."

"Peace has been concluded, the emperor has abandoned
his Tyrol, the Tyrol is lost!" cried Andreas, in a loud outburst of grief; and his long-restrained tears streamed from his
eyes. Andreas was not ashamed of them. He threw himself
on a chair, buried his face in his hands, and wept aloud.

"The Tyrol is lost," he sobbed; all my dear countrymen
are in profound distress, and, moreover, in the utmost danger;
our beloved, beautiful country will have to shed rivers of blood,
and nothing will be heard but wails and lamentations. For
the emperor has abandoned us, the enemy will re-enter the
country, kill and burn, and wreak a terrible revenge upon our
people!—Lord God," he exclaimed all at once, "can I not do
any thing, then, for my dear country? Tell me, my friends,
can I not do any thing to avert this great calamity and save
the lives of my dear countrymen?"

"Yes, Andreas," said Baron von Wörndle, "you can do a
great deal for the Tyrol and your countrymen. You can prevent bloodshed, soften the vindictiveness of the enemy, and
induce him to spare the vanquished and wreak no revenge on
the disarmed. Write a proclamation to the Tyrolese, admon-
ish them to keep quiet, and order them to lay down their
arms. Return yourself to your home, your inn, and you will
have done on this mournful day more for the Tyrol than you
have been able to do for it up to this time; for you will thereby save the Tyrol from untold disasters, which will surely befall the country if you resume hostilities against enemies
who are a hundred times superior to us. It is impossible for
us to withstand them successfully. Their columns, well provided with artillery, are moving upon all sides, and the
whole Tyrol, as the Viceroy of Italy writes, is surrounded.
We have no course left but submission. Order the Tyrolese,
therefore, to submit, set a good example to them yourself, and
the Tyrol is saved, and no more blood will be shed."

"No more blood will be shed!" repeated Andreas Hofer, joyously. "Well, then, I see that you are right, and that we

have no course left but submission. It is true, the emperor has abandoned us, but the good God will still stand by us ; and on seeing that we are humble and submissive, He will have mercy upon us. Sit down, Cajetan ; I will dictate a letter to you. To whom must I write on behalf of my beloved country ? "

"Write to General Drouet," said Döninger. "It was he who wrote to you yesterday from Innspruck, informing you of the conclusion of peace, and promising that, if you and all the Tyrolese would submit, no harm should befall any one. You refused to answer his letter because you did not believe him."

"I did not believe him," said Andreas, gently, "for I still believed in my emperor. But I see now that General Drouet was right ; I will, therefore, write to him, and recommend my country and the good and brave Tyrolese to his mercy. Take up the pen, Cajetan, and write."

And Andreas Hofer dictated in a low, tremulous voice, often interrupted by sighs which issued from his breast like the groans of a dying man, a letter to General Drouet, in which he promised in touching words that the Tyrolese would lay down their arms, and said they would trust, for pardon and oblivion of the past, to the magnanimity of Napoleon, whose footsteps were guided by a superior power, which it was no longer permitted them to resist.

"There," he said, after convincing himself that Döninger had written exactly what he had dictated, "now give me the pen, Cajetan. I will sign it myself."

He bent over the table, and wrote quickly what he had so often written under his decrees, "Andreas Hofer, commander-in-chief of the Tyrol."

But then he gave a start, and contemplated his signature long and musingly. Heaving a profound sigh, and casting a mournful glance toward heaven, he took up the pen a second time, and added the word "late," slowly and with a trembling hand, to his title "commander-in-chief of the Tyrol." *

"Now come, Cajetan," he exclaimed, throwing down the pen, as if it was a viper which had wounded him, "come,

* "Gallery of Heroes : Andreas Hofer," p. 173.

Cajetan. I will go to my sharpshooters and exhort them to disband, and afterward I will return with you to my inn in the Passeyr valley, in order to set a good example to all, and show them how to submit quietly and patiently."

And Andreas Hofer acted accordingly. He ordered his men to disband, and after they had obeyed his order in sullen silence, he himself, accompanied only by his faithful Cajetan Döninger, went back to his home.

But neither the joyous welcome, with which his wife, faithful Anna Gertrude, received him, nor the jubilant shouts of his children, could arouse Andreas Hofer from his mournful brooding, or bring a smile to his lips. He did not rejoice at his return to his dear ones ; he paid no attention to his business, he did not go to the stables and barns as he used to do ; but he sat hanging his head, his hands folded on his knees, staring at the floor, and sighing from time to time, "My poor country ! How could the emperor abandon us ?"

Only when Cajetan Döninger was not with him, Andreas Hofer became uneasy ; he glanced around anxiously and called for his secretary ; when the latter hastened to him, he held out his hand and said in a low, tremulous voice, "Cajetan, do not leave me. I always think I may have something to write yet, and it seems to me as though what I dictated to you at Steinach, declaring my readiness to submit, were not the last of my official papers. Something else must come yet, —yes, something else. I know it, for this state of affairs cannot last. Therefore, Cajetan, stay with me that you may be ready and able to write when the hour has come."

Cajetan stayed with him ; both sat together in silence, and absorbed in their gloomy reflections, and the days passed slowly and mournfully.

It was on the afternoon of the fifth day, and Andreas Hofer sat in silence, as usual, in the gloomy room. Every thing was still without. All at once this profound silence was broken by a hum of many voices and loud noise.

Hofer looked up and listened. "That sounds as if we were still at war, and as if my sharpshooters were marching up," he said.

"Andreas Hofer, commander-in-chief of the Tyrol!" shouted loud voices under the windows.

Hofer jumped up. "Who calls me?" he shouted, in a powerful voice.

At this moment the door was thrown open violently, and four mountaineers, armed with their rifles, came in. Hofer saw through the open door that the yard in front of the house was thronged with peasants, and all looked with flashing eyes through the door at Hofer ; and they shouted now, " Andreas Hofer, commander-in-chief of the Tyrol, come with us, come ! "

Andreas Hofer seemed all at once animated by new life ; his eyes shot fire, his form was drawn up to its full height, and his head rose again proudly between his powerful shoulders.

"What do you want of me, my dear countrymen ?" he asked, going to meet them.

One of the four sharpshooters who had entered the room now came forward, and placed himself with a defiant face in front of Hofer.

"We want you," he said. "Three thousand French soldiers are marching across the Janfen. There is great excitement in the Puster valley, and some fighting has taken place. Anthony Wallner has driven the Bavarians long since across the frontier, and Speckbacher and the Capuchin have marched to the Mühlbach Pass in order to attack Rusca. And why are we to keep quiet, then ? Why are we to allow the French to enter the Passeyr valley ? "

" We will not allow them to do it ! " shouted the peasants outside. " No, we will not allow the French to enter the Passeyr valley."

"You hear it, commander-in-chief," said the first speaker. "We are all ready and determined. Now say what we are to do with the French. Will you do any thing or not ? "

" Yes, will you do any thing or not ? " repeated the peasants, penetrating with furious gestures into the room.

"If you do not want to do any thing," cried the peasant, raising his rifle menacingly, "my rifle is loaded for you as well as for any Frenchman. You commenced the insurrection, now put it through." *

"But you know, countrymen, that I cannot ! " cried Hofer. "The emperor has made peace with Bonaparte and abandoned us. What course have we left but that of submission ? We must yield, or the Tyrol will be ruined entirely."

"But we do not want to submit," shouted the peasants, furiously. "And the whole country is of our opinion ; no one is willing to submit. We will die rather than submit."

"Issue another proclamation calling out the able-bodied men ! " said the first speaker.

"Yes, issue another proclamation, commander-in-chief," shouted the crowd. "We will fight, we must fight ! "

"And you shall and must be our leader ! " exclaimed the peasant, laying his heavy hand on Hofer's shoulder. "We will compel you to go with us or kill you as a traitor. Issue another proclamation. We men are still the same as before, and so is our cause ; now you must likewise be the same Andreas Hofer, commander-in-chief of the Tyrol ! "

"Yes, exclaimed Andreas, with a radiant face, drawing a deep breath, as if relieved from an oppressive burden, "yes, I will be the same as before. This state of affairs cannot continue. We must fight ; we had better die than lead such a life. Go, Döninger, go ; write a proclamation ! "

"Hurrah ! Long live our commander-in-chief," shouted the peasants, triumphantly ; "long live our dear faithful Andreas Hofer ! "

"I thank you, my dear countrymen," said Andreas ; "I am your leader now, and we will fight again. But do not hold me responsible for the events of the future. You must never forget that you compelled me to resume war. I intended to submit humbly and patiently, but you would not allow me to do so, and dragged me forcibly from my retirement. The bloody struggle will commence again—God grant us protection, and further victories ! We are not going to fight from motives of pride and arrogance, but only for the sake of our country—because we want to remain Germans,

* Loritza, "Bilder und Erinnerungen aus Tyrol's Freiheitskämpfen von 1800," p. 14.

and do not want to become French subjects, and because we
want to keep our God, our liberty, and our constitution.
Amen !"

CHAPTER XLI.

BETRAYAL AND SEIZURE OF HOFER.

WAR was now resumed at all points ; but the forces brought
from all sides against the Tyrol were so immense that no hope
remained to the inhabitants but by deeds of glory to throw a
last radiance around their fall. The Tyrolese fought with
desperate valor, but their heroism was unavailing. The superior forces of the enemy were everywhere victorious. The
artillery of the Bavarians and French thinned the ranks of the
mountaineers from day to day ; whole ranks of the Tyrolese
being mowed down by the balls of the enemy. They fled
panic-struck into the mountains. The victorious invaders
penetrated farther and farther into the interior of the country ;
burning towns and villages marked the route which they followed, and wails and lamentations rent the air wherever they
made their appearance.

Before the middle of December all resistance had been
overpowered. The enemy stalked in a merciless manner over
the gory, reeking, groaning Tyrol, and pursued relentlessly all
who had dared to rise against him. He had promised oblivion and forgiveness in return for peaceful submission ; but
as the Tyrolese had not submitted, but continued the struggle,
the enemy now threatened to revenge himself and punish the
vanquished.

A furious chase now commenced. Every one who had
been seized with arms in hand was shot ; every one who concealed one of the pursued patriots in his house was executed,
and his house was burned down.

The leaders of the Tyrolese had fled into the mountains,
but the French generals promised large rewards for the heads
of the most influential patriots ; and the soldiers traversed the
country, impelled by thirst for revenge and gain, spying

everywhere for the outlawed mountaineers, and ascending even to the snow-clad summits of the mountains in order to obtain the large rewards. As yet, however, they had not succeeded in seizing one of the pursued chiefs. The French generals had vainly promised a reward of ten thousand florins for the apprehension of Andreas Hofer, and rewards of five thousand florins for the seizure of Joseph Spechbacher, Anthony Wallner, and Joachim Haspinger. They had disappeared, and the patrols and soldiers, who were hunting for them, had not yet been able to discover the hiding-place of any of the four great chiefs of the insurrection. The mountains, those natural fortresses of the Tyrol, protected the outlawed commanders ; and in the Alpine huts, amidst the chamois and vultures, which alone saw and knew their hiding-places, there were no traitors.

Retiring to his native valley, Andreas Hofer long eluded the search of the victors. His place of concealment was a solitary Alpine hut, four leagues distant from his home, in general inaccessible from the snow which surrounded it. Love had accompanied Andreas to this inhospitable spot. His wife and his son John were with him, and so was Cajetan Döninger, his faithful secretary. Love had accompanied him to the Alpine hut of his friend Pfandler ; love watched over him in the valley below. Many peasants there were well aware of Hofer's place of concealment ; but no one betrayed him, no one was tempted by the reward of ten thousand florins which Baraguay d'Hilliers, the French general, offered for Hofer's apprehension. They often saw Pfandler's servants, loaded with all sorts of provisions, wending their way slowly and painfully up the snow-clad Alp ; but they averted their heads, as though they did not want to see anything, and prayed God in a low tone to protect the messengers who conveyed food to Hofer and his dear ones. The peasants in the valley forbore carefully to speak among each other of what they knew ; only they treated Pfandler with reverential tenderness, shook hands with him quietly, and whispered, " God bless you and him !" At times, on a clear winter day, when thin smoke curled up suddenly from the Alp, the peasants in the valley looked up sighingly and whispered compassionately, "They

have built a fire in their hut. The cold is so severe. God
bless them !" But whenever one whom they did not trust
stepped up to them, wondering at the smoke, and saying that
somebody was concealed up there, and had built a fire in order not to freeze to death, the others laughed at him, and said
there was no smoke at all, but only snow blown up by the
storm.

One day, however, a stranger arrived in the valley, and
asked whisperingly for Andreas Hofer, to whom, he said, he
would bring assistance and safety. At first no one replied to
him ; but he showed them a paper, bearing the name and seal
of the Archduke John, and containing the following words,
written by the prince himself : "Help my messenger to find
Andreas Hofer, and bring him assistance and safety."

On reading this, the peasants distrusted him no longer.
They glanced furtively up to the Schneeberg, pointed to the
two wanderers, loaded with baskets, who were toiling up the
mountain through the snow, and whispered almost inaudibly,
"Follow them !"

The messenger did so. He climbed after the two servants,
and ascended with them the inhospitable, dreary, and deserted
heights. At length he arrived in front of the Alpine hut : he
knocked at the door, and asked admittance in the name of God
and the Archduke John.

The door opened immediately, and on the threshold appeared Hofer's tall, bearded form, as erect and vigorous as it
had been in the days of his splendor, and his mild, honest eye
greeted the new-comer.

"He who comes in the name of God and the Archduke
John will not deceive me," said Andreas, kindly. "Come in,
therefore ; for you must have good intentions toward me, inasmuch as the severe cold did not deter you from coming up
to me."

"Indeed I have good intentions toward you," said the messenger. "Do you not know me, then, Andy ? I am Anthony
Steeger, the Archduke John's gunsmith."

"Oh, yes, now I know you !" exclaimed Andreas, joyfully.
"I saw you in Vienna at the time we were there to devise
plans for the deliverance of the Tyrol. Well, come in, An-

thony Steeger ; come in to my wife, my son, and my secretary."

He conducted Anthony Steeger into the room, where the three greeted him, and made room for him in front of the hearth, on which large billets of wood were burning.

Anthony Steeger looked around in this wretched room, which contained nothing but a few rickety wooden chairs, and a rough-hewn pine table, and the walls and windows of which were protected from the cold by thick linings of hay and straw.

" Yes, you may well look around in my palace," said Andreas, smilingly ; " it is not very gorgeous here, but the good God is with us, and He will help us to get along."

" And the Archduke John will help you also," said Anthony Steeger. " Listen to me, Andreas. The archduke sends me to you. He sends you his greetings, and entreats you to come with your family to him and stay with him all your life long, or, if you should not like to do that, at least until you can live again safely in the Tyrol. The archduke has already fitted up a house for you in a village which belongs to him ; you shall live there with your whole family as the beloved and honored guests of the archduke. He implores you to accept his invitation. I have with me every thing that is necessary for your flight, Andy. The archduke has given me money, a passport for you and your family, and safeguards issued by the French generals. I am familiar with the roads and by-paths in this vicinity, and will convey you safely through the mountains. The archduke has thought of every thing and provided for every thing."

" It is very kind in the dear Archduke John not to have forgotten me," said Andreas, deeply moved ; " it is honest and faithful that he should like to take care of me and reward my love. And it is very kind in you, too, Anthony Steeger, to have acted in this spirit of self-denial. You have come from a great distance to save us, and are not afraid of venturing with us upon this most dangerous flight."

" And you accept my offer, Andy, and consent to accompany me, do you not ? "

" And what of them ? " asked Andreas, casting a tender

glance on his wife and his son. "The route across the glaciers is impassable for a woman and a child."

"First save yourself, my Andy," exclaimed Anna Gertrude ; "save yourself for us and the country. After you are
gone and have arrived at a place of safety, the enemy will
hardly trouble us any more, and I will follow you then with
the children."

"You need not be anxious, so far as your wife and children
are concerned," said Döninger. "I will not leave them, but
bring them to you."

"Pray do not hesitate, Andy," said Anthony Steeger, urgently. "The archduke implores you not to grieve him by
rejecting his offer, but to relieve his conscience from the heavy
debt which he has hitherto been unable to discharge to the
Tyrol. You shall escape for his sake and for the good of the
fatherland, and save your life for better times, which will
surely dawn upon the Tyrol. Do it, Andreas. Let us go to
work immediately. See, I have with me all that you need,
and wear two suits of clothes ; one is destined for you, and
you will put it on. And here is the razor, with which we
shall shave off your beard ; and when it is gone, and you have
put on the new clothes, no one will scent the Barbone in the
man with a foreign dress and a smooth chin. Come, now,
Andy, and do not hesitate."

"I am to make quite another man of myself," said Andreas,
shaking his head, "merely to save my miserable life ? I am
to deny my dear Passeyr ? I am to shave off my beard, which
I have worn so long in an honorable manner, and by which
every one knows me throughout the Tyrol ? No, Anthony
Steeger, I will never do that ! "

"If you do not, Andreas, you are lost," said Anthony Steeger. "I am afraid the French are already on your track. A
peasant said he had seen you up here the other day."

"Yes, it was Raffel. He came up here to look for his
cow, and met me here. But I gave him money not to betray my secret, and he promised me solemnly that he would
not."

"He must have violated his pledge already, Andy ; for he
told Donay, the priest, about it, and the latter boasted pub-

licly yesterday that he was aware of Andreas Hofer's place of concealment."

"It is true, Donay is a bad and mean man," said Andreas Hofer, musingly ; " but I do not believe he will be so mean as to betray me, whom he always called his best commander-in-chief and dearest friend."

" He is mean enough to do it," murmured Döninger. "The magnitude of the price set on your head will induce him to betray his benefactor."

"Andy," cried Anna Gertrude, bursting into tears, and clinging to her husband, "save yourself ! If you love me and the children, save yourself ; cut off your beard, put on the new suit of clothes, and escape from your bloodthirsty enemies. Save yourself, for the sake of your wife and your poor children ! "

"I cannot," said Andreas, mournfully, embracing his wife tenderly ; "no, so help me God, I cannot leave my dear, un-hap.. country. I know full well that I shall not avert any calamities from the Tyrol by staying here, but I will at least share its misfortunes. I was unable to save my native country ; I will therefore suffer with it. A good captain does not desert his shipwrecked vessel, but dies with it ; and thus I will not desert my country either, but die with it. I will do all I can to save myself, but I will not leave the Tyrol ; I will not cut off my beard nor put on other clothes. I will not mask and disguise myself, but will remain in adversity what I was in the days of prosperity, Andreas Hofer, the Barbone. State that to the dear archduke, Anthony Steeger, and tell him also that I am very grateful to him for wishing to save me in *his* way, and that I hope he will not be angry with me for being unable to accept his kind offer, or for wishing to live and die with my country. If he wishes to do any thing for me, let him go to the Emperor Francis, and tell him I am well aware that he himself would never have forgotten us, but that his bad ministers did it all, and betrayed the poor Tyrol so perfidiously. Let him beseech the emperor to intercede vigorously in behalf of the Tyrol and of myself, but not to separate me from the Tyrol."*

* " Gallery of Heroes : Andreas Hofer," p. 188.

"Andreas," cried his wife, despairingly, "you are lost—I feel it here in my heart—you are lost, if you do not flee with Steeger this very night."

"And I feel it here in my heart that I must stay here, even though I should be lost," said Andreas, firmly. "Well, you must weep no more, Anna Gertrude ; and you, Anthony Steeger, accept my cordial thanks for your kind and generous intentions."

"Then you have made up your mind, Andy, not to go with me ?"

"I have, Anthony. But if you will do me a great favor, take my wife and my boy with you, for the enemy threatens them as well as me. Take them with you, Anthony, convey them across the mountains, and conduct them to the Archduke John."

"It is impossible," said Anthony Steeger, mournfully, "the roads are so full of snow that they are utterly impassable for women and children."

"And you would advise me to leave them here ?" asked Andreas Hofer, reproachfully. "I am to leave here my most precious treasures merely to save my miserable life ? No, my friend, I shall stay here with my wife and child and Döninger there. But you must go now and save yourself ; for, if the enemy should really come, it would be bad for you to be found here."

"I will go, Andy, not to save myself, however, but to convey your message speedily to the archduke, that he may save you in another way by the emperor's intercession. In the valley I shall tell every one that you are no longer in this Alpine hut, but have already succeeded in escaping to Vienna, so that it will be unnecessary for the enemy to pursue you any longer."

"Do so, Anthony Steeger ; and if they believe you, I shall be glad of it. But go now ; I am anxious on your account, and think something might happen to you here. Go, my dear friend."

He drew Steeger to the door, and, not permitting him to take a long leave of the others, conducted him out of the hut, and then embraced him tenderly. "Now listen to what I wish

to tell you," he whispered, in a low voice.   "I must stay here
to save my wife and my boy. The two cannot flee now, as
you yourself admitted to me.   If I should escape now, and
leave them here, the enemy would spy out their place of concealment and revenge himself upon them ; he would torture
and kill them in his rage at not having captured me. But if
I stay, and the French should find me, I believe they would
release my wife and my son and do no harm to them ; for
then they would have got me, and they are entirely innocent.
Go, then, my dear friend ; tell the archduke all I have said to
you, and greet him a thousand times from his faithful Andy.
Now farewell, and go with God's blessing ! "

He nodded once more kindly to Anthony Steeger, and returned quickly into the Alpine hut. He found his wife in
tears ; little John, her son, was kneeling before her, with his
head against his mother's knees, and weeping also. Döninger
stood at the hearth and stared into the fire.

Andreas Hofer went to him and laid his hand gently on
his shoulder.   "Cajetan," he asked, mildly, "did I do right ? "

"Yes, commander-in-chief, you did," said Döninger, solemnly.

"I want to tell you something more, Cajetan," added Andreas.   "What Steeger said about Raffel and Donay may be
true ; the French may have discovered my place of concealment, and may come up here. Hence, dear Cajetan, you must
leave me and escape, lest they should seize you, too."

"A good servant leaves his master no more than a captain
deserts his shipwrecked vessel," said Döninger, firmly. "You
refuse to leave your native country in its adversity because
you love it. I refuse, likewise, to leave you in the days of
your adversity, because I love you. I shall stay here."

Andreas Hofer encircled Döninger with his arms and folded him tenderly to his heart. "Stay with me, then, my Cajetan," he said, affectionately. "God knows my heart would
have grieved had you consented to leave me. And now, Anna
Gertrude, do not weep any longer. Make haste, dear wife,
pack up all your things, and let us go early to bed. For early
in the morning we will leave this hut. I know another Alpine hut at no great distance from here ; I believe we will be

able to get thither, and we will take with us as many things as we can carry. Make haste, therefore, dear Anna Gertrude !"

Anna Gertrude dried her tears, and, flushed with new hope, packed up their things in four small bundles, so that each might carry one according to his strength.

Night came at last—the last night which they were to pass at this hut. At the break of day they were to set out for their new place of concealment.

They went to bed at an early hour. Andreas Hofer had sent the two servants down to Brandach, where they were to get some articles necessary for the trip on the morrow. Hofer and his wife slept in the room below. Cajetan Döninger and little John Hofer lay in the small hay-loft, to which a ladder led up from the room.

But Döninger did not sleep. He thought all the while of Raffel, who had come up there three days ago and seen Andreas ; he thought of Donay, the priest, to whom Raffel had betrayed Hofer's place of concealment. He knew that Donay, who, up to the days of adversity, had always professed to be Hofer's friend and an extreme partisan of the insurrection, had suddenly, since the enemy had reoccupied the Tyrol, changed his colors, become a preacher of peace and submission, and an ardent adherent of the French, with whose officers he held a great deal of intercourse. He knew Donay's avaricious and treacherous character, and, therefore, he trembled for Andreas Hofer's safety. He lay uneasy and full of anxiety on his couch, listening all the while for suspicious sounds. But nothing was heard but the storm howling and whistling about the hut, and the regular respirations of the two sleepers in the room below.

Hour passed after hour ; all remained silent, and Döninger felt somewhat relieved, for day would soon dawn, when the hour of flight would be at hand. Döninger dropped his head slowly on the hay to sleep an hour and invigorate himself for to-morrow's trip. However, no sooner had he done so than he gave a start, lifted up his head again, and listened. He had heard a sound outside. The sound, as it were, of many approaching footsteps which creaked on the frozen snow.

Döninger crept cautiously to the small hole in the roof and looked out. The moon shed her pale light on the white snow-field around the hut, and Döninger could see and recognize every thing. He saw a detachment of soldiers coming up yonder. He saw them halt at a short distance from the hut. He then saw two forms approaching the hut. Now they stood still in front of it. The moon shone brightly into the face of one of them ; Döninger recognized him him at once ; it was Raffel, the betrayer. The other was a French officer. The latter stood still at a distance of some steps from the hut, but Raffel went close up to the door, applied his ear to it and listened.

"They are here," he then said to the officer in a low voice. The officer immediately lifted up his arm and shouted "Forward !" The soldiers advanced and surrounded the hut. All was lost !

Döninger awakened the sleeping boy. "John," he said in a low voice, "let us go down to father. The French have come."

The boy uttered a loud cry. "The French have come !" he exclaimed, despairingly ; "they want to arrest my father !"

"Come," said Döninger, imperatively ; and he took the boy in his arms, and hastened with him down the ladder into the room below.

"Awake," he said, bending over Andreas Hofer ; "the enemy has come.

Andreas started up and stared incredulously at Döninger ; but his wife rose, uttering low lamentations, and dressed herself hurriedly.

"Let us flee," she murmured ; "quick, quick, let us escape by the back door."

"The hut is surrounded," said Döninger, assisting Hofer in dressing. "We can no longer flee."

"Is that true ?" asked Andreas, calmly.

"It is, commander-in-chief."

"Well, then, as it pleases God," said Hofer, crossing himself ; and, traversing the room quickly, he opened the front door.

The soldiers stood four files deep, shouldering their muskets. Andreas advanced fearlessly close up to the enemy.

"Is there one of you, gentlemen, who speaks German?" he asked, with entire calmness.

"I do," said the officer, stepping rapidly forward.

Andreas greeted him with a proud nod of the head. "Well, then," he said, "I am Andreas Hofer, late commander-in-chief of the Tyrolese. I ask for quarter and good treatment."

"I cannot promise any thing to a rebel," replied the officer, contemptuously.

"But you have come to seize me, and none but me," continued Andreas, in a gentle voice. "Well, then, here I am; do with me as you please. But I ask you to have mercy upon my wife and my son, and this young man, for they are entirely innocent." *

The officer made no reply. He signed to his soldiers, and ordered them to bind Andreas Hofer and the others in such a manner as to render it utterly impossible for them to escape.

The soldiers rushed furiously upon the defenseless captives, tied their hands on their backs, and wound the ropes round their necks, so that they could drag them forward like oxen. And after binding Andreas Hofer, so that they were no longer afraid of his strong arms, they surrounded him with scornful laughter, tore handfuls of hair from his beard, and said they would keep them "as souve irs of General Barbone." Blood streamed from his lacerated face, but the cold froze it and transformed the gory beard into a blood-red icicle, which pricked the numerous wounds in his chin every moment, and inflicted intense pain.

Andreas did not complain; he looked only at his wife, his son, and his friend, who, bound like himself, scantily dressed and barefooted like himself, were dragged down the mountain, which was covered with snow and ice, into the plain below. His hands, into which the rope was cutting all the while, were very sore; his bare feet swelled from walking on the snow and were torn by the icicles. Still Andreas did not com-

* Andreas Hofer's own words.—See "Gallery of Heroes."

plain ; but on hearing the low wails of his son, on seeing that
every footstep of his wife, who was dragged along before him,
left a bloody spot in the snow, he burst into loud sobs, and two
tears rolled slowly down his cheeks into his beard, where they
froze in the blood.

The dreadful march was continued to Meran. French generals, staff-officers, and soldiers awaited the tottering prisoners
at the gate. The soldiers greeted the captured " bandit chief
Barbone " with loud cheers and scornful laughter ; and Andreas Hofer and the others entered the city, preceded by a
band which played a ringing march. The French were overjoyed, but the citizens stood in front of their houses, and, regardless of the presence of their cruel enemies, greeted Andreas
Hofer with tears and loud lamentations.

The journey was continued on the following day to Botzen ; only the prisoners, whose bleeding and lacerated feet
refused to carry them any longer, had been laid on a common farm-wagon, and some clothing had been thrown over
them.

At Botzen Andreas Hofer received cheering news. A noble
German lady, the wife of Baron de Giovanelli, had dared to
implore the French General Baraguay d'Hilliers to have
mercy on Hofer's unfortunate and innocent family ; to save
them, she had knelt down before the general and besought
him with heart-rending lamentations. Baraguay d'Hilliers
had been unable to withstand her supplications, and consented
to release those for whom she pleaded.

" The viceroy's orders," he said, " are only to the effect that
the Sandwirth Hofer be conveyed to Mantua. I yield to your
prayers, therefore, madame ; his companions shall be released,
and shall not be molested again. His wife may return with
her son to her home, and carry on the inn as heretofore ; but
she must be cautious and not expose herself to new dangers
by imprudent words. The young man may go wherever he
pleases."

This was the cheering intelligence which Andreas Hofer
received on the third day of his captivity in the jail where he
and his dear ones lay on wet straw.

" See, Cajetan," he exclaimed, joyfully, " it turns out just as I said. My seizure releases my wife and my child, and relieves them from all dangers."

"But I will not leave you," cried Anna Gertrude, embracing him tenderly ; "I will stay and die with you."

"And is our son yonder to die too ?" asked Andreas, pointing to his boy. "And our three little girls, are they to become entirely helpless, and have neither father nor mother to protect them ? Anna Gertrude, you must be father and mother to them ; you must not leave them and our boy. You must preserve their small inheritance to them, bring them up in the fear of the Lord, and teach them, also, to love their poor father and honor his memory."

"Husband, dear husband, I cannot leave you, I cannot !" sobbed the poor woman. "Do not thrust me from your heart, do not leave me behind, all alone and without consolation."

Andreas lifted his arm and pointed up to heaven. "There is our Consoler," he said ; "He will help you. Confide in Him, Anna Gertrude. Go to your children, be father and mother to them, and love them in my and your name."

At this moment the door of the prison opened, and the jailer, followed by soldiers, came in.

"Andreas Hofer," said the jailer, imperatively, "come ! The wagon which is to convey you to Mantua is in readiness. As for you others, begone ; you have no longer any business here. Come, Andreas Hofer, come !"

"Let me first bless my wife and my son, my friend," said Hofer, and, laying his hands on the heads of his wife and child, he blessed them in a loud voice, and commended them to the protection of the Lord. Döninger knelt behind him, and Andreas Hofer laid his hand on his head also, blessed him, and thanked him for his love and fidelity.

"Come now, come !" cried the soldiers ; and they seized him with rude violence and dragged him forward.

Anna Gertrude burst into loud lamentations in her grief and despair, and clung to Hofer in the anguish of her love.

"Do not lament any longer," said Andreas, mildly ; "bring your grief as an offering to the crucified Redeemer, and show now that you are Hofer's wife. Farewell, love ! Kiss our children ! Forward now !"

And he led the way with a rapid step. Anna Gertrude, pale as a corpse, trembling and tottering, seized her son's hand and rushed after her husband. Cajetan Döninger followed them resolutely and with a defiant expression of countenance.

At the street-door stood the farm-wagon, covered with straw, which was to convey Andreas Hofer to Mantua. Ten soldiers with loaded muskets stood upon it, and a crowd of sol-diers surrounded it.

Andreas Hofer walked calmly and with head erect through their ranks to the wagon. His wife had knelt down ; she wept and sobbed bitterly, and embraced convulsively her son, who gazed in dismay at his father.

Andreas Hofer had now ascended the wagon. The soldiers stepped back, and the driver whipped up the horses.

Suddenly, Cajetan Döninger elbowed his way to the wagon, and signed to the driver to stop.

" I shall accompany Hofer," he said, grasping the side-rail-ing of the wagon in order to mount it.

" No, no," cried the jailer, hastening to him. " You are mistaken, you are free."

Döninger, still clinging to the railing of the wagon, turned to him. " What said the general's order ? " he asked.

" It said, ' the young man is free, and can go wherever he pleases.' "

" Well, then," said Döninger, mounting the wagon, quickly, " the young man will accompany Andreas Hofer to Mantua. Forward, driver, forward ! "

The driver whipped up the horses, and the wagon started for Mantua.*

---

* Donay, the priest who betrayed Andreas Hofer, according to the general belief of the Tyrolese, was soon afterwards appointed imperial chaplain at the chapel of Loretto, by a special decree of the Emperor Napoleon, and received, besides, large donations in lands and money.—See Hormayr's " Andreas Hofer," vol. ii., p. 507.—The peasant Francis Joseph Raffel, who had betrayed Hofer's place of concealment to Donay, was afterward called Judas Iscariot throughout the Tyrol. Every one turned his back upon him with the ut-most horror, and the men of the Passeyr valley told him they would shoot him if he did not hang himself within a week. Raffel fled in great dismay to Bavaria, where the government gave him a small office in the revenue de-partment.—See " Gallery of Heroes : Andreas Hofer," p. 191.

CHAPTER XLII.

THE WARNING.

THE French hunted throughout the Tyrol for the unfortunate men who had hitherto been the heroes of the fatherland, but who, since their cause had succumbed, were called rebels and traitors. The soldiers who were in search of this noble game, for which large rewards were offered to them, had already succeeded in arresting one of the heroes of the Tyrol ; Peter Mayer had fallen into their hands, and, having been tried by a military commission at Botzen, was shot. But they had been unable as yet to discover the hiding-places of the other insurgent leaders, despite the large prices which the government had set upon their heads. Joseph Speckbacher, for whom the soldiers were hunting most eagerly, had disappeared. The French and Bavarians ransacked every house where they suspected he might be concealed ; they inflicted the heaviest fines and most cruel tortures on the friends of the fugitive chief, because they would not betray the place where their beloved commander was concealed ; but all was in vain. Joseph Speckbacher had disappeared, and so had Father Haspinger and Anthony Wallner.*

* Speckbacher had fled to the higher mountains, where, on one of the summits of the Eisgletscher, in a cavern discovered by him in former times when pursuing the chamois, he lay for several weeks in the depth of winter, supported by salt provisions, eaten raw, lest the smoke of a fire should betray his place of concealment to his pursuers. Happening one day, in the beginning of March, to walk to the entrance for a few minutes to enjoy the ascending sun, an avalanche, descending from the summit of the mountain above, swept him along with it, down to the distance of half a mile on the slope beneath, and dislocated his hip-bone in the fall. Unable now to stand, surrounded only by ice and snow, tracked on every side by ruthless pursuers, his situation was, to all appearance, desperate; but even then the unconquerable energy of his mind and the incorruptible fidelity of his friends saved him from destruction. Summoning up all his courage, he contrived to drag himself along the snow for several leagues, during the night, to the village of Volderberg, where, to avoid discovery, he crept into the stable. His faithful friend gave him a kind reception, and carried him on his back to Rinn, where his wife and children were, and where Zoppel, his devoted domestic, con-

General Broussier was especially exasperated at the last named, the valiant commander of Windisch-Matrey, and he had promised a reward of one thousand ducats to him who would arrest "that dangerous demagogue and bandit-chief, Anthony Aichberger-Wallner," and deliver him to the French authorities. But Wallner and his two sons, who, although hardly above the age of boyhood, had seemed to the French authorities so dangerous that they had set prices upon their heads, were not to be found anywhere. Schröpfel, Wallner's faithful servant, had taken the boys into the mountains, where he stayed with them; after nightfall he went down to Matrey to fetch provisions for the lonely fugitives.

Anthony Wallner's fine house was silent and deserted now. Only his wife and his daughter Eliza lived in it, and they passed their days in dreary loneliness and incessant fear and anguish. Eliza Wallner was alone, all alone and joyless. She had not seen her beloved Elza since the day when she was married. She herself had started the same night with Haspinger for her father's headquarters. Elza had remained with her young husband in Innspruck, where her father died on the following day; and after the old Baron had been buried, Elza had accompanied her husband to Munich. From thence she wrote from time to time letters overflowing with fervent

cealed him in a hole in the cowhouse, beneath where the cattle stood, though beyond the reach of their feet, where he was covered up with cow-dung and fodder, and remained for two months, till his leg was set and he was able to walk. The town was full of Bavarian troops; but this extraordinary place of concealment was never discovered, even when the Bavarian dragoons, as was frequently the case, were in the stable looking after their horses. Zoppel did not even inform Speckbacher's wife of her husband's return, lest her emotions or visits to the place might betray his place of concealment. At length, in the beginning of May, the Bavarian soldiers having left the house, Speckbacher was lifted from his living grave and restored to his wife and children. As soon as he was able to walk, he set out, and, journeying chiefly in the night, through the wildest and most secluded Alps, by Dux and the sources of the Salza, he passed the Styrian Alps, where he crossed the frontier and reached Vienna in safety. There he was soon after joined by his family and liberally provided for.

Haspinger succeeded in escaping into Switzerland, whence he travelled by cross-paths through Friuli and Carinthia to Vienna, where he received protection from the emperor.

tenderness to her beloved friend, and these letters were the
only sunbeams which illuminated Eliza's cheerless life ; these
letters told her of her friend's happiness, of her attachment to
her young husband, who treated her with the utmost kindness
and tenderness.

Eliza had received this afternoon another letter from her
friend ; with a melancholy smile she read Elza's description
of her domestic happiness, and her eyes had unconsciously
filled with tears which rolled slowly down her pale cheeks.
She dried them quickly, but her mother, who sat opposite her
near the lamp and seemed to be busily sewing, had already
seen them.

"Why do you weep, Lizzie ?" she asked. "Have you got
bad news from Elza ?"

Eliza shook her head with a mournful smile. "No, dear
mother," she said ; "thank God, my Elza is happy and well,
and that is my only joy."

"And yet you weep, Eliza ?"

"Did I weep, then ?" she asked. "It was probably a tear
of joy at my Elza's happiness."

"No, Lizzie, it was no tear of joy," cried her mother,
mournfully. "I see you often in tears, when you think that
I do not notice it. You are grieving, Lizzie, do not deny it ;
you are grieving. You sacrificed your love and happiness to
Elza, and she does not even know it ; she does not thank you,
and you will pine away. I see very well how sad you are ;
and you become paler and more emaciated from day to day.
Yes, yes, you will die of grief, for you still love Ulrich von
Hohenberg."

"No," cried Eliza, vehemently, blushing deeply, "I do not
love him. I have buried my love in my heart, and it reposes
there as in a shrine. It is true I think of it very often, I pray
to it, but I have no unholy thoughts and feel no sinful desires.
I am glad that my Elza is so happy ; yes, I am glad of it and
thank God for it. But how can I be merry and laugh, mother,
so long as my dear, dear father has not returned to us ? He
must hide like a criminal ; they are chasing him like a wild
beast ; he is always in danger, and we must constantly tremble
for his safety. And I cannot do any thing for him, I cannot

share his dangers, I cannot be with him in the dreadful solitude on the Alp above. I must look on in idleness, and cannot be useful to any one, neither to my father, nor to my brothers, nor to you, dear mother. I cannot help my father and brothers, and cannot comfort you, mother; for I myself am in despair, and would—what was that, mother? Did not some one knock at the window-shutter?"

"Hush, hush!" whispered her mother; "let us listen."

They listened with bated breath. Eliza had not been mistaken; some one knocked a second time at the window-shutter, and the voice of a man whispered, "Mrs. Wallner, are you in the room? Open the door to me!"

"It must be a good friend of ours, for the dogs do not bark," said Eliza; "we will let him come in."

She took the lamp and went out courageously to draw the bolt from the street-door and open it.

Yes, she had not been mistaken, it was really a good friend of theirs; the man who entered the house was one of the few friends who had not denied Anthony Wallner, and who had not turned their backs upon his family since it was outlawed and in distress.

"You bring us bad news, Peter Siebermeier?" asked Eliza, anxiously, gazing into the mountaineer's pale and dismayed face.

"Unfortunately I do," sighed Siebermeier, stepping hastily into the sitting-room and shaking hands with Eliza's mother. "Mrs. Wallner," he said, in breathless hurry, "your husband is in the greatest danger, and only speedy flight can save him."

Mrs. Wallner uttered a piercing cry, sank back into her chair, wrung her hands, and wept aloud. Eliza did not weep; she was calm and courageous. "Tell me, Siebermeier, what can we do for father? What danger threatens him?"

"A bad man, I believe, the clerk of the court, has informed the French that Anthony Wallner is still on one of the heights in this neighborhood. General Broussier intends to have him arrested. A whole battalion of soldiers will march to-morrow morning to the mountain of Ober-Peischlag and occupy it."

"Great God! my husband is lost, then!" cried Eliza's mother, despairing; "nothing can save him now."

"Hush, mother, hush!" said Eliza, almost imperatively; "we must not weep now, we must think only of saving him. Tell me, friend Siebermeier, is there no way of saving him?"

"There is one," said Siebermeier, "but how shall we get up to him? A friend of mine, who is acquainted with the members of the court, informed me quite stealthily that, if Aichberger could be saved yet, it should be done this very night. Now listen to the plan I have devised. I intended to set out to-morrow morning to peddle carpets and blankets, for money is very scarce in these hard times. I procured, therefore, a passport for myself and my boy, who is to carry my bundle. Here is the passport—and look! the description corresponds nearly to Wallner's appearance. He is of my stature and age, has hair and whiskers like mine, and might be passed off for myself. I am quite willing to let him have my passport, and conceal myself meanwhile at home and feign sickness. The passport would enable him to escape safely; of course he would have to journey through the Alps, for every one knows him in the plain. However, the passport cannot do him any good, for there is no one to take it up to him. I would do so, but the wound which I received in our last skirmish with the Bavarians, in my side here, prevents me from ascending the mountain-paths; and, even though I could go up to him, it would be useless, for we two could not travel together, the passport being issued to two persons, Siebermeier, the carpet-dealer, and the boy carrying his bundle. The boy is not described in the passport; therefore, I thought, if one of your sons were in the neighborhood, he might go up to his father, warn him of his danger, and accompany him on his trip through the mountains."

"But neither of the boys is here," said Mrs. Wallner, despairingly; "Schröpfel took them to the Alpine hut near Upper Lindeau, and is with them. We two are all alone, and there is, therefore, no way of saving my dear husband."

"Yes, mother, there is," cried Eliza, flushed with excitement. "I will go up to father. I will warn him of his danger, carry him the passport, and flee with him."

"You!" cried her mother, in dismay. "It is impossible! You cannot ascend the road, which is almost impassable even for men. How should a girl, then, be able to get over it, particularly in the night, and in so heavy a snow-storm?"

"You will be unable to reach your father, Lizzie," said Siebermeier; "the road is precipitous and very long; you will sink into the snow; your shoes will stick in it, and the storm will catch your dress."

"No road is too precipitous for me if I can save my father," exclaimed Eliza, enthusiastically. "I must reach him, and God will enable me to do so. Wait here a moment, I will be back immediately. I will prepare myself for the trip, and then give me the passport."

"She will lose her life in the attempt," said Mrs. Wallner, mournfully, after she had hastened out of the room. "Alas! alas! I shall lose my husband, my sons, and my daughter too! And all has been in vain, for the Tyrol is ruined, and we have to suffer these dreadful misfortunes without having accomplished anything!"

"And the enemy acts with merciless cruelty in the country," said Siebermeier, furiously; "he sets whole villages on fire if he thinks that one of the fugitives is concealed here; he imposes on the people heavy war-taxes, which we are unable to pay; and if we say we have no money, he takes our cattle and other property from us. Wails and lamentations are to be heard throughout the valley; that is all we have gained by our bloody struggle!"

At this moment the door opened, and Eliza came in, not however in her own dress, but in the costume of a Tyrolese peasant-lad.

"Heavens! she has put on her brother William's Sunday clothes," cried her mother, with a mournful smile; "and they sit as well on her as if they had been made for her."

"Now, Siebermeier," said Eliza, holding out her hand to him, "give me the passport. The moon is rising now, and I must go."

"But listen, my daughter, how the wind howls!" cried her mother, in deep anguish. "It beats against the windows as if to warn us not to go out. Oh, Lizzie, my last joy, do not leave me ! I have no one left but you ; stay with me, my Lizzie, do not leave your poor mother ! You will die in the attempt, Lizzie ! Stay here ; have mercy upon me, and stay here ! "

"I must go to father," replied Eliza, disengaging herself gently from her mother's arms. "Give me the passport, friend Siebermeier."

"You are a brave girl," said Siebermeier, profoundly moved ; "the good God and the Holy Virgin will protect you. There, take the passport ; you are worthy to carry it to your father."

"And I shall carry it to him or die on the road," cried Eliza, enthusiastically, waving the paper. "Now, dear mother, do not weep, but give me your blessing ! "

She knelt down before her mother, who had laid her hand on her head.

"Lord, my God," she exclaimed, solemnly, "protect her graciously in her pious effort to save her father. Take your mother's blessing, my Lizzie, and think that her heart and love accompany you."

She bent over her, and imprinted a long kiss on her daughter's forehead.

"I must go now, it is high time," said Eliza, making a violent effort to restrain her tears. "Farewell, friend Siebermeier ; God and the saints will reward you for the service you have rendered us."

"My best reward will be to learn that Wallner is safe," said Siebermeier, shaking hands with her.

"Now, a last kiss, dearest mother," said Eliza. She encircled her mother's neck with both her arms, and kissed her tenderly. "Pray for me and love me," she whispered ; "and if I should not come back, if I should lose my life, mother, write it to Elza and to *him*, and write that I died with love and fidelity in my heart. Farewell ! "

She disengaged herself quickly and hastened out of the room, regardless of the despairing cries of her mother, and not even looking back to her. It was high time for her to set out.

She was in the street now. The snow rushed furiously into her face ; the howling storm dashed madly against her cheeks until they became very sore, but the moon was in the heavens

and lighted her path. It was the same path which she had
ascended with Ulrich when saving him. She was alone now, but
her courage and her trust in God were with her; strengthened
and refreshed by her love for her father, she ascended the
steep mountain path. At times the piercing wind rendered
her breathless and seized her with such violence that she had
to cling to a projecting rock in order not to fall from the narrow path into the abyss yawning at her feet. At times avalanches rolled close to her with thundering noise into the
depth and enveloped her in a cloud of snow; but the moon
shed her silver light on her path, and Eliza looked up courageously. Forgetful of her own danger, she prayed in her
heart only, "God grant that I may save my father! Let me
not die before reaching him!"

CHAPTER XLIII.

THE FLIGHT.

ANTHONY WALLNER sat in his lonely Alpine hut on the
height near the village of Ober-Peischlag, and listened to the
storm, which howled so loudly to-night that the hut shook and
he was unable to sleep on his couch of straw. He had lighted
his lamp, and sat musingly at the pine table, leaning his head
on his hand, and brooding mournfully over his dreary future.
How long would he have to remain here in his open grave?
How long would he be chased yet, like a wild beast, from
mountain to mountain? How long would he be obliged yet
to lead an idle and unprofitable life in this frozen solitude, exposed to the fury of the elements, and in constant dread of
losing this miserable life? These were the questions that he
asked himself; intense rage seized his heart, tears of bitter
grief filled his eyes—not, however, at his own misfortunes, but
at the miseries of his fatherland.

"What am I suffering for? What did I fight and risk my
life for? What did we all shed our blood for? What did
our brethren die for on the field of battle? The fatherland

was not saved, the French defeated us, and our emperor abandoned us. We were brave defenders of our country, and now
they call us criminals ; we intended to save the fatherland,
and now they call us rebels and traitors ! The emperor gives
us away like a piece of merchandise, regardless of his sacred
pledges, and the French are chasing us as though we were
thieves and murderers ! And Thou sufferest it, God in heav-
en ? Thou—Hark ! did not that sound like a shot ? Is it the
wind that is knocking so loudly at my door ? "

He sprang to his feet, took up his rifle, cocked it, and aimed
at the door.

There was another knocking at the door ; no, it was assuredly not the storm that was rapping and hammering at it so
regularly. No, no, it was the enemy ! He had spied him out,
he had discovered his track, he had come to seize him !

"I will sell my life dearly," murmured Anthony Wallner,
grimly. "I will shoot down the first man who opens the
door ; then I will force a passage through the ranks with the
butt-end of my rifle, and—"

"Father," cried a voice outside, "father, open the door ! "

"Great God !" murmured Wallner, "did not that sound
like my Lizzie calling me ? But that is impossible ; it cannot
be she ; she cannot have ascended the mountain-path ; the
storm would have killed her, and—"

"Father, dear father, pray open the door," shouted the
voice again, and somebody shook the door.

Wallner laid down his rifle and hastened to the door.
"May God protect me if they deceive me, but I believe it is
Lizzie."

He threw open the door ; the little Tyrolese lad rushed in,
embraced him tenderly, kissed him with his cold lips, and
whispered, "My father ! thank God, I am with you ! "

"It is Lizzie !" cried Wallner, in a ringing voice. "She
has come to me through night and storm ! It is my daughter,
my dear, dear daughter ! Oh, joy of my heart, how were you
able to get up here in this terrible night ? No man would
have dared to attempt it."

"But I dared it, father, for I am your child, and love you."

"You love me, and I thank God !" he exclaimed, folding

her tenderly and anxiously to his heart; "I thank God for saving you, and—"

He faltered and burst into tears, which he did not try to conceal. He wept aloud and bitterly, and Eliza wept with him, and neither of them knew whether they wept for joy or grief.

Eliza was the first to overcome her emotion. "Father," she said, raising her head quickly, "the enemy is on your track, and early to-morrow morning the French are going to occupy the mountain in order to arrest you. That is the reason why I have come up to you, for you must flee this very hour."

"Flee!" he cried, mournfully. "How can I? The first Bavarian or French *gendarme* on the frontier, who meets me and asks me for my passport, will arrest me. I have no passport."

"Here is a passport," said Eliza, joyfully, handing him the paper, "Siebermeier sends it to you."

"The faithful friend! Yes, that is help in need. Now I will try with God's aid to escape. You, Lizzie, will return to mother, and bring her a thousand greetings from me; and as soon as I am across the frontier, you shall hear from me."

"I must go with you, father," said Eliza, smiling. "The passport is valid for Siebermeier, the carpet-dealer, and his son. Now you see, dear father, I am your son, and shall flee with you."

"No," cried her father, in dismay; "no, you shall never do so, Lizzie. I must journey through the wildest and most secluded Alps, and you would die in the attempt to follow me, Lizzie."

"And even though I knew that I should die, father, I should go with you," said Lizzie, joyfully. "You cannot flee without me, and I do not love my life very dearly if it cannot be useful to you, dear father. Therefore, say no more about it, and do not reject my offer any longer; for if you do, it will be in vain, because I shall follow you for all that, and no road is too precipitous for me when I see you before me. Therefore, come, dear father; do not hesitate any longer, but come with your little boy. You cannot flee without me ; therefore, let us try it courageously together."

"Well, I will do so, my brave little boy ; I believe I must comply with your wish," exclaimed Wallner, folding her tenderly to his heart. "You shall accompany me, you shall save your father's life. Oh, it would be glorious if God should grant me the satisfaction of being indebted for my life to my dear daughter Lizzie !"

"Come, now, father, come ; every minute's delay increases the danger."

"I am ready, Lizzie. Let me only see if my rifle is in good order and put on my powder-pouch."

"You cannot take your rifle with you, nor your powder-pouch either. You are no longer the brave commander of the sharpshooters of Windisch-Matrey, but Siebermeier, the carpet-dealer, a very peaceable man, who does not take his rifle and powder-pouch with him on his travels."

"You are right, Lizzie. But it is hard indeed to flee without arms, and to be defenceless even in case of an attack by the enemy. And I do not want to let my rifle fall into the hands of the French when they come up here. I know a hole in the rock close by ; I will take it there and conceal it till my return. Come, now, Lizzie, and let us attempt, with God's aid, to escape from the enemy."

He wrapped himself in his cloak, took the rifle, and both left the hut.

Day was now dawning ; some rosy streaks appeared already in the eastern horizon, and the summits of the glaciers were faintly illuminated. Eliza saw it, but she did not rejoice this time at the majestic beauty of the sunrise ; it made her only uneasy and sad, and while her father concealed his rifle carefully in the hole in the rock, Eliza glanced around anxiously, murmuring to herself : "They intend to start at daybreak. It is now after daybreak ; the sun has risen, and they have doubtless set out already to arrest him."

"Now come," said her father, returning to her ; "we have a long journey before us to-day, for we must pass the Alps by hunters' paths up to the Isel-Tauerkamm. We shall pass the night at the inn there ; in the morning we shall continue the journey, and, if it please God, we shall reach the Austrian frontier within three hours."

And they descended the mountain, hand in hand and with firm steps, and entered the forest.

Nothing was to be heard all around ; not a sound broke the peaceful stillness of awaking nature ; only the wind howled and whistled, and caused the branches of the trees to creak. The sun had risen higher and higher, and shed already its golden rays through the forest.

" I would we had passed through the thicket and reached the heights again," said Anthony Wallner, in a low voice. " We were obliged to descend in order to pass round the precipice and the steep slope ; we shall afterwards ascend the mountain again and remain on the heights. But if the soldiers from Windisch-Matrey meet us here, we are lost, for they know me and will not pay any attention to my passport."

" God will not permit them to meet us," sighed Lizzie, accelerating her steps. They kept silent a long while, and not a sound was to be heard around them. All at once both gave a start, for they had heard the noise of heavy footsteps and the clang of arms. They had just passed through the clearing in the forest and were now again close to the thicket, by the side of which there was a small chapel with a large crucifix. They turned and looked back.

" The enemy ! the enemy !" cried Anthony Wallner, pointing to the soldiers who were just stepping from the other side of the forest. " Lizzie, we are lost ! Ah, and I have not even got my rifle ! I must allow myself to be seized without resistance !"

" No, we are not yet lost, father ; look at the chapel. Maybe they have not yet seen us. Let us enter the chapel quickly. There is room enough for us two under the altar."

Without giving her father time to reply, Eliza hastened into the chapel and disappeared behind the altar. In a second Wallner was with her, and, clinging close to each other and with stifled breath, they awaited the arrival of the enemy.

Now they heard footsteps approaching rapidly and voices shouting out aloud. They came nearer and nearer, and were now close to the chapel. It was a Bavarian patrol, and the two, therefore, could understand every word they spoke, and every word froze their hearts. The Bavarians had seen them ; they were convinced that they must be close by ; they exhorted each other to look diligently for the fugitives, and alluded to the reward which awaited them in case they should arrest Anthony Wallner.

Both lay under the altar with hearts throbbing impetuously, and almost senseless from fear and anguish ; Eliza murmuring a prayer with quivering lips ; Anthony Wallner clinching his fists, and firmly resolved to sell his life dearly and defend himself and his child to the last drop of blood.

The enemies were now close to them ; they entered the chapel and advanced to the altar. Eliza, pale and almost fainting from terror, leaned her head on her father's shoulder. The Bavarians struck now with the butt-ends of their muskets against the closed front-side of the altar ; it gave a dull, hard sound, for the fugitives filled the cavity.

"There is no one in there, for the altar is not hollow," said one of the soldiers. The footsteps thereupon moved away from the altar, and soon all was silent in the chapel. Wallner and Lizzie heard only footsteps and voices outside ; they moved away farther and farther, and after a few seconds not a sound broke the silence.

The fugitives lay still behind the altar, motionless, listening, with hearts throbbing impetuously. Could they dare to leave their place of concealment ? Was it not, perhaps, a mere stratagem of the enemy to keep silent ? Had the soldiers surrounded the chapel, and were they waiting merely for them to come out ? They waited and listened for hours, but their cowering position benumbed their blood ; it stiffened their limbs and made their heads ache.

"Father, I can no longer stand it," murmured Eliza ; "I will die rather than stay here any longer."

"Come, Lizzie," said Wallner, raising himself up and jumping over the altar, "come ! I, too, think it is better for us to die than hide thus like thieves."

They joined hands and left the chapel, looking anxiously

in all directions. But every thing remained silent, and not a Bavarian soldier made his appearance.

"They are gone, indeed they are gone," said Wallner, triumphantly. "Now we must make haste, my girl; we shall ascend the height; the footpath leads up here in the rear of the chapel; within two hours we shall reach the summit, and, if our feet do not slip, if we do not fall into the depth, if no avalanche overwhelms us, and if the storm does not freeze us, I think we shall reach the Isel-Tauerkamm to-night, and sleep at the inn there. May the Holy Virgin protect us!"

And the Holy Virgin did seem to guard the intrepid wanderers—to enable them to cross abysses on frail bridges; to prevent them from sinking into invisible clefts and pits covered with snow; to make them safely escape the avalanches falling down here and there, and protect them from freezing to death.

Toward dusk they reached at length the inn on the Isel-Tauerkamm, utterly exhausted by fatigue, hunger, and frost, and entered the bar-room on the ground-floor. Nobody was there but the landlord, a gloomy, morose-looking man, who eyed the new-comers with evident distrust.

When the two wanderers, scarcely able to utter a word, seated themselves on the bench at the narrow table, the landlord stepped up to them.

"I am not allowed to harbor any one without seeing his passport," he said. "There are all sorts of fugitive vagabonds prowling around here to hide from the Bavarians, who are searching the whole district to-day. Give me your passport, therefore."

Wallner handed him the paper in silence. The landlord read it attentively, and seemed to compare the two with the description in the passport.

"H'm!" he said, "the carpet-dealer and his son—that corresponds to what the passport says; but where is the bundle of carpets?"

Anthony Wallner gave a slight start; he recovered his presence of mind immediately, however, and said calmly, "The carpets are all sold already; we are on our return to Windisch-Matrey."

"See, see how lucky you have been," said the landlord, laughing; "the passport says you started only yesterday morning, and to-day you have already sold all your carpets. Well, in that case, you are certainly justified in returning to your home. Your passport is in good order, and the Bavarians, therefore, will not molest you."

"As my passport is in good order, I suppose you will give us beds, and, above all things, something to eat and drink."

"You shall have everything, that is to say, every thing that I can give you. I am all alone here, and have nothing but a piece of ham, bread, and cheese, and a glass of wine. As for beds, I have not got any ; you must sleep on the bench here."

"Well, we will do so ; but give us something to eat now," said Wallner, "and add a little fuel to the fire, that we may warm ourselves."

The landlord added some brushwood and a few billets to the fire, fetched the provisions, and looked on while the wanderers were partaking of the food with eager appetite. All at once he stepped quickly up to them, seated himself on the bench opposite them, and drew a paper from his pocket. "I will read something to you now," he said. "There were Bavarian soldiers here to-day ; they gave me a new decree, and ordered me to obey it under pain of death. Listen to me."

And he read, in a loud, scornful voice :

"Know all men by these presents, that any inhabitant of the German or Italian Tyrol, who dares to harbor Anthony Wallner, called Aichberger, late commander of the sharpshooters of Windisch-Matrey, or his two sons, shall lose his whole property by confiscation, and his house shall be burned down." *

"Did you hear it ? " asked the landlord, after reading the proclamation.

"I did," said Wallner, with perfect composure, "but it does not concern us."

"Yes, it does. I believe you are Anthony Wallner, and the lad there is one of your sons."

Anthony Wallner laughed. "Forsooth," he said, "if I were Wallner I should not be so stupid as to show myself. I be-

* Loritza, p. 130.

lieve he is hiding somewhere in the mountains near Windisch-Matrey. But I think I resemble him a little, for you are not the first man who has taken me for Anthony Wallner. And that the lad there is not one of Anthony Wallner's sons, I will swear on the crucifix, if you want me to do so."

"Well, well, it is all right, I believe you," growled the landlord. "Now lie down and sleep; there is a pillow for each of you, and now good-night; I will go to my chamber and sleep too."

He nodded to them morosely, and left the room.

"Lizzie, do you think we can trust him?" asked Wallner, in a low voice.

Eliza made no reply; she only beckoned to her father, slipped on tiptoe across the room to the door, and applied her ear to it.

There was a pause. Then they heard the front door jar.

"Father," whispered Eliza, hastening to Wallner, "he has left the house to fetch the soldiers. I heard him walk through the hall to the front door and open it. He has left, and locked us up."

"Locked us up?" cried Wallner, and hastened to the door. He shook it with the strength of a giant, but the lock did not yield; the bolts did not give way.

"It is in vain, in vain!" cried Wallner, stamping the floor furiously; "the door does not yield; we are caught in the trap, for there is no other outlet."

"Yes, father, there is; there is the window," said Eliza. "Come, we must jump out of the window."

"But did you not see, Lizzie, that the house stands on a slope, and that a staircase leads outside to the front door? If we jump out of the window, we shall fall at least twenty feet."

"But there is a great deal of snow on the ground, and we shall fall softly. I will jump out first, father, and you must follow me immediately."

And Eliza disappeared out of the window. Wallner waited a few seconds and then followed her. They reached the ground safely; the deep snow prevented the leap from being dangerous; they sprang quickly to their feet, and hastened on as fast as their weary limbs would carry them.

It was a cold, dark night. The moon, which shone so brightly during the previous night, was covered with heavy clouds ; the storm swept clouds of snow before it, and whistled and howled across the extensive snow-fields. But the wanderers continued their journey with undaunted hearts.

All at once something stirred behind them ; they saw torches gleaming up, and Bavarian soldiers accompanying the bearers of the torches. The soldiers, headed by the landlord who had fetched them, rushed forward with wild shouts and imprecations. But Wallner and Eliza likewise rushed forward like roes hunted down. They panted heavily, the piercing storm almost froze their faces, their feet bled, but they continued their flight at a rapid rate. Nevertheless, the distance separating them from their pursuers became shorter and shorter. The Bavarians, provided with torches, could see the road and the footsteps of the fugitives in the snow, while the latter had to run blindly into the night, unable to see whither their feet were carrying them, and exhausted by the long journey of the preceding day.

The distance between pursuers and pursued rapidly diminished ; scarcely twenty yards now lay between them, and the soldiers extended their hands already to seize them. At this moment of extreme peril the storm came up howling with redoubled fury and drove whole clouds of snow before it, extinguished the torches of the Bavarians, and shrouded every thing in utter darkness. The joyful cries of the pursued and the imprecations of their pursuers were heard at the same time.

Wallner and Eliza, whose eyes were already accustomed to the darkness, advanced at a rapid rate : the soldiers followed them, but blinded by the darkness, unable to see the road, and calling each other in order to remain together. These calls and shouts added to the advantages of the fugitives, for they indicated to them the direction which they had to take in order to avoid the enemy. Finally, the shouts became weaker and weaker, and died away entirely.

The fugitives continued their flight more leisurely ; but they could not rest and stand still in the dark, cold night, for the storm would have frozen them, the cold would have killed them. They did not speak, but advanced breathlessly and hand in hand. All at once they beheld a light twinkling in the distance like a star. There was a house, then, and men also. They walked on briskly, and the light came nearer and nearer. Now they saw already the house through whose windows it gleamed. In a few minutes they were close to the house, in front of which they beheld a tall post.

"Great God!" cried Anthony Wallner; "I believe that is a boundary-post, and we are now on Austrian soil."

He knocked hastily at the door; it opened, and the two wanderers entered the small, warm, and cozy room, where they were received by a man in uniform, who sat at the table eating his supper.

Anthony Wallner went close up to him and pointed to his uniform.

"You wear the Austrian uniform?" he asked.

"I do, sir," said the man, smilingly.

"And we are here on Austrian soil?"

"Yes, sir. The boundary-post is in front of this house. This is an Austrian custom-house."

Anthony Wallner threw his arm around Eliza's neck and knelt down. He burst into tears, and exclaimed in a loud, joyous voice, "Lord God in heaven, I thank Thee!"

Eliza said nothing, but her tears spoke for her, and so did the smile with which she looked up to heaven and then at her father.

The custom-house officer had risen and stood profoundly moved by the side of the two.

"Who are you, my friend?" he asked; "and why do you weep and thank God?"

"Who am I?" asked Wallner, rising and drawing Eliza up with him. "I am Anthony Wallner, and this is my daughter Lizzie, who has saved me from the Bavarians. The good God—"

He said no more, but leaned totteringly on Eliza's shoulder, and sank senseless to the ground.

Eliza threw herself upon him, uttering loud cries of anguish. "He is dead," she cried, despairingly; "he is dead!"

" No, he is not dead," said the officer ; " the excitement
and fatigue have produced a swoon.   He will soon be restored
to consciousness and get over it.   Careful nursing shall not be
wanting to Anthony Wallner in my house."

He had prophesied correctly.   Anthony Wallner awoke
again, and seemed to recover rapidly under the kind nursing
of his host and his daughter.

They remained two days at the custom-house on the frontier.   The news of Anthony Wallner's arrival spread like
wildfire through the whole neighborhood, and the landed
proprietors of the district hastened to the custom-house to see
the heroic Tyrolese chief and his intrepid daughter, and offered
their services to both of them.

It was no longer necessary for them to journey on foot.
Wherever they came, the carriages of the wealthy and
aristocratic inhabitants were in readiness for them, and they
were greeted everywhere with jubilant acclamations.   Their
journey to Vienna was an incessant triumphal procession, a
continued chain of demonstrations of enthusiasm and manifestations of love.

Anthony Wallner, however, remained silent, gloomy, and
downcast, amid all these triumphs ; and on arousing himself
sometimes from his sombre broodings, and seeing the painful
expression with which Eliza's eyes rested on him, he tried to
smile, but the smile died away on his trembling lips.

" I believe I shall be taken very sick," he said, faintly.
" My head aches dreadfully, and all my limbs are trembling.
I was too long in the Alpine hut, and the numerous previous
fatigues.   The excitement, grief, cold, and hunger, and last, the
long journey on foot, have been too much for me.   Ah, Lizzie,
Lizzie, I shall be taken sick.   Great God! it would be dreadful
if I should die now and leave you all alone in this foreign
country!   No, no, I do not want to be taken sick, I have no
time for it.   Oh, listen to me, my God!   I do not want to be
taken sick, for Lizzie must not be left an orphan here.   No,
no, no ! "

And he lifted his clinched fist to heaven, screamed, and
wept, and uttered senseless and incoherent words.

" I am afraid he has got the nervous fever," said Baron

Engenberg, who was conveying Wallner and Eliza in his carriage from the last station to Vienna. "It will be necessary for us to take him at once to a hospital."

"Can I stay with him there and nurse him?" asked Eliza, repressing her tears.

"Of course you can."

"Then let us take him to a hospital," she said, calmly. "He will die, but *I* shall be there to close his eyes."

And it was Eliza that closed her father's eyes. The violent nervous fever which had seized Anthony Wallner was too much for his exhausted body. He died five days after his arrival at Vienna, on the 15th of February, 1810, at the city hospital.

Many persons attended his funeral; many persons came to see Eliza Wallner, the young heroine of the Tyrol. But Eliza would not see anybody. She remained in the room which had been assigned to her at the hospital, and she spoke and prayed only with the priest who had administered the last unction to her father.

On the day after the funeral the Emperor Francis sent one of his chamberlains to Eliza, to induce her to remain in Vienna. He would provide for her bountifully, and reward her for what her father had done. The chamberlain was also instructed to conduct Eliza to the emperor, that he might thank and console her personally.

Eliza shook her head, gravely. "The emperor need not thank me," she said, "for I did no more for him than he did for the Tyrol. He is unable to console me; God alone can do that, and He will also provide for me. I cannot see the emperor, for my heart is too deeply afflicted. But if you will give me money enough, sir, to return quickly to my dear Tyrol and my beloved mother, I shall accept it and be grateful to you. I must return to my mother and weep with her; and my dear home, my dear mountains will console me."

"You can set out as soon as you please," said the chamberlain. "The emperor has interceded in your behalf and obtained this safeguard for you in case you wished to return to your native country. No one will molest you, and you and your family can live quietly at your home."

"If the emperor had done as much for my father as he does for me, my father would not have died," said Eliza, gravely, accepting the paper. "Now he has no longer need of an emperor. He is with God, and I would I were with him above! But I must not leave my mother. I must console her and stay with her as long as it pleases God." *

CHAPTER XLIV.

ANDREAS HOFER'S DEATH.

THE court-martial at Mantua had passed sentence of death upon Andreas Hofer for fighting against the French after the last proclamation of Eugene Beauharnais offering a general amnesty. But the court-martial had not adopted this decision unanimously; several members had voted for long confinement, and two had had the courage to vote for his entire deliverance. By a singular revolution of fortune, the same General Bisson, who had been taken prisoner at Innspruck at the outbreak of the insurrection, and with whom Major Teimer had made his triumphal entry into Innspruck, was now governor of Mantua, and president of the court-martial which tried the commander-in-chief of the Tyrolese. The general, in consideration of his captivity among the Tyrolese, wished to act mildly and impartially, and sent a telegraphic dispatch to the viceroy at Milan to inquire what was to be done with Andreas Hofer, inasmuch as the sentence of the court-martial had not been passed unanimously. An answer was returned very soon. It contained the categorical order that Andreas Hofer should be shot within twenty-four hours.

---

* Eliza Wallner returned to Windisch-Matrey, and lived there in quiet retirement. She never married. After the death of her mother she yielded to Joachim Haspinger's entreaties and went to live at his house. The Capuchin was ordained and appointed pastor of Jetelsee, and afterward of Traunfeld. Eliza lived with him as his adopted daughter, and was still with him at the time of his death, which took place in 1856, at Salzburg.—See Schallhammer's "Joachim Haspinger," p. 184.

Commissioners of the military authorities, therefore, entered Andreas Hofer's cell on the 21st of February, and informed him that he would suffer death within two hours.

He listened to them standing, and with unshaken firmness. "I shall die, then, at least as a soldier, and not as a criminal," he said, nodding his head gently. "I am not afraid of bullets, nor of the good God either ; He was always kind to me, and it is even now kind in Him to relieve me from my sufferings here. I am ready to appear before the judgment-seat of God."

"If you have any special wishes to prefer, communicate them to us now ; and if it is possible, they shall be granted," said one of the officers, profoundly moved.

"There are some wishes which I should like to prefer," replied Hofer, musingly. "In the first place, I wish to see once more my dear Cajetan Döninger, who was separated from me and confined in another cell ; and then I wish to dictate a letter and my last will, and would request that both be sent to my dear brother-in-law."

"These wishes shall be complied with ; I promise it to you in the name of General Bisson. Do you desire to prefer any additional requests ?"

"I wish further that a priest be sent to me, that he may receive my confession, and grant me absolution ; and finally, I should like to see once more my dear countrymen, who are imprisoned in the casemates here, and take leave of them in a few words."

"A confessor will be sent to you, but your last request can not be complied with," was the reply. "An exciting and perhaps disorderly scene would ensue, and such things must be avoided."

"Well, then," said Andreas, sighing, "send me my dear secretary, and afterward the priest."

A few minutes after the officers had withdrawn, the door opened, and Cajetan Döninger came in. He burst into tears, rushed toward Andreas Hofer, and folding him to his heart, exclaimed mournfully : "Is it true, then, that they intend to kill you ? Is it true that they are going to assassinate the noblest and best man like a criminal ?"

"Hush, hush, Cajetan," said Andreas, gently, pressing Döninger tenderly to his heart; "do not scold, but submit as I do. I die gladly, for it is better that I should sacrifice myself for my native country than that others should die for my sake, or for the fatherland." *

"Oh, would that I could die for you!" sobbed Döninger; "my life is worthless without you. Is it possible that you must suffer now so ignominious a punishment for all your noble deeds and aspirations?"

"God alone knows what is good," said Andreas, mildly, "and I have doubtless committed many errors, for which I have to suffer now. But, Cajetan, will you fulfil my last request?"

"Name it, and I will comply with it."

"Then weep no more, my dear friend, for your tears give me pain. Be, as formerly, manful and firm."

"I will," said Döninger; and he dried his tears and forced himself to be calm and composed.

"And now, Cajetan, be my secretary for the last time," said Andreas, gently. "I will dictate to you a letter to my brother-in-law Pöhler, at Neustadt. The jailer has already laid paper, pen, and ink on the table. Sit down, therefore, and write."

Cajetan went to the table and seated himself. "I am ready, commander-in-chief," he said; "dictate to me now."

Andreas walked up and down several times musingly; he then stood still near the table; a wondrous expression of serene calmness and peace beamed from his face, and he dictated in a clear, quiet voice, which did not once tremble with emotion.

"Dearest brother-in-law : It was God's will that I should exchange here at Mantua my earthly life for a better one. But—God be praised for his divine mercy!—it seems to me as little painful as if I were to be led out for another purpose. God in His mercy will doubtless be with me to the last moment, where I shall ascend to that eternal dwelling-place where my soul will rejoice for evermore with all the chosen spirits,

* Hofer's own words.—See "Gallery of Heroes: Andreas Hofer," p. 195.

and where I shall pray for all, and particularly for those to whom I owe my intercession ; above all, for you, too, and your dear wife, on account of the book which you presented to me, and of other kind acts. Let all my dear friends and acquaintances pray for me too, and help me to rise from the devouring flames, when I have to expiate my sins in purgatory. My beloved wife, Anna Gertrude, is to have masses read for me at *St. Martin's Zum rosenfarbnen Blut*. She shall have prayers read in both of the parish-churches, and treat my friends at the lower inn to soup and meat, and give every one half a bottle of wine. The money I had about me will be distributed among the poor of this city ; for the rest, settle with my debtors and creditors as honestly as you can, lest I should have to atone for it also. Farewell, all of you, for this world, until we shall meet in heaven and praise God for evermore. Dearest brother-in-law, repair to the Passeyr valley, and inform the landlord of the lower inn of my instructions. He will make all necessary dispositions. Let all the inhabitants of Passeyr, and all my acquaintances remember me in their prayers. Dearest brother-in-law, tell my wife, Anna Gertrude, not to grieve for me. I shall pray to God for her and for all. Adieu, beautiful world ! Dying seems to me so easy that there are not even tears in my eyes.

"Written at nine o'clock ; at ten I shall ascend to God with the aid of all the saints.

"Your ——.

"Mantua, February 20, 1810." *

"I will write the signature as I always did," said Andreas Hofer ; and, taking up the pen quickly, he wrote :

"Your Andreas Hofer, from Sand in Passeyr, whom you loved in this life. I will set out on my last journey in the Lord's name." †

"I thank you, Cajetan, for rendering me this last service," said Andreas, kindly. "And now, my dear friend, let us take

* "Gallery of heroes : Andreas Hofer," p. 197.
† "Gallery of Heroes."

leave of each other. The confessor will be here soon, and then
I must no longer speak to any one but God."

Cajetan came to him with a tottering step, and leaned his
head silently on Hofer's shoulder. He did not speak, he
wanted to be firm, but he was unable to restrain the sobs and
sighs which issued from his breast.

"My dear Cajetan, why do you weep?" asked Hofer, pressing Döninger's head gently to his heart. "Did you weep
when I went into battle, where the enemy's bullets might have
hit me at any second? You did not weep then. Think, therefore, that I am going into battle to-day too, and that it is better for me to be hit by the bullets than suffer any longer in
this manner."

At this moment the door opened, and the priest, Giovanni
Giacomo Manifesti, dressed in full vestments, came in. The
guards who followed him led away Döninger, who obeyed
them in silence, as if stunned by his terrible grief.*

Andreas Hofer remained alone with his confessor.

At eleven o'clock the doors of the prison were thrown
open, and Andreas Hofer was led out to execution. His face
was serene, and in his hands he held the small crucifix which
he had always worn on his breast. His confessor, Manifesti,
walked by his side, and a battalion of grenadiers followed
him.

Andreas Hofer walked along the ramparts of the fortress
with a firm step. As he passed by the barracks of the Porta
Molina, where the Tyrolese prisoners were confined, they fell
on their knees and wept aloud. Andreas turned quickly to
Manifesti, the priest. "Your reverence," he said, "you will
distribute among my poor countrymen the five hundred
florins, my last property, which I gave to you, will you not?"

"I will, my son."

"And take my greetings to all," said Andreas Hofer, in a
grave, loud voice, "and tell them not to be disheartened, nor
to think that all is lost, and that we have fought and bled in

---

* Cajetan Döninger was taken immediately after Hofer's execution, from
his prison, and sent to the Island of Corsica, as a private in a regiment of light
infantry. He succeeded, some time afterward, in escaping from thence, and
returning to his native country.

vain. Better times will dawn upon my beloved Tyrol, and one day it will be again a free German country. Tell them to hope and believe in this prediction."

On the broad bastion, a little distance from the Porta Ceresa, the grenadiers formed a square, open in the rear. Andreas Hofer entered this open space with the priest, bowed kindly to all sides, and prayed aloud with the priest.

"Now, farewell, dear reverend father," he then said, "and accept this crucifix as a souvenir from me. I have worn it on my breast for twenty years past, and it will remind you of Andreas Hofer. Inform my wife that I suffered death joyously, and that I know we shall meet again above. You promised me to do so, and you will redeem your promise, reverend father, will you not?"

"Certainly I will, my beloved, pious son," said Manifesti; and with tears in his eyes he embraced and blessed Andreas Hofer for the last time.*

The priest thereupon left the square, while twelve men and

---

* Manifesti redeemed his promise. He sent to the Tyrol the following letter regarding Hofer's death:

MANTOVA, li 21, Febrajo, 1810.

"Ieri poco primo del mezzo giorno è stato fucillato il Signore Andrea Hofer, gia commandante del Tirolo. Dalla commissione militare, che l'ha sententiato, fu invitato ad assisterlo, e sebbene fossi convalescente per una maladia pocchi giorno avanti sofferta, ho volonteri assento l'impegno, e con somma mia consolazione ed edificatione ho ammirato un uomo, che è andato alla morte d'un eroe Christiano e l'ha sostenuto di martire intrepido. Egli con tutta segretezza mi ha consegnata una carta di somma importanza per l'orfona sua famiglia, incaricando mi dirigerla a V. Sig. Rio M.—Sono con perfetta stima,

"Di V. S. Rio M.

"Divotissimo,

"GIOV. BATT. (ARCIPRETE) MANIFESTI."

"MANTUA, Feb. 21, 1810.—Yesterday, a few minutes before twelve, Mr. Andreas Hofer, late commander of the Tyrol, was shot here. The military commission which tried him requested me to attend him, and although I had recovered but a few days since from sickness, I gladly complied with the request, and admired, to my consolation and edification, a man who went to death as a Christian hero, and suffered it as an intrepid martyr. Under the seal of profound silence he intrusted to me a paper of the highest importance to his family," &c.—See Hormayr's "Lebensbilder," vol. i. p. 224.

a corporal stood forth with loaded muskets. The corporal offered Hofer a white handkerchief to bandage his eyes.

"No," said Hofer. "I have often already faced death ; it
is a dear friend of mine, and I want to see it, therefore, when
it comes to me."

"Kneel down, then," said the corporal.

"I shall not," replied Hofer, gravely and almost imperiously. "I am used to stand upright before my Creator, and
in that posture I will deliver up my spirit to Him. But pray,"
he added in a milder voice, "aim well. Come, corporal, I will
give you yet a souvenir ; it is my whole remaining property.
Look at this Zwanziger ; I had it coined when I was commander-in-chief of the Tyrol ; and it reminds me now of my
beloved country, and it seems to me as though its snow-clad
mountains were looking down on me and greeting me. There,
keep it as a remembrancer, and aim well !"

The corporal stepped back and commanded in a voice
tremulous with emotion, "Fire !"

"Fire !" shouted Hofer. "Long live the Tyrol !"

Six shots rang out, but Andreas Hofer was not dead ; he
had sunk only on one knee and leaned on his right hand.

Six shots crashed again. They struck him to the ground,
but did not yet kill him. He raised his bleeding head once
more.

The corporal, filled with pity, stepped now close up to him,
put his musket to Hofer's forehead, and fired.

This thirteenth shot dispatched him at length !

The grenadiers raised the corpse and carried it on a black
bier to St. Michael's church, where it lay in state during the
requiem, that the people might convince themselves of the
death of the beloved and feared commander-in-chief of the
Tyrol, *Le Général Sanvird*, Andreas Hofer, the Barbone, and
of the final subjugation of the Tyrol.*

---

* Hofer's remains were buried in Manifesti's garden. A simple slab on
his grave bore the following inscription : "Qui giace la spoglia del fu Andrea
Hofer, detto il Generale Barbone, commandante supremo delle milicie del
Tirolo, fucillato in questa forterezza nel giorno 20 Febrajo 1810, sepolto in
questo luogo." ("Here rest the remains of the late Andreas Hofer, called
General Barbone, commander-in-chief of the Tyrolese militia, shot in this for-

This occurred on the 20th of February, 1810 ; and on the same day on which Andreas Hofer was shot at Mantua, because he had loved his country and his Emperor Francis too faithfully, almost at the very hour of his death, the booming of artillery was to be heard on the ramparts of Vienna.

It proclaimed to the Viennese the joyful news that the Archduchess Maria Louisa, the emperor's daughter, was the affianced bride of the Emperor Napoleon !

tress on the 20th of February, 1810, and buried in this place.") Fourteen years afterward Hofer's remains were disinterred by three Austrian officers, who had obtained Manifesti's consent, and conveyed to Botzen. The Emperor Francis gave orders to transfer them to Innspruck, where they were buried in the church of the Franciscans by the side of the monument of the Archduke Ferdinand and his beloved Philippina Welser.—See Hormayr's "Andreas Hofer," vol. ii., p. 539.

THE END.